ENIGMA

ROAD TO THE BREAKING
BOOK 2

CHRIS BENNETT

Enigma is a work of historical fiction. Apart from well-documented actual people, events, and places that figure in the narrative, all names, characters, places, and incidents are the products of the author's imagination, or are used fictitiously. Any resemblance to current events, places, or living persons, is entirely coincidental.

Enigma

ISBN: 978-1-7331079-5-2 (Trade Paperback)
ISBN: 978-1-7331079-6-9 (eBook)

Publisher's Cataloging-In-Publication Data
(Prepared by The Donohue Group, Inc.)

Names: Bennett, Chris (Chris Arthur), 1959- author.
Title: Enigma / Chris Bennett.
Description: [North Bend, Washington] : [CPB Publishing, LLC], [2021] | Series: Road to the breaking ; book 2
Identifiers: ISBN 9781733107952 (trade paperback) | ISBN 9781733107969 (ebook)
Subjects: LCSH: United States. Army--Officers--History--19th century--Fiction. | Slaveholders--Virginia--Fiction. | United States--History--Civil War, 1861-1865--Fiction. | Vendetta--Virginia--Fiction. | Man-woman relationships--Fiction. | LCGFT: Historical fiction.
Classification: LCC PS3602.E66446 E55 2021 (print) | LCC PS3602.E66446 (ebook) | DDC 813/.6--dc23

To sign up for a
no-spam newsletter
about
Road to the Breaking
and
exclusive free bonus material
visit my website:

http://www.ChrisABennett.com

DEDICATION

To my father
Craig A. Bennett, M.D.;
I miss you Dad,
and I know you
would've loved
seeing this in print.

Enigma [uh-**nig**-muh] noun:
1. A person of puzzling, inscrutable, mysterious, or contradictory character, 2. A perplexing or inexplicable occurrence or situation, difficult to understand or explain, 3. Obscure speech or writing, containing a hidden meaning: a riddle.

Contents

"I'm not particularly keen on doing what's normal. I much prefer doing what's right."

– Nathan Chambers

CHAPTER 1. PRINCES, STRANGE BEASTS, AND MAGICAL GIANTS

"Let the sleeping dogs lie,
but rise up!
You sleeping giants."
– Bernard Kelvin Clive

Monday June 11, 1860 – Greenbrier County, Virginia:

They walked their horses slowly down the dirt lane, fields of tobacco tumbling away into the distance on either side. Further off they could see other crops—okra and sweet potatoes, among others. But one crop dominated the view, the king of all: cotton. It covered a vast acreage with endless rows of knee-high, bright-green, bushy plants, gently rising and falling with the lay of the land.

A lush green valley spread before them, backed by heavily wooded hills, rolling off as far as the eye could see. The hooves of their horses kicked up but little dust. A brief morning shower had wetted the road earlier. But now the sun shone strong and bright in a cobalt blue sky, dotted only sparsely with puffy white clouds that did nothing to diminish the late-morning heat.

Nathan could smell the dampness of the earth as they rode. Looking down into the valley ahead, he saw a cluster of buildings—slave quarters, sheds, barns, and various storage buildings. And last, deep in the valley, a great, white house. The *Big House*, Nathan reminded himself.

Nathan's granddaddy, Daniel Chambers, had built it in the classic Greek style. Four large, two-story columns lined the peaked front entrance, which was flanked by a veranda wrapping entirely around the house, lined by smaller, single-story columns that mimicked the front. The first floor sat five feet off the ground, with a set of broad, stone steps leading up to the veranda from the drive. Daniel Chambers had harvested timber from the site to build the structure of the house and to provide the white-painted wood siding and trim. He'd done it mostly because he

1

appreciated the economics it afforded him; he'd avoided the expense of hauling in the huge quantity of bricks required to build a red-brick manor house of the style popular in Richmond. Nathan thought the effect of the pure white house, sparkling in the sun against an emerald green background, was truly magnificent.

Home. It seemed strange and surreal—a dream from which there would be no awakening. Back home to his new life. He sighed a heavy sigh. This would take some getting used to, he decided.

A lone rider trotted toward them from the valley below. Nathan raised his hand, and the small troop immediately pulled to a stop. They awaited the rider in expectant silence.

The men from Texas had endured a journey of twenty-five hundred miles to come here, with little idea what they'd find once they arrived. Nathan had invited the men to stay and enjoy the hospitality of his home for a week or two before they headed off to their final destinations. Happily, all had agreed.

The rider pulled up in front of them, doffed his wide-brimmed felt hat and said, "Captain Chambers, I presume?"

"Yes, that's correct. And who might you be?"

"Well, sir, I am Allen Sickles, head overseer of Mountain Meadows. Welcome home, Mr. Chambers, sir. I am entirely at your service, of course."

"Thank you, Mr. Sickles. It is good to be home again."

Nathan's response was proper and formal, as the occasion demanded, but there were mixed emotions behind it.

"My traveling companions ..." he gestured toward the men, "are also from the Army out in Texas. They'll be guests enjoying the hospitality of our home for a spell. Please see to it they are made welcome."

"Yes, sir. Certainly! Most welcome, most welcome gentlemen, one and all. Welcome to Mountain Meadows Farm of western Virginia." He nodded his head toward the men, while squeezing and crumpling his hat nervously. When he glanced at Billy Creek, he appeared startled, but said nothing.

"No need to ruin your hat, nor burn your face in the sun, Mr. Sickles. Lead on, if you please. I'll make individual introductions once we're safely in the shade of the house."

"Yes, Master. Certainly, sir." Sickles whipped his hat back on his head and pulled the reins of his horse back toward the valley.

Nathan's instinctive gut reaction was to dislike the man. There was something disagreeable about him. He was a little too polite and obsequious. And he rarely made eye contact, giving him a nervous, guilty look, while also tending to glance at a person out the side of his face, as if silently passing judgment.

But Nathan scolded himself, *not fair to judge a man so suddenly, on nothing more than first impressions and instincts.* And yet … such instincts were usually correct, he counterargued. He decided to let the matter rest and think on it later.

As they reached the valley floor, and the road flattened out, they saw ahead of them a row of people standing still, lining both sides of the drive. Men, women, and children of all ages and sizes—with black faces—the slaves. Nathan swallowed a lump in his throat. This was the moment he'd thought about, dreamt about, and dreaded the entire journey.

How would they react to his return? Were they anything like he remembered? It was all so hazy in his memory. His world had changed since he was last here. It'd been another lifetime, another person—not himself. And yet … he could remember sneaking off to the river with a couple of the young black boys to swim and go fishing. Running, climbing, swinging from a rope into the water, laughing uproariously! And the boys suffering punishment later while he was forced to watch. Was it a dream, or had it really happened oh, so long ago?

The men on horseback leaned forward, looking around with curiosity. At a time when an adult slave might sell for fifteen hundred dollars or more at auction, this group represented more wealth than most men would earn in a lifetime.

Tom whistled quietly, turned to Jim and whispered, "I knew the Captain's family had wealth, but this?" He shook his head. Jim nodded and grunted his agreement.

But for Nathan, the economic value of these people was the furthest thing from his mind. As they walked their horses between the rows of people, he looked down at their faces. None looked back. In the days before their arrival, he'd replayed this moment in his mind a hundred times — the expectant faces looking up at their new master with curiosity, wondering what he'd become in his years of absence. Maybe a shy smile or two, or a look of recognition, which he might return in an encouraging manner.

But *this* ...

He felt his earlier excitement draining away. Face after face looked straight at the ground, never looking up at him, never meeting his eyes. Too afraid, too humbled, too downtrodden to even glance up to see how their new master looked, or what his demeanor might be.

He suffered a growing sadness, a wave of depression and hopelessness that threatened to darken the otherwise bright day of his homecoming. After the last two days of hard travel by horseback, Nathan had pulled out his dress clothes this morning for his arrival. He wanted to make an impression on his new "employees," both black and white. But now he felt foolish for the thought. These people didn't care how he looked; they had no reason to.

His decision to sell the farm and move Miss Abbey to a new home in Richmond hit hard against the realization of what that would mean to these people. Unless someone bought the whole thing, including all the slaves, they'd be sold off individually and scattered to the four winds. Families, such as they were, would be separated. Some might end up with better masters, others with worse. But in the end, even if they all stayed here, every single one, down to the tiniest tyke, would still be ... a *slave*.

Oh, my dear God. What have we done? He had a sudden sick feeling like being kicked in the gut. *What am I to do?* He fought down the tears welling in his eyes.

As they moved along the row of slaves, Nathan looked up and surveyed their surroundings. To their right stood rough-looking, low-roofed buildings: the slave cabins. They'd built them using

4

unpainted logs cut square-sided, not round. He noticed several cabins were missing wooden shingles in places, which must be a huge annoyance whenever it rained.

Past the slave quarters were several better kept buildings: storage and utility sheds. He scowled. They kept the farm's tools and equipment in better buildings than its people. He expected the same was likely true of the livestock, though he hadn't yet seen the barns or pens.

Looming ahead of them on the road was the Big House. He remembered it well from his childhood. A bright green lawn, neatly cropped by a small flock of sheep, surrounded a large white house. The gravel road ran straight toward the house, then looped around just in front of a broad set of stairs leading up to the columned veranda. More evenly trimmed grass filled the island at the center of the circle the roadway created. A neat row of flowers lined both the inner and outer edges of the circle; pink, white, and yellow, their colors sparkled in the sunshine. It was a beautiful and picturesque scene, he had to admit. But all he could feel was an overwhelming sadness.

ಬಿಕೊಅಗಿ಄ಬಿಕೊಅಗಿ಄ಬಿಕೊಅಗ಄

They brought their horses to a halt in front of the house by a long hitching post. Three young black men and one older one came trotting forward to take their reins, and to relieve them of the pack animals and all their baggage. The men on horseback dismounted and stretched their limbs.

Nathan gazed up toward the front door of the house. He'd expected to see Miss Abbey standing there to greet him. But the front of the veranda was empty. He turned and gave Sickles a questioning look.

Sickles seemed uncomfortable meeting his intense gaze and looked down at his boots, "Miss Abbey is … well, sir she's …"

Nathan felt a knot forming in his stomach.

"What is it, man? What's wrong with Miss Abbey?"

"Miss Abbey hasn't been well lately, sir … she took ill about a week ago and …"

5

Nathan's eyes widened, and he turned back toward the house, "Momma ..." he whispered and started toward the stairs. The growing anxiety that had dogged his steps the entire journey now seemed to be coming home to roost. *No ... dear God ... don't let it be ...* he thought, slowly shaking his head, fighting down a cold fear that threatened to overwhelm him.

But as he reached the bottom of the stone stairs leading up to the veranda, the front door opened, and a woman stepped out. She was dressed in a long white cotton gown trimmed in gold-colored satin and lace. To the newcomers it was clear she was the lady of the manor, an older woman, in her early fifties, but still attractive and vigorous; not the least frail-looking, showing no sign of her recent illness. Tall and thin, she carried herself with an easy, natural grace.

Nathan breathed a deep sigh of relief and smiled. His men politely held back, removing their hats respectfully.

When she came forward, three dark-skinned female servants followed in her wake. These were dressed in much nicer clothes than the people lining the roadway — these were house slaves.

The woman walked to the veranda's edge at the top of the stairs. She paused and looked at Nathan, an unreadable expression on her face. Nathan looked back at her with curiosity — Abigail Chambers, his mother, whom he hadn't seen or spoken to, except in letters, for almost twenty years! He decided she was still a beautiful woman, just as he had always pictured her in his mind. An odd thought then occurred to him; the last time he'd seen her she'd been the age *he* was now. *My God ... has it been that long?*

Then she suddenly covered her mouth, and her eyes teared up. She fell to her knees, and her servants rushed forward to catch her.

Nathan took the steps three at a time, and was soon kneeling next to her, holding her upright. "Momma! Are you all right? I heard you've been ill ..."

"I'm fine now ... *perfect* even ..." she whispered, voice choked with emotion, "Oh, my dear boy ... oh my precious *God*. You're really *home* ... you are ... *finally* home! After *all* these years, my little boy … is finally … home," she reached out and grasped him by the shirt collar, thrusting her face into the crook of his neck. Then she sobbed, long, and hard.

He put his arms around her shoulders and held her gently. "It's all right, Momma. I'm home now … home for *good*. Don't worry Momma, your little boy is home." They knelt on the veranda, and he held her close, softly patting her back, feeling suddenly helpless, not knowing what to do.

But after several minutes, she gathered herself, stood, and stepped back to gaze at him. "I'm all right. It's true, I've been ill of late and feeling unsteady. But today … today my son is home! So all is right with the world! And … look at you! You have become such a fine, handsome *man*, Nathan, dear. As I knew you would."

It was true; he was now a grown man, truly. His thirty-third birthday would be in less than a month. And while he was away, he had grown from a gangly teen into a tall, muscular man. She gazed at his face for several seconds, as if trying to see the little boy in the man. Then she flashed a smile, warm and genuine, though she still blinked back the tears. Nathan smiled brightly in return.

"It's so good to see you, Momma," he said sincerely. He'd not decided how he truly felt about her until this very moment. He'd always had such mixed emotions about his father, and about his home—it'd been difficult to separate out his feelings for his mother.

"I've stayed away too long. I'm … *so sorry.*" He felt a surge of emotion, his earlier sadness about the slaves momentarily forgotten. He could feel tears welling and he suffered a sudden vision of the endless years this fine woman had spent waiting for her only child to return.

She choked back another sob, "Yes … it's been too long. But I know you had to be *free* … free to be happy … free from … your Daddy…" She paused, struggling with her emotions, searching for the right words to say. "He was a *hard* man … a difficult man to understand … difficult to love …"

She gazed up at the sky for a long moment and took a deep breath. Then she looked back at him, clapped her hands together, and clutched them to her breast, "But now you're finally home! Hallelujah!"

She smiled at him again and took him by the arm, leaning in against his shoulder.

Then she looked over at the men and smiled brightly, "Oh, my goodness! My apologies for such a display! My Momma would be appalled at such manners, were she alive to see them! Please forgive me, young gentleman, and welcome! Welcome most sincerely to my home! And … thank you from the bottom of my heart … for bringing my son safely home to me!"

She turned to the black woman on her left, and said, "Will you please escort Nathaniel and his men into the house and give them shade and refreshment. They must be hot from riding all morning in the sun and tired after their long journey."

"Yes, Miss Abbey. Please, do come inside, masters." The maid stepped forward and gestured for the men to come up into the house.

Nathan had been so focused on Miss Abbey he noticed the black woman for the first time. She was also a fine-looking woman, tall and lean. She appeared to be about the same age as Miss Abbey. She had a few wrinkles, and a little gray in her hair that hadn't been there before, but hers was a face he would *never* forget. "Hello, *Megs!* It's so very good to see you again, after all these years!"

He looked her in the eye, and was pleased she was not intimidated, and didn't look away like the other slaves had. It raised his spirits after the reception he'd received back on the road, and it made him smile.

She returned the smile, "Welcome home, Master. And … it's very good to see *you* as well."

"My goodness, Megs … now I think on it, you were the one always looking after me, teaching me my lessons, and whatnot when I was a boy. I don't suppose I ever thanked you or showed the least appreciation. So … *thank you*, twenty years late …"

She seemed surprised by this, and he thought he saw a little moisture forming in her eyes. She smiled, and bowed her head, but was suddenly unable to speak.

"But, if I recall, you were none too soft on me there toward the end. Said I was 'an uppity and spoiled young princeling,' if I remember." He shook his head and smiled at the memory.

"Yes, Master Nathaniel. You remember it rightly," she answered, finding her voice again. "Do you disagree with how I saw you then?" He could see she was now smiling with her eyes, a playful expression he remembered from so long ago.

He thought back for a moment, remembering when he was a young boy, running through the house, causing no end of mischief, noise, and destruction, without a care for who it affected. And when he was older, getting into fights and arguing with anyone who had a tongue to speak!

He laughed, "Right you were, Megs! An uppity spoiled prince I was. Well, now you can judge for yourself whether or not I've changed."

"Oh *no*, sir! You're the master of this house; it ain't my place to judge you, nor to question your behavior."

"Hmm … well, we'll see about that, Megs. Anyway, I'd appreciate it if you would continue to let me know if I'm behaving as an uppity brat, or a haughty prince. You may consider it an order, if that makes it easier." He gave her a warm smile.

"Well, master, all's I can say about that is … be careful what you wish for!" She gave him a mischievous smile, then turned and headed back into the house to fetch refreshments for the men.

ঝঞ৻৵৶ঝঞ৻৵৶ঝঞ৵৶ঝঞ৻৵৶

Nathan turned to escort the men inside, when he heard a loud commotion coming from around the corner of the house. It sounded like a wild animal howling and snarling, mixed with men's voices, shouting frantically.

He came quickly down the steps, and strode past the corner of the house, "What on earth …?"

An enormous, hairy beast was howling, growling, and snapping at two of the black grooms, who had apparently been trying to put a rope around the creature's neck. It snarled, showing a jaw full of enormous, sharp teeth.

Nathan and his men stopped and stared in wonder.

It was a gigantic hound, appearing to weigh somewhere around two hundred and fifty pounds, broad of chest, and long of leg. He had a huge head with a long, wide mouth.

The grooms backed away in obvious terror of the hound. The beast eyed them threateningly, snarling fiercely, showing his teeth. "Look out, masters!!" one of the grooms yelled, "He's a mad beast—like to kill someone!"

Then the hound stopped, lifted his head, and sniffed the air. He seemed to have gotten wind of the newcomers, watching the action only a few yards away. He turned and looked at them with spooky-looking, beady yellow eyes. After sniffing the air once again, he let off a tremendous howling bark—a noise to make men cover their ears for the painful, explosive sound of it.

He came bounding toward Nathan and his men. Jamie and Georgie, the only two still wearing gun belts, reached for their pistols. But Nathan held up his hand and commanded them, "Peace!" They obeyed their captain's word without question, but kept their hands at the ready, and their eyes locked on the great, snarling beast.

When the hound came closer, Nathan reached into his jacket pocket and pulled out the small Colt, but otherwise made no movement. He held the gun straight down at his side. The creature seemed to single him out, coming straight toward him howling madly, bouncing up and down on its front legs threateningly, baring its ferocious teeth.

Nathan pulled back the hammer with a click and raised the pistol. But when the hound got to within about ten feet of him, a most singular thing occurred: instead of launching himself at the Captain, the beast dropped to the ground on his belly, his great head resting on his paws. He made no sound, but merely stared silently up at the man standing over him.

For a long moment, nobody moved in a breathless silence. Nathan lowered the hammer on the Colt and returned it to his pocket. He stepped toward the hound, knelt, placed the palm of his hand on top of the enormous head, and scratched. The beast let out a low growling sound, and the men again reached for their weapons. But the hound simply rolled over, its great paws in the air, displaying its belly to its new master.

The groom who'd shouted the warning, named Phinney, whistled softly, "I'd never've believed it, if'n I ain't seen it with my own eyes!"

But the second groom, named Cobb, shook his head and said, "I seen it before … one other time; it's the master. The hound—he knows the master. He never let nobody touch him, and never let nobody tie him, 'cept the master. The *old* master tamed him."

"He's right," said a woman's voice. They turned and saw Miss Abbey walking toward them across the lawn.

"What's he talking about, Momma? What's the story about this dog, anyway? The grooms act like he's the devil incarnate, but he seems as soft as a feather pillow to me." He emphasized the point by scratching the hound's enormous chest, to which he received no objection.

"It's because nobody has ever done what you're doing now … except your father. It was … three, maybe four years ago … when he showed up on the lawn. Nobody knew where he came from. But when the servants went near him, and tried to throw a rope on him, he set in to snarling and snapping, and howling something awful. Well, you know, like you heard just now.

"Anyway, your Daddy heard the commotion and looked out an upstairs window. He saw the grooms trying to restrain the beast and clearly fearing for their lives. So he loaded a pistol and strode out onto the lawn meaning to make an end to the creature. And he would have done so, only the strangest thing happened; the hound came and bowed down to him, same as he did just now to you! He's never done it with anyone else until now.

"And your Daddy, stern as he was, didn't have the heart to shoot the animal, groveling before him as it was. So instead, he ordered the servants to feed him, turned, and walked back into the house. From that day Harry the Dog has been a permanent fixture around this house."

"Harry?" Nathan asked.

"Harry *the Dog*," she corrected him. "Your father once said he was 'as stubborn as old Harry,' who was the head groom at the time. So people called the hound 'Harry.' But it was too confusing to figure out who they were talking about, the man or the beast; so they started calling him 'Harry the Dog' to keep it all straight, and the name stuck. Anyway, the poor thing has hardly eaten or slept since your Daddy passed; at night, if it's hot and I have the bedroom window open, I can hear him pacing around the house and whimpering. It was so sad I was thinking of having the overseer put him down, but I hadn't the heart to do it."

She sighed, "Anyway, there seems to be something about the hound makes him recognizes the master of the house and will only submit to him. Lately he's been extra aggressive toward strangers—overly protective of the house. I was afraid he might attack you or one of your men. So I asked the grooms to tie him up; I can see now it was a mistake. The poor thing will suffer no one to confine him, other than his own master. But now *you* are here, I expect he will be *just* fine!"

"All right then, go ahead and feed him, but otherwise let him be and *for God's sake*, don't try to tie him," Nathan instructed the grooms. "I think he'll be all right now, if you just let him alone."

"Oh, yes, Master! We will certainly be happy—*very happy* to leave him alone," answered Cobb with a grin.

Phinney nodded his head in enthusiastic agreement, then added, "After we feeds him, of course, sir."

Nathan stood up, "Well, Harry, guess I have myself a dog."

The hound rolled back over and looked up at Nathan. He suddenly looked relaxed and happy. His tongue lolled out to the side of his mouth, and he panted contentedly in the midday heat.

"But … what *is* that beast, anyway?" Georgie asked, scratching his head up under his hat. "Ain't never seen the like."

"Cross between an English Mastiff and an Irish Wolfhound, I would hazard to guess," William answered. "But bigger than either, I believe. See there … he has the large broad head and floppy jowls of a Mastiff, but a long snout full of teeth like a Wolfhound. And he has a Wolfhound's wooly, curly gray fur mottled with brown speckles—a coat commonly called brindle. Either that or he's covered in mud … hard to tell which."

"English and Irish mix," Jamie said and laughed, "now there's a deadly combination for you, lads."

"Maybe we should call him '*Stan* the Dog' on account of him bein' foreign and all, plus him being so gosh-awful big!" Georgie said.

This got a chuckle from the others. Then Georgie leaned in a little too close, and the dog showed his teeth threateningly. But Nathan gave the dog a sharp command, and the teeth clamped back shut with a click.

Stan looked down at the dog, smiling and rubbing his chin thoughtfully and as he did so. He seemed to notice for the first time the considerable growth of whiskers he'd never had in the Army. "Hmm … maybe must be calling me 'Harry the Person.' With no shave and no bath I am looking … and *smelling* … worse than big crazy dog!"

He let loose with one of his tremendous laughs, which the other men echoed.

"'Harry the Human' would be more accurate," William corrected.

"Or maybe just 'The Hairy Human,'" Georgie got out between giggles.

The dog seemed amused now, looking from person to person as they laughed. He appeared especially interested in Stan. Every time Stan let out a loud spasm of laughter, the dog would look at him and cock his head curiously, before letting out a howl—this one somewhat comical and musical in quality, rather than ear-splitting.

"Look, Stan lad …" Jamie said, hardly able to breathe between gasps of laugher, "he's after knowing his own kind …" which led to more peals of laughter from the group.

By this time, the infectious laughter had spread to all the bystanders, including the grooms, the household servants, and Miss Abbey.

The dog watched as they made their way back to the house, seemingly content to stay where he was on the grass.

Nathan was pleased; the sudden, unexpected intervention of the great, strange hound had swept away the awkwardness of the long-overdue homecoming. Everyone now seemed relaxed and at ease, conversing in a light-hearted manner—all except the overseer, Sickles, who still looked nervous and out of sorts.

When they stepped inside, Nathan took a deep breath, and the memories flooded back in. The house was just as he had remembered it.

English-style furniture—fine, elegantly carved wood covered in horsehair, soft leather, or beautiful brocades; huge, beautiful chandeliers in the common rooms, and intricate rugs over sparkling, polished wood floors throughout; elaborately carved armoires, marble-topped side tables and desks; richly embroidered drapery over and above the windows; fireplaces in nearly every room, most lined with marble. There were many rooms downstairs—and many more bedrooms upstairs. Topping all was a large library, filled with books both ancient and contemporary—another clear sign of wealth. A glossy-black grand piano dominated one side of the great room. Nathan remembered his Momma playing it when he was a boy. He had nearly forgotten that pleasure and had a sudden desire to hear it again.

The maids led the group into a large dining hall, where they'd already set the table with food for the midday meal.

Nathan and his men had spent the previous evening at the fine new hotel at White Sulphur Springs, less than ten miles east of the turnoff to Mountain Meadows. Having arrived there late in the evening, Nathan had decided to stay the night at the hotel rather than pushing ahead in the dark. He'd sent word ahead to inform Miss Abbey they'd be arriving the following day but had received no reply.

And this morning, he'd not been in a hurry to get underway, for once, taking the time to bathe, shave, and otherwise make himself presentable before heading out. He'd also wanted to give

Miss Abbey time to make any preparations she wanted to make, so had told her they'd arrive midday.

He could now see his plan had paid dividends in the form of a nicely prepared meal!

Everyone found a seat, and there were plenty to spare; the huge dining hall and table could easily seat twenty. On this occasion Sickles joined them, though he usually took his meals out in the barracks with the hired hands. The hungry men quickly set upon the meal, the like of which they'd not enjoyed since they started their long train ride from New Orleans. The meal was like a Christmas feast, featuring a baked ham, a roast goose, sweet potatoes, fried okra, and freshly baked rolls, with plenty of butter. Whenever a platter began to run low, one of the black serving maids would quickly whisk it away to the kitchen. Another maid would instantly replace it with a full one.

Megs was ever present with a quick word of instruction, a glance, or a nod, keeping the staff and the meal flowing smoothly. Her skill and dedication impressed Nathan. He always enjoyed seeing someone performing a job they did well, and he suspected she could do this one better than most anyone. At one point she caught him watching her, as she corrected a maid for reaching in front of one of the men to retrieve a tray. She flashed him a grin, before turning back to her duties.

And then it occurred to him to wonder what would happen to *her* if he sold the farm, and it darkened his mood again. Of course, he could keep her as Miss Abbey's personal servant, along with a few others to run her household. He could even free them and pay them a small salary without breaking the law.

But what of the others? Were they any less deserving simply because he didn't know them personally? Were they really all that different from Megs because they were anonymous faces working out in the fields?

He pondered these thoughts for the rest of the meal, and as it was winding down, an idea came to him.

He turned toward Sickles and said, "Mr. Sickles, I would like you to conduct me on a tour of the farm tomorrow morning at sunup. All you men are welcome to join me, of course, if you wish."

"Certainly, sir. It will be my honor. I shall have the horses saddled and waiting in the drive at first light."

"No. No need for horses. We shall have our tour afoot, if you please. I want to see everything up close, and to meet everyone and speak with them at eye level as they go about their work. And please make sure everyone is going about their usual workday. I want to see the working farm, as it is every day, *not* the spit and polish of an inspection tour. Do you understand me?"

"Oh, yes sir, completely, sir. I will instruct the crew to make sure everything is run in the normal manner. We'll be sure it is *especially* normal tomorrow for your tour, sir."

Nathan gave Tom a look that said he didn't think Sickles quite got the spirit of what he was asking for, but he let it drop. *Can't expect too much from the man so soon,* he decided.

"But I was thinking," Sickles said, "it will be a mighty long day of walking, if you want to see it all." He trailed off, in a tone Nathan took to mean he didn't relish the thought of all that walking, obviously not something he did regularly.

"You forget, Mr. Sickles, I was raised on this farm, so am familiar with every inch. And yes, you can assume it will be a *very* long day of walking."

Sickles looked like he might be ill, now that he knew the new master meant to walk the tour, rather than ride. And clearly there could be no shortcuts taken, on account of the master already knowing the extent of the property. "Well then, if you'll excuse me, Master Chambers, I will just go and pass along your instructions to the crew. Then I'll be going back about my business of the day. Thank you ever so kindly, Miss Abbey, for the lovely supper. I am much obliged."

"You are most welcome. And, good day to you, Mr. Sickles," she responded. Her tone with him was formal and cordial, but Nathan noted there was no special warmth in it.

"Yes, good day, Sickles," Nathan added. "See you at sunup."

Sickles nodded and departed the company.

Then Nathan turned to his guests, "Now, young gentlemen, you have traveled long and hard to get here, and you all look … and *smell* the part." He couldn't help but smile, recalling the joking outside about Stan smelling like the dog. It was not far from the truth; they had become a scruffy bunch during their travels.

"I'm sure Momma has laid out rooms and prepared hot baths for you. And after you've finished your bathing and shaving, just do put on whatever you have that's the least dirty. Leave the rest in a pile in the hallway to be laundered."

The men were well used to obeying their Captain's orders; in an instant they'd pushed back their chairs and were rising to their feet. Miss Abbey rose with them.

"And don't become accustomed to being bratty, spoiled little princelings … like *I* used to be around here," he said, giving Megs a wink. "You can all help haul bath water, so Megs and her ladies don't have to do all the heavy lifting."

"Yes, sir, Captain!" Jim snapped a salute and grinned. "We all will make damned sure *you're* the only spoiled-rotten prince in this-here household … *sir!*"

"Dismissed, gentlemen. Once you're cleaned up, please do me the honor of joining me on the back veranda for a smoke and perhaps a sip of whiskey, if there's any to be had in this house."

They filed out of the room, led by one of the maids.

"Momma, it's such a pleasure seeing you looking so well! I've been … *worried* about you lately … though I haven't been able to figure out *why*. It has felt as if … there was something *amiss* with you, but I could never think what it might be.

"But now I can see it isn't so. It seems all my worrying has been for naught."

She looked at him a moment before answering, and he noticed a dark frown cross her face before she suddenly smiled brightly again. "Things have been … *interesting* … here of late, and … not in a *good* way. But I … I don't wish to speak of it today …

"Shall we speak of it on the morrow … *please?* Today I'd love to just revel in the pleasure of your homecoming; I'd not allow any clouds to darken the sunny skies of my delight."

He raised an eyebrow, "Oh … I see. So … *not* entirely my imagination after all?"

"No … not your imagination, say rather … your *intuition*, maybe? But please, dear … let us speak no more of this today."

"Very well, Momma, as you wish. Tomorrow then."

Then, to break the sudden awkward moment of silence between them, he said, "Momma, will you walk with me in the gardens while the men are cleaning up? I would very much enjoy seeing how your flowers are coming along this year," he smiled and offered her his arm.

She took the proffered arm enthusiastically, a bright smile lighting her face. "It would be my great pleasure, Nathan, dear." They strode down the hall toward the back door, leading to the garden path, arm in arm.

ಬಿಐಂ೧ಖಐಂ೧ಖ

The next morning dawned bright and clear, without a cloud in the sky. It was still early summer, so it promised to be a warm day, though not so terribly hot as it might be later in the season.

Nathan walked out the front door, across the veranda and down the steps to the drive, just as the sun was peeking above the mountains on the eastern horizon. His men from Texas followed close behind. They were military men, so being up and dressed before daylight was perfectly routine for them. Sickles, likewise, being a farmhand since his youth, was used to rising with the sun, so he was already waiting there to greet them, appearing well refreshed.

After a brief "good morning," the group set out on their tour. As they moved down the driveway, Tom nudged Nathan with his elbow, and motioned back with his head. Nathan looked back. The sun was still creeping over the horizon and had not yet illuminated the lawn around the house, so at first Nathan could not make out what had caught Tom's eye. Then he saw it; a great hulking four-legged shape in the shadows, moving along behind them, keeping pace at a short distance—Harry the Dog.

Nathan turned back to Tom and smiled in acknowledgment. He had a feeling Harry would be his constant shadow from that day forward.

He turned to Sickles, and said, "Tell me about your crew as we walk, Mr. Sickles."

"Well, sir, we currently have five men, plus myself. A bit short-handed, if you don't mind my saying so … oh, not counting your *new* men, of course, begging your pardon, sir. No offense intended."

"None taken, Mr. Sickles. The men who came with me from Texas, except for Mr. Clark, are only here as guests, so can't be considered part of the crew. And I don't expect Mr. Clark to work the fields."

"Oh. Thank you for clarifying that for me, sir … anyway, as I was saying, sir, five hands. We were planning on adding two or three more for the spring planting, but then the master … your father, the *old* master, I mean … passed away. And … well, your mother didn't want to hire anyone new until you arrived …"

"Ah … and the count of the black slaves?"

"One hundred twelve, of which sixteen are considered too young or too old for serious labor, and eight who are assigned duties in the Big House." He answered this query easily, clearly expecting the question.

"Mr. Sickles, as we go along, I would like you to introduce me to everyone we meet."

"Yes, sir. But the hands are presently scattered about the farm supervising the work, so it may take a while to meet them all."

"No … Mr. Sickles, I mean *everyone* we meet."

"You mean … the negro slaves, sir?"

"Of course. I am their new master. I would know their names."

"Well, yes … certainly, sir. It's just, well, you see … I don't generally work with *all* of them on a regular basis. So … would it be all right if I have them introduce *themselves* … sir?"

Nathan suspected Sickles was feeling out of his element and had *not* expected *this*. The old master likely showed no interest in the names of the slaves. They were just … property … like the cattle or the horses… but even horses have names …

"Yes, that'll be fine. If you don't know the names, we'll just ask them to introduce themselves."

They walked a short distance to where a group of slaves hoed a large vegetable garden. This garden was several acres planted in a mixed variety of vegetables: the household subsistence crops. Nathan looked at Sickles, who blushed, then turned to the slaves and said in a loud voice, "Listen up, y'all ... this here's your new Master. As he comes 'round, you will stop your work, and tell him your name." He looked back at Nathan and shrugged his shoulders apologetically. Nathan smiled, nodded his head, and walked toward the nearest of the workers.

He could see the man was young, probably in his late teens or early twenties. When Nathan stepped up, he stopped hoeing, clasped the tool in front of his chest and said, "Tony, Master." He spoke in a monotone voice, devoid of any emotion, staring straight at the ground in front of his feet.

"Nice to meet you, Tony," Nathan answered in a kindly tone. "Now, will you do me the honor of looking up from the ground, and meeting my eye?"

The other slaves continued working as if nothing out of the ordinary were happening. Nathan found the noise distracting, so he turned from Tony and called out, "Everyone within sound of my voice ... stop working now ... just for a moment ... *please.*"

Slowly, almost reluctantly, the work came to a stop, and a silence fell over the garden.

"Thank you. Please stay where you are now while I will come around to meet each of you. I wish for y'all to look me in the eye and tell me your name. *Please.*"

He turned back toward the young man in front of him. Tony was still looking at his feet, but slowly looked up and met his new master's eyes.

"How old are you, Tony?" Nathan asked quietly.

"I ... doesn't rightly know, Master," Tony answered in a quiet voice, as if he could barely force the words out.

"That's all right, Tony. I expect nobody has ever told you. Perhaps later we can see if we have your birth records in the old master's books. Perhaps we can learn your birthday." He smiled.

Tony smiled back. It occurred to Nathan he probably didn't even know what a "birthday" was, but likely would understand the kindly tone of the offer.

"Yes, sir. That would be … very good, Master …"

Nathan smiled again, "Tony … it was good to meet you."

Nathan continued around the garden, interacting with the other slaves similarly. Most were quiet and shy like Tony, apparently intimidated by their new master. But a few met his eye more easily, a couple of whom even managed a slight smile. This he found encouraging and heartening. He was feeling a little more hopeful.

After he'd finished with the introductions, he began an inspection of the crops in the garden, his men and Sickles in tow. String beans, beets, onions, and cabbages. All looked abundant and healthy, in full early summer growth. It'd been a warm spring, and the plants were responding accordingly. As he moved between the rows, he asked the workers specific questions about the various crops: how they were progressing compared to other years, what the yield might be, if there were any problems with pests, and so on. He stopped and listened respectfully to their answers, often asking additional questions. Occasionally he'd quietly tell the person he was speaking to, "It'd be all right if you'd look at me while we speak … if you wish." To which he sometimes received a shy peek between sentences. This pleased him immensely whenever it happened.

ༀༀༀༀༀༀༀༀༀༀༀༀ

They left the garden and moved on. Nathan turned to Sickles and asked, "Tell me … how is the morale and … *discipline* on the farm?"

"Oh, sir, the men are in most excellent spirits … now *you* have arrived, of course. They were a bit downcast at first, after your Daddy's … er, I mean, after the old master's passing, you understand. But once Miss Abbey informed us of your imminent arrival, why … all the men perked right back up—myself included. And, to answer your other question, no discipline problems among the hands. I don't allow no hard drinking nor carousing, and they're all hard-working lads of good repute."

"Yes, yes, no doubt they are. I'm sure my father would hire no other kind, nor would he put up with any ne'er-do-wells." He smiled recalling his father using that term to describe *him* when he was a young lad. Probably well deserved, he decided, after a moment's reflection.

"But ... what I meant was, what is the morale amongst the *black* workers?"

"The negroes, sir?" Sickles seemed confused. He paused for moment and then gathered himself.

"Well, I guess I never rightly asked them about how they was feeling about things. Never really *occurred* to me, if you excuse my saying so, sir. They seem ... always ... the *same* to me. Never too happy, and never too sad. Just ... always ... the same."

"And discipline?"

"Ah, yes. Discipline is maintained most scrupulously, sir. We have hardly no discipline problems whatsoever, sir. And the few we have are dealt with efficiently and religiously, if I may say so, sir. Your father, the late master, was a stickler for discipline ... as you no doubt already know ..."

"Just so," Nathan answered.

He'd witnessed firsthand that form of *discipline* and the suffering it caused while still just a child. It'd made a strong impression.

They crossed a great field of waist-high cotton to where another group of men worked. These men were on their hands and knees in the dirt between the rows of cotton, pulling out weeds missed by earlier hoeing. A short distance away, another small group could be seen, and yet another further on. One of the white overseers stood near the third group, and there were more workers beyond them.

But Nathan's mood had changed, and this time he strode up to within a few yards of the group and stopped, hands on hips. "I am your new master, please stop working now, and stand where you are."

The men in front of him immediately stopped working and slowly rose to their feet. The other groups in the distance continued their work.

They were a dozen or so men, ranging in age from late teens to men with gray hair. They all turned toward him but stared down at the ground. Nathan said nothing for several moments, but looked them over, one at a time.

"Turn around now, and face the other way, if you please."

They did as ordered.

"Now, remove your shirts please … but hold them; you need not drop them in the dirt."

Obediently they all peeled off their shirts—rough linen homespun, sewn by the black women, Nathan assumed. He stepped closer and examined their backs. His first impression was of the obvious strength in those well-muscled backs; these were clearly men used to a hard day's work. But he'd not had them expose themselves so he could inspect their strength; he had a different purpose in mind.

He walked down the row, examining each man's back closely. Nearly all showed smooth, unblemished skin, shining with the sweat of their labors in the bright spring sun. But three of the men had skin less smooth than the others, and of an uneven color, a more mottled appearance. Leaning closer, Nathan could see this discoloration was caused by raised marks, crisscrossing their broad backs—scars from a whipping. To a soldier, the sight wasn't shocking; the Army knew how to apply the whip when deemed necessary, and Nathan had seen it done many times. He'd even ordered it done a few times, when an offense was so heinous nothing else would serve.

But he knew these men had never committed a crime. They'd done nothing to deserve punishment so severe. He felt the familiar cold hard anger growing and paused a moment to get a firm grip on it.

"Turn around, and face me, please," he said quietly, as he approached one of the men with marks on his back. The young man turned around but continued gazing at the ground.

"Please look me in the eye," he said, in an even voice. The man still bowed his head, and trembled, in obvious terror.

"I'm not going to hurt you, I just want to speak with you ..." Nathan said, in a softer tone.

This seemed to calm the man, and he cautiously looked up and met Nathan's eyes. What he saw there seemed to reassure him. "How can I serve, master?" he said in a soft voice.

"First, I would know your name... and then ... I would know how you came by those marks on your back."

"I's called Ned, sir," he answered the first question, then bowed his head again.

"And the marks ...?"

"Yes, sir ... it was ... I reckon three seasons ago, now. I was feeling sickly, sir, of a morning ... cramping in my middle parts and all ... and not being able to keep down my food, if you understands, sir."

"Yes. And ..."

"Well, sir, I must've not been in my best right mind, what with feeling poorly and all. So instead of going out to the fields, I just crawled myself under the bed and hid so's I wouldn't have to go out and work."

"And...?"

"And ... next thing someone's got ahold of my leg and's dragging me out from under the bed. Don't remember much more, sir. I's not much a mind of remembering the whipping," he shot a quick glance at Sickles, who glared back. Nathan had a strong suspicion about who had laid on the whip, but he let that drop.

Nathan thanked him and moved on to the next man who told a similar story, a moment of indiscretion leading to a back striped and bleeding. A man left incapacitated for several days. The third man's story was not much different.

Nathan noticed Sickles never tried to correct their stories, nor to deny the truth of them, despite a sour expression, like a man who'd just eaten a lemon.

After the third man finished his story, Nathan thanked him, and turned straight toward Sickles, locking eyes with him.

"Mr. Sickles," he said in a firm, tightly controlled voice, "you will instruct the crew there will be no more corporal punishment on this farm from this day forward. Is that clearly understood?"

Sickles nodded in agreement.

"Oh, yes sir … as you say, sir. No more whippings, just as you say … *but …*"

"No whippings, no beatings, no punching, kicking, stabbing, shooting, biting, dragging, nor any other form of physical mistreatment! Is that *quite clear*, Mr. Sickles?"

Nathan was now becoming red in the face with the effort to control his pent-up wrath.

"Yes sir, it will be exactly as you say, sir!" Sickles answered, backing away.

Nathan turned then, head bent as if deep in thought, and started striding away toward the next group of workers. The men filed in behind him, dutifully following along. Then, almost comically, he halted suddenly in mid-stride, and the men following had to react quickly to keep from bumping into him, and each other.

"Oh, sorry! Excuse, me! I nearly forgot something…" he said, and immediately turned and walked right through the middle of the group which quickly divided to get out of his way. With puzzled looks they watched as he walked back toward the row of black men who continued standing in place, obediently, having not yet been told to return to work.

"Just another moment, if you please!"

He went down the line, looking each man in the eye and asking his name before finally dismissing them to their labors.

"I nearly forgot to ask their names," he said by way of explanation, not even noticing the look of amusement on the faces of his men, especially Stan; he had a wide grin and was shaking his head, as if the day was shaping up to be very entertaining.

ᴤᴥᴐᴕᴈᴥᴤᴥᴐᴕᴈᴥᴤᴥᴐᴕᴈ

In the end, it was a *very* long day of walking, talking, and meeting groups of black workers. Of course, they also met the team of white overseers, most of whom seemed earnest, and eager to please their new master.

As the sun was setting, the weary, foot-sore group made their way down the same gravel road they'd arrived on the day before. They could see the Big House in the distance, glowing in the twilight, its oil lamps shining out through many windows. On their right was the first of the slave quarters. Nathan turned aside and walked straight up to the first cabin, stepping up onto the small, covered front porch held up by four posts. It was well within his right as owner and absolute master to simply open the door and walk in. But he stopped and politely knocked.

After a moment, the door opened. The dark face of a middle-aged woman looked out. Her expression instantly changed to shock and surprise as she realized who was standing at her door.

"Excuse me for interrupting your evening, ma'am. Would it be too great an inconvenience if we came in?"

"Oh! Oh my!" she said, covering her mouth. "Oh dear, yes. Please, please come in, masters ..." she answered, backing into the room. "Please masters, forgive the mess, we's just working on the dinner." She tried in vain to straighten the mess on the simple sturdy wooden table in the center of the room, the leavings from preparing the evening meal. Men and women would soon come in from the fields for the humble meal these women had been preparing.

"Please, don't bother yourself, ma'am ... we're not here for an inspection," Nathan paused, realizing she didn't understand the military lingo. "Please, leave off your work a moment, so I may speak with you."

The cabin's inside was just as Nathan remembered from his childhood. A single room with a fireplace on one end for both heat and cooking, a table and four chairs in the middle, and beds around the sides. He knew now the Mountain Meadows cabins were nicer than most, on account of their wooden floors, rather than just dirt. And each cabin had a single, one-paned window on the north side to let in light. Also, they'd built the walls tightly to keep the weather out. The inside walls had been whitewashed to make the room relatively bright, despite just the one window. A row of large nails along one wall at about head height served as hooks for hanging various items, including everything from cooking utensils to straw hats.

Despite the mess from preparing the meal, the cabin was generally in a cleanly state, the floors having been recently swept.

Three women were currently in the small cabin, and six young children huddled together in one of the corners, wedged in behind a bed. The children appeared startled and frightened by the sudden appearance of all these large, white men.

Nathan repeated the now-familiar pattern, talking with each of the women, asking them to look him in the eye and give their name. Then giving them a friendly smile, asking a question or two and then thanking them before moving on to the next.

Stan, meanwhile, had approached the group of children. He knelt down on the opposite side of the bed from where they'd gathered and leaned across, putting his elbows on the bed. They'd covered the bed in rough, homespun cloth, like the clothing the men wore out in the fields. But the bed was neatly made, and the few holes in the blanket had been carefully patched. He nodded to himself in approval. He'd stayed in much worse quarters and appreciated when people who had but little made the best of what they had. Then he grinned broadly at the children, showing his great wide smile. Stan was so huge, and his smile so comical, the children all smiled.

"So tell me how it is the beautiful young children are doing this evening?" he asked, with another wide grin.

A small girl who looked to be about four years old immediately laughed out loud. She grinned brightly and said, "Why do you talks so funny, Master Giant?"

Stan laughed, interrupting the Captain mid-question with one of the women. Nathan looked over, and seeing it was just Stan up to his usual tricks, shook his head, and went back to his business.

"I will tell you sweet little children what it is makes us *giants* talk in the funny way. You see, long time ago, when I was little giant, like you, I was living in faraway place … hmm … *magic* place people in America call 'Russia.' Is far away across *big* water and is of great coldness; much ice and snow … not so warm as here. There in Russia all peoples ... giant, *and* normal size, are talking funny, like me!"

The little girl who had first spoken replied with a broad smile of her own, "Master Giant, I ain't never heard of no place called ... what was it again? *Rushy?*"

"Russia."

"My Granddaddy once did tell me about a faraway place acrossed the big oceans. He was calling it 'Africa'. He was saying it was where all of us black-skinned peoples come from, and he says there ain't no white people there. You ever hear of such a place as that, Master Giant?"

"Oh, yeah ... sure, little missy, I have heard such tales of Africa. But never have I been there. Perhaps one day. And your Granddaddy told it a-rightly ... all the black folks are from there ... but white men are there now, too they say. Too bad, I say."

"Well, Master Giant, I reckon if'n all the white men was as friendly as you, then it'd be all right for them to be in ol' Africa."

By now the soldiers had gathered around the bed and seemed to enjoy the exchange between Stan and the little children.

"Hey ... you children must be knowing we giants can do the magic? *No?* Well, then I must show you ..."

Stan looked over and winked at the men. They had seen his favorite "magic" tricks enough times to know exactly what was coming.

William said, "Oh, Stan. You're not going to do *that* old trick, are you?"

But Stan just nodded his head, and said, piously, "Now, William, these young children ain't never before seen *real* giant-magic, from faraway land of Russia. So it will be pleasure for them, no?"

"Sure, sure, Stan. If you must ... it's just we've all seen it a thousand times before."

But Tom encouraged him, "Go ahead, Stan. Show them the *giant-magic.*"

"Yes, *sir!* Children, this man is special kind of master called *sergeant*. This means even us *giants* must do as he says!" He snapped a salute at Tom, comically, prompting a giggle from the children, and a roll of the eyes from Tom.

Stan put on a serious face and leaned in toward the first little girl. "So sweet little girl … oh, excuse my very much rudeness … we have not been properly acquainted … what is your name being, please?"

"I'm Susie. Pleased to meet you master, sir!" she said, in a nicely polished manner. Clearly, she'd been coached on it. One of the older women looked over at her and gave a nod of approval. Stan chuckled, and the other men smiled appreciatively.

"It is very happy I am to be meeting you too, Susie. I am called Stan."

"So now you see, little girl called Susie, from all the traveling in faraway lands we giants have learned much magic. I will show you a little of such. Like …" he suddenly leaned forward and stuck his fingers in one of her ears, "we can make monies appear in the very strangest places …"And he showed her a small coin he had pulled, from all appearances, directly out of her ear. "Like little girl's ears!"

He made a great flourish, handing the girl the coin. It was a bright silver coin, with some king's head on one side, and frilly looking leaves and flowers on the other. The girl gasped as she held it in her palm. It was the most beautiful and interesting thing she'd ever seen. The other children gathered around to stare in amazement.

A young woman who'd been watching, immediately said, "You give that right back, Susie! That don't properly belong to you."

But Stan held up his hand, "No, is all right, madam. The coin is from little-girl Susie's ear, so by rightful laws of magic … and of giants … the coin is now belonging to Susie." Then he stood and made a bow.

"Well, all right, if you say so, master. But it don't seem right to me, a little girl taking coins she ain't never earned."

"Is okay, madam, is coin from the *magic*, not from the *man!*" Then he once again smiled that broad, irresistible grin, and the woman couldn't help but smile in answer. Stan then pulled coins from all the *other* children's ears. By the end of it all were laughing and squealing with delight, mingled with Stan's loud laughter echoing around the room.

Nathan concluded his interviews, and turned to the men, "Well, clearly I've been one-upped by our resident magician, and giant. So on that note, I'd say it has been enough of a day. Let's head back to the house. We will meet the rest of the women and children tomorrow."

He turned toward the women, said "Good night," and headed for the door.

Stan stood up from where he'd been kneeling next to the bed on the floor. The children looked up at his gigantic stature with pure awe and joy. Clearly, they'd never imagined a man so enormous, so jolly, and so *magical*.

ঙ৵৯৩৩৪ঙ৵৯৩৩৪ঙ৵৯৩৩৪

The men headed toward the Big House. Sickles took his leave politely, saying, "Good night, master. Thank you for spending the day with me."

"Thank you very kindly for the tour, Mr. Sickles."

Sickles departed for the barracks of the white farmhands.

Nathan and the rest of the men walked down the road in the fading light, gravel crunching beneath their boots, toward the welcoming lights of Mountain Meadows' manor house. Slinking along in the tall grass at the side of the road a few paces behind was a now familiar, four-legged shadow.

Chapter 2. Talk of Many Things

"The time has come,
the Walrus said,
to talk of many things;
of shoes, and ships,
and sealing wax,
of cabbages, and kings!"
– Lewis Carroll
(Through the Looking Glass)

Wednesday June 12, 1860 – Greenbrier County, Virginia:

After their meal, the men once again relaxed on the veranda, sipping whiskey and smoking cigars.

But this time Nathan didn't sit with them, explaining he wanted to get caught up on all the family news with Miss Abbey. So mother and son sat at their own table on the veranda, a dozen yards away from where the other men sat. But while the men chatted and joked in boisterous good humor, Nathan and Abbey had a much darker, more serious conversation.

First, Nathan told a brief version of their various adventures since leaving Texas, expecting and receiving motherly chastisement for risking his life in Mexico rescuing the girl. She made him pull up his shirt and show her the wound he'd received from Gold-tooth's knife. And though it was now almost completely healed, and only a long, bright pink scar, it still made Miss Abbey gasp and flinch involuntarily. He shrugged his shoulders and smiled, pulling the shirt back down.

Then it was Abbey's turn to tell Nathan about her rough treatment at the hands of their unfriendly neighbor. He scowled darkly when she finally described how Walters had taken away her preferred seats at church.

"The *scoundrel* … I can't believe a man would behave in such an ignominious manner right in front of all his neighbors. Well,

31

I'll soon put a stop to *that* nonsense, I promise you!" A dark frown creased his brow.

"Yes, I know you will dear, I have never doubted it. But it's a shame you had to return to this ridiculous *feud*, which you had no hand in starting."

"Yes … and I truly knew nothing about it. Daddy never wrote me, and you never spoke of it in your letters. I can only vaguely remember ever meeting the senior Walters when I was a very young child, and have no recollection whatever of the younger one. Which is odd, since I typically remember anyone I've ever met in great detail."

"It's probably that inscrutable, bland expression of his. Since he never shows any emotion, there was probably nothing interesting about him to stick in your memory."

"Maybe … could be. Anyway … though I don't intend to put up with any more of his foolishness, I also don't intend to continue the feud. Perhaps now that I'm home he'll be open to a compromise over the silly property-line issue, and we can be done with it."

"Yes … let's hope so …" Her brow furrowed as she paused in reflection. "Nathan … I can't tell you why, but … he *scares* me. I mean in the very *physical* way … like a man who'd hurt you on purpose and enjoy it. I've begun to believe he's a very dangerous man. Don't ever turn your back on him or trust him, Nathan dear. I would die if anything bad happened to you, after you've come all this way at my request."

Nathan sat back and chuckled, shaking his head. "Momma … I've spent the last twenty years fighting. Firstly, in a real war where men died in droves. Then dealing with Indians and outlaws, some of whom would rather kill you slowly and painfully than shake your hand. And for nothing more than the sick pleasure of it.

"I hear you, Momma, and I believe you; he very well may be a *very dangerous* man. But *really*, Momma … you needn't fear for *me*. *He's* the one who ought to be afraid. I am also a *very dangerous* man. I know you won't want to hear this but … I've killed *many* men in my lifetime, Momma. And most were far more dangerous than Walters, believe me. I'm … no longer the skinny, innocent, hot-headed thirteen-year-old boy who left here twenty years ago …"

She smiled, unshaken by his revelations. She wasn't entirely naïve and had always had a pretty good idea the type of life-or-death adventure he'd been living out in Texas. But his obvious strength and dauntless courage buoyed up her spirits, "Yes … *that* I can clearly see, Nathan, dear … That I can clearly see.

"I *knew* all would be well once you returned home. And never have hopes and wishes proven more true!"

⚜⚜⚜⚜⚜⚜⚜⚜⚜⚜

While Nathan sat on the veranda talking with Miss Abbey, he had no inkling of the effect his little "inspection tour" had had across the farm. Except for those staying in the Big House, the inhabitants of Mountain Meadows were abuzz with talk and activity, triggered by the many startling happenings of the day.

For the white farmhands in the worker's barracks, it was a mixture of anxiety, curiosity, and confusion about what it all meant.

"I'm tellin' y'all, them're his exact words 'No more beatin's, no-how!'" Sickles repeated, getting heated by the continued questioning from the other hands.

"But, Mr. Sickles," complained Dan, a skinny, freckle-faced and red-headed young man, "how's we supposed to enforce discipline if'n they's to be no beatin's? T'aint natural, I say."

Two of the others nodded their agreement.

"Well, that may well be, but them's the new master's orders, and we best be carrying them out or there'll be hell to pay. He may seem kindly and all, but I seen a fire in his eyes. He's got a temper, I tell you, like the rumors said. And that big foreign fellow he has with him scares the devil out of me."

It was a statement to which they could all agree.

"I'm more a'feared of that tame Injun he done brought back with him," said Frank, another young farmhand, who'd been at Mountain Meadows for several years now. "I've heard all kind of

33

tales of them wild savages, eating the flesh off'n captive men, and such. He's got a mean, killer look, that one."

"Well, then I suggest you don't go and do anything to anger the new master, or he's like to turn his Injun loose on you."

Sickles decided he could at least use the fear of the newcomers to get his men to shut up and accept the new orders.

"Don't worry, boys. Once he's a bit settled in, I reckon he'll see the need for sterner measures. Things'll be back to normal in no time, y'all just wait and see. But for now, *DO AS HE SAYS!* Y'all understand me?"

"Yes, Mr. Sickles ..." they all answered, respectfully.

Though he'd been disappointed when Miss Abbey recovered from the arsenic he'd put in her tea, Sickles figured it hadn't been a total disaster. *At least no one's the wiser,* he thought, *so I still have my job and can continue collecting my pay. But this new master ... seems like he could be a problem. Maybe Walters will offer even more to get rid of him.* It was a happy thought that made the odd happenings of the day easier to accept.

The white farmhands continued to discuss the odd behavior of their strange new master, and his unusual companions, well into the night. It made for a very groggy-eyed crew in the morning.

ಐ೮೦೧౩ಐ೮೦೧౩ಐ೮೦೧౩

Nathan's "inspection tour" also affected the slaves, of course. But amongst them it was a muddled confusion of bewilderment, skepticism, fear, and even a little hope — generally scoffed at.

Rumors ran like wildfire through the cabins that night. Men ran from cabin to cabin to discuss the day's events with others who may have heard or seen something other than what they had.

The stories were muddled after being passed around from mouth to mouth; it was unclear what the new master might turn out to be. Was he what the rumors had made of him before his arrival, or was he ... something *different?*

"Those eyes, those eyes ..." was the most commonly repeated phrase, along with "It felt like he looked right into me." Many found the experience terrifying and mistrusted the new master's motives. They thought him some kind of devil trying to give them "the evil eye," or to discern their thoughts by staring them down.

But there was one singular event witnessed by nearly a dozen men, all of whom gave a similar story no one could deny: the new master had become enraged at the sight of whip marks on the backs of the slaves. And he'd commanded the white overseers, "No more beatings, never, ever!"

But most of those who hadn't seen the new master's fury and heard his words in person wouldn't be swayed. This majority still believed the new master was up to something—a man to be feared, despite his kindly seeming act. Ironically, even Ned, the man whose whipped back had started the whole "no more beatings" incident, was a skeptic. He scoffed at the idea the new master would change things. "All's just talk. Ain't nothin' gonna change. White master still holds the whip, and uses it whenever he pleases," was all he'd say on the subject.

Other than the one cabin Nathan had visited the evening before, the women, children, and a few old men who stayed in the cabins during the day hadn't yet met the new master face to face. To them, the talk going around was amazing and almost unbelievable. One of the new master's men was a great giant, like Goliath, from some foreign land across the sea who worked magic spells. Another was a captive Indian from the wild lands away out West who could freeze a man's heart with a stare. Those who'd been left out of the day's excitement awaited the new dawn with feelings of trepidation and dread … mixed with a hint of excitement.

Throughout the camp at every cabin, they continued to discuss the odd behavior of their strange new master, and his unusual companions, well into the night. It made for a very groggy-eyed group of workers in the morning.

ЖОЮCЖОЮCЖОЮCЖОЮCЖ

It was a much shorter "inspection tour" the next morning. The only part of the farm they'd not yet visited were the remaining slave cabins.

Sickles did not join them this morning, returning to his regular duties. Nathan had told him his services would not be required on today's tour. The foreman seemed relieved.

This time, their appearance at the slave quarters was *not* unexpected. The firestorm of discussion, conversation, and speculation raging the evening before had concluded two things for certain. One—for good or ill, the new master was cut from a *whole* different cloth than any white man they'd yet experienced. And two—he was set on personally meeting every slave, looking them in the eye, and asking their name! Old men, women, and young children were not exempt from his attention—as they generally *were* with the other white overseers.

So when the men arrived at the first cabin, they were surprised to find the inhabitants, all women and children, standing outside, lined up neatly in a row. Nathan thought they looked cleaner and dressier than anyone had the day before. Several even wore shoes!

This time as Nathan approached them, each woman raised her head, looked him straight in the eye, and stated her name, "Betty, master. Suzy, master. Jenny, master," and so on. Nathan glanced over at Tom and raised an eyebrow. Tom shrugged and smiled.

The children behaved the same, clearly having been coached. But a few of them smiled and looked over at Stan expectantly. Obviously, word had gotten around. But Nathan had warned him there'd be no "magic" this morning, so he could finish the tour without undue delay. But that didn't stop him from grinning and winking at the little ones, triggering several bouts of giggling.

The reception at the remaining cabins was much the same, with everyone neatly lined up outside, names stated like clockwork, and the occasional bright smile from the children.

When it was over, Nathan felt encouraged. It seemed to him these people were responding positively to the little bit of attention and kindness he'd paid them. *My God, what have we done to these people?* he thought once again … *that they should be so pleased by the simplest acts of kindness and respect …*

Later, after another excellent and filling midday meal, Nathan called a meeting of the men who'd come with him from Texas. They pulled two tables together on the veranda, and enough chairs for all to sit.

"Gentlemen, I've said it before, but I wanted to thank you again for escorting me here from Texas, ensuring a safe return to my home and Miss Abbey."

"Well, hell, Captain … it seemed more like you were the one doing the 'escorting' than the other way around! Us fellas seemed determined to get into mischief just so's you could pull us out again!" Georgie said, grinning and looking around at the others, who nodded agreement.

Nathan smiled.

"Y'all are good men, and I was very grateful and honored having you with me every step of the way. There's nothing beats knowing the man next to you will kill for you when necessary and knows you'll do the same for him."

There were serious looks now, and several nods of agreement.

"And it also gave me pleasure to pay you a small wage during our travels, though several of you protested that it wasn't necessary. I thought it'd be good if you had a little pocket money when you got where you were going.

"But now … I'd like to put a new proposition to you. Since coming home I've discovered things are … not exactly as I'd hoped. It seems there's trouble with one of our neighbors. He's been … hmm … let's just say he's been treating Miss Abbey with less respect than I would expect and demand. And it seems he's intent on causing further mischief."

This news brought dark looks from the men, Miss Abbey's joyful kindness and warm welcome having completely won them over from the first. They were already feeling a motherly affection for her.

"So I'd like to ask you men to stay on a while longer, if you'd be willing. Tom and Jim have already agreed to it, but I'd like you others to stay as well, if you would. I intend to pay y'all twice the wages you were earning in the Army, if that'll help sway you.

"Men ... I know some of y'all are eager to see your own families and homes, and I promise if you want to do so, there'll be no hard feelings. Right now, it's ... one of those times a man could use a few good hands at his side in case things turn ugly. You can think on it a while if you'd like ..."

William gave his answer before the Captain had even stopped speaking. "Captain, even if I had family waiting for me, which I don't since my father passed away a few years back, I'd still say 'yes.' If you need me, it would be my honor to help you."

"Yes, yes ... of course, Captain!" Stan butted in. "As William says ... if you are needing us to do little things for you, like ... hmm ... kill someone, maybe?" He shrugged, "Who am I to say 'no'?" He grinned broadly, and Nathan couldn't help grinning back.

He turned to Georgie and Jamie, "Georgie, I know you have a large family back in Pennsylvania. If you feel the urge to get back to them, I'll understand."

"Heck, Captain ... I'm the middlest of seven children—four boys and three girls!" He laughed, "I doubt my folks'll even notice if I show up at home or not."

Jamie elbowed him in the ribs, "Hell, Georgie lad, they ain't *yet* noticed you been gone these two years past!"

They laughed, and Georgie nodded his agreement.

Then Jamie spoke for them both. "Captain, we're after hoping you'd ask us to stay on longer. So ... we're your men, as ever we been."

"Yep, he says it true, Captain," Georgie nodded.

Their loyalty touched Nathan, and he could feel his eyes start to bead up, but he fought down the urge.

Finally, he turned to the last of their company, "Billy?"

But Billy looked at him as if he didn't understand what was being asked of him, "Yes, Captain?"

"Will you stay on and ... help out as needed?"

He seemed confused, tilting his head as if trying to puzzle out what the Captain meant. Then he shrugged, "I never thought about going anywhere else than where you and the other men go, Captain ... if that's what you're asking."

Nathan smiled, and leaned over patting Billy on the back with affection, "Good man!"

"Thank y'all, men. It means a lot to me. And … I must admit … I'm happy it postpones having to say goodbye." He could feel the tears building up again, so he looked away from their earnest faces for a moment.

Then, in typical military fashion, Nathan laid out his plans for the next day, and his more general plans for the near future. Tom and Jamie were to saddle up horses and the mule and ride into town at first light—Tom to visit the county clerk to deal with some kind of "paperwork" the two had apparently discussed before, and Jamie to go with him, but for a different purpose.

"When we were still in the hotel at White Sulphur Springs, while you were bathing and shaving, I took the liberty of drawing up the papers you wanted," Tom said. "So if the clerk approves them without too many changes, I should be able to conclude my business in short order."

"Excellent, Tom! I want to get that taken care of as soon as possible so we can get about … doing what needs to be done. Jamie … I want you to take the mule along in hopes you'll be able to purchase something for me."

"Yes, sir. And what would I be after buying?"

"Guns."

At *that* word, the interest of the rest of the men perked up, and they listened intently for the explanation they knew was coming.

"Look, I know y'all traveled a long way to leave the Army behind. But for better or worse, it did teach you some useful skills, one of which was how to shoot a rifle. I don't expect any *real* trouble, mind, but it seems to me a man who is prepared for trouble is best able to avoid it. And I think it'd be a shame to let all that valuable army training go to waste and let your shooting skills deteriorate. I'd like Jamie to go into town and see if there are any serviceable rifles to be found, along with powder and bullets, of course. I've been thinking we'd set up a regular target-shooting regimen, say one or two times a week for a couple of hours, to keep the skills sharp. I would even encourage the occasional hunting expedition, which will provide some entertainment, as well as food for the larder. And of course … if there *is* any trouble, we'll be ready!"

The men seemed well pleased with this idea. Billy Creek said nothing, but smiled knowingly, as he looked at the Captain.

"Do you find something amusing, Billy?" Nathan asked.

"No, Captain. Just … not surprised. You can take a lion to a farm, but that don't make him a sheep!"

Nathan felt a little twinge of guilt, wondering if he was overreacting to Miss Abbey's revelations about their unfriendly neighbor. And the purchase of rifles and enough ammunition for regular target practice might be an unnecessary expense for the farm. It could also be a sign of his unwillingness, or inability, to give up his soldierly lifestyle and habits. But then he shrugged, inwardly rationalizing, *need to keep the men's morale up, and this is as good way to do it as any. And … there's also Walters, and whatever he's up to …*

Turning back to Jamie he said, "Let's do a quick survey of what my old Daddy has accumulated around here before you leave in the morning. There may still be a few serviceable firearms."

He didn't hold out much hope. His father had never shown much interest in guns, probably because they wouldn't help bring the crops in. And he'd had little interest in hunting—not from any compassion for the game animals or anything of the like. To him it was simply an inefficient way of putting food on the table. The energy spent on that activity was better spent raising chickens, hogs, or cattle, which made much better eating than any wild game animals. As for sport, he had no use for the idea. And as a result, young Nathan had never been much exposed to guns, other than the occasional hunting expedition with one of the neighbor boys. That was, until he enrolled in the military academy at West Point. There, and later in the regular Army, it was a whole different story; guns of all types and sizes were as much a part of everyday life as eating or sleeping.

He also went over the near-future roles he envisioned for each of the men in turn.

Georgie, with his experience as a blacksmith, would be responsible for maintenance of all the farm tools and equipment,

with the help of Jamie, when he wasn't maintaining firearms —
which Nathan pointed out, would *not* be a full-time occupation,
to which Jamie responded with a pout.

Jim would oversee the upkeep and maintenance of all the
buildings on the farm. William and Stan would serve as his
construction workers. Stan shrugged his shoulders good-
naturedly, saying "Well, is better than the pulling out of weeds."
To which William readily agreed.

William would also serve as farm doctor when needed. And
being a scholar, he might be called upon to help Tom on various
business-related projects from time to time.

"Jim, I want you to start with those slave quarters … it seems
to me they are in a rather shabby state of repair compared to the
other buildings."

"From what I seen yesterday, I'd have to agree with you there,
Captain," Jim responded agreeably.

Everyone already knew Tom would continue to play the role
of the Captain's right-hand man. He'd take care of the business of
the farm and make sure the Captain's plans and ideas were
properly implemented, so nothing was said on *that* subject.

"For now, I'll let the old crew continue the day to day running
of the farm. They have more knowledge and experience in that
regard than the rest of us. But eventually it may make sense for
each of us to become more acquainted with the farming activities,
so we can assist as needed and fill in when necessary."

The men were agreeable, and relieved he'd assigned them
tasks they already knew how to do, rather than immediately
immersing them into the unknown realm of agriculture.

But then it came time for Billy Creek. Nathan turned to him
and said, "Billy, I'm honored and pleased you've come with us
and agreed to stay. But I must admit, I've been puzzling over what
it is you will do here. What will a *scout* do, on a farm in western
Virginia?" He had almost said "Indian scout" but had thought
better of it. No need to point out the obvious; Billy was now
probably the only Indian within hundreds, if not thousands of
miles of this place.

"He will *scout*," Billy answered easily with a shrug of his shoulders, as if it were the most obvious thing on earth. "You said it yourself, Captain—and you are sometimes wise, for a white man. 'A man prepared for trouble may not find any.' The scout will explore the woods and the hills, until every tree and bush is known, and the surrounding farms and towns, until every enemy is also known."

"Well, that sounds fine to me, Billy. But I'm praying we won't have *that* kind of trouble here in civilization, though I agree it's best we be ready for it."

"Ha!" Billy snorted a short, derisive laugh. "Already I have heard things said in the towns. Men in the East are killers, same as the West. Same as anywhere. They try to fool themselves they are not. They say 'civilized,' as if that makes them a *different* kind of men. But I have seen them. I have looked in their eyes. Civilized or not, *killers* ... all the same." He folded his arms and leaned back in his chair, contentedly blowing puffs of smoke into the air from his cigar.

Nathan nodded. "Oh ... one more thing," he added, "since y'all have agreed to stay on as employees, it won't do for y'all to continue staying in the Big House after tonight. I can't be seen showing such favoritism, and it wouldn't be proper. Out to the workers' barracks for you, then. As Mr. Sickles said, we are currently short-handed, so there are spare bunks enough for all." But as soon as he said it, he knew Billy Creek would never stay in the barracks with the others. He had never done so in the Army, always finding his own place to sleep; no one was sure quite where.

"I should add, however, Tom will stay in the Big House. I need him with me in the evenings to work out the business and financial aspects of the farm. It'd be too inconvenient otherwise."

Nobody seemed surprised or put-off by any of this; they were soldiers, and were used to rough living. With the possible exception of William, the soldiers felt uncomfortable and constrained inside Miss Abbey's beautiful white house, feeling obligated to act a bit too formal and polite, like children forced to wear neat, uncomfortable clothes to church on Sunday, sitting quietly and still on hard benches. The workers' barracks would be more relaxed, and more suitable to their preferred manner of living.

Thursday June 14, 1860 – Greenbrier County, Virginia:

The next morning, the men gathered on the front steps of the veranda. William and Stan were blowing on cups of steaming hot coffee they'd acquired in the kitchen. The sun was coming up in a crystal-clear blue sky, promising another warm early-summer day. But for the moment, the morning air was still cool and moist from the night, the dew sparkling faintly on the grass. There was a pleasant, earthy smell that the men appreciated after their long tour in the scorching dryness of West Texas.

Tom and two grooms, Sampson and Phinney, walked up the drive with a pair of horses and the mule. The horses were saddled and bridled, and the mule rigged up with a pack saddle. The others greeted them with a friendly "good morning."

They were still missing the Captain, plus Georgie and Jamie. They weren't surprised, knowing from the plans of the previous evening they were even now conducting their audit of the household firearms, such as they were.

Billy Creek found this incredible; a place holding hundreds of people in a perpetual state of bondage against their will, had no serviceable firearms—at least not any loaded and readily available to the white masters. In fact, no weapons were generally in evidence at all during the normal working day, beyond the sour looks and sharp tongues of the white overseers. After some thought, it occurred to Billy that the black men could simply walk away whenever they wished, and no one could stop them. But then, he wondered, *But, where will they go?* Wherever they went white men would hunt them down and bring them back, with whips and chains. It actually seemed a very effective system, now that he thought on it. White men didn't have to do a thing to hold the slaves, as long as they all stuck together.

Today Billy, unlike the others, dressed in his rough travel clothes, freshly washed and pressed, to his amusement. It would take a while to lose the human scent of soap now clinging to them. He carried an ash bow, and a quiver of arrows on his back, along with a small backpack—the barest essentials for the expedition he had planned. Conspicuous in its absence was his gun holster and Colt revolver. None of the white men would've ever ventured off into the wilds on their own without a firearm and plenty of powder and ammunition, but Billy was indifferent about it. He much preferred the stealthier weapons he could use without so much "smoke and noise." Toward that end, he also carried his small hunting knife in a brown leather sheath at his waist.

The other men had also abandoned carrying their sidearms after their arrival on the first day. Each now carried a knife in a sheath, same as Billy. There were two reasons for this. First, carrying a loaded pistol every day involved a lot of maintenance. In this humid climate the powder would quickly become fouled if they didn't fire the gun occasionally. And cleaning caked-on powder from the cylinders was a tedious and time-consuming activity. Even in Texas, where the climate was drier, just the sweat from a full day in the saddle or hiking through the brush could foul the powder. That was why they'd ideally fire off any unspent rounds at the end of the day if they could do so—much easier to let the gun do the work!

But the second, and probably more important reason, was they felt a little foolish going about fully armed in a place so civilized and pacific. It wouldn't do to have such supposedly fierce fighting men look as if they were afraid of their own shadows. Like Billy, they had opted to carry hunting knives on their belts instead. No shame in that. A knife was not just a weapon, but was also a convenient all-purpose tool, especially on a farm.

Even the Captain now carried his great Bowie knife on his belt. They were a little surprised at that; it was *not* a typical hunting or working knife, but rather a large, serious fighting weapon. Someone, probably Stan, had nick-named it "the Captain's tail." Nathan often carried it with the sheath all the way around at his back out of the way, where it hung straight down like a tail. They had given him a little good-natured teasing about it the first day he wore it on the farm. But he'd shrugged and said he felt naked without it, which ruined their fun.

"So ... fixing to go hunting today, Billy?" Jim asked curiously, noticing the bow and arrows for the first time.

"Scouting."

"Ah, yes, of course. And when shall we expect your return, mister?"

"Before five suns, I reckon."

"And when shall we send a party to recover your body, and where shall we look for it?" Jim asked, in the grim, humorous, nonchalant manner of the Army. But the question had a serious point; if a scout didn't return when expected from a mission in the wilderness, it was most likely a body recovery mission, rather than a rescue.

"Hmm ... maybe ten suns ... and this time I shall be up those mountains to the east, maybe so far as to see the other side."

"Very well. Good hunting, scout." Jim gave the standard response, the other men echoing the same, "Good hunting, Billy."

Billy nodded, turned, and trotted across the grass, kicking up little wisps of dew with his boots. He quickly disappeared into the trees surrounding the house, heading out toward the rising sun and the mountains looming in the east.

A few moments later, the front door opened and the Captain stepped out, followed by Jamie and Georgie.

"Where's Billy?" Nathan immediately asked, scanning the group. The men appreciated his habit of noticing the smallest detail, and it had not slipped since leaving Texas.

"Scouting," Jim answered.

"Ah, yes, of course. Which way did he go?"

"East."

Nathan stood for a moment, looking toward the rising sun, as if absorbing the answer.

"Yes ... that makes sense. The *mountains* ... that *would* be the most interesting thing to him, having spent his whole life in Texas. Hills, and ravines, and such there ... but nothing like our

45

mountains here in western Virginia. I'm sure he's been itching with curiosity."

"Yes, I expect you have the right of it, Captain. Expects to be out for five days, ten at the outside."

"Very good. Thank you sarge ... er, Jim."

"Any luck, Captain?" Tom asked, inquiring about their audit of the farm's firearms.

"Not much. A very nice Kentucky long-rifle, a fine firearm for sure—thin and elegant looking. They were used very effectively in the first war against the British. 'Able to shoot the eye out of a squirrel at four hundred yards,' if you believe such things. But not really a military weapon; can't take any kind of abuse. Very slow to load a ball in the old days because of the rifling—before they invented the Minni ball. And, of course, no way to mount a bayonet!"

He made the last statement as if it put an end to any arguments in favor of the weapon.

"Still, a very pretty thing. It's engraved—apparently a gift from Governor Wise! I knew my father had been in the state legislature but didn't know he'd been close with the former governor. Daddy never wrote letters, and Momma never mentioned it in any of hers."

"Oh! That's impressive. Anything else?" Jim asked.

"A couple of fowling pieces—very old and worn. Flintlocks, if you can believe it, lads," Jamie answered this time, stepping up to get into the conversation. Flintlocks had been replaced by the more reliable percussion cap technology more than thirty years earlier.

"And an old flintlock dueling gun," Georgie put in, not wanting to be left out of the report. "The only pistol we found."

"Yes ... my Daddy was apparently braver than I knew," Nathan said with a smile. "He faced down Harry the Dog with only *that* old thing in hand!"

They shared a laugh. The flintlock pistol was notoriously unreliable; smooth bored, it was extremely inaccurate past a few yards, if it bothered to fire at all when the trigger was pulled. They'd been used for dueling in the not-too-distant past, and typically both shooters would miss their mark at twenty paces—everyone's honor satisfied, and no one the worse for the wear! But there'd been a few well-publicized cases in which at least one of the duelists had *not* missed, the tragic death of the great founding father Alexander Hamilton at the hands of Vice President Aaron Burr being the most infamous. This had eventually put an end to the practice.

"Speaking of the dog," William said, motioning his head back toward the north corner of the house. There the great beast was, yawning and stretching.

Tom chuckled. "Your new shadow, Captain." And with that comment, he swung himself into the saddle. Jamie handed his now-empty coffee cup to Georgie and strode forward to take the reins of the other horse from one of the grooms. He too swung up into the saddle. The second groom handed him the lead for the pack mule, which he looped around the saddle horn.

"Good day to you, gentlemen … Captain," Tom said, tipping his hat.

"See you this evening, Tom … Jamie," Nathan answered.

The two turned their horses and trotted up the drive, the mule following along behind.

"Jim, take Stan and William and go down to the shed we saw yesterday with the spare lumber and tools, and see what you can do for these cabins. Start thinking about what else you will need and make a list for Tom. Next time he goes into town he can take a wagon and get more materials."

"Captain!" Jim said with a salute, immediately pivoting on his heels and striding out in the direction of the utility buildings. "Volkov, Jenkins … with me," he said by way of an order as he strode away, never bothering to look in their direction. They looked at each other briefly, smiled, shrugged their shoulders, and turned to follow "Sergeant" Jim.

"Georgie, go on down to the sheds as well, and start your inspection of the equipment and tools to see what might need maintenance, repair, or replacement. Like I said to Jim, start a list of any supplies you might need from town."

"Yes, sir." Georgie resisted the urge to salute, and instead flashed a smile, one Nathan happily returned.

He was proud of his men and pleased with the way things were going so far. But the decision on what to ultimately do with the farm ... and the slaves ... still loomed large.

Once Georgie had departed, he realized he'd made plans for everyone but himself. He thought for a moment and decided he hadn't yet inspected the barns and pens where the livestock was kept, so he turned and headed in that direction. A dozen yards behind, a large, four-legged shape got up off the ground from under a lilac bush and followed along.

A few minutes later, Nathan was leaning on a wood railing. Inside the pen, a half-dozen good-sized hogs rolled in the dirt or rooted in a trough for any food they might have missed at the pre-dawn feeding. A dozen or so little piglets scampered about between the adults, adeptly avoiding being trampled by their gargantuan elders.

As he gazed at the hogs Nathan heard a commotion around the corner of the barn connected to the hog pen—dogs barking furiously, and *not* Harry this time.

He walked around the corner to see what all the noise was about. There he found Harry the Dog sitting on the ground staring into a pen with a higher fence, and tighter slats than the pen holding the hogs. Inside, five large hounds barked energetically at Harry, who stared them down, baring his huge teeth in a silent snarl.

"Sorry for all the noise, master. They does this all the time—old Harry baiting the others, and them worked up to a lather, howling back at him in great fury. I ain't yet figured any way to put a stop to it."

It was one of the grooms he'd first met trying to throw a rope around Harry.

"Cobb, isn't it?"

"Yes, sir. That's right, Cobb, master." He smiled, as if pleased the new master had remembered his name so quickly.

"Well, Cobb, it appears there's no great love between Harry and these other hounds. Why are they kept caged like this, anyway?"

"Oh, sir … they's caged because … well, they ain't too friendly like. I's afraid if they was loose … well, it'd be likely someone'd get his-self bit … and most likely that'd be *me!*"

"Well, if they're so fierce and unfriendly, why're they here? What did my Daddy keep them for?"

"Well, sir … they's *hunting* dogs, you see."

"Hunting? I never knew my Daddy to do any hunting. What kind of animals did he hunt with these hounds?"

Cobb was silent for a minute, gazing at Nathan, as if not sure how to answer. Finally, he said, "Well, sir … they's *not* for hunting the *four-legged* kind of animal … if you take my meaning, sir."

"*Oh!* Oh, I see …"

Nathan stared at the barking dogs for a moment longer, then said, "Thank you, Cobb. Please, carry on with what you were doing." He turned and strode off.

Harry walked up to the pen, lifted a leg and urinated. Then he turned his back on the caged hounds, kicked dirt at them contemptuously, and trotted after his master, ignoring his adversaries' infuriated barking.

❧❦☙❧❦☙❧❦☙

As the sun was setting, Nathan, Jim, Stan, and William made their way slowly up the drive. They'd put in a long hard day on the construction work and had made a good start on patching up the first of the cabins.

They were wearied from labor their muscles weren't used to doing regularly. Nathan, having completed another circuit of the fields, had found himself in mid-afternoon with nothing better to do. So he had joined his men in their construction project for the last several hours, swinging a hammer, nailing new wooden shakes on the roof.

As they approached the house, they saw that Tom and Jamie were already there, having returned from their expedition into town.

"Successful mission?" Jim asked as they neared the house. The grooms nodded politely as they passed them, heading in the opposite direction toward the stables. They were leading away the horses and the mule to put them up for the night.

"Yes, I would say so. Have fun banging nails?" Tom responded with a grin. He could see the stiffness and weariness in Jim's stride, and couldn't resist a little good-natured ribbing.

"Yes … never had more fun … except for Stan's incessant joking. If I'd had my pistol with me, I'd've shot him and put him out of *my* misery!"

"Oh? Say you so? *Now* you are for *shooting* Stan, but *before* … you laugh so hard at jokes, like to fall from roof!" and he let out another of his thunderous laughs. The others smiled and shook their heads. Stan was Stan, tired or not, and there was no doing anything about it!

"Hey, Captain! C'mere and lookie what I got!" Jamie motioned enthusiastically. He gestured toward a large canvas bundle sitting up on the veranda. They moved up the stairs and circled around to have a look at what Jamie had brought from town.

He unwrapped the bundle with a flair, like a magician unveiling a magic trick. And the men's reaction did not disappoint. Jim immediately reached down, lifted out a rifle and held it up in the light of the setting sun.

"'55 Springfield, *by God!* Very nice piece, Jamie!" he said, holding it up for a closer examination. It was new and clean, and the well-polished black walnut stock and steel hardware sparkled in the sunlight. It was a state-of-the art military rifle, or rifle-musket as some people still called them, on account of their strong resemblance to the earlier, now obsolete weapon. This, however, was no smooth bore musket, nor was it a delicate hunting firearm like the Kentucky long-rifle. This was a sturdy, well-made *military* weapon. The inside of the barrel was rifled for excellent accuracy at long range, but it had an overall length not so excessive as to be unwieldy in combat. Also, it could be fitted with a standard eighteen-inch, military-issue, needle-sharp bayonet.

"Yep, and I got me three more just like it! Can't believe the luck. I walked into the general store, and it was after looking

50

pretty dull and depressing, I can tell you. Old flintlocks, hunting rifles, and such. Nothing much better'n what we'd already got here on the farm. Then, what do you know?! Of all the good luck, just then a wagon pulls up full of goods. They was unloading it when I noticed me a small crate of a very interesting shape. I looks closer and sees the words *Springfield Armory* painted on the side; well I can tell you I was near to salivating, lads! The proprietor was most annoyed on account o' how insistent I was he open that crate first; probably thinking I was just a lookie-loo and not a buyer. Anyway, soon as he pries off the top he says 'Damn it, they sent me the wrong thing! I asked for hunting rifles, but these here are military muskets—why look at here, bayonets and all!' and I nearly jumps into the box to see what's inside.

"I says, 'I'll take 'em!' He says, 'what do you mean? You ain't even seen what they are yet!' To which I answers, 'I knows exactly what they are! I seen one once when we was out West in the Army, and that's what I want … bloody damned bayonets and all!" So I wraps them up right there, and straps them on the mule. Then I was after goin' back through his stock and picking out the best of what was left; a few fairly serviceable hunting rifles. And I made him a deal on a couple more in a sorry state of repair, figuring I could fix 'em back up later. I got eight rifles in all, six of which can be used straightaway. I suppose if we count the governor's rifle upstairs that makes seven usable, and the hunting rifle we brought from Texas, eight."

"You did well, Jamie," Nathan said, nodding his head. "Those Springfields are better than anything I'd hoped for, and the others'll do just fine for keeping our skills up, and maybe a hunting trip or two. Thank you!"

Jamie beamed brightly, enjoying the praise.

"My pleasure, sir! My great, good pleasure, to be sure!"

The others gathered around, snatching up the various guns for closer examination, and patting Jamie heartily on the back.

"Oh, and I almost forgot, sir … he was pretty well stocked with Minni balls and powder, so I got me a goodly supply of ammunition as well. The grooms already carried that into the house and put it in the closet with the other old guns."

Just then Georgie came up at a trot and took the stairs two at a time. He'd finished up his work for the day, surveying the various farm implements. He was walking up the drive when he saw the others gathered on the veranda and wanted to have a look himself. "What'd you get, Jamie?"

He leaned in between two of the others to have a better look. "Ooooo … Springfields, ain't they? Nice, Jamie, very nice!"

"And you, Tom … how was your mission?" Nathan asked, pulling Tom to the side while the rest of the group continued to ogle the rifles.

"Excellent, sir! The papers were nearly perfect. The clerk made a few minor changes to make sure it was all proper and legal, which is why we are a little longer getting back. That and Mr. O'Brien's enthusiasm for all things concussive! He insisted on showing me every firearm in the store, so he could give his expert opinion on each!" Tom rolled his eyes and shared a grin with the Captain.

"Good, good … excellent. Well done, Tom. Let's get together in the library after dinner. I've been giving everything a lot of thought, and I want to discuss my ideas with you before we meet with Momma—Miss Abbey, that is."

"Yes, certainly, sir. I've been … looking forward to it … since before we started our journey, actually," Tom said, cryptically. Nathan raised an eyebrow but didn't want to press the matter further in front of the others.

Megs stepped out onto the veranda and said, "I was told you great soldier-men were going to sleep in the farmhands' barracks tonight. So I had your things moved over earlier today. Come on in now, sirs, and have your dinner."

"Why Megs, I was going to have the men move their own things," Nathan said in mock reproach. "You're going to turn them into spoiled little princelings if you keep waiting on them!"

"Yes, I remember, master; you said we could only have *one* of those 'round here 'bouts."

She gave him a smirk, then pivoted, marching back into the house.

Nathan chuckled.

"Well, men, go ahead and bring those rifles in. Stack them in the closet with the others, if you please. Jamie will show you the way. Then wash up for supper."

The mention of food was all it took to get them moving, and soon the veranda was clear, men, rifles, canvas bag, and all.

𝔈𝔬𝔬𝔯𝔠𝔰𝔈𝔬𝔈𝔬𝔯𝔠𝔰𝔈𝔬𝔈𝔬𝔯𝔠𝔰

Hours later, Tom and Nathan sat alone in the library. They'd dined earlier with Miss Abbey in the great hall while the rest of the men had eaten in the kitchen, where the old farmhands were invited to join.

Nathan opened the window to the outside, and the two men sat smoking cigars. Nathan leaned back in a soft leather chair, slowly blowing smoke up toward the ceiling, as if lost in thought.

Tom did likewise, enjoying the familiar warm sensation and smell, all the while watching the Captain out the corner of his eye. He suspected Nathan was working up to discuss something serious, probably about the future of the farm. But Tom was content to smoke the cigar in silence and let him take his own time on coming out with it.

"You know … when we left Texas, I'd convinced myself the right thing to do was to sell the farm, and move Momma to Richmond …"

Tom nodded, but said nothing, not wanting to interrupt the Captain's flow of words, now he'd finally started.

"But then, on the road … these … *things* seemed to keep happening."

"Things?"

"Yes. *Accidents … incidents …* whatever you want to call them. They kept happening on our journey, through no forethought or intention on our part."

"Firstly, there was the young girl, Sue. Taken hostage, *held in bondage*, as it were, through no fault of her own. A complete innocent who'd likely have been sold off for a slave in some God-forsaken brothel south of the border, if we hadn't rescued her …

"Next, we stayed with Mrs. Schmidt, whom I have … *dearly loved* … as you know …"

He was silent for a moment, as if deep in thought. Tom could see his eyes become a little misty when he added softly, *"God bless her, and keep her …"*

"Anyway, there was dear Alisa scolding me for returning to Virginia to become a slaver. I started to deny it, but then realized … it was *true.*"

He became silent again, taking another deep drag on the cigar. He blew the smoke out again, then continued.

"Then those absurd boys trying to rob the train … risking a lengthy imprisonment for a handful of coins. And likely would've suffered it if not for my uncharacteristic leniency.

"And, as if by pure chance, we end up on a steam ship whose first mate is, of all things, a free black man. And think about this, Tom … if not for that sudden, *unexpected* storm, we'd have left the boat never seeing Mr. Harvey's exemplary skills as a seaman; navigating the ship out of danger as neatly and flawlessly as *any* man could possibly do. And to have seen the respect the rest of the crew had for him, including the ship's captain."

"True … all very true, sir."

"To top it all off … our experiences in New Orleans. The undeserved jailing of our own men, another form of *bondage.* And the encounter with the warehouse foreman, brazenly beating a slave for a simple stumble. Leading to our meeting with the despicable black slaver Dubuclet, who cared nothing for his fellow man, only his money. The man didn't even have the decency to bother with the *excuse* of nobly employing ignorant African savages."

"Yes. Now you say it *that* way, I *am* seeing the pattern here, Captain."

"Of course, Tom! Even a blind fool could've seen it … *but not me!*"

"That's going a bit hard on yourself …"

He shook his head, "All that time traveling, and it didn't hit me until we were riding down the road into this farm. The black people lining the road were so downtrodden they didn't even bother glancing up and see what their new master *looked* like."

His voice choked with emotion, and his eyes watered up. He reached over and took a sip from the whiskey glass on the side table before continuing.

"It was at that very moment, looking down at those sad faces, a voice seemed to speak in my mind," he shook his head, and smiled ironically. "It spoke most *eloquently*, Tom. It said, *'Chambers, you damned fool! Can't you see what you're doing to these people … and to your own soul, slaver? These are God's own children, whom he has made 'In His Own Image!''*

"Damn it, Tom! Our journey has been nothing but one lesson after another … laid out for my edification. By the Lord God Almighty himself, I now have no doubts …"

He was quiet for another moment, then added, "As the great song says, *'I once was lost, but now am found; was blind … but now I see.'*"

Tom nodded his agreement. He wasn't especially surprised Nathan had come to this conclusion, but he hadn't thought about the lessons learned along the road until just now. The way Nathan laid it out, it all made sense.

"So what will you do, sir?"

Nathan leaned back and took a few more puffs on his cigar before responding.

"Tom, I am reminded of Matthew chapter seven, verse twenty-four. It says, *'Therefore whosoever heareth these sayings of mine, and doeth them, I will liken him unto a wise man, which built his house upon a rock.'*

"To me, this passage means … now I have clearly heard the teachings of the Lord, I must use his lessons to the very best of my ability, as a wise man … or my house will fail. But if I use these teachings wisely, my house will prosper. I will 'build my house upon a rock,' as it says."

Tom again nodded, "Sir … if I understand you rightly, you're now thinking you ought to free these slaves, rather than selling them along with the farm."

It was a statement, not a question, and Nathan nodded his agreement, "Yes, but … I can't think how to get around this onerous *law*. You know the one … a master can't free his slaves all at once."

"Ah … yes. I'd been thinking about that law ever since we left Texas. And when I was in at the county clerk's office, I borrowed his law book and read through it. It's an interesting law … very thorough and heavy-handed, I'm afraid. Airtight, seemingly. Except …"

"Yes?"

"Except … I may have figured a way around it."

Nathan raised an eyebrow.

"You see, the law specifically addresses lifelong slaves of African descent."

"Yes, of course … so?"

"So … it mentions nothing about *indentured servants* …"

Nathan's eyes widened, and he leaned back in his chair, stuck the cigar in his mouth and stared up at the ceiling.

"Oh … I see where you're going with this, Tom. There's no law against converting a lifelong slave into an indentured servant. Masters do it all the time as a reward and incentive for an especially favored individual, or for any number of other reasons."

"That's right," Tom said, "and … by definition, indentured servants must serve a specific period of time, after which …"

"After which they are by law free men! Brilliant, Tom! We can convert them all to indentured servants, give them all a short time to serve, and then …"

"Yep … then they'll be free, all legal and proper, and nothing anybody can do about it!"

Tom leaned back, put his cigar between his teeth, folded his arms across his chest and grinned.

Nathan likewise sat back in his chair, and puffed on his cigar, a thoughtful expression on his brow.

"Tom … I thank you for that. You're … I don't know how to say it … 'a good man' seems so far short of the mark."

"Happy to help, sir."

After another pause, he said, "You know, besides the slavery issue … ever since arriving, and seeing this place again after all these years—its peaceful natural beauty, the grand old house, and the way Miss Abbey's eyes light up when she's touring her flower garden …"

"You're having second thoughts about selling the place?"

Nathan didn't answer but leaned back in his chair, picked up the whiskey glass, and stared into it, slowly swirling the contents. This time the pause was so long Tom wondered if Nathan was nodding off from exhaustion.

But Nathan suddenly leaned forward and looked Tom hard in the eyes, "Tom, do you think it's possible to figure a way to run this farm without slaves? To use all the modern knowledge, science, machinery, fertilizers, and whatnot, to make it profitable … *without* slave labor?"

The earnestness in his eyes, almost pleading, nearly took Tom's breath away. But fortunately for Tom, he'd been thinking on this very subject, long and hard, even to the extent of making specific plans in his mind, ever since he'd first heard of his Captain's "dilemma" back at Fort Davis, Texas.

"Of course, it is, sir," he answered simply, grinning again. "I've given it a lot of thought, in case you decided you wanted to keep the farm. I have dozens of ideas already. And I'm sure I can come up with more … now I'm in one place for a few days and have time to look into it. And I can recruit our resident scholar, William to assist me, if he's agreeable."

Nathan seemed shocked by this answer and stared at Tom open-mouthed. Then his features softened, and he returned the smile, "Good man! And … God bless you, Tom. God bless you!"

He clapped his hands and laughed, a sound of pure joy. Tom could see Nathan's eyes were watery again and felt his own doing the same.

ༀༀༀༀༀༀༀༀༀༀༀ

Nathan and Tom discussed the outlines of a plan for another hour or so, before asking one of the servants to find Miss Abbey that she might join them.

They sat together in the library, the men sipping whiskey while Miss Abbey held a small glass containing just a splash of

57

brandy. The other men had long-since retired to the farmhands' barracks, laughing boisterously as they went.

"Well, I must say, I've never before had a meal in the dining hall where one couldn't hear what was being said across the table, on account of the noise coming down the hall from the kitchen!" Miss Abbey laughed with amusement. "Your Stan is really quite remarkable. I don't believe I've ever met, or ever even *heard* of, for that matter, anyone so great big and jolly as he! My goodness! His laugh practically shakes the house! And if I'm not mistaken, the *old* farmhands joined in the laughter as well … something we haven't heard around here in a very, very long time …" She trailed off as if thinking back. "*Never*, as a matter of fact … *never* have we had such laughter in this house! Your father wouldn't have liked it."

"Daddy never had to contend with Stan," Nathan answered with a chuckle.

Miss Abbey grinned, and shook her head, "Imagine your small, stern, serious father looking up and trying to scold the great, boisterous giant, Stan! That would've been a sight to see."

There followed a short, awkward silence. Then she said, "So, young gentlemen, you didn't invite me in here to talk about good-humored giants. You are obviously up to something, so you might as well be out with it." She leaned forward, looking Nathan and Tom in the eye, each in turn.

"Yes, Momma. I do have some business I want to conclude. Then we can return to discussing whatever you please. You will recall, Momma, our agreement about my coming home, what I insisted upon when I telegraphed you from Texas?"

"Yes, of course, Nathan, dear. Although it is entirely unnecessary; the farm is yours, and you are the master. No one will dispute that, now or ever, least of all me!"

"Yes, I know you mean that, Momma. But I have reasons for what I'm doing, good reasons you will understand in a moment."

He now had her complete attention, and curiosity. She leaned closer.

"As agreed, I need you to sign papers granting me complete and indisputable ownership of the farm, and all of its property—

except for your personal belongings, of course—so no one can ever dispute the legality of any decisions I make concerning this farm. In return, I have written out a will making you my sole heir, so you would retain everything should I pass before you."

"Of course, dear. But why is this necessary? What decisions are you planning to make? What is it you are planning on doing?" Her curiosity was now piqued, but a feeling of dread had come over her.

"Momma, I will now tell you something so you will know I'm being totally honest with you. That I'm not taking ownership of this farm under any false pretenses. And when I tell you what I am planning, you may say 'no' and I will hold no ill will against you. I will return to my career in the Army, and everything will be as it was before."

She had a sinking feeling about where this was going. She feared he intended to sell the farm and move her to some place easier to maintain, in a town or city. For years she'd wished for that very thing, feeling isolated and alone out here in western Virginia, far away from the more interesting life and all her friends and family in Richmond.

But over the years, Mountain Meadows had become her home. She loved her flower gardens, her pond with its frogs and its ducks. And the big, beautiful house. She never tired of the magnificent sunrises over the mountains, and the lovely sunsets into the mists of the fields in the west. Her heart suddenly ached at the thought of leaving this place. How could she bear it?

She choked back such thoughts, bracing herself for what was coming, and said "Yes, dear. Tell me what you're planning to do …"

"I'm going to free the slaves, Momma."

ಶಿಶಿಂಡುಶಿಶಿಂಡುಶಿಶಿಂಡು

After a stunned silence, Miss Abbey finally said, in a quiet voice, "I can understand the sentiment; I've never felt good about it, either. But, Nathan, dear … we'll lose the farm. Our home, your inheritance, everything your father … and your granddaddy, worked for their whole lives, will be … *gone.*"

"I don't think so, Momma. At least, that's not my intention. I mean to free the slaves *and* save the farm. In fact, I mean to make the farm prosper like never before!"

"But how, dear? Without the workers, the crops won't be planted, or tended, or … harvested!"

"Yes, of course, I know all that, Momma. I may *not* be a farmer, but I do understand the gist of it."

"Oh, yes, certainly you do … I didn't mean to insult you, dear. It's just … I don't understand."

"We'll still need to have farm workers, but not slaves. We'll use paid labor."

"But if you turn all the slaves out, where ever will you find enough workers?"

"Well, unless I miss my mark, I think they'll be the very same workers we have now!"

Miss Abbey looked puzzled, so Nathan said, "Tom and I have been working out a plan for how the farm can prosper *without* slavery. Other people have been doing it since the beginning of time, and they didn't have all the modern science and industry we have! It's the middle of the nineteenth century, after all, not the dark ages! The more we've talked about it, the more excited I've become. And if it works, we can make an example for other farms to follow. Then perhaps slavery in this country can finally come to an end!"

"Well, that sounds more hopeful, but … the workers?"

"After we free the slaves, we'll offer them jobs, if they'll continue to work the farm. We'll pay them a wage, so they'll be working for their own benefit and by their own choice rather than by force and compunction. Men free to choose will work harder, and better than a person who's compelled. And we'll use all the modern science we can to make the crops grow hardier and stronger. We'll also plant crops able to bring more profits to the farm with less need of labor."

"But dear, you can't change the world in a day! They say even the great Caesar couldn't do *that*!"

"I believe the saying is, 'Rome wasn't built in a day,' Momma," Nathan said with a smile. "Don't worry, I'm not going to set them free *tomorrow*. I wouldn't be doing them any favors if I did. What good would it do to cast them adrift on the great sea of the world, with no knowledge about what they'd face? Freedom isn't much use if you're starving to death with no roof over your head!

"They'll need to learn what it means to be free; how to survive in the world outside this farm—how to get a job, how to handle money, pay rent, all the things free people do.

"I honestly believe they are capable of accomplishing anything a white man can accomplish, if given the opportunity. Learning a trade, going to school and becoming a professional, owning their own land or business—all these things are possible in the future. On our journey from Texas, Tom and I met an impressive young black man who was a highly skilled navigator and first mate aboard a steamship. Believe me, there is no man alive who could've steered that ship more confidently in a frightful storm than that fellow.

"But for many of our slaves, their most immediate chance for prosperity in their freedom is the prosperity of this farm and their employment here. Farming is the skill they know best, and it's the obvious first choice for a good home and a stable life once they're free.

"Tom and I have just been discussing it, and I'm thinking it will take at least two … maybe three years to put all of our plans in place."

"Oh … that makes me feel a little better, dear. So … when do you mean to tell *them?*"

"Sunday. But I have no idea how they'll react to it …"

"Well … from the rumblings I've heard, they're still very fearful of you, and skeptical. It'll take a while to convince them you're truthful, and sincere."

"Hmm … yes, I can see why they'd not be inclined to believe anything their white slave master tells them. It'll take time and following through on promises. But … I have to start somewhere, and 'there's no time like the present,' as they say. That is … assuming you're still willing to sign the papers …"

"Oh! Oh, yes, the papers ... of course, of course. You know I trust you completely, dear. I would sign anything you like—but I *am* happy you have a plan to keep the farm alive."

She took the papers from Tom, leafed through to the last page, dipped her pen in the inkwell, and signed. There were two identical copies—one to keep on the farm with the other important papers, and one to file with the county clerk. She immediately signed the second copy also. Tom blotted her signatures and handed the papers to Nathan to countersign. Once he'd finished, Tom also signed as the witness, making it all legal.

"You know, when I was a young bride, I *hated* this place ... so far away from everything I'd ever known. My family, my friends ... all left behind in Richmond. And living with a man who ... well, let's just say your Daddy was not the warmest person, nor the most talkative.

"But now, after all these years ... for whatever reasons, it has become *home*. I've come to love this place like nowhere else. I don't ever want to leave here."

"Then you never shall," Nathan answered.

Tom raised his glass and said, "A toast ... to the breaking of bonds!"

But Nathan shook his head. "We're not there yet, Tom. We still have a long way to go. But ... we're at least now on the right road."

"All right then ... here's to being on *the road to the breaking*, anyway!"

"Okay ... I'll drink to that."

Miss Abbey smiled and raised her glass in answer. They all three clinked their glasses together and had another drink.

But even as he was taking his swallow, Tom had a sudden uneasy premonition. It came into his mind, sharp and clear—Billy had used the same word ... "breaking" ... to describe the terrible time when the world had nearly ended, when the Comanche and Tonkawa became enemies and started their never-ending war. He shuddered involuntarily, *God forbid we're on the road to that kind of breaking*. But he said nothing to the Captain or Miss Abbey, unwilling to dampen the otherwise happy mood.

They set down their glasses. Tom stood, bowed, said his good nights, and departed with the papers, leaving mother and son alone.

"Nathan, we have not really had much time alone since you first arrived. I want you to know how truly happy you've made me, coming home after all these years. And, I also want to tell you how proud you've made me. *My goodness!* Look at you ... so tall, so handsome! A war hero, and a leader of men," she smiled brightly.

"Momma, it is such a *true* pleasure to be with you again. I really don't have words to express it. I had such ... *strong* ... feelings about Daddy ... I couldn't imagine ever coming home again. And it hurt too much to think of *you*, so I'm afraid I got into the habit of *not* thinking about home at all. But now ... I realize how much I've missed all these years, being away from you."

Then he sat up straighter, and once again held up his glass, "I mean to make amends, Momma. We shall live here together always. 'Happily ever after,' like in the old story books! What say you to that?"

"I say that will be absolutely lovely, dear. As lovely as it can possibly be!" And as she answered, tears flowed freely from her eyes, which were quickly echoed by tears of his own. She leaned her head into his chest, and they embraced.

After she sat up and wiped her tears, she said, "But you know, Nathan, dear, you and I here alone is not enough." She gazed at him with an odd, unreadable look with just the hint of a smile.

"What do you mean, Momma?"

"Nathan, on the fourth of July you'll turn thirty-three. It's time you were married and started a family. If not for you, then for me. It's high time I became a grandma!" she grinned.

He rolled his eyes. "Really, Momma! I just got home. I have so many things to deal with right now. Finding a bride is the last thing on my mind. I'm not saying you're wrong, but give it a little time, please."

"Okay, whatever you say, dear. I'll let it drop for now, but this isn't the end of it."

He chuckled, "I'd be shocked if it was."

She smiled and nodded. "You go ahead and deal with all the business of the farm," but in her mind she completed the thought, *and I'll worry about finding you a bride!*

She had intended to share the letter she'd recently received from the friend of a friend in Richmond. It was from a woman named Harriet Hanson who said she was planning a trip to western Virginia with her lovely young daughter, Evelyn. Harriet inquired if they might stop in for a social call on account of her and Abbey having many mutual friends and acquaintances in Richmond. She said she felt it was unfortunate they hadn't previously been better acquainted when Abbey lived in Richmond, and she wished to rectify that. And she understood Abbey's son was returning from the West and perhaps he and Evelyn might also enjoy meeting each other.

Of course, to Abbey the purpose was clear; it was a thinly veiled offer to introduce Evelyn to Nathan with the eventual goal being a mutually rewarding matrimonial engagement.

No need to bother Nathan with the details, she decided. *I think I'll just pen an answer to Miss Harriet myself …*

Chapter 3. Rough Wooing

"Put all to fyre and swoorde …
as there may remayn forever
a perpetual memory
of the vengeaunce of God
lightened upon them
for their faulsehode
and disloyailtye."
– Henry VIII
(Instructions to his army for the
"Rough Wooing" of Mary, Queen of Scots)

Wednesday May 16, 1860 – Richmond, Virginia:

Her tears continued to fall, and she could not seem to stop them. Nothing before in her young life had prepared Evelyn Hanson for such utter and complete loss.

Her father … the man had been everything to her. Now he was suddenly gone. Not gone for a week, nor for a year. Those temporary partings would've been hard enough to bear. No, he was gone *forever*, and she would never again see his loving face on this earth.

She was vaguely aware the preacher was saying words … words from the Bible, she assumed. But she couldn't focus on them; they had become droning noise in her ears. That noise, blending with her own sobs and the steady dripping of rain, seemed to soak into everyone and everything at the funeral. Evelyn stood next to her mother in a small, dreary cemetery on the edge of Richmond, Virginia. The dark, lowering clouds and drizzling rain mirrored her own feelings.

When it was finally over, men quickly shoveled dirt into the hole containing a great wooden box. Under different circumstances she might have felt relief, eager to get out of the wet and cold. But today she just felt numb.

"Pull yourself together, child! You're making a spectacle," her mother whispered in an angry hiss as they walked across the lawn between the headstones. Attendance at the funeral had been light—fewer than a dozen friends and neighbors. And these now seemed most concerned about getting warm and dry as quickly as possible.

"Well, there's not much of anyone here to notice," Evelyn said between snuffles. "Where are all the men who claimed to be Daddy's friends?"

"Gone! Along with the farm and money. Those tend to go together!"

"You mean they only *pretended* to like him because he had money?"

"Wake up girl! Time you learned about the *real* world. It's not your Daddy's imagined world of goodness and light! Might as well believe in *fairyland*. *Pah!*"

"But Daddy was a *good* man. People liked him. The men in town were always happy when he visited, I saw it with my own eyes. Are you saying they were play-acting? That they never *really* liked him? I don't believe it."

"Believe what you like, child; the truth is men respect a man if he's able to prosper and take care of his own. If he can't ... they toss him out like last night's bath water."

"But what happened to the farm ... it wasn't his fault!"

"Wasn't it? While the neighbors were making a fortune off cotton, your Daddy planted tobacco and beans. Beans?!" she shook her head.

"Well, yes, I guess Daddy didn't have much of a mind for business. But he knew *so* many other things. We used to talk for hours about the most interesting things ..."

"Lot of good it did either of you! Did his long-winded philosophizing bring any money into the farm? Did it pay for next year's seeds? Did it cover our expenses? Did it make good on the bank loans he kept taking out every year? Of course not!

"And did his coddling the slaves benefit *them* in any way? Keeping slave families together, even at the cost of thousands of dollars we'd have earned by splitting them up? I'll tell you what it did for them: *nothing!* They're now scattered all over seven counties, and not a child is with his mother, you can bet your last dollar! But some other man reaped the rewards of that sale, not *us!*"

"Oh, Momma, don't you have anything good to say about Daddy? Not even on *this* day, of all days?"

"No. And you shouldn't either! He did you no favors, you know. Raising you like you were … like you were a *boy!* Shameful! But nothing I could do or say would sway him—or *you* for that matter. You must accept some blame in this too, you know. You never would behave like a proper young lady. Always running around the farm in bare feet, hob-knobbing with the slave children; riding horses, fishing, hunting, and whatnot with your Daddy. What a way to raise a girl!"

"But, Momma … you make it out like something sinful. I enjoyed doing things with Daddy. You always wanted me to stay home and learn how to behave *ladylike*; how to stitch and … *decorate* … and whatnot. I *did* learn about music, and dancing, as you wished …"

"Yes, because you *liked* doing those things. What a stubborn child you were … and your Daddy always took up for you and kept me from doing for you what I should have done. But *NO MORE!* From this day forward, you will learn to be a lady!"

"Oh, Momma … that sounds so …"

"Never you mind how it *sounds*. It is what you *will* do … what you *MUST* do. For us … for your family … or what's left of it. You must become a lady and restore the family's standing and honor, if it's not too late."

"But … I don't know how to do any of that!"

"*I do*. I will teach you everything you need to know, starting today. Today, everything changes. Today, you're a *lady*. Your childhood is over!"

Evelyn had no argument for her mother on that score. She was already nineteen years old. Most of her friends were already married. If it'd been up to her mother, and her father hadn't kept her isolated on the farm, she'd have been married off long ago.

She ducked into the waiting carriage for the ride back to their new, small house in Richmond. She sat with a heavy sigh. *Daddy's gone, and so is my childhood. I wonder what tomorrow will bring, and who I will become. If I'm no longer Daddy's little girl, then … who am I?*

ᘒᘓᘔᘕᘒᘓᘔᘕᘒᘓᘔᘕ

Saturday June 2, 1860 – Richmond, Virginia:

"Evelyn! I swear, you haven't heard a word I've been saying!" Belinda said, covering her mouth in mock reproach. "If I didn't know better, I'd say you were in *love* with the handsome young gentleman who brought you." She spoke teasingly, drawing out the word *love* for emphasis.

"Sorry, Bel. Just thinking … NO, oh *no!* Not *love*, oh heavens *no!*" Evelyn replied, coming out of her reverie and realizing what Belinda had been suggesting. "I hardly *know* the man, and to tell the truth I … I've been having a hard time *getting* to know him. I really can't decide what kind of man he is."

"The rich and handsome kind!" Belinda laughed. "What else matters?"

"Well, I suppose being kindly, and gentle, and … easy to talk to … might be good." Evelyn struggled to put into words the thoughts she'd been wrestling with before Belinda's interruption.

The young women sat on a bench on one side of a great hall, filled with well-to-do revelers. The dance hall was the largest and most elegant room in a very large and elegant house. It featured a row of three massive, beautiful chandeliers down the middle of the room, a dazzling array of crystals lit by multiple levels of white candles. The floor was of a dark wood polished to a mirror-like shine. Opulent white panels with gold leaf accents covered the walls and ceiling. Between the panels, the walls were lined with floor-to-ceiling windows, each with a lush, multi-layered, gold-colored drapery. Between the windows were low, gilded benches, softly padded and covered in red velvet. It was upon one of these that Evelyn and Belinda sat.

On one side of the room was a huge white marble fireplace, intricately carved and adorned, its hearth filled with profuse displays of fresh flowers. On the opposite side was a broad alcove that housed a white lacquered grand piano, with room for four or five musicians. This evening the alcove was being used for that very purpose, and a Chopin waltz filled the room with its complex, sophisticated notes.

This was a formal ball, in the southern tradition, with all the attendants dressed in their finest. Evelyn felt somewhat self-conscious about that. Her "finest" was barely passable amongst such company. Her family's recent financial troubles had forced her mother, Harriet, to tighten the purse strings to an uncomfortable level.

This had necessitated creativity. The gown she wore was a hand-me-down from her mother. The dark blue satin with velvet trim was still in fashion, but the cut was a little dated. Also, she wasn't *exactly* the same size as her mother had been when she'd worn the dress in her youth; Evelyn was several inches taller, and a bit thinner in the waist. They had no trouble taking in the waist. But when they tried to let out the hem, the wear on the soft velvet was too noticeable. So they'd had to add a second layer of black velvet all along the bottom, overlapping the original. For this they had to cannibalize another gown, which meant Evelyn's options were now even more limited. They'd also strategically added a little ribbon, and a touch of lace in just enough measure to disguise the original outdated cut. When they were finished, and she tried it on, Harriet had scowled and given it an unenthusiastic, "Adequate." Evelyn prayed it'd be too dark at the event for anyone to notice. And so far, no one had made any derisive remarks or given her any sideways looks, so she guessed it was working.

Two other young ladies sat on the next bench over, ignoring Evelyn and Belinda, discussing typical "ladylike" topics—the latest style of dress from Paris, which hats were in fashion, how the ladies up north were arranging their hair, and so on. Women were expected to talk of such things, and to enjoy it. Evelyn found such talk boring and tedious, although she knew she should pay more attention (for self-defense in such company, if nothing else.) She wanted to join the men, smoking their cigars and sipping their whiskey out on the veranda. Debating everything from philosophy to horse-racing, as she used to do with her father.

It was one reason she liked Belinda. Her friend was also not much interested in the latest fashion trends, and found the "man talk" more interesting, although she unfortunately knew little or nothing about it.

"Yes, yes, but I'm sure he will pamper you once he's wedded you! Why wouldn't he? I know you don't believe me, but you are truly the most beautiful woman at this ball, or any other, for that matter. Look at you! You're an absolute angel in blue satin and lace! What man wouldn't treat you like *gold?*"

"I hear men beat gold with a hammer after setting it on fire." Evelyn made a wry smile, and Belinda laughed out loud in a very unladylike manner, covering her mouth to stifle it.

But she knew Bel was right. She had the looks men admired — slim waist, long legs, and curves in the right places. And a nice face — good-looking but not too "fancy" or petite, with wide, baby blue eyes, and a bright smile. A face that would wear well over time, she supposed.

But her best physical feature, she suspected, was her hair. Naturally wavy, with a little work it would hang in long curvy strands that shone with a subtle gold color. Not a bright yellow color, like many men preferred, but more like gold with years of wear on it — old, and rich. She liked the color and the effect it afforded her. Elegant and sophisticated, not gaudy and showy. The navy-blue satin gown had just a hint of cleavage to complete the air of understated elegance.

Bel, by contrast, chose gaudy and showy whenever possible. Tonight, it was a bright yellow and white dress with plenty of ribbons, and lace trim. *Well, at least she's not a bright yellow blonde,* Evelyn thought as she took in Bel's dark curls, cut just past shoulder length. And such a bountiful cleavage, Evelyn had a hard time not staring!

Bel caught her looking and laughed, answering the unspoken question, "The men seem to like it, so why not? May as well use what the Good Lord's given me to get a good husband."

"But, Bel ... do you really think it's the most important thing in a woman's life; finding the right husband? Momma seems to think so, but I don't know ... maybe there should be more ..."

"Of course it's the most important thing, silly! You need a husband to have a household to run and children to raise and to take care of you in your old age. And ... well, I've heard the married women say it can be a great *pleasure* to be with the right man."

Evelyn blushed.

"So if you must have a husband, you may as well have the most wealthy, important, and handsome one you can get. What could be more important than that?" Bel continued.

"I ... I don't know, it's just so ... *boring* isn't quite the right word for it, but something close. Men are always riding off to battles, writing new laws or giving speeches and we ... we're stuck raising children and running a household. It seems ... *strange*, somehow."

Bel smiled, and shook her head, "Your Momma may be right. No disrespect to your Daddy, God rest his soul, and you know how I loved him, but ... he did put a lot of odd thoughts in your head."

"Yes, you may be right ... maybe as I grow older, I'll see things in a different light."

"Of course, you will, that's the spirit! In fact, you two make a *fine* couple! Maybe he's finally *'the one,'*" Bel said with a wink.

"I don't know, Bel. He seems ... how can I put it ... *cold?* He smiles, but not with his eyes, if you understand what I mean. Like he doesn't really mean it, somehow. Oh, I'm probably just confused and making things up."

"Don't worry, Eve. I'm sure you just need to get better acquainted, and then it'll be fine, you'll see! Come on, now. Stop worrying so much. And put on that dazzling smile that so charms all the men!"

71

Evelyn rolled her eyes and made a humorous face. They shared a laugh and then she smiled as Bel had instructed, despite herself.

"Our escorts are returning." Belinda said, nodding her head toward the far end of the room. True enough, her escort, Stanley Finch was crossing the room toward them, with Belinda's escort, Oliver "Ollie" Boyd in tow. Stanley was in the lead, walking with a brisk air of authority as he strode across the room, Ollie shuffling along behind.

"Ladies …" Stanley said, bowing his head slightly.

"Hullo, Miss Belinda, Miss Evelyn. We're back," Ollie said.

"Well, that we can clearly see!" Bel responded, teasing Ollie. He blushed but did not seem displeased at her witty retort.

"Miss Evelyn," Stanley continued smoothly, "would you do me the great honor of accompanying me on a short walk outside? The moonlight is particularly stunning this evening, and I'm sure you would enjoy the view."

"Oh, but Mr. Finch, it doesn't seem right abandoning my friend Miss Belinda when we were just having such a stimulating conversation."

"Nonsense," Belinda blurted out, ignoring her friend's subtle hint. "You two go gaze at the moon. I'm sure Mr. Boyd will be so kind as to keep me from any harm … or any loneliness …" She gave Ollie a sly smile. As if on cue, he blushed again.

"Oh, very well, if you're sure you'll be all right …"

"I'm sure she is in good hands," Stanley said. "Mr. Boyd is, no doubt, capable of keeping up his end of the conversation." He spoke in a manner bordering on facetiousness. This time when Ollie blushed, it was *not* from pleasure.

They left the ball room, and Evelyn collected her wrap in the foyer before they stepped out of the wide front doors onto the veranda. The house was on the outer edge of Richmond, in a more rural area, located at the end of a long lane crossing well-tended fields.

True to his word, Stanley lead her down a gravel pathway rounding the house, heading out toward the garden, with moonlight streaming down to light their way.

"A full moon!" Stanley announced, gesturing upward with his arm, as if Evelyn couldn't clearly see it for herself.

"Yes … it's lovely, as you said. Why … it's nearly as bright as day!" Despite her earlier hesitance, she found herself enjoying the beautiful scene.

"Yes, it is quite a sight," he agreed.

She looked at his face. He was handsome, as Belinda had said, in a lean and stately way. He was clean-shaven, with short, neatly cut dark hair—his face perhaps a bit too thin for her taste. Then she scolded herself for such *shallow* thoughts. Surely there was so much more to a person than *that*. But still … a little more … *softness* … to his features, would be nice …

His eyes were a pale blue, and despite the bright moonlight illuminating his features, once again she found his expression unreadable.

"Come, my dear, there's a very pleasant place to sit and admire the scenery, over yonder beyond that rock wall." He gestured toward a low garden wall crossing the gravel path a short distance ahead.

Evelyn wasn't yet comfortable with this man and didn't want to be alone with him out here in the darkness. But it would seem rude to refuse his invitation.

The garden path passed through a gap in the rock wall. A few steps further they came to an intersection where the path led left or right along the garden wall. Evelyn caught a strong fragrance of lilacs wafting on a warm, spring breeze. She had to admit it was a most romantic setting, so why wasn't she in a romantic mood?

They soon came to a place where the gravel widened out into a shallow "bay" next to the rock wall, and in it sat a stone bench. The bench was decoratively carved with vines and flowers, and though it was well aged, it was clean and in good repair.

"We have arrived at our destination," Stanley motioned toward the bench.

Though she didn't really want to sit, she could think of no reasonable excuse to decline. Mr. Finch had neither done, nor said, anything to deserve a reproach or refusal, so it seemed only polite to agree.

They settled down on the bench, only a hand's breadth apart, and Evelyn had to admit the view was spectacular. A short distance away was a small stream, musically churning by, the moonlight shining across the small ripples. Further off in the distance were small rolling hills covered with dark trees, and further still she could see … something long, and flat, sparkling in the moonlight. "Why, you can see the river from here!" she exclaimed, once again caught up in the scenery, despite her misgivings.

She had arrived earlier in the evening by the front gate, stepping from a covered carriage straight up the stairs onto the veranda and in the front door. She'd not seen anything outside the house until now.

Stanley smiled, pleased with her reaction. "You see? I knew you would be pleased. It is really lovely, and breathtaking … very much like *you*, my dear."

"Very kindly of you to say, Mr. Finch," she responded demurely, in the manner her mother had drilled into her during endless lessons on manners and social protocol. She was nervous and couldn't think of anything else to say.

"The evening is cooling; would you allow me to hold your hand?" he asked, extending his right hand, palm upward in a polite, inviting manner.

Once again, she could not refuse—he had proceeded most properly. So she complied, placing her left hand in his right. Her hands were cold, despite the warmth of the evening, which she attributed to nervousness. But she was surprised his hand felt even colder, and clammy, an unpleasant, cold, moist sensation. She resisted the urge to flinch at the touch. His hand was lean, like the rest of him, but there was a hard strength in it.

After a brief silence, he said, "I find myself quite attracted to you, Evelyn. You are really a lovely young woman." He leaned closer and looked into her eyes.

She couldn't think of what to say in answer. Obviously, Stanley would like her to respond in kind, but she didn't feel that way toward him, at least not yet; after all, she hardly knew him. They'd met before socially, and she'd occasionally seen him around town, but they'd only briefly spoken. Evelyn's mother had made all the arrangements with Stanley's mother for this evening's rendezvous. It was the first time they'd been in each other's company for an entire evening. And he'd spent half of that on the back veranda with the other men.

Drinking whiskey, and smoking cigars, she said to herself, silently. She could smell the telltale odors on him now as he leaned in toward her. Ironically, she did not find these smells disagreeable. On the contrary, they reminded her most strongly of sitting on her father's lap when she was a young girl, listening to him explain his latest theory. It was one of her very favorite childhood memories …

Stanly interrupted her pleasant daydreams by leaning over and planting his lips on hers! *Oops! Should have seen that coming. Shouldn't have let my mind wander so,* she scolded herself.

But it was *not* entirely unpleasant, so she allowed him to continue, thinking it would soon be over. But then he became more insistent. Instead of pulling back, as decency and decorum would prescribe, he pushed in harder, forcing her lips apart with his and grasping her shoulders with his strong hands. Now she resisted, trying to push him away. But his strength was much greater, and he had caught her by surprise. She was out of breath and leaned backward, about to lose her balance.

He continued leaning forward and pushed his hard chest up against her breast. She tried to squirm out of his grasp but felt like she was smothering and could barely move. Then his left arm released its grip on her back, and he cupped her right breast. It was offensive and disgusting, but just the distraction she needed to extricate herself from his embrace. With his left arm removed from her back, he had relinquished his control over her, and she had leverage with her back against the stone bench. She pushed and twisted with a sudden ferocity that surprised him and slid him sideways off the bench onto the gravel beneath.

He fell with an exclamation of surprise and pain. She sprang to her feet and ran for the path before he could react. She grabbed her long dress in both hands to free her legs as she ran. But a strong hand grasped her right arm from behind, in an iron grip.

She braced herself to pull away but Stanely cried, "Wait!" in a stern, commanding voice.

Just then another couple emerged from around the corner of the path, also out for a stroll in the moonlight, but clearly taking pleasure in it. The couple stopped in surprise, sensing something was amiss.

"I say … is everything all right?" the man asked, his concern apparent. He seemed unsure whether they'd stumbled on a clandestine but pleasurable rendezvous, or something more nefarious.

Evelyn just starred at them, mouth open, not knowing what to do or say. She wanted to call out Stanley for his despicable behavior, but at the same time felt an overwhelming sense of embarrassment and shame. "Everything is *fine!*" she said in a voice that made clear it was not. She jerked her arm from Stanley's slackening grasp and dashed back down the path toward the house.

ဪ၏ဢ၆ဪဪ၏ဢ၆ဪဪ၏ဢ၆

"All right, now … tell me what happened," her mother demanded as the carriage rolled along, bumping up and down on the uneven gravel surface. "And for God's sake, Evelyn, stop sniffling and collect yourself! You're not a simpering school girl! You're a *high-class young lady*, please act the part!"

It was a familiar haranguing to Evelyn, "act the part." Why must she act a part? Why must young ladies *act* at all? Instead, why not be … she didn't know *what* exactly. But not this. *And if I'm always acting a part, then … who am I?* Suddenly she felt self-conscious about the way she was dressed.

"Momma, he behaved in a most beastly manner. He invited me outside …" she managed between sobs, "and then he kissed me, and …"

"Well, I warned you not to let things go too far, too soon," her mother interrupted in a scolding tone.

"It wasn't like *that* Momma, I didn't encourage him, he was just so … so, forceful! I didn't know what to do, and then he was

76

on top of me and his hands … his hands. Then he … he … *ohhhh*, Momma!"

Uncontrollable sobbing prevented her saying anything more for a long time.

"All right, all right, child … I understand. It's all right," her mother said, finally taking a more consoling tone. But they sat on opposite sides of the carriage, and her mother offered no physical comforting; she'd never been *that* type of mother.

They rode along for a long time without speaking. The lights of Richmond appeared as they came back into the city. Evelyn had regained control of her emotions and sat staring out the window.

"It may be for the best," Harriet said, breaking the long silence.

"The … *best?*"

"Oh, sorry … not *best* the way he treated you, of course. *Beastly* man … shameful, inexcusable behavior. Obviously *not* a proper gentleman. I shall be sure all the ladies hear about *him*. It will be a cold day in hell before he escorts another *proper* lady to a ball!"

"But Momma, you won't tell all the ladies what happened? They'll think it was all my fault, that I … *encouraged* him …"

"No, no, of course not! *Your* name will never come into it. That's the beauty of spreading rumors. They don't have to be true; they just have to be intriguing, and plausible. People will believe what they wish to believe!

"What I meant was, it's for the *best* because I heard some *very* interesting news tonight. News that may work out well in our favor."

"News, Momma?"

"Well, it was all the talk at the party. That a certain eligible, single young gentleman has recently retired from the Army out west and is on his way back to Virginia to inherit his father's considerable estate. So naturally he will need a beautiful young bride. And the best part is …" she paused as if for dramatic effect.

"What, Momma?"

"Their estate is just over the mountains, outside the circle of local gossip, and so it's very likely they've not yet heard anything about our family's troubles. So if we pounce, they may never learn … at least not until it's too late!"

"Too late for what, Momma?"

"We'll see, Evelyn. We'll see …" Harriet smiled.

Chapter 4. The Book of the Earth

"Earth and sky, woods and fields,
lakes and rivers,
the mountains and the sea,
are excellent schoolmasters,
and teach some of us more
than we can ever learn from books."
– John Lubbock

Thursday June 14, 1860 – Allegheny Mountains, Virginia:

Billy trotted along, his legs feeling the strain after so many weeks of sitting on a horse, on the seat of a train, or the deck of a boat. Higher and higher he climbed into the mountains, weaving his way between bush and tree. It was an alien landscape to him, no bare dirt anywhere, every part of the ground covered either with green or with hard rock. Even on the rocks there was green — moss and lichen. He didn't know the names for such things, so he made them up as he went along. *"Mupashn"* he called the green sponginess filling the spaces between the other plants, and *"rupugphan"* for the strange lacey growing things clinging to the sides of trees and rocks. Even the trees and bushes were strange; nothing like the scrub and mesquite in Texas. So he invented names for these as well. Later he'd ask the Captain or William the English names.

The alien plant life was not the only interesting thing, however. There were also different types of animals. He enjoyed watching strange, red-colored squirrels that scrambled up the nearest tree as he approached, and then scolded him from above. One even dropped cones and pine needles down on his head, to his amusement. He was tempted to draw out the bow and bring one down for a noonday meal. But he'd found them so humorous and entertaining he decided not to kill one of these "little brothers."

But at the moment he was giving little thought to his belly — he was worrying about a much bigger problem — in this place, he had lost his ability to read the land.

He scanned the ground constantly as he moved along, looking for any sign of animals, both human and otherwise. He quickly became befuddled and confused. Nothing was as it should be. He'd spent his whole life in the dry desert climate of the West. There, if a man had walked along the ground a month ago, assuming none of the infrequent thunderstorms had passed since, you could still make out every detail — how much he weighed, how tall he was by the length of his stride, whether he was well fed or hungry, tired, or refreshed, and on and on. You knew if his horse was healthy and freshly shod or worn down and ready to collapse.

But here, the earth was moist and spongy. Everything was covered with old, decaying leaves, branches, and pine needles. It was like looking at the world through a dust storm; nothing was clear and precise; all was fuzzy and unclear.

He sat down on an old, moss-covered log, feeling frustrated with himself. It occurred to him the tracking skills he'd learned out west were like a child's first steps in *this* country. He'd always taken pride in his abilities, lessons taught him in early childhood by his grandfather which he had honed to a fine skill in the years since. He enjoyed how easily he could impress his white companions, who rarely read any sign beyond the most grossly obvious: a herd of cattle had passed, or ten men had been riding hard on horses! Or if they happened upon a dead body riddled with bullets or filled with arrows — they usually wouldn't miss reading *that* one! He grinned at the thought.

But now he was floundering in a strange land, where his skills seemed to count for nothing. He closed his eyes and took a deep breath. What would he tell the soldiers now? That he no longer knew how to scout? *No, never, never ever that! Somehow, I must learn this ... learn how to read this new country. I thought I knew how to read the earth, but I knew nothing. Now I need to learn a whole new way of reading. I have been a child, playing at reading the earth. Now I must become a master. But ... how?*

He didn't have long to ponder; suddenly he felt a series of sharp, stinging pains all over his lower legs, hips, and back. He shot to his feet, in shock at the pain coming from so many points of his body all at once. He looked down and his vision seemed to swim, blurry, and confusing. Then he realized—bees! In his distracted reverie, he had sat down on a hollow log inside of which was a large hive of bees. The unhappy residents were now swarming around him like a Texas dust tornado, which accounted for his blurred vision. He scolded himself for his foolishness. If he hadn't been so distraught about his lack of skills, he never would have fallen into such a trap.

But even as he was thinking these thoughts, his body's natural instincts kicked in. He launched himself off into the woods at full speed to distance himself from the nest.

In a short while, the bees gave up the chase, content to have run off the invader, and happy to return to their familiar hive. Billy, however, still felt the aftereffects of the bees' displeasure. Now having had time to think about it, he realized they'd been hornets, after all. Each sting was not quite as potent as a honeybee, who forfeited his life in the assault. But the hornet could sting again and again, only gradually running out of the painful venom.

He made his way to a nearby creek and dug into the edges to scoop out handfuls of mud to rub into the throbbing redness around his ankles. The pain eased as the mud absorbed the venom and its coolness helped to numb the throbbing. Billy smiled at the realization—at least some of his skills were still useful. Maybe he was not a *total fool* after all!

ಬಿಎಂಾಃ೦ಬಿಎಂಾಃ೦ಬಿಎಂಾ೦

Billy Creek looked down from a high ridge. He overlooked the pass through the Allegheny Mountains between Greenbrier County and Richmond, the great city of Virginia he'd heard the Captain speak of. He knew he couldn't see Richmond from such a distance, even if there hadn't been endless hills and ridges in between. From where he stood, the city was hundreds of miles away, lost in the haze.

Still, to Billy it was a magnificent sight. He'd never stood on anything so high before, and he felt like he could see forever, like a soaring eagle. It was inspiring and invigorating. And he felt much better about himself. After the hornets' nest, he'd stopped pitying himself, and started learning his new craft, the woods craft he would need to be a scout in this strange new country called *Virginia*.

He had decided he needed to start at the beginning with the simplest things. Like what did a boot print look like in these woods? So he found a small meadow, where there were not too many trees or bushes and plenty of light, and then he purposefully strode straight across it. When he reached the far side, he stopped and turned around. Then he got down to the ground on all fours. There he closely observed what his boot marks looked like. After a few minutes gazing, he shook his head in frustration, *still like looking through dust, or muddy water*, he thought. But he moved on, looking at more prints, until he began to pick out the pattern. Then he expanded his attention upward, observing how his movement had affected the grass and other plants of the meadow—how the stems were bent or broken, how quickly they sprang back to their original position and shape, how many remained broken and still detectable a few minutes later. He also tried to pay attention to a new aspect that had rarely been a factor in Texas—the moisture. He noticed his boots had displaced the dew to the sides of where he'd stepped, and it took some time for it to reform as it had been. He had earlier seen how the dew clung to the undersides of the grass all day long, even in relatively bright sunlight. And now he realized this was one more aspect he could read.

It occurred to him then: if a man were smart, persistent, and observant there was actually much more to read from *this* book, than from the dry book of the West. For starters, there were many more pages in this book, such as the dew, and the bending of the grass, that would tell the reader *when* a thing had happened, not just *what* had happened. This was a revelation to Billy, and his excitement grew. This place was not *just* a harder place to read; if mastered, the reader would learn so much *more* than he'd ever learned before!

With a newfound sense of wonder, he attacked his subject with a passion, spending hours at a time crawling around on all fours. He observed the marks a snake made when moving through deep leaves, and the subtle footprints a column of ants made when walking along the edge of a stream. Searching the woods for any moving creature, he'd observe how it behaved, and study the tracks it left behind.

He'd become so absorbed in his observations he didn't notice the sky clouding over. A sudden rain shower caught him out in the open and threatened a thorough drenching. Though he didn't know much about this country, he knew it was never good to get soaked out in the wild, especially with night approaching. A man might freeze to death if wet, even in Texas. So he quickly made his way from tree to tree, trying to stay as dry as possible, as he looked for any kind of shelter—a thick bush, or rocky overhang; anything to keep the rain off. As he moved along, he scolded himself, for the daylight dropped suddenly, as it did in the mountains when night began its approach. It was becoming difficult to see much of anything ahead of him. He continued moving uphill, even as his situation became more desperate. He didn't want to backtrack and lose any ground. Besides, he couldn't recall seeing any shelter back the way he'd come.

He gave up hope and decided to make the best of it huddled up next to the trunk of a fairly large tree with a good number of overhanging branches. But then he noticed a dark spot against the hillside a short distance ahead, like a darker patch of shade. Dark shade offered at least the chance that whatever was causing it— tree, bush, or large rock—might keep him dry. So he made for it as quickly as possible, trying to avoid stumbling in the dark.

However, when he got closer, he realized it was neither bush nor tree, but a small cave. Although this was the best possible shelter a man might find, a cave held its own problems. Wild animals also liked to shelter from the rain, and they knew where all the good caves were. He would have to approach cautiously.

He crept up to the edge of the cave, as quietly as possible. Keeping off to one side so as not to make a target of his silhouette, he approached the entrance. He considered drawing his bow, but then realized he wouldn't be able to see if he did. He needed a free hand to hold a light. So he drew out his hunting knife instead, and taking out a match, struck a light. He hurried into the cave, holding the match up above his head to illuminate the opening.

The walls were rough and uneven. But the floor was fairly level, mostly filled up with rocky, sandy dirt, the tiny pieces of the cave roof slowly falling and accumulating over the years. The cave was small, less than ten feet wide, and barely five feet at the highest, so Billy had to stoop as he entered. The dirt floor held animal tracks—fox or coyote, possibly—but nothing fresh. He noticed the cave wound back some ways, too far for the light of the match to reach, and he had to let it drop when it had burned down to his fingers. He resisted lighting another; the matches were precious, and he didn't want to waste any.

Of course, he could light a fire the old-fashioned way; any self-respecting Indian could. But he had to admit the white man's way was much quicker and easier in a pinch, and he didn't wish to waste time and energy lighting fires. So, still being fairly dry, and not especially cold, he decided to do without a campfire for the night.

He felt around until he found a relatively smooth spot, moved a few of the larger stones out of the way, and settled himself down on the floor. He pulled a small wool blanket out of his pack, wrapped himself up in it, and laid down. Up to that moment he hadn't realized how tired he was. And before giving it much thought, he was fast asleep.

In the middle of the night, he awoke to the sound of snuffling and moving feet at the cave entrance. It was dark as coal, so he couldn't see his midnight visitor. He slid the knife blade from its sheath at his belt. The snuffling continued a few more minutes, then was gone. *Apparently didn't like my smell,* he thought, *might need another bath!* He laid back down and quickly returned to sleep. The knife, however, remained clutched in his hand.

Billy had spent most of his life sleeping outdoors, and had gained the ability to sleep deeply while his mind stayed alert to any threatening sound or smell. Conversely, he would ignore the normal, non-threatening natural sounds. In the early pre-dawn hours, still mostly asleep, he was aware of, but not especially alarmed by, the sound of tiny wings moving about the entrance of the cave. Birds, he thought at first, but then as he became more aware, he puzzled out what kind of birds would fly around a cave entrance. *Bats*, he realized, as his sleep-fogged mind cleared. But this didn't worry him. Bats were harmless unless you stumbled into a large group when they were sleeping or tried to hold one in your hand; then they could deliver a painful bite. It was even said such a bite might turn deadly, the victim eventually being driven to madness by the pain. He'd never seen such a thing, however, so didn't pay it much credence.

He rolled over slowly onto his back and could see the small creatures flitting about, just over his head. If he sat up, he knew they'd be swirling around his head, but they would never hit him. He remembered when he was a young boy and lived near a cave filled with bats.

One day some older boys had dared him to walk into the cave when the bats were returning from their night-long foray. Bats terrified him, but he dared not show any fear, neither to duck his head nor to wave his arms. He knew if he did, he'd suffer endless taunting, and very likely a beating from the older boys. So he strode straight in, head held high, sure the creatures would instantly bump into him and attack him mercilessly in their startled displeasure.

But a most amazing thing had happened instead. As he walked forward, the storm of bats seemed to part around him, and he found himself entirely surrounded, but unharmed and untouched within the living maelstrom. Working up his courage, he raised one of his arms above his head, curious what would happen. And the creatures, despite their numbers and the great speed of their whirling flight, somehow, miraculously, avoided hitting his upraised arm. What had started as a terrifying ordeal had turned into a wondrous miracle of nature. It'd given him a newfound admiration for these incredible creatures. And it had earned him the amazed respect from his peers as he calmly walked out of the cave sometime later, a smile on his face. The stunned looks on the older boys' faces had made the experience all the sweeter.

So now as he lay flat on his back, watching these amazing creatures flowing into their cave. He felt no fear and thoroughly enjoyed the spectacle.

He remembered William saying some foreign people had a special word for them—*fledermaus*, which meant "flying mouse" or "flitting mouse." Billy thought it a good name for them. He found both the Tonkawa and English words lacking; they bore the negative connotation of an annoying pest, an opinion he did *not* share.

As the daylight slowly grew, and the flow of the living stream diminished to a trickle, Billy sat up and stretched. The few remaining stragglers easily dodged his now upright form. He looked back into the cave, curious where they'd all gone. It was then he noticed he could see farther back into the cave, and not by any reflected light from the entrance—there was a source of light somewhere inside. He quickly gathered up his things, stowing the blanket back in his pack and returning the knife to its sheath.

He briefly considered stopping to have a quick bite of something from his pack; his belly was rumbling from hunger pangs. He'd been too tired last night to think about eating anything before fading off to sleep. But his curiosity got the better of him, and he decided breakfast could wait a few more minutes. He moved cautiously back into the cave. It was still very dark in this part of the cave, and the growing light ahead actually made it harder to see where he was going in this darker section.

He walked hunched over beneath the low ceiling. Once again, the agility of the tiny bats amazed him—able to fly at great speed through this dark, narrow cave, avoiding ceiling and walls and all other obstacles, including each other, with apparent ease.

The cave wound around several twisting turns, and then as he rounded another corner, a light coming from high above dazzled his eyes. Sunlight was streaming in great beams, lighting the walls and floor of a vast cavern. Billy looked up in awe at the ceiling, at least a hundred feet or more above his head. Then he looked down, and saw the floor sloped steeply down from where he stood to a dark pool of water, probably fifty feet further down. It was an amazing sight; one he'd never seen before. The caves in the West were dark, dry holes in the ground, barren and uninteresting, though sometimes a useful shelter from the weather or enemies. This place was a waking dream—long spear-like rock formations covered the ceiling, water dripping down from the pointiest end of each spear. And amazingly, more of these rock spears pointed directly up toward their brothers on the ceiling, as if some meticulous god had lined them up precisely. And through some unfathomable miracle, the drops of water from the spears on the ceiling fell exactly onto the tips of the upward-thrusting points!

On the far side of the cavern, several hundred feet away there appeared to be another narrower opening, leading further back into the hillside. He guessed this was where the *fledermaus* slept.

He carefully scanned the room, looking for a way to get around to the far side. But the dark pool spanned the entire floor of the cavern, except for the places where sharp rocks covered the sloping ground near the sides. He decided he *might* be able to cross over without swimming, but it would be slippery and dangerous; so he'd save that exploration for another day. Prudence suggested he ought to tell the Officer of Scouts before he tried it. Otherwise, should he take a bad fall, they'd likely never find him, dead or alive.

It was then he recalled the Captain saying something about there being a lot of caves around where he grew up. But that had been several years ago, well before Billy had any idea he might someday visit the place, so he'd forgotten about it. Now he knew the Captain had been telling the truth, as he was in the habit of doing. Billy guessed this was one of many such caves spread all over these mountains. The prospect excited him. Ha! Let the white soldiers dig in the dirt back at the farm; Billy would enjoy this "Virginia" much more than they!

He turned and walked back to the entrance, stepping back out into the daylight. Once again, the day had dawned bright and clear, the rain of the evening before apparently just a passing shower. Billy had to squint for a few moments while his eyes adjusted to the bright light of day.

He sat cross-legged under a large bush—an old habit. In the wild he always rested under cover, so neither potential hunters nor potential prey would see him.

He sat on the west-facing slope of the ridge, so there was no direct sunlight on him yet. But he could see the tops of the ridges farther off to the west were brightly lit.

He reached into his pack and took out a piece of the hard salted pork he'd brought with him. After sniffing it briefly (another old survival habit) he then bit off a hunk and chewed. He hadn't hunted yet on this trip, concentrating instead on learning his new reading skills, but today he decided he should secure fresh meat. Not good to become too dependent on packed-in food—you never knew how long it'd have to last, and when you'd have nothing else. But these hills supported abundant game. He knew he'd have good success hunting.

The sudden onset of rain the night before made him think about how one might navigate in these heavily wooded hills. He had a good natural sense of direction. But he knew it was easy to get directions slightly skewed working through difficult terrain, especially without the sun in the sky, or clear stars at night. And directions slightly off might lead to long, fruitless delays before getting back on course, or worse, becoming totally lost in an unfamiliar wilderness. *One more thing to learn*, he decided.

Out in the dry, sunbaked West, he could always tell north from south by examining the vegetation. In the springtime, plants to the north of any tree or tall rock wouldn't grow quite as quickly because of the shade. Conversely, later in summer these same plants would look slightly more vigorous, and keep their green color longer, not being constantly cooked by the sun.

But here everything was lush and green everywhere all at once. There was never a lack of moisture, and the sun didn't have the same effect, positive or negative, it had out West. Time would tell if the plants would show differences as the summer heated up, but that did him no good this time of year. No … there must be some other way to tell.

As he chewed on the dried pork, he scrutinized the surrounding plants, paying special attention to those growing on the north side of rocks, trees, and large bushes. But the more he looked, the more baffled he became. Grasses and other small plants grew just as vigorously on the north side as any other. Soil, slope, and other factors seemed to affect them more than sun or shade. He decided he'd need to give it more thought and study as he went along.

The salty pork had made him thirsty, and it suddenly occurred to him he'd seen very little flowing water—only the tiny ant-stream since he'd sat on the hornet nest. He puzzled over this for a few minutes. Then it came to him. He smiled at his own foolishness. He'd seen the answer this very morning. The cave, and the water flowing into it! What if such caves filled these hills? Then much of the water normally flowing on the surface, in streams, and sitting in ponds, would seep into the ground and fill the spaces below. Just as he'd seen in the *fledermaus* cavern. Thinking it a good theory at least, he returned to the cave and refilled his water skin before venturing further on.

All that day he continued to work on his tracking skills as he moved along. He scanned the ground for signs of any earlier movement, animal or human. A clear boot mark in the earth rewarded his efforts in the middle of the afternoon.

He crouched down and inspected the ground in a slowly widening circle. He scrutinized each blade of grass, every rock, and each indentation in the earth. Satisfied he was now reading this story correctly, he moved forward along the trail of the boot marks. Two different men walking along together had made these tracks.

He decided the tracks were more than a day old, probably two or three days. Their makers had clearly passed here *before* the rain shower that'd chased Billy into the cave.

He followed the trail as it wended its way up the hill, several hundred yards in a nearly straight line. Then the marks angled off at forty-five-degrees to the left from the original path. This new development excited him. The men now moved swiftly and with purpose directly toward a large pine tree some twenty paces away from the previous track. What had made the men change direction and increase their pace?

He stepped up to the tree and surveyed it, looking slowly up the rough bark, at the outstretching branches with their long, pointy green needles. He looked for any recent signs an animal or human had climbed it but saw nothing of the kind. Then he moved closer to the base of the tree, following the boot tracks with his eyes as he walked. Something caught his eye: a deep mark pressed down hard into the grass next to one of the boot tracks very near the tree trunk. Getting down on all fours, he examined this new mark more closely. There he noticed small, dark dots on blades of grass and small plants growing low to the ground. When he reached out and touched one of the spots, it rubbed off onto his finger. He held the finger up to his nose and smelled. *Ha!*

He smiled, *now the story becomes clear! Two men out hunting. They notice something further up the hill that excites them. A deer, or elk, likely. So they swiftly move up behind the tree for cover. There they load their rifles. The butt of one rifle makes a deep mark in the grass as the hunter loads it from the muzzle. In his hurry and excitement, he spills tiny bits of gunpowder, leaving dark spots on the grass.*

He pored over the ground around the tree to confirm his findings. He soon found what he'd been seeking, another identical mark in the ground—the second rifle! This man had loaded his rifle more neatly, though; Billy found no sign of spilled gunpowder this time.

He continued reading the signs—stealthy movements as the men emerged from tree cover. They carefully moved from tree to bush to rock as they made their way up the hill and ever closer to their prey. Billy could now tell these were experienced hunters.

He appreciated the obvious skill with which they had stalked their prey. Envisioning the thrill of the hunt, he became ever more excited, almost holding his breath with anticipation of what would happen next.

He wondered if he'd be able to tell whether the men had fired their guns. Probably not, he decided. Unless … if the shooter were near a tree, bush, or other tall plant when he fired, the flash from the muzzle might leave behind a telltale scorch. And then he saw it and nearly laughed out loud with delight. The leaves on the top of a waist-high bush were curled and slightly darker than those further down its sides. When he plucked them, they were dry and brittle, not soft and supple like the others. *So at least one gunshot from here,* he thought. He looked to see how the man was standing to determine which way he was likely aiming when he fired his shot, and with the help of the scorched bush, he made a fairly confident determination. He gazed out in that direction, and less than a hundred yards away was a small, grassy draw mostly clear of trees. *Good grazing for deer,* he decided. *If he had a true aim, I should find the evidence there.*

He noted the hunters had hurried again, this time to find out if they'd hit their mark. When he came to the grassy draw, he saw clear signs that deer had indeed been grazing here. Even a child could read these signs—hoof marks, chewed off grass, and plenty of dung, not all of it fresh. Clearly the men had stumbled upon a regular, favored grazing spot for the deer. Just a few yards further, he found blood upon the grass, and signs of a sudden, violent movement of several deer—five he guessed, although they had been so closely packed it would have taken a while to sort out all the marks. One deer had not run far; only a few paces away the grass was beaten down. The men's tracks covered the ground all around the spot. They'd cut the deer open and removed the inner organs to lighten the load for the long haul back to camp. Other tracks—many, many small tracks, also covered the grassy area—coyote and fox for sure, and other smaller ones. Rats most likely. Between them they'd cleaned up the entrails of the deer almost entirely; nothing remained but a dark, greasy stain on the grass and in the dirt underneath.

Billy sat and admired the scene with great satisfaction. More so, he thought, than if he'd been on the hunt himself. He'd read the whole thing from the book of the earth. As if he'd been there to see the kill with his own eyes! It was an exhilarating feeling; one he could never explain to another person. Well, at least not to the white men. They had no patience nor understanding for such things. Oh, they appreciated when he used his skills to their benefit, that was true. And even expressed admiration for his keen abilities. But they would never understand the thrill, the utter excitement of correctly reading the tales the earth had to tell.

Most important, he now knew he *could* learn to read this new book, given enough time, diligent practice, and patient attention to every detail. It would take months to be even a fraction as confident as he was back in Texas, and likely years to thoroughly master the skills. But it was a start!

෫෮෮෮෮෮෮෮෮෮෮෮෮෮෮෮

Toward the end of the day he stood at the crest of a ridge. It was the third such ridge he had crossed that day, traveling generally west to east, while the ridgelines flowed in a southwest to northeast direction. And he could see no end to them, as if a tremendous giant had folded all the land. He'd spent the morning scrambling up a tall ridge and back down the other side. He'd repeated the same thing again, and then once again.

Now he looked down from the ridgeline into the valley below and saw a road. This must be the road crossing the mountains to the far side, eventually leading to the sea. The road made a distinct line cutting through the trees into the distance. His eyes followed its wandering course and he soon recognized that it cleverly wove its way so the ups and downs were as minimal as possible. They'd not built it to blindly forge from west to east in a straight line over ridge after ridge, like *he* had just been doing, he chided himself! Instead, they'd found a way *around* the ridges. The builders had wisely taken advantage of gaps in the ends of the ridgelines where they faded down near the level of the valleys. He nodded his head appreciatively.

Then he turned away from the road. He wasn't going *that* way this time. Instead, he looked to his more immediate surroundings. He now stood on top of a large rock outcropping at the top of the ridge which ran away almost straight in a line to the northeast. If he headed in that direction, he'd have an easier time of it, he realized. The top of the ridgeline never varied much in elevation—no great peaks or dips as far as he could see. But if he continued to the east, he'd counted at least five more ridgelines just as high as the one he stood on. He grimaced thinking of scrambling up and down over all those ridgelines. No, not a good way to go! Tomorrow, he would move along the top of the ridgeline and see what he could see.

☜☞☜☞☜☞☜☞☜☞☜☞

The next day he was up with the dawn, covering all remaining signs of his small campfire and the impression in the earth where he had slept. After a bite of crusty bread and hard cheese from his pack, he had a quick swig of water from his water skin. Then he headed out across the crest of the ridgeline, heading in a northeasterly direction.

It was much easier going this way. Not only was there much less elevation gain and loss, but wide, smooth rocks covered the ridgeline and it had fewer trees and less underbrush to contend with. By midday he had reached a point he'd been aiming for over the last several hours. It seemed to be the highest point along the entire ridgeline, though still he would not call it a peak.

He sat on an old stump and enjoyed the panoramic view to the east as he had another bite of the dry food. As he sat, idly swinging his feet, bumping his heels against the side of the stump, he noticed his left leg hit something soft—not the hard wood of the stump his right heel was knocking against. He looked down and noticed the green spongy plant that seemed to grow everywhere in these woods—on rocks, on trees, between bushes and clumps of grass—pretty much any space where other plants weren't already growing. Then a sudden thought struck him—*not* any space; some places did *not* have this green covering … like the other side of this stump. He jumped down and inspected the stump. Sure enough, the greenness only covered half. And not evenly either; toward the edges it got thinner and thinner until it no longer grew at all. In fact, it was clearly …

"Thickest on the *north* side!" he said out loud and laughed. He shook his head slowly and smiled, thinking, *"I've been too clever by half," Sergeant Jim would say. The answer was in front of me all along. Not the things growing in the shade, but the thing growing on the shade!*

He continued staring at the stump in wonder. As he turned his gaze toward his surroundings, it became as plain as the sun in the sky; the green, spongy plant *always* grew best on the north side of any tree, rock, or other plant. He sat back down and finished his meal, a contented smile on his face.

Well, time to start heading back, he decided when he'd finished. *Told Sergeant Jim five suns, and it will be just that by the time I get back.* It was another good survival skill for a scout—do what you told your officer you would do and return when you told him you would return. That way if you were late it was much more likely he would notice. And more likely he'd know where to send someone to find out *why*.

Or where to find the body. He grinned and shook his head, enjoying the thought of Sergeant Jim's grim soldier's humor. It was Billy's favorite kind as well.

Instead of heading back along the ridgeline the way he'd come, he headed down the slope and made his way along the valley for a while. Maybe he'd go far enough to meet up with the road. He didn't much care for roads, and didn't intend to travel along it, but he was curious about its condition, and how it was constructed. He considered it part of his duties as a scout to know about such things. If an enemy or friend were to use this road, what conditions would he encounter? How quickly could he move along it, and how much would the weather affect his progress? Was it so hard as to yield little information about a person's passing, or softer material willing to tell a more interesting tale? If he wished to know these things, he'd have to go see it for himself. He *could* ask the soldiers his questions, but he knew they'd just say, "It's a road. Dusty in summer, and muddy in winter. Bumpy when you ride on it. What else do you need to know?" Useless, but not surprising.

He had made it about halfway down the slope toward the valley when he drew to a sudden stop. His ever-scanning eyes had noticed a set of tracks crossing the direction he was going at an angle heading back up the hill in a northerly direction. When he crouched down for a close look, he became puzzled. Clearly human tracks, but … not *boot* marks. He moved slowly around looking carefully at each mark. The signs were all muddled. More than one person … two, or … no, maybe three or more different people. But walking in single file, almost as if … as if, to befuddle a tracker! Single file made it much harder to tell the numbers in a group, or to tell much detail about any individual.

And he kept coming back to the fact none of these people wore boots. But they weren't barefoot either, as a group of slaves might be. The soles of their shoes were flat and smooth with no boot heel. This puzzled him greatly. He'd never seen white men walking out in the wild without wearing boots.

And yet, here they were, walking through the woods, moving in single file so no one could track them, apparently.

And … *not wearing boots!* Like … like *Indians?* It made no sense, and he could not puzzle it out. If he were still in Texas, the answer would be simple: a group of Indians out hunting and not wanting to give away their numbers or nature to any other Indians happening by.

But the Captain had assured him there were no longer any Indians in Virginia, nor anywhere near it for a thousand miles or more. They *had* lived here once, years ago. And they'd fought great battles with the white men, and with each other, before being driven out to the West.

And yet … he could think of no other explanation. He considered following the tracks back up the mountain, but then thought better of it. For one, these tracks were older than the hunters' tracks he'd seen earlier, so the trail had likely gone cold. He wouldn't be able to track whoever it was all the way to their final destination. But the other consideration he had was, *What if they are Indians? They probably won't like me tracking them, and I might end up alone and outnumbered amongst hostile enemies.*

Through long, hard experience, the Tonkawa mistrusted and disliked all other Indian tribes. It was part of the reason they'd thrown in their lot with the white soldiers, the soldiers being the only humans who valued their abilities and didn't try to kill them on sight!

Finally, he shrugged his shoulders at the mystery, turned, and continued down the hill. He'd ask the Captain again if there might still be any stray Indians in these mountains.

೩ೞೞೞೞೞೞೞೞೞೞೞ

Billy reached the crest of another ridgeline as the afternoon sun was westering. He felt a weariness deep in his muscles from his long exertions of the day.

It was time to find shelter, make a fire, and cook the pair of healthy young rabbits he'd felled with his bow earlier in the day. He decided he would much rather eat them than continue carrying them, dangling from the back of his belt, bouncing along as he walked.

He found no great caves this time, but he did find a large, dry area under an overhanging rock, which suited him just fine. Better for a fire anyway—in a cave the smoke might become oppressive. And tonight, he saved the matches. He found a handful of nice, dry tinder, courtesy of a mouse nest in the crack of a rock, and used his more primitive fire-lighting implements. Soon he had a nice little fire going, the rabbits roasting happily on spits above. It was a lovely evening, and the stars filled the sky as he picked the last of the rabbit meat from the bones. No *fledermaus* this evening, but he did see an owl sail by on silent wings, only visible via its silhouette darkening out the stars behind as it flew.

He settled down happily to sleep, pulling the small wool blanket over his shoulders as the fire slowly died. His last thoughts before drifting off were of his newfound liking for this place called Virginia. A very interesting country; a person could spend a lifetime learning to read its ways.

Chapter 5. The Winds of Change

"For they have sown the wind,
and they shall reap the whirlwind."
– Hosea 8:7

Sunday June 17, 1860 – Greenbrier County, Virginia:

Nathan decided he would *not* attend the local church service this Sunday morning, as was Miss Abbey's usual habit. For one, he wasn't ready to confront Mr. Walters over the ridiculous front-row church seats matter. He'd rather meet with the man in private first to see if he could smooth things over, ending the feud in a gentlemanly, civilized fashion, if possible. Walters' ill-treatment of his mother would be difficult to forgive and forget, however.

But more important, today he had in mind giving a "sermon" of his own and didn't want to wait until later in the afternoon. Also, he wanted to start a new routine, recognizing the Sabbath in the traditional way: no work, not even for the slaves, from sunrise to sunset. He knew he'd have to be there to see to its enforcement. Since he had just returned home after twenty years away, he figured another week's absence from the local church service would be of little matter.

"But dear, Reverend Blackburn has been coming to the farm once a month to preach to the slaves, at your Daddy's request, for years now. And *this* Sunday he's scheduled to come again."

"Hmm … have you listened to any of these sermons, Momma? No? Well, I have and am not much taken with the idea. It's common practice for slave owners to bring in preachers who tell the black people how fortunate they are to be slaves. And there are plenty of positive references to slavery in the Bible, I'm sorry to say. But also, just as many opposing the practice …

'Servants, be obedient to them that are your masters according to the flesh, with fear and trembling, in singleness of your heart, as unto Christ,' Ephesians chapter six, verse five.

97

'*Stand fast therefore in the liberty wherewith Christ hath made us free, and be not entangled again with the yoke of bondage,*' Galatians chapter five, verse one.

'*Servants be obedient unto your own masters, and please them well in all things,*' Titus chapter two, verse nine.

'*And he that stealeth a man, and selleth him, or if he be found in his hand, he shall surely be put to death,*' Exodus chapter twenty-one, verse sixteen.

"And so on, and so forth. There are dozens more of the same."

"Nathan, dear—however do you *do* that?"

"Do *what*, Momma?"

"Remember all those Bible verses like that? My goodness! I've been going to church my entire life, and I couldn't quote even a single one."

"Oh, *that*. Well, I seem to have a good memory for such things … I don't know why. For instance, I can glance at a room full of people, and later recall every detail—where everyone stood, who they were talking to, what they were wearing, the expressions they had on their faces, and so on. It's the reason I wanted to look at each of the slaves as they said their own names. Even now I see each face clearly in my mind, and each is speaking his own name to me.

"And being in the Army, I've had plenty of times when I had little to do, and nothing to read but the Bible. I have to confess, I don't know *every* chapter and verse … but the ones I've found interesting seem to … *stick* in my memory, somehow."

"That's amazing! I wonder where you get it from. Certainly not from me … I can't remember what I had in the morning for breakfast! And I never saw your Daddy show anything like it."

Nathan shrugged his shoulders. "A gift from God, I suppose. Given for reasons only *He* knows. Anyway, I can't reconcile the idea of a just and loving God, who created *all* the people, with the notion of keeping some of them in perpetual slavery. I can't imagine God caring what country they came from, nor the color of their skin.

"I will talk with Reverend Blackburn this afternoon when he comes and tell him his services at Mountain Meadows are no longer required."

"*Oh …*"

"What is it, Momma?"

"Well … it's just … the pastor is … well, a very *strong-willed* man. I imagine he'll not take kindly to the change."

"Oh, is that all? Well … the pastor will find I can also be … *very strong-willed.*"

Miss Abbey laughed, shook her head, and rolled her eyes. "Yes … I have known *that* since the day you were born!"

ഇരുഇരുഇരുഇരുഇരു

It had been four days since the new master made his now famous—or infamous, depending on who you talked to—first walk around the farm. And Tony found himself, to his surprise and discomfort, a minor celebrity among the other field workers. He'd been the first to come face to face with the new master, the first forced to look him in the eye and give his name, and the first questioned by him. As the talk had continued to circulate, the new master had taken on a mystical and, in Tony's opinion, unrealistic stature, both good and bad. Because of this, many of the slaves now assumed there'd been premeditated purpose in everything the master had done and said on that day. And so Tony, being the first slave the master had singled out and spoken to, now took on special significance in their eyes.

At first, he found the attention novel, and even enjoyable. But now it had become an annoyance—people looking at him differently when he walked by and whispering amongst themselves. Others seeking him out and pestering him with endless questions and even more endless, nonsensical speculation on the meaning of it all.

To Tony, it had been nothing more than pure dumb luck the master had spoken with him first. And now he wondered whether it had been good luck, or bad. The simple truth was, he happened to be the person working the closest to the house when the master started his walk that morning. But he had given up trying to explain it to people, in pure exasperation. The people wanted to believe what they wanted to believe, and the *truth* had nothing to do with it.

Tony himself was more of a skeptic. After he'd recovered from the shock and excitement of that first meeting with the master, he sank back into old, hard thoughts about his life. He'd decided this new young master was just trying to impress the people upon his arrival. To make them work harder, be more loyal, or whatever other reasons of his own. Soon the newness would wear off, things would return to their normal routine, and nothing would change.

But now, several days later, Tony found himself forced to question his earlier notions and entertain the idea he *might* be wrong. It was a Sunday morning. The sun was already up and shining on the bright green lawn, a place he'd never expected to be on this day. He wouldn't generally have even been aware what day of the week it was, each day being much like the others—up before dawn, work till dusk, eat, sleep, and do the same the next day. Occasionally, the local white pastor, named Blackburn, would come preach a sermon to the slaves an hour or so before the end of the normal workday. But that always seemed to take Tony and the others by surprise. There was so much time in between sermons they lost track of when the next would be.

But yesterday evening the white overseers had called them in from the fields an hour earlier than normal, not yet sunset. At first Tony assumed it must be for the preacher's sermon, but it was not so.

Instead, the overseers gathered them all together on the road in front of the slave quarters, much as they'd done on the day of the new master's arrival. Sickles, the head boss man, told them in a matter-of-fact tone that the next day was Sunday, and the master had declared they would all celebrate God's Sabbath. There would be no work in the fields or the pens, or anywhere else, *all day* tomorrow, from sunrise to sunset.

This was shocking enough, but Sickles also announced everyone should dress in the nicest clothes they had. Tony found this order puzzling, and slightly amusing; he had no such clothes.

Finally, he told them they must all, even the smallest child or babe in arms, gather on the lawn in front of the house at first light. There the master would speak to them.

"That is all," Sickles concluded abruptly. He turned around and strode away, followed closely by the other white farmhands.

Now it was Sunday morning, and here Tony stood, with all the other slaves, men, women, and children. He noticed some of their clothing did look a little cleaner and whiter than usual. Either they'd stashed away some clothes to keep them nicer, or some late-night washing had occurred. As for him, he wore what he always wore: a worn and stained rough-spun cotton shirt and wool trousers, with a short length of rope for a belt. He had work shoes back at the cabin, but he never wore them in the warm weather because they made his feet hot. Besides, he'd rather not let them get worn out, so he'd have them when he needed them during the cold winter weather.

The group had followed Sickle's instructions to the letter; they'd gathered on the lawn in front of the Big House. But they'd all bunched up at the edge of the lawn, the farthest they could be from the house while still being where they were told. Most of them had been there since before the sunrise, not wanting to be late for whatever was going to happen. There was nervous chatter, mostly small talk, but some speculation about what may happen. Those who were better versed in the teachings of the Bible, mostly the elders, were explaining what the Sabbath meant. A few people were reciting the seven days of the week to those who'd never learned them, never having had any reason to.

It was now about an hour after sunrise, and Tony was becoming impatient. Not that it bothered him to stand for long periods of time, he was well used to that, working all day on the farm. They only allowed the workers to sit for a few minutes to eat a small bite and have a quick drink of water at lunch time. There were otherwise no rest periods during all the long day. No, it was not the standing, but the anxious anticipation of the unknown that troubled him. He wasn't used to the unknown.

His entire life up until now had been the most mundane, repetitive routine possible. Other than changes in the weather, and the occasional swapping out of individual white overseers—who were all pretty much the same, in his opinion—nothing ever changed. There was never any reason to be anxious, worried, or excited about what would happen in the next hour, the next day, the next year, or … ever. But now, suddenly, things *had* changed. For one, never in his whole life could Tony remember a day, except for Christmas once a year, when they weren't made to work in the fields. There were days during the hardest winters when they had little *productive* work to do, with snow covering the ground, and a chill, biting wind howling through the air. But still the masters roused them from the warmth of their beds and forced them outside to do whatever they could do—shoveling snow from the walkways and road, clearing ice from the livestock's fodder and water troughs, hauling firewood to the cabins, barracks, and the Big House. And so on, and so on.

Even when the old master died, they marched the workers out to the fields to do their normal work routine, as if nothing at all unusual had happened. They only learned about it at the end of the day, in the same way they'd learned about the Sabbath; Sickles announced it, matter-of-factly, as they gathered outside the cabins.

But this day there was to be no work at all. And Tony had come to understand it was for no better reason than because it was the seventh day of the week, called "Sunday," but also called "Sabbath." The elders explained it was to honor God by resting on the seventh day as He had rested on the seventh day after creating the heavens and the Earth. Tony shook his head at the wonder of that. *God must be mighty powerful to create all the things there were in only seven days. No … six*, he reminded himself; *on the seventh day God didn't work at all. Yes, sir, mighty powerful, all right!*

Tony was anxiously gazing at the entrance to the great white house when the front door suddenly came open. A hush fell over the group as a figure stepped out. There was an audible groan of disappointment when they saw the figure was Megs, the head of the household slaves.

Ned nudged Tony with his elbow, "Damned house slaves … traitors … *whores!* … worse'n slavers."

Tony nodded his agreement. He had little use for the slaves working the Big House. The field slaves all knew anything said to them would go straight to the master's ears. They lived in the comfort of the Big House and ate its fancy meals; kissed the white men's babies, and, if the rumors were true, the women slept in the white men's beds. The slaves who worked the fields had nothing but contempt for them.

But Megs didn't seem to know, or else just didn't care about the ill will from the other slaves. At least, she didn't acknowledge it. She was smug and bossy, from what Tony had seen, and it didn't seem to matter who she bossed. He decided he really *despised* her.

She looked out at the group and strode forward to the edge of the veranda at the top of the broad stairs leading up from the drive. There she stopped, and cupping her hands around her mouth shouted, "Come on over here closer to the house, y'all. Master wants to talk with you, and you're gonna give him a hoarse sore voice if'n you stands all the way back there and makes him shout!" She waved her arms in a beckoning motion indicating they should move up closer.

At that moment Sickles and the other white overseers arrived, including all the new ones who'd come from the West with the new master. Even the strange wild "Indian" man had come. He was a source of much speculation and mystery amongst the workers. They could not fathom why the new master had brought him here, nor what he did with himself during the day. People said they wouldn't see him for days at a time, and then suddenly he would be there. But he did no work at all, just sat under a tree or bush and watched the other men work. A very strange man.

"The maid's got the right of it. Move on up, y'all, so's the master don't have to shout," Sickles commanded in his loud, stern voice.

Tony found it telling Sickles and the other white men were arriving just now, an hour or more *after* sunrise, when they'd ordered all the slaves there at dawn. They clearly knew there would be nothing happening so early, and there was no need to have the people gathering then, but they had ordered it anyway.

Why? Tony wondered. *Just pure meanness, I guess.* He had no love for Sickles and needed no more reason to dislike the man.

They walked in a group up toward the veranda. Megs stood at the top of the stairs gazing down at them, hands on hips, like an annoyed mother.

"Well, that's better, but you needn't bunch up so tight. It's a nice warm morning, so there's no need to huddle together like frozen sheep. Spread out a bit and try to look more ... oh, I don't know ... *comfortable-like.*" As the group slowly spread a little, she gave them one last look, shook her head in apparent exasperation, shrugged her shoulders, turned, and went back into the house.

This time the small talk did *not* resume; there was too much nervous anticipation. The white men moved over to stand next to the veranda, looking out toward the gathered slaves. Tony noticed they chatted amiably with one another, smiling and laughing quietly amongst themselves. He also saw Sickles and two of the old hands had separated themselves from the others, and did not appear to be smiling, or talking much. They looked as anxious as Tony was feeling. It suddenly occurred to him—Sickles didn't know what was going to happen either! That was an eye-opener. He'd never considered they might not be in the know about all the master's plans and intentions. It was a revelation. He decided he would have to give it some thought later.

But not now; the door suddenly opened again. This time the master himself stepped out, followed closely by the younger master called Tom, and Miss Abbey. Megs and all the household slaves soon followed, gathering around the doorway. The master turned and said something to Megs and the others. They quickly made their way past him, coming briskly down the stairs to stand next to, but slightly apart from, the other slaves.

The master stepped up to the edge of the veranda and looked out over the assembly. He'd dressed in his fine black suit and hat, the same as he'd worn on his return to Mountain Meadows. The entire farm had gathered before him. It was the first time in Tony's memory *that* had happened. Even the crazy big dog was there, he saw. It was lying on the grass by the corner of the house, tongue hanging out to one side, gazing at the master intently, as were they all.

"Good morning," the master began, in a clear, deep voice, "and good *Sabbath* to you. I know y'all have been taught the word of the Lord, our God from his own good and holy book, the Bible. Y'all are proper Christians, believers in the one true God, whose son he sent to this Earth long ago to do good for us simple men. Some of you may have learned to read and so have seen the words in this great book for yourselves. Others of you may have been told the words by visiting preachers, or others. Either way, you will know … when Moses came down from the mountain where God spoke to him, he carried a tablet stone, on which God had written his Commandments: the laws for his people. I'm not going to name all ten today. But I would like to remind you about *one* of these Commandments, of which Moses said:"

> *Remember the Sabbath day, to keep it holy. Six days you shall labor, and do all your work, but the seventh day is a Sabbath to the LORD your God. On it you shall not do any work; you, or your son, or your daughter, your male servant, or your female servant, or your livestock, or the sojourner who is within your gates. For in six days the LORD made heaven and earth, the sea, and all that is in them, and rested on the seventh day. Therefore, the LORD blessed the Sabbath day and made it holy.*

The master paused in his speech, as if to let it sink in.

"Today I will talk to you about many things, and many changes I am going to make at this farm. If you believe my return means nothing more than changing an older master for a younger one, after which life will go on, the same as before, *you are greatly mistaken!*

"Whether you be field worker, animal tender, or kitchen maid, you are, even now, enjoying one of the simplest of those great changes. As you've already been told, we are today celebrating the Sabbath in the way God intended and instructed his people, by *not* working this day. We will instead, use this day today ... and *every* Sunday while I'm master of this farm ... to come together to talk. To learn the lessons God would have us learn from his good book, and to learn other useful skills and lessons, which I will talk more about later."

When the master said, "... today, and *every* Sunday ..." there were many wide-eyed looks passed between the people in the audience. Tony saw Big George turn toward his wife Babs to catch her eye. He grinned at her and winked. She rolled her eyes in response.

"I am *very* happy to stand here before you today and tell you the things I'm about to tell you. For you, the people of the dark-colored skin, the people in bondage, this is a *great* day—a day you'll remember the rest of your lives. I asked even the smallest babe in arms be here with us today, so someday when they're old and gray, with grandchildren on their knees, they'll be able to say, 'I was there on *that* day and heard *those* things with my very own ears.'

"Those of you who have read or have heard the words of God's Holy Bible will know the truth of what I'm about to say. When God finished creating the Earth, the stars, and all the creatures that walk, swim or fly, he made the *people*. He made them to be his own *special* children.

"And when he made the people, the Bible says he made them '*in his own image*.' It means, he made us people to look like *Him*. And do you know what the Bible says was the *color* of God, that he used when he made the people to look like Him? No ... you don't ... and neither do I. The truth is, *nobody* knows the color of God. And the Bible does *not*, even once, in all its thousands of pages, say what color the people were when God created them.

"And while men may argue, and say this, or that, or the other, as suits their own purposes, *I believe* God made ALL the people. And He made them in all the different colors the people are, *because* he made them '*in his own image*.' You see, God is too great to be of only one color, for he is of no color at all, and of all colors ... both at the same time. And so, whether we be white, or black ... or red," he nodded toward the Indian, who nodded back, "we

106

are *all* the children of God. And He made us to look exactly like *Him*. Together, we are as brothers in God's eyes.

"Now … I am the master and leader of all the people here on this farm. But I have this role, not because of some great skill or intelligence I have shown, nor any great things I have done. Nor because the people of this farm have taken a vote and chosen me to be their leader. No … I am the master because of the fortune of my birth alone, nothing more. My father was the master of this farm, and I was born his son. It is as simple as that.

"Likewise, *you* who are held in bondage as slaves on this farm are not here because you've committed some crime or sin, nor because you owe a debt, nor because you are in any way unworthy to be free men. No … you are slaves held in bondage for no other reason than you were born to parents who were also slaves. And *they* were slaves because hard, cruel men with guns, whips, and chains captured one of your people sometime in the past in faraway Africa. They put them on a ship and sailed them away from their African home to America. Once here, they forced them to work hard, or they'd be beaten, and starved. Whatever you may have heard other people say … *this is the simple truth!* You are *not* lesser men. You are *not* less smart, nor less capable of doing great things, nor of being free men.

"On our recent journey here from the West we also sailed on a ship across great waters. When a terrible storm blew, it was a free black man who steered our ship out of harm's way with great skill, saving us from a terrible, watery death. No white man could have done better.

"You've been born into bondage. You've been purposely kept ignorant, and poor, and dependent upon your masters for your every need, and for your very survival. None of this is your fault, and it does not make you less than other men.

"We live in the greatest land in the world. Nay, not just the greatest land in the world, but rather the greatest land *that has ever been* in the whole long history of the world. Greater than Athens, greater than Rome … greater even than England's mighty empire, though it spans the entire Earth. Never have men enjoyed a land of such wealth, and opportunity, and … yes, *freedom*.

"But it's the great, damning shame and disgrace of our people. We who enjoy the bounties of freedom are depriving a whole group of fellow human beings—of fellow *children of God*—of the fruits of that freedom. It is unconscionable, and unacceptable to men of good will and character, *men of God* … to take part in this travesty.

"And yet … here am I, master of a farm holding one hundred and twelve souls in bondage, through no fault of their own. How can I call myself a pious man of God, a righteous man, a man of good conscience, when I myself am no better than a *slaver*?

"I can tell you this question has sorely troubled my soul, and given me many sleepless nights, until I have finally decided what I must do."

He paused, and looked down, as if collecting his thoughts. No one made a sound, as if transfixed, or collectively holding their breath, hanging on every word.

Tony didn't recognize some words in the speech; "unconscionable" and "travesty" were words he didn't know, among others. But there was no mistaking the general meaning of what the master was saying …

"But before I tell you what decision I've made … I want to talk to you about this *place* where we all live; this place we call Mountain Meadows Farm, in western Virginia.

"To most of you it's just the place you live and work every day. Most of you have been here your whole lives and know nothing else. I was born here, but left this place as a young boy, and traveled all over the land. Up north to Washington, and to New York, Philadelphia, and Boston—to all the great cities of America. And I traveled south. Down a great river called Mississippi, all the way to a strange and beautiful city called New Orleans, where they speak the language of the French people. There I boarded a boat with other soldiers, and sailed away to a land called Mexico, where they talk in yet another foreign language. After that I traveled way out to the West, out past where the sun sets to a place called Texas. There everything is wild, including the people, white, brown, and red," he shared a look with the Indian again, who smiled back at him.

"I tell you this story because I want you to know—though this place is just normal, ordinary, and everyday to you, who have known nothing else—this is a very special place on this Earth. It's a place of exceeding beauty, of clean, pure water, bountiful game in the woods, and fish in the streams. It is of mild weather, not unbearably hot in the summer, nor deathly cold in the winter. And the soil generously brings forth bountiful harvests, year after year. I can honestly tell you, in all my travels, I have seen no other place as good, as this place, *our* home.

"I have seen beautiful sights, to be sure, and many wonderful things!

"But I have also seen horrible places, where the people suffer terrible cold or heat, thirst or hunger. Where all manner of pests— insects, snakes, wolves, and deadly diseases—plague the people. Where men are wicked, and cruel to each other. Where robbery and murder are a part of everyday life, and a man may not raise his family without constant fear for their lives.

"Thankfully, we do *not* live in that kind of place. This beautiful farm is *our* home—*all of us!* When I left and saw the wider world, I came to appreciate just how fine, how *special* this place is. I came to cherish it, and to wish no harm or evil would *ever* befall it. I came to know one thing for certain: as long as I live, this will always be my beloved home."

He looked back at Miss Abbey and smiled, and she smiled back, and Tony could see tears freely flowing down her cheeks.

"And though you're in bondage, this is still *your* home, too. It has nurtured and sustained you throughout your life; though it must be said … it has demanded *hard labor* in return.

"But now we come to the heart of my dilemma. How can this place survive without all of *you* to keep it thriving? You provide the labor, every day, every year that makes this farm possible. Without your hard work, *our* home, yours and mine, would soon fall to ruin; would soon return to a wilderness where wolves would freely roam, and no man could live. And we, who once lived here, would be left to wander the wide world, homeless, like *'strangers in a strange land,'* as the good book says."

Again, he paused, and looked out at the people. Not past them but seeming to meet their eyes. Tony was sure he now looked directly at him.

"But what if you don't care about any of that? What if you truly don't care about this farm or what happens to it? What then?

"What would happen, if by some miracle, like those in the good book, God Almighty were to suddenly appear before us, and set you all free with his mighty hand? And tell you to go forth into the world and be free? What would you do? Where would you go?

"You couldn't stay here in the south. The people here don't wish the dark-skinned people to be free. And even if they allowed it, they wouldn't *pay* you to work, so you'd have no money. And without money, no food, no clothes, and no roof over your head. You'd quickly perish from hunger and cold.

"So what if you went north? I'm sure you've heard the people up north think kindlier toward you ... they'd not force you back into slavery. And some might even shelter you for a time and give you food, out of pity. But you have no skills they need in the North. You only know how to work a farm. They already have all the farm workers they need. And only a few of you can read or write, few of you have the skills to build things, or to work the machines in a factory. You would become pitiable, pathetic, and dependent upon the good will of others. Beggars in a cold, hard land.

"Well then ... what about Africa? Y'all have heard the stories of how your people came from there. That they lived there for age upon age ... free from the whips and chains of the white men.

"I'm sorry to say, you can't go back that way. For one, the ships that brought your people here take no one back. And even if they did, no one would ever take such a horrible journey of their own free choice. Many and many died on those horrible, death ships before ever reaching these shores. Then what if you were to pay for a journey on a normal passenger ship back to Africa, if you could find one? It would cost more than you could earn in *years* of hard labor, if you could save it all and didn't have to eat, buy clothes, or pay to live under a roof.

"And even if you could somehow make it back to Africa, what would you find there? You would find people that may look like you, but speak a different language, have different customs, live in a strange country filled with dangerous animals, and deadly diseases. And you would find the people worship the old African gods, and have never even heard of the Christ, Our Lord and Savior.

"I'm afraid you would be unwelcome strangers in the land of your fathers. You have become *Americans*, for better or worse, and *here you must stay.*

"And if you *were* all gone, and there was no one left to work this farm, then what? I will tell you. There aren't enough white workers in the South to hire, since most farms use slave labor, so I'd have no choice but to sell the farm. And the only ones who could afford it would be men who use slaves for labor. And the cycle of bondage would continue on this farm for others."

He paused again, and looked at them, long, and hard.

"I will tell you now what *we* are going to do. Myself, and the other white men here, will teach *you* … all of you … the things you'll need to know to become *free men.* And when we've finished teaching you … *I AM GOING TO SET YOU FREE!*"

There followed a dead silence, as if the listeners were in a state of shock. Tony felt the shock himself. This was so far beyond anything he'd ever considered; he didn't know what to think. Not joy, nor elation, nor anxiety, nor fear. Just numbness. As if the words were being heard by someone else. For some reason, he looked over at Sickles, and saw him leaning over toward one of the other men, shaking his head, and whispering something. The other man nodded in response. *Trouble,* Tony thought.

"And *when* I free you, it is my hope many of you will choose to stay here and help run this farm—not as slaves, but as free men and women. Paid money like the white men are paid, and free to come and go as you please, and to leave whenever you like. And if you choose to leave, I will wish you well; and I'll trust in the training we've given you to carry you forth into a world you'll be prepared to enter. A place where you'll be able to find work, and a wholesome place to live."

And despite these great words, words Tony had *never* expected to hear in his life; still … there was a deathly silence. No one spoke, no one whispered, no one looked at anyone except the master, as if they'd been transfixed and stripped of their ability to think and speak.

The master seemed surprised, and unsure for a moment—as if he had expected some other reaction. Tony felt a momentary twinge of guilt and sympathy for him. Maybe he'd expected clapping and cheering. But instead he received cold silence.

"Well … I expect it will take some time to sink in …" he said, hesitantly. He looked over toward the group of white men he'd brought with him from the West: the soldiers. Tony looked at them for the first time since the master had started speaking. They were smiling at the master, as if giving him encouragement. It occurred to him then … the Captain's speech had *not* surprised these men. *They* knew what would happen, but Sickles didn't. *That* was interesting …

And then the master seemed to take heart from the looks of his men and continued with more confidence. "So, along with the Sabbath and the teachings, we shall make other changes starting today. I know some of you overheard me telling the white farmhands there shall be no more beatings, whippings, or any other kind of cruel punishment. I am saying it now again so all will hear. There shall be no more on my farm, now and forever. This I swear on the Holy Bible.

"Further, to begin the change from slavery to freedom, starting today … starting *now*, you will no longer address the white men as 'master.' From now on you will address them as 'Mister' followed by their name, either first name or last as they prefer, it matters not to me. So, for example, our very large, jolly fellow over there," he said, waving his hand toward Stan, "you may call 'Mister Stan,' rather than 'master,'" and with this Stan bowed; a grand, formal bow and then he gave a great, toothsome grin. This seemed to finally break the spell of silence, causing a twitter of giggles from the young children.

"As for myself, you may call me 'Mister Chambers,' or … you may just call me 'Captain,' as my men from the Army do, if you wish."

There was now a buzz of conversation; the idea of no longer referring to the master as "master" was so novel and unheard of, it immediately triggered a flurry of nervous laughter and conversation in the group.

The master then raised his hands, "One more moment, if you please. I have one more thing to say."

The chatter instantly died back down.

"I want you to know … you don't *owe* me anything for these things I intend to do. You *deserve* to be free, and you have worked long and hard to the great benefit of this farm, and of my family. So I don't want you to feel I am, like those Northerners I spoke of a moment ago, giving you things because I *pity* you. Or because I believe you are helpless and cannot do for yourselves. I want you to know I think you have *earned* these things—earned them through the labor you've already done, and the labor you *will do* from now until the time of your freedom. You are *not* pitiable, but strong, intelligent, capable people, who *will* succeed as free men when given a fair chance.

"Now, I must be honest with you, we must work hard, all of us, *together* to change this farm so it can thrive without slave labor. I have already been working long and hard with Mr. Tom to plan how we can change things for the better. We'll use the very latest in modern science—planting crops to grow with more abundance and less need of labor, so we all may enjoy the fruits of this land. This will not all happen in a day, or even in a season. But I believe it will happen soon, if we all work together. While you're learning to survive in the world as free men, we'll be working to change this place into a new kind of farm. I intend us to serve as a shining light for rest of the South. To show our friends and neighbors what people can do if they work together as free men.

"Thank you for listening to me today. Please, go out and enjoy this beautiful Sabbath day the Lord has made for us. And … God bless you all."

Then he turned and walked back into the house.

113

For a moment, everyone stood as if stunned. Sickles immediately turned and strode away without a word, followed by two of the farmhands.

Slowly the group broke up, moving off toward the cabins. Tony didn't know what to think about this. If true, it was a thing unbelievably good—beyond anyone's wildest imaginings. But was it true? To the natural born skeptic in him it was nothing more than pretty talk; intended to make the slaves work harder, striving toward some magical dream that'd never happen.

But then … he reminded himself, Sickles had been *surprised* and angry. *He* believed it, at least, and clearly didn't like it. What did *that* mean? And would Sickles be able to stop it? He tried to envision Sickles standing up to the master. He smiled and shook his head in amusement at the image—Sickles was mean, and hard, and not a man to be crossed. But the new master … he was something *else* altogether. Somehow Tony knew, instinctively, Sickles wasn't half the man the master was. *The Captain*, he corrected himself. *That'll be hard to get used to!* he decided.

All these thoughts ran through his mind as he walked. Some wanted to speculate on what it all meant, but he didn't feel like talking. He wanted time to think, to absorb it all. His mind wandered on into the future … what would it be like to be free? To decide what to do with no one telling you what to do? He had a hard time deciding what he would do if he was free. Would he leave this place? Strike out for faraway lands? Maybe he would, if it came down to it.

But could it really be true? His mind raced on and on. It felt like an endless circle as he walked back toward the cabins. And … what would he do with the rest of today? He'd never had a day when he didn't have to work—other than Christmas when it was too cold to do anything anyway. It was a puzzling question, and he pondered it as he strode along.

࿐ಞ࿐ಞ࿐ಞ࿐ಞ

When Tom entered the library, Nathan was sitting there with Miss Abbey, and they looked up as he entered.

"Well, that wasn't exactly the reaction I was expecting, Tom," Nathan said as Tom took a chair. It was soft, made of dark, beautifully carved wood, padded and covered with leather. Tom liked the feel of it and sank down in.

"No, I expect not, Captain. An enthusiastic 'hurrah!' would have been nice. But instead you got silence. Hard to read how they felt about it. You know … they're probably just having a hard time believing it."

"Yes, I can understand they don't yet know me, and may not trust what I say."

"I think they're just not going to be able to believe you for a while," Miss Abbey offered, "not until they've seen more concrete changes. The Sabbath is a good start, but the rest is just words at this point."

"True, much as it galls me to admit it. I've gotten used to people accepting my word unquestioningly in the Army. This skepticism is a new thing for me."

"Cheer up, dear. If you keep showing them your sincerity, teaching them how to be free men, and such … they'll eventually see it's really going to happen. Speaking of … when *will* you do it?"

"Do what, Momma?"

"Free them, of course. When do you plan to free them? You said more than a season, but you didn't say how long. And I'm sure if I'm wondering, they are too."

"It'll take at least two more harvests after this next one to get things changed over to the way we need them to be: better crops, better methods, other sources of income. But no more than three. Not that we couldn't use more time, God knows. But I feel badly enough making them wait that long."

"But if all goes well, we can make it worth the wait for them. I haven't told them yet, but for those choosing to stay, I intend to give them each a small parcel of land of their own to cultivate. So they'll not only be free and paid a wage for their work, but they'll be landowners as well. What do you think of that?"

"I think that will be just lovely, dear. Hopefully they'll be truly pleased and grateful … when the time comes."

"Sir ... not to change the subject but ... I couldn't help noticing the reaction of Mr. Sickles and some of the other hands. Well, truthfully, I was specifically looking to see how they would react to your speech. It seems to me they were none too pleased with your plan, and went off in a huff, after you were finished. Do you think there might be trouble from that direction? I don't really trust the man."

"Yes, I've felt the same way about him from the beginning. But ... you must admit I did take him by surprise with this whole announcement, so I suppose he could be miffed about that. In hindsight, I probably should have shown him the courtesy of telling him what I had in mind first, before announcing it to the whole world. I should have a talk with him and apologize for that, and to feel him out about how he's taking it."

"Well, sir, I understand what you're saying. But if I know you like I think I do, you *did* consider telling Sickles beforehand, but decided against it because ... well, because you just don't trust him, same as me."

"Hmm ... there's some truth to that ..."

"Oh, my ..." Miss Abbey interjected, "Mr. Sickles has been a good, loyal employee of long standing. Your Daddy was always pleased with him and used to say Mr. Sickles kept the farm in 'ship-shape.' Which I take is a nautical term for 'running well.' And he has been a great support to me with suggestions and advice as to what to do since your father's passing. I hate to sit here and listen to you disparaging the man."

"Sorry, Momma. I stand corrected. You are quite right, he has done nothing wrong since I have been here, so I have no reason to speak ill of him. It's just a ... well, an *uncomfortable* feeling I get around him, like ... well, like he's not quite on my side, that's all. So for your sake, Momma, I will give him every benefit of the doubt. I'm sure your confidence in him will prove well-founded."

This answer seemed to please her, and Nathan silently decided any further discussions with Tom about Mr. Sickles would take place in her absence.

There was a knocking sound near the doorway. Nathan looked up and saw Megs standing at the entrance to the library. The door

116

wasn't closed, but she was standing next to it, and knocking on the doorway out of courtesy. She had a serious look on her face.

"Yes, Megs? Come on in. What can we do for you?"

"I want to know if all you said today is true. I reckon plenty of the others don't believe it, but I … I *want* to believe it. So … is it true? You really gonna to free us all?"

"I meant every word, Megs. And I mean to carry out my plans, just as I said them, so help me God."

"Well, that's enough for me, *Captain*. Thank you."

He saw there were tears welling up in her eyes.

"And … and … I want to say one more thing. I want to say I am *very* proud … very, very proud, I had some small part in helping to raise such a … *fine* … man."

Her tears were now flowing in earnest.

Nathan answered in a quiet, humble tone, "Thank you, Megs. And … thank you for everything. I know I wasn't the *easiest* child. I remember treating you cruelly just before I left here … I was … ungrateful and angry. Please accept my heartfelt apology. You deserved better from me."

Now Miss Abbey was also tearing up, and she smiled up at Megs fondly, "Well, I certainly couldn't have done it without you, Megs. As he says, he was a real handful!"

She laughed, and Megs laughed as well. Nathan and Tom smiled.

After a moment Nathan said, "Only God knows what the future will hold, but I mean to carry through with my plans. And though I've no control over God, of course, I mean to let no *man* stop me."

"Yes, Captain. I believe you mean that, too. But I fear men may *try* to stop you. There's plenty of folks round here-bouts that thinks the black people ought to be slaves forever, and ain't good for nothin' more. They won't like what you're trying to do here and may think to force you from doing it."

"Well, Megs, have no fear of *that*. These soldier boys from Texas aren't here because they're good at slopping hogs and pulling weeds. If there's trouble, they know how to handle it, you can be sure of that."

"Yes, well, I believe what you say, Captain. I can well see they's some fine, tough young men you brought with you.

"But ... speaking of slopping hogs, and such ... the other thing I came in here to say was ... I do believe you been away from the farm too long, Captain! What with all this talk of no work on the Sabbath I fear you have clean forgot about the livestock. Poor things ain't ate a thing yet today, and they's used to getting fed at first light. And the chickens and geese as well ... and the cows need milking, and the eggs need collecting. Captain ... Sabbath may be good for us *people*, but them critters don't know nothing 'bout such. They still needs tending to, but you have gone and told off all of your workers for the day! Now what you going to do about that, sir?"

She looked at him and grinned, knowing she'd totally caught him off guard this time.

"Well ... *damn it!* Right you are, Megs! I was so proud and pleased with myself I completely forgot about the livestock. I thought, 'Well, no harm done if the weeds aren't pulled for a day, and it's not so hot it'll harm any crops to go without water.' Never considered the animals.

"Come on, Tom! No rest for us yet." He jumped up, stripped off his fine jacket and laid it across the chair. He was rolling up his sleeves as he strode for the front door. Tom stood up and scrambled after him.

He burst out the front door onto the veranda, Tom in tow. He saw the men were still standing around the edge of the house, leaning up against the porch, talking animatedly. They turned and looked up as he came out across the veranda.

"Come on, men! No rest for us yet. We've got hogs to slop, and cows to milk!"

Nathan strode down the stairs.

"But Captain ... what about Sabbath ... not doing the working, and whatnot?" Stan asked, in a mock pouty tone.

"Well Stan, I did say we would use this day for *education* ... so you can consider this your education on how to work a farm!"

"Just what I am needing to learn ... how to feed piggies," Stan rolled his eyes.

But the Captain was already striding away in the direction of the animal pens.

"Well, y'all heard that officer, lazy loafers! Let's hop-to," Sergeant Jim prodded. Soon they were all moving along in the Captain's wake.

As he strode along, Nathan turned his head back over his shoulder. "And I was thinking, as a reward for doing a little labor on the Sabbath, when we're done, we'll go try out those new Springfields!"

As he walked on, he detected a bit more enthusiasm in the men's strides.

☙℘ℨℭ℘℘ℨℭℨ℘℘ℨℭ℘℘ℨℭℨ

Later that afternoon, the sound of gunfire echoed across the farm. The men had scouted out, for their purpose, a meadow back beyond the duck pond on the far side of Miss Abbey's flower garden. It was a slightly undulating stretch of ground with knee-high grass, ending in a slight rise, a perfect backstop for the bullets. They'd made targets from white cloth rags stretched between four boards crudely nailed into a frame. On these they'd painted a circle with some red paint Jim had found when looking for materials for repairing the cabins. They set a target at fifty and one hundred yards, and a third at two hundred yards. They rarely took a shot at anything farther out than that in the Army, considering it a waste of ammunition.

But today they were finding these new Springfield "rifled muskets" were superbly accurate and rugged, so they were starting to re-think the placement of their targets. The Captain had brought along his brass spy glass, and was reading out where each shot hit, as the men took turns firing off their rounds. They soon found the fifty-yard target was ridiculously easy, so they quickly abandoned it in favor of the one hundred-yard target. But this too proved no challenge for the men. So now they fired every shot at the two hundred-yard target, and still, they were greatly successful.

The Captain had also brought along the Kentucky long rifle, or the "governor's rifle," as the men had taken to calling it. It proved to have even better accuracy. Nathan had no trouble hitting the two hundred-yard target with great regularity, once Jamie showed him the odd way it was designed to be held when firing.

Nathan had noticed it had a strange, crescent moon shape to the butt of the stock. He'd thought it'd be extremely uncomfortable to hold up against one's shoulder when firing. But Jamie explained it was meant to be held instead in the crook of one's elbow, where the curved, crescent moon shape fit perfectly. The shooter stood with the target to his left, rather than straight in front. Then he laid the rifle across his chest, with the left arm holding the sight in front of his eyes, his head turned to the left. Once he got used to the novelty of it, Nathan concluded it was an ingenious design, giving the shooter greater control over the long, and otherwise unwieldy, weapon.

It was no surprise Jamie was the best shot of the bunch, him being the gunsmith and biggest shooting enthusiast. But they all shot well, even Billy Creek, whose duties in the Army hadn't included using a rifle regularly.

Nathan thought to compliment Billy on his fine shooting and turned to say something between shots. But Billy was no longer there. Nathan looked around and couldn't see him anywhere. He did see Harry the Dog, laying in the shade under a nearby bush, his tongue hanging out as he panted in the heat. He seemed to be watching the activity with interest. It occurred to Nathan the dog was comfortable around guns, the noise apparently not bothering him in the least. Likely, it meant he'd been a hunting dog when he was younger.

"Hey, has anyone seen where Billy went?" he asked.

"No, sir," Jim answered, also looking around. "He was here a minute ago."

"Perhaps he had to answer the call of nature, Captain," Georgie offered.

"Yes, I suppose you're right, Georgie," Nathan responded, uncertainly. He'd never known Billy to be weak of bladder, or to disappear in the middle of an action.

Billy had reloaded his rifle, and was waiting his turn at the target, when he got that itchy feeling something was amiss. For reasons he didn't entirely understand, his instincts were never truly off duty, even when he was asleep. It was the main reason he never had more than one or two drinks of alcohol whenever the rest of the men were indulging. If he had more it made him feel strangely. Like he had lost that little edge. It was *not* a feeling he enjoyed.

Right now, the instincts were telling him someone uninvited was watching, and it was *not* that great, ugly dog, whom he could plainly see off to one side. No, this watcher was back behind them in the tall brush and thicket of trees just off the edge of the field. He realized it was probably not a *real* threat here on the farm, but still, the challenge of turning the tables on the spy was always one he enjoyed. So he casually set his rifle down, in an open space obvious enough no one would accidentally kick it or step on it. Then he slowly scanned the ground behind him, all the way from where he stood to the bushes. Through long practice he could make these observations so someone watching wouldn't be suspicious. Just a man gazing about at the scenery while awaiting his turn at the target.

He strolled over to the spot he'd picked out and sat down in the grass as if simply tired of standing. The place he'd picked was not particularly interesting or noteworthy. To the casual observer there was no special reason he would have chosen that spot. But Billy had a good reason for the choice; in a direct line between that spot and the copse of trees was a slight rise in the field. And on that rise was a tuft of grass slightly taller than the surrounding grass. So from where Billy now sat to the place where the unknown observer was, the view would now be blocked. As soon as he was sure all the soldiers and the Captain were absorbed in their business, he dropped to all fours facing toward the bushes and trees. He quickly scrambled to his left, keeping his head below the level of the grass. Then he moved toward a slight dip in the field he'd seen there, a low dry gully that drained off excess water in a hard rainstorm. As he moved, he was careful not to bump any tall tufts of grass. In this way, someone watching from a distance would not detect any motion. When he reached the small gully, he realized he was now only a short distance from where the great hound lay. He knew his tricks would never fool a dog. Their senses were much keener than his. He just hoped the beast wouldn't react and give him away. He risked a quick look in that direction, and, sure enough, the hound was staring directly at him. It took a few sniffs, tilted its great head curiously, then opened its mouth and … rolled out its great tongue and panted from the heat. Billy let out his breath, not realizing he'd been holding it. The dog turned his big, shaggy head back toward where the Captain was standing, apparently deciding Billy was not interesting enough to pay any mind.

Billy moved out again. He soon reached the edge of the field, and the start of the tall brush and small trees. He "knew" the observer was now off to his right, although he wasn't entirely sure *how* he knew it. So he worked his way further back into the bushes, in the same low, careful manner, until he was sure he was now well behind. Then he circled back around so he would come up directly behind the unknown observer. He crept up to within five feet of the man before he quietly rose to his feet. It was one of the black field workers, crouched down behind a bush, looking out at where the men were shooting the guns.

He realized he didn't know the man's name, title, rank, or anything else about him. So he said the first thing that came to his mind, "Hey … black man!"

The man jumped in a manner Billy found both amusing and satisfying.

"Oh! You 'bout scared the pants right off of me!" he said, clutching his chest. "How you get back there? Wasn't you out in yonder field just now?"

"Sure. But now I'm *here*. Why are *you* here? What are you doing there behind that bush?" Billy asked. He wasn't much of one to give orders and was not especially forceful with people. But he had captured plenty of enemy spies and combatants over the years, so he knew how to clearly state his business.

"Well, sir … I wasn't meaning no harm by it. I was just wonderin' what I was to do with myself on a day where I gots no work to do. And then I heard these-here loud noises and didn't know what they was. But some of the other fellas says, 'the soldiers is shooting off big guns.' So I … I guess I done got curious, sir, is all. Never seen nobody shoot guns before, and I … I was curious is all, meant no harm, sir."

Billy could see and hear the truth in what the man was saying. He always knew when men were telling lies, or not, but didn't know how he knew *that* either.

"Not for me to decide. Come. We'll see what the Captain says."

"But … I still can't believe it. You's got to tell me how you done got back there behind me. You was right out there in plain sight in front of my nose not more'n a heartbeat ago."

Billy thought for a moment, then shrugged his shoulders, and gave the answer that had always satisfied the white men. He figured it might also work on a black one: "Old Indian trick."

The man gave him a skeptical look, which made Billy wonder if maybe black men had more sense than white.

"They say your name's Billy. That right? Mine's Tony."

"Okay, Tony, let's go see the Captain."

"Wait, before we go … can I asks you a question? I been curious, and nobody I asks knows. What kind of slave is you anyway? You don't seems to do any kind of work round here, and yet the master … er, *the Captain* … he don't seem to care."

"I'm not *any* kind of slave. I'm an Indian."

"But what is it an Indian is supposed to do around this-here farm, anyways?"

Billy thought a moment, and said, "I guess … whatever he wants to do."

"You mean you's a free man? Like the white folks? I heard the master was out West killin' your people … but they ain't made you be a slave when they catch you?"

"Captain hasn't been killing *my* people. My people are Tonkawa. We fight *beside* the great white soldiers, *against* other Indians, our hated enemies. The Comanche, the Apache, the

Navajo, the … well, many, many others. Hmm … pretty much *all* other Indians."

"Oh, so them *other* Indians … they make *them* be slaves?"

"No … just fight them, run them off, force them into camps … or *kill* them. No Indian slaves."

"Why not? If they make the black men be slaves, why not the Indian men?"

Billy tilted his head and thought about this. He'd never considered it, but now he decided it had to do with the realization he'd come to earlier, about the white slavers not needing any weapons. "Maybe because Indians would *never* stop fighting … they'd just kill their masters and run back into the wild lands, any chance they got. I guess nobody wants a slave who's gonna kill him."

"No … I reckon not," said Tony, with a thoughtful look on his face. The Indian's words seemed to echo in the back of his mind, *Nobody wants a slave who's gonna kill him …*

𝕭𝕺𝕮𝕭𝕺𝕮𝕭𝕺𝕮𝕭𝕺𝕮𝕭𝕺𝕮

The mystery of Billy's sudden disappearance was solved when he came striding back across the field from a nearby copse of small trees. A young black man walked beside him.

The men stopped shooting, and those who'd been prone on the ground stood to see what this was all about.

Billy said, "Noticed someone was watching us, Captain. So I went to see who."

The young man acted nervous and guilty, looking down at his feet as the Captain stepped up to him.

"So … 'Tony,' isn't it?"

"Yes, Master … er, *Mister* Chambers, sir." He didn't look up, continuing to stare at his own feet.

"Well, Tony, what were you doing over in the bushes?"

The tone was friendly, but firm; he didn't believe Tony was up to anything nefarious, but wanted the man to answer for himself.

"Wasn't meanin' no harm, sir. Was just … curious, is all. Heard the loud noises and … well, I ain't never seen no guns before, and I … I just wanted to see it. I's sorry, Master, if I done wrong, sir."

124

Nathan was quiet for a moment, watching the man's movements and expressions, as much as listening to what he was saying. While the words sounded genuine, and innocent enough, something in his demeanor made Nathan uneasy. Maybe he was speaking the truth … but maybe he wasn't saying everything on his mind. The man had clearly been drawn to the sound of the guns.

Visions of Nat Turner's infamous, bloody, slave revolt back in 1831 came unbidden into his mind. He was sympathetic with slaves revolting against their masters. Spartacus had famously led a slave revolt against the Roman Empire back in ancient times and was now considered something of a hero.

He believed in giving any man the benefit of the doubt. And he was confident the changes he was undertaking would ultimately make believers of all those held in bondage. But he'd seen too much evil and violence in his lifetime to be naïve about it. Men were not sheep, despite what some people wanted to believe. Rather like wolves. No … wolves could never match men for senseless, brutal violence against their own kind. Civilization was ultimately a thin veneer over the violent nature of man, a nature always lurking just beneath the surface. He had to admit he had no way of knowing what these enslaved men were really thinking, as he had never walked in their shoes. They might be thinking he was a genuine, kind man, determined to better their lot—or just as easily thinking he was a cold, calculating liar and they should strike him down at the first opportunity.

He sighed a heavy sigh. It would take time for trust to build on both sides. But it had to start somewhere.

"Well, no harm done, I suppose. You can stay and watch if you wish."

ༀༀༀༀༀༀༀༀༀༀༀༀ

Two hours later they were on their way back to the house.

"Oh, Jim …" Nathan called out over his shoulder, "next week make sure we invite the other farmhands as well. Won't hurt to have everyone trained up on the guns, and I never even thought of it until now."

"Yes, sir! I will muster them out just as you say, sir."

"No, you will *invite* them … nicely and politely, Mr. Wiggins. Especially our Mr. Sickles—I think he's already starting to feel a bit displaced by all you newcomers."

"Nicely and politely it shall be, Captain!"

The former army privates found Jim's response amusing, and several shared smiles and knowing looks. They'd been on the receiving end of Sergeant Jim's *invitations* … and "niceness and politeness" was not typically part of it.

When the Captain and his men turned toward the house, Tony headed out across a tobacco field on his way back to the cabins. He stepped out of the field onto the grassy area just before the road. There he saw Sickles and two of the other farmhands sitting at the large, sturdy wooden table under the shade of an oak tree growing there. The white farmhands often gathered there to eat their lunch or to plan the day's activities.

Tony was hoping to pass by without being seen. He wanted no part of Sickles on this day, of all days. Sickles might come up with some kind of work that needed doing, despite the Captain's wishes. So he kept his head down, and walked at an even pace, heading toward the cabins.

But just as he pulled even with the table, a few dozen yards away, Sickles looked up, and said, "Hey there, boy! What you been doin' over that a-way? Nobody said … just because you wasn't workin' you could be wanderin' all over the place, see?"

Tony had a pretty good idea Sickles wouldn't be pleased, not pleased at all, if he knew the truth, that Tony had spent the afternoon watching the soldier men shooting guns. So he made up something that sounded likely enough it could have been true. "Yes, sir. Sorry, sir. But one of the master's new men, he asks me to fetch them soldiers some water. They was mighty thirsty on account of firin' off them guns and all. So I was just on my way back to the cabins after fetching them their water, sir. Meaning no offense, Mr. Sickles, sir."

Tony was pleased with himself for the story he'd come up with. It not only sounded plausible, but it would be hard for Sickles to punish him for doing something specifically asked for by one of the Captain's new men. But the reaction he got was both surprising and shocking, all on account of *one* thing he'd said.

"What did you call me, boy?! You will address me as 'Master,' do you hear?! I'll be Goddamned if I'll allow some sassy darkie to call me 'Mister.' After all these years of hard, loyal service ... 'Mister?!'

"If the master wants to degrade himself, allowing his slaves to call him 'Captain,' that's his business, but I'll have none of it, you hear me, boy?"

There'd been several other slaves sitting on the other side of the road, talking happily. Now there was a deathly silence.

Tony burned with anger. After the speech earlier by the Captain, this degrading tirade by Sickles was even more hurtful. But he just lowered his head and answered, "Yes, Master. I is most sorry, Master. It won't happen again, sir."

"You see it don't, *boy!* And you may as well tell the others, too." Then he raised his voice so those across the road could also hear, "And also ... I don't care what the new master says about the beatings, neither! If'n any of you deserves it, you can bet me and the boys here won't spare the whip just so's to not offend the new master's sensibilities. Y'all are still *slaves*, and we are still the *masters*, and y'all will behave as such. Is that understood?!!"

"Yes, sir, Master. Very well understood sir," Tony said, continuing to stare at his own feet.

"Then get on over to the others, and don't let me see you wanderin' around no more, you hear?"

Sickles turned back to the other farmhands, having already dismissed Tony from his mind.

Tony crossed to road and headed back toward his own cabin. The day had started with such promise, but now it had been soiled by the hard revelation that some things had *not* changed.

He saw Ned and Johnny sitting in the grass, so he walked over and plopped down next to them.

Ned looked at him, and seeing his sour expression, said, "Master done talked a pretty talk. Don't matter none. White men's still white men. Ain't about what he say. Ain't nothin' gonna change. When we does what they ain't likin' … they's gonna beat us."

"Well then, maybe we's just gotta be makin' our own changes!" Tony said, and buried his face in his hands.

Johnny looked over at Ned and shrugged. Ned looked at Tony, then back at Johnny, and shrugged in answer.

CHAPTER 6. THE MAKING OF MISS EVELYN

"Learning without thought is labor lost;
thought without learning is perilous."
– Confucius

Friday June 15, 1860 – Richmond, Virginia:

"Must we go through it again, Momma? We've already gone over it a hundred times," Evelyn said.

"And we'll go over it a hundred more times if need be," Harriet answered. "We'll go over it until it's so ingrained you can do it without thinking. Until it comes out naturally from your memory without pause or reflection!

"We must get this right, Evelyn. There can be no missteps this time, no mistakes. Too much is at stake. I've done my checking, made inquiries all over Richmond. And I've learned all there is to know about the Chambers family, and the young heir Nathaniel. I tell you it's perfect and couldn't be better. So we must make sure everything works out perfectly."

"*We*, Momma? Aren't *I* the one supposed to marry him?"

"Of course, *you*, of course. But I'll help you do it and make sure you're prepared. You've had too many disasters lately, Evelyn. We must leave nothing to chance this time."

Evelyn had to admit her mother was right about one thing; her recent courting experiences had been a series of calamities and mismatches, culminating with the horrible episode with Mr. Stanley Finch! She shuddered with disgust.

"Well, *sir*, I've never paid much mind to such matters …" Evelyn launched herself into the response her mother had been prodding for.

Harriet played the role of a young gentleman suitor. Evelyn switched into full "Southern Belle" mode, her voice coming out in sweet melodic tones. Her movements—batting eyelashes, head-tilting, delicate fanning, even breathing in a manner emphasizing cleavage and bosom—were designed to encourage and entice a potential paramour, all choreographed to perfection.

"But from what I understand, the rights of the individual states aren't to be subjugated by the federal government. That government derives its just powers from the will of the people in those states. Don't you agree, sir? And, as for those beastly Northerners calling themselves *abolitionists* ... why it seems to me they are nothing but criminals, aiding and abetting fugitives, wouldn't you say? And though I rarely dwell on such matters, aren't we really just showing Christian charity to the black man? We've brought him out of the heathen darkness of Africa and into God's holy light in this land of abundance. We've given him food, shelter, and a healthy occupation. Why, I've been told the so-called 'slaves' of the south live in much better conditions than the so-called 'free laborers' working in Northern factories. Wouldn't you agree, sir?"

She leaned slightly forward, smiling brightly and continuing to wave the small, lacey folding fan she held in her right hand for the perfect affect.

"All right, all right. Yes, you've now got it down, I'll admit. For such a bright, pretty girl it's surprising how difficult it's been teaching you to attract the right kind of man. I swear, it's your father's fault—all that time he wasted with you when you were younger. Running all around the countryside—him treating you like you were a *boy*! Disgraceful! I've had the devil's own time making a lady out of you. But maybe ... just maybe ... it will finally stick this time!"

"Oh, Momma ... it's hard for me because it doesn't seem natural ... it seems like, oh, I don't know ... like memorizing lines for a play. Like putting on an *act*. Like it isn't really *me* talking." And then she silently added, *and didn't Daddy teach me things that were ... almost the opposite? Who's right about all this?*

"Of course, it's *you*, or will be if you work at it enough. Listen, Evelyn, a young man wants a wife who's a perfect lady—doing and saying all the things perfect ladies do and say. If he engages you in a discussion about politics, or economics, or religion, he isn't asking for a debate. He doesn't want a dissertation on the topic. He wants you to listen, nod, and agree with everything he says. And occasionally interject something perfectly innocuous and in total agreement with what he's already said. Do you understand? The last thing a man wants is a wife who's smarter than him. Or more capable, or liable to start running his life for him ... like I was with your father ..."

"But Momma ... I'm sure Daddy appreciated everything you did for him ..."

"No, he didn't! Once I stuck my nose into his business affairs, we were never warm or close again. Not that it didn't *need* doing. And I would do it again. But still ...

"Anyway, you need to entice the *right* husband, one that's strong and capable so you'll never have to worry about dealing with such things.

"And speaking of ... by all accounts, young Nathaniel Chambers is such a man. He's been an army officer—a man used to taking charge and being master of his own affairs. And the family has amassed a sizeable estate, which he's now inherited.

"And, you may be happy to hear, the rumor is ... he is *exceedingly* handsome, and a proper gentleman in every way."

"I wouldn't take much stock in such rumors, Momma. Every man who's come courting has been rumored to be 'exceedingly handsome.' And I suppose their *mothers* think so, but I haven't been so greatly impressed. Besides, you said Mr. Chambers has been a soldier most of his life. I expect he's become terribly bossy and used to everyone jumping and saluting whenever he barks! How will such a man treat his wife, I wonder?"

"Like she deserves, no doubt!" Harriet folded her arms across her chest and scowled.

"And, Momma ... if he fought in that long-ago war, he must be awfully old by now, and I'm only nineteen!"

"Haven't you listened to anything I've said? He was a *very* young man, just out of school when he left for that war in Mexico. That makes him only ..." Harriet thought a moment and seemed to be adding up numbers on her fingers, "a little over thirty years old. Still vigorous—in the prime of life. And you, young lady, will turn twenty next month! Which is well past the age when you should be married and chasing after little brats running around under your feet!"

"Momma, you make me sound like an old spinster, but I feel like I'm still only a child. I really know nothing of men, or marriage, or the big, wide world. And you're not so very old yourself—why … not much older than Mr. Chambers, really. How *ever* did you become so wise and know so many things?"

"Because I *had* to," Harriet snapped back, "I had a much harder childhood than you and was not nearly so pampered and indulged. And then the way your father ran the farm, or rather how he *didn't* run it, forced me to do things a woman oughtn't have to do. I learned a lot of things about the world that way. Many of which I wish I'd never needed to know!"

"I'm sorry, Momma. I didn't mean to offend you, just the opposite. You seem so knowledgeable, and I feel so … *ignorant.*"

"Never mind, child. We will keep working on getting you prepared, so when the time comes, you'll know what you need to know about men and marriage and running a proper household. And *none* of the things you *don't* need to know, thank God!"

ॐᏋᎧᏇᏇᏇᏇᏇᏇᏇᏇᏇᏇ

Later that day, Evelyn found herself in Miss Ava Dupree's dress shop in downtown Richmond. Miss Ava specialized in the latest fashions from Paris. And she also had the requisite firsthand experience and knowledge, being a Parisian herself.

Her dresses were always among the most expensive in town. All the upper-class ladies felt obligated to pay her a visit from time to time to keep conversant on the latest trends. Even if they bought nothing, they'd still browse the dresses and discuss fashion with Miss Dupree.

She welcomed Evelyn and Harriet with an enthusiastic, "*Bon jour! Bon jour* my dear ladies! *Entrez s'il vous plaît!* Please, won't you come in?"

Although Harriet *was* planning on buying at least one elegant new gown for Evelyn, she was also intending to get her money's worth in the education department. So she grilled Miss Ava mercilessly on all the latest trends—even more so than was typical. What the various fashion "experts" were saying about this or that; when she expected certain fashions to go in and out of favor in the coming year; which colors were the trend — and which weren't; materials, lengths of sleeves, necklines, etc., etc.

Soon, Evelyn's head was swimming from trying to absorb it all. But absorb it she did. Harriet would grill her on each new subject after discussing it with Miss Ava, to the proprietress's baffled amusement.

After the fashion lesson, they spent hours trying on various gowns. The popular style was for dresses that emphasized a small waist, forcing most women to resort to corsets. Fortunately for Evelyn, her waist was already thin enough she didn't need the added reinforcement, for which she was very grateful. She envisioned such devices as extremely uncomfortable.

Most of the dresses they looked at had high necklines, often with a removable white collar, although some were low-cut, and off the shoulder. Evelyn preferred these, as she found the stiff, stuffy high collars to be uncomfortable and hot.

Many of the gowns had center front buttons. These were typically very fancy, made of mother-of-pearl, glass, bone, leather, or ceramics. The skirts were very full, with hoops or starched petticoats. Pleats ran from the waist up the bodice and down the skirt, to further emphasize the waist.

Sleeves were full and wide at the elbow, but narrow at the wrist, when long-sleeved. The bodice often used whalebone to get everything narrowing down to the waist, and the shoulders were broad and sloping. Decorations on the dresses often included ruching or braid, but lace was used only sparingly.

Gowns were made from silk, linen, velvet, and even cotton and wool. There were solid colors, stripes, and plaids.

They finally settled on a lovely gold-colored formal gown that seemed to suit Evelyn's hair color and figure perfectly. It was low-cut, off the shoulders, as Evelyn had preferred, and of a light-gold silk, with darker-gold velvet trim and accents. Between the silk and velvet were bright gold braids. These made a swirling pattern around the hem of the dress at the sleeves just below the shoulders, and across the front of the dress at the bustline. Two broad, velvet sashes hung down at the back, from the waistline extending about halfway to the ground.

She decided on using the starched petticoat underneath rather than the hoops—the latter always seemed so ridiculously impractical and awkward to her. She also picked out two less-formal gowns, more appropriate for walking around during the day. These cotton dresses weren't nearly so fancy, although one featured colorful embroidered flowers around the edges.

Once they'd finished with the gowns, Evelyn had to try on hats. No proper lady could be seen in public without one, especially outdoors, and Miss Ava had a wide variety. Some were not much more than a lacey bonnet, while others had a wide brim, covered in lace, ribbons, silk flowers, and even bird feathers.

She decided to lean toward practicality, or at least as much as one could, given the clothing they were buying. On Mr. Chamber's farm she might have to wear the gown outdoors, so she ought to have something with a brim to keep the sun off her face. But not one with a brim so wide the wind would blow the hat away.

The one she chose was shaped like a bonnet. It had a brim extending in front and featured a wide ribbon for tying under the chin to secure it outdoors. This hat matched the formal gown she'd selected, covered in the same silk and velvet, but it also included a few black and white accents to give it a little contrast.

Then she picked out two more casual, straw hats, with wider brims for walking around in bright sunlight. She could wear these with the less-formal gowns.

Thinking about the sun reminded her she would also need a parasol. They chose three of these.

Next came shoes. She already had several pairs of casual shoes but needed something to go with the new formal gown. Miss Ava had plenty of these. And there was an educational component to this exercise as well, but Evelyn found the subject matter much simpler. The variety of styles and colors available was much more limited than with the other items. And, having already selected a gown, it was only a matter of finding shoes that were a good match, rather than trying on every pair in the store!

Evelyn felt relief when they finished selecting the shoes. At last, they could leave the dress store and go home. She was tired out from getting dressed and undressed so many times, and from the endless stream of fashion details she was trying to memorize.

But then she suppressed a groan when her mother turned to Miss Ava and said, "Now … let's talk about makeup…"

"Ah, the makeup, *oui, oui, mademoiselle!* The forbidden topic! Most taboo to admit one would use it, but also most essential for the elegance, no?"

"Yes. A lady must use it to look perfectly elegant, but she mustn't seem to be using anything at all. It's quite a nuisance, really, but it's an unfortunate necessity. We must do it because everyone else is doing it. If we don't, we'll appear ordinary by compare," Harriet said.

"Are you sure this is necessary?" Evelyn asked, trying not to sound pouty.

"*Oui, oui,* Miss Evelyn! *Most* necessary! But, don't you concern yourself, *ma cherie.* Miss Ava will teach you how to do it *just so* — soon you will be master of your own face! When we finish, you will be the most *beautiful* young lady in the world!" She spoke with such enthusiasm and sincerity, Evelyn almost believed it.

Miss Ava took Evelyn by the hand and led her down a hallway, into a back room. Harriet followed. There, Ava lit a whole row of lamps, so the room was brightly lit even though it had no windows. There were several chairs, and a small table covered with a white cloth, what the French called a *"toilette."* The table was next to a wall on which hung a large mirror which, despite its tarnished brass frame, was clean and sharp, providing a perfect reflection of the person seated at the table — in this case, Evelyn. Miss Ava opened a cupboard and brought out bottles, cans, and brushes of varying sizes and shapes. She pulled up a chair next to Evelyn, sat down, and then she went to work, starting with a white powder from a jar, applied with a short, wide, round brush.

Harriet sat in a chair on the other side of Evelyn so she could study the operation and mentally take note. She'd need to learn how to repeat the whole process later at home. Once again, at each step she quizzed Miss Ava on every detail: What was in the concoction? How was it made and what was its purpose? Were there any alternate methods of doing the same thing? How long had this been the fashion? And on and on. Miss Ava patiently answered every question, and even when not prompted, provided a running commentary, instructing both mother and daughter on specific techniques to the best of her abilities. Evelyn noticed Miss Ava had perked up and become much more enthusiastic once she realized Harriet intended to buy one of her expensive gowns, with all the accoutrements.

Miss Ava applied a hint of blush to Evelyn's cheeks with a reddish powder—rouge, the women correctly guessed. Then a darker substance above her eyes and on her eyelids. With a very tiny brush, which she dipped in a black liquid—not ink, but nearly as dark—she delicately outlined Evelyn's eyes and eyelashes. Miss Ava worked efficiently and with obvious expertise.

In just under an hour it was finished. Miss Ava stood up from the chair, taking a step back to admire her handiwork, saying "There you are, darling. Even as I said: *the most beautiful lady in all the world!* Is it not so?"

Evelyn gazed at the mirror in astonishment. It was true. The person looking back at her was a truly stunning woman—elegant, sophisticated, with an air of mystery. And something else … seduction, maybe? The change shocked her. She'd always considered herself attractive; it was natural for young girls to compare themselves to their friends and acquaintances and make mental assessments. She'd rarely felt herself lacking in that regard. But compared to this woman now staring at her from within the mirror, her normal face looked plain, and uninteresting.

"Why, it's me, but … it's … *not* me," she said, struggling to find the words to express what she was seeing.

"Exquisite! Absolutely lovely," Harriet said with enthusiasm. "She's perfect, like a China doll!"

Miss Ava beamed with pride.

"Oooo … I am almost forgetting. She is needing one more thing for making all a perfection. She must smell as beautiful as she looks, no? And Miss Ava has just the thing!"

She hurried back to the cupboard and brought back a small, clear bottle with a brass top. She unscrewed the top, stuck one finger over the opening, and flipped the bottle over and back again. Then she resealed it. She stepped up to Evelyn and gently touched her on the neck behind each ear, and on each arm inside the elbow. A wonderful aroma enveloped Evelyn. She'd worn perfume before, but this was especially nice. Not too overpowering, just a very light, sweet smell … like lilacs, or lavender, or something … like a sweet pastry baking in the oven off down the hall.

They left the store with a package containing the shoes, perfume, and various bottles and brushes. The gowns they left behind, along with the parasols and hats. Miss Ava needed to alter the gowns; Evelyn was slightly slimmer in the waist and hips, and a little larger in the bust than the dress model had been. They'd left the other items so they'd not have so much to carry. They'd come back in a carriage to collect their purchases in a few days.

Miss Ava smiled happily and wished them a most heartfelt, *"Merci beaucoup! Au revoir!"*

After the ladies left, Ava hummed an old French love song to herself as she pulled out the broom. And though it was only late afternoon, she decided to close up shop for the day.

ঝ৯৹৻ৠ৹ঝ৯৹ৠ৹ঝ৯৹৻

They made their way down the street, and Evelyn felt slightly self-conscious. Although she was back in her normal, everyday clothes, which were nice—simple and feminine, but not elegant like the gowns she had spent the afternoon trying on—she still had on the makeup. And it seemed to her the gentlemen *were* paying more attention to her than usual—friendly smiles and greetings, tipping of hats, and slight bows. She thought her imagination must be running away with her, but Harriet noticed it too, "You see? The men can tell the difference, but they don't understand why …"

The women also seemed to notice, but their greetings were generally not so friendly. A few seemed entirely *un*friendly, especially if the men escorting them paid too much attention.

"Never mind *them* dear. They're just jealous they don't look like you!" Harriet chuckled.

Evelyn didn't know what to think. True, it was still her, still her own face, but somehow it didn't seem real, not *really* her at all. *Like acting in a play,* she realized, once again.

Their house was not far, only about ten blocks west of the dress shop on Jefferson Street. But for Evelyn it had been a long day, and she felt exhausted. Harriet seemed done in as well; she went straight to her bedroom.

Evelyn assumed Harriet was going to take a nap, but after a few moments she came back out carrying a small wooden box. She set it on the table, opened the lid, and started looking inside. Evelyn's curiosity soon got the better of her. Despite her exhaustion, she got up from the cushioned chair and moved over to the table for a look.

Inside were various items of jewelry. Rings made of silver, and of brass. A silver broach shaped like a flower and a necklace of silver and pearls. A bracelet of gold wound like a braid, and an intricately wrought gold hairpiece, with a sparkling green stone at its center.

"Momma!" Evelyn gasped, when she looked in the box. "I never imagined you owned such things."

"They belonged to your Daddy's mother, your grandmother. And probably a few of these older pieces came from her mother before her, I don't know for sure. When things were going badly with the farm, I was tempted to sell them. But then … it became too late. It wouldn't have been enough to make any difference. So I saved them for another time when I might need the money. But we may as well put them to good use. When we get the gown back, we'll try these on and see what suits you. With this jewelry, and what we purchased today, you will look like a princess. No man will be able to resist you!"

Evelyn nodded her agreement, but thought, *But I'm not a princess. I'm … I don't know what I am, or who I am. I don't know if I'm even me anymore. Who am I?*

"And best of all, today I received a reply from the letter I penned to Mrs. Jacob Chambers—'Abigail,' Nathaniel Chambers' mother," Harriet grinned. "In it I offered to introduce you to Mr. Chambers and asked if we might come for a visit to their farm. She has accepted and has extended us an invitation to stay at their estate as long as we wish."

"Oh! But what about *him*, Momma? Shouldn't you be asking *Mister* Chambers if we can visit?"

"Nonsense! Of course not! What does a man know about arranging such things? Leave it to the mothers. We'll have the betrothal signed, sealed, and delivered, before he even knows you exist! You wait and see. If I know anything about mothers, and I should certainly hope I do, she will be as eager to see him married as I am you. Now that he has retired from the Army and moved back home, it's the most natural thing on earth to find a bride and marry her straightaway. And we must pounce, and get there first, before anyone else thinks of it!"

She closed the box and returned to her room. This time she did not return. After a time, Evelyn heard soft snoring coming from the room.

Chapter 7. Dark Clouds Beneath the Silver Lining

"Even in evil, that dark cloud
which hangs over the creation,
we discern rays of light and hope
and gradually come to see
in suffering and temptation
proofs and instruments
of the sublimest purpose
of wisdom and love."
– William Ellery Channing

Sunday June 17, 1860 – Greenbrier County, Virginia:

"Well, what you be a-thinkin' of the new master now, Phin? Don't seem like such a toothsome monster as we's led to believe."

"No, I reckon not, Cobb. He do talk a good talk, and say some fine, sweet things, that's certain. And it do seem he ain't got much of a mind for the beatin's, which is mighty all right to me. But do you figure he gonna really go through with it?"

"With what? You mean settin' all us colored folks free and all?"

"Yeah ... it sure do sound like a fine dream ... but ... I don't know ..."

"What, Phin?"

"Well, I was also thinkin' ... maybe he somehow found out about ... you know ... The Way, and all, and just wants to make us all works harder for him."

"Could be ... could be. It's somethin' to think on, that's certain. I reckon we's just got to keep our ears open and see what we can see."

"Cobb! You damned fool. You can't *open* ears, and you sure as sin can't see out of 'em!"

Cobb smiled, rolled his eyes, and made a foolish, comical face, pulling on his ears as if seeing out of them. He shrugged his shoulders, and they shared a laugh, leaning back against the rough boards of a cabin, on the cool, shady side. The simple, unexpected luxury of having no work to do was something they had rarely experienced before, except on Christmas when it was too cold to enjoy it.

ᘓᘯᘓᘔᘓᘔᘓᘯᘓᘔᘓᘔᘓᘯᘓᘔᘓᘔ

Later that Sabbath afternoon, a small, black carriage arrived, drawn by a single horse and driven by a gray-haired black servant dressed neatly in a simple, black suit. He got down and gazed around, as if bewildered. After a moment's pause, he walked over to the carriage door, and opened it.

Another elderly gentleman took the hand of the driver and stepped out. This man had white hair, and white skin, and wore a black suit, with a white tie of the style particular to preachers. He was more heavy-set than the first man, and had a round face, with slightly drooping jowls.

"I's sorry, Master Reverend, sir. Can't understand where them grooms has got to. Mountain Meadows usually runs a 'tight ship,' as they say."

"Well, never mind that, Benny. The old master has passed away, and there's a new master here now … perhaps things have … slipped a bit? It is of little matter, if the son is anything like the father, I'm sure he'll have things straightened out in short order."

The driver tied the horse and carriage to a hitching post, then took the arm of his master to help him up the stairs. When they were about half-way up, the door to the house opened. *Good, the groom's here at last to give an old man a helping hand,* the driver thought. But instead of grooms or a butler, they saw Miss Abbey, the mistress of the farm. The men paused in their climb and gazed up at her.

"Reverend Blackburn. So very good to see you, won't you please come in and enjoy our shade and refreshment?"

"Thank you kindly, Miss Abbey. It will be greatly appreciated after the hot carriage ride I've just endured."

Miss Abbey held the door open politely as Reverend Blackburn moved across the veranda, still holding Benny's arm. At the entrance, he turned and dismissed the servant.

"Please, Reverend, won't you be seated and find your comfort in the library while I go fetch Mr. Chambers?"

She noticed now that he was no longer holding the arm of his servant he did not appear so feeble. He'd always seemed vigorous before, so she'd been wondering if he'd suffered an illness or injury.

"Certainly, Miss Abbey. Most gracious of you."

The pastor settled himself into a comfortable seat to wait.

In a few moments, a tall, vigorous looking young man entered the room with Miss Abbey.

"Reverend Blackburn, may I introduce my son, Mr. Nathaniel Chambers, the master of Mountain Meadows Farm."

The pastor stood and extended his hand, which Nathan reached out and shook firmly. Their eyes met, and Miss Abbey noted the look was intense, and neither man was smiling.

"Welcome to my home, Reverend. It is a pleasure and an honor to meet you."

"Oh, but the pleasure is all mine, Mr. Chambers. I was very fond of your father, and most saddened when he passed away. My condolences to you, sir, on your loss."

"Thank you, Reverend."

Nathan gestured for the preacher to retake his seat and then took one just opposite.

"We missed you at the morning service ..." the pastor prompted, looking over at Miss Abbey with a raised eyebrow. It had been more of a question than a statement.

"Yes ... well, it couldn't be helped, I suppose ... I'm sure Mr. Chambers will explain. If you'll excuse me, I'll just go see about some refreshments."

The men stood again, politely, as Miss Abbey left the room.

"Is aught amiss at Mountain Meadows, Mr. Chambers?"

"No, Reverend, everything is well. Why do you ask?"

"Oh ... well, it's just ... Miss Abbey hasn't missed a Sunday church service since ... well, *ever*, I suppose. And when we arrived your grooms did not greet us, as is the usual custom. And further, I have seen no household servants, and Miss Abbey has just now left to see about refreshments herself."

"It is my fault Miss Abbey missed the service this morning. I asked her to stay here while I conducted some important business. You see, I was actively implementing my very sincere desire for a strict observance of the Sabbath, from sunrise to sunset, today and every Sunday from this day forward."

"Ah ... very commendable of you, Mr. Chambers. I had ... *suggested* ... the notion to your father on several occasions, but he was ... *unmoved* ... by my arguments. I'm happy to see you are of a more pious persuasion."

"Yes, I think you will find I am a man of God, a follower of the Christ our Lord, and a man of very strong convictions. My father was ... well, as I understand it, more of a *secular* frame of mind."

"Yes ... I would agree with your assessment of your father, and I can see you're clearly cut from a different cloth.

"And are there other changes you intend to make at Mountain Meadows, now you are the master, if you don't mind my asking?"

"Oh, as for that ... I have *many* ideas for improvements, as one might imagine, being a younger man than my father, and having ... a somewhat different perspective on things."

"Ah yes ... one can imagine your years up North, and out West, not to mention your military service, may have effected your view of things."

"Just so. But I did want to reassure you our absence from your services this morning was a one-time event. Miss Abbey and I, and several other of our people I expect, will attend next Sunday, and thereafter."

"Oh, that is very heartening to hear, Mr. Chambers ... though I had no doubts about it."

"But ... speaking of changes ..."

"Yes?"

"Well ... you must excuse me if you find I am direct, and to the point. I'm afraid my military training and experience has drilled the habit into me, and I'm led to understand some people may find it a bit ... off-putting."

"Never fear, Mr. Chambers ... I am entirely at your service, of course, and open to whatever you have to say, no matter how blunt."

"I'm happy to hear it," Nathan smiled. It occurred to him the pastor likely expected him to complain about Walters' annexation of Miss Abbey's front row seats at church. But he had no intention of doing so. It felt too much like complaining to the headmaster at school about the actions of a playground bully. Better to deal with that sort of thing directly and personally, at the proper time and place.

"I have decided to discontinue your monthly sermons to the servants here at Mountain Meadows, an arrangement of long-standing, as I understand it, between yourself and my late father."

The pastor's face betrayed a look of surprise at this pronouncement, and it turned a light shade of red.

"Oh ... I see. Well, of course, the welfare of your slaves is entirely your concern. But as a man of the cloth, I feel it is my duty to protest your decision. Though these negroes may be lesser men, and may be but servants in our eyes, our Lord tells us to proselytize to the lowliest among us, even to the heathens out in the wild lands."

Nathan smiled, but there was no humor in it. "Oh, I still mean to have *my people* taught the word of the Lord ..."

Now the pastor's face became a darker shade of red.

"But, Mr. Chambers ... a moment ago you indicated you and Miss Abbey would continue to attend my church services. Now ... well, it sounds as if you've replaced me with another."

"No ... I do not intend to replace you, Reverend."

"Then ... who will teach your slaves the word of the Holy Gospels?"

Out of habit, Nathan reached into his suit pocket and pulled out a cigar, sticking the unlit cigar in his mouth before responding. But he resisted the urge to reach for a match and light it. "*I* will teach them."

"You? But, sir ... as far as I know, you are not an ordained minister, nor have you any of the requisite training. Have you studied at seminary, then? Did the military teach you how to minister to your flock?"

"No, no, and no."

"Mr. Chambers, it says in the Bible, *'I will give you pastors according to mine heart, which shall feed you with knowledge and understanding.'*"

"Yes … that would be *Jeremiah* chapter three, verse fifteen, I believe. And in *Mark* chapter sixteen, verse fifteen, Our Lord Jesus Christ said, *'Go ye into all the world, and preach the gospel to every creature.'*"

Reverend Blackburn sat back in his chair, a look of incredulity on his face. "I see you have some knowledge of the Bible, sir; then you will know those words of Our Lord in the book of *Mark* were directed specifically at the eleven remaining apostles …"

"Yes, of course. But in Ephesians chapter four, verse eleven, speaking specifically of Our Lord the Christ, it says *'And he gave some, apostles; and some, prophets; and some, evangelists; and some, pastors and teachers.'* Although I don't claim to be any of the former, I do consider myself a teacher. And as you say, I do have 'some knowledge.'

"I also believe I am best suited to minister to my own *flock*, regardless of my lack of formal training."

Then he leaned forward and gave the pastor a hard look.

"I may not have formal religious training, but I am a pious man, a God-fearing man, and have studied the Bible extensively. I also know that no man, nor group of men, regardless of ordination or title, has a monopoly on the Word of God. This was the cornerstone of the Protestant Reformation, and countless men fought and died for that very belief."

But Reverend Blackburn was not easily overawed and was now becoming worked up.

"Don't presume to teach me theology, sir! I have studied the subject my entire adult life, while you have been studying military matters to the greatest extent, and the Bible presumably as something of a hobby."

Nathan did not answer this but continued to lock eyes with the revered while slowly chewing on the unlit cigar.

At that moment Miss Abbey returned with a tray containing cups of tea and small, sweet biscuits. She walked into a silent room. Two forceful, intense men stared at each other, not speaking. She wished she had simply stayed in the kitchen, but now she was here it would be even more awkward to turn and walk out again.

"Here we are, gentlemen. Reverend, will you have milk and sugar with your tea?"

She set the tray down on a side table and looked over at the pastor with a polite smile, as if nothing untoward were happening.

The pastor's features softened, and he said, "Thank you, my dear. Both, if you please. Mr. Chambers, won't you join me?"

"Yes, certainly ... why not? Nothing in mine, thank you, Momma." Nathan detested tea but didn't wish to be impolite.

After serving the men, Miss Abbey served herself and took a seat.

Reverend Blackburn lifted his cup and held it up toward Nathan. "To your homecoming, Mr. Chambers. May it be all the things you would wish."

"Thank you, Reverend."

They took a sip of the hot tea, after which Miss Abbey took over the conversation with small talk; she prodded the pastor for any news of the surrounding neighborhood she might have missed at the morning service. After another hour or so, Reverend Blackburn excused himself and left in the carriage. Nathan and Miss Abbey watched his departure from the top steps of the veranda.

Miss Abbey looked up at Nathan and frowned. He shrugged his shoulders apologetically, but said nothing, so she turned, and walked back into the house. He stood a moment longer, watching the carriage roll away, then reached into his pocket, pulled out a match, and finally lit the cigar he'd been chewing on.

☙❧☙❧☙❧☙❧☙❧☙❧

The next day, late in the afternoon, Mountain Meadows once again received visitors. These visitors, however, were both unexpected, and entirely unwelcome.

Nathan was standing in a tobacco field talking with Sickles when he noticed several slaves had stopped hoeing to gaze back over toward the road. Curious, Nathan and Sickles looked that way as well.

"What the ...?" Nathan began. He saw a man on a horse, plodding slowly along the road, moving in the direction of the Big House, followed by another man driving a small wagon drawn by a single horse. Between these two white men walked eight black men and one black woman in single file, chained together at their necks. They shuffled along with heads down as if either exhausted, or utterly hopeless and downcast. Or both.

"Slave traders, sir," Sickles said. Looking back at his own charges, he growled, "All right, then ... nobody told you to stop working." The men immediately got back to work, paying no more attention to what was happening back on the road.

It crossed his mind to correct Sickles for being overly harsh, but by then Nathan was already moving off toward the house to deal with the new arrivals. Further, he decided, it wouldn't do to call Sickles out in front of the workers. It would be unfair, for one; he was only trying to do his job. And it would undermine his authority over the laborers, for another.

Nathan took the shorter route to the house, cutting through the tobacco fields. He moved at an easy trot and arrived just as the grooms were taking charge of the horses and helping the riders down.

He stepped across the gravel drive even as they were stepping down onto it.

"I am Mr. Chambers, the owner of this farm. How can I help you men?"

It was not exactly a proper greeting; Nathan hadn't bothered to honor them with the title "gentlemen," as he normally would have, addressing strangers and guests. He knew enough about such men he could not bring himself to denigrate the title by applying it to their like. It was all he could do to feign a polite

147

manner when what he really wanted to do was send them packing immediately.

But a quick glance told him their charges were parched and exhausted. Some of them appeared near collapse, and several showed signs of bruises or lash marks.

"Mr. *Chambers?* We were last here two years back, and as I recall, we dealt with an older gentleman, who also called himself Chambers."

"Yes, certainly. That would've been my father, who has recently passed. Please state your business on my farm."

The men seemed surprised and confused, both by the person, and by the reception.

"Well, Mr. Chambers, we've come to offer our services in the 'trade,' so to speak. I am Mr. Miller, and this is Mr. Bright. We've done business in the past with your father. Our condolences on his passing, of course; we had not heard of it before. Since we were passing by this way, we wished to extend him the courtesy of stopping by to see if we might be of service once again. May we come in out of this hot sun, sir, and discuss some potentially profitable business?" Surprisingly, Miller spoke with a northern accent, and seemed to be well-educated.

Nathan again looked over at the row of exhausted slaves. His heart went out to them. If he ordered the slavers off his property, as was his wish, there'd be no respite for these poor souls. They'd be forced to march right back down the road they'd just finished toiling up, in the heat of the day.

"Very well," he said. Then he called out to the grooms, pointing toward the row of chained slaves, "Cobb ... Sampson ... lead these men over under the shade of the house there. And then fetch them water, and food if they'll take it."

"Thank you kindly, Mr. Chambers. Right hospitable of you," Miller said.

But Nathan gave him an angry glare. "You've driven your charges to exhaustion, without mercy, in the hot sun. Simple Christian charity demands I give them what solace I may."

"Regardless, you have possibly saved us from grievous loss of profit, due to our negligence and poor planning, forgetting to bring along our water skins. For that we do thank you."

"I care nothing for your *profits*, sir."

Even as the words were coming out of his mouth, Megs poked her head out the front door.

"Oh! I'll see to food and refreshments, right away, Master," and darted back inside.

But before the door could even swing shut Tom stepped out.

"Everything, okay, Captain?"

"Yes, Tom, thank you. It seems we have unexpected guests." Tom noted Nathan's lack of decorum, not even bothering to introduce the newcomers. They were not only unexpected but also clearly unwelcome.

"Oh … yes, I can see that. Is there anything I can do for you, sir?"

"No, I don't think so, Tom. I—"

But even as he said these words, and before he could finish his sentence, something whispered in the back of his mind, *But … what have they got in the wagon?*

He'd initially assumed the wagon was just for hauling supplies, and possibly a little fodder for the horses. But now he strode around the back of it and looked inside.

"Damn!" He looked over at Mr. Miller, and scowled, "Give my man the keys to these shackles, sir! Tom, get his keys and come here at once."

Without hesitation or question, Tom strode down the stairs and held out his hand in front of Mr. Miller.

"Oh …" Miller responded, "I'd rather you didn't do that, sir. No telling where they'll wander off to."

Nathan looked over at him with a glare that could have melted wax. "Give him the keys, sir. This is my land, and I will not be gainsaid!"

Miller reached in his pocket and pulled out a ring of keys. He fumbled for a moment and then handed the ring to Tom with one specific key extended. Tom grabbed the key ring and trotted over to where the Captain stood at the back of the wagon.

"*Damn* is right!" Tom said, as he looked in and saw the contents of the wagon. Five young black children sat on a bedding of hay between stacks of luggage. They'd been shackled together, each at one ankle. A length of rusty chain ran through the shackles and was bolted to the frame of the wagon. There were three boys and two girls and appeared to range in age between four and eight years.

"Bastards ..." Tom said under his breath, and immediately jumped up into the back of the wagon, hurrying down the row, using the key to remove the shackles.

"Cobb, just leave those men to Sampson for the moment, and come over here, if you please."

Cobb trotted over and looked up in the wagon. His reaction, however, was not as strong as Nathan and Tom's had been; he'd seen it before.

"Yes sir, the children. It's always hardest on the little ones ..."

Nathan gazed at him a moment, shook his head, and turned back toward Tom. "Just hand them down to me, Tom. Cobb, once they're all down, you lead them inside the house and find them a cool place to lie down, and give them water, and food. Then come back here and see to these horses. They'll be needing water first, then fodder shortly thereafter."

"Yes, Captain, sir. Us'll bring 'em right in to old Megs. She'll know just where to put 'em, and how to feed 'em, and such. And don't you worry none about them horses ... soon they'll be thinking they's in horse heaven!"

Tom had just finished with the shackles, and scooped the children up, handing them down one at a time to the Captain. As Nathan held each, he said, "We'll get you shade, water, and food in the house ..."

He could think of nothing else to say. He couldn't tell them everything would be all right, or they were safe now, as he wished to. It wasn't true, and he couldn't bring himself to lie to them, who had already suffered so much, and had so much more to come.

Tom handed him down the last child, the smallest—a young girl who appeared to be about four. When he lifted her, she looked him right in the eyes, and he could see she was crying.

He set her gently on the ground and knelt down in front of her. She continued to gaze straight into his eyes as if she held no fear of him.

"Why are you crying, little one?" he asked. "Nobody here will harm you. We will give you shade, water, and food."

"I miss my Momma."

Nathan took a deep breath, and thought, *Damn! Damn it all to hell!*

"Yes … yes, I understand, little one. What is your name?"

"Lonna, Master."

Nathan took another deep breath, fighting down a deep aching pain building in his chest.

"These men say I won't never see her again. But I want to, Master. I want to see my Momma! More'n anything." The tears streamed harder now, but she didn't look down or turn away.

Nathan fought down the emotions threatening to choke the breath out of him, and he could feel his own tears welling up.

"Let me tell you something, Lonna … 'never' is a very, very long time. So long these men that told you 'never' don't really know how long it is. Even I don't know, and I'm much smarter than they."

She smiled slightly at this, but the tears continued to flow.

"Only God knows how long 'never' is, and what may happen before then. Let me tell you a little story, Lonna. When I was very young, I was also taken away from my Momma."

"*You* were, Master?"

"Yes … and at the time it seemed like I would never see her again."

"And did you cry?"

"Yes. I cried … like you. But a wise man came and said I needed to be strong, to stop crying, and to *do my best*. And if I did, then maybe someday I would be with her again."

"Like what you're telling me now, Master?"

"Yes … that's right, Lonna. You've just gotta be strong now and do your best at whatever you've got to do. And believe in your heart … someday you will see your Momma again. Then when you do, she'll be proud of you … because you did your best. And never stopped believing."

"Did you ever get to be with your Momma again, Master?"

"Well yes … yes, I did, Lonna. We live together again now, right here on this farm."

She sniffled back the tears and tried to smile. He resisted the urge to hug her; it would only make the whole thing harder. He looked up at Cobb and nodded.

"Come along, children. Old Cobb's gonna find you some cool shade, and somethin' to eat and drink up at the Big House."

Nathan looked over at the slave traders, fighting down a strong desire to order them seized and whipped. But then, for the first time, he noticed they were also hot and nearly exhausted. Clearly, they had also suffered from their own lack of planning, failing to bring water with them on their long, hot march. Christian charity demanded he also show mercy to these men, no matter how despicable he found them.

"Very well, come sit and take your rest in the shade on the veranda, while I have food and drink brought round."

It was as much courtesy as he could bear to extend them. He would not have them in his house. He had no desire to tarnish the good feelings of his home with their ill presence.

"Most kindly offered, sir. Most kindly," Miller said, and Bright nodded in agreement.

The maids served out drinks and a simple meal of bread and cold meat to the slave traders, same as they'd offered to the bound slaves. The slavers were seated at one of the outside veranda tables on the shady side of the house. Nathan came and sat across from them.

Miller once again spoke for the pair, "Mr. Chambers. Thank you again for your hospitality. We are much obliged."

Nathan said nothing, just gazed at him and pulled a cigar from his pocket and stuck it in his mouth to chew on.

"We're currently offering top dollar for healthy, adult field workers. They're presently in high demand down in New Orleans, on account of a general shortage of workers in the sugar production business. If you have any surplus of laborers, we're prepared to pay handsomely for the trade. And we have a goodly supply of the highest quality bank notes to offer in payment.

"Conversely, if you are in need of additional labor, we are in a position to accommodate you there as well at a reasonable price. If we can sell our assets here it clearly saves us the expense of the long transport to the South. In fact, we have a very nice pair of slaves, a man and a woman, we will sell you at a considerable discount due to the requirement they be sold as a pair."

"Requirement?" Nathan couldn't help asking, though he had no intention of dealing with these men. He'd never heard of any such restriction, and his curiosity was piqued.

"Yes ... you see, in an apparent moment of weakness, their former master granted their wish to be allowed a real wedding, performed by an ordained minister and sanctioned by the church. As you know, slave weddings are typically ... hmm ... *informal*, shall we say? No legal standing nor church recognition. 'Jumping the broom,' it's often called, I believe. But on *this* one ... well, we have a legal and moral obligation to honor it, I'm afraid.

"Of course, we recognize it affects their value. But if you'll just have a look at them, you'll see they are each in prime condition—healthy, young, and strong. You'll never regret acquiring the pair, I can assure you of that, sir.

"And, as you can see, we also buy and sell surplus children as we travel ... more as a service than any real profitable endeavor, you understand."

Nathan looked hard at them, then said, "I have just recently come from New Orleans, and I have seen how they treat their slaves. I would *never* send any of my people there, even if I *were* of a mind to sell them ... which I'm not.

"And I'm not interested in acquiring any more slaves, married or otherwise. As for buying and selling children ... I find the very idea detestable. I'm afraid you have wasted your time coming here, and your long, hot climb up our road has been for naught."

"Oh, never you worry about that, Mr. Chambers. We are happy to come and see if we can be of service, anytime, even though it may have been, as you say, of wasted effort this time."

"You misunderstand me, Mr. Miller. I find your trade highly despicable, and will *not* take part in it now, or ever. Further, I find your treatment of these people disgraceful, in this specific instance. Easy enough for you to say, 'don't worry' about the long, hot climb when you did the whole thing on horseback. Rather ask those who had to walk the entire way in shackles whether or not it was worth the bother."

Miller was so taken aback by this unexpected speech and Nathan's thoroughly intimidating presence and manner, he could find nothing to say in response, nor did he dare utter a word. He looked down at his plate, and slowly stirred his food with his fork. Bright also gazed at his food. He hadn't said a word yet and didn't appear inclined to start now.

"For the sake of the children, and those poor shackled men, and the woman, who've already suffered enough for today — and even for you two, who are clearly also done in, I have to admit — I'll allow you to spend the night in one of my barns. I'll have my men bring round food, and water at first light in the morning. Also, I'll give you additional water skins to carry on your journey tomorrow, so you'll not run dry again.

"After you have broken the fast, you must leave this farm straightaway, and I'll ask you politely not to return. To be blunt, you are *not* welcome here. And if you speak to others in your trade, you may kindly tell them the same. Good day to you."

Then without another word, he pushed back his chair, stood, and strode away, still chewing on the unlit cigar.

Later, after his own dinner, he sat on the veranda at a table with Tom and Jim. They could see the events of the day troubled him deeply. He smoked one cigar after another, with little talk, and sipped the whiskey without seeming to notice it.

"That last little girl sure did tug at the old heartstrings, Captain," Tom finally said, risking bringing up the topic he guessed was most troubling Nathan's mind.

He looked over at Tom and nodded.

"Yes … that she did. Damn those slave traders! They casually tear children from their mommas, husbands from their wives, with no more thought than of earning a few dollars. Cobb came over and told me one of the shackled men, a fellow named Henry, had pleaded with him to ask me to buy him. He was desperate to stay close to his wife, rather than letting them take him away to New Orleans. She lives just to the east over in Lynchburg. The man said they'd pulled him out of the field, shackled him to the others, and marched him off without even letting him tell her goodbye."

"It's a damned sorry, miserable business, that's for sure," Jim concluded, shaking his head sadly, and taking another sip of whiskey.

"Well … you *could* buy that man … and the little girl as well, for that matter," Tom suggested.

"No!" Nathan shot back, slamming his open palm on the table with such force and emotion, it startled the other two.

"That's the damned, torturous shame of it all! I *can't* buy them, nor any others. If I do, then I'd not only be giving money to my enemies, but every slaver in Virginia would be knocking on our door from now 'til perdition. And every slave they'd bring would have another sad story, like to bring a man to tears! Can I buy them all? Can I save them all?"

He leaned back in his chair and puffed on his cigar. Gazing up at the sky, he blew great clouds of smoke high above his head. For several minutes he continued to do the same, not saying a word.

His companions knew him well enough when to leave him to his thoughts, so they just sat, and said nothing, continuing to sip their whiskey.

"No … I can't even buy that one little girl, and it breaks my heart. Unless I'm willing to murder those men and bury them deep where nobody will ever find them … and believe me, I've considered it. Otherwise, as sure as the sun rises in the east, the word would get around, 'Chambers has a soft spot for the little children, deprived of their mommas.' And next thing you know there's a steady stream of wagons rolling up to Mountain Meadows, and I've become the very cause of the practice I most despise and wish to prevent.

"No, gentlemen, I'm afraid this is the cross I must bear. And dear, sweet little Lonna must leave in the morning with these despicable men, shackled like a beast. And there's not a damned thing I can do about it.

"No … we must be resolute, and stick with our plans, no matter the temptations the *enemy* puts before us. God willing, others will follow our lead, and this evil can be ended for good and all."

He sat in silence for a few more minutes. Then he stood, raised his glass to them, and said, "Gentlemen, I find I'm feeling very low this evening.

"In the Psalms it says, *'He healeth the broken in heart, and bindeth up their wounds.'* So I will trust in the word of the Lord and choose to believe … tomorrow will be a better day. Good night."

He downed the last swallow, set the glass down on the table, and strode away. Tom could see there were tears in his eyes.

ஐௐ௯௧ஐௐ௯௧ஐௐ௯௧

That night the cabins were once again abuzz with talk and wild rumors, this time surrounding the arrival of the slave traders and their human cargo. That the Captain had apparently welcomed them and allowed them to stay the night, rather than sending them away, only fueled the fires. The speculation ran the gamut, from those few who'd already developed a belief in their new master, the Captain, to the majority who were still skeptical of anything white men did or said. These figured him for the worst sort of liar and fraud, though admittedly not as cruel as originally feared.

The former argued the master was buying up more slaves just so he could free them later. There was even talk of young children being seen among those he was going to "rescue" from the slavers.

On the other, more pessimistic side, were Tony and his friends, among many others. To them, the Captain's dealings with the slave traders was proof he was not all he'd claimed to be. That he would sell off his surplus slaves, most likely the littlest children, who weren't yet productive. And maybe a few of the more vigorous young men, who were in highest demand and would bring in the most money.

Babs was again distraught and tearful, as she hadn't been since before the Captain's arrival. When she tucked the little girls into bed that night, she lay down with them, holding and rocking them. And once again, George could think of nothing to say or do to console her. In the end, he ate his dinner cold and alone at the table. When he finished, he said a little silent prayer … *Dear Lord, whatever else may be, please just grant our two sweet little girls ain't taken away in the morning. Nor Babs, neither. And if'n somebody gots to go, then let it be me instead. Thank you most kindly for listening, sir. Amen.*

ಬಿ೮ೡ೮ೖಬಿ೮ೡ೮ೖಬಿ೮ೡ೮ೖ

By midmorning the next day, the occupants of the cabins were feeling much relieved. Though there were no new faces, as some had predicted, they saw the slavers leaving at first light with no additions to their human chain. Those with small children, like Babs and George, were especially happy to know the slave traders had left the farm, apparently having conducted no business with the Captain.

Still, it had been a puzzling incident, and it'd left many with an uneasy feeling. Why had he welcomed them in if he never intended to buy or sell any slaves? Maybe the prices just weren't right, or they couldn't agree on a deal. Maybe they'd come back again another time when conditions were more favorable for a trade. And on and on.

Nathan was conversely curious what the people were thinking and saying about the slave traders, but wasn't privy to any of their discussions. So around noon time he sought out Megs to see if she'd heard anything. He understood she somehow had a very good sense of what was going on around the farm, even though she only worked in the house.

He knew about the traditional mistrust between house and field slaves; it was the same on every farm. But he sensed she had somehow figured out a way to keep the pulse of the outside workers without ever being seen speaking with them. He guessed she must have her own private network of people whom she got the news from.

157

"Megs, I was wondering if you'd heard anything … you know … about the slave traders."

"Heard anything, Captain? I know they left at first light with the same folks they came with … *exactly* the same ones, and no others, if that's what you mean."

"Well, yes, there's that, but … I was wondering … well, how the people in the cabins are feeling about the slavers being here."

She was quiet a moment, staring at him. He wondered if she knew he'd guessed she had some clandestine means of getting the news from outside.

"I … I ain't never out in the cabins, Captain. So how would I know a thing like *that?*"

"Oh, well … I just thought one of the maids … hmm … out collecting eggs or fetching milk or something … may have overheard some talk."

She looked at him again for another long moment, "Well, now you mention it … I *did* hear some talk back in the kitchen this morning."

"And?"

"And … well, let's just say it didn't do you no favors. Them that's inclined to misbelieve you see it as proof they're right."

"Even though I never invited them in the first place and never even discussed any business with them?"

"Well, sir … I reckon them out in the cabins don't know nothing about any of that. Alls they know is, the slave traders came, they met with you, and you welcomed them to stay the night. It don't … *look good* … whatever the truth may be."

"*Damn it!* I was afraid of that. How it galled me, suffering their presence here! And I did it only for the sake of those poor captives, who were about to collapse from thirst and fatigue. And now no one knows how badly I wanted to send those slavers packing straightaway … preferably at the end of a cracked whip!"

She looked at him another long moment, then finally said, "*I know* … now."

&⅋⅋∞(⅋⅋∞(⅋⅋∞(⅋

On the afternoon of the day the slave traders departed, another unexpected visitor arrived at Mountain Meadows. He arrived an hour past noon in a coach, much more formal and elegant looking than the simple one Reverend Blackburn had arrived in on Sunday.

And if Stan was the biggest man in height and muscular build any of them had ever seen, this man had to be the biggest in girth. Nathan could see the coachman straining to assist the man as he stepped down from the coach. He wore a formal, black suit, much like the one Nathan had worn on that first day back at Mountain Meadows. And he had a matching black, bowler style hat. He carried a small black leather bag, such as businessmen might use to carry legal papers, and carried a walking stick, highly polished black lacquered wood with a silver knob on top.

Nathan was just heading back out to the fields having had his midday meal, so he stepped up to the coach to greet their unexpected guest. The man looked up and said, "Do I have the pleasure of addressing Mr. Nathaniel Chambers, sir?"

"That you do, sir. But you have me at a disadvantage; it seems you know who I am, but I have not had the pleasure of your acquaintance."

"Quite so, Mr. Chambers, though I was very well acquainted with your Daddy, the late and honorable Mr. Jacob Chambers. My name is Templeton, sir. Wilfred Templeton, at your service."

"Good to meet you, Mr. Templeton." Nathan extended his hand. Templeton took the hand in a firm, if slightly sweaty embrace. His hand, like the rest of him, was large and meaty.

"As I assume you are not from around here, you must be tired and hot from your journey. Won't you please come in and take shade and refreshment in my home?"

"Yes, thank you most kindly, Mr. Chambers. Though I have only come as far as White Sulphur Springs this day, the journey, as a whole, has been long and wearing, and the day is already hot."

Nathan gestured toward the stairs, and as they climbed, he saw Megs looking out the door. "Megs, would you be so kind as to get Mr. Templeton some refreshments? Thank you kindly."

"Yes, Master, right away," Megs responded, and quickly turned to go arrange for the needs of the guest. Nathan noted she'd switched from calling him "Captain" as she had done all week, to "Master" in front of this unknown guest. Wise woman, he thought. We don't know who this man is, nor what he is about, so best to be cautious. She'd subtly reminded him of that.

"Please, won't you join me in our library? I find it the most cool and comfortable room in the house. Megs will soon bring us refreshments."

"That is most kind of you, Mr. Chambers. Most kindly."

Templeton was soon easing himself into a large, padded leather chair. Nathan wondered when the screws had last been tightened on it and felt some relief when the chair held without even a creak.

After a few moments, Megs and Sarah entered the room holding trays. They swiftly set out glasses of cool lemonade and small sweet biscuits on the side tables next to the chairs where the men sat. Then they withdrew from the room, closing the double doors behind them.

"So you were saying you knew my father," Nathan prompted, to start the conversation on a casual note. Friendlier, he thought, than just asking, "Why are you here, and what do you want?"

"Yes, yes, in fact, I have known your father for several years. A fine gentleman, and a very stand-up fellow. Oh! And my most heartfelt condolences on your loss, *of course!*" he said, as if he had forgotten his manners by not saying this initially.

"Thank you—most kind of you."

After a long sip on the glass of lemonade, Templeton said, "Ah … delicious. Please give my compliments to your kitchen staff."

Nathan nodded in appreciation, but said nothing, waiting for Templeton to continue.

"Well, Mr. Chambers, I'm sure you're wondering just who I am—besides my name of course—and why I'm here. And how it is I know your father so well."

Nathan just smiled and shrugged his shoulders.

Templeton continued, "Well, it just so happens I am the chief aide to Mr. Letcher … that is, his honor Governor John Letcher of the great Commonwealth of Virginia. And, I know your father because he was, of course, one of our state senators. And a great support and comfort to the Governor, in all his good works, as he was to Mr. Letcher's predecessor, Mr. Wise."

With this pronouncement, Nathan sat up and was suddenly much more interested in his new guest. He had expected Mr. Templeton was a salesman, peddling some new kind of farm equipment or implement. But ... here was a man who'd come straight from the Governor's office!

"Well, I am honored to know you, sir. And may I ask what brings you all this way from Richmond to western Virginia?" Nathan was genuinely curious now, no longer just making polite conversation.

"Well, you do come straight to the point, sir, I must say! They warned me you were a career army officer before returning to your Daddy's farm, so I guess it is to be expected."

But Templeton was clearly not put off by Nathan's abruptness; he'd responded in good humor and with a smile.

"Sorry, sir. It's just you now have my curiosity fully piqued. It's not every day someone from the Governor's office drops by for a visit."

"Just so, just so, Mr. Chambers. Yes, yes ... so I will get right to the point of my visit."

He set the half empty glass down on a side table and settled back comfortably into his chair.

"As you know, your father was a sitting state senator when he passed away ... may God rest his soul. So that means his position in the state senate is presently vacant. As such it is the duty, and prerogative, of the Governor to appoint someone to fill his seat for the remainder of his term which is ... nearly another three years."

"And you would like my opinion, or blessing, or some such, on the new person to fill his seat? Is that why you're here?"

"Well, you could say that ... but not *exactly*."

Nathan raised an eyebrow at this cryptic answer but waited for his guest to elaborate.

"You see, the Governor has been struggling to find a suitable replacement for your father. So when his honor heard Mr.

Chambers' grown son, an army officer of excellent reputation—a war hero even according to the *official* accounts. Well, anyway, when he heard the son of Jacob Chambers was returning, he thought, 'who better to fill out the father's term than the returning son?' So he has sent me here to ask if you would consider finishing out your father's term as state senator."

Templeton leaned forward to gauge Nathan's reaction to this pronouncement.

Now it was Nathan's turn to sit back in his chair. He looked up at the ceiling and tried to digest this new development.

"Before I answer, I'll have to admit I know very little about being a state senator, sir. For instance, what is it a senator does, and when does he do it? How much time is he expected to spend in Richmond, and so forth? I'm afraid I've been away in the Army most of my adult life, fighting wars, outlaws, and Indians. I've not paid much attention to the workings of civilian government. And I've been quite out of touch with any recent developments or issues in Virginia, as far as that goes."

"Oh, don't concern yourself about any of that, Mr. Chambers. You are a gentleman of high education, with years of experience leading men, and working within the machinations of government, albeit of the *military* persuasion. You will have no difficulty mastering the duties required of a senator, and we shall quickly teach you all there is to know. And, you'll only need be in Richmond two months out of the year. So you'll have plenty of time to oversee the proper running of your family estate here in western Virginia."

"Well, I am honored, though I expect the honor all goes to my father. I'd simply be serving as his stand-in, as it were."

"Oh, say not so, sir! Certainly, it is well-earned on *your* part as well—no doubt, sir, no doubt. If not for your stellar military service and exemplary reputation, I'm sure the Governor should be forced to look elsewhere, regardless of how he felt about your father."

"Yes, I suppose that's true. And thank you so kindly for saying so. But as I said, I feel like I know almost nothing about the issues the Governor must even now be wrestling with. Still, I suppose it would be good to have a say—a *voice*, so to speak, in the future of Virginia, now that I'm back. And I'm sure I would have opinions on various topics once I became better informed. Did his honor instruct you to ask me any questions about my opinions on any *particular* subjects?" It suddenly occurred to him the Governor might not agree with his plans for Mountain Meadows and its workers, or his opinions in general about the institution of slavery!

"Oh no, certainly *not!* The Governor is … a man who believes strongly in serving *all* the people of the Commonwealth. As such, he is open to the wants and needs of *all* its citizens, as opposed to having a specific agenda, as some political candidates will espouse."

No specific agenda … or no strong opinions? Nathan wondered. *Hmm … wonder if our governor is some kind of mugwump?*

"So he would welcome any suggestions or ideas you might bring to the legislature. And, of course, he is well aware you have just arrived back in the Commonwealth after a long absence, honorably serving our country. He has every confidence you'll quickly grasp the issues we must deal with. And he has people, such as myself, who'll be more than happy to work with you in that regard once you arrive in Richmond. Nothing to worry about there, Mr. Chambers. You will be in very good hands. You'll agree then? To fill out your father's term of office?"

Nathan thought about Templeton's question for a long moment. Should he tell Templeton his thoughts about slavery, and his plans to set an example for how to replace it with an economic system that would end it? How would Templeton react? And how would the Governor react? Templeton said Mr. Letcher was an open-minded man … so he might be open to Nathan's ideas and suggestions. But no telling what Templeton might do if Nathan explained his plans now. What to do? Finally, he decided it would be best to have a voice in the government if he wanted to promote his ideas. And since Templeton had asked no specific questions, not volunteering any thoughts wasn't exactly being deceptive …

"Well, I suppose it is my duty as a citizen, to serve my country when called, just as I did when I was a soldier. So, *yes*, Mr. Templeton, I will do it!"

"Excellent! Excellent! Thank you, Mr. Chambers."

Templeton grinned broadly and leaned forward to grasp Nathan's right hand in both of his. Nathan's hand all but disappeared in the great, broad hands of Mr. Templeton.

"So what happens now?"

"Oh, it is quite simple, Mr. Chambers. I have brought the necessary papers with me to swear you in, already signed by the Governor. Of course, there will be a formal ceremony with the Governor when you come to Richmond, but these papers I brought with me will make it all official. I will just need a pen and ink, and a suitable witness in addition to myself, and then we shall be able to conclude our happy business."

Nathan stood up and walked to the library doors, opening one door, he called out, "Megs, would you come here, please?"

She quickly arrived and did a small curtsy. "Yes, Master. How may I be of service to you, sir?"

"Would you please locate Mr. Clark and ask him to bring pen and ink with him to the library?"

"Yes, Master, I believe he is just upstairs, sir."

Megs hurried down the hall toward the back stairs. Nathan imagined Tom must be upstairs in the business office, once again going through the records, planning and plotting the many improvements needed on the farm.

A few minutes later there was a low knock on the door. "Come," Nathan responded.

Tom entered and said, "Megs said you wanted to see me, sir … with pen and ink?"

"Thank you, yes, Tom. Tom, this is Mr. Wilfred Templeton. Mr. Templeton, this is my right-hand man, Mr. Tom Clark. Tom served me as a master sergeant and quartermaster at Fort Davis out in Texas."

Templeton started to rise, but Tom could see that would be a great effort because of his size. So he immediately leaned forward, extending his hand, "Please … don't bother yourself with rising … it is very good to meet you, sir."

Templeton nodded gratefully and took Tom's hand, "Likewise, Mr. Clark. A great pleasure to meet you as well and please accept my heartfelt gratitude for your past service to our country out West."

"Thank you, sir."

"Tom, Mr. Templeton has come from Richmond. He is from Governor Letcher's staff. He's come on behalf of the Governor to ask me to finish out my father's term as state senator, and I have accepted."

"*Oh!* Well, many congratulations on that, sir! And greatly deserved, if you don't mind my saying so!"

"Well, we shall see about that," Nathan gave a wry smile. "Anyway, Mr. Templeton has some papers we need to sign to make it legal, and I would like you to sign as witness."

"I would be honored, *of course*, sir!"

𝕦𝕦

Later, they stood on the veranda, smoking cigars and sipping glasses of whiskey Nathan had provided to celebrate the momentous event. Miss Abbey joined them. She had met Templeton several times before in Richmond when Jacob was serving in the senate and was happy to pay her respects.

"Are you sure you won't stay to dinner, Mr. Templeton?" Miss Abbey asked.

"Oh, thank you, no, Mrs. Chambers. I've had a long, difficult trek from Richmond, and I have a room waiting for me back at the hotel in White Sulphur Springs. I shall need a good night's sleep before boarding the coach in the morning for the long ride back to the train station, and beyond. But thank you most kindly for your hospitality, and on behalf of Mr. Letcher, thank you for letting us borrow your son to help in the running of the government!"

"Oh, well, I guess I shouldn't be surprised. It seems to run in the family," she answered smiling, with obvious pride in the honor being paid to her son, on behalf of her late husband.

"Well, I expect you are very proud of your men, ma'am. You certainly have every right to be. And let me say, it has been a great pleasure to see you again, Mrs. Chambers. As I recall, the last time you and your husband were in Richmond it was quite a merry gathering—even before Mr. Letcher had been elected Governor, I believe. Mr. Chambers, I recall Colonel Robert Lee, a fellow Virginian whom you likely served under in Texas, was there as well. Am I remembering it rightly, Mrs. Chambers?"

"Oh, yes. You are quite correct, Mr. Templeton. I do recall meeting Colonel Lee and speaking with him about our dear Nathaniel."

"Yes, that's right! And now I recall Colonel Lee spoke very highly of your son, '*Captain* Chambers.' I had nearly forgotten that, before you brought it to mind just now!"

Then Nathan put his hand to his forehead, and said, "Oh, my! Now I am feeling like quite the cad, Momma. Colonel Lee specifically requested I give you his highest regards, and condolences, of course … before I left Texas! With everything that's happened since my arrival back home, I had completely forgotten it! My apologies, Momma!"

"Oh, never mind that, Nathan. What did the dear Colonel have to say?"

"Oh … well, he called you a 'lovely and gracious woman.'"

Miss Abbey smiled at the compliment.

"As I recall, your Colonel Lee was quite the handsome and gallant gentleman and looked very striking in his officer's uniform," Miss Abbey said with a wistful look. "I believe your Daddy was … well, *jealous*, might be the right word for it."

Nathan blushed. The thought of his mother being attracted to Colonel Lee, a man he'd looked up to and admired most of his adult life, felt a bit awkward.

"Ahem … yes," Templeton said, glancing from mother to son. "Well … anyway, I'm sure I speak for the Governor when I say I sincerely hope you'll be able to accompany your son on occasion when he comes to Richmond. And I hope you will grace us with your lovely company when you do so," he bowed.

"You are too kind, Mr. Templeton. I shall certainly endeavor to return such courtesy with the same. I hope and trust you will have a safe journey home, sir. And do give my kindest regards to his honor, Mr. Letcher."

Templeton was soon loaded back into his coach and on his way back to his hotel, and from there on to Richmond, having successfully completed his mission.

Later in the day Nathan and Tom sat on the veranda sipping whiskey.

"Well, now I suppose I'll have to learn how to be a senator as a well as a farmer."

"So it would seem, sir. So it would seem."

Chapter 8. By the People, For the People

"Democracy is two wolves and a lamb
voting on what to have for lunch.
Liberty is a well-armed lamb
contesting the vote."
– Benjamin Franklin

Tuesday June 19, 1860 – Greenbrier County, Virginia:

"So ... I suppose a senator just goes over to Richmond and votes on this or that proposal the governor or somebody else proposes ..."

"Well, Captain, if I remember my civics lessons from grammar school, ours is not a 'true democracy' where every citizen votes on every issue, like the old Greeks had. It's a 'representative' democracy, or 'republic.' Which means the people don't vote on every law, but instead vote on someone to *represent* them and then that person votes on their behalf."

"Yes, yes, I know all that, of course. What I don't know is any of the day-to-day details about being a state senator ..."

"Yes, of course you do, sir. But the point I was getting at is, as a representative of the people the most important thing is to *represent* them!"

"And just how do you expect me to do that, when I have *no idea* what any of them are thinking about, or what they would like me to do?"

"Ah, ha! There you have it ... that's exactly my point! How can you represent the people if you don't know what they're thinking? So my suggestion is ... go forth, meet with your 'people' and ... *ask them!*"

Tom leaned back in his chair triumphantly, folded his arms across his chest, and smiled like the cat who had just eaten the cream, cigar firmly planted between his teeth.

"Ah ... yes ... once again 'I was blind but now I see.' That is exactly the thing to do. I was so wound up in my own affairs and about how I would find time to learn this whole senator business, I nearly forgot the whole point of it!

"Thanks, Tom. Thank you kindly for clarifying things. In fact, first thing tomorrow morning, we'll set out to meet our neighbors, and ask them how they would like me to represent them."

"*We?*" Tom envisioned the pile of paperwork he still needed to wade through.

"Of course, *we*, Tom! After all, it was *your* idea, wasn't it? And it seems to me a proper senator should have an assistant with him, to jot down ideas, and suggestions, and whatnot. Don't you agree?"

"Yes … certainly, sir. It should prove very *entertaining*, I'm sure. Remind me again, sir, which of us *volunteered* for this duty?"

"Oh, come now, Tom. Cheer up. It'll do you good to get out of the house and go for a ride. Your stack of papers will still be there when you return."

"Yes, that's what I'm afraid of, sir. Well, I suppose William will continue making progress in my absence."

The next day just after sunrise, they were trotting their horses up the drive with the large dog steadily following along behind. They rode the four miles to the junction with the main east-west road. To the east the road ran over the Allegheny Mountains and all the way to Richmond. To the west it led to Lewisburg and eventually to Kentucky beyond. They turned east.

Their first stop was several miles east along the main road, then north on a winding side path up into the hills. Nathan's closest physical neighbor was a subsistence farmer. He occupied a small, one-story house made of logs on a sloping farm of several acres cleared out of the wooded hills. Jonathon Greene was the man's name. He grew just enough crops to feed himself and his livestock, plus did a little trapping and hunting to provide pelts and meat to trade for other staples. He'd lived in that same place since Nathan was a boy, and Miss Abbey had confirmed he lived there still. As they rode along, Nathan tried to imagine what opinions Mr. Greene might have about the government of Virginia. He was reasonably sure this was a waste of time but was determined to carry it through. He now considered it his duty to learn what the people wanted, and since Mr. Greene was one of the people ...

When they neared the cabin, a small brood of hens scurried noisily out of the way as their horses approached. Before they could dismount, the cabin door opened, and a small, wiry, gray-haired man came out. He was cradling a double-barreled shotgun in his arms. He held it casually, not pointed at them, but Nathan noticed he'd cocked both hammers, so it was likely loaded and ready for immediate use.

"Hello, Mr. Greene," Nathan called out in a friendly manner, "I'm your neighbor, Mr. Chambers, and this is my assistant, Mr. Clark ..."

But before he could explain the purpose of their visit, the old man interrupted.

"No ... you ain't Chambers! I've know'd Chambers all my life. He's an older fella, like myself, not a young tough like you. Aside from which I heard a rumor he was dead these past few months."

"Sorry, Mr. Greene. Right you are. I should have said ... I am Mr. *Nathaniel* Chambers. Mr. *Jacob* Chambers, whom you have known, was my father. I say *was*, as you are correct; my Daddy passed away several months ago. I have returned from out West to take over the family farm."

"Well, all right then, Mr. *Nathaniel* Chambers ... that makes a might more sense. And now you mention it, I *can* see a family resemblance."

He seemed to relax a little. "And what is it I can do for you, Mr. Chambers, and Mr. Clark?"

"Well actually, sir, I'm here to see what I can do for *you*. You see, the Governor has asked me to finish out my father's term as a state senator, and I've agreed. The problem is, I've been away off in the Army so long I've no idea what concerns folks here 'bouts. I need to learn, so I can be their 'voice,' so to speak, when I go over to Richmond."

"Y'all are here just to ask me what I think about things?" Greene was wide-eyed. "Your Daddy never once stopped by to ask my opinion about nothing, and he's been going off to Richmond for ... oh ... I reckon ten years or more now."

"Well, Mr. Greene, I expect you will find I'm different from my father in *many* ways. May we come in, sir?"

"Very well, I guess it won't do no harm … but I doubt you'll like anything I have to say. You can just tie your horses to yonder tree. Then come on in."

They dismounted and looped their reins over the low-hanging branches of a small tree growing a few yards from the house. Nathan looked around for Harry the Dog but couldn't spot him. No doubt he'd already found himself a comfortable, shady spot to lie down, just out of sight. They followed Greene into the cabin, Nathan having to duck his head to keep from bumping it on the low doorway. Greene sat at a small, crude table, and he motioned them to come sit in wooden chairs on the side opposite him. Nathan noted Greene had hung his shotgun up on the wall between two hooks placed there for the purpose. He also noticed Greene had lowered the gun's hammers. He took that for a positive sign!

"So now, what's it you're wanting to know, Chambers?" Greene asked after they had pulled up their chairs to the table.

"Well, that's the problem, you see … I don't rightly know what it is I *should* ask. So I guess I'd just like you to say anything that's on your mind—anything the government ought to know, or do, that is."

"Well, for the most part I don't got much to do with the gov'ment, Mr. Chambers, which is danged all right by me. I pretty much keep to myself here, and mostly nobody much bothers me."

Nathan listened politely but Mr. Greene seemed to confirm his assumption this would not be very productive or informative.

But then Greene changed his tone, "But I'll tell you what does bother me, that you won't like to hear, Mr. Chambers: the unfairness of the property tax!"

"The property tax, Mr. Greene?"

"Yes, sir. That's just what I said. Well, I don't pay much, what with my small plot of land, and no large livestock to speak of, but still, it's the *principle* of the thing. I'd like to hear your opinion, if you disagree."

This statement completely stumped Nathan, so he looked at Tom for help. But Tom just shrugged his shoulders and smiled back. He was no help!

"I'm sorry, Mr. Greene, but you must forgive me, but I am truly at a loss here. I'm unaware of what you're referring to concerning the property tax. *Why* is it unfair?"

For a moment Greene looked from one to the other in amazement, his mouth wide open. Then he shook his head and said, "The *slaves*, Mr. Chambers! All property in Virginia is subject to the property tax based on its fair value, except for them slaves! They're the one piece of 'property' treated different for the tax! No tax on slave children under age twelve, and the value of adults is capped at $300, even though I hear they're selling for more'n a thousand dollars!

"So a man such as myself, who does all *for* himself, without no help from nobody … well, he pays tax for *all* his property. But the man who makes his riches on the backs of them unwilling workers … he don't pay even half the tax for his so-called 'property.' Now you understand what I'm talking 'bout, Chambers? And you being one of them that's benefiting from the tax, I expect y'all won't agree with me on this one."

Greene sat back with arms folded on his chest.

"As a matter of fact, I *do* agree with you, Mr. Greene. I think you're right, and those owning slaves and treating them as property, ought to pay fair property tax on them, same as anything else."

Again, Greene stared at Nathan in open-mouthed disbelief. "You're saying you *agree* with me, Chambers?"

"Yes, sir. That's exactly what I'm saying. Thank you for bringing this matter to my attention. I will be sure to discuss the issue with the Governor when I see him. What else is on your mind, Mr. Greene?" Nathan asked, warming to his new role.

"Well …" Greene considered for a moment, apparently surprised his first issue had been so well received. "I'd like to see the road better maintained. It ain't bad in the summertime but come winter the mud gets so thick it's near impossible to get into town. Makes it might hard to get my necessities. I expect that'd be to your benefit too, Chambers, since you're just down the road from me."

"Sounds like a reasonable suggestion, Mr. Greene."

Greene finally broke into a smile and leaned back in his chair. "Well, after all these years, it's good to have a *neighbor*, Mr. Chambers!"

"Likewise, Mr. Greene!"

They spent a few more minutes on general small talk about goings on in the local area, Greene doing his best to bring Nathan up to date on the status of the various neighbors here on the east side of Lewisburg. Then they were back outside preparing to saddle up.

After he swung up into the saddle, Nathan said, "Oh, Mr. Greene … if you see a large dog roaming about, I would greatly appreciate you not shooting him. He seems to belong to me … or could be I belong to him. Either way I'd prefer he didn't get himself shot for a trespasser."

"Well, so long as he don't eat my chickens, I'll have no cause to shoot him."

"Oh, he'll not bother your chickens—never pays any attention to 'em. Too small to notice, likely. He might take down a mule deer, or a small elk, however," Nathan smiled, an unlit cigar now clenched between his teeth.

"Well, in that case he's welcome to 'em. Damned critters is always getting into my cabbages and pulling up my turnips. Ever since my old hound died and don't chase 'em off no more!"

Greene turned, and spat in disgust. "They's good eating, though…" he added as an afterthought, and then gave Nathan a little smile and a wink.

"Say … now you've reminded me of it … I seem to have inherited a crew of hunting dogs I've got no particular use for. Would you like one or two to replace your old hound? They probably need a bit of attention, and some gentling though …"

"Hmm … might be nice to have one around, now you mention it. Always worried I'll step out in the morning and run into a bear in my garden. Having a dog around eases that sort of concern."

"Tell you what, Mr. Greene ... I'll have one of my men bring a couple of those dogs 'round tomorrow. If you take a liking to them, you keep them. If not, just send them on back, no harm done."

"Well ... that seems more than fair. Mighty kindly of you, Chambers. Much obliged."

"Don't mention it, Mr. Greene. If you take them, you'll be doing me a favor, as I'll no longer need to be caring for them. A good day to you, sir!" Nathan tipped his hat.

"Yes, a very good day to you, sir, and thank you for the hospitality," Tom added.

"Thank y'all kindly, Mr. Chambers ... Mr. Clark. Y'all come back anytime, now."

They turned their horses and moved down the drive. A large brown and gray animal sprang up onto the road from under a bush it had been laying under, startling Greene and nearly making him jump.

He quickly recovered from his shock. "My *goodness*, Chambers, you wasn't kidding about that hound taking down a small elk ... maybe a *big* elk even, from the looks of him!"

Nathan and Tom turned around, and laughed, tipping their hats again toward Mr. Greene, then continuing down the trail, Harry the Dog trotting along behind.

They visited several other small farms scattered about the hills between Mr. Greene's cabin and White Sulphur Springs, the nearest town east of Mountain Meadows. The reception they received at these other homesteads was like that they'd received at Greene's farm, cautious and skeptical at the beginning, gradually growing warmer and friendlier as they came to understand Nathan's sincere interest in what they had to say.

Dark, heavy-looking clouds had covered the sky all day, and just as they made their way back onto the main road from a side trail it began to drizzle. After a few miles they were dripping wet, so they changed their plans. Rather than riding on to the next neighbor, whose turnoff was several miles further east, they turned back toward Mountain Meadows. Their mission wasn't urgent or time-sensitive; it could certainly wait for another day, and better weather. Even the great hound seemed annoyed with the change in the weather, stopping every few hundred yards to shake the water off his coat in a great, flopping display, water flying off him in all directions creating a cloud of mist.

They reached home and stabled the horses. Before heading inside to get out of the weather, Nathan stopped by the place where the hunting dogs were kenneled. Along the way they saw Zeke, one of the original white farmhands, supervising the various activities around the pens, and asked him to come along. When they reached the hounds' cage Nathan picked out two slightly less mean looking dogs and told Zeke to take them to Mr. Greene's place on the morrow.

"Yes, sir. I'll get 'er done first light tomorrow."

"Good man … just give him a little time to get comfortable with them and let him decide if he wants to keep them … one, or both. But if he doesn't want either, just bring 'em on back."

"It will be done just as you say, sir. But, if you don't mind my asking … why're we giving away these good hunting hound dogs to Mr. Greene, anyway?"

"Well, Zeke … for one, I don't much care for keeping things caged up and never free. And for another—I don't expect we'll have a need for the type of hunting *these* hounds have been trained for …"

He gave the farmhand a meaningful look.

Zeke smiled, shrugged his shoulders, and said, "Yes, sir. I reckon not, neither."

৪৩৩৩৪৩৩৩৪৩৩৩৪৩৩৩

The next day the gloom had set in even harder, and a steady rain pelted the rooftop. Nathan donned his oiled long-coat and wide-brimmed felt hat and headed out into the rain. He had nothing in particular he needed to do. But the field workers would be out, along with the hired hands and his own men—still working to repair the cabins. So he felt it was important to be seen out among them. He spent the day making the rounds from one group of workers to the next. Chatting with the men, offering a kind word here, a little humor there—generally doing what he

175

could to boost morale on an otherwise miserable day. Even Sickles seemed to appreciate the effort, commenting he had never seen the old master outdoors in such inclement weather.

The next day was much the same. But the clouds started breaking up by evening, and the rains slowed to a spotty drizzle. Nathan hoped the worst of the weather was over.

ಬಿಖಿಖಿಖಿಖಿಖಿಖಿಖಿಖಿಖಿ

The next morning followed through on the previous evening's promise of better weather. The rains had stopped, although there was still a patchy cloud cover and a chill breeze in the air. Not perfect, but good enough for another neighborly visit, Nathan decided.

But today he was uneasy and anxious about the reception he might receive. He'd decided it was time to visit Elijah Walters and try putting an end to the long-running feud.

Just after sunrise, he and Tom saddled up and once again headed down the drive. As expected, Harry the Dog came popping out from underneath a large bush and trotted after them as they passed.

Walters was the nearest neighbor in the westward direction, toward Lewisburg. Walters Farm, like Mountain Meadows, was a sprawling plantation of many hundreds of acres. And dozens of "unpaid laborers" worked this farm as well. Walters, like Nathan, had inherited the estate from his father, who had passed away several years earlier. Besides the feud, the senior Walters and Chambers had also shared an unstated rivalry for supremacy in the section of Greenbrier County east of Lewisburg. Nathan hoped they could also put a stop to that nonsense. He had enough things to deal with and worry about, without trying to outdo his neighbor in every regard.

The most challenging part would likely be keeping his own anger in check. He'd laid in bed the previous night in prayerful contemplation of today's meeting. He was still at a low, simmering boil from the man's treatment of Miss Abbey, and it would take very little to set him off. But he was determined to keep control this time and had left his weapons behind. But

176

remembering Miss Abbey's dire warnings about the man, he'd given Tom the small pocket Colt to bring with them … just in case.

He found himself curious about *Mrs.* Walters. As far as Miss Abbey knew, nobody in Greenbrier County had ever seen the new Mrs. Walters since her arrival from Richmond. The rumors said she was very shy, or possibly sickly, so never left the Walters' estate, not even to attend church on Sundays. It was possible she traveled back to Richmond to visit her relatives from time to time, but no one knew for sure. Nathan hoped to at least do a little reconnaissance in that regard and report back to Miss Abbey. She'd be thrilled with any news or gossip he could provide.

As they plodded along down the main road toward Lewisburg, Nathan recalled what Mr. Greene had said about the road turning to mud whenever it rained. That was certainly proving true today. The horses struggled to keep from slipping and sliding, especially on the long, twisty, sloping, track from Mountain Meadows Farm to the junction. And the main road was even worse; the slick and mucky surface quickly left the horses' hooves caked in a thick layer of sticky brown sludge. Harry the Dog wisely kept off the road entirely, preferring to work his way through the tall grass and underbrush at the side.

After several miles, they were happy to take the side road leading to Walters Farm. The road branched off in a southerly direction, and the improvement was immediate. It seemed Walters or his father before him had put some effort into adding crushed rock to the dirt, giving it a firmer surface. They had done much the same on the side road leading to Mountain Meadows, but not as extensively nor as neatly. Nathan wondered how much it might improve travel if they did the same on the main road itself. *Maybe old Mr. Greene was right,* he thought, *though it'd be quite a job to run it all the way from Lewisburg to Richmond!*

The main road paralleled Howard Creek on the north bank for the several miles between Mountain Meadows and Walters Farm. Now Walters' side road crossed the creek in a shallow, rocky ford. The two days of rain had swollen the creek somewhat, but it was still only a foot or so deep, so the horses crossed without trouble, and the accumulated mud was washed from their hooves. Harry the Dog strode briskly across behind them without hesitation.

In less than a mile they came to cultivated fields, cotton and tobacco, looking very much like Mountain Meadows. They saw field workers out amongst the crops. This farm, like all the others in the area, had a slightly undulating surface making it impossible to see a great distance in any direction. They came up over a slight rise and suddenly saw before them the great house at the center of Walters' plantation. They'd built the Walters Farm manor house in the colonial style, rather than the Greek style used on the Chambers' house. It was of red brick, with windows trimmed in white, outlined with black painted shutters. Though it did not have the grand columns lining the veranda, like Mountain Meadows, it was still an imposing and impressive presence dominating the surrounding countryside.

As they approached, Nathan noted the house had a wide, rectangular graveled area in front of the main doors, rather than the circular drive at the Chambers' house. A black servant, neatly dressed in white, came quickly out of the house to greet them, another following in his wake.

"May we take your horses, masters?" the first man asked.

"Yes, certainly, thank you ... but, just don't try restraining the dog, mind you. He'll have none of it."

"Oh, *no*, master! We'll not bother your great hound-dog," he looked at the dog fearfully. "He can just make hisself right to home as he pleases, master."

As the first servant was leading the horses away, the second was already ushering the guests into the house. "Please masters, won't you step into the house and rest yourselves? We will bring you refreshments presently."

"Thank you, kindly. Lead on, my good fellow."

They followed the man up the stairs to a wide porch. *Not too different from the great veranda back home,* Nathan thought. Then they entered the house through large double-doors. He led them across a broad foyer floored in marble from which a broad, curved stairway ran up the left side to a landing above. They entered a formal sitting room, filled with cushioned chairs and highly polished side tables for serving food and drink.

"Please masters, do take your comfort in this room now, while's I announce y'all and just fetch y'all refreshments. Who shall I tell the Master is calling?"

"I am Mr. Nathaniel Chambers, Mr. Walters' neighbor, and this is Mr. Clark," Nathan answered.

"Very good, master. I will announce y'all at once," he bowed and quickly exited the room.

Nathan and Tom took seats and settled down to wait. The room, and everything they'd seen about the house, was immaculate and elegant, almost to an extreme. He thought the interior of this house made the Big House at Mountain Meadows seem almost ordinary. Marble floors shined to a high gloss, and dark, intricately carved wainscoting ran along the hallways. Floor-to-ceiling paneling painted white with gold leaf accents, or dark, highly varnished wood paneling covered the common rooms. Sparkling chandeliers of crystal, shining with the light of hundreds of candles hung from the ceilings. Rich, heavy brass fixtures appeared on all the doors and windows, and beautiful, wrought-iron banisters on the stairways. Draperies of highly embroidered velvet covered the windows. It seemed they'd decorated every square inch of the house in some fashion, and all of it cleaned and polished to sparkling perfection.

He was suddenly very grateful they'd never had to dismount on the muddy road, tracking mud into this immaculate house.

In a few moments, the servants returned with a pot of tea, and a tray of small cookies, which they set on a side table. Both men declined the offered tea. Being Army men, they had little use for tea, but would never start a morning without coffee, unless it couldn't be helped.

The servants left the tray and departed. A few minutes later a white man stepped into the sitting room. Tom and Nathan rose to greet him.

"Chambers," the man said, matter-of-factly. He was shorter than Nathan, but burlier—strong looking, rather than fat. He had dark brown hair and a full beard, neatly trimmed. He had an inquisitive look on his face but didn't smile at his guests.

Nathan immediately stood and extended his hand in greeting. "Walters, good to finally meet you. This is my man, Tom Clark," he said gesturing toward Tom. Nathan suddenly felt very awkward, though, as Walters ignored the outstretched hand as if he hadn't seen it.

"We've met before, you know … though you clearly don't remember it," Walters said, in a low, almost monotone voice. "You were just a child. Five … maybe six. I was … just a young man. Daddy and I came to your place for a visit with Mr. Chambers. Seem to recall you running into the house covered in mud, and the maids snatching you up, dragging you off for a bath or something."

Strangely, Walters delivered this story, which most people would have considered humorous, in such a serious deadpan tone and with such lack of facial expression, it was really quite uncanny. Nathan was unsure how to respond.

"Well … that sounds like my typical childhood mischief," he smiled. The smile was not, however, returned by their host, who simply looked at Nathan with the same blank expression. *Odd*, Nathan thought. He also noticed Walters had never acknowledged Tom at all, as if he wasn't there. *Very odd*.

"I heard of your daddy's passing. My condolences to you. And your mother … she is well?" Walters asked, in the same flat tone, which projected an utter lack of interest, despite the kindly words.

"She is well, thank you for inquiring, Mr. Walters," Nathan answered, resisting the urge to add, "no thanks to you!"

"And your wife? I trust she is also in good health," he hoped this would be the opening for Walters to call for her, that they might be introduced. It would've been the proper response.

But Walters simply answered, "Yes, certainly … thank you," and seemed disinclined to discuss the matter further. So Nathan let it drop.

"So, Chambers. It has been a long time since anyone from your house has visited. Our daddies didn't see eye to eye at the end and never spoke. You come here on a peace mission?"

"Well, yes, I suppose. Though I'm not sure there's need for a peace mission. I've personally held no ill will toward your father, or you, or your family. Whatever grievances our fathers had with each other can stay buried with them. Wouldn't you agree?"

"Maybe … there's still the unresolved boundary between our properties. Never has been settled all these years. Since our daddies wouldn't speak, it was … *difficult* to come to a resolution."

"Yes, I would imagine so. As for that, my father was always rather tight-lipped about his business affairs, so I was entirely unaware there even *was* a boundary dispute until just recently."

"It's but a small matter, Chambers, a mistake made when recording the property lines causing a small overlap between our two parcels."

Nathan nodded, biting back the temptation to bring up Walters' recent logging in the section without regard to the Chambers' claims on it. But he'd decided not to pursue the matter just yet, hoping they could work out an agreement instead.

"Yes … well, I'm sure we'll have no difficulty resolving the matter, Walters. Dividing down the middle, or something like, should resolve it, don't you agree?"

"Yes, very possibly. If you're agreeable, I can have one of my men draw up a new proposed boundary and bring it round to your house for your approval. Perhaps early next week?"

Walters now finally settled himself into a chair, though he sat upright and looked stiff and uncomfortable. Nathan and Tom sat down in their chairs, but taking the cue from their host, didn't sit back and relax.

"So, Chambers, since we've agreed to end the dispute … *amicably* … is there anything else you wish to discuss?"

Nathan considered this question borderline rude, being the equivalent of a dismissal, but he chose to ignore it. He was also tempted to bring up the matter of the church seats but decided against it. Better to wait and see if the new ·more amicable relationship would serve to resolve it naturally without a confrontation.

"Well, in fact, yes there is. As you are no doubt aware, when my father died, he was the sitting state senator for this area, leaving a vacancy in Richmond. Last week the Governor sent a man out to ask on his behalf if I would fill out the rest of my father's term of office. I have agreed. But the problem I have is I've been away from home so long I'm unaware of the issues concerning the people hereabouts. So I've been visiting the neighbors asking what concerns them."

As soon as the words came out of his mouth, he knew it was a mistake. He realized Walters would expect his opinions to be especially valuable and weighty, and now Nathan had made him out to be just "one of the neighbors."

Walters' brow furrowed, and he got a dark look. "So you want to know if I have any thoughts worth taking back to Richmond? Seems like the Governor might have wanted to appoint someone better informed."

"Sorry, that didn't come across at all the way I intended," Nathan said, trying to think of a way to extract himself from his verbal misstep. "Of course, it goes without saying; you *are* one of the most influential and well-known men in the county. Your thoughts and opinions are of particular interest to me and ones I would *most* highly value."

This seemed to mollify Walters somewhat, and he appeared to relax a little. He was quiet for a moment, then said, "I'm concerned about this fellow from Illinois running for president. I'd like to hear what the Governor thinks about him."

"Sorry, I must apologize for my ignorance. I've paid little attention to national politics since my return. I'm not familiar with anyone running for president. Who is this man, and what is it about him that concerns you?"

"His name is Lincoln. He's heading up a new party called 'Republican.' Bunch of Goddamned radicals. Abolitionists, though they claim they're not. Worst thing is, they say he's popular up North. May even win. I want to know what Mr. Letcher will do about *that.*"

"Well, this is all news to me. As I said, I've been away a long time. I've never heard of this *Lincoln*, nor his *Republicans*. Why do you say they're abolitionists, if they say they aren't?"

"This Lincoln spends half his time preaching about the evils of slavery—how it is an 'abomination,' and on and on. Gets big crowds up North, according to the newspapers. A man like that, all puffed up with himself gets elected, no telling what he'll do."

"So if that's true, and he wins the election, what do you expect Governor Letcher to do about it?" Nathan was genuinely puzzled. After all, what could a governor do if he disliked or disagreed with a president?

"Well, I guess that's why he's the Governor. To figure out things like that. All I know is *something* must be done about this Lincoln."

"Clearly you don't like the way this Lincoln feels about it, but what do *you* think of slavery?" Nathan inquired. Again, he thought this was probably a mistake, but he needed to feel out his neighbors and get a sense of their commitment to the institution.

Walters looked at him, as if confused by the question. "What do you mean? What do I *think* of it? It is necessary … it is a good thing. These negroes would be nothing but heathen savages back in Africa. And up North where the damned abolitionists pretend to be holier-than-thou about it, they'd be starved, frozen, or worked to death in factories. Here, they're clothed, fed, and taught the Word of God. It's a well-known, scientific fact these people are incapable of taking care of themselves in a civilized country. It is our burden and duty to watch over them. If they must do a little work to earn their keep, there's no harm in that.

"What about *you*, Chambers? Since you ask … what is *your* opinion on slavery?"

Nathan knew he'd stepped both feet into it now.

"Well, to be honest, I've come to greatly dislike the institution. I believe we're in the wrong to continue it, long-term," he decided to say the bare minimum he could. The less the better. He certainly wasn't going to disclose his bigger plans to the man.

Walters had a cold, blank look on his face, but his face had turned a darker shade of red. "Does Governor Letcher know about this? Does he know what kind of man he has asked to perform the duties of state senator?" Walters' typical cold tone had grown even colder.

Nathan struggled to baton-down his own rising temper, "Seems to me, Walters, gentlemen may have friendly discourse, without becoming *uncivil* ..."

But Walters was no longer in a conciliatory mood. "Can't believe the son of Jacob Chambers is ... is ... an abolitionist!"

"Look here—I'm *not* an abolitionist. Sudden abolition would be an economic disaster of *epic* proportions. It's not just people like you and me who'd lose everything; the entire economy, even up North likely, would suffer terribly from a collapse of Southern agriculture. And, ironically, the people they'd tried to help would suffer the most. With no jobs, no homes, no means of making a living or feeding themselves the black men would go from slavery to abject poverty and starvation. And, they would no doubt suffer the open hostility of those who, fairly or not, blamed them for the downfall. No, the fiery, wild-eyed radicals preaching immediate abolition are impractical idealists. I'm convinced if they had their way, they would do more harm than good to their own cause."

"Hmm ... that sounds more sensible. But what about what you said earlier? At least those abolitionists—*may they all rot in hell*—have the courage of their convictions. I'm wondering if you know your own mind on this, Chambers ..."

"Then allow me to explain my thinking to you ... maybe you'll even agree with me on it. You see, the course of history is against us on this; all other *civilized* nations have abolished slavery years ago. We are the last holdout. It can't last forever."

"Humph! I don't give a good Goddamn what those prissy Europeans think of us. They can all go to hell with the other abolitionists for all I care. And if you had any self-respect, you wouldn't care what they think either."

"Look, Walters. I'm trying to be civil here ... no need to cast aspersions on me.

"You seem to forget, *sir*, I marched with the Army that planted the American flag on top of the very capitol building in Mexico City! And not a man among us cared one whit what the rest of the world thought about it. Our country told us it needed doing, so we did it, *by God!* So don't speak to me of self-respect!" Nathan could feel his heat rising and was losing patience with the man.

"Hmm ... quite right on that score. Quite right. Planted the flag—*showed them.* Yes, that was well done, Chambers." Walters had a far-away look.

"Anyway," Nathan continued, trying to finish his explanation, "as I was saying, I believe we're against history on this one, and the reason you *should* care, is this: right now, cotton is king in the South, as everyone knows. From what I understand, the South makes more money from the sale of cotton than all other crops combined.

"But who are our two largest consumers, after which all others pale to insignificance? The northern states, and England! Now, what would happen if either one of those, or God forbid both at the same time, stopped buying our cotton on account of their opposition to slavery?"

If he'd hoped this line of reasoning would get through to Walters, he was quickly disappointed.

"I'd say it would be time to plant another flag in another capital!" Walters was red in the face now. "They wouldn't *dare!* It would mean red war, that's what."

"Look, Walters, all I'm saying is ... wouldn't it be better if we *controlled* the thing? If we decided for ourselves when and how it went away. Planned, and gradual, rather than sudden and catastrophic? Don't you agree that'd be better for all concerned?"

"No! I don't! I don't agree negro slavery is wrong, or bad, or immoral, and I see no reason why it should *ever* be abolished, either planned or forced! As I said before, those black men are much better off now, serving us, than ever they were as savages back in the jungle. And free they'd be no better than useless, starving beggars. You said so yourself a moment ago!"

"I don't believe *that* ... they're just *people*, same as us, only kept in ignorance and poverty. If they were just taught ..."

"I've heard *enough*, Chambers! I'll never agree with what you say, so you're wasting your breath, and your time ... and mine. You may as well go see what the *other neighbors* have to say."

He stood and walked from the room, never looking back.

Nathan and Tom shared a look. Nathan shrugged. They stood and followed in Walters' wake, across the foyer and out the front door. Walters was already standing on the porch awaiting them.

"Good day to y'all, sirs." Walters had resumed his blank expression and dispassionate voice. Nathan noticed the plural in "sirs" was the closest Walters had come to acknowledging Tom's presence since they'd arrived, though he still hadn't looked at him.

Nathan and Tom went down the stairs with no further discussion. The grooms led their horses up and handed them the reins. After they'd mounted, Harry the Dog lifted himself up off the grass where he'd been resting, and Walters seemed startled, noticing him for the first time.

"What the devil is *that?*"

"I'm told he is half Irish wolfhound, and half English mastiff."

"What an ugly mongrel. Pity nobody shot him years ago."

"Yes, I believe it *was* pity kept my father from shooting him, years ago."

Nathan smiled, and couldn't resist adding, "And *yet* ... he has proven himself strong, smart, and capable, regardless of what anyone says about his ancestry! Good day to you, sir."

Nathan tipped his hat, turned his horse and trotted away, not waiting for a reply.

ഔഏരൃഔഏരൃഔഏരൃ

When they crested the first rise on their way back to the main road, Nathan pulled a cigar from his pocket and lit it. He turned to Tom, "Well, that didn't go so well."

"No, sir. But now I can see why Jacob Chambers and the elder Walters didn't get along, if the son is any indication. From what you've described, they must have been just alike!"

"Yes, I expect you've got the right of it, Tom. Two stubborn, mean old men, each unwilling to admit he might be wrong about anything. And the son seems just the same, if not worse. Well, hopefully I at least have broken out of that rut!"

"Oh, yes, of course, sir! You're nothing like *that* one. Nor like your father, from all I've heard. Nothing to worry about on that score, Captain."

"Well, now we know where we stand with Mr. Walters. At least I resisted the temptation to commit violence on his person …

"But I guess we can expect him to oppose everything we're planning on doing."

"Yes, I fear you're right, sir. Makes me happy we bought those Springfields."

"Oh, you don't think it would come to that, do you? Not to *actual* violence—here, in Virginia? Amongst civilized men? Seems too … *unthinkable*. And I'm still hopeful, despite our differences of opinion, we might put this ridiculous feud to rest."

Nathan took another drag on the cigar.

"I hope you're right, sir. But I didn't like the look in his eye when you were talking. I don't trust the man."

"Me neither, Tom. Me neither. Well, he was right about one thing."

"What's that, sir?"

"Time to go hear what the other neighbors have to say."

They rode along in silence for a while, then Nathan said, "Now I'm wondering about this candidate, Lincoln, Walters was complaining about. You heard anything about him?"

"Not much. Just the name, mostly. Some folks were talking about him in town when I was down there, but they didn't know much about him either. Just curious and not knowing what he might be all about."

"Well, now *I'm* curious … and wondering whether I should be hopeful, or fearful of the man."

"He's sure got one good thing going for him," Tom said with a sly grin.

"Oh?"

"Yeah, I reckon if Walters doesn't like him that must be a pretty good recommendation!"

"Guess you're right about that, Tom … based on that alone Mr. Lincoln must be good man!"

Back at the manor house, Walters was again in the sitting room, brooding on his conversation with young Chambers.

Bob poked his head in at the door, "Everything okay, sir? What did Mr. Chambers want, if you don't mind my asking?"

"Seems Chambers fancies himself an abolitionist. Apparently came here to lecture me on the evils of my ways, Bob. So I sent him packing."

"Good for you, sir. I'd say that was pretty cheeky of him. Anything I can do for you, sir?"

"Yes … pack my things, and yours. We're going to Richmond."

"Richmond, sir? Not that it's none of my business, of course, sir. But … if I knew the length of our stay, and the purpose, why … it'd be easier to decide which things to pack, if you get my meaning."

"You should plan on us staying there a week or so. And as for the purpose … I reckon it's time I had a talk with Mr. Letcher. So I'm fixing to pay him a visit."

"Mr. Letcher?"

"Yes, you know, *Governor* Letcher? Of the Commonwealth of Virginia."

"You're going to meet with the *Governor*?" Bob asked in surprise. But even he'd finished the question, he knew his knee-jerk reaction had been a *big* mistake.

Walters turned toward him with a hard look. "What? You don't think I'm important enough to meet with the Governor, Bob?"

He spoke in that low, cold voice Bob knew well and dreaded. It meant trouble. Big trouble if it couldn't be deflected in a hurry.

"Oh, *no* sir, that's not what I meant at all, not at all! It's just you've never talked with the Governor before, and, well, frankly sir, I think it's long overdue. Why … you are surely the most important man in Greenbrier County … maybe even all of western Virginia."

This seemed to calm Walters. "Yes, you're right, Bob. It *is* long overdue. Have the carriage loaded and waiting at the door at first light tomorrow and we shall be on our way."

"Yes, certainly, sir. I'll take care of everything."

"And just go ahead and stash that cash box in my trunk. I'm fixing to deposit those new bank notes in the bank in Richmond while we're there."

"Yes, sir. That was sure a timely visit by them slave traders."

"Yes, good to be rid of those surplus slaves. I've no patience for those young brats. Feeding, clothing, and putting up with their commotion and nonsense for years and years, just waiting for them to grow into something useful. *Pah!* Let someone else foot the bill, I say."

"Yes, sir. I agree. And we got one good, strong field hand out of the deal too—a slave named Henry from a farm over in Lynchburg. That'll help come the cotton harvest.

"And, sir … is there anyone else you'd like to take with us, you know, to see to your personal needs and such once we get there?"

"Hmm … yes, I suppose we should bring Josiah along to wait on me. Have him ready as well. That will be all, Bob."

"Yes, sir. I'll have Josiah ready to go. Thank you, sir." But then Bob felt the familiar twinge of guilt when he thought of the lonely woman of the house. He steeled his nerves and asked, "And Mrs. Walters, sir?"

"What about her?"

"Well, I just thought … since her family is there and all …" Bob answered lamely, knowing he was treading on dangerous ground. She was still a virtual prisoner in her own bedroom, as she'd been ever since Walters had lost his temper when she'd overheard them plotting against the Chambers' widow. For reasons he didn't completely understand, he felt badly for her and thought it worth the try, as unlikely as it was to succeed.

"Mrs. Walters has no need to travel to Richmond. Her *delicate constitution* would not agree with such a long, difficult journey."

Bob made his withdrawal and soon had the servants scurrying to prepare for their master's journey.

Margaret Walters quickly retreated down the hallway and ducked into her bedroom, closing the door quietly behind her. She sat in a chair next to her dresser, and tried to catch her breath, and stop her heart from pounding. It was not just the sudden exertion of running down the hall that had her out of breath; she had also been in a state of great excitement mixed with anxiety.

Earlier, she had seen two horsemen arriving from her bedroom window. She knew every inch of terrain she could see from that window, to the smallest detail, having spent countless hours, days … months even, gazing out it. So anything new immediately caught her eye. And these men were not field hands, nor casual travelers. She could tell by their attire, the way they held themselves as they rode, and the high quality of their horses and tack, that they were men of means and importance.

This piqued her curiosity. Who were they? Why had they come? How would Walters receive them? And, the question she almost dare not think: might her family have sent them to check on her well-being, having not heard a word from her since her arrival in … *this place?* She had little hope of that. She was the youngest of three daughters in a family that could ill-afford to support any. Her father had been almost giddy at the prospect of marrying her off to a rich man.

The wedding had been seven months ago now. Seven months that seemed like seven years—or a hundred.

Walters had seemed pleasant enough when she'd first met him. Polite and well-mannered. And, more important, to her parents he was clearly a man of considerable wealth. He initially lavished her, and her family, with expensive gifts.

He had seen her dancing at one of the many formal balls in Richmond. Apparently, he'd liked the look of her, though she'd always considered herself plain looking and too willowy thin for most men's taste. Though intelligent, she was shy, and quiet, feeling awkward in social circumstances. In Richmond high society, this typically left her feeling insecure and lacking in confidence around other people, especially young men.

But Walters had never approached her, nor made any attempt to talk to her. Instead, he called on her parents, and proposed the marriage to *them*, to which they heartily agreed. That Margaret might have a different opinion on the matter never entered into it. They'd informed her of the arrangements after the fact. And being the good, polite, obedient daughter, and also being insecure about anything to do with an actual courtship, it never occurred to her to question it or to disagree.

She now regretted most *bitterly* her obedience, and her complete lack of conscious thought about the man she would marry. Walters had proven himself cold and cruel, with no human warmth or kindness she could discern. On their wedding night he had taken her with a force and urgency that was frightening and not in any way gentle, loving, or romantic. He'd left the room immediately after he'd finished, and did not return the rest of the night, leaving her alone in the bed, softly crying. Any childhood dreams she may have had about marital love and romance had been completely shattered.

For the first several months, he'd repeated this behavior regularly. But, thankfully, he seemed to have eventually tired of it, so now it was an infrequent occurrence, for which she was grateful. Through all that she had never conceived, for which she was also grateful. Though a child might prove a comfort and company at least for her, she couldn't imagine the anxiety of raising a child in this place, with this man. And it also occurred to her Walters might divorce her if she couldn't give him children. But he said nothing about it, nor had he ever mentioned anything about having children. Perhaps he simply didn't care about that either.

And now she feared Walters, in a very real, physical way. From what she could tell, the same was true for everyone else at the plantation, even the white farmhands. It went well beyond just being cold and stern. He was clearly a very dangerous and unpredictable man. She had watched him murder slaves on two occasions, with his own hands. She'd witnessed both beatings out on the front drive from her window, making her wonder if he'd made sure she would see it. It had been the most terrible thing

Margaret had ever seen. After a few moments she had turned away and covered her ears. Walters beat the men to death, one with a club, and the other with a whip. It was a shock and horror that still brought her to tears and shakes when the thought crossed her mind. And she'd overheard the servants saying there'd been others over the years. The household slaves lived in constant fear of him, making it nearly impossible to turn them to her side. They feared getting close to her, or treating her too kindly, lest it anger the master.

And now, ever since the incident where she'd overheard him plotting to murder one of their neighbors, he forced her to stay always in her room. He'd even had her windows nailed shut, afraid she'd escape through them, or maybe jump to her death to end her misery. Either way, it made for very hot and stuffy summer evenings.

So now, seeing the strange riders approach, she could stand it no longer; she risked Walters' wrath to eavesdrop on their conversation. When she cracked open her door, she couldn't see anyone loitering in the hall. Maybe the sudden arrival of unexpected guests had so stirred up the household everyone had forgotten about watching her, for the moment. So she crept quietly to the end of the hallway and sat at the top of the stairs. There she could overhear any conversation taking place in the foyer or the sitting room where Walters entertained their infrequent guests.

And there she sat and listened as young Mr. Nathaniel Chambers discussed property lines and slavery with Walters. Margaret felt an unexplainable thrill hearing *that* voice—a voice different from those she'd heard every day for the last seven months with no variation. And unlike Walters, Mr. Chambers sounded like a real, warm, interesting human being. Margaret could not get enough of his flow of words—strong, sure, and forceful, but with an undercurrent of kindness and decency. She instantly knew this was a man she would like. A strong, admirable man who treated other people as human beings, rather than possessions or nuisances. She teared up listening to him, not even caring what he was saying.

Then, suddenly it was over. The visitors were leaving. Though fear of being caught gripped her, still she hesitated, wanting to hear more.

Then she heard Bob's voice. He was a puzzle to her, a seeming contradiction. The head overseer of Walters Farm, and Walters' co-conspirator in his nefarious plots, he'd also been the one person to show her anything approaching human kindness. Maybe he felt guilty about how she was being treated.

Bob had asked Walters if he would take her with him to Richmond. For one breathless moment she prayed Walters might agree, but wasn't surprised when he said "no." Maybe Walters feared if she ever returned to Richmond she'd never come back to his farm.

But now, back in her room, the more she thought about going to Richmond, the more determined she became. To confront Walters, to ask him to take her with him, even if she had to promise to return with him. It'd be worth it just to talk to *other* people. Real, interesting people. Not slaves. Not farmhands. And not Walters.

So once her heart stopped pounding, and her breathing returned to normal, she walked to the door and opened it. This time, unlike the last, one of the house slaves met her almost immediately, as expected.

"How can I help you, Mistress?" the woman asked, stepping in front of the door, preventing her from exiting the room.

"I wish to speak with Mr. Walters. Please tell him."

"Yes, Mistress. Please go back into your room, and I will send someone to tell the Master you wish to speak with him."

"All right. Thank you," she said, and retreated into the bedroom. She had a sudden thought. What would happen if she pushed her way out into the hall? Would the black woman—a *slave* after all—dare to lay hands on her, to prevent her by force? She was the mistress of the house, wasn't she? She sat and pondered this question for a long time, imagining all the possible scenarios. But she couldn't come to any definitive answer.

She sat, thinking about the day's happenings, and nearly jumped when there was a quiet knocking at the door.

"Come in," she said.

The door opened, and to her surprise, Walters entered the room. Surprise, because he normally didn't knock when he entered her room, but also, because he'd never before appeared before dark. If he wanted her for anything other than ... well, other than to have her ... he usually just sent one of the slaves to fetch her.

She looked, up, screwed up her courage and determination, and said, "Hello, Mr. Walters."

"Hello, Margaret. The maid said you wished to see me. I am very busy, so please tell me what it is you wish to speak with me about."

As usual, abrupt and to the point. No smile, no warmth whatsoever.

But despite this, she took some hope from the fact he'd come in person, rather than sending one of the servants.

"Oh ... well, thank you for coming, Elijah." It seemed odd to use his given name, but she did it purposefully, hoping it might help soften the conversation.

But he said nothing, simply giving her his usual blank stare.

"I've come to understand ... from overhearing talk among the servants ... you are preparing to leave for Richmond."

"Yes. What of it?"

"Well ... I was wondering if you might consider taking me along ... for a ... um ... *holiday* of sorts. I haven't seen my family, and ... friends, and such ... well, you know ... since the wedding."

"Mrs. Walters, I am going to Richmond on serious business. This is not a 'holiday,' as you call it. There will be no social calls, and the like. There is no place for you on this trip."

"Oh ... I see. But ... I promise I would be no trouble to you, Mr. Walters. I would just like to pay my respects to my Momma and Daddy, I'm sure you understand ..."

"No. There will be no time for such. Is that all?"

"Well, yes ... I suppose ... if you're sure you couldn't ... *accommodate* my wishes ... just this once?"

"No, Mrs. Walters. This is a serious, business trip. I have no time to ... 'accommodate' you on it. Good night."

194

Then he turned, and walked out the door, closing it gently behind him.

Margaret sat and shook for several minutes. It was the first time she'd so forcefully asked Walters for anything. And it had taken all her fortitude to do so. But he had still rejected her request out of hand.

She sat and mulled over her situation for a long time. She was feeling utterly alone, forlorn, and desperate. Then a voice seemed to speak in the back of her mind, *But … what will it be like when Mr. Walters is not in this house? When he is hundreds of miles, and a week's travel, away?*

The more she considered this, the better she felt. And then she thought about the two gentlemen who'd come calling today. A plan began to formulate in her mind. *What if …?*

ഇജ്ഞ്ജരജ്ഞ്ജഇജ്ഞ്ജരജ്ഞ്ജഇജ്ഞ്ജരജ്ഞ്ജ

Henry saw the same riders Margaret Walters saw that afternoon, coming to and going from Walters Farm. But his perspective was slightly different. Not a high window in a gilded prison; his personal prison was a bit lower down, hoeing weeds in Walters' okra field, along with a dozen other field slaves. And in contrast to her keen curiosity about the visitors, he had little interest in two unknown white masters riding horses along the road. Just two more slavers; no concern of his.

What did concern him was the sun beating down on his bare back. He'd lost his shirt the first night after his arrival at Walters Farm, just three days earlier, and now his back was burning and itching from the sudden exposure. His first day shirtless, it'd been overcast and rainy, so other than a chill he'd not suffered the loss. But today the stolen shirt was all he could think about. He realized the simplest thing, the lack of a shirt, had now become the most important thing in his world. He shook his head and fought down a growing feeling of gloom and hopelessness.

He'd felt relief and hope when they'd bought him off the traveling slave traders' caravan, shortly after his arrival at Walters Farm. And it had happened relatively quickly, after less than a week of travel. To get out of the galling iron shackle around his

195

neck was a blessing in itself—chafing his skin with every step, unbearably heavy, and scorching hot in the sun. And avoiding the endless trek to a place the slavers called New Orleans, countless miles away, was yet another blessing.

But to still be within reasonable distance of his wife—left behind at the last master's farm—that was clearly the greatest blessing of all. It kept alive the possibility he might see her again one day. He prayed to Jesus for it every waking hour of the day and dreamed of it at night.

But soon after they'd removed him from the line of chained men, and led him away to the cabins, he'd discovered the harsh reality of his new world. It was just getting dark, and the field workers were returning for the night. His immediate impression looking at their faces wasn't good—a very downcast lot; frightened looking even. They wore ragged clothes; several men had no shirts, and others had no pants. None had hats, not even the simple homemade straw ones all workers wore on the last farm. After dinner, a pot of cornmeal with bits of salted herring, it shocked him when a dozen or more men and women settled themselves around the floor to sleep. At the last farm, a cabin this size would've held five at the most.

And a shabby, disgraceful cabin it was, too, made of roughhewn logs with a dirt floor and no windows. But the lack of windows was no problem, the gaps between the logs let in plenty of light and air. It surprised him when the people stretched out to sleep on plank boards laid out on the floor. Seemed awfully hard to him. He'd had a rough, straw bed at the last place, and that'd been plenty uncomfortable.

But as he was pondering these dismal accommodations, a bare-chested young man stepped up to him and said, "I wants your shirt. Give it t'me."

Henry looked at him but didn't think he'd heard rightly. "What you be saying?"

For answer, the young man punched him hard in the jaw, knocking him back into the wall where he bumped his head hard and blacked out.

He woke up fuzzy headed, slumped against the wall on the floor. And the shirt was gone. He briefly considered retaliating, but when he moved to get up, his head pounded so hard the room spun, and his vision got blurry. *Maybe tomorrow …*

The night brought more urgent concerns. It rained, and with a slight breeze, the cabin became bitterly cold and wet. Water streamed down from the leaky roof and blew in through the gaps in the logs. They'd not given him any bedding, and now he had no shirt, so he shivered uncontrollably, and his teeth chattered. It suddenly occurred to him why the people lay on boards. As the rain dripped in, the floor turned to a sticky, slimy, nasty-smelling muck. It was a long, miserable night, the worst he could remember.

And then a horn blew. It was still pitch black out, but everyone jumped up out of bed, and immediately headed out the door. They knew there'd be nothing to eat until lunch time, and being late to the fields would guarantee a harsh beating. Henry was eager to get up and going. He was miserably cold and had slept only fitfully. Being up and moving seemed preferable.

But now, three days later, the sun beat down like a hammer, and sweat rolled off him in streams. He paused a moment to wipe off his brow with the back of his hand. He felt a sudden, stinging pain on the back of his legs, followed by a *snap!*

"This ain't leisure time, boy! Them weeds ain't fixin' to hoe they-selves, so keep at it!"

"Yes, massa …" he said. But he really wanted to strangle the man! *Tomorrow … then I'll pay him back …*

ଧ୭ଈଔଃ୭ଈଔଃ୭ଈଔଃ୭ଈଔଃ

Instead of turning east toward home when they reached the main road, Nathan and Tom continued into Lewisburg, since they were already more than halfway there. The town, by far the largest in the county, had around a thousand residents. So Nathan wouldn't be able to call on and speak with every one of them.

Instead, he'd decided to "borrow" the county courthouse and hold a meeting. He'd had Tom draw up a notice inviting the townspeople to come and meet their new state senator and to give him their thoughts. He set the date for one week from today, which would make it Friday, June 29th, 1860.

They stopped in and paid their respects to the county clerk, Albert Johnson, whom Tom had met when handling Nathan's earlier deed paperwork for Mountain Meadows. The clerk had no objections to Nathan using the courthouse for the meeting and suggested where to post their sign so the most people would see it.

Nathan also inquired if he knew anything about the property line dispute between Jacob Chambers and Percival Walters. Albert said he could only recall there *was* some kind of dispute. It had all played out when he was just a young apprentice, so he could recall no details. He promised to go back through all the records, and when they returned in a week's time for the meeting, he'd be able to answer their questions on it.

They thanked him kindly and departed, hanging the notice in the spot the clerk had recommended before saddling up and heading for home. As they passed the Lewisburg Inn, which also served as the local watering hole, Tom asked if Nathan wanted to stop off for a little refreshment before the ride back.

"It's a thought, Tom. But a couple of whiskeys, and I'll be nodding off in the saddle on the ride home. Tell you what, we'll have that drink out on the veranda when we get back to the farm. Then it'll be a nice short trip upstairs to bed after!"

"Sounds fair, Captain."

Chapter 9. To Do What Must Be Done

"Just do what must be done.
This may not be happiness,
but it is greatness."
– George Bernard Shaw

Sunday June 24, 1860 – Greenbrier County, Virginia:

The next morning was Sunday, and as promised, Nathan accompanied Miss Abbey to the community church Jacob Chambers had helped finance, where Reverend Blackburn ministered his flock. Tom, Jim, and the other men from Texas accompanied them, along with three of the original farmhands. Sickles declined, saying it was his turn to stay and mind the farm. The rest of the farmhands stayed home also, citing the same reason. Nathan wasn't convinced, since there'd be no work to supervise, but he wouldn't force anyone to go who didn't wish to.

Nathan drove Miss Abbey in the shiny, black formal carriage, which he drove himself, refusing to let Cobb drive as he normally would. "No, Cobb. Since this is part of your duties, I must consider it *work* for you, and that I will not allow on the Sabbath."

"Yes, Master, er … *Captain*, sir. But if you drives it, sir, ain't it the same?"

"No, certainly, *not!* It isn't *work* for me!" He gave Cobb a grin, and a friendly pat on the back.

The other men rode their own horses, which they saddled themselves, taking their lead from Nathan and refusing the grooms' offer to do it for them.

Since Nathan was driving the carriage, Abbey felt odd about sitting inside by herself, so she climbed up next to him on the driver's seat. When he told her she should sit in the back where it was more comfortable, she just smiled and said, "I will when you will," which ended the argument. It occurred to Nathan he hadn't gotten *all* his stubbornness from his father's side.

On the road to church, Abbey thought Nathan was driving the carriage more slowly than was normal or necessary. When she asked him about it and expressed concern they might arrive late for the start of the service, he shrugged his shoulders and smiled.

"Momma, I'm already twenty *years* late, so a few more minutes is of little concern."

Still, she thought it odd, and finally decided he was purposely making them late, though she couldn't reckon why.

When they arrived at the church, the doors were already closed. As Miss Abbey had predicted, the service was already underway. But Nathan seemed unconcerned, as he helped her down from the carriage.

Rather than wait for them and follow behind, as she had expected, the former soldiers quickly dismounted, tied their horses, and trotted over to the church steps. Something was up, she decided, looking at Nathan inquisitively. But he'd suddenly become more serious.

The farmhands stood by Miss Abbey, as they normally did, waiting to follow her lead. They looked confused about what the soldiers were doing. But none felt inclined to ask the Captain about it. The look on his face didn't encourage inquiry.

Abbey took Nathan's proffered arm, and they strolled toward the church. His men lined up in a neat single file at the bottom of the stairs, except Tom who stood by the door, peeking in. He came back down the stairs and stood in front of the others, awaiting Nathan.

"Tom?"

"It is as you feared, Captain, the same as Miss Abbey reported from her *last* visit. But … oddly, Walters himself appears to be absent."

"I see. Zeke, please escort Miss Abbey into church from here. I'll enter first with the other men. Once we're inside, you and the other hands follow with Miss Abbey. But stay in the back and stand out of the aisle, if you please. I'll tell you when to come forward. Do you understand?"

"Yes, Captain."

"Nathan, dear … what are you up to?"

"Taking care of a little church *housecleaning*, Momma. Please do stay back … and watch what happens."

She shook her head, and rolled her eyes at him, but this time he ignored her and was no longer smiling.

Nathan strode forward to the front of his men and turned toward them. His face carried a stern expression. Turning back to the church door he said, "Tom … *now*, if you please."

Tom barked out, "Forward … *march!* Left … left … left …"

To Miss Abbey's shock and surprise, the men, including Nathan, marched up the stairs of the church, opened the door, and entered, Tom still chanting out the steps. And though they were not in their blue soldier uniforms, they did *look* uniform, Abbey noticed. Nathan was wearing his nice black suit, and Tom his fine gray one. The rest of Nathan's men, however, wore identical brown wool trousers and fine long-sleeved white cotton shirts, and thin black bow ties. Nathan had hired a tailor to make the men something suitable for church, since they'd only brought rough clothing from Texas. It'd been a rush order, but the tailor had come through just in time for today's service.

"Come, Miss Abbey," Zeke said, extending his arm toward her and smiling for the first time. "I reckon we'll not want to miss *this* show!"

She shook her head and muttered, "Oh dear …" but took his arm.

By the time she entered the church, Nathan and company had marched down the center aisle all the way to the front. Pastor Blackburn stood wide-eyed at the front of the nave, staring at Nathan as if in disbelief. Most of the parishioners did likewise. Only Walters' men refrained from staring. They were studiously ignoring the interruption, as if they'd been instructed to do so.

Nathan's men stood in a perfect row, stock still as if at attention for an officer's inspection, their faces expressionless. The church was silent, all eyes now on Nathan.

"I apologize for the interruption, your reverence, and for the lateness of our arrival. But I do have a little *church business* to conduct before you continue, if you don't mind."

The pastor returned a puzzled look but said nothing, only nodding and gesturing for him to carry on.

Nathan returned the nod, then turned toward the six parishioners seated in the right-side front row. He could see they were a tough looking bunch of young men—Walters' farmhands, even as Miss Abbey had described. "Excuse me, gentlemen, I am Mr. Chambers, and these seats are rightly reserved for use by my family. Please, kindly go find others."

The man in the seat closest to the aisle looked up and scowled, "Our master said we could sit where we pleased ... and it *pleases* us to sit here." He was a large, surly looking man with a long unkempt dark beard. He spoke to Nathan in a sarcastic, mocking tone.

Nathan stared down at him for another moment then sighed, "Very well."

He stepped back and said, "Mr. Volkov ... if you please ..."

Stan flashed a quick grin, then resumed his stony expression. He took one step forward, snapped his heels together, neatly pivoted and marched down the aisle to the front. He stood in front of the Captain and snapped a salute which Nathan returned smartly. Then Stan turned and stepped up to where Walters' man sat.

"Captain says ... *move!*"

"Look here, fella ... our boss says we ain't gotta—"

But before the man could finish his sentence, Stan leaned down, grasped him with both hands by the front of his shirt, and lifted him bodily off the bench. It happened so quickly the man hadn't been able to react or resist. Then, with Walters' man still sputtering in shock, Stan stepped back into the aisle. He twirled the man around so his back was to Stan and he was facing the front door of the church. The big Russian now had his left hand grasping the back of the man's shirt, and his right the belt of his trousers, holding him up so the tips of his toes could not quite reach the floor. The man's arms flailed back toward Stan but couldn't reach him, and his feet kicked back ineffectually. He vainly attempted to pry loose the iron grip, but all his efforts went for naught. None of Walters' other men moved, shocked looks on their faces.

Stan strode briskly down the aisle toward the door of the church. When he was almost there, he looked over at Joe, the Mountain Meadows' farmhand closest to the exit, and said, "Open door … *now*, please."

Joe jumped to comply, and pushed the door open, holding it wide while Stan approached.

When he reached the doorway, Stan stopped, and with one mighty heave hurled Walters' man out the opening. He stepped up and stood in the doorway, hands on hips watching the man tumble down the stairs, coming to a stop at the bottom. The farmhand sat still where he'd landed, slowly rubbing his head with one hand. As he didn't seem inclined to cause further trouble, Stan pivoted, marched back to his spot and, clicking his heels again, stepped back into line. He snapped another salute at the Captain and stood at attention next to the others.

Miss Abbey felt appalled and could feel her face blushing a bright red. She saw shock on the faces of several parishioners. But she also noticed several others smiling, nodding, and whispering to one another.

Nathan again stepped in front of the men remaining in the front row. None had moved, nor tried to intervene as Stan manhandled their comrade. "Gentlemen … if you please …" he said, gesturing toward the outer aisle. All five immediately stood, and moved to the outside aisle, then continued to the back of the church. But when they reached the back row, they continued out the door, rather than taking other seats.

The four of Walters' men on the left-side front row stayed seated. But they stared straight ahead and offered no objections. As Tom had reported, Walters himself was not in attendance. Though he didn't know if that was coincidental, Nathan decided it may have been for the best. It had likely prevented a larger, more serious confrontation.

He gestured for Zeke to bring Miss Abbey forward. They walked straight up the aisle to the front row where she joined Nathan. Nathan sat in the aisle seat with Miss Abbey next to him.

203

Zeke, Joe, and Benny took their normal seats in the front row, with Tom taking the last open seat. But when Nathan's "soldiers" looked back to find empty seats, the people in the second row stood up and offered their pew to the newcomers. Nathan turned and told them it wasn't necessary, but one gentleman said, "Don't mention it, Mr. Chambers. It's our pleasure ... and honor."

Nathan thanked him, and his men seated themselves in the second row.

Once everyone was seated, Nathan turned back toward Reverend Blackburn and said, "My apologies again for the interruption, your reverence ... pray, *do* continue."

Despite their disagreement back at Mountain Meadows, and the rude interruption, the pastor smiled. Then he resumed his sermon exactly where he'd left off, as if nothing unusual had just happened.

ဆယ်ဆော်ဆော်ဆော်ဆော်ဆော်ဆော်ဆော်

When the sermon was over, Nathan was surprised to find his attentions much in demand. He was surrounded and prevented from exiting the church by parishioners curious to meet and speak with the returning Chambers son. He met dozens of people, each of whom gave him their names and welcomed him warmly. He also greeted several people he and Tom had visited and spoken with earlier, on their senatorial ride around the county. No one seemed put out by his little show earlier, and several mentioned it appreciatively. It didn't greatly surprise him the parishioners seemed to have no love for Walters.

Nathan also noticed that Miss Abbey seemed to be going out of her way to introduce him to the unmarried young ladies. That shouldn't have surprised him, he decided, given their earlier discussion on the topic of finding a suitable bride. He caught her eye and gave her a wry smile.

Nathan returned all their greetings with a firm handshake, and an unforced, sincere warmth. To his surprise, he was enjoying this homecoming very much. Miss Abbey beamed with delight, despite his sideways looks at her each time she introduced one of the prospective brides.

Through it all, Nathan smiled when he thought of how pleased they would all be next Sunday, when he readily remembered every name, as was his custom.

The other men from Texas also attracted a lot of attention from the flock. New faces were rare at this small country church, so having more than a half-dozen all at once was a novel thing. Stan was the center of much excitement. Nathan grinned when he noticed a large group of young adults gathered around him, and the young ladies seemed especially interested in what he had to say.

Billy was also the source of much curiosity, particularly among young boys and older men. Nathan smiled when he overheard an interesting conversation Billy had with one of the men.

"Now, sir, are you a Christian, or do you still hold with the Indian gods, whatever those may be?"

Billy answered, "I believe the white men's God must be the most powerful god; his people are the most numerous and prosperous."

"But, sir … we believe there is only *one* God …"

"Hmm … and all other beings are mortals, as you and I?"

"Yes, that's right …"

"But what of your 'angels,' and what of the one you call 'Satan' and his soldiers you call 'demons?' Are these creatures humans like us, or … *something more?*"

"Well, no … I suppose they ain't mortals like the rest of us … they're … *special* in some way, I reckon."

"And what of your 'saints?' I've heard people pray to them … but are they just men after all, like you and I and all the others standing in this church?"

"Uh … no … I reckon they're also … *special* somehow …"

"Hmm … my people, what you call 'Indians,' know many gods. Maybe these 'Indian gods' are something like your saints, angels, and demons; not so almighty as the most-high God you call Jehovah, but still, something more than men."

The man looked thoughtful, then his eyes went wide, "Yes … maybe so! I never thought of it that way before."

Nathan finally made his way out the front door, and found Reverend Blackburn was there, greeting the members of his congregation as they exited. He took Nathan's hand and shook it warmly, and they exchanged a friendly smile.

"So, Mr. Chambers, did you enjoy the sermon?"

Nathan was a little surprised the pastor didn't mention his rude interruption of the service. He paused a moment, and tilted his head in thought, before answering.

"I found it ... *interesting*, Reverend."

"Oh, how so?"

"Well, firstly, I thought it was quite a ... *coincidence* ... maybe? On my first visit to the church, after nearly twenty years away, the sermon was *'The Prodigal Son.'*"

"Yes, now you mention it ... I can see how it *might* seem like something of a coincidence."

"And I found your particular ... *interpretation* ... of the parable, a little ... *unusual? Unorthodox* even, perhaps, Reverend?"

"Oh, do you think so?"

"Well, from what I've seen, they usually say the parable means the Holy Father will always welcome his sons home, no matter how badly they've strayed and sinned. But this morning you have made it sound more ... hmm ... as if maybe the father should *not* have so readily welcomed back his strayed son. That the returning son might bring with him 'foreign' ideas and might introduce sinfulness into his father's house."

"Well, theology is a not an exact science, as I'm sure you are aware, Mr. Chambers. We theologians are always trying to glean new meaning from Bible passages, to make sure God's message is thoroughly understood. Do you ... *disagree* with the message of my sermon?"

"Did I say so? No ... I just found it ... *interesting*, is all."

He smiled, but otherwise gave the Reverend an unreadable look.

"Speaking of interesting, and unusual, Reverend, I was surprised our neighbor, Mr. Walters, was not in attendance today. I'd been led to understand he is a regular parishioner. I pray nothing is amiss with him?"

"Oh, did you not *know*, Mr. Chambers? Mr. Walters has undertaken a business trip to Richmond. He left yesterday morning and sent word he would miss the service today. But, my dear Mr. Chambers … I was under the impression it was some sort of business dealing in which you had a part."

"Oh, why do you say that?"

"Well, the message he sent said … something to the effect … he had business to attend to in Richmond … on account of the *new* Mr. Chambers."

⬥⬥⬥⬥⬥⬥⬥⬥⬥⬥⬥

That afternoon, the workers once again gathered in front of the veranda to listen to the Captain speak. Tony appreciated they'd not ordered them to arrive at first light this time. Even Sickles, apparently, couldn't stretch the truth that far.

And they gathered as close to the veranda as they could, with a reasonable amount of room between them.

Tony noticed Sickles and the two hired hands Frank and Dan were *not* in attendance this time. The Captain's soldiers were there, however, and the other white overseers.

He also noticed there was a chair placed at the top of the veranda stairs this time. The front door opened, and Megs came out followed by the other household slaves. This time they came straight down the stairs to join the group on the grass. The Captain's man, Mr. Tom was with them.

A few moments later, the Captain came out, along with Miss Abbey. She also walked down the stairs and out into the middle of the slaves where she turned to face the Captain. Tony was shocked; he never would've imagined Miss Abbey coming out and casually mingling with the slaves. And yet here she was. She seemed to have a slight smile on her face.

The Captain stood and faced the assembly.

"Once again, we are gathered together, in the sight of the almighty. We are reminded of His great presence by the beauty of this land and the warmth of the sun on our faces. We, who are as brothers and sisters in His eyes. As I said last week, 'He is the God of all colors, and no color at all.'"

207

"Amen!" someone within the crowd said, clearly one of the Captain's enthusiasts. Tony scowled and noticed others doing the same.

But the Captain smiled, "Yes, *amen* indeed! Thank you."

There were a few giggles, and several smiles on faces in the audience.

"In the Bible, it tells us how the people of old Israel were held as slaves in bondage. But Moses faced down the mighty Pharaoh, King of Egypt, and said, 'set my people free!' And when the Pharaoh refused, the Lord God visited upon Egypt many punishments, until Pharaoh finally relented and let the people go. So too shall the Lord our God set all of *you* free. But instead of punishments and a great man like Moses, he will use myself, Miss Abbey, and the men working for me as the instruments of your freedom. We will teach you all you need to know to live as free men and women in *this* Promised Land."

There were no "amens" this time, but he had the audience's attention. There was complete silence, and every eye was upon him.

"So today I'm going to teach you the first part of the first lesson you will need to learn. Today we will talk about … *money*."

Nathan sat in his chair and asked his audience to also sit. The day was already warm and the grass mostly dry, so sitting on it was not uncomfortable. They all sat, including Miss Abbey, and leaned forward attentively, as the Captain began his talk.

Tony listened at first, but his mind quickly began to wander. Not that it wasn't interesting, and not that he didn't *want* to learn. Despite his continued skepticism, Tony could see the Captain was a good teacher. He explained things carefully and slowly, pausing to give meaningful examples. He also took time to interact with his audience, singling people out by name to use in his examples and encouraging questions.

He had Tom show the proper way to raise one's hand, wait to be acknowledged, and speak the question out in a clear voice so all could hear. He said this was exactly the way they did it in the white men's schools.

But though Tony had to admit the Captain was teaching a good lesson, his mind was wandering for an unrelated, and unexpected reason. Soon after sitting down, he found himself behind and to one side of the young girl Rosa. He knew everyone on the farm and had known her his whole life. And though he liked her and thought her pleasant enough, he had never really *noticed* her before. Now, suddenly, sitting this close to her and looking at her for an extended time with no interruption, he realized something was different. Sometime or other she had changed from a pretty little *girl*, into a *very* nice-looking *young woman*. It made him realize he was no longer a young boy. She made him feel … *uncomfortable* in a way he didn't fully understand. Now he wanted to look at her more, and maybe, later … talk with her a bit …

The lesson lasted only an hour. It could have gone on all day without Nathan teaching all he intended to on the subject. But he knew whether you were a schoolboy, a soldier, or a farm slave, after two hours or so the body would take over, and then the mind could no longer stick to the task. So he thanked them and sent them on their way to enjoy another blessed Sabbath day.

Today Nathan's men would not have to slop the hogs and feed the chickens after the Sabbath talk. He'd planned ahead and organized work crews to tend to the livestock before sunrise and immediately after sunset while there was still light enough to see. The crews, made up of about twenty people, would trade off week to week so everybody could enjoy a whole Sabbath day off most weeks. And even those with livestock duty would enjoy the entire Sabbath day off, from sunrise to sunset, in the traditional manner.

He also made sure there was enough food prepared ahead of time, so no one need wait on anyone in the Big House during the whole day of the Sabbath. Miss Abbey was very supportive and said she was quite content to nibble on this or that on Sundays rather than having a large formal meal.

ᔕᕮᘏᑫᏗᔕᕮᘏᑫᏗᔕᕮᘏᑫᏗ

In the afternoon, Tony watched the soldiers carry their rifles out to the shooting range. This time he saw three of the original

209

white farmhands going with them, although Sickles wasn't among them.

He had a strong desire to watch again. He hadn't quite figured out the why of it, but … something told him it was important. It was a thing he *should* learn how to do. From watching the last time, he had a pretty good idea how it all worked, but he wanted to see it done again to … *fix* it in his mind. But how could he do it?

Then he smiled, and chuckled to himself, remembering the little lie he'd told Sickles last time about fetching water for the soldier-men. Why not make truth out of the lie? No one would think anything amiss if he brought the men drinking water. He'd be able to stand around while they slowly emptied the bucket. With any luck that would take most of the afternoon. And this time he'd be extra careful to avoid Sickles on the way back!

This afternoon when the men staked out their targets, they extended them out to three hundred yards, though they also left targets at one hundred and two hundred yards for the new men. Three of the seven original farmhands had agreed to join them, with the others politely declining, including Sickles. The three that joined them were Ezekiel "Zeke" Benton, Benjamin "Benny" Johnston, and Joseph "Joe" Mercer. That Zeke and Benny had joined in was no surprise. These two had seemed to hit it off with the newcomers from the beginning, and likewise didn't appear especially enamored of Sickles. Joe was a surprise, however; he'd seemed more neutral in preference between the new hands versus the old. Nathan took this for a good sign—maybe one more individual who'd turned to his way of thinking.

Jamie, Georgie, and William each took charge of one of the new arrivals. They were soon all down to business, chatting and laughing as they fired off each round. The newcomers took to it quickly. They'd all been raised in rural areas where hunting was a regular pastime, so were already familiar with handling a gun. They were, however, appreciative of the finer points the soldiers shared with them. Jamie showed them how to load a gun efficiently and consistently while in various odd positions, as behind cover, or laying prone. William taught them how to calm the breathing and time the trigger pull so it came between heartbeats. And Georgie went over the proper way to clean and oil the gun, along with various tricks for keeping the powder from fouling while marching in poor weather.

When it came Stan's turn, he soon had them all laughing hysterically. He demonstrated, in typical humorous Stan fashion, the finer points of the bayonet. How to mount and dismount it in proper military manner—and how not to. How to poke it into a deserving opponent and how to prevent sticking it into your buddy when out on the march. And so on … all acted out with great vigor and humor.

No one seemed surprised when Tony showed up, this time carrying a bucket sloshing over with water, and a tin drinking cup. "Thought you men might be getting thirsty out here in the hot sun. So seein's how I had nothin' needed doing, I thought I'd bring you some water to drink."

Nathan gave him a friendly smile, and Tom said, "A very handsome *thought*, Tony. Thank you very kindly for that."

Tony nodded his head in acknowledgment and returned the smiles. The others thanked him as well. It was already a warm afternoon, and they greatly appreciated the refreshment.

❧❧❧❧❧❧❧❧❧❧❧

At the end of the afternoon, as they headed back toward the Big House, Tony split off to head to the cabins. He had only gone a few steps when the Captain suddenly stopped, and turned toward him, saying, "Oh, Tony … it was December twenty-seventh, 1841."

"What's that, sir?" Tony asked.

"Your birthday. The first time we met I told you I would see if I could discover your birthday. I asked Tom to search through the old records, and he found it. That means you're eighteen years old, and will be nineteen this December, two days after Christmas!"

"Well … I'll be …" Tony said, his eyes wide with surprise. "Two days past Christmas. And I'm eighteen years. My, my.

211

Thank you, sir, thank you most kindly. That is right-good to know about, I reckon."

He walked away shaking his head. Nathan smiled with satisfaction watching him go.

Tony felt a twinge of guilt, feeling like he'd spent the afternoon spying on men doing their best to treat him kindly. He was still skeptical of the new master, and suspicious of his intentions … but he had to admit, the man was making it hard to hate him.

This time Tony went back the long way around, to avoid Sickles. And maybe, just maybe … catch a glimpse of *Rosa*.

ༀསྒྲསྒྲༀསྒྲསྒྲༀསྒྲསྒྲ

Walters had departed Saturday morning at first light, as announced. He didn't bother saying goodbye to Margaret, which didn't surprise her. She'd *not* been expecting it and was relieved not to speak with him again.

She was, however, surprised how quickly she felt his absence—positively, of course. As soon as the carriage drew out of sight, she felt she could breathe a little easier. As if there were less tension in the air. She wondered if everyone in the household felt the same.

Almost from the instant Walters left her room the previous night, she'd been thinking about how to take advantage of his impending absence. She was a quiet, thoughtful person, whose usual habit was to plan her actions to the smallest detail and envision all potential outcomes to the last possible variation. She'd done this all her life, even with the most seemingly trivial matters. In this case, however, the stakes were much higher— possibly even to the level one might consider life or death.

So this time she would make her very most careful, well-thought out plan, commensurate with the seriousness of the situation. She would leave nothing to chance, if possible, to ensure her ultimate success.

Margaret had already decided to leave the farm while Walters was away, so the next question became, how?

She'd never learned to ride a horse, so that was out of the question. Large and powerful, they made her feel small and insignificant; their great brute physicality frightened her.

And from what she could remember, it was a very long and hilly walk from Walters Farm to even the nearest neighbor, let alone to a town of any size.

So her only options were to ride *with* someone, or to take the carriage. The thought of clinging to a strange man while bouncing along for miles on horseback was so repellent it gave her the shivers—that was out!

Which left only the carriage. But Walters had taken that to the train station. Would he order the driver to stay and await his return, or would he send it back? Everything hinged on the answer. Without the carriage she could think of no means of escape.

She'd watched as they'd departed and noted the carriage held four persons: the driver who was an older slave, Walters, Bob, and Josiah, Walters' personal servant. One of the white farmhands had also left with them on horseback.

The rider was clearly the escort who would keep an eye on the carriage once Walters left on the train. But when would the carriage and its escort return to the farm? They might wait in Covington for however long it took Walters to reach Richmond, conduct his business, and return. Or they might immediately come back to the farm, with orders to be back at the train station on a specific date, by a specific time.

Hmm … which would it be? She remembered Walters telling Bob to plan on them being in Richmond for a week. That'd require him to pay the white farmhand's room and board for something like nine or ten days. The driver, being a slave, would sleep in the carriage.

From what she'd seen, Walters was not one to spend money he didn't have to. Also, he certainly wouldn't care if his servants, black or white, had to suffer the long ride twice. On top of which, it would probably gall him to have two of his workers idling about for more than a week, paid or not.

So logic said Walters would send them back with the carriage.

But what if she was *wrong* about that? She considered the question for only a few moments before deciding. She may as well plan the whole thing out as if she were correct about the carriage. If she was incorrect, all she'd have lost was the time spent planning a scheme she'd never be able to carry out. And *time* was one thing she had plenty of, and to spare!

She figured about ten hours' ride to the train station. That meant they'd arrive around sunset on Saturday. She thought back to her own journey from Richmond, traveling to the end of the line east of the small town of Covington. The train had departed the Richmond station at first light and had arrived at … approximately 4:00 in the afternoon. And she recalled the engine had turned around and departed almost immediately once the few waiting passengers had boarded. Though she supposed that if it had to take on cargo it would take longer.

Well, no way to be sure, she decided. She'd just have to assume Walters wouldn't make the Saturday train. That meant he'd spend the night near the train station and catch the Sunday afternoon train. She also had to assume he wouldn't send the carriage back until he was safely on the train. Trains sometimes broke down, or derailed, so he'd not leave himself stranded with no means of transportation, just in case.

And … he wouldn't have the carriage return in the dark, risking damage to the vehicle or injury to the horses. That meant the driver and his escort would spend Sunday night in Covington and start back to the farm at first light Monday morning. So the carriage and its single escort should arrive early to midafternoon on Monday.

And she had a very strong feeling she should be outside to greet that carriage, and to turn it around at once, herself aboard. That would make her getaway swift and simple. If she had to order the carriage readied, the horses rigged, and whatnot, and to wait around for that to happen, it might give someone the idea of trying to stop her.

Now she had to figure a plan to get from her room to the driveway to greet the carriage, and how to convince the driver to take her where she wanted to go while making sure the escort didn't interfere. No easy task, considering Walters' had ordered his servants, both black and white, never to allow her out of her room. And they all lived in grave fear of him, with good reason.

So … what to do about *that* …?

ᛊᛟᛖᛟᚲᛊᚲᛒᚢᛊᛟᚲᛊᚲᛒᚢᛊᛟᚲᛊᚲᛒ

When she woke Monday morning, Margaret dressed in one of her nicer informal dresses. Not an elegant, flowing gown like one would wear to a formal ball or dinner; rather, a pretty, feminine dress like a woman might wear to attend a church service, or to go visit a neighbor. She tried to stay calm and do everything in the normal, routine manner. But she found herself wound as tightly as a clock spring. She couldn't keep her hands from shaking when she picked up the brush to work on her hair.

Once she finished dressing and brushing her hair, there was nothing to do but wait. She tried sitting at the window and watching in her normal manner, but soon couldn't help but stand and pace about the room, looking up at the clock on the dresser every few minutes. She'd launch her plan at precisely 3:30 p.m., but the clock read 6:34 a.m. She sighed. The maid hadn't even brought breakfast yet. She decided this would be the longest day of her life.

When the big hand on the clock reached the "6" with a *click*, finally 3:30, she rose from her seat and walked to the door. She opened it, and said, "Willona, will you step into my room for a moment, please?"

"Yes, Missus," came the reply from down the hall. The maids took turns sitting in a chair watching her door. By now, she knew their routine exactly. It was now Willona's shift.

A black woman stepped into the room. She was about ten years older than Margaret, taller, and of a much heavier build. But if Margaret's escape plan depended on any kind of physical strength, she knew it'd be an utter failure before it ever started.

"Please close the door and come sit. I wish to speak with you about something."

"Yes Missus," she replied, and did as requested, choosing a seat positioning herself between Margaret and the door.

215

Margaret smiled inwardly at this. Her plan certainly did *not* require slipping past the maid in an athletic manner!

"Willona, as you know, the Master is now away from the house on business."

"Yes, Missus."

"And you would agree, I am the mistress of this house, the Master's wife, and in his absence, I must be obeyed, even as he would be?"

"Well ... Missus ... normally I'd be for sayin' that was the truth, but ..."

"But, what?"

"But, Missus ... the Master, well, he done left all us household servants some ... *orders* like ..."

"Let me guess; you are to continue watching me, as you have done while the Master was in residence. And you are *not* to allow me out of my room, same as when he was here. Do I have it right?"

"Yes, Missus ... I's awful sorry t'not allows y'all to do as you pleases, but the Master ... well, he done said how it should be, even when he be gone."

This didn't surprise Margaret. She had totally expected it and had counted on it in her plan.

"Yes, Mr. Walters is a very stern master. In fact, he is a very *frightening* person, wouldn't you agree, Willona?"

"Oh *no*, Missus. It ain't my place to say any such things about the Master. No ma'am."

"You needn't agree Willona, but you *know* it's true. You know he has *killed* several slaves with his bare hands, in his anger.

"Let me ask you something else, Willona ... do you know *why* Mr. Walters keeps me always shut up in this room?"

"No, Missus. The Master ain't told us no reason for such. He say 'do this,' and 'don't do that,' but he don't *never* say why. And we ain't *never* gonna ask."

"Oh, I can't blame you for that, Willona. Like I said, Mr. Walters is a very frightening, dangerous man.

"So let me tell you why the Master keeps me in this room. Mr. Walters is so obsessed with me, so ... *in love* with me ... he can't bear the thought of an injury or hardship of any kind befalling me.

He fears I may fall down the stairs, suffer a snake bite, get kicked by a horse, or experience any number of other calamities.

"It sounds foolish, but believe me, I've tried to reason with him about it. But he refuses to hear my pleas. He lives in great fear of anything *bad* ever happening to me. Do you understand what I'm saying, Willona?"

"Yes, Missus. I guess that does sorta help explain the *why* of it."

"But though the Master has good intentions, I have begun to tire of this room. And I've especially lost patience with you servants disobeying my commands."

Willona gazed at her feet, looking embarrassed.

"So listen carefully, Willona. This is how it will be from now on …"

Willona looked up and met her eyes with a curious expression.

"From now on, you will do *exactly* as I say, even if it goes against the Master's wishes."

"Oh *no*, Missus, I couldn't …"

"Silence!" Margaret hissed, in her very best, angry mistress tone. It took all her willpower to play such a forceful role, so against her true nature.

"What do you think the Master would do to *you*, a simple house slave, if I told him you had laid hands on me? And you had struck me with your fists, doing me an injury?"

"Oh, but, Missus … I would *never* do such a thing."

"Well … *I* know that, and *you* know that, but … what do you suppose the *Master* knows? And who would he believe, the slave, or the wife he obsessively protects? Especially if she had the bruises to prove it?"

Willona stared wide-eyed, fear and shock on her face.

"Let me make it clear, so there will be no mistake. Either you will obey my every word from this day forward, or I will do myself an injury, and will tell the Master it was *you* who did it. Do you understand me?"

Willona looked down at her feet, and now could not meet Margaret's eyes. *Good*, Margaret thought, *finally the tables are turned. This may actually work!*

"Yes, Missus."

"Good. You may just save your own skin after all. Now, when you leave this room, you will tell all the other house slaves the same thing I have told you. They *will obey me*, or I will tell the Master they have injured me. And he will ... well, I will leave it to your imagination what he would do in such a case."

"Yes, ma'am. I will tell them, just as you say."

"Good. See that you do. If any of them disobeys me, I will assume it was *you* who failed to tell them. And I'll tell the Master *you* held me down while the other slaves hit me."

"Oh no, Missus! Please don't do that! I'll be tellin' 'em all straight'way, as you say. None of us'll disobey you, ma'am!"

"All right, good. Now ... what I need to know is, who's in charge of the white overseers with Master Bob being gone?"

"That would be Master Stenson, Missus."

"Then go find Master Stenson at once and tell him I must see him in my room, without delay. Tell him it is *most* urgent. Do not fail me in this, Willona!"

"Yes, Missus. I'll be sendin' for Master Stenson with all due haste."

"And one more thing ... tell Mr. Stenson I wish to speak with him *alone*—no one else is to come with him, not even you, Willona. Do I make myself clear? Good. Go now. If Mr. Stenson is not here within the next half hour, it will go hard on you."

"Yes, ma'am!" she said, and hurried out the door.

Margaret closed the door behind her and sat down on the bed.

She let out a deep breath and looked down at her hands—they trembled. She felt her heart pounding and suppressed a strong urge to weep—or to run out the door and apologize to Willona, assuring her she would never in life do any of the cruel things she'd just threatened. But she calmed herself with a force of will.

She'd done nothing remotely like *that* before. Never had she ordered anyone to do anything, much less threatened their life if they didn't. But fortunately, she had *seen* it done, and read about it, enough times that she was able to pull it off.

Now all she could do was sit and wait for Mr. Stenson to arrive. Then, she could start the next part of her plan ...

A white woman wouldn't so easily fool or intimidate the white foreman Stenson, so this part called for more drastic measures. She tried to calm herself, and to steel her nerves for what she *must do* next.

In twelve minutes by the clock, there came a quiet knock on the door. She forced herself to sit and wait. After a half minute there was a second knock, this time slightly louder. She rose and walked to the door at a steady pace. No good being in a hurry. It would be suspicious and smack of desperation.

She opened the door and gazed out. A tall, thin man, with dark hair and mustache, but no beard, stood in the hall, clutching his hat. He'd clearly come in from the fields—his clothing had a workmanlike appearance. *Good, he'll be out of his element.* And also, a good thing for her purposes that he didn't have a full beard …

"Come in, Mr. Stenson … I don't wish to stand in the hallway when speaking with you. You may leave the door open if it makes you more comfortable."

"Yes ma'am, I think I'll do that."

She turned and walked toward her bed but motioned toward a chair she had placed between the bed and the door. "Please, have a seat."

"Thank you, ma'am."

Stenson sat carefully in the chair and turned to look at her, an inquisitive expression on his face.

But she didn't immediately sit on the bed opposite him, as it seemed she would do. Instead, she stepped forward and struck Stenson hard on the side of his face with her right hand. More than just a slap, she'd led with her nails, leaving behind four parallel gouges on his cheeks. She retreated to the bed and sat facing him.

"*Ow!* Whatcha wanna go'n do *that* for, ma'am?"

He rubbed his face and looked at his hand. It was streaked with blood.

"That, *sir*, is what a woman does to a man, not her husband, who dares come into her bedroom and lay hands on her!"

"But … *Mrs. Walters* … I never did *any* such thing, and you knows it!"

219

"Yes ... *I* know it, and *you* know it. But I wonder what Mr. Walters will say when I tell him my little tale, and you have the marks on your face to prove it true. Even if the scratches heal by the time he returns, everyone will have seen them on you, so there will be plenty of witnesses to corroborate my story."

Stenson turned pale, an expression of utter shock and confusion on his face.

"But ... but ... *why?* Why would you wanna do such a thing, ma'am, when I ain't never done you no harm no-how? Mr. Walters ... well, I reckon he'd skin me alive for somethin' like that!"

"Yes, I agree, Mr. Walters would likely skin you alive ... unless he could think of something even worse. And ... now that you clearly understand the situation, I will tell you *why*.

"The *why* is I'm sick and tired of being kept in this room. And ... *how dare you* say you've done nothing to harm me? *That's a lie, and you know it!* You, and all the rest, have kept me a prisoner in my own home ... *in my own bedroom!* How would you feel toward a man who'd helped keep you captive? That is plenty and enough *harm* for me, thank you very much!"

Stenson didn't have an answer for this, but it seemed to touch him. He looked down at his feet and appeared shamed by it.

"So, Mr. Stenson, here is how you can save your own neck, and the others as well. In a few minutes time I will walk out of this room, down the stairs, and out the front door. Then I will walk around the grounds for a bit of fresh air. You will make sure nobody tries to stop me or tries to follow me. In fact, I recommend everyone simply look the other way, so if asked, they can honestly say they saw *nothing*.

"You will also make sure everyone knows never to tell Mr. Walters I left my room. If they know what's good for them, they will lie shamelessly, if necessary. Not only will Walters be angry if he knows you let me out, but if he ever finds out, I promise I'll spin my *nasty* little tale. And I'll be sure he believes every, *lying* word of it! He's insanely jealous, you know ... that's why he keeps me locked in this room. He can't abide another man even *looking* at me. Imagine what he'd do if another man actually … *touched* me?"

Stenson turned pale and looked like he might be ill. "It'll be done as you say, ma'am … I'll be sure nobody bothers you none. But … please ma'am … please do come back safely to your room later, or Mr. Walters will have my neck, lying story, or no."

"You may go now, Mr. Stenson. I expect *not* to see you again today."

"Yes, ma'am."

After Stenson departed, she turned and walked to the window. This time she was not shaking so badly, and her heart did not seem to be pounding quite as hard as it had before.

Now, to wait for the carriage to arrive. She had used four o'clock as her beginning point, assuming it could arrive at any time thereafter. It was now sixteen minutes to four, by the clock.

She'd prepared for a wait of several hours, but in the end, it wasn't as long as she'd feared. At 4:37, she saw the carriage coming down the road at the farthest point visible from her window, the escort rider directly behind.

She stood and strolled to the door. Opening it, she stepped out into the hall, where down a ways she saw the chair, normally occupied by one of the maids, was now empty. She smiled, *so far, so good.*

She walked to the stairs and started down. When she reached the foyer, she paused again and looked around. No one in sight. Good.

She walked across the broad, marble foyer, past the sitting room, to the front door, and through it out onto the veranda. She paused, looking from side to side and out across the front drive to the fields beyond. Margaret smiled again. Stenson had taken her at her word. Not even a field slave was in sight for as far as her eyes could see. And no grooms appeared to meet the carriage.

She strode across the veranda, down the front stairs, and out across the drive, heading toward the building where they kept the carriage. They'd go there first to unhitch and put away the vehicle. After that, the horses would be unbridled and ready for a drink and a rub-down.

Sorry, horses, your day's not done yet, she smiled.

She waited outside the doors to the carriage barn. She heard it coming before she saw it, but it was suddenly directly in front of her, heading straight at her. But following through with her plan, she stood still where she was, potentially in harm's way, and held up her hands, signaling the driver to stop.

"Whoa, whoa, there!" he called out. The two horses brought the carriage to a sudden halt. And by a stroke of good luck the escort wasn't there, apparently peeling off earlier to take his horse straight to the stables. So much the better.

"Oh my, Missus! Y'all startled me something fierce! Y'ought not be out here where y'might get yourself runned over."

"It's not your place to tell me where I should or shouldn't be!" she snapped, once again calling up her best "angry mistress" voice.

"Oh, *no*, Missus. I's most sorry, ma'am. I was startled is all, a-feared I'da runned you over with the team, ma'am."

"Never mind that now. Turn them around, I wish to go out."

"But ... Missus ... the Master, he ain't never told me to take y'all out in the carriage. I ain't s'posed to give nobody no ride w'out the Master saying so."

Margaret had been expecting this. So for answer she strode over to the carriage, stepped up onto the front bench, and sat next to the driver.

"Fine. Then step down, and hand me the reins."

He looked at her in complete puzzlement, so far out of his element he didn't even know what to say.

"But ... but ... Missus ..."

"Well, which is it going to be? Either drive, as I have ordered you, or give me the reins, and I will drive the carriage myself. There is no other choice ... unless ... Well, unless you intend to lay your hands on my person and *force* me from this carriage. You *could* do that ... you are much larger and stronger than I. But ..."

"But what, Missus?"

"But I wouldn't recommend it. What do you imagine Mr. Walters would do, if he heard one of his male slaves had laid hands on *his wife*, and used his force on her?"

"Oh, Missus … I reckon he'd … I reckon … well …"

"He'd skin them alive …" she hissed, remembering Stenson's words.

"Yes, ma'am, I reckon he would, at that."

"So … then you must choose. Either drive me or let me drive the carriage myself. But I must warn you … I've only driven a carriage once before, and that was with my Daddy sitting next to me. So it is possible I might drive the team off into a ditch somewhere out there. And … well, I can imagine Mr. Walters wouldn't be happy about *that* either, wouldn't you think?"

"No, ma'am, I reckon the Master would be some kinda terrible angry on account of something like that.

"Ma'am … how abouts I drive you wherever it is you wants to go, and then, later …"

"Yes?"

"Well ma'am, I's just to-thinking. Maybe the Master … well, he being out over to Richmond and all. Well, maybe he don't needs to know nothing about this-here ride."

She smiled.

"Yes, I agree. Do then just turn this carriage around and head back up the road, if you please … what was your name?"

"Samuel, ma'am."

"Well, Samuel, do please drive back up the road."

"Yes, ma'am. But … does the Missus knows where we's fixing to be going?"

"Yes, Samuel … take me to the house of *Mr. Nathaniel Chambers.*"

ഇൽൽൽൽൽൽൽൽൽൽൽൽൽ

Miss Abbey sat in the library, reading a book.

Megs poked her head in the door, "They's a carriage in the drive, Miss Abbey."

"Oh? Do you know whose it is?"

"No, ma'am. Ain't never seen it before. There's a young lady in it, but I ain't seen her before either."

"Really? Well, I wasn't expecting any guests. My, but it does seem we've had a lot of unexpected visitors lately!"

"Yes, ma'am. It does at that."

She stood and walked with Megs out the front door and across the veranda to the head of the stairs. An elderly black driver was helping a young lady down from the carriage. She was thin, and pale, with a rather plain-looking face, to Abbey's way of thinking. But she wore a fine, new-seeming dress, and the carriage was of the highest quality, as were the horses. And the driver's garb was first-rate as well. Clearly, she came from a house of means, but Abbey was at a loss as to whose it could be. Her curiosity was absolutely piqued.

"Good afternoon," Abbey said, in a cheerful, welcoming voice. "Welcome to Mountain Meadows Farm. I am Abigail Chambers, but you may call me Abbey. Please, may I offer you shade and refreshment in my home?"

The young lady wore a serious expression when she answered, "Yes … thank you very sincerely, Miss Abbey. It would be an honor and a pleasure."

She came up the stairs without further ado, so Abbey smiled, and gestured for her to enter the house. *Odd … she didn't even give her name,* Abbey thought.

They were soon seated comfortably in the library. Their guest removed her hat, handing it to Megs, who took it with a bow, and left to go fetch refreshments.

"Miss Abbey, I apologize for showing up on your doorstep uninvited, and for my seeming rudeness just now, not introducing myself. But … I … well, I think you'll understand better when you've heard my whole story. You see, my name is Margaret … but, if you've heard of me at all, you would probably know me as … *Mrs. Elijah Walters.*"

Abbey had to suppress a gasp of surprise. Walters' mysterious wife had been the subject of much conjecture, rumor, and gossip in the county since Walters unexpectedly returned with her from Richmond over half a year ago.

"Mrs. Walters! What a pleasant surprise. Welcome … most welcome, indeed!"

"Oh … please, I beg of you … call me Margaret. I … I don't wish to be called anything other."

What an odd thing to say, Abbey thought. But what she said was, "Of course, it would be my pleasure to use the more familiar term, *Miss Margaret,* seeing's how we're neighbors and all."

"Well, yes, I agree with that, Miss Abbey, but … well, I didn't exactly *mean* it that way. You see … I have really come to *despise* the name Walters."

"*Oh!* Oh … I see. As you say, I guess I'll have to hear your story to understand the 'why' of that."

"Yes, ma'am. And I've come here to do just that … tell my story, that is, only …"

"Yes, dear?"

"Well, to tell the truth, I came here to speak with Mr. Nathaniel Chambers, your … *husband?*"

Miss Abbey laughed, a delighted, musical kind of laugh, "Oh, bless you, my dear! You are too kind to suggest such a thing, but Mr. Nathaniel Chambers is my *son,* and the master of this house since my late husband's passing this spring."

"Oh … truly? My sincere condolences on the passing of your husband … I did not know of it. And please excuse my ignorance. It's just … please forgive me, Miss Abbey, but … you're so very beautiful and young-looking; you don't seem old enough to have a full-grown man for a son."

"Well … I'll not *forgive* you for that, but I will *thank* you! But yes, it's true. Did you meet Mr. Chambers when he recently paid a visit to your husband at your farm? Odd he never mentioned it. He knew how … *curious* … I was to know more about you. And how eager I've been to make your acquaintance."

"Miss Abbey, it is a … *complicated* story. And … please don't take this in any way disrespectful, but I came here hoping to tell my story to *Mr.* Chambers. I'm very happy for you to hear it also, but … to be honest, it is difficult and … painful … for me to speak of. So I'd rather not have to tell it twice, if you don't mind. Would it be possible to have an audience with Mr. Chambers? And you too, of course."

"Certainly, my dear. I understand completely and take no offense, never fear. I will call for Mr. Chambers straight away."

"Oh, thank you ever so kindly, ma'am."

Abbey rose and left the room. Margaret sat back and gazed around the library. It was beautiful, and elegantly furnished, though not nearly so large and grand as the sitting room back at Walters Farm. *But the books!* She'd never seen so many before in one place outside a public library. Walters had very few books, and most of those were informational, such as books on different crops or agricultural implements. The Chambers' books seemed to be on a wide variety of topics, both fiction and non-fiction. Old books, and many newer ones. If she'd had access to this many books, she might never have felt inclined to leave Walters' place. Not true, she realized ... but it certainly would have made her *incarceration* more pleasant.

Miss Abbey soon returned.

"I have sent for Mr. Chambers, but he is presently out in the fields somewhere, so we may need to wait a few minutes. The maids are preparing tea and cookies, so shortly we shall have something pleasant to pass the time."

"Oh, thank you kindly, Miss Abbey. I am much obliged."

"Never mention it, my dear. I am so pleased you've come for a visit, whatever the reasons."

"Thank you ... but ... you've been so gracious, and understanding of me already ..."

"What is it dear?"

"I have ... been forced to spend a lot of time indoors of late. I would dearly love to sit outside on your veranda in the fresh air while we await Mr. Chambers, if it would be possible."

"But of course, dear! And I'm so sorry to hear you've been *ill*. I trust you're feeling better now?"

For reasons Abbey didn't quite understand, Margaret smiled brightly at this question as if she were about to laugh.

"Oh, Miss Abbey ... you have *no idea* how wonderful I feel right now, compared to just a very short time ago!"

ⅢⅢⅢⅢⅢⅢ

The two ladies were sitting at a table on the shady side of the veranda, sipping tea, and exchanging small talk when Nathan arrived. Miss Abbey was doing most of the talking, describing how her flowers were progressing and sharing some local ladies' gossip she'd picked up at church this past Sunday.

She was careful, however, to avoid any subject touching on Mr. Walters and his doings, and she didn't feel inclined to say anything about Nathan either. He should speak for himself in front of this woman. She was, after all, the wife of a man whose father had had a long-standing feud with Nathan's father. And who now gave every sign of continuing the dispute.

Nathan came walking around the corner of the veranda, stepped up to the table, removed his hat, and made a slight bow.

"Mr. Chambers, may I introduce Miss Margaret. Miss Margaret is our neighbor and is …"

"Mr. Chambers, it is a pleasure to meet you," Margaret said, rising to her feet and presenting her hand. Nathan took her hand in his, keenly aware of the sweat and dirt covering his own rough hands. Her dainty hand, by contrast, was pure white, and soft as silk.

"Miss Margaret, the pleasure is all mine. Welcome to our home … most welcome, indeed. We are always pleased and honored when one of our neighbors pays a visit. Please excuse my ignorance, having been away so many years, but which neighboring farm is yours?"

"Well, as for that, Mr. Chambers, you've been there yourself very recently. You see, I have come from Mr. Elijah Walters' farm."

"*Oh!* Oh, I see …"

Nathan pulled out a chair and sat at the table, and Margaret resumed her own seat.

"To what do we owe the pleasure, Mrs. Walters?"

To Nathan's surprise, when he said this, the young woman winced as if in pain.

"I beg of you, Mr. Chambers … please, call me Margaret."

"Very well … to what do we owe the pleasure, *Miss Margaret?*"

"I … I'm afraid I've come to your home, uninvited, to beg a favor of you, Mr. Chambers. I know it's most rude of me, but I … could think of nothing else to do."

"Oh, think nothing of it, Miss Margaret … if it is within my power to help you, I shall be more than happy to do so."

"Thank you, Mr. Chambers. It is so kind of you to say. But it may be, once you've heard my tale, you may change your mind, and no blame if you do. Your dear, sweet Momma, Miss Abbey, has been the very picture of patience with me. But I really wished *you* to hear my story, sir, and I couldn't bear the thought of telling it twice."

"Tell it to me? But why *me*, if I may ask, since we have never before met?"

"Well, to be perfectly honest, Mr. Chambers, it is partly because I overheard you talking with Mr. Walters … I *eavesdropped*, as it were. I thought you sounded … well, *kindly*, among other things. And, also, well … I blush to say, but … when I left Walters Farm today, yours was the *only* name I knew among the neighbors. I truly had nowhere else to go."

Nathan could see she was distraught. And he found it passing strange she'd heard his voice in her own home, but had never been introduced, nor had attempted to make his acquaintance. He suspected there was quite a tale here and found his curiosity thoroughly aroused.

"Well then, perhaps you should tell us your tale, madam. I'm sure I can also speak for Miss Abbey when I say you have our full, and undivided attention."

Miss Abbey smiled and nodded in agreement.

"Very well and thank you both very kindly for listening to what I have to say …"

She began at the beginning, when she'd first heard about Walters from her parents, and then met him. She tried to recite the story in as matter-of-fact terms as she could, trying to speak calmly, without becoming overwrought. But at times during the tale, her voice cracked, and her eyes welled up with tears. Even so, she never stopped, and doggedly continued her tale, leaving nothing out. Despite her earlier hesitance, once she started the telling, she found it felt good to let it out, to tell other human beings what she'd experienced, and endured, and how she'd felt about it.

Nathan gazed at her as she spoke, a serious, unreadable expression on his face. Miss Abbey shook her head and had to wipe her eyes from time to time as Margaret described especially painful or emotional incidents.

Margaret told of Nathan's recent visit to Walters Farm, and of Walters' decision to go to Richmond, and how it had instigated her plot to escape.

"That was another reason I wished to talk with you, Mr. Chambers. I wanted to warn you about Walters' intention to speak with the Governor about you. He intends to undermine your standing with his honor before ever you arrive in Richmond."

Nathan rubbed his chin and looked thoughtful for a moment. "Hmm … that explains the odd thing the Reverend Blackburn told me on Sunday, when I asked about Walters' absence."

"Reverend Blackburn? He's the only person from outside the farm I've seen all these long months. He comes to the farm once a month … to preach to the slaves … afterward he pays me a visit, reads from the Bible, and says a prayer over me. I've asked him to help me, to at least convince Walters to take me to church service on Sundays. But he says it's not his place to come between a man and his wife. That we must work these issues out between us. The last time I spoke with him about it, he became short-tempered and stern with me, and told me not to speak of it again. So I no longer mention it to him, and just let him read his verses and say his prayers."

"Thank you for the warning about the Governor, Miss Margaret. I shall give it some thought. And, sorry … I didn't mean to interrupt your tale. Pray continue, if you please."

"Well, as you can see, your visit started events in motion, which have led me to be here today. Almost as if … well, I hesitate to say it, for fear it makes me sound more important than I believe I am. But … it almost seems as if *God* sent you that day, so I could listen to your voice, and take hope from it."

"In the Lord's eyes you are as important as the greatest queen who ever walked the Earth! Never doubt *that*, Miss Margaret! And … well, now I'm the one to fear sounding too self-important. But

… it seems God, for whatever reasons of his own, has used me recently for the betterment of others. I can't explain it, but lately I seem to be in just the place I need to be, through no forethought or intention. It has happened too many times of late to be mere coincidence, as one might otherwise believe."

"Then perhaps it's true, after all … but I digress. I wish to finish my tale, that you may judge for yourselves whether or not I'm worthy of your aid … or of God's."

She described, in every detail, her situation, and her reasoning as she worked out the best way to make her escape, taking advantage of Walters' temporary absence. She described the events of the day, her encounters with each person she had to get past to gain her freedom, and everything she'd said and done to turn things her way. She left nothing out. She wanted these good, kindly people to understand what kind of wicked, lying, cruel person she had become. So if they agreed to help her it would not be under any false pretenses.

As she told this last part of her story, Mr. Chambers startled her when he suddenly got up from his chair. He paced back and forth on the veranda as he listened to the rest of her tale. It seemed her story had stirred a passion inside him, and she feared he had become angered by her misbehavior. But she was determined to finish her tale, in all its ugliness.

She concluded with her arrival at Mountain Meadows, describing her feeling of delight seeing the beautiful white house in the distance, and the even more beautiful mistress of the manor who greeted her warmly at the door.

She looked up at Nathan expectantly, anxiously awaiting his response.

He stopped his pacing in mid-stride, pivoted toward her, and slammed his right fist into the palm of his left hand, making her jump. For a moment she feared the worst.

"*My God*, Miss Margaret! If you were one of my soldiers, I'd pin a medal on you, and grant you a field promotion on the spot! That was as neatly planned, and handsomely run an operation— completely surrounded and unarmed, in hostile enemy territory—as I've ever seen or heard of! Excellent strategy, and flawless tactics. Well planned, to a fine level of detail, but also just enough latitude in the execution to allow for the vagaries of warfare. Used your weakness for a strength and used the enemy's greatest strength against him. I especially liked how you used an entirely different tactic on each of your *jailors*, based on the situation and their position, to achieve the same end.

"And … never in life have I heard of a completely unarmed prisoner convincing the jail guards to stand aside and let her walk right out the front door. And then to top it off, having them offering her a ride to wherever she wished to go! *Absolutely brilliant!*"

He stepped over and took a knee in front of her, holding out his right hand, palm up and gazing into her eyes. She slowly placed her right hand in his. He bent down and gently kissed the back of her hand.

"I salute you, madam, and I also wish to say … I am *very proud* to know you!"

"Oh! Oh, thank you Mr. Chambers. Thank you, for your very kind words. I'm certain no one has ever said anything half so kind to me before. But … sir, if all that's true, why do I feel so … so *horrible* and guilty for what I've done? I have lied, threatened, and berated poor servants who really didn't deserve it. And I've even gone so far as to purposely injure a man who has never before harmed me in any way."

Nathan was quiet and seemed thoughtful, before answering.

"Being a military man, I've often struggled with those same questions. I've committed terrible, bloody acts … upon people who may or may not have deserved them. I've killed and wounded many men and have ordered it done … men for whom I held no particular ill will."

"Oh, truly? And how have you lived with yourself after?"

"By realizing I have always done *what I had to do* … to protect myself, my men, or my country and its citizens. Those men I killed may never have personally done anything to me, but they were threatening harm to me or to those I hold dear. Sometimes a man … *or woman* … must do what must be done, though he personally finds it distasteful, or disheartening. I believe that is exactly what you've done today, Margaret. You've done what you *had* to do.

"You wouldn't have done those things if you'd not been forced into a desperate situation by an evil man. And those serving this man, either through their own free will, or through fear, or even by force, are still aiding him. They *must* be opposed, even with violence when necessary.

"Don't be too harsh on yourself. You know in your heart you aren't that person you've pretended to be today. And I suspect those you've ill-treated know, deep in *their* hearts, you were justified in your actions. No one deserves to be held against their will, and *everyone* knows it, whether they'll admit it or not."

"Thank you very kindly, Mr. Chambers."

Nathan nodded.

"Thank you for confiding in us, dear. That was bravely done. But ... what's next for you?" Miss Abbey asked. "What will you do, and where will you go, now you've gained your freedom?"

"Well, there's the favor I wished to ask, if you're still willing."

"Of course, of course, dear. Anything you wish!"

"Thank you. I wish to borrow writing paper and implements so I might pen a letter to my father in Richmond. Two letters, actually, to be certain he gets one. And I beg of you to put them in the mail. One as soon as may be, and the other ... about a week later, in case the first doesn't go through for any reason."

"Of course, certainly dear. Then, will you return to your parents' home in Richmond, or do you have another place you wish to go?"

Margaret didn't immediately respond and gazed down at the table.

"I ... I must return to Walters Farm."

"What?!" Nathan jumped to his feet again. "Surely *not!* After all you've been through, you would go back to that place ... to that ... *man?*"

"Oh, please hear me out ... I don't *wish* to go. In fact, I wish to be anywhere else in the world. But ... I've thought about this even longer and harder than I thought about my escape plan. First, if I leave now and never return, it will go very hard on those who have, willingly or not, aided in my escape. I fear he may kill some of the slaves in his anger, maybe even that old man out there who drives the carriage and has never harmed a soul in his life. And second, if I simply return to my parents' home, he will come searching for me, of that I have no doubt. And he may harm my parents if they try to stand in his way. I don't want to live my life always looking over my shoulder, fearing to see *him* standing there. Never having peace. Can you understand?"

"Well yes, but then … *what?* Just go back to being a prisoner the rest of your days?"

"I hope not to, Mr. Chambers. The letters to my father are to tell him I wish to divorce Mr. Walters. That he holds me prisoner against my will, and that I wish him to come to Walters Farm and bring me home. I will also warn him to bring an officer of the law with him to make sure Walters doesn't oppose him by force. That way, if I'm taken away, properly and legally by my own father, witnessed by a lawman, perhaps Walters will accept it and let me go."

Nathan was quiet for a moment, and looked over and met eyes with Miss Abbey, who had tears in her eyes.

"Once again, I find myself so thoroughly impressed by you — almost beyond words, Miss Margaret. It is a very brave and selfless thing you're proposing. But … you are *not* responsible for the lives of those people back at the farm … Walters will do with them as he will, and *that* is not your fault. You *must* save yourself, I beg you!

"And, as for Walters hunting you down … you're welcome to stay here … for as long as you'd like. I promise you Walters would never touch you here. I have no fear of him. I've had long years dealing with nasty characters who'd make your Mr. Walters seem like a petty schoolyard bully."

"Oh, thank you most kindly, Mr. Chambers — again for your kind words, and for your generosity inviting me into your home. I can't tell you how much that means to me. But I must decline. Even here I would be a prisoner. Oh, it would be a much larger and nicer cell, with jailors who would treat me better than I deserve, no doubt. But still a prison. I wouldn't dare leave your property ever, for any reason.

"And … I *know* Walters. Though now I've met you I can truly believe you have no fear of him—it is clear you're *that* kind of man—still, unless you mean to steal his carriage and his driver, he'll know I'm here. And he would use force if necessary, to get me back. I don't want to be the cause of a battle in which good men could be hurt, or even killed. I could not live with myself if that were to happen."

Nathan turned and paced again, and Margaret could tell her plans troubled him deeply.

"You are such a very clever woman … can you not think of some way out of this? Now I've met you, and have heard your tale, it grates on me terribly to think of you willingly going back there."

"I'm sorry, Mr. Chambers, but I can think of no other way. Will you send the letters to my father?"

"Yes, yes, of course. And if he's able to get you out of there, then have him bring you straight here. We will provide you a proper escort to the train station to ensure Walters doesn't try any nonsense out on the road.

"And when I travel to Richmond, sometime after the New Year, I will come visit you to be sure you're still safe. But what if your father isn't able to get you out?"

"Well, then … I ask you to pray for me."

"That I will do, regardless. All right … I will agree to help you and send your letters. But I can't promise I won't take more … *extreme measures* … if your plan fails to bear fruit."

"Oh, thank you Mr. Chambers … Miss Abbey. You've been more kind to me than I ever could have imagined. And I want you to know … I would rather stay here with you forever, than go any other place I can think of … if I had a choice."

ᔕᕮᗡᘛᘔᔕᕮᗡᘛᘔᔕᕮᗡᘛᘔ

The following Friday, Nathan and Tom rode their horses slowly across the Greenbrier River bridge on their way to the county courthouse for the scheduled town meeting. Tom found he enjoyed the sound the horses' hooves made on the heavy wood planks inside the covered bridge—a pleasant, echoing sound.

But he pulled his mind away from that thought, back to the topic he'd been discussing with the Captain.

"So Mrs. Walters told you …"

"Margaret," Nathan corrected him.

"Well, yes, of course, my apologies—I now understand why she prefers going by her given name. Anyway, you were telling me Margaret confirmed our suspicions—Walters went to Richmond to speak to the Governor about you?"

"Yes, I'm afraid so, Tom."

"Why … that crusty old son-of-a-bitch!"

"Oh no, Tom. I must disagree with you on *that* point … he's really not all that *old!*"

They shared a smile.

"So what do you intend to do about it, sir?"

"Do about what?"

"About Walters talking to the Governor."

"I don't intend to do anything."

"What? You're just going to sit here while he tells whatever lies about you he pleases, to the most important man in the state?"

"All right … what would *you* suggest I do, Tom?"

"Oh, I don't know … maybe send a letter or … no, a telegram—that would get there quicker—to warn him about Walters. That he's not to be believed or trusted."

Nathan didn't immediately respond, instead blowing a long plume of smoke from the cigar he'd been working on the last few miles.

"Tom, think about it this way: if I send a telegram to the Governor, firstly, he doesn't know me any better than he knows Walters, so why should he take my word over his. And secondly, it would make it seem I am overly worried about what Walters has to say. That would tend to have the opposite effect from what we would wish. The fact I'm acting concerned about it lends it some credence, as if whatever he's saying *might* be true.

"If, on the other hand, I adopt an air of indifference, it tends to indicate I have no concern about what Walters says. As if it is of little moment, and being patently untrue, of little concern. Do you see what I mean?"

"Yes, I think so … when you put it that way, my suggestion seems rather … *foolish*, really."

"No, no, not at all, Tom. Many people think the way you've suggested. That they should stifle their enemies, and not let them say what they wish to say, for fear other people might be swayed to their way of thinking. Or take a liking to them, or what have you.

"But Tom, I'm a firm believer in freedom of speech. And not just for you and me, and other people we like and generally agree with, but also for those we dislike, and disagree with. In fact, *especially* for them. If fools like Walters were never allowed to speak, someone might start thinking more highly of them than they deserve. But allow them to speak freely, to express their views as loudly and as often as they like, and they quickly show themselves for the lying, foolish, blowhards they are.

"I'd go so far as to say our First Amendment, granting us that treasured freedom—along with freedom of religion, freedom of the press, and freedom of assembly—is the single greatest law ever passed in the whole long history of civilization! And that's not something to be taken lightly.

"So getting back to your original question, I would *not* stop Walters from talking to the Governor even if I had the power to do so, which thankfully, I don't. He has the right to have his say, no matter how much I might dislike and disagree with what he says."

"Yes, I see your point, sir. But … if Walters talks to the Governor, and he starts thinking ill of you, what then?"

"Well, Tom, that's the flip side of the freedom of speech; you must trust the listener has the wisdom, or at least the good horse sense, to separate the truth from the lies. We must have faith our governor would not be in the high position he is if he weren't capable of doing so.

"Once we get to Richmond, when the moment is right, I will have a quiet, casual conversation with him about it, as a matter of little concern, a minor curiosity on my part concerning one very odd neighbor, and what he might have had to say to his honor, the Governor."

Tom shook his head and smiled. "Once again, sir, I am humbled by your wisdom."

"Well, Tom, some things I know well, and about which am confident in my convictions. Others …? Well, I reckon we shall see what we shall see at this little town meeting."

"Yes, sir, that we will."

"I'll tell you what I *will* do about Walters, however …"

"What's that sir?"

"He can *talk* all he wants, but I'll not let him get away with murdering his slaves, not to mention all the trouble he's caused Miss Abbey and Margaret. As soon as Margaret is free, I will encourage her to go before a magistrate and testify against him."

"Do you think it will do any good? Aren't slave masters allowed to do whatever they wish with their slaves, up to, and including murder?"

"Well, technically, yes, but judges tend to frown on that type of extreme misbehavior. Makes us all look bad, especially in the current political climate. It's likely he would at least be called in to face charges, which would make it into the Richmond papers and cause him considerable embarrassment, if nothing else."

"Then why not do it now? Go to a magistrate, I mean. Tell the judge Walters is holding his wife prisoner, and he's been murdering his slaves?"

"Believe me, Tom, I would if I thought it'd do any good. But without Margaret to testify, there's only my secondhand word against his. And my word would be tainted by the long-standing feud between our fathers. More importantly, it would put her in grave danger. If the law confronted him, he might start digging into who had given him away, and that might lead to Margaret. I shudder to think of what he might do to her in such circumstances."

"Yes … I can see your point on that, sir. From what you say, she is such an admirable woman, it would be a shame if anything bad happened to her."

"Plenty bad has *already* happened to that fine woman, Tom. I just pray nothing more does. And I promise I'll do all in my power, legally ... or *otherwise* ... to prevent that from happening."

"Amen, sir. I'm with you on that."

When they entered the courthouse, they sat in chairs up front while people filed in and took their seats. Some came forward and politely introduced themselves, while others, a bit shy perhaps, entered and went directly to their seats.

Being a military man, schooled in punctuality, Nathan referred to his pocket watch, and when the watch ticked onto the top of the hour, he started the meeting.

"Thank you so very much for coming here today to meet with me. I am Nathaniel Chambers, son of the late State Senator, Jacob Chambers, and current owner of Mountain Meadows Farm east of town. His honor, Governor John Letcher, of the great Commonwealth of Virginia, has graciously asked me to take up my father's seat in the senate, and finish out his term. I have humbly agreed to accept this honor and undertake this duty.

"You may know I've been away from Virginia for a very long time. In fact, my entire adult life. So when the Governor asked me to fill this position, I quickly realized I knew very little about what matters are of concern to the people of Virginia, and more specifically in this, our western part of Virginia. And that's why I've invited you here today. Not to give you a grand speech, but rather to ask for *your* instructions. For, you see, when I go to Richmond, I am going on *your* behalf, to make sure your thoughts and opinions are presented to the government of the Commonwealth. So I am here today to ask you ... well, in the Army we'd ask our commanding officer for our marching orders. So I guess I am asking you for my marching orders when I go to Richmond." He finished with a smile, and several people chuckled at that.

"I've spoken to some of my close-by neighbors already, and I have heard complaints about roads, and taxes. But, please, don't be shy to speak up. And don't assume I already know about this or that, as I can assure you I most likely do *not!*"

He could sense a positive reaction from the audience for his candor, and light-hearted manner. They were clearly more used to political figures being more formal, and more inclined to talk, than to listen.

"So let's open it up to any questions or comments you may have. Please raise your hand if you wish to speak, and we will take each in turn."

A half-dozen or so hands shot up. Nathan pointed to a middle-aged woman seated toward the front. She asked about better schools. Several other people chimed in agreement while she was talking. Others nodded.

Another man brought up the roads, like Mr. Greene, to which there was general, and universal agreement. Nathan thought it interesting there was little dispute about what the government "over to Richmond" ought to do, and it was not anything amazing, or unreasonable.

Then somebody raised the property tax issue, and this time Nathan expected it and was prepared with his answer. His response—once again he agreed they should tax the slave owners fairly—was met with nods of approval, but no other comments.

It also didn't catch him by surprise when someone asked him about the presidential election, and what he thought about Mr. Lincoln.

"Well, to be honest, I had never even heard of Mr. Lincoln before a week ago. But since then I've been reading everything I can get my hands on in the newspapers concerning his candidacy. From what I can tell, he has made it quite clear he is morally opposed to slavery. And has made no secret this new 'Republican' party of his will work to prevent the expansion of slavery into any territories or new states. But he's also said he'll take no action to abolish slavery, nor to interfere in the internal affairs of the Southern states. So I see no reason why we should have any concerns about him being elected. And frankly, even if he does get elected, I don't see there's anything the government in Richmond can do about it, anyway."

He felt good about his answer. Reading between the lines of the Southern newspapers, which generally vilified him, Nathan thought Lincoln sounded like a rational, reasonable man who wasn't about to do anything rash. He could see no reasonable objection to the man being president, except for the fact he was from the north, and wasn't an outright pro-slavery candidate.

So just as he was feeling smug about his preparedness for this meeting, he was again caught off guard by a question.

"Well, Mr. Chambers, if what you say is true about Mr. Lincoln, then what do you think about all this talk of secession?"

Nathan was bewildered and at a loss. He looked over at Tom for help, but Tom shrugged his shoulders. He had no idea either.

Nathan finally had to admit defeat. He replied, "I'm sorry, as I said before, I've been away a long time ... I don't know what you specifically mean by 'secession.' Who would be seceding from what?"

There were a few snickers, but the man who'd asked the initial question puffed up, as if he took pride in being the one person who had stumped the senator with a question. "Secession, as in the Southern states seceding from the United States. There's some people saying the South ought to secede if this Lincoln fellow gets elected, on account of him going to take away the rights of the Southern states. I heard it's all the talk in Charleston ... the one in South Carolina that is ... anyway, now you know what it's about. I'd like to hear what you think on it."

Nathan was flabbergasted. He was sure his mouth must have been hanging open in total disbelief.

"Secede from the United States ... because of one man? Why, that would be unconscionable ... unreasonable ... nonsensical. Why would anyone in their right mind consider such a notion? After all we've been through as a nation ... defeating the British ... *twice!* Creating the great Constitution of this land, something never done before. The Bill of Rights, guaranteeing each of us our freedoms! Why would we throw all that away because we don't happen to agree with what a president has to say? That's why we have elections. If we don't like him, we elect someone different next time!"

But despite Nathan's growing vehemence, the man stood his ground. "Well, on account of there's a whole speck more of them northerners. So once they decides to all band together to elect someone, the game's up here in the South. And then, whatever he says now, once he's elected, he can do as he pleases, and the states down here ain't got no more say. That's what folks is saying, anyway," he concluded, and sat down, folding his arms, a satisfied look on his face.

"Well, I don't agree. This Lincoln doesn't strike me as a person to force his opinions on others, nor to do anything unreasonable or rash. To separate from our great union on account of a single election … why, it is beyond imagining. Maybe the people of South Carolina might entertain such thoughts … I don't know, not having ever lived there. But I know Virginians have more sense than that. My God, man … George Washington … Thomas Jefferson … James Madison! They were *Virginians!* They'd roll over in their graves at such talk. They built this country. I … I just, can't imagine it, I'm sorry."

Nathan realized he'd become heated in his response and could feel his anger rising. Only this time, there'd be no one to vent it on but one old man who'd only asked a question. He willed himself to cool his temper.

He turned and looked at Tom, who rolled his eyes, as if to say, *"You're right, but you're losing control …"*

Nathan took a deep breath, let out a heavy sigh, and turned once again toward the audience. "I apologize for my heated response. That was impolite of me. It's just … well, you must understand … I have marched in the armies of this country, with the stars and stripes leading the way, into a foreign land. They had us outnumbered and outgunned … thousands of miles from home with no hope of reinforcement. But the love of our country and everything it stands for carried us forward, and we won the day, against all odds. To think of anyone wanting to tear down *that* country … it is … difficult for me to countenance."

His talk of fighting for his country seemed to win over the audience. There were smiles, and nodding heads throughout the room.

He decided it would be a good note to end on. "Thank you all very much for coming. You've given me much to think upon, and to discuss with the other representatives when we meet in Richmond. Thank you, and good night."

With that he stood, and Tom with him. Most people headed for the door. But a few came up to shake his hand and thank him for listening to them and for his service to the country.

When he and Tom climbed into the saddle to head back to Mountain Meadows, he couldn't shake a sinking feeling in the pit of his stomach. *Secession?* he thought ... *they can't be serious...* But by the time they'd reached home he'd convinced himself it was just idle talk. After all, it made no sense, and people were clearly more sensible than that.

‣‣‣‣‣‣‣‣‣‣‣‣‣

"Mr. Templeton, sir, sorry to disturb you, but the Governor sends his compliments, and wishes to see you straightaway."

A young man stood in the doorway of Templeton's office. He looked up from his papers, his eyes peering up over the top of his reading glasses to get a better look at the man.

He stopped what he was doing and pushed back his chair from his desk.

"Thank you, Mr. Reed. Did his honor give any indication as to what this meeting might be concerning?"

"No, sir. He did *not* mention it to me, however ..."

"Yes?"

"Well, sir ... he was just visited by a man from western Virginia. A wealthy land-owner I believe, but no one I had ever seen here before, nor ever heard of."

"Go on ..."

"Well, if I may be so bold as to offer an opinion, sir, I'd say this gentleman was particularly *unpleasant*, and ungentlemanly. And whatever he had to say to the Governor was somehow ... *upsetting? Unsettling* ... maybe?"

Templeton digested this bit of interesting information. He also ignored the man's amusing contradiction—referring to the visitor as a "gentleman" on the one hand and then accusing him of being "ungentlemanly" on the other.

"Very well, Mr. Reed. Lead on. We shall soon see if your guesses are correct."

When he arrived at the Governor Letcher's office, Templeton stood patiently in front of the large walnut desk behind which the Governor sat. The great man sat with his back to his visitor, gazing out the window beyond as if lost in thought. Templeton cleared his throat, and without looking, the Governor waved a hand over his shoulder and said, "Please be seated, Templeton."

Templeton gratefully lowered his bulk into a padded leather chair on the opposite side of the Governor's desk. After a few moments, the Governor swung back around, and locked eyes with him. They'd worked together for more than a year now. And though well used to dealing with politicians and government officials, Templeton still found the intensity of the Governor's gaze intimidating.

"Templeton, I was just visited by a most unpleasant gentleman. His name was Walters, *Elijah* Walters from Greenbrier County over in western Virginia. Have you heard of him?"

"No, sir. Can't say I have," Templeton answered after a few moments of searching his vast memory. "It seems to me there *was* a *Percival* Walters, who was a wealthy landowner in those parts, at one time."

"Yes, that was the father. I met him once, and he was also a disagreeable sort. Our old friend, the late Jacob Chambers had some sort of long-standing feud with him, which is probably where you heard the name."

"Ah … I'm sure you have the right of it, sir."

"Anyway, the son has, for reasons of his own, seen fit to pay me a visit, and it would appear the Chambers–Walters feud has been inherited by the sons. At least that's how it appears to me after listening to Mr. *Elijah* Walters."

"Oh? What exactly did he have to say about the younger Chambers, if you don't mind my asking?"

"Not at all, Templeton. That's why I asked you here; to tell you what he said, and to ask your opinion on it."

"As always, I am entirely at your service, sir."

243

"Yes, yes. I know full-well you are mostly at your *own* service, Templeton. But, be that as it may, I respect your deep knowledge of Virginia's affairs, and appreciate your opinions."

Templeton nodded his head in acknowledgement but didn't see fit to disagree with the Governor's statement.

"Anyway, as I was saying, Mr. Walters is a thoroughly unpleasant fellow—arrogant, unfriendly, and disinterested in other people's opinions, as far as I can tell. He also never smiles, talks in a slow, monotone manner, and rarely makes eye contact. He entirely ignores the administrative helpers, as if they don't exist at all, or at best are a distracting nuisance."

"Anything else, sir?"

"Yes, on top of all that, he dresses in a slovenly manner, and smells bad!"

Templeton raised an eyebrow at this last statement, it being well beyond the Governor's typical rant about those he disliked. But he said nothing, knowing the Governor would soon come to the heart of the matter.

"But putting personal feelings aside, he had some *unsettling* things to say about our young Mr. Chambers."

"Oh, how so?"

"Well, it seems Chambers has been going about meeting his neighbors and asking their opinions on various topics in his official capacity as their new state senator."

"That seems perfectly reasonable and appropriate, sir."

"Yes, of course it is. But according to Walters, Chambers is spouting *abolitionist* ideas! Saying slavery is an abomination and ought to be abolished, and whatnot!"

"Walters said *that*? Oh, sir, I doubt very much it's true. Why, Mr. *Jacob* Chambers was a true Southern gentleman, as you well know. As was his father before him, I understand. Their estate has become quite extensive and hugely wealthy on the backs of slave labor, and is still highly dependent upon the peculiar institution for its continued profitability. And from all accounts Mr. *Nathan* Chambers is a gentleman of highest repute, excellent education, and great intelligence. Surely, he would be well-aware of the economic disaster abolition would mean to his very own estates!

I've no doubt your very disagreeable Mr. Walters is simply trying to slander the man, on account of their long-standing family feud."

"I had concluded the same, but I wanted to hear your opinion on it, since you were the one who met with young Chambers in person. Good … good! That is reassuring. Not that I care a whit about slavery, per se, but I as you know, I simply detest radicals, and legislators with strong, personal agendas. And if it were true, the Slave Power would be livid, and I'd not soon hear the end of it."

"Yes, sir. I know when Jacob Chambers passed you would have preferred to replace him with someone more … *moderate* in his leanings, but the Slave Power …"

"Yes, they were most *forceful* in their insistence he be replaced with one of their own—especially my predecessor, that detestable Henry Wise, *damn him!* Acts like he still runs this state; that he still sits in this chair and not me!"

"Yes, your honor. It is most … *inappropriate* of him. But unfortunately, the Slave Power legislators still take their lead from the man, despite him no longer holding any public office."

"Well, as long as Chambers isn't some kind of radical, I'd not be displeased if he turned out to be less than solidly in the Slave Power camp. After all, they agreed with his selection when we suggested it, so if he turns out to be something other than what we all expected, they can hardly blame me.

"Anyway, we'll write all this 'abolition' talk off to a vindictive neighbor. And once Mr. Chambers arrives for the legislative session, we shall take him under our wing, and all will be well."

The Governor leaned back in his chair, now looking more at ease.

"I agree, your honor. Will that be all, sir?"

"Yes, yes. That will be all Templeton. Thank you for coming to see me so promptly."

"Think nothing of it, sir. It is my pleasure to serve."

As he stepped toward the door, the Governor said, "Oh, one more thing, Templeton."

He paused and turned. "Yes, sir?"

"Did you happen to *ask* Mr. Nathaniel Chambers his opinion on slavery or abolition when you were there on his farm?"

"Well, now you mention it, I don't believe the subject ever came up. But, honestly, sir ... why *would* I ask such a question when surrounded by the obvious and abundant fruits of that labor?"

"Yes ... why indeed?" the Governor answered, nodding.

But when Templeton once again turned toward the door to leave, Mr. Reed poked his head in. "Excuse me, your honor ... Mr. Templeton ... but there are two gentlemen here to see you. They aren't on your calendar, sir, but they plead for an audience."

Letcher looked at him and raised a questioning eyebrow.

"Oh, their names, yes, of course, sir. The first is one of *our* legislators, Mr. Lewis Harvie of Amelia County, and the other is a gentleman from South Carolina, a former U.S. Congressman, Mr. John McQueen."

Letcher groaned. "You may as well stay for *this*, Templeton. It will save me the trouble of telling you about it later."

"I assume from your reaction, sir, you already know what they wish to discuss? I can hazard a guess ... based on the second gentleman being from South Carolina, given the current political climate there."

"Your guess would probably be right, Templeton. They likely intend to try bending me to their way of thinking on this whole *secession* idea. I find the whole matter very unsettling. It seems to me we have enough to do handling the people's business without spending our time worrying about things that may never come to fruition."

"I couldn't agree more, sir," Templeton said. He moved to a different chair, one that strategically positioned him on the Governor's side of the desk, symbolizing his position as his honor's right-hand man.

"Show them in, if you please, Mr. Reed."

"Yes, your honor."

Templeton rose to his feet, but the Governor remained seated as the two men entered. They approached the desk and stood politely, waiting for the Governor to speak first.

"Welcome, gentlemen. Mr. Harvie, you know Mr. Templeton, of course."

The two exchanged greetings and shook hands.

"And, most welcome, Mr. McQueen, we are honored. May I introduce Mr. Templeton, my chief aide."

"An honor, Mr. McQueen."

"A pleasure to meet you, Mr. Templeton."

"Gentlemen, please be seated, and do tell us to what we owe this *unexpected* pleasure?"

Although his tone was cordial, the Governor's emphasis made it clear he did not appreciate an unscheduled interruption in his schedule, and it had better be important.

"My apologies, your honor, for coming to your office without an appointment," Harvie said. "But a group of us Delegates just met with Mr. McQueen, and we felt it was a most interesting and informative discussion. We concluded … er, *voted*, really, we would like you to hear what Mr. McQueen has to say."

Letcher raised an eyebrow at Harvie. "Highly irregular, don't you think, Mr. Harvie, conducting legislative meetings out of session, and unannounced?"

"Oh, *no*, sir! This was not any kind of *official* meeting. No, not at all, sir! Just … well, an informal gathering of … concerned citizens, who just happen to be legislators."

"Hmm … still, such a meeting might smack of following the letter of the law, while avoiding the spirit. Please do tell your … *fellow citizens* … to exercise more discretion in the future, to avoid any appearance of impropriety, Mr. Harvie."

"Yes, your honor, I will be sure to pass along your … *wise advice* … to my associates."

"So now that I have granted you an audience, you may as well tell me what it is you wish me to hear. Mr. McQueen?"

"Yes, your honor. And thank you again, most kindly for agreeing to see me on such short notice."

Letcher nodded his head in acknowledgment but said nothing.

"Ahem … well, as you are no doubt aware, sir, many people are concerned about the upcoming presidential election and its potential effect on the Southern states. To be more precise, about what might happen if this Lincoln is elected."

"Yes, of course, I've heard the talk. And what earth-shattering cataclysm do you expect Lincoln to instigate if he is elected, pray tell? He has already stated publicly, on multiple occasions from what I understand, he won't make any effort to change the legal status of slavery in the South. Or make any other drastic changes, for that matter. What are you concerned he might do, exactly?"

McQueen was quiet for a moment, meeting eyes with Letcher, as if deciding what to say next.

"Your honor, may I speak frankly and … *confidentially?*"

He glanced toward Templeton as he said this.

"Mr. Templeton's reputation is impeccable, have no fears in that regard. If I ask Mr. Templeton to keep a matter between us, I am certain no other living soul will ever hear of it."

Templeton nodded his head toward the Governor in appreciation.

"But as for myself … I am the *Governor of the Commonwealth*, gentlemen. I have sworn an oath to conduct the people's business according to the dictates of the law, and to the best of my abilities. I do not take such oaths lightly. So I can promise you nothing in that regard. You can either speak your mind, or not, but I will be the ultimate arbiter as to whether or not such discussion should remain confidential."

McQueen turned to look at Harvie, who just shrugged his shoulders, indicating it was McQueen's decision to make.

"Very well, your honor. I will trust to your judgment in this matter, believing you will recognize the importance of being able to have these kinds of … *high-level* … discussions, in confidence."

"Proceed, then, if you will."

"Yes, your honor.

"I have already spoken with many powerful men in the South—governors, senators, legislators … even some influential newspapermen, known to be trustworthy. Especially in my home state of South Carolina, of course. And they are in agreement … this presidential election is about more than just the election of one man. This *Lincoln* ultimately is of little significance … it is the fact he is a northerner … a relative unknown, from a newer, industrialized western state, Illinois … that is so troubling. As you know, from the beginning of this country, men from the agrarian South, and your state of Virginia, in particular, have been the driving force in this country. In fact, if I remember rightly, four of the first five presidents were from right here, in Virginia! Most presidents, in fact, have been from the South. And those few early presidents who weren't from the South generally won their election on their personal reputations, like the two Adams. Or based on some kind of heroic military service, as with Harrison.

"And, though admittedly our last three presidents have been northerners, only one of those was openly anti-slavery — the other two being very much pro-Southern in their political leanings. But now comes this Lincoln, and his new party called *Republican*. Clearly anti-slavery, pro-Northern, and with the strong backing of the industrial North.

"Gentlemen, those I represent see this as the beginning of the end for the political power and influence of the South in this country. The North becomes more populous, and more industrial daily, and we can foresee nothing to stop that trend. We believe we must act swiftly, while the moment in history is right, or the South will slowly fade to insignificance, and our way of life with it. It may well be this Lincoln will not try to abolish slavery or take away rights from the South. But he is just the start of an endless stream of Northern, industrial presidents who will slowly erode our position."

McQueen paused in his speech, and looked up at the Governor, gauging his reaction. Letcher had leaned back in his chair, looking up at the ceiling, as if deep in thought. When McQueen paused, he sat up, and leaned forward over his desk.

"Do I hear you correctly, sir … you and your … *associates* … don't actually believe this Lincoln will take any action against the South? That he may well be every bit as innocuous toward us, as he claims he will be? If that's the case, sir, then why have you been publicly vilifying him, making him out to be the very precursor to the proverbial apocalypse?"

249

McQueen looked over at Harvie, then glanced at Templeton before continuing. Templeton gave him a bland, non-committal look, which was not exactly encouraging for his discourse.

"Well, sir ... that is the ... *ahem* ... *confidential* ... part of this discussion. You see, those I have spoken with, who are in a position to be the most powerful proponents of the secession idea, see this as a ... *strategy* ... of sorts."

"A *strategy*? I don't understand what you mean."

"We think secession is the means to preserve the prestige of the Southern states, in a new, independent nation. With the ability to elect our own president, to pass our own laws, and run our own affairs. We can then decide on the matter of slavery. Its eventual demise, if necessary, and the ... *disposition* ... of the former slaves ... under our full control. Not having it forced down our throats by Northern abolitionists."

"Yes, I can appreciate the concept, but I'm still confused by what you're saying. If you believe Mr. Lincoln may *not* take any action against the South, then why is this 'the right moment in history,' as you say, to pursue secession? Wouldn't it be better to wait and see if Lincoln goes back on his word—proves himself deceitful and untrustworthy?"

"Ah ... now you have touched upon the heart of the matter, your honor. There is currently a great fear throughout the general populace in the South about Lincoln, and what he *might* do. We can use that fear to stir up the passions of the people ... to ensure their backing for the secession, and their absolute loyalty for the resulting new government. While the election is still being run, we can *claim* Mr. Lincoln intends to free the slaves, and to take away our 'states' rights.' You see, because we are saying this is what Mr. Lincoln *is going to do* when elected, it is impossible for anyone to prove us wrong. If we wait until Lincoln is elected, and takes office, he may prove to be competent, honest, and *God forbid*, a good, reliable president. Then all hope for secession will be lost."

"Hmm ... to be honest, gentlemen, this seems to me a most cynical strategy. What you *say* you fear, that Lincoln will harm the South when elected, is actually the *opposite* of what you really fear he will do, which is ... *nothing at all?* I really don't see how this strategy can succeed. For one thing, most Southerners own no slaves at all, and are really quite ambivalent about what happens to slavery in the long run. It's certainly not a concept they'd think important enough to break the country apart over, nor to risk a general war over.

"Nor would the abstract notion of a gradual decline in the national influence of the South give them much concern. Such a thing would have little impact on their daily lives. To be honest gentlemen, I hear much more from the people about improving roads, extending the railroads, and building more schools, than about any matters of national significance."

"We agree with you on that, sir, and believe me, there has been much discussion about how to get the common, ordinary Southerner firmly on our side. But I believe we have an answer there as well, sir. You see, we will take advantage of Mr. Lincoln's rhetoric about slavery—how it is an abomination, immoral, an outrage, and whatnot—to play on the people's baser fears and instincts. We will make them fear what Lincoln will do, not by ending slavery, but by making the negroes their equals. The common Southerner may care little about slavery per se, but the idea of negroes being made his equal ... living in the house next door, attending the same schools as his children, voting, holding public office, and—*God forbid*—marrying his daughters! These things will arouse his greatest fears and his most vehement passions. That, sir, is a thing he *will* fight for, we believe."

"Hmm ... yes, I can see how that might be more effective ...

"But to be honest, gentlemen, I find the whole concept very distasteful, and verging on deceit, hypocrisy and disingenuousness."

"Yes, that is understandable, your honor, and I can respect your feelings on the matter, believe me. But I also believe men of good conscience must sometimes do things that are ... distasteful ... in the short term, for the long-term benefit of the people they represent. To do what *must* be done, so to speak. Wouldn't you agree, sir?"

"Please don't insult my intelligence, Mr. McQueen. A man in my position is well aware of the personal trade-offs and sacrifices

251

sometimes required for the common good. I need no lecture from you, *sir*, on the subject."

"Yes, of course. My apologies for my presumptuousness, your honor."

Letcher waved his hand dismissively to show he accepted the apology.

"Gentlemen, if you'll excuse me, I have other matters requiring my attention."

"Yes, of course, your honor. Thank you for your time. And can we … count on your support when the time comes?"

"I will … take it under advisement and will give it all due thought and consideration. Good day to you, gentlemen."

After the two men had departed, Letcher shared a hard look with Templeton. He said nothing, but Templeton could tell the direction of current events troubled the Governor. And Mr. McQueen's revelations had only increased those feelings.

Finally, he shook his head and said, "Templeton, the time is coming soon, I'm afraid, when we'll be forced to choose sides on this matter."

"That very well may be, your honor, but please allow me to give it more urgent attention and thought. Never forget, sir, you are the Governor of the most important and powerful state in the South, and as such may exert the *most* influence over events. Perhaps we can come up with a strategy of our own, possibly something that can head-off this impending … *train collision?*"

"Yes … yes, *good*, Templeton! Please do give it some thought, and I will do the same. Perhaps between the two of us we can think of something … as you say, *our own* strategy."

Despite his optimistic words to Mr. Letcher, Templeton was feeling unsettled over the whole secession matter as he made his way down the corridor back toward his own office.

He also had a tiny prickling doubt about the situation with Mr. Chambers. He mulled over the details in his mind. Young Chambers had been educated in the North, served years away in the Army, never returning home until his father's death. Could it be Walters was right? Finally, he decided it was nothing but fruitless conjecture at this stage. No point losing sleep over something he could, for the time being, do nothing about. But before he closed the book on that topic, he wrote himself a note in his datebook:

Meet with Mr. Nathaniel Chambers upon his arrival in Richmond … before the Governor does!

Chapter 10. Hard Lessons

"Experience is a hard teacher
because she gives the test first,
the lesson afterwards."
– Vernon Sanders Law

Friday June 29, 1860 – Greenbrier County, Virginia:

The others who'd lived their whole lives at Mountain Meadows hadn't yet grasped the true joy of a Sunday morning's Sabbath, but George did! He'd been at other farms that let slaves off work on the Sabbath. And though the day off was a great pleasure to be sure, the real gift it afforded was … *Saturday night!* The gift of not having to hear the overseer's horn, come dawn. This meant there was no need to be in bed early the night before. And from George's point of view, having that Saturday night to experience some of life's pleasure made all the difference — the difference between being a human being, and being just another work animal, like a horse, or a mule.

But now, he had to convince the others. He'd spent the evening the previous night turning Babs to his way of thinking, and he was making the rounds to the other cabins to convince more people. It was Friday after dinner, so he had little time to get around before everyone would be asleep.

"Lookie, here … we ain't gotta be up before first light. So we can have us some fun, like we all used to have over at the other farms where I been. The folks'd slip off into the woods of a Saturday night, and light a big ol' fire, then dance, and sing, and laugh, like they's no tomorrow! Come on now … we ain't never done nothing of the like here-abouts. And now Master's given us the Sabbath … well, it's our chance to live life a little."

"But Master won't like it. Don't matter what he says in them fancy Sabbath talks, when it come right down to it he ain't gonna like us black men running around in the woods, makin' music and whatnot! And what if them overseers catches us? They's gonna be

254

powerful angry … and maybe they makes us work on the Sabbath after all. They'll give us a whipping for sure if they catches us …" and on and on, went the naysayers.

"Come on, now … Master said they'd be no more beatings, didn't you hear? And I, for one, believes him. And … he never said we couldn't go out and have fun the night before the Sabbath, did he? Come on now … are y'all mules? Are y'all cattle? Or are y'all actual, human *people?* Come on! Whatcha gonna do, just work 'til y'all die, and never enjoy nothing of life? Lookie here what I done made already … you others can make something of your own too."

He pulled something out of an old burlap bag he'd brought with him. It was half of an old discarded whiskey barrel; he'd cleaned it up and stretched an animal hide across until it had dried nice and tight. Holding the homemade drum in front of him, he sat cross-legged on the floor of the cabin and proceeded to pound out a rhythm with his hands. The rhythm was from a song he remembered from his days at the last farm. He'd enjoyed playing the drum back then and had gotten pretty good at it. He began singing in a clear deep bass voice. The song had no particular words … George just made them up according to whatever he was thinking about at the time.

> Master says he free us,
> But I don't know,
> 'Cause Master need old fire stoked,
> And mebbe it gonna snow …

George had a quick, clever mind for such rhymes, and could easily come up with one after another without missing a beat. Soon the others were smiling, laughing, and clapping to the rhythm of the drum.

Then one of the other men, jumped in with his own verse …

> Master gives the Sabbath day,
> And says the darkies get to play,
> But next day come, as sure as rain,
> And then ol' Sickles, bring the pain …

When George finished playing, all agreed to recruit others and meet at the back of the cabins the next night.

Before he left, George met eyes with the other men.

"Maybe Master will free us … and maybe he won't—only God knows for sure. But tomorrow we starts being humans around this farm … no longer beasts!"

The others nodded at him. And then he turned and left, headed for another cabin where some other young folk stayed.

ᏦᏌᎣᏣᏋᏦᏌᎣᏣᏋᏦᏌᎣᏣᏋ

The following evening Nathan, Tom, and William were in the upstairs office. They were going over ideas Tom and William had come up with for boosting profits, including possibly harvesting timber, now that the train came all the way to Covington. They might buy a small steam engine and a circular saw and have their own production site right here on the farm. Nathan's granddaddy had put together a crude, mule-powered lumber mill way back when he built the house. But he'd only used it to produce enough lumber for his own needs. It'd been too difficult and costly to ship the lumber to market. But now, with the railroad …

There was also mining; several caves up the hillsides on the east side of the property offered the possibility of coal, lime, saltpeter, and whatever else they might find. And without requiring extensive mine works.

They were discussing the mining possibilities when Jeb, who was a cook, poked his head in the door.

"Excuse me, Captain, sir. But Mr. Sickles is downstairs and asks you to come speak with him. He says to tell you it's an important matter that can't wait. And …well … I'm only passing on what he says, sir …"

"Yes …?"

"Well, Mr. Sickles says, '*And tell the Master to bring along his pistol, as there may be trouble,*' his words, not *mine*, Captain, sir."

"*Oh* … I see. Tom, William, will you join me? Let's stop off at my room and I'll just grab that small Colt, in case Mr. Sickles is correct in his concern."

"Of course, sir. Shall I grab a weapon as well?" Tom asked.

"Hmm … I doubt that'll be necessary. If it were all that serious, I'm sure Sickles would've come upstairs himself, etiquette be damned!"

"Yes … I'm sure you're right, sir," Tom said, and William nodded agreement.

After stopping off at Nathan's room long enough for him to pocket the small Colt revolver, unloaded, they headed down the back stairs, following Jeb.

When they reached the back door, they found Sickles waiting for them.

"Mr. Sickles. What seems to be the trouble?"

"Sorry to disturb you, sir, so late on a Saturday night and all. But one of the men thought he heard noises, and saw strange lights out in the east woods, back toward the hills. So he went to investigate. And … well, it seems several slaves have taken it upon themselves to light a fire and hold some kind of gathering. Well, I can tell you, sir, nothing of the kind has ever happened here before. Your Daddy … uh, I mean, the old master, he … well, anyway, it ain't never happened before. Of course, we know all 'bout that Nat Turner uprising, and whatnot. Anyway … I just thought you should know and might want to come with me as we … er … *investigate* the matter."

"Very well, let's go see what all the noise is about, shall we? Please, lead the way, Mr. Sickles."

"Yes, Captain."

Dan, the man who'd discovered the gathering in the woods, joined them when they came out onto the veranda. He led them off through the dark to the edge of the lawn, then into the woods on the east side. There was a trail of sorts, probably made by deer coming to graze on the grass or raid the vegetable garden. The moon was at half full, giving off just enough light to keep the men from straying from each other.

At first, they could hear nothing beyond the sound of their own movement. But soon they heard voices, talking, and singing mixed with a pounding noise like a drum. Then they began seeing shafts of a bright, orange light ahead through the trees.

They came to a stop, and Sickles put a finger to his mouth to signal they should be quiet. He motioned the Captain to come forward.

When Nathan looked out, he saw a small clearing in the forest—a meadow of grass and small bushes. In the middle of this open space a good-sized fire was burning, putting out little smoke, and only the occasional spark.

But it was not the fire that captured his attention. Seated on the ground, with his back toward Nathan, was a large, black man beating on a drum with his hands. A woman sat next to him, leaning her head on his shoulder. Two other men played musical instruments of a sort. One appeared to be the jawbone of an animal—mule, or cow likely—and the man was making a very pleasant rasping sound by running a stick across the row of teeth. A third man was clacking together what looked like two hollowed-out sticks, making an interesting echoing sound.

Between these musicians and the fire, a dozen or more people danced, and sang. The majority were men, but four women danced among them. It was a performance such as Nathan had never seen before, being raised on the formal, traditional European-style dances. But what it lacked in structure and synchronization, it made up for in originality, energy, and athleticism! They were jumping and twirling, more than stepping. The dance moves appeared improvised, the song much the same. A singer would sing out a humorous verse, seemingly made up on the spot, and the others would echo it back, accompanied by grins and laughter.

> The Captain tell us Moses say,
> They be no work on Sabbath day,
> So Big George, he up and say,
> Is Saturday night, so men should play!

And then …

> All week we digs, and works the hoe,
> But come a Saturday we works no mo'e,
> And dance and sing, out on the floor,

'Round hot ol' fire 'til feet are sore!

And several other verses of a similar nature.

Nathan waited until there was a break between songs, then stepped out into the clearing and strode up to the fire, followed by Tom, William, Sickles, and Dan.

Everything went quiet, and all stood still where they were. The only sound now was from the crackling fire.

Nathan reached into his jacket pocket and pulled out a cigar, lit it, and blew a puff of smoke high into the air.

The large man who'd been playing the drum stood up, and walked over to the Captain, standing in front of him. Nathan recognized him as George—"Big George" he'd heard the other slaves call him, and for good reason; he was a very large, strong-looking man, as tall as Nathan but much heavier. George looked him in the eye, rather than down at his feet as he'd expected. That pleased him.

"Master Captain … this here … well, this is all *my* doing … on account of the places I lived before. You see, since we all didn't have to be up 'fore dawn of the Sabbath day, we could stay up a tad the night before. And have a bit of fun. Well, sir, when I thought on having the day off of work, it just seemed … natural-like to play some music, and dance; meanin' no harm, sir. So if they's any punishment, I begs it to be all on my own back, and none on these others."

He had a serious look, and though he spoke bravely, Nathan knew a look of fear in a man's eyes when he saw it.

But he didn't immediately answer George. Instead he tilted his head back toward the men behind him, "Mr. Sickles … did the old master have a rule against singing and dancing of a Saturday night?"

"Well, no sir, but—"

"And did he have a rule about lighting fires for warmth and … entertainment?"

"No sir, not that I can recall, but—"

"And … did he have a rule about what time a person had to be asleep in bed by?"

"No, Captain, I don't reckon he ever needed such a rule before. But ... he *did* have a rule again' sneaking out of the slave quarters at night without proper permission!"

"Oh ... *I see.*"

Nathan looked back at George, who still met his eyes, but now seemed even more concerned. Then Nathan grinned and George looked surprised.

Then Nathan turned to William, caught his eye, and winked. "William, you're our expert musician ... tell me, what is your opinion on the performance we just witnessed?"

"Well, sir ... they've an excellent percussion section, that's certain. And some fine baritone voices, though entirely lacking in tenors, and light on sopranos, I find. They're also devoid of strings, or any other melodic instruments. Though likely I might provide ... *some assistance* ... in that regard."

"Yes, I'm sure you could. Anything else?"

"Hmm ... well, I'd say what the music, lyrics, and dance lack in proper form and structure, is more than made up for by creativity, unadulterated enthusiasm, and unbridled energy!"

"Well said, and I agree."

He looked back at Sickles, who returned a puzzled look. "Well, Mr. Sickles ... I reckon I can easily resolve the rule-breaking issue by going ahead and granting permission for this gathering. Tonight, and *every* Saturday night from now on. But ... George ..."

"Yes, Captain, sir?"

"These woods get pretty dry this time of year ... best y'all be moving your fire over by the lawn and away from the trees for next Saturday. Besides which, it'll provide more room for all the others. I shall look 'round in the next day or two and pick out a suitable spot."

He stuck the cigar back in his mouth, and grinned broadly at George, who returned the Captain's smile with a small, hesitant one of his own.

"Uh ... thank you ... thank you, sir. That's most decently kind of you, Captain, sir," George said, sounding unsure he was comprehending what he'd just heard.

"No, no, not at all, George. Y'all work hard all week and deserve to have a bit of fun. Thank *you* for reminding me. That was well done … yes … well done, indeed, George."

He turned around and looked at the men who'd come with him. Tom and William were grinning at him, but Sickles had a sour expression. Dan looked confused. He, like George, seemed unable to comprehend what had just happened.

"Gentlemen, I believe everything is in good order here, so we may as well return to our own business. Dan, be so kind as to lead us back to the house, if you please?"

"Yes, Captain, sir."

⁘⁙⁘⁙⁘⁙⁘⁙

On Sunday, Nathan and his men once again accompanied Miss Abbey to church. This time, Sickles and the other farmhands who'd stayed behind the previous week came with them, trading places with three others.

Based on what Margaret had told them, it didn't surprise him to see Walters still absent. She'd expected him to arrive early to midweek. He couldn't help but think of Margaret and wonder how she was getting along.

Before she'd left Mountain Meadows to return to Walters Farm, she'd said she intended to take full advantage of her newfound leverage over the servants—to enjoy the freedom afforded her while Walters was still away in Richmond, and any time after that when Walters was away from the house.

This week the preacher's sermon was relatively innocuous, and not specifically directed at Nathan personally, for which he was grateful.

The other members of the congregation greeted him warmly again as he made his way out the door. And, as he'd expected, he amazed them by recalling each person's name, down to the smallest tyke. Miss Abbey smiled knowingly.

Then, once again, Nathan stood face to face with Reverend Blackburn.

"Good morning, Mr. Chambers. Did you find today's sermon more to your liking?"

"I liked it just fine, Reverend. And it seemed a bit more … *traditional* … than last week's."

The preacher just smiled and nodded.

ℬℰℭℭℬℰℰℭℭℬℰℭℭ

The next day, Nathan was riding out beyond the far edge of the target practice field. It was an unused section of the farm — rolling ground covered with tight thickets of small trees and scrub brush, interspersed with more open areas of waist-high grass. He couldn't remember much about this northwest corner of the property from his childhood. Probably because there was nothing there. At least nothing of interest to a young boy — no ponds or streams, no barns or other outbuildings, no crops. He had a mind to explore it today, to see if it might have some future use for agriculture. He was thinking ahead to granting the freed men plots of land for their own, and he wanted to make a plan for where that might be.

He had ridden today, rather than walking, as had been his regular habit, for two reasons. One, he knew from an earlier quick look this area had tall grass and a rolling landscape, so he would get a better picture from higher up. And also, his mare, Millie, whom he had brought with him from Texas, needed exercise, as she hadn't been ridden since the meeting at the courthouse. She was just over three years old but had proven her worth on many occasions. So when it had come time to leave for Virginia, he exercised his officer's privilege and purchased her from the Army. She was high-spirited, but not high-strung, and had proven herself sure-footed on all different kinds of rough terrain. She did not shy from loud noises, snakes, dogs, or other distractions. And he'd trained her to take care of her master, even to the point of lashing out with hooves and teeth when necessary. She was an animal you could take into battle and not find her wanting in any regard.

Of course, Harry the Dog followed, a constant shadow — weaving in and out of the light and shade like a restless ghost, always following, but never coming too close. Nathan was looking back toward the main farm when he noticed something

262

unusual. The dog was trotting along casually, then stopped mid-stride, perked up his ears, and looked back toward the distant house. Curious, Nathan turned Millie, and trotted back to where Harry stood, stopping just a few feet away. The great hound stood motionless, ears pricked up, tilting his head from side to side as if listening to something in the distance. Nathan held Millie still and listened as well. Finally, he heard it; a distant, high pitched noise that sounded like … like a woman's voice calling … for him …

"Captain! Mr. Chambers, sir! Are you out there?"

The voice sounded desperate, frantic. Nathan kicked Millie into motion, and she instantly responded with a satisfying lurch forward. She was fleet of foot, and they quickly crested a rise, with a view of the whole target practice field, the pond, and house looming behind. Across the field he could see a figure running toward him. A slave woman—heavy of build, but running as fast as she could—yelling, "Captain, sir! Oh, Captain! Please come …"

He was soon pulling Millie up, just short of the woman, who halted, leaning over, hands on knees, panting.

"What is it? What has happened? Betsy … isn't it?" he asked, her face causing the name to come into his mind.

"Yes, Master Captain, sir. Betsy, that's right sir!" she gasped, still trying to catch her breath.

"Well, what is it? What's the matter?" he prodded again.

"Sir … did you mean it when you said they'd be no more beatings?" she got out between gasps.

"Of course, I meant it, every word!" he felt a sinking feeling something had gone terribly wrong back at the farm while he was out riding.

"Well then, sir … you'd best get over to the cabins. They's fixing to give that girl Rosa a beatin' for sure …"

He didn't wait to hear the rest but gave Millie another kick, this time more urgent, and she responded in kind. If she'd been fleet before, now she fairly flew. She soon crossed the target practice field, and he briefly debated whether to take the shorter route across the fields. But he decided the crops might slow the horse down as she beat a path through them. So he took the slightly longer route of skirting the pond, rounding the house, and heading up the drive toward the cabins.

As he came up the road, he could see the cabins and a group of people gathered in front, next to a large walnut tree. As he got closer, he took in the whole scene: a figure with hands bound above her head, hung on a hook embedded in the tree. The sweat on her bare back gleamed in the sun but her smooth brown skin was not yet marked by the large, braided leather bullwhip Sickles held in his right hand where he stood about ten feet behind her. The slaves, mostly women and children, gathered round to watch at a distance, their expressions unreadable. Billy Creek was there as well, sitting cross-legged on top of the sturdy wooden table under an oak on the opposite side of the drive.

Sickles was not, however, focused on the bound girl. Instead, he faced off with Jim Wiggins, who stood only a few feet away. The men shared hard looks, a building storm of deadly violence on the verge of being unleashed.

When Nathan pulled up and dismounted, he could hear Jim shouting.

"I *said* … drop the whip Sickles, or I swear by God, I'll beat you like the stinking, poxy, whore's son you are!"

Jim rested his right hand on the handle of his belt knife but had not yet pulled it out.

As far as Nathan knew, Jim wasn't afraid of anybody or anything, so the whip in Sickles hand was little deterrent.

But Sickles was also fired up and not backing down. "You'll not tell me my business, soldier boy! Get away, or I'll mark your hide as well. This ain't none of your concern!"

"Well, it is *my* concern!" Nathan growled, as he stepped forward toward the two men. "Explain yourself, Sickles!"

At the sound of Nathan's voice, Sickles seemed to deflate. Facing down the ex-soldiers, whom he disliked and distrusted, came easily to him, and only stoked his fires. But standing up to the Master was a whole different thing.

"Sorry, sir …" he stammered, letting the whip slip from his hand and settle to the ground. "I … I guess I got caught up in the heat of the moment. You know, old habits, and all. Anyway, the little bitch … uh, the young woman was intentionally disobeying my instructions, and when I tried to correct her … nicely, and polite-like, that is … she was … disrespectful, willful, and contrary-like, if you get my meaning, sir. Well, it didn't sit too well with me, sir, not well at all. And … I reckon I must've forgot your earlier instructions about the beat … uh, the disciplinary actions, sir." Sickles tone had turned whiney and deprecating.

Jim scowled at him, a look of disgust on his face. He glanced over at Nathan then turned his head to the side and spat on the ground. He pivoted and marched off through the cabins.

Just then Stan and William came trotting up to see what was happening. They'd been up on a roof fixing wooden shakes. Sergeant Jim had gone to fetch more boards and nails. But then they saw him trotting back across the camp with a young black woman trailing along behind. They knew something was up, but it must not be serious enough for Sergeant Jim to call for their help, which he could have easily done. Still, their curiosity was up, so they clambered down the ladder and followed along.

As they came to a stop, still catching their breath, Nathan turned and addressed them. "Stan, William. Please escort Mr. Sickles to the Big House and there meet with Mr. Clark. Tell him Mr. Sickles is to be cashiered, effective immediately."

"Cashiered?" Sickles stammered. "You're … you're turning me out? After all these years of service, over … over *one* slave?" He looked shocked, and his face suddenly turned pale.

"I was very clear and explicit in my instructions, Mr. Sickles. I am a military man, and as such I expect strict discipline and obedience from my men. Be happy we aren't in the military, Mr. Sickles. The Army is infamous for coming up with creative and *uncomfortable* punishments for willful disobedience. But, unfortunately, for my wishes, this isn't the Army. My only recourse is to end your employment. So that's what I'm doing."

He seemed calm, but his voice was stern. His face had turned a red color, and there was an underlying tone of anger, of violence contained by force of will. It was clear to Sickles any argument or further appeal would only make matters worse.

"Well, your Daddy would never've approved such a thing …" was all he said. He turned toward the house, Stan's large hand gripping his upper arm.

"I am *not* my father."

Sickles departed, Stan leading the way, and William bringing up the rear, as if they were escorting a dangerous prisoner.

Nathan stepped over to the tree and knelt down in front of the young woman. Her hands were tied together with a leather strap which was looped over an old, rusty iron hook embedded in the tree. Although her arms were stretched above her head, she could kneel on the grass. She was bare to the waist, the remains of her torn dress hanging to the ground. Her head was slumped forward, and she was sobbing great heaving sobs.

Nathan leaned his head in close to her and said softly, "Rosa, do you know who I am?"

Between sobs she whispered, "Yes, Master," and she looked up at him. Tears streamed down her face.

Then she gasped as a large knife flashed in front of her eyes. For an instant, she feared the Captain would finish what Sickles had started, using his great knife. But just as quickly she found her wrists free, and she was slumping to the ground. The knife had sliced through the thick leather thongs as easily as if they'd been made of twine.

The Captain looked over at the people gathered round, "Quickly, bring something to cover her."

A moment later someone handed him a rough-spun blanket, and he wrapped it around her shoulders, instructing her to hold it together in front.

But he did not immediately help her to her feet, nor send her away to her cabin.

He needed to know *exactly* what had happened, and he'd never have the true story from Sickles. So he meant to get the truth from the girl and was prepared to be stern if necessary. He feared there might be truth in what Sickles had said, feared his changes in the treatment of the slaves, the prospect of their eventual freedom, the teachings, all might have had an unintended negative effect. He had staked everything on a belief: men treated with understanding, kindness, and respect would respond in kind. But he was not naïve; he'd spent years dealing with hardened killers and criminals, men who respected only brute force and punishment. Men who'd stab you as soon as you turned your back, no matter how much kindness you'd shown them. He had a sinking feeling the slaves might stop taking directions, refuse to work or to cooperate with his plans since the threat of severe punishment had been taken away. He didn't *want* to believe it, but he had to admit it was a possibility. He *had* to know.

So instead of sending her away, he knelt in front of her. Leaning his head in close to hers he said, "Rosa, are you harmed?" He knew she'd not been whipped, thanks to Jim's timely intervention. But she *had* been roughly handled, and the thongs around her wrists could not have been comfortable.

"No, Master," she whispered again, the sobs now calming and becoming long sniffles.

"I'm happy to hear it … and no harm *will* come to you, Rosa. But I want you to calm yourself and tell me *the truth* about everything that happened. I need to know why you were tied to this tree. Do you understand me?"

His voice was calm, but firm and commanding, conceding no possibility for disagreement.

"Yes, Master," she whispered again.

"Good, Rosa. Now, listen to me, and do as I say … close your eyes and take three deep breaths—as deep as you can. Think only of breathing in, and then out again. In and out."

She took a deep breath, holding it for a moment, and then exhaling again. The air came out in a rush, like a heavy sigh.

Nathan waited for her to take two more deep breaths. By the time she'd finished, the sobs had ceased, and only a slight sniffle remained.

"Good. Now, open your eyes, and look at me, Rosa. The same as you did on the day we first met, and you told me your name."

❧❧❧❧❧❧❧❧❧

Rosa opened her eyes and looked at the face in front of hers. It was a stern face, with dark intense eyes that could not be denied.

And yet, she felt a kindness and compassion in the voice. It was an entirely overwhelming experience such as she'd never imagined. Made the more so by the sudden, inexplicable change from being roughly man-handled, tied to a tree, and threatened with a whipping. Now, with no time in-between, she found herself ... swimming ... sinking ... into *those* eyes. The eyes of ... who, or *what?*

"Rosa ... Rosa, do you hear me?" the voice came insistently. She realized he'd been speaking, and she hadn't been responding, lost in a deep, dark place.

"Yes, Mast ... Captain." This time she remembered his preferred title.

"Rosa, I need you to tell me exactly what happened today. Everything Mr. Sickles said and did, and everything *you* said and did. I want the *truth*, Rosa. The *exact truth*. Do you understand me?"

He continued to speak in the hard, insistent voice that would brook no argument.

"Yes, Captain. It started this morning when I went to fetch wood from the woodshed for the cooking fire ..." she began. And in a calm, almost dreamy voice, she told him her story. To those watching it was a strange sight. The girl described every detail matter-of-factly, devoid of all emotion, as if she were reciting something she'd read in a book.

She described how she'd gone into the woodshed to gather an armload of wood, but when she turned toward the door, Mr. Sickles was standing in the entrance. At first, she couldn't tell who it was because the light behind made him appear as a dark silhouette in the doorway of the darkened shed. He told her to set the wood down; he needed her to do something before she returned to the cooking. She complied obediently, placing the wood on the floor in a neat pile. But instead of instructing her on other duties, he approached her and gripped her hard by the upper arms, forcing her backward, and down. "I've been watching you, and you ain't no longer a child. It's time you became a woman," and he shoved her the rest of the way down to the floor of the shed.

Although she was still young and innocent, she understood what grown men and women did in bed together at night. In the cabins, there was little or no privacy; and though the adults tried to be discreet, by the time they were teenaged, the young people knew all about such things.

And so, she realized what Mr. Sickles intended to do to her, and the thought gave her a sudden shock and revulsion spurring her into action. As he was unbuckling his belt, she seized a piece of firewood and hurled it at his head. She leapt from the floor, climbed over the woodpile and ran out the door.

But Sickles had reacted quickly, throwing his hands up in time to prevent the firewood from hitting him in the face, though it likely gave him a painful bruise on his arms. With a curse he came after her, and she'd not made it ten steps from the shed when he caught her and shoved her hard to the ground. He was much bigger than her, and immeasurably stronger. Her struggles met with firm, unbreakable resistance. This time there would be no escape.

She remembered all the beautiful dreams for the future she'd been thinking—thoughts she'd had ever since the Captain had come to the farm and had changed everything with his beautiful words and his kind voice. And now it all seemed a lie; nothing had *really* changed. They were still slaves, and the white masters still owned them, and could do with them as they wished. And … and … suddenly the pain of the lost dream and the horror of what was happening welled up in her and … she screamed. She screamed again, and again.

"Shut up, you ungrateful bitch!" Sickles growled and slapped her hard across the face. But she didn't care; it occurred to her this was the one thing he did *not* want her to do. So it was now the thing she wanted to do *most!* She screamed again, as loudly as she could.

She braced herself for the blow she knew would come. But instead he jerked her up off the ground. Sickles now looked around at the black faces appearing in cabin windows, and in the lanes between the buildings. He cursed again, and held her wrists tightly together with one hand, pulling a leather strap from his

269

pocket with the other. The strap already had a loop in it, as if made for the purpose. He quickly slipped it around her wrists and pulled it tight. She gasped with the pain, but he looped it around a few more times before tying it off.

Then he spoke in a loud, projecting voice, as if addressing the larger audience watching, "You have left me no choice. I will teach you what happens to those disobedient and disrespectful of their betters!"

Sickles pulled her along by her bound wrists, dragging her to a nearby tool shed. He opened the door and entered, pulling her staggering in behind him. For a moment, she thought he would finish what he'd started in the woodshed. But he reached up and took something down from a hook. Unreasoning fear gripped her when she saw what it was, and she nearly blacked out. In his hand he now gripped the thick, braided, leather coils of a bull whip!

She knew all her resistance and struggling had only made her situation worse. It was a hard lesson. Instead of Sickles "making a woman of her," which would've been demeaning, disgusting, and likely painful, he would beat her with the whip. Strong men beaten with the bull whip might take weeks to recover. Some died. Those who survived were scarred for life, both physically and mentally; they were never the same after.

And she wasn't a big, strong man, only a slight young woman. She shook with panic, felt wobbly in the legs, and sick to her stomach. She could barely walk and thought she might faint. So Sickles half dragged her to the tree, there he looped the bound wrists over the hook, and let her sink to the ground. She bowed her head, her thoughts swimming with fear of the pain about to come—pain unthinkable and unbearable, such as she had never experienced. She knew she would die; she wasn't strong enough to bear it.

When he ripped open her dress to expose her back, she barely noticed. She sobbed uncontrollably, and her mind drifted far away. Then she became vaguely aware of voices ... Sickles voice was there, but also *another* man ... a loud, angry voice yelling, cursing ... but not at her. This voice was cursing at Sickles. And Sickles was cursing back.

"… and then you were here talking with me, Captain," she concluded, still gazing into his eyes as she'd done during her whole recitation.

It was then she noticed something strange about the eyes she'd been staring into. They were different from before, somehow … more liquid, watery even. She realized the Captain had tears welling up in his eyes. This was almost as shocking as anything else she'd experienced. Why would the Master be crying? His kindly but stern face now was turning red and looked angry. Very angry …

The Captain was suddenly up and moving away from her. He spoke to the people gathered round, "You women get her up and take her to her cabin. Then put her into bed."

Several women came forward. Soon she found herself in their warm embrace, soothing voices cooing in her ears, "You did good, child. You gonna be just fine, now. All's okay now, poor little dear …" and on, and on.

But as they got her to her feet, and started bundling her off to her cabin, the Captain's voice commanded, "No, stop! Wait. Keep her here a moment longer."

She turned toward his voice and saw him reach down and scoop up the whip from where Sickles had dropped it. She no longer feared he would use it on her, but she was curious. What was he going to do with it?

He strode purposefully across the drive toward the big wooden table on the other side. For the first time, she noticed the Indian sitting atop it, cross-legged, as if watching a show. As the Captain approached the table, he made a sweeping motion at the Indian, who immediately jumped to his feet and clambered off. The Captain walked around to the far side of the table. He turned to face the people standing on this side of the road, clutching the whip in his left hand. Rosa saw he still held the great knife in the other. He started doing something on the table, but she couldn't tell what. She realized he was spreading the whip out on the tabletop.

When he finished, he looked up. She could see his face was a dark storm, red with anger. "Let there be no doubt. There will be *NO MORE BEATINGS* on my farm! Now or ever!"

He raised the knife above his head and brought it down with great force on the table. It made a great *thunk* sound, and the whip neatly parted in two. But he was not finished; he struck the table over and over. Pieces of the whip flipped up in the air with each stroke.

Then he paused, and Rosa could see him breathing heavily. He turned and threw the knife at the nearby oak tree, where it stuck hard, embedding several inches into the trunk. Then he scooped up an armful of the leather whip pieces from the table and strode over to the edge of the cotton field. He tossed the pieces into the wind, as far as he could. No one moved during this whole display, and not a word was spoken.

He walked back across the road. Rosa could see his face was now calm, his anger apparently spent. "There will be no more beatings," he said calmly, and turned to retrieve his horse, who was cropping grass a short distance away.

It occurred to Rosa this must be what it was like in one of those old Bible stories; like when Christ cleared the moneylenders from the temple in his wrath. Though the Captain was wrathful, she no longer feared him, knowing his anger was righteous and had been spent on her behalf.

☙❧☙☙❧☙❧☙☙❧☙❧☙☙❧

Nathan decided he'd best *not* see Sickles again. He still didn't entirely trust himself under these circumstances—visions of Moat Kangly, a neat bullet hole through the center of his forehead, and Gold-tooth, pinned to the wall with a Bowie knife, flashed through his mind. So he decided he'd only briefly stop in at the house to let Tom know what had happened, and put him in charge, before returning to his earlier explorations with Millie. Better to let Tom deal with Sickles, he decided.

As he walked over to retrieve Millie, he was reminded of how much he appreciated her; she was an exceptional war horse he'd spent years training. When he'd arrived at the scene of the whipping, he'd leapt from the saddle and strode forward, without a backward glance or second thought about the horse. But he'd not needed to tie her; he'd trained her to stop where she was and watch her master to see if he needed her. If anyone had paid attention to the horse during the incident, they'd have seen her standing patiently, watching the Captain. She'd have intervened if needed, with teeth and hooves; her feisty temperament was well-suited to it. But this time, she'd decided there was no immediate threat to her master. So she'd taken the opportunity to crop the lush green grass at the roadside, never straying from sight.

When he got back in the saddle, Billy came up and handed him the knife, handle first. "Tree will most likely live," Billy said, grinning.

"Thanks," Nathan said, returning the smile, and slipping the knife back into the sheath on his belt. Billy's dry sense of humor often caught him a little off guard.

"Billy, please go find the other soldiers, and tell them what happened. Have them round up all the original farmhands and inform them of Sickles' departure. Then bring them to the house and have each speak with Tom. Tom will decide who should stay and who should go."

"Yes, Captain."

Nathan knew it was properly his own job to decide about the farmhands. But right now he needed time alone to think and calm down. Besides, Tom would know exactly how to handle it.

But as Billy turned to go carry out his orders, a question occurred to Nathan. "Billy, when I arrived you were sitting on the table watching. Why?"

Billy shrugged and said, "I'm Tonkawa. We love a good fight. Was figuring to see one until you came and spoiled the fun."

Nathan shook his head in amusement. "And what would you have done if Sergeant Jim had *lost* the fight?"

Billy tilted his head and paused for a moment. "Don't know … never seen Sergeant Jim lose a fight before. Didn't reckon the farm boy would be the first."

Nathan laughed. Billy's unique view of the world was helping to clear away the lingering effects of his anger.

"Captain ... you really shouldn't have stopped the fun, you know."

"Why is that, Billy? You think I should've let Sickles whip the girl?"

"Ha!" Billy laughed his short, intense laugh—more like a snort than a musical laugh. "No chance of that with Sergeant Jim standing there! No, I was thinking it would've been a good lesson for that farm boy—what an iron-hard beating *feels* like. Maybe then he wouldn't be so ready to deal one out. Sergeant Jim makes a good teacher in that school. Maybe then you wouldn't have murdered a perfectly good whip!"

Billy laughed again.

"Billy ... there's much wisdom in you," Nathan said with new appreciation of his companion. "And, in case I haven't said it before, I will say it now ... I am *very* happy you're here."

Billy smiled, and said, "Thank you, Captain. This *Virginia* is turning out to be more interesting than I'd feared."

☯☯☯☯☯☯☯☯☯

The fallout from the whip incident was swift. Nathan's men quickly rounded up the other farmhands and brought them to the Big House. Tom made Sickles wait in a room by himself, with the others in a separate room, supervised by Stan and William. Tom had instructed the hands to sit and not speak among themselves about what had happened until he could speak with each of them individually.

He didn't want the hands making any group decision about what they intended to do or say. And he wouldn't allow Sickles to have any more influence on matters.

So he brought them into his office one at a time and made sure they knew exactly what had happened—Rosa's version, *not* Sickles'. Then he grilled them about their thoughts and feelings, everything from how they felt about Sickles to what they thought of the Captain's plans, and the changes he was bringing to the farm. Finally, he asked each man if he'd stay and get on board with the plans or take his payoff and leave, either with Sickles or on his own.

In the end, it didn't surprise him two of the men, Frank and Dan, the ones most often seen conversing with Sickles, decided to accept their pay and leave. He was pleased, however, the remaining three men wished to stay on. And they generally seemed appreciative of the changes the Captain was making and enjoyed working with the new men he'd brought with him. A couple of them even said they would *not* be sorry to see Sickles go; he had a mean streak they didn't appreciate.

It was a surly group departing the farm that afternoon. This time Georgie and Jamie got escort duty. Tom gave each of the three departing men the option to buy one of the farm's horses, the cost to be deducted out of their final pay. Or they could simply borrow one for the ride to Lewisburg. They had opted to borrow the horses, so Georgie and Jamie were going along to bring the horses back. They had also brought along the pack mule as it made it easier to load up the departing men's personal effects. Much easier than trying to strap them onto a horse's saddle behind a rider.

Sickles spoke not a word the entire two-hour ride to town, and the others little more. The Captain's men were relieved to finally leave them off in town after unloading the mule.

They decided it had been a thankless task, and a thirsty one. l they stopped off at one of the local watering holes for a little refreshment on their ride back.

They'd never been there before, but the proprietress, Mrs. Caldwell, told them its official name was "Elmhurst." The locals just called it "the Caldwell Place," after the owners. They'd built it on the east bank of the Greenbrier River, only a few yards from the covered bridge where the main road crossed over to Lewisburg. A two-story red brick building, it featured four square columns in front, capped by a white ornamental stepped gable. It served as both an inn for travelers, and a tavern for anyone hungry or thirsty; the two Mountain Meadows men qualified as the latter. The men found it nicely furnished, looking like a manor house rather than a typical roadside inn. This gave it the feel of visiting neighbors and not just the local saloon. Jamie and Georgie enjoyed their visit, having a few refreshments, and striking up a pleasant conversation with a young couple—travelers from Richmond on their way west to Kentucky to visit relatives.

And so it was a much more congenial and jolly return trip.

"Well, at least the company on the ride has improved now Sickles and those other two yokels are gone. Ain't that right, Molly?" Georgie said, addressing the mule which made them both laugh. They'd taken to calling her "Molly the Mule," a humorous counterpoint to the Captain's horse, "Millie the Mare."

"Aye lad, she's certainly better company than old Sickles, and I have t'say, the dear lassie makes for a more intelligent conversation," Jamie agreed with a chuckle.

"And she's much better looking, too!" Georgie added, making a screwed-up, humorous face—his rendition of Sickles. They shared another laugh.

"Aye, old Sickles has a face like a blind cobbler's thumb! You know, the only thing I'm sorry after is missing out on all the day's fun. I hear Sergeant Jim cursed out Sickles like to curdle milk."

"Yep, but too bad he never got to give him a proper Texas whuppin'. But I heard the Captain had a dandy temper tantrum like he ain't had since we left New Orleans."

"Aye … that would've been a right-fine sight to see, boyo … a right-fine sight."

"Yep … and too bad we was back in the workshop, fixing that damned broken wagon axle the whole time. If it hadn't been for Billy coming 'round, we'd have never knowed anything had happened at all."

"True … and then we'd have missed out on Mrs. Caldwell's fine whiskey, and that'd been a damned shame, to be sure. A damned shame."

"I'll drink to that … or … I would if we had any more whiskey …"

ༀༀༀༀༀༀༀༀༀༀༀༀ

Nathan rode back out into the field where he'd been when Harry the Dog had first heard the woman Betsy shouting. During all the commotion, Nathan had never thought about the dog, nor worried about where he might be. But there he was once again, following at a short distance, as usual. It made him wonder if the dog, like the mare, was watching to see if his master was in harm's way. He was curious if the hound would have intervened had there been a fight. He'd shown no sign of it so far, but dogs were strangely protective and loyal in that way, instinctively, even with no training.

But at the moment, Nathan had bigger things to worry about, more than anyone might suspect. There were the obvious things—Sickles' reprehensible behavior, Jim's quick intervention preventing a tragedy, the commendable actions of the slave women, and the admirable, indomitable courage of Rosa.

But it was the young girl who'd unwittingly triggered the firestorm of thoughts and emotions presently swirling through Nathan's mind. In fact, she was the main reason he felt the need to be alone with his thoughts. The girl had, through no conscious actions of her own, given him a great shock—one neither she nor anyone else present could have suspected.

He'd successfully kept a tight rein on his volatile temper right up to the moment Rosa finished taking her three deep breaths and looked up, meeting eyes with him. In that instant a shocking thought flashed through his mind. Like a match struck in a dark room, this revelation was so sudden and unexpected, it nearly took his breath away. He realized she had very distinctive facial features: narrower nose, and thinner lips than the other black women. And for the first time he realized her skin was a very light brown—not black at all. He immediately knew … her father *had to* have been a white man.

And … he was already aware, from going through the records with Tom, the slave girl named Rosa had been born *on the farm*. And on *this* farm, where Jacob Chambers ruled with an iron fist, would any of the white overseers have dared to have done what Sickles had tried?

These thoughts went through his mind in a fraction of a second. And in the next second, he wondered, *could it have been Daddy? If the mother had been as lovely as the daughter is, it would've* been a sore temptation for a man with God-like power over his slaves. *Could it be? Could Rosa be ... my sister?*

Those watching had seen nothing more than a polite pause, the Captain allowing the girl to catch her breath, before proceeding with his interrogation. But Nathan had felt his heart stop. He listened to Rosa's words with emotions in heaving turmoil. He couldn't stop thinking it was possible a sister he'd never known had nearly been raped and beaten to death on his own farm. By the time she'd finished her tale he was filled with a fiery wrath he could not easily contain. He'd had to vent the rage ... somehow ... or ...

He recalled his old schoolmaster, Mr. Wilson, who'd taught him to use little tricks to safely vent his rage and keep from killing someone when he could feel it heating to the boiling point. Like chopping up the whip. He smiled. Mr. Wilson would've liked that one!

He let out a heavy sigh. Nothing terrible had happened *today*, for which he said a silent prayer of thanks.

Again, his thoughts turned to Rosa. How could he learn the truth? *Momma doesn't know, that's for sure. No use asking her about it. It would only hurt her. And where is Rosa's mother? Is she dead?* He was sure she was no longer on the farm. What had become of her? He'd have to ask Tom to investigate.

And should he confide in Tom about his suspicions? He debated this question for only a moment before coming to the obvious conclusion, laughing out loud and shaking his head. Millie tossed her head back and eyed him, as if wondering what the sudden unexpected noise was all about.

Of course, I should tell Tom! He figured out the whole thing about my father's death, my dilemma about returning to Virginia, and my struggle about what I intended to do when I got here, without me saying a word. He'll figure this one out whether I tell him or not. Might as well save him the bother.

Then he wondered, *And ... how do I feel about it? A young girl ... no, that's not right. A young woman! But a half-black slave woman might be my half-sister.* He mulled it over for a few minutes, before deciding. *Damn it ... she's clearly smart, resourceful, beautiful, and courageous … any man should be proud to call her sister. If true, it'd be a wonderful, unexpected gift from God.*

In that moment he knew for sure, without any doubt, the words he'd been preaching were true and he believed them to his core—that one's color didn't matter. *We are all brothers to God, who is of all colors … and no color at all.*

He felt a calm come over him, and a deep-down feeling of joy and goodwill. As if God had listened in on his thoughts and smiled at the outcome.

He stood in the stirrups and gazed about, taking in a satisfying, deep breath. His own lands spread out before him, as far as his eyes could see all the way to the far distant hills, a magnificent vista. He was young, strong, and wealthy, with good, loyal men at his command. He was doing great works, in a great land. And, just maybe, unexpectedly, he now had a *sister* he'd never known!

And a fine horse under me, he added, reveling in all the good things in life, despite the upsets of the day. He turned Millie toward home and kicked her into action. They raced for home, his mind now at ease.

☙℘ℭ℞℘℘ℭ℞℘℘ℭℜ℘℘ℭ℞

Later that evening Nathan and Tom sat on the veranda, sipping whiskey and smoking cigars. Miss Abbey had retired for the evening a few minutes earlier, and Nathan had just finished explaining to Tom his suspicions about Rosa.

"Whew…" Tom whistled, "That'd really be *something*, Captain! A sister? But … how do you *feel* about that, sir? To find out at this age you may have a sibling, and a half-black slave girl, at that. And … what does that say about your father? It must be very … I don't know … *conflicting?*"

Nathan smiled. "Well, firstly … having met the girl and spoken with her at some length, I can honestly say I would be thrilled beyond words if it were true. I've searched my heart and I tell you … I care nothing about her being a half-black African. She's *not* of the *African* race, she's of the *human* race, same as you and me!"

279

Tom looked thoughtful for a moment, then nodded his head and raised his whiskey glass, "Well said, sir. I couldn't agree more."

"But yes, to answer your other question, I *have been* struggling with the question about my Daddy, Tom. And though you were polite enough not to say it, I imagine you were wondering whether it was forced or consensual."

"Well, yes ... I have to admit, the thought had crossed my mind."

"Mine too. But it makes no difference—it's wrong *either* way. White men have too much power over the slaves to allow it. Tomorrow I'm calling a meeting of *all* the white men on this farm, including those from Texas. I mean to put the fear of God into them ... there will be no more *relations* with the black women on my farm, period! At best, the offender will be immediately cashiered and escorted from the property. But if I'm in a particularly foul mood I expect they'll feel the sting of a whip first!" Nathan scowled darkly at the thought.

Tom nodded, but decided it needed no response; likely any further discussion would only add to the Captain's agitation concerning the matter. But fortunately, he was saved from a potentially uncomfortable silence when something caught the corner of his eye.

"Oh ... I see Jim coming," Tom said, sitting up and nodding in the direction of the outbuildings.

"Ah, good. I asked him to come join us on the veranda after dinner. Please see what you can find out about Rosa's mother, Tom. In the meantime, let's keep this matter between us for now."

"Jacob's records concerning the slaves are very exact and detailed. I should have no trouble finding everything there is to know about her."

"Good! Thanks, Tom."

"Hullo, Jim! A fine evening for a smoke and a bit of refreshment," Tom called out genially, waving his cigar in the air for emphasis.

"Yes, it appears so," Jim responded with a grin, "but it also appears you two ungentlemanly fellows have not been polite enough to wait for me."

"Well, sir, come on over and we shall attempt to make amends," Nathan answered in good humor. "We shall let you have two sips for every one we partake until you feel your honor has been satisfied."

He raised his glass toward Jim in salute.

"Well, now, sir. That seems more than fair! I'm feeling more kindly disposed towards y'all already!"

Jim took the stairs two at a time and pulled up a chair beside them.

Nathan poured him a glass from the bottle sitting at the table. Jim wasted no time catching up, taking his first swallow.

"Mmm … that's *good* whiskey! A little sweeter than usual, ain't it? What kind is it?"

"I picked up a barrel earlier in the week when I was over in town getting supplies," Tom answered. "The store clerk said it was a new batch from over the border in Bourbon County, Kentucky. I guess he's right—it has 'Bourbon County' stamped right on the side of the barrel. The Captain and I were commenting on it before you arrived."

Jim took another sip, and this time swirled it around in his mouth a minute before swallowing. "Yep, I reckon I'm gonna like this new Bourbon whiskey!"

He flashed them a smile. Tom and Nathan raised their glasses in agreement. Jim helped himself to a cigar, lit it, and leaned back in his chair contentedly, blowing a great puff of smoke into the air.

"Yes, sir. A man from Texas could get used to this *Virginia* place. No dust, biting flies, or belligerent Indians. Nor much of any outlaws to speak of!"

He leaned back, with a smile on his face and the cigar between his teeth.

"Except maybe Sickles," Tom teased, eliciting a snort of laughter from Jim.

"Speaking of," Nathan interjected, "I wanted to thank you for your timely intervention today, Jim. That was handsomely done."

"Think nothing of it, sir. It was my great, good pleasure staring down that rascal Sickles. *By God, sir!* The man blatantly disobeyed your *direct* orders! Right in front of *me*, no less! Even our *stupidest* private back in the Army knew better'n to do *that!* No sir, I can't abide a willfully disobedient soldier!"

He turned his head to spit, as was his habit when making a point, only to realize it wouldn't be proper on Miss Abbey's nice, clean veranda. He swallowed it, to the silent amusement of Nathan and Tom.

"Well, now you mention it … what *would* you have done if I *hadn't* given the order against whippings?" Nathan asked, out of pure curiosity.

Jim leaned back in his chair and blew another puff of smoke, considering his response.

"Well, sir. As you probably know, I ain't exactly the squeamish type. I seen plenty of no-good scoundrels was practically *begging* for a good whipping. And I've been more'n happy to oblige them on occasion, if y'all catch my drift.

"But that-there little slip of a girl today … why … that whip'd like to cut her in half I expect! No, sir, I wouldn't've stood by and watched *that*, orders or no. No, I reckon I'd've given him a proper thumping, either way!"

He sat back and grinned.

"Glad to hear it, Jim. But I can't say I'm surprised. Beneath that gruff exterior lives the very soul of chivalry, I believe," Nathan nodded his head to Jim before taking a puff on his own cigar.

"Well, sir, ain't never studied such things in school myself, but if you say so, I'll have to take your word on it."

Jim took another sip of whiskey. "Yes sir, it was quite my pleasure putting a stop to such nonsense. Only …"

"Yes?" Nathan asked, with a good idea of what was coming.

"Well, after it was over, I started thinking it was too bad Millie hadn't throwed a shoe on the way over … just to slow you down a bit …"

Jim had a sly grin touching the edges of his mouth.

282

"Hmm … Billy said much the same earlier. I reckon it's the first time I've ever been accused of being *too* punctual!" Nathan laughed.

"Well, it ain't we don't appreciate your company, sir! But I have to admit it would've been more satisfying-like, to've been able to give him a good-old Texas thrashing for his troubles."

"And you weren't worried about getting whipped?" Tom asked, just to prod him, knowing full well what the answer would be.

"*What?!* That farm boy never fought a *Texan* before! Oh, I might've got a welt or two, but he'd've had an aching head that wouldn't've *knowed* when to quit! Not to mention a few less teeth, and a might prettier-looking nose, unless I miss my guess!"

They shared a good laugh at that, but then Nathan had an uncomfortable image flash through his mind. His old schoolmate, the bully Johnny Miller, huddling on the ground, whimpering and bleeding. He shuddered, and it gave him a more sobering thought about the day's events.

To clear away the evil image, he asked Jim a question he'd been curious about for some time, "Tell me, Jim, how *did* you come to love fighting so much? Sure, Tom and I enjoy a good tussle now and again, but I don't recall ever meeting a man, except maybe Big Stan, who loved fighting more than you."

Jim snorted a short laugh and took another sip of whiskey before answering. "I can tell you *exactly* when it happened, sir. I remember it like it were yesterday.

"It was on my fourteenth birthday, as a matter of fact, nearly ten years ago now. Believe it or not, I'd been a scrawny kid up 'til then. The kind the other boys picked on. Especially my older brother, Jeb. He was only a year and a half older'n me, but always way bigger 'n stronger. He loved to wrestle me to the ground and sit on me, then punch me, tickle me, or stick something disgusting in my face, or make me eat it.

"And to make matters worse, he'd gone to school and learned readin' before Pa got hisself kicked by a horse and went lame so's he couldn't work no more. After that we all had to work and couldn't afford no more schoolin'. So Jeb called me 'stupid' ever' chance he got, on account o' I couldn't read nor write.

"But in the past year I'd begun to fill out some and had growed a good inch or two. So's he was no longer so much bigger and stronger'n me.

"The day I turned fourteen I woke up feelin' my oats and was finally fed up with takin' his nonsense. I figured if he called me 'stupid' one more time, I was fixin' to let him have it, come what may.

"So that morning we went out to milk the cow and gather the eggs, as was our usual chores. We'd finished up with the cow and was ready to go get them eggs when he says, 'Come on, *stupid*, let's get done with it.' That was his mistake!

"I steps right up and punches him in the nose. Well, despite my piss and vinegar, he was still bigger'n me, and way meaner. So of course he punched me back, hard, knocking me to the ground.

"But as I sat there rubbin' my sore head I decided so long as I was still breathin', I was gonna keep gettin' up, and punchin' him as hard as I could, square in the nose. So I did.

"And he knocked me down again.

"So I got up again, and wacked him.

"And again, he knocked me to the ground.

"We kept at it for several minutes—him knockin' me down, and me gettin' right back up and whangin' him in the nose.

"Until finally, I gets back up, for the umpteenth time, only this time he says, 'Damn it, *Jim!* Stop *doin'* that!'

"It was then I noticed he was bleedin' bad from nose and mouth. And it shocked me to see him cryin' like a baby. So I says, 'Don't call me stupid no more!' and I turns and stalks back into the house, him followin' along like a whipped cur.

"Of course, Momma asked what'd happened, as we both looked like we'd been run over by a wagon. So of course we lied and said the cow'd kicked us. But Momma didn't much care. She weren't never much of a mother, and ever since Pa got crippled she'd taken to beating us with a switch pert-near ever' day,

284

whether we needed it or no. So she says, 'drop yer britches, and bend over so's I can give y'all a whuppin'.'

"But right then and there I decided I'd had enough o' her, too. So I says, 'No, I ain't. I'm all growed up now, and you ain't whippin' me no more!'

"She got all flummoxed, and said, 'Well, you can just get your sorry, ungrateful hide outta here then.'

"So I did—walked right out the door with nothin' but the clothes I was wearin'. Ain't never gone back. Walked straight down to the local Army fort, which was only five mile or so, and signed up right there on the spot."

"At age fourteen?" Tom asked.

"Well, of course I lied and said I was seventeen. Either they believed me, or they was so desperate for men they didn't care. Anyway, they took me in and … well, you can figure the rest."

"So that's when you decided you liked to fight, on account of whipping your ornery brother?" Nathan asked, grinning with amusement.

"Yep. I know some folks say fightin' don't solve no problems, but it sure did for me. And after that when the older soldiers tried to give me grief, I just gave them a taste of the medicine I'd served up to old Jeb. *Ha!* They never seemed to like it any better'n he did!"

"I'd imagine not!" Tom said and they shared another laugh.

Then Nathan got a more serious look. "Gentlemen … I'm afraid I learned a hard lesson today. No amount of logic, nor intellect, nor compassion can win over *everyone*. I truly believed Sickles would come 'round to my way of thinking, once he saw it was for the good of all."

"Well, if you want to know what I think," Jim offered, the whiskey making him wax philosophical, "some men are just plain *mean*. They'll do what's cruel and wicked even if doing the right thing's more to their benefit."

"Then, what do you *do* with such men?"

"Here's what I believe, Captain. God put good men like us on the Earth to deal with men like that. Fight 'em or jail 'em when needed … and when necessary … go ahead and *kill* 'em!"

Nathan considered Jim's words. Good men, and bad men. Good, hard men to keep the evil bad men in check, so normal people could lead their lives unmolested. Jim's simple philosophy was no more complicated than that. After a few moments' reflection, Nathan could think of nothing better. So he nodded his head to Jim, raised his glass, and took another drink.

ಐಐ಄಄ಐಐ಄಄ಐಐ಄಄

The next day, Nathan came into Tom's office and sat in the extra chair. Tom set aside his papers and turned to look at his Captain.

"Have you found out anything more about Rosa's mother?"

"I'm afraid I've dug out everything there is in the paperwork. Her name was Lilly. She came to the farm as a young girl of eight years, part of a large influx of slaves Jacob brought in around that time. The prices at auction had been rising steeply, and ... well, to be blunt, young girls were brought in mostly for their ability to ... you know ... reproduce?"

"Humph," Nathan responded with a snort of disgust.

"Looks like she was not much older than Rosa is now when she gave birth to the girl. She was sixteen ... no, let's see ... just turned seventeen rather," Tom said, referring back to some notes he'd written out on a piece of parchment. "No mention of who the father was, although that's not all that unusual. And then—this is the strange part—when the child was only two years old the mother was sold off the farm, but the toddler remained behind. That was not so unusual *in general*—separating parents from young children, I mean—but doesn't appear to be typical on *this* farm. And Jacob sold Lilly at a time when he was steadily increasing his numbers.

"I've looked back through the records for several years each side of that transaction and can find nothing similar. No case where Jacob sold off a parent with a young child. And no record of selling a slave during a time when he was otherwise buying slaves."

"Hmm ... the evidence is *telling*, but not completely conclusive, I'm afraid. Does it say who she was sold to?"

"No, only the date and the name of the auction house — Davenport and Company, 15th and Cary streets in Richmond. Oh, and the price, of course. After that the trail runs cold on this end. No further entries about either the mother or the child."

"So what now? I would dearly like to learn the truth of the matter."

"Yes, of course, sir. I've been considering that and can think of two different approaches from here ... one I can pursue, but the other is going to require your personal intervention. The next step from the historical record perspective is to visit that auction house in Richmond. See if they still have a record of the transaction, and if they'll let us have a look."

"If I know anything about such places, I'm sure a few well-placed dollars will get you the information you need. If it's there to be had."

"My thinking exactly, sir. When we go over to Richmond for your senatorial duties, I can start looking into it."

"We? Tom, you're acting like the dog — can't leave you behind if I try!"

They shared a laugh.

"Someone has to look after you, sir. And I doubt they'll let that great hound into the assembly hall!"

Nathan tried to picture the huge dog roaming the marbled halls of the capitol building and shook his head in amusement.

"And the other line of investigation? The one requiring my intervention?"

"Well, some of the slaves *must* know what happened. If you can get them to confide in you, it may provide an answer more quickly than trying to track down the mother."

"Hmm ... I see your point. I'll have to give it some thought. I'd have to be very careful about how that was handled. I'd need to make sure I was getting the truth, rather than what they might think I want to hear, rightly or wrongly. And further, true or not, I'd rather not place Rosa in an uncomfortable position with the others."

That Friday, Nathan once again entered Tom's office first thing in the morning. He strode in with a purposeful air and immediately sat in the extra chair.

"Tom … I've been thinking …" he began.

"Good morning, sir," Tom said, with a wry smile.

"Oh … yes … good morning, Tom. Sorry … my mind was preoccupied, and I seem to have misplaced my manners. How are you this morning …?"

"It's all right, sir. I was only teasing you … I could see you had something serious on your mind, so you may as well have out with it."

"Thanks, Tom. Yes, I have an idea I want to discuss with you."

By way of answer, Tom set down his pen and paper and turned his chair toward Nathan, giving him is full attention.

"As you know, I've been trying to think of various ways to make the lives of our people better while working toward the ultimate payday, when they receive their freedom."

Tom nodded but allowed Nathan to continue.

"So far, it's been a lot of simple things, easy to implement — putting an end to corporal punishment, giving them the Sabbath day off, fixing the leaky roofs on the cabins, better food and clothing. Teaching them practical lessons, and so forth."

"Well, those may be simple, but they're fairly profound from a slave's point of view, I should think," Tom said.

"True, true … and I don't wish to diminish their importance. It's just … I've been wanting to do something … bigger."

"Bigger, sir?"

"Yes … something they'll be talking about for months. Something that will make their lives … I don't know … more hopeful? More pleasurable?

"Anyway, I'd been wracking my brain and not coming up with anything. But then yesterday I got to thinking about the poor wretches those slave traders dragged up here a couple of weeks ago. Of course, it made me angry again, as it always does when I think on it. Only this time I remembered something that'd been pushed to the back of my mind, mostly because of that poor little girl, Lonna."

"Ah, yes … I remember her plight touched you deeply."

"Yes … but what I was getting at was, I recalled the traders saying they had a married couple in their group and that they were legally and morally bound not to split them up."

Tom got a curious look, "Oh! I hadn't heard about *that* before. But, sir … slave traders break up married couples all the time. What was different this time?"

"Yes, it's true; they do it all the time, with little thought or hesitation," Nathan scowled at the thought before continuing.

"From what I understand, some slaves have their own marriage ceremony of sorts; they call it 'jumping the broom.' But it has no legal standing, and the white masters give it little credence. Nor does the church, I'm afraid. So, legally and theologically, none of the black couples, even those with children living together as a family, are actually wedded."

"Then, what was different about *this* couple?"

"It was different because … for some reason they'd been legally wedded by an ordained minister, using all the proper, sacred wording. Tom, their marriage had been officially sanctioned by the church—blessed by God, as it were. As such, the law recognized it as a legally binding contract.

"Someone forcibly breaking up such a union could, theoretically, be subject to punishment under the law. Not to mention chastisement by the religious authorities."

"Hmm … interesting," Tom said, looking thoughtful. "So … what do you have in mind, sir?"

"Well … you realize the slaves on this farm have never been allowed to have any kind of wedding, even 'jumping the broom,' unless they did it in secret. From what Megs tells me, my Daddy thought it so much nonsense and wouldn't allow it."

"From what I've heard, that sounds like Jacob Chambers, all right, sir. So you're going to announce the slaves can now get married if they wish? That should make them happy, I'd think."

"I mean to do more than that, Tom. I am going to announce a wedding on this farm. A real, honest-to-God *legal* wedding for any couple that wants to take part. Then, as the sacred words say, *'whomever God has joined together let no man put asunder!'*

"I intend to give them a wedding they'll never forget. Maybe the biggest nuptials ever held in Virginia!"

"Whew …" Tom whistled, leaning back in his chair, a smile lighting his face.

ᛒᚢᛋᚫᚲᚷᛒᚢᛋᚫᚲᚷᛒᚢᛋᚫᚲᚷ

On Sunday, when Nathan and Miss Abbey arrived at church, Walters and his men were already seated in their usual place in the first two rows, on the *left* side. He'd apparently withdrawn from the field in the "Church Pew Battle" of the past several weeks, conceding Nathan the victory.

For Margaret's sake, he was determined to force down his true feelings and greet Walters cordially—neither overly warm, nor noticeably cold. Either might cause him to suspect Nathan knew more about his business in Richmond than he should. And that might start him wondering how he knew it. But he had to at least acknowledge Walters trip to Richmond, since the pastor had told him about it, and it was likely general knowledge in the community by now.

Once again, his thoughts turned to Margaret, and he couldn't help but worry about her. Doubtless, she was now feeling her incarceration more acutely, after her relative freedom while Walters was out of town. But then he remembered she'd said she intended to take advantage of *any* time Walters was absent from the house. *Like now*, Nathan thought, and smiled.

Miss Abbey leaned into him and whispered, "What are you smiling about? I'd think you'd have nothing but scowls for our unsavory neighbor."

"True. But just now I was thinking of our friend 'M,' and how at this very moment she must be enjoying a bit of fresh air!"

Abbey gave him a knowing look, nodded her head, and returned his smile.

When the sermon was over, and people began to file out, Nathan stepped into the aisle at almost the same moment as Walters.

"Hello, Walters. We have felt your absence the last two weeks. The pastor tells me you had business over in Richmond. I trust you had a productive trip?"

"Chambers. Yes, the trip went as expected. Thank you for asking. And I suppose welcomes are in order … to our congregation, I mean. Though clearly you've been here already in my absence."

"Thank you, Walters. I've been made to feel most welcome by the *other* members of the pastor's flock, and by his reverence as well, of course."

He smiled as the image of Big Stan throwing Walters' man out the front door flashed through his mind.

"I am most gratified to hear it, Chambers. Mrs. Chambers. A good day to you both." He nodded and quickly left.

Nathan noticed he did not exchange words with anyone else in the congregation and only had a brief word with the pastor. Then he and his men walked straight to their carriage and horses and immediately departed.

"Well, not overflowing with warmth, but at least he was civil," Miss Abbey said.

"Yes … as was I, and it took all my self-restraint to pull it off. I'd much prefer sticking a knife in him."

She smiled and patted him on the arm affectionately.

This morning, after the usual exchange of pleasantries with the pastor, Nathan said, "Reverend, I'd like a word with you in private before we leave, if you have a moment."

"Of course, Mr. Chambers. Once I've finished greeting the flock, I will seek you out. Will you be found by your carriage, sir?"

ༀༀༀༀༀༀༀༀༀༀ

"Reverend, I wish to grant my slaves the opportunity for a real church wedding. I worry the current … *informal* … arrangement, 'jumping the broom,' as they call it, goes against the commandments of God. It causes persons who are otherwise inclined toward a serious, familial relationship, to live in sin."

"Hmm … it's an admirable idea, Mr. Chambers. Of course, you know, many slave owners allow their slaves to marry, so it's not anything *new*."

"Yes, I'm familiar with the practice. But I'm also aware the slave owners, the state, and the church, for that matter, don't recognize these unions as legally binding, allowing the marital partners to be sold off separately, should it be convenient. In fact, I am told, they've changed the vows to read 'til death or distance do us part.' Words not exactly conducive to eternal love and faithfulness, I'd say."

"Yes … it is a … *difficult* situation, the persons involved being the legal property of their masters. So if this is not the kind of arrangement you're speaking of, what exactly is it you're proposing, Mr. Chambers?"

"I wish to conduct a real, proper wedding for my slaves, presided over by an ordained pastor, using the proper, legally recognized vows. So the individuals will be married in the eyes of God, and the state, and may *not* be parted, legally or morally."

"*Oh* … I see. And … do I understand correctly you are talking about performing this … *type* of wedding … for multiple couples, simultaneously?"

"Yes, certainly. For any couples who wish to go through with the ceremony. Why do you ask?"

The Reverend was quiet for several moments before responding.

"Mr. Chambers … you must understand the … *delicate sensibilities* of your fellow parishioners. A quiet, simple wedding of this nature, involving a single couple … might be arranged, and no one be the wiser. But a large wedding, with multiple couples, well … that will be almost impossible to keep quiet. People will talk."

"*Talk?* And what of it? Am I not their master? Are they not my *legal* property—as you say—in the eyes of the law, to do with as I see fit?"

"Yes, of course, that is true, but still …"

"Still?"

"Still, your friends and neighbors would not like to see you setting such a precedence with your slaves. Word might get around. Others might do it too, and very soon the ability to ... *conveniently* trade slaves ... might be called into jeopardy."

"Honestly, Reverend, I care nothing for the business of trading in slaves. I've seen it in action—children stripped from their mothers, husbands from wives—and I find the practice entirely deplorable. I've no wish to subject my slaves, nor any others, to such inhumane treatment, now, or ever."

"Well, that may well be, Mr. Chambers, but others will *not* agree. And they may feel threatened by the precedence you would be setting."

"Hmm ... well, I can see we may be in strong disagreement on this matter. I had intended to ask you to perform the ceremony ..."

"I am honored, of course, Mr. Chambers, but I must decline. Despite your obvious good intentions, a large, church-sanctioned slave wedding of this type would not be ... in the best interests of all concerned."

Nathan was quiet for a moment, then reached into his jacket pulled out a cigar, and lit it.

"Let me tell you what I *will* do, Reverend. I *will* find a pastor willing to perform this ceremony. I *will* make sure it is legal, and proper. And what I will *not* do, is care one whit what you, or anyone else thinks about it. Good day to you, sir!"

He turned on his heels, and strode back to the carriage, where he immediately climbed up into the seat beside Miss Abbey. Without pause, he picked up the reins, and snapped the horses into motion.

"How did it go, Nathan, dear? What did he say?"

Nathan turned toward her and frowned. "He said, *no!*"

"Oh *dear* ... and ... I trust you were polite and thanked him for giving the matter due consideration?"

She looked at him through a frown of her own.

He looked back at her, and then grinned, the cigar in his teeth, "Of course, Momma! Have you ever known me to do otherwise?"

She rolled her eyes and shook her head.

"Whatever am I going to do with you, Nathan, dear?"

"God only knows, Momma. God only knows …"

ಬಬಿಬಿಬಿಬಿಬಿಬಿಬಿಬಿಬಿ

Reverend Blackburn stood where he was and watched the Chambers party leave. He was steaming on the inside but would never display such temper in front of his flock. *Such an impudent upstart! Just because his father helped build this church, he thinks he can march in here and lord it over me. I will not stand still for such treatment! Hold a wedding without me, and against my wishes? We'll see about that! By the time I've finished making the rounds to the local pastors, nobody will give him the proper time of day, let alone conduct a wedding ceremony for him.*

What next? Replace me as pastor of my own church? No … he will never get away with that. Not over my dead body!

As he continued to stew on such thoughts, his servant, Benny, stepped up to him.

"Master Reverend, your carriage be all hitched up, an' ready, sir."

"Carriage? Oh … yes, thank you, Benny. Good. And … is it not our day to ride out to Walters Farm? Yes … good. As it turns out, I have a … *matter* of some importance I wish to discuss with Mr. Walters."

"Very good, Master Reverend. We's ready to go whenever you wishes it."

ಬಬಿಬಿಬಿಬಿಬಿಬಿಬಿಬಿಬಿ

It was late morning, and Margaret had assumed her favorite spot at the top of the stairs in the foyer. It was the place from which she eavesdropped on all Mr. Walters' conversations. He liked to sit in a particular chair in the large sitting room off the foyer at the bottom of the stairway. And there he discussed business with Bob, his foreman, or with guests such as Mr. Chambers.

She couldn't figure out exactly what it was—the shape of the foyer, or the hard marble floor—but she could hear even soft talk in the room below, even down to a whisper. She'd taken to sitting

294

at the top of the stairs any time Mr. Walters had company in that room.

Ever since she'd forced her will upon the house slaves, they no longer kept her confined to her room when Walters wasn't watching. And in the time since her escape, she'd come to an understanding with the maid Willona, such that they were now on reasonably good terms.

Unfortunately for Margaret, the guest was not Mr. Chambers this time, but Reverend Blackburn on his regular monthly visit. She was none too fond of the pastor, given his refusal to intercede on her behalf with Walters. But more than that … for some reason she didn't entirely comprehend, she didn't trust the man. There was something … *insincere* about him. He gave her an odd feeling. Like he was playing the role of a goodly man without truly being one.

So, more than ought to be the case with a member of the clergy, she was curious what he might have to discuss with Walters. And once again, her curiosity seemed to pay off.

"Mr. Walters … it is really none of *my* concern. But a man in your position might feel … *threatened* by his actions," the Reverend was saying just as Margaret took her seat.

"Chambers! The man infuriates me with his smugness," Walters said, momentarily loosening the tight rein he normally held on his emotions.

Mr. Chambers! Margaret thought with a sudden thrill. *What could they be discussing about him?* She listened intently.

"Yes, I can understand the feeling. He is … very sure of himself, to put it mildly."

"Humph! A monumental ego would be closer to the mark. Sitting up on that hill, lording over the valley like he owns the whole place!" Walters continued in a heated tone.

"I agree. He is a man who … expects to be followed and obeyed, to be sure. Now … about this matter I mentioned …"

Walters growled, "Having a preacher marry a whole pack of savages at once? A disgusting farce, certainly, but why should it concern me? I care nothing about what Chambers chooses to do with his own slaves. He can kiss or kill the whole lot; I care *not* either way."

"Well, the reason you *should* care is this ... he intends to give them a real, binding, legal church wedding. Meaning legally these couples can never again be sold off separately."

"So?"

"So ... as you have said yourself, Mr. Chambers is very influential in this county, for better or worse—not to mention his position as a state senator. If he carries this ... *business* off ... others may follow suit. Who knows how far such an idea might carry. Soon it may be impossible to buy or sell most adult slaves singly, which could have a serious economic impact. But, as I said, it is no concern of mine ... I just thought *you* might want to be aware."

Walters growled, "Yes ... this scheme of Chambers has gone from a farce to something more ... *nefarious*, it would seem."

"One might say so. It would be ... unfortunate ... if men of honor, such as yourself, sat idly by while this precedent was being set."

Margaret didn't hear Walters response, but imagined a dark scowl, unless he had reverted to his blank, emotionless stare.

"Well, I must stop in and say a prayer over Mrs. Walters before I depart. Good day to you, sir."

"Good day, Reverend." Walters said, blandly.

Margaret rose and moved quickly back down the hallway to her room in preparation for Reverend Blackburn's visit. If she had been able to stay longer and continue her eavesdropping, she would have heard Walters call for Bob, and the two of them discuss plans well into the evening.

As it was, Margaret felt a growing anxiety for the welfare of Mr. Chambers and Miss Abbey, wondering if Walters would take the Reverend's bait.

ᔕᘊᕉᖋᏟᔆᔕᘊᕉᖋᏟᔆᔕᘊᕉᖋᏟᔆ

That afternoon, Nathan moved his "sermon" to a new location. Rather than the veranda, Nathan decided he'd stand atop the same table where he'd cut up the whip and have the people sit on the lawn thereabouts. He chose the site for the obvious tie-in to

296

the events having just occurred there, now well known around the farm to one and all. He wanted to re-emphasize his new rule against white men having relations with the black women, which had been announced earlier in the week. But also, the summer weather was setting in, and the lawn next to the veranda offered no shade from the heat of the sun. The large oak tree next to the table, and the old walnut on the side of the drive opposite, provided ample shade for all. Nathan noticed, with satisfaction, the old rusty hook Rosa had been tied to no longer protruded from the walnut. More good works by Sergeant Jim, no doubt.

He also noticed Miss Abbey was absent. Odd. So too was Megs. *Very* odd. He would have to ask them about it later. Perhaps they'd tired of his preaching?

"Good Sabbath to you all, and God bless you."

This time several people responded, "God bless, you Captain, God bless you Master, God bless …" to which he smiled, pleased it seemed a few more had turned to a favorable opinion of him.

"The good book tells us God decreed a man and a woman should come together in the holy bonds of marriage. Within such a blessed union, love and peace may flourish. And it is this love that brings forth the blessings of children. In the sacred, matrimonial bonds God has decreed, relations between a man and a woman are a great joy and blessing.

"Now, I have been made to understand, the old master of this farm disapproved of such bonds for his servants. He never would allow marriage between black couples on this farm.

"And yet, I know there are loving bonds between many of you. Bonds both strong and familial. Lifelong commitments that have brought forth children in a loving and faithful manner.

"Well, unlike the old master, I mean to recognize these admirable family bonds among you. In fact, I mean to make them stronger.

"And so, from this day forward, you will not only be allowed, but will be encouraged to marry when love flourishes.

"And I have decided—what better way to honor and celebrate God's good word, than to hold a very special wedding—a *great* wedding—for all the couples who've wanted for years to be married but have never been allowed.

"And, unlike other slave marriages you may have heard about, I intend for this wedding to be performed by a real, ordained minister. And I will make sure it uses all the proper, legal vows, such that man and wife may *never* be parted by anyone, for any reason, *ever*. Even the most vile slave trader will fear to break these sacred bonds, blessed by God.

"So in a few weeks' time, or as soon as may be arranged, we will hold a wedding right here on this farm, with white dresses, flowers, and all. For any and all couples who wish to be married!"

These words caused an immediate stir. He could see shocked looks, smiles, laughter, and a few tears. Several couples leaned together and embraced, right there where they sat on the grass. He decided this was as good a time as any to end the sermon. He was pretty sure nothing further he could add would beat this reaction. If it came off as he hoped, it would not only improve their lives, but should dispel any remaining doubts about the honesty and sincerity of this future plans.

"Any couples wishing to be married, please come to the Big House any time the rest of the day and speak with Mr. Tom. He will record your information in the plans he's making for the event. Thank you, and God bless." He stepped down from the table and strode away toward the house. He heard an eruption of talk behind him and smiled.

As he walked, listening to the distant babble of voices, another sound came to his ears—the sound of horse's hooves, and the wheels of a carriage. He turned to see a formal black carriage coming up the drive, making its way between the now standing congregation, which parted to allow the unexpected vehicle to pass. A black coachman in formal dress steered its single horse.

Nathan stood to the edge of the roadway to let the coach pass, looking on with curiosity. He'd dressed much less formally than on earlier Sabbaths. Due to the heat and the longer walk to the table across from the cabins, he'd decided to forgo his more formal attire. He wore riding boots with britches and a plain white shirt, his old felt hat on his head. As the carriage approached, he imagined he looked anything but the farm's master, so it didn't surprise him when it continued on past at a trot.

He did, however, catch a glimpse of the passengers within: an attractive older woman in formal traveling attire and, seated across from her, a *very* striking young woman. She had golden hair hanging down in long curls from beneath her hat. She looked back at him, and their eyes met. His breath caught. If she wasn't the most beautiful woman he'd *ever* seen, he couldn't imagine who was.

It suddenly occurred to him why Miss Abbey had been absent from the sermon. She would *not* be surprised by the visitors because she had arranged their visit.

Despite agreeing to let the matter drop, Miss Abbey clearly intended to find him a bride, regardless of what he thought about it. She really had no shame concerning the matter! He laughed at the thought, shaking his head even as he tipped his hat to the young lady. She smiled in return.

Well, I suppose a man who thinks he can control his own mother is no better than a damned fool, he thought and laughed again, following in the carriage's dust as it continued toward the house.

Chapter II. An Unexpected Courtship

*"A modicum of discord is
the very spice of courtship."*
– Nicolas Chamfort

Sunday July 8, 1860 – Greenbrier County, Virginia:

Evelyn was filled with mixed emotions. The shiny black carriage bounced along the gravel road leading to the Chambers' farm. It had been a tiresome journey from Richmond. A full day on the train, and then another full day riding in a coach with her mother and two other passengers, finally reaching the hotel at White Sulphur Springs, where they'd spent last night.

But today's two-hour journey from the hotel was more pleasant. The early morning sun had not yet heated the air to the extent it would later in the day. And the mode of transportation was also much improved—Harriet had rented a carriage and driver at the hotel. As a result, their arrival today was more formal and proper.

But despite the beautiful day, Evelyn couldn't suppress a growing trepidation about the meeting to come. For one, Mr. Nathaniel Chambers did not even know she was arriving. She had pried *that* much information out of her mother. Harriet and Abigail Chambers had arranged the whole thing through an exchange of mailed letters. And they'd decided it would be best not to "bother" Mr. Chambers with the information ahead of time, him being busy with the running of the farm, and all.

In addition, Evelyn had stopped believing her mother about how "handsome, kind, and gentlemanly" her suitors were. She had learned the hard way these were exaggerations at best— mostly outright lies. She assumed Harriet had come up with this latest match based on economics and availability alone. The man was wealthy and not yet betrothed or married. In her mother's mind, all other considerations were secondary, if not completely immaterial.

But to Evelyn, still young and filled with notions of love and romance, those "other considerations" were everything. In her mind's eye she pictured an older gentleman—after all, Nathaniel Chambers was in his early thirties! And he was an army officer, so likely used to shouting out orders all the time. She pictured a small, round, bossy man with thinning gray hair. She sighed a heavy sigh. *If only …* she began, for the hundredth time.

As the carriage crested a rise, she could see a large farm spread out below. Rolling fields of cotton and tobacco, various buildings, with a great white house at the end of the gravel road they were following. Between them and the house she saw a gathering of people beginning to move off in different directions. Black faces mostly: the slaves. So many! She wondered why they'd all been together in one place; but lacking any ideas, she let the matter drop.

As they approached the small house-like buildings—clearly the slave quarters—they passed between groups of slaves who were walking along casually or gathered in small groups talking. This she also found strange; slaves were rarely allowed to be idle. Unless they were eating or sleeping, farm slaves worked constantly. Even in the middle of winter when they had little productive work. These slaves, however, seemed in no hurry to do anything. *Odd … I must ask Momma about it later…*

As they passed through the group of slaves and came closer to the main house, Evelyn could see a lone man striding along the road ahead of them. He was walking toward the house with his back to them. But he must have heard the carriage approaching, as he glanced quickly back and then stepped to the left side of the drive, allowing them to pass. He wore a plain white shirt with long, full sleeves, brown pants, a broad-brimmed felt work hat, and what appeared to be well-worn riding boots. *One of the hired hands, no doubt,* Evelyn decided.

As they approached, the man turned toward the carriage, as if curious about who was arriving. He was tall, but well-muscled, with dark hair and mustache but no beard. She was aware of an instinctive reaction—a stirring inside herself; this was a *man!* And those eyes! Dark and intense, staring hard into her own eyes as the carriage passed. She stared back. Then suddenly, he laughed. *How odd,* she thought. But then he politely tipped his hat, and smiled, so she naturally smiled back.

What was that about? she wondered. Harriet hadn't noticed the man, nor the look they'd shared; the fast-approaching house had captured her full attention.

But Evelyn's emotions were in turmoil. Never had a man stirred her feelings like *that!* He was clearly one of the farmhands. Her heart sank as the image of old, stodgy army officer Nathaniel Chambers flashed into her mind—the man she was supposed to entice into marriage. She steeled herself for the task at hand, but a wild thought crossed her mind. For the first time, she understood the rumors she'd heard—of fine, high-class, married ladies dallying with handsome, young gentlemen. If she were married to old Mr. Chambers, and this handsome young farmhand were always lurking about, would she be able to resist *that* temptation? It might prove a hard test …

The carriage arrived and circled the round drive, stopping in front of the broad stairs leading up to the front entrance. The driver stepped down but looked confused. He gazed about, surprised at the lack of a reception.

But as he walked to the door of the carriage, two young black men came up at a full run and motioned him to step aside.

"Most sorry, ma'ams. We was … away from the house for a moment, on account of we wasn't expecting no visitors this morning. But when we saw y'all's carriage we come a running, ain't that so, Phin?"

"Yessir, Cobb that we did! Welcome, welcome, to Mountain Meadows Farm, Misses," Phin said between gasps for breath.

Cobb went around to secure the horses to the hitching post, while Phin came and opened the door, assisting the ladies as they stepped down out of the carriage.

The women stepped onto the gravel of the drive, and Evelyn felt the sun beating down on her hat and the cloth of her dress. She was happy to be wearing a light-yellow-colored dress with lacy white trim rather than something dark, or the heat might prove oppressive. Then she chastised herself; what a trivial thing to think of at a time like this!

As they walked toward the house, a woman appeared on the veranda at the top of the stairs. She was tall and thin, and older than Harriet, as Evelyn knew from what her mother had told her. But she didn't look older, Evelyn decided. She still looked elegant—*beautiful* even, for an older woman. And she moved with a natural grace, reflected in her smile that seemed to touch the corners of her eyes. *Well, the mother is handsome enough—that's something at least,* Evelyn mused hopefully.

"Welcome! Welcome, my dear ladies! It is such a perfect pleasure to have you here. I am Abigail Chambers, as you've likely guessed. But please do just call me Abbey," she said with what appeared to be genuine warmth and enthusiasm. Her voice had a sweet, musical quality.

Evelyn liked Miss Abbey from the first moment, despite her earlier trepidation.

"Very pleased to meet you in person, Abbey, after getting to know you a little through your most engaging letter," Harriet responded. "I am, of course, Harriet … and please allow me to introduce you to my daughter, Evelyn Hanson."

"I am pleased and honored to meet you, Miss Abbey," Evelyn said, bowing her head and making a quick curtsy.

"The pleasure is mine, dear!" Abbey responded, smiling even more brightly. "Oh *my*, Harriet! I can see you did not need to exaggerate in the least the charms of your daughter! Why, my dear Evelyn, you are just … *absolutely lovely*, if you'll excuse my being so forward!"

"Thank you, Miss Abbey. And may I say, whatever beauty I might possess, is surely dimmed in your most-elegant presence."

"Oh, my—yes, you may say *that*, if it pleases you! Although I doubt very much it's true!"

Abbey laughed, obviously appreciating Evelyn's compliment. Harriet flashed her daughter a discreet smile, clearly appreciating it as well.

"But where are my manners? Keeping you talking out here in the hot sun! Please, please ... do come in my dear ladies and find shade and refreshment in my home!"

Abbey gestured for them to come up the stairs and enter the open doors of the house.

As she walked up to the veranda, Evelyn looked around at the row of broad, white columns, impressive in their grandeur. They entered the front doors into a broad, round foyer. On the left side, a set of double doors made of glass panes set in a dark wood led to a room that appeared to be a library. Miss Abbey gestured them to enter the room.

Inside it was cool, and dark—richly appointed with thickly padded chairs covered in soft cloth or leather. A tremendous collection of books filled its shelves. The room simply oozed of wealth. Evelyn had to admit, maybe this time her mother had been right—about the Chambers family wealth at least.

"Please, be seated and at ease," Miss Abbey said, gesturing toward the comfortable chairs spaced around the library's walls. "My maid Megs will be here shortly with refreshments. In the meantime, let us get better acquainted. Please, do tell me, how was your journey? And, of course, I would love to hear the latest gossip ... *oh* ... I meant to say 'news' out of Richmond," she giggled. "It's been so long since I've had the company of ladies from the city; I have to confess—I've been terribly excited awaiting your arrival."

Miss Abbey's warmth and infectious enthusiasm helped Evelyn relax and begin to enjoy herself.

Harriet launched into a narrative of their travels, and all the latest happenings among the upper-class ladies of Richmond. Miss Abbey listened attentively and asked various questions about people she knew.

But Evelyn listened distractedly. She kept wondering, *but ... where is Mr. Chambers? When shall we meet him?*

Then she heard a commotion in the foyer—a man's voice and then a woman's—a maid, she assumed. Then suddenly a man stood outlined in the library's doorway. The darkness of the room and the relative brightness of the foyer beyond made it impossible to see anything more than his outline. A deep voice came from that form and said, "Momma, it seems we have guests. I suppose it slipped your mind to mention it?"

The words sounded like scolding, but the tone was good humored. *Mister* Chambers at last!

"Oh, Nathan dear! Yes, I suppose I forgot to tell you we were expecting visitors today. Do forgive me, my dear. An old lady is forgetful sometimes," she smiled coyly, betraying she did not expect him to believe her story in the least.

The man stepped forward into the room, and the lamps of the library lit his features. Evelyn nearly gasped from the sudden shock … and *thrill*.

"Ladies … I am Nathaniel Chambers, at your service. I am master of this farm … though clearly I don't order *all* things here-abouts."

He said this last part with a smile, and a sideways glance at his mother. She returned the smile.

"Nathan, dear, may I present my dear friend Harriet Hanson."

Nathan took Harriet's extended hand and made a slight bow, "A pleasure to meet you, ma'am. Any friend of my Momma is, of course, most welcome in this house."

Harriet nodded her head politely in response.

"And, her daughter, Miss *Evelyn* Hanson," Abbey continued.

Nathan turned toward her, and their eyes locked once again.

"And it's a pleasure to meet you, as well, Miss Evelyn," he said smoothly.

Evelyn's heart was pounding so hard she was sure everyone else in the room could hear it. She was afraid she wouldn't be able to speak. Or if she tried it would come out in an embarrassing squeak. Then she recalled him laughing when their eyes first met out on the road, and she felt saved, suddenly having something to say.

"Mr. Chambers. We did see each other briefly as our carriage arrived on the road. Please, do tell me what it was you found so humorous when you first saw me?"

This unexpected response and question seemed to catch everyone off guard. An embarrassed silence came over the room. Evelyn could see Harriet scowling out of the corner of her eye.

But then Nathan laughed, and said, "My apologies for that, Miss Evelyn. Please let me assure you, there is nothing humorous or untoward about your appearance, or that of your lovely mother," he turned toward Harriet and nodded. She smiled and returned the gesture.

"It's just … your sudden, *unexpected* appearance," he looked toward Miss Abbey giving her a wry smile, "caught me by surprise. I'm afraid it brought an unrelated humorous notion to mind. I sincerely apologize if I have offended you by it—I can assure you—causing you insult was the furthest thing from my mind."

He smiled at her warmly, and she felt relieved she could breathe again.

"No apology is necessary, Mr. Chambers. I was just curious, is all. I don't normally elicit *that* response from gentlemen."

She was regaining her composure.

"No, I wouldn't imagine so, Miss Evelyn."

"Please, do excuse me, ladies. As I said, I did *not* expect company, and so am not properly dressed or presentable. And … I'm afraid I have promised my men I would go out target-shooting with them, so I must depart for the moment. But, please, be most welcome in my home—I will be looking forward to seeing you at dinner." He bowed politely and departed.

Evelyn's head was swimming. This … is *Mr. Chambers*? Suddenly the short, gray-haired, red-faced, dumpy army officer she'd envisioned sailed away like smoke on a breezy day.

Again, her heart was pounding, and her thoughts reeling. *Get ahold of yourself, Evelyn!* she scolded, *isn't this what you wanted?* But it was overwhelming and dreamlike … the sudden appearance of the man by the road … stirring feelings in her she'd never known. And brooding over having to marry a stodgy old man, and then suddenly the old man turned into the beautiful young man and …

"Evelyn! Evelyn, dear!"

She looked up, and the two older ladies were staring at her.

"Yes? What is it?" she asked.

"Oh my, Harriet! I fear the heat and all the travel has been too much for her. I shall have Megs come take her to her room so she might lie down for a spell.

"Oh, no, Miss Abbey. I am perfectly fine," Evelyn said, but as the words were coming out, she knew they weren't true. She felt light-headed … like she might *need* to lie down …

"No, no, Miss Evelyn. You're pale as a ghost! You must go lie down … Megs! Megs!" Abbey shouted.

A thin, older black woman appeared at the doorway. "Yes, Miss Abbey? I do apologize for the delay in the refreshments; several of the maids were a bit slow getting back from the Captain's sermon."

"Oh, never mind about that now, Megs. Miss Evelyn is feeling quite peaked from her travels in the hot sun! Please take her to her room and lay her down. Then bring her something cool to drink."

Megs looked over at Evelyn and then hurried over to her. "I see what you mean, Miss Abbey. She don't look so well. I'll take care of her, don't you worry. Come dear, come with old Megs …" she cooed, putting a hand under Evelyn's arm and helping her up.

The journey upstairs to the bedroom was a blur. Soon she was stripped of her fine dress and lay in a soft bed. The room was warm, but not stifling. The black woman … Megs … was standing over her, looking down, handing her a glass of cool lemonade. "You's gonna be just fine, dear. Here … have a little drink of this then just relax and sleep. You'll feel better soon. Old Megs will take good care of you, don't you worry none. Just sleep now … sleep … I'll be close by to check in on you …" the words faded away into a dream.

ಬಿಎಲಿಛಿಅಬಿಎಲಿಛಿಅಬಿಎಲಿಛಿಅ

She awoke sometime later, and for a moment was completely disoriented, not knowing where she was or how she'd gotten there. She stared up at a strange ceiling.

"You feelin' better, dearie?" a kindly voice asked.

She looked down and saw Megs sitting on the edge of the bed. Suddenly it all came back in a rush—the carriage ride, meeting eyes with the man on the road, Miss Abbey. And then learning, to her shock, the mystery man was in fact Mr. Chambers. Only now, lying comfortably in bed, out of the heat, it no longer seemed so disorienting and overwhelming.

"Yes, much better. Thank you, Megs. How long have I slept?"

"Oh, not long dear. An hour … maybe a little more."

Evelyn sat up and realized she really did feel better now. *It must've just been the heat, or the tightness of the dress,* she concluded. And then she realized the only one she was lying to was herself. *Or the excitement …* she admitted.

"Tell me, Megs … what's he like, your master?"

She asked sincerely, but as soon as the words were out, she remembered a slave was unlikely to tell her anything she wanted to know about their master.

So it surprised her when Megs became thoughtful, as if pondering the question. She finally answered, "I don't rightly know how to describe Master Nathan, dear. He's not like any man I ever knowed before, that's for sure. He's … well … he was a terrible bad handful when he was a youngster, I can tell you that. Oh *my* … remembering some of the tricks he done pulled, and the troubles he got hisself into! It's downright amazing he lived to be growed up at all!"

She smiled and shook her head, as if recalling the scenes. Evelyn smiled with her, trying to imagine Nathan as a small boy.

"But you know … when he came back from the Army … he was changed-like; a *different* man. A man in control of himself and other men. A leader—the kind men want to be with and follow. And a kindlier man, more patient-like. And yet …"

"Yet?"

"Well, there's still a hardness there. Like if he don't want to budge from a spot, he won't budge for no man. And heaven help the man that crosses him in a *bad* way … I guess that's what a *real* man is about, ain't it dear? A kindness and a gentleness on the outside, but iron-hard on the inside … maybe?

"Oh, what do I know? I'm just an old woman and know little enough about the ways of men."

"You seem very wise to me, Megs. Thank you for speaking honestly with me. Your Mr. Chambers at least seems an interesting person to get to know. Hopefully I'll get to do that."

"Oh, yes. He's an *interesting* one, all right. But I've said enough. Best you discover the rest of what there is to know on your own.

"Come now, child … let's get you dressed and back downstairs with the other ladies. I'm sure they'll be starting in to worry 'bout you now. It'll do them good to see you with some color in your cheeks."

"Yes, thank you Megs."

She stood so the maid could help her back into her dress.

ॐৡৈৣৠৡৈৣৠৡৈৣৠ

During a lull in the shooting, while the men were out checking the damage they'd just inflicted on their targets, Nathan pulled Tom aside. He told him about the two ladies arriving from Richmond.

Tom smiled and said, "So Miss Abbey has arranged it all without a word to you? I'm surprised she hasn't already scheduled the wedding."

"Don't joke about it—she probably has! And she doesn't seem to need my opinion on it either!

"On the other hand, a man could do worse from what I've seen so far. She is definitely a *fine*-looking young lady. No … that's not quite fair … I should say she is *strikingly beautiful*. And charming too … from what I could tell."

"From what you could tell? Didn't you talk with her?"

"Well, yes … and … no."

"Yes, and no?"

"Well, she arrived so unexpectedly, and … I was caught off my guard by it all, and … couldn't seem to find my words. So I quickly made my excuses and withdrew."

Tom couldn't help but chuckle at his Captain's discomfort, which earned him a scowl from Nathan.

"What's so humorous about it?"

"Well, you have to admit, there is a bit of irony in it, sir. A professional soldier, and veteran of countless battles, fearless in the face of murderous outlaws and Indians—intimidated by a proper young lady?"

"Yes, I see your point ... but you don't have to enjoy it so much. Anyway, what do you suggest I do?"

"Do? Well, you must *court* her, of course, sir!"

"Court her?"

"Yes, sir. Miss Abbey wouldn't have arranged the visit if she hadn't already vetted the young woman and her family. And, you must admit, you *are* over thirty, so it's time you thought about a wife and children. On top of which, we are a bit isolated out here in western Virginia you know. That's got to make it more difficult to meet the right woman. So here you sit, your potential bride handed to you on a silver platter! Of course, you must court her, Captain! It's the only sensible plan of attack."

"Okay, Tom. I can see you're right, as usual. It's just ... it's taken me by surprise, and I feel ... well ... as if they've *conspired* against me somehow. As if I have no say in the matter. Hmm ... kind of like when you and Jim decided you were coming with me to Virginia, before I even knew I was going!"

He chuckled and slapped Tom hard on the arm. Then he turned and strode back to where the others were lined up to continue shooting.

"Well, that was for your own good as well, sir!" Tom shot back, rubbing his sore arm.

ༀ๏ﾒﾒﾒ๏ༀ๏ﾒﾒ๏ༀ๏ﾒﾒ

That evening, Nathan sat through an awkward meal with the ladies, filled with polite small talk. They prompted him with questions: the outlook for the crops, how the weather had been since his arrival, if he found the farm much changed from his youth, and other mundane and innocuous topics. He thought the conversation rather dull, and he could sense a nervous tension at the table, not least of which was emanating from his own seat.

Evelyn was lovely and charming. Her smile was bright, and there was a sparkle in her eyes difficult to ignore. But the words

310

coming from her mouth seemed trite and rehearsed. He wondered if this reflected her personality, or she was just nervous, and this was her way of dealing with it.

As the meal was winding down, he realized his courting campaign would never get very far with the two mothers present. Since the ladies were guests of the household, making them technically "friends of the family," he decided it would be acceptable for them to spend time alone, as long as it was in full daylight and out in the open where nothing untoward could possibly happen.

So he took the cold plunge into the dark, swirling waters of potential romance. When they stood from the table, he said, "Momma, would you be offended if I were to conduct Miss Evelyn on a tour of your flower gardens? With your permission, of course, Miss Harriet. And assuming you would be interested, Miss Evelyn."

"Certainly not, dear! That's a wonderful idea. The columbine and hollyhock are in full bloom and very lovely just now. But the dahlias and roses aren't blooming yet and won't be showing any color for another week or two—depending on the weather of course."

Nathan had expected nothing less from his mother, but gave his guests an inquisitive look. Evelyn turned to her mother for approval, which was entirely appropriate under the circumstances.

"Yes, certainly, Mr. Chambers. I'm sure Evelyn would enjoy Miss Abbey's flower gardens. Please, you two young people do go and enjoy the evening air. Miss Abbey and I have plenty more news of Richmond to discuss, having only just scratched bare the surface earlier today." She finished with a bright smile which her daughter mirrored.

Evelyn added, "Yes, that would be lovely, Mr. Chambers. I'm sure I would enjoy seeing it."

They stood, and for the first time she placed her hand on his arm. To Nathan she seemed surprisingly strong, but he felt a slight tremble. *Yes, I'm nervous too*, he thought, with immediate empathy for her.

They walked down the broad hallway which lead to the large foyer and front door in the one direction, and past the kitchens to the back door in the other. Nathan led Evelyn back toward Miss Abbey's flower gardens. As they passed down the hallway, Evelyn looked through a large open doorway on her left and saw the kitchen. There were tall, well-used counters for cutting and preparing food, and a large, simple table over in the far corner surrounded by chairs. This was where the household servants and the white farmhands ate their meals, though not at the same time. At the moment, the faces surrounding the table were all black ones, and Evelyn recognized the maid Megs among the group. They were enjoying each other's company amiably, though there was no loud talk or laughter; the master of the house wouldn't typically tolerate such an outburst. The servants didn't seem to notice as Nathan and Evelyn passed by the room.

"They use the kitchen inside the house for *preparing* the meals, but not for the cooking. This house, like many others I'm sure you're familiar with, has a separate building for cooking, all made of brick, just outside the back door.

"As you no doubt already know, they did this to prevent a runaway cooking fire destroying the main house. Not to mention the awful cooking heat inside a house on a hot summer day."

Since he hadn't been prepared for Evelyn's visit, he was at a disadvantage describing the workings of the house and farm, not knowing if he'd be telling her something new and interesting, or insulting her by telling her things she already knew. He was walking an awkward middle road with her.

"Yes, I'm familiar with the practice, Mr. Chambers. The house I grew up in had a similar arrangement." But, detecting her host's discomfort, she added, "But it was not nearly so grand and beautiful as this house."

She smiled up at him encouragingly.

Nathan opened the back door, and they paused a moment while Evelyn tied on a wide-brimmed straw hat with a sash of a lacey, silk-like material. The sun was still high, and without a hat its direct rays would burn the delicate skin of her face. Nathan put on his fine black, wide-brimmed hat from San Antonio. He'd collected it from a hook in the hallway as they'd walked to the door. They crossed the veranda to the back stairs.

Before they went down, Nathan glanced over to where several tables with chairs were arranged off to one side of the veranda. But neither Tom nor Jim were there, as was the norm after dinner, sipping whiskey and smoking cigars. The men were nowhere in sight this evening. Then he remembered Tom's excuse about feeling "indisposed" at dinner time. *Hmm ... another conspiracy apparently*, Nathan thought, and smiled.

The gravel path lead across the wide, neatly cropped lawn. When they had walked about half of it, they passed beneath the shade of a tree. It had mottled gray bark, and many thick, twisted branches covered with large, oval-shaped leaves of a bright green shade. "Oh, my!" Evelyn exclaimed when she recognized what it was. "This can't possibly be a magnolia, can it? I've never seen one so big before!"

Nathan smiled in appreciation. "Yes, it's a magnolia. In the spring it's entirely covered in beautiful, lavender and white flowers, shaped something like a tulip. My granddaddy brought the seedling with him when he came out here from Richmond. He planted it in the middle of a field of wild grass, long before there was any house or lawn. It seems the soil and climate has agreed with it, as you can see. I can remember when I was a child being amazed at the covering of flowers, thicker than the stars in the summer sky, like nothing else anywhere. In all my travels since, I've never seen the like, even in Richmond where they're quite common. In fact, when I planned my return home several months back, I remember feeling disappointed when I realized I would arrive too late to see it blooming this year. Oh well, there's always next year."

Evelyn looked up at him with curiosity. His description of the tree, and his feelings about it were sincere, serious, and heartfelt. It didn't seem like something he was saying for her benefit—some clever attempt to impress an impressionable young lady. When he spoke, he had a far-away look, as if seeing the tree through the eyes of the young boy—eyes filled with wonder at the glory of a beautiful, living thing. *What kind of man goes forth to war, committing murder and mayhem on the one hand, but gets all misty about a flowering tree on the other?* she wondered.

When they turned away from the tree to continue down the path, Evelyn noticed something large moving out of the corner of her eye back toward the house. When she turned around to look, she gasped, "My word, Mr. Chambers! What on earth kind of animal is *that?*"

Nathan turned to see what she was looking at, and laughed, "That, believe it or not, is a *dog*. Or at least that's what we assume he is, since he doesn't seem to fit the description for any other animal."

"But ... but, he is so ... *huge!* I've never seen a dog even remotely that size. More like a pony, except much stronger looking. Where did you come by him, and how?"

"No one rightly knows. He just showed up on the farm one day when I was away out West. He was growling and snarling at the workers. But when my Daddy showed up with a pistol to put an end to the menace, the beast groveled at his feet. So Daddy didn't have the heart to kill him. At least that's how the story goes. Then when I showed up, he repeated the trick, as if he somehow instinctively recognizes the master of the farm. Now he follows me everywhere I go, like a distant shadow. He'll never come much nearer, unless I force the issue, and he won't let anyone but me touch him."

"What's his name, or doesn't he have one?"

"Everyone calls him 'Harry the Dog.' My Daddy had a servant named Harry and for some reason the one reminded him of the other."

"Well, I think he's kind of cute—in a *very* large, and ugly way ..."

She took a step in his direction, holding out a hand. The dog had been sitting up, ears pricked up in their direction as if listening in on their conversation. He now lowered his head, turned, and slunk back into the shade of a bush growing near the house.

"That's odd," Nathan said, scratching his chin. "Never seen him react *that* way. Normally he growls and bares his teeth when

314

anyone tries to approach him. He's never been driven from the field in full retreat before."

"Well, perhaps he knows when he has met his match!" Evelyn responded with a laugh.

Nathan looked at her with a new appreciation. Perhaps there was more to her than just beauty and charm … "Maybe so … maybe so."

They turned and continued along the path. It led toward a decorative arbor of white-painted wood, thickly overgrown with wisteria, forming an archway of green leaves and purple blossoms. To either side was a tall hedge row of lilacs, their dark, lavender blossoms wafting a sweet smell across the lawn in the slight breeze. As they passed under the arbor, they entered Miss Abbey's flower garden.

Evelyn quickly realized Miss Abbey's was no ordinary flower garden. Rather, it was a testament to what one could accomplish with almost unlimited time, money, and … inexhaustible, free labor.

Evelyn guessed it covered more than an acre. The gravel path, neatly lined with square-cut cobblestones, meandered throughout the garden, splitting apart here, coming back together there. In stark contrast—perhaps intentionally so—to the straight rows and perfectly square corners of the commercial crops on the farm.

Also, in contrast to the farm's other crops, Miss Abbey had *not* arranged the flower garden by plant variety. With an artist's keen eye, she had arranged her garden as a visual feast for the eyes. She had sections with flowers of differing kinds, but similar colors, as in various shades of yellow, or pink, or red. In other areas she'd planted flowers of the same kind, but varying shades, arranged in a pleasing array. In yet other areas, the blossoms seemed to explode in every different vivid color, size, and style, like fireworks on the Fourth of July.

As they moved along, Evelyn realized Miss Abbey had not only artistically used the horizontal spaces of the garden—the areas defined by the meandering path—but had also made use of the vertical space, mixing plants of differing heights and textures in various interesting patterns. She also included plants simply

315

for their interesting colorful or textured leaves, though they had no blossoms.

Evelyn recognized many of the flowers: columbine, hollyhock, lavender, daisy, lily, iris, and many, many others. Still others she'd never seen before and didn't know their names.

And the scents! They nearly overwhelmed her olfactory senses. She'd thought the lilac blossoms out by the arbor pungent, but inside the garden the various flowers competed to see which scent would dominate the others. The result was extraordinary.

Honeybees buzzed about everywhere, as if trying to decide which scent was most enticing. *Poor things must not know where to turn next!* Evelyn thought.

And then something buzzed past her ear at great speed, and she flinched. At first, she imagined it must be the greatest bumblebee ever seen, but then she realized it was a hummingbird.

She watched as the tiny bird poked its long, thin beak into a blossom, hovering just in front.

"Oh! Mr. Chambers ... they are so ... *precious.* Do they come often to the garden?"

He laughed, and said, "Look for yourself!" gesturing out across the garden.

She'd been so focused on the beauty of the sights right in front of her face she hadn't gazed across the entirety of the garden until now. She looked up and gasped. Dozens upon dozens of the tiny birds hovered and flitted from flower to flower, seemingly covering every part of the garden.

"Oh my goodness! So many! I've never seen more than one or two at a time, and those but rarely. Oh! They're so lovely, and so cute ... oh, *oh!* They're just ... *darling!*"

"Yes, they are. But don't let their small size and delicate features fool you—they're feisty little creatures, and as tough as they are small. Those little fellows are out here feeding on these flowers in weather that would drive any other beast in under cover. Wind-driven rain coming down sideways, thunder and lightning ... none of it matters to them.

"And if one has a flower he particularly likes, he'll fight off all comers to make sure he gets the lion's share of its nectar."

He smiled wistfully as he talked, and once again she imagined she was getting a small glimpse of the little boy inside the man. It made her smile with genuine pleasure.

"Here, let me show you a trick I used to enjoy when I was a boy. Pick a large, red-colored flower, then hold it up above your head, as high as you can."

"All right."

She looked around a moment, then found a huge, red amaryllis, with five blossoms on top, and picked one flower.

"Hold it up with two fingers and spread the other fingers out wide."

She gave him a bemused expression but did as he said.

She held the blossom up above her head. For a minute, nothing happened, and she looked over at him, with a raised eyebrow.

"Give it a moment," he grinned.

She waited another moment, then just looked down at him again when she felt something touch one of her fingers. She looked up, and saw one of the tiny birds, perching on her finger, its long beak poked into the amaryllis.

"Oh!" she exclaimed, covering her mouth with her other hand. She turned toward Nathan, and smiled such a dazzling smile, it took his breath away. He couldn't help smiling back.

Then she looked back up at her tiny visitor. He had a sparkling, iridescent red throat, grayish-green vest, and a long, straight, thin bill. He also had white underparts, and a black tail with white spots at the tips of the feathers. But as she was examining her little guest, another arrived, and perched on a different finger. This one had totally different colors—a female, she guessed. She had a green back, and a black mask with just a touch of white behind the eyes. But before Evelyn could look back at Nathan, another male landed on the next finger. And then another landed, and still another.

She had to stifle a squeal of delight, for fear she would frighten off her little guests. To Evelyn, the sight of the tiny birds perched on her own hand feeding was a thing of unimaginable wonder.

To Nathan, watching her, the look on her face—her pure, girlish joy—warmed his heart in a way he'd rarely felt.

And then, as quickly as they'd arrived, something startled them, and all launched themselves from her hand at once.

She lowered her arm.

"Whew … I was afraid I couldn't hold my hand up there much longer!

"Oh, Mr. Chambers! That was so … *wonderful!* I've never held a wild bird in my hand before, let alone a half-dozen! Thank you so much for that!"

"It was my pleasure to see it. I learned that trick back when I was a boy, and then I showed Miss Abbey. She was so pleased it made her cry, of course."

"She is so sweet, and kindhearted. And this garden is so beautiful. Why … I've never seen the like! Miss Abbey is truly an artist in floriculture!"

"Thank you. Yes, I agree. It's truly amazing what she can do with a few seeds and a little dirt," he said with a laugh.

"And sunshine, water … and fertilizer, I suppose," she added, smiling up at him.

He returned the smile easily.

Then it occurred to him Miss Abbey had created this beauty with slave labor. The thought momentarily dimmed his bright mood, like a cloud passing over the sun. To break the uncomfortable train of thought, he said, "Come, I have something else I would show you. I think you'll enjoy it. Feel free to come and wander about the flower garden at your leisure whenever you please. I find it takes several hours to take it all in. And every day there is some new blossom to see."

"That I can well believe," she said with great earnestness, once again taking his arm. She found she enjoyed the feel of it: strong as iron, but also soft and warm, somehow.

They left the garden on the opposite side from the wisteria arbor. Here was another white arbor, this one covered in clematis, a pink and purple explosion of star-shaped flowers covering dark green vines. Rather than lilacs to form its walls, this arbor made use of Miss Abbey's dahlias.

"They're her pride and joy. When they're in bloom, they're the highlight of the garden, which is why she places them at the very

318

back," Nathan explained. "Women come from all over the county to see them when they're blooming. Some even make the trek from Richmond, I'm told."

Here they grew thickly, some as tall as Nathan, and many with blossoms as large as his head. But as Miss Abbey had warned, they weren't quite yet in blossom, their large "heads" swelling with the colorful petals within, nearly ready to open ... but not yet.

"Miss Abbey says a few more weeks, but it seems to me they're ready to burst at any moment," Nathan said, and once again laughed in his easy manner.

Evelyn was enjoying that sound. "I *would* agree with you, but I think it would be ill-advised to bet against Miss Abbey, when it comes to flowers."

"Yes, you have a good point there, Miss Evelyn."

They passed through the archway, and now the path wound through tall, unkempt grass—a wilder area of the gardens, with shrubs and small plants more randomly and naturally propagated. In the near distance Evelyn saw they were approaching a large weeping willow. Though the magnolia back on the lawn had been overly large for its kind, this huge, gnarly old willow dwarfed it. As they approached its welcoming shade, Evelyn noticed a sturdily built swing of a light-color, varnished to a high gloss, hanging beneath a great branch, suspended by sturdy ropes.

Beyond the tree and its swing, she saw a pond. It wasn't overly large, a little less than two acres in size, but she found it a truly beautiful sight. Cattails and bulrushes, along with bright yellow water iris, lined the edge. The pond had large areas of open water, interspersed with areas covered in lily pads, their pointy purple and pink blossoms providing a splash of bright color to an otherwise blue and green pallet. Vibrantly colored ducks swam in small groups out on the water, like fleets of small ships, creating ever-widening "V"s in their wake. When Evelyn stepped up close to the water, a large, bumpy, gray-green bullfrog expressed its annoyance with a loud "croak," and an even louder splash into the water. Evelyn jumped at the sudden noise and motion, then laughed. "Sorry, Mr. Toad! I'm afraid we startled each other!"

She smiled brightly, and Nathan smiled back. He was feeling a warmth toward this young woman as welcome as it was unexpected—as if he hadn't realized what he was missing in life until it was thrust suddenly in front of him.

"Will you join me for a rest in the shade on the swing?" he gestured toward the tree and its suspended seat.

An uncomfortable memory of Stanley Finch and the bench in the garden back in Richmond flashed through her mind, and she shuddered. Then she shook off that memory, looked up at Nathan and smiled, "Yes, of course. That would be lovely."

She could tell without the slightest doubt Mr. Nathaniel Chambers was a real, honest gentleman. He had no more in common with Stanley Finch than he had with that bullfrog in the pond!

Once they'd settled onto the swing, Nathan gave the ground a gentle kick to start the seat into motion. They rocked back and forth for a few moments in silence. Evelyn took in the idyllic scene, the cool shade, the lovely pond, and the ducks slowly paddling by. She relaxed and leaned back, enjoying the pleasant motion of the swing. It seemed to her nothing could be better than this. She closed her eyes and breathed in deeply. And though this area by the pond didn't have the sweet smells of the flower garden, she nevertheless thought it a very pleasant smell—the smell of life in all its richness.

When she opened her eyes again, Nathan was gazing at her with a curious expression. "Do you like this place?"

"Oh, Mr. Chambers ... *like* is not a strong enough word for it. It's lovely. No ... *lovely* is too common a word. I don't have words for how wonderful it is ... along with this whole farm ... the grand old house, Miss Abbey's gardens, this pond. Everything about your home is just ... *perfect*? *Beautiful*? Oh, I don't know how to describe it ..." she trailed off. She struggled to find words for the feelings she was having about the farm, this moment ... and this *man*.

Nathan smiled, clearly pleased with her reaction.

"Yes, this is one of my favorite places. I often come here to think. This place … it's more than just a pretty picture … it's *alive*, somehow. All the living things, the plants, the ducks … ha! Even the ugly old bullfrogs, make it something more. Somehow it has an energy that fills me … makes me invigorated. Like after a few hours of being here I can go back into the world and do great things. Sorry … that must sound silly …"

"Oh no, I see what you mean. I feel it too. This is such a special place … full of life and …" she trailed off, realizing she was about to say, "and full of love …" *Too soon for that!* she chastised herself.

They were silent for a few more moments, just taking in the sights and the sounds, enjoying the gentle rocking of the swing, creating its own cooling breeze. Evelyn was reluctant to break the silence, but worried if it continued it might become awkward, so she said, "Mr. Chambers, I do believe if there is such a thing, this farm must be heaven on earth."

She thought it was a nice continuation of their earlier talk, and it would be an easy way to restart the conversation.

But she was surprised when he abruptly stopped the swing and turned toward her with a serious look.

"Not heaven. *Almost* heaven, but *not* heaven," he said in a more serious tone.

"Whatever do you mean, Mr. Chambers? What could possibly be amiss in this glorious place?" Evelyn asked, genuinely curious what he could mean by it.

"It *would* be heaven, if it weren't for the slaves."

"I don't understand. What's wrong with the slaves? Don't you *like* them? Do you dislike being around the black people?"

"No, no, you misunderstand. It's not that I dislike the black people … I like them just fine … as *people*. I just don't like them as *slaves*."

Evelyn's mind reeled, rudely pulled from the idyllic dream of the garden, pond, and swing. She found herself suddenly, unexpectedly thrust into rough, uncharted waters.

What was Mr. Chambers' trying to say? What was his *real* opinion on slavery? Harriet had said nothing about that. She'd assumed since the Chamber's plantation had many dozens of slaves his opinions would be nothing but pro-slavery and anti-abolition. Was he really saying he opposed the very idea of slavery? Or was this a *test*—a test to see where she stood on the subject?

Her mind worked quickly, almost in a panic, trying to recall her mother's training—the long hours going over, and over what to say, how to act. How quickly she had forgotten all of *that* under the influence of this overwhelming man!

And then it came to her. She could hear the voice of her mother as clearly as if Miss Harriet were sitting next to her on the swing.

"They will test you, Evelyn. They will say things to get your reaction, to see if you are a true Southern lady. They will say things like 'I'm thinking the abolitionists may have a point. What do you think, my dear?' and you must stay firm. You must remember the words we practiced. You must say what a proper Southern lady would say, or they will reject you as someone corrupted by Northern influence. Mark my words, Evelyn! Don't forget."

"Well, surely Mr. Chambers, the black men are much better off on this beautiful farm than ever they were back in the dark jungles of Africa? Surely, they had to work just as hard there to scratch out a meager living, and had worse living conditions? And undoubtedly chiefs, or kings, or some such, were much harsher task masters?"

She found the words flowed easily now she had calmed herself.

"Well, yes, I have to admit it's a possibility. But it's really not the point. The slavers didn't bring them out of Africa to do them a favor. They stole them from their homes and sold them for money. They can never justify that using twisted logic—that somehow, we did it for their own good.

"Besides, how they got here, and why, is in the past, and no longer something we can do anything about. I believe we must accept moral responsibility for what we're doing *now*, at this very moment. Not for what our predecessors did years ago."

"But, Mr. Chambers, are we not giving them food, shelter, and clothing? Are we not providing them with steady employment? It seems to me it's not so very different from how they treat immigrants from Ireland, and other parts of Europe in the North. Why, I've heard those Northern factory laborers work harder and longer hours. And they're forced to live in company-owned houses and buy their own food and clothing from their meager wages. At the end of the day they have no money left over to spend on what they wish. So even though they are supposedly 'free men' paid wages, they are no better off than our so-called 'slaves,' and likely worse."

Evelyn was feeling more confident in her role.

"Hmm … yes, I've heard such arguments before. But it seems to me a man should not justify his own actions by arguing they are no worse than those of his neighbor. My neighbor may *also* be wrong, and his house may also need repair. That does not absolve me of the responsibility for the condition of my *own* house."

"And what about their souls, Mr. Chambers? Have we not brought to them the enlightenment of the teachings of our Lord Jesus Christ? Are they not now able to attain the blessings of the afterlife forever denied them in heathen Africa? Why, Miss Abbey tells me you yourself preach to them from the Bible every Sunday, which I find most admirable, if I may say so."

"Well, yes, I must admit I struggle greatly with that argument. Our Lord teaches us to bring his word to all the people of the world, or their souls will not be saved. Without it they will suffer eternal damnation in the afterlife."

Nathan then went quiet as if deep in thought. He kicked the swing back into motion, and they were silent as the seat gently swayed back and forth.

"It may be the one true benefit they've received from all this."

He'd lowered his voice and seemed to have lost some of the passion of a few moments earlier. This time he had not stopped the swing but spoke as it gently swung.

"I've debated *this* question the most with myself. I am a *true* believer and must trust in the Word of our Lord. The Bible says saving their souls is worth any price, is worth any worldly sacrifice on their part. But even so, I must believe there's a better way. I have heard of men called 'missionaries' who go out into Africa, and other foreign lands, to spread the Word among the heathen. I'm sure it's slow progress, and dangerous work. But it seems like it's the *right* way to do it. It is asking great sacrifice of the *teacher*, rather than the *student*. Somehow that feels more *right* to me. I can even imagine myself going on such a mission one day."

Once again, he fell silent and seemed thoughtful.

Evelyn was having doubts. This was no longer feeling like some sort of test. He seemed so earnest and sincere. Could it be he truly believed the things he was saying? Could her mother be wrong about this? She couldn't decide what to do, which direction to go. Should she continue playing her expected part, or seem to give in, and agree with him? What was the right course of action?

And ... what do I really think about all this? It hit her like a bolt of lightning from the clear blue sky—the most disturbing notion of all. She really didn't know her own mind on the subject. Or *any* subject, for that matter. She'd spent so many years being told one thing by her father, and sometimes the total opposite by her mother, she felt like she'd lost her own, independent mind.

Evelyn fought against a rising panic. She knew she should say something, but her mind was in such disarray she was nearly overwhelmed. *No ... calm yourself, Evelyn,* she scolded, *it won't do to have another fainting spell! You won't make a very impressive future wife that way!*

Then it came to her. The safest course of action was to stop giving opinions, and simply ask questions. It was another trick Harriet had taught her; if in doubt, stop talking and just ask questions, listen, and nod attentively.

"So if you believe all of what you've just said, you must be ... conflicted? About being the master of this place?"

She breathed a sigh of relief she'd been able to come up with *something* to say.

"Yes, that would be a fair statement. I was content as an army officer out West and had no thoughts of returning home until Daddy passed away. It was difficult to resign my commission and return here. I doubt I would've done so if it weren't for worry about Miss Abbey running this place all by herself, or trying to sell it on her own, with no experience in business."

"So you decided to return home?"

"Yes, in the end I decided I *must* return home, and take responsibility for my family affairs," he answered. He'd decided not to mention his decision to free the slaves ... yet. Not until he knew her better and knew he could trust her.

Nathan was feeling conflicted. He was greatly attracted to this beautiful young woman on many levels. More so than any woman in a very long time ... maybe *ever*. She was intelligent, charming, and the very picture of a perfect lady. Her passionate, heartfelt reaction to the beauty of the gardens, the birds, and the pond had touched him deeply—it was clearly something they held in common.

And yet, she seemed so entrenched in the Southern tradition she was almost immune to his arguments about slavery. Her responses were the same old tired reasoning he'd come to expect from people simply spouting what they'd been taught from birth: the negroes were inferior, we were doing them a favor, etc., etc. It frustrated him he couldn't really talk to her, to somehow get beneath that hard, Southern armor and appeal to the human being underneath.

"And now you're here, and conflicted about slavery, what do you intend to do to resolve your dilemma?"

Her tone was still pleasant, and unemotional. But Nathan noticed she had never given her opinion on all this, other than to throw out the typical arguments. He wondered if she was just asking questions to avoid having to do so, not because she was truly interested in what he had to say.

"I don't know," he answered curtly, and once again stopped the swing. "Shall we return to the house? I'm sure Miss Harriet and Miss Abbey will be anxious for our return."

"Yes, certainly," she responded mildly, and they rose from the seat. Yet inside she knew somehow this conversation had *not* gone well. Even though she'd followed her mother's training, and hadn't slipped up, it didn't *feel* right. She would have to think on it later to decide how she could have done better. Maybe when they were alone, she could discuss it with Miss Harriet and see if she had any ideas.

They made their way back through the flower garden, this time taking a different course to see other parts of the garden. Evelyn continued to hold Nathan's arm, but now he felt tense somehow. He didn't talk much, and when he did it was terse, and seemed devoid of the earlier emotion.

When they returned to the house, the two older ladies greeted them. They were sitting at a table on the veranda, on the side away from the strong rays of the westering sun. They seemed to have been enjoying themselves, smiling and chatting easily as Nathan and Evelyn approached.

"Oh, hello, my dears," Miss Abbey said brightly, "back so soon? How did you enjoy my flower garden, Miss Evelyn?"

"Oh, Miss Abbey! It is wonderful beyond my wildest imaginings! Momma, you really must see it! The finest gardens I've seen in Richmond pale by comparison. My most heartfelt congratulations, Miss Abbey. You are truly an artist in the medium of growing, blossoming flora. Truly, truly, beautiful … and wonderful—oh! I said *that* already," she said with a quick laugh. She went on to describe the wonders she'd seen there, especially the delightful little birds.

Once again Nathan felt himself relaxing. And again, he enjoyed Evelyn's almost child-like wonder and enthusiasm as she described the gardens to Harriet. But when he glanced at Miss Abbey, he could see her watching him, with a concerned look. She was keenly perceptive of people's moods and feelings, and he knew she could tell something was slightly amiss with him.

When there was a pause in the talk, Nathan interjected, "If you ladies will excuse me, I'd like to check in on Tom to see how he's feeling. If you recall, he skipped dinner because he was feeling unwell. I have farm business to discuss with him and would like to see if he's up to it."

"Of course, dear," Miss Abbey responded. "We shall just sit here a bit longer and enjoy the setting sun before retiring for the evening."

Nathan wished them all a good evening and went back into the house.

Although it had been a convenient excuse to remove himself from the company of the ladies, he did want to speak with Tom, though not about farm business.

Nathan used the back stairs—the "servant's stairs"—which were narrower, and less showy than the grand, curving stairway in the foyer. He took the stairs two at a time up to the second floor, and then down the hall to the small office where Tom usually held forth.

As expected, Tom was sitting at the desk, going over a stack of papers, ink pen in hand. He didn't appear ill, which did not surprise Nathan in the least.

"Well ... on the mend I see, Mr. Clark!" Nathan said with a smirk.

Tom turned around in his chair and smiled, "Yes; feeling much better, sir. Thanks for asking."

"Had a slight bout of discretion, no doubt?" Nathan asked in a mock-serious tone.

"Yes, something of the kind. But nothing a little hard work—and perhaps a sip of whiskey later—won't cure, I'm sure," Tom responded in good humor. "So, Captain, how goes the wooing?"

Nathan sat down heavily in the seat opposite Tom and let out a heavy sigh.

"Ooh ... that doesn't sound good, sir."

"I seem to be out of practice in the fine art. Can't recall struggling this hard with it when I was younger. I remember being more relaxed and confident around the young girls. And they usually responded appreciatively."

Tom nodded, but didn't interrupt, allowing Nathan to finish his thought.

"But now ... for some reason I'm fumbling for things to say. And when I do say something it isn't the *right* thing. Just now I turned what should've been a perfectly romantic moment into a serious, political discussion, utterly spoiling the whole show. I feel out of sorts, confused, and unsure of myself.

327

"Well, don't just sit there enjoying my discomfort ... out with it, Tom! What's the matter with me?"

Tom chuckled.

"The explanation is really quite simple, Captain. You felt relaxed with those girls in the past because you had nothing to lose. If they responded in kind, fine. If they didn't, well ... you knew there was always the next one, no harm done.

"Now, it's different. You're older, and more serious in your intentions. You're looking at this young lady as a potential bride, not as a happy roll in the hay. The stakes are higher, and also ..." he trailed off, as if thinking of the right words.

"Also, what?"

"Also, I'm not sure why but ... it seems like this *particular* girl is different somehow. Of course, I don't know her, and have barely talked to her, but when I see the two of you together, I *feel* something. It's hard to put into words, but it feels like it's a good fit."

"Hmm ... maybe you're right, Tom. She's beautiful, that's for sure. But a lot of those other girls were also. And charming, and witty, and all the other good things. But again, nothing extraordinary ... I don't know. There is *something* about her ... I must admit I'm excited by the possibilities. Maybe that's what's putting me off my stride.

"But I'm also a little frustrated with her. It feels like she's not being honest with me ... that there's something just under the surface she's not letting me see. Something she's guarding and keeping to herself."

"Well, maybe she's just nervous, and being reserved. Sometimes it takes people a little while to open up to strangers. She doesn't know you yet, so doesn't feel free to be herself with you. Give it some time."

"Yes, of course! You're absolutely right, Tom. On all counts ... as *usual*, I should add!"

Nathan was now feeling much better. He stood and slapped Tom on the shoulder in appreciation before heading to the door, "Thanks, Tom. You've been a great help.

"You're welcome, sir."

Tom then said a quick, silent prayer he was right about all this! After all, he'd not done so well himself in his most recent romantic affair.

And then, for the thousandth time, he thought of Adilida, and felt a familiar knot in the pit of his stomach. He hadn't told the Captain it was the other reason he'd skipped the dinner; the sight of Nathan with Miss Evelyn brought back painful memories of his own recent romance. Memories he still could not shake from his mind, along with the lingering doubts. Had he been mistaken about her? Had he done the right thing, leaving without telling her goodbye? That pain in his stomach didn't seem to think so …

ᔡᏇᏻᏇᔡᏇᏻᏇᔡᏇᏻᏇ

Later that evening, Evelyn and Harriet had excused themselves from Miss Abbey's company to retire to their rooms for the night. They now sat on the edge of the bed in Evelyn's room and quietly discussed the day's events. Harriet demanded a complete and detailed description of Evelyn's walk with Nathan—everything they saw, everything they did, and everything they said. Evelyn didn't hesitate telling her mother every detail. It felt like they were in this together—co-conspirators of a sort—and she desperately needed her opinion and counsel on the matter.

At the end of her narrative, which Harriet frequently interrupted to ask questions and to offer various opinions, Evelyn said, "I believe I did and said everything correctly. And yet … it feels like it didn't go so very well. Oh, for a while it felt *really* fine, like everything was going just beautifully. But then … then after we'd been talking for a while, I felt like he wasn't pleased with me. Should I have been more agreeable, do you think? I was afraid to fall into one of those traps you warned me of. But maybe … maybe he really meant what he said, and I disappointed him by not agreeing?"

"No, no … you did just fine. Listen … I wasn't wasting my time in idle gossip while you were out sightseeing. I was using the time to our best advantage—prodding Miss Abbey for every

329

bit of useful information I might gather about your future spouse. So I'm not at all surprised by the things he said to you."

Harriet spoke in quiet, conspiratorial tones, as if someone might be listening at the door, which was entirely possible in a house full of servants.

"You're not? Oh, you mean you expected him to test me?"

"Well … yes … and no," Harriet answered cryptically, causing Evelyn to raise her brows in confusion.

"You see … he wasn't exactly testing to see if you were sympathetic to the abolitionists, but rather if you could be sympathetic to the negro slaves. You see, Miss Abbey explained to me Mr. Chambers is rather young and idealistic—naïve, I might call it. But even so, it seems he is trying to improve the lot for his slaves. Preaching sermons on Sundays, learning their names, fixing up their cabins, treating them with all Christian kindness, that sort of thing. Why, I understand he even fired his head foreman in a dispute about whether or not a young Negress should be whipped for being sassy!"

And though Harriet described Mr. Chambers' actions in a tone that said she did *not* approve, to Evelyn this sounded very admirable of him. But she said nothing and let her mother continue with her explanation.

"So you see, he is not especially concerned about your opinions on abolition—by now I'm sure he is quite sure on that score. What he wants to know is whether or not you can have his same kind of … compassion? *Empathy*, maybe? Anyway, if you are capable of showing kindness to the slaves. So here's what you will do …"

𝕰𝖚𝕰𝖚𝕮𝖀𝕰𝖚𝕰𝖚𝕮𝖀𝕰𝖚𝕰𝖚𝕮𝖀

The next morning at breakfast, Nathan seemed cheerful once again, easily making small talk with the ladies and Tom. Nathan continually made eye contact with Evelyn, to her great pleasure, and seemed to have completely recovered from his glum mood of the evening before.

As the servants were clearing away the dishes, he rose and said, "Miss Evelyn, would you do me the honor of accompanying me once again on a little tour?" He made a slight bow in her direction.

"It would be my great pleasure, Mr. Chambers," she replied with genuine enthusiasm, flashing him her best smile.

Without further ado, he held out his hand to her, which she accepted as she stood from the table.

"Ladies … Tom … if you will excuse us … I will wish you a very good morning!" Nathan said with a smile and another slight bow.

After all the "good mornings" were properly exchanged, Nathan offered Evelyn his arm once again, and together they strode out the front door.

It was another glorious summer morning. Evelyn was feeling much more confident after her talk with Harriet the night before, aided by the apparent good humor of Mr. Chambers. She was determined today there would be no mistakes. She would do and say everything just so … she would make him want to continue their unspoken courtship.

While Evelyn was thinking these thoughts, Nathan was also determined there would be no repeat of the evening before—no uncomfortable political discussion. Just an easy walk around the grounds, meeting and talking with whoever they should meet, with no particular agenda.

"This building, now only a tool shed, was the original manor house when my granddaddy first settled this land!"

They stood in front of a small, square, one-room building with a single, small window on each side.

"Oh, my!" Evelyn responded with genuine surprise. "And … how many people lived in that tiny house?"

"Four. My granddaddy and grandma with my father, and his sister—my Aunt Annie—who now lives in Richmond."

Evelyn stopped and looked back at the grand house they'd just come from, with its wide lawn surrounding.

"Isn't it amazing what people can do when they set their minds to it? It is truly incredible that this amazing plantation started from such humble beginnings, not so very long ago."

"Yes … it never ceases to impress me what my granddaddy, and my daddy after him drew forth from raw wilderness, just … hmm … fifty or so years ago."

Then the thought of the slave labor it had required to accomplish it flashed through his mind. He suppressed it through an effort of will, so as not to spoil the mood.

"Beautiful. Just beautiful … but I said that yesterday," Evelyn said, wondering if it was the right time to explore the touchy subject of the previous day. She decided to plunge in and test the waters, "but you said you were uncomfortable about the slaves who made all this possible?"

"Well, yes, that's true. But I don't want to spoil the mood of this beautiful day by discussing anything that might be … controversial."

"Oh, don't trouble your mind, Mr. Chambers. I am nothing if not open-minded when it comes to any philosophical discussion. For example, I do believe we should treat the negro slaves with all Christian kindness and charity. And we should appreciate their labors on our behalf to the greatest degree possible," she intentionally flashed him her most charming smile.

Nathan had to suppress a strong desire to embrace her. He found when she spoke to him in this way and smiled in that utterly irresistible manner, she was surely the most desirable woman in the world. He turned away to avoid her intoxicating gaze.

"Yes, I agree. They are … most admirable in their hard work … and their contribution to the success of this farm is … immeasurable. I believe this deserves the utmost respect and appreciation on our part. Shall we … meet some of them?"

"Certainly, Mr. Chambers. Please … lead on."

Before they had gone far, she stole a quick look over her shoulder, and saw what she was expecting: a large brown and gray animal padding along behind at a safe distance. She turned to Nathan and caught his eye, motioning backward with her head and smiling. He turned his head to see what she was motioning toward and let out a chuckle.

"Yep, wherever I go, my shadow is never far behind!"

332

They shared a laugh.

He led her to the nearest field. It was a field of tobacco, and in the middle was a group of black men hoeing weeds, supervised by one of the white farmhands. To keep out the sun, Evelyn wore a white, wide-brimmed hat, trimmed with lace hanging down at the sides and carried a white, lace-trimmed parasol. Nathan wore his formal, black hat, which also had a wide brim. Despite the protection on their faces they could feel the sun beating down on their clothes, and they began to sweat in the heat. Evelyn wondered how it must be for the black workers, out in the full sun all day with no respite.

When they got close to the workmen, the white farmhand stepped up to greet them. He was young, probably not even as old as she. And he was thin and gangly looking, with long, scraggly looking reddish hair sticking out from under his wide-brimmed felt hat. "Good morning, Captain … Miss," he said, bowing his head slightly toward Evelyn. He smiled self-consciously and was obviously shy around upper-class women — he was having a hard time looking at her directly. She'd found this typical of working-class men. Upper-class gentlemen, on the other hand, had no such troubles, though sometimes she wished they had!

"Zeke, this is Miss Evelyn. Miss Evelyn, please meet Ezekiel Benton. Miss Evelyn and her mother Harriet are here for a visit."

"Very nice to meet you, ma'am," he responded, removing his hat, and unconsciously crushing it in his hands.

"The pleasure is all mine, Mr. Benton," she replied politely, giving him a slight nod, rather than a full curtsy, as was proper given their differences in station.

"Oh, no ma'am, nobody ever calls me 'Mr. Benton.' Just 'Zeke' will do, if you have a mind to call on me at all," he responded, blushing.

"All right … Zeke it shall be!" she said and smiled. "But please, Zeke, put your hat back on … you'll catch your death from this hot sun!"

"Thank you kindly, ma'am—worrying about my health and such. Well, best be back to work, unless y'all are needing me for something, Captain?"

"No, thank you, Zeke ... just do call the men over for a moment, if you please. I would like to speak with them."

Zeke turned and called out, "All right fellers, y'all listen up! Just be setting down your hoes and come on over. Captain wants a word with you." He then tipped his hat to Nathan and Evelyn and moved away toward where the men had just laid down their hoes.

The group moved over to where Nathan and Evelyn stood.

The demeanor of these workers surprised Evelyn, not the surly, downcast looks she was used to seeing from farm slaves. Several of these men actually smiled. And rather than looking at their feet, as she remembered from when she was a young girl walking the rounds with her father, these men looked up at Mr. Chambers. They seemed relaxed, even happy at the unexpected intrusion on their labors. She wondered at this, but couldn't decide what to make of it.

"Gentlemen, I would like to introduce you to Miss Evelyn, who is a guest in our home."

Evelyn was shocked when the black men looked right at her and several of them said, "Hello, Miss Evelyn," almost in unison!

"Hello," she answered, not knowing what else to do or say. She found it most odd. Even with her father, whom she had considered most sympathetic to the slaves, there had never been such ... *familiarity*.

Warning bells were ringing in her head once again from her mother's training. Was he testing her again? Did he want her to express an opinion? To react to the seeming familiarity of the slaves?

Nathan then introduced each by name, which surprised her, but seemed to please the men immensely.

He seemed pleased with the exchange as they continued on, so she decided to play it safe with an inquiry, rather than a statement.

"Have your workers always been so … *familiar* … with their masters?" she asked, hesitantly.

"Oh, no, not at all! That's all *my* doing. My Daddy would've never allowed it! It comes partly from my military training, I suppose … in the Army men aren't allowed to hang their heads and look pathetic. It's always, 'chin up, and chest out,' in the ranks. So when I arrived back home and saw all those downcast, dejected looks, and shuffling feet … I was downright appalled! Guess I'd forgotten the way it was back here after being gone so long. Anyway, it seems to me if a person wants respect, he must stand tall, and meet the other man's eye. So that's what I've been teaching them to do."

"Oh … I see," she said, noncommittally.

"You don't approve, I can see." It was a statement, not a question.

"Oh, no! Did I say so? No … it's just … just hard to get used to, is all. I've been around the negroes my whole life, and … well, I've never seen them act *that* way before. It is … a little … shocking, that's all. They've always seemed so … *subservient*. Like they aren't comfortable with us and would rather not look at us directly."

"Hmm … yes, it is their usual manner, for sure. But I believe you'll find it's a learned behavior, rather than something in their nature. Despite all the teaching and preaching to the contrary, they are *real* men underneath all the bowing and scraping. With the same thoughts, wishes, and needs as us. Believe me, Miss Evelyn, the crack of a whip across a man's back can have a very strong effect on his behavior, no matter the color of his skin! I have seen it myself frequently."

Nathan was warming to his topic, and was speaking more emphatically now, gesturing broadly as he talked.

Despite her trepidation at doing or saying the wrong thing, Evelyn was enjoying hearing the man speak in this manner—so direct … so forceful! So sure of the things he was saying. His strong, handsome countenance had a more serious and determined expression than any she'd seen up until now. She smiled as he spoke, which, unexpectedly, she quickly regretted.

"Do you find something humorous in what I've said, Miss Evelyn?"

His tone sounding offended, mistaking her smile for something other than appreciation.

"No, no, Mr. Chambers. It was just …"

"You think me naïve … or ignorant maybe, since I've been up North, and then out West for so long?" he was getting a little heated.

"Please, Mr. Chambers! Don't put words in my mouth." She was feeling a touch of heat herself. "I was … simply appreciating the firmness with which you were expressing your convictions."

"But you disagree …" he shot back, still not completely mollified.

"I never said *that*, Mr. Chambers. I've been raised of a different viewpoint, that's all. I'm not used to such ideas … I … I was raised to see the negroes as nothing more than servants—*property* even. Now you say they are men like us … in some circles that would be considered … oh, I don't know, 'blasphemous' isn't quite right, is it? But something like it, anyway. There are many people in the South who would be highly incensed by such words."

She was carefully skirting around stating a firm position, one way or the other. Harriet's strong words of warning continued to echo through her mind. But on the other hand, Mr. Chambers seemed so sincere, so certain of what he was saying. Surely this was not a test, but his real, true feelings? Should she agree with him? Would he think her fickle and easily swayed if she did? Or would he believe her incapable of sympathy for the plight of the negroes if she didn't?

Once again, playing it safe won out.

"I'm sorry if I have offended you, Mr. Chambers. It was not my intention. Shall we continue our tour?"

"Yes, certainly. And no, you have not offended me. Think nothing more of it," he said, and once again held out his arm for her to hold as they continued their walk. But once again she felt a stiffness in his touch.

They walked along for a while without talking. He was now leading her back out of the tobacco field, toward what appeared to be a group of small houses or cabins. She recognized them as the slave quarters they had passed by on the day she had arrived in the carriage. They left the neat rows of cotton plants behind and walked across a narrow strip of neatly trimmed grass lining the roadway into the welcome shade of an oak tree. Near the base of the tree was a large, solidly built table with matching benches — the very table where Nathan had earlier chopped up the bullwhip, although Evelyn knew nothing of that. To her, it was simply welcome shade from the hot sun.

"May we sit for a moment in the shade, Mr. Chambers?"

"Yes, of course. The day is heating up. It seems like we're in for a warm summer this year."

He pulled out one of the benches for her to sit on.

They sat in silence for several minutes, looking out across the road at the row of small, rough houses on the other side. Evelyn could see the signs of recent repair: new shakes on the roofs in patches, new siding boards among the old, weathered ones. A new shiny doorknob on a door where the hinges were old and dull. The handiwork of Stan, William, and Sergeant Jim, although she didn't know it, and had not yet met any of Nathan's men other than Tom.

"It seems you've been busy since your arrival," she offered.

"Oh? What makes you say so?"

"Well, I was just noticing the worker's cabins have been recently repaired in many places."

Nathan looked over at the cabins and with his typical keen eye took in the same details she'd been seeing. "Yes, I suppose it's quite obvious now you mention it." He responded with a slight smile.

She found his grin a hopeful sign, so she pushed her luck a bit, "No, *not* so obvious, Mr. Chambers. I'll bet a hundred women could sit in this very spot and not a single one would notice it … but *I did.*" Now it was her turn to smile up at him.

He looked up again at the cabins, and then down at her smiling face and felt his earlier chilliness thawing.

"Yes, I believe you're right! You *are* quite observant, and clever … I will grant you *that*, Miss Evelyn."

"Thank you, Mr. Chambers! Now, shall we continue our tour? I'm feeling much refreshed now."

They continued on in better spirits. The pathways between the cabins were dirt paths, smooth and packed down to a shiny hardness by the passing of countless bare feet over untold years. On the edges of the paths grew more of the bright green grass, also neatly cropped. No flowers or ornamental plants grew here, however. Those were the purview of the white masters only.

There was no one outside, although Evelyn knew from experience many of the cabins would be bustling with the activity of the elderly, and the very young—those not fit for the fields. They'd be making and mending clothes, patching shoes, and preparing meals for the field workers.

Nathan led Evelyn through the rows of cabins, and after passing straight through several rows, turned to the right and led her to the second cabin on the left. He said, "there is someone here I want to check in on. She … had a bit of trouble recently and I wish to see about her health. You may as well meet her and the other women in this house since we're here."

He stepped up onto the low porch projecting a few feet from the front door. There were no steps or railings, the porch serving as both patio and front step. The door was right in the middle of the front wall of the house. As far as Evelyn had seen, all the other cabins were nearly identical, as if the builders had made one single plan and then repeated it over and over. Nathan knocked politely and waited, although Evelyn knew nobody would've expected him to.

In a moment the door opened, and an older heavyset black woman in an apron looked out. When she saw Nathan standing there, she lit up a large smile. Evelyn had never before seen such a genuinely warm, unrehearsed reaction of a slave to a master. "Master Captain, sir!" she said with enthusiasm, "Please do come in, if it pleases you, sir."

"Hello, Betsy. I find you in good health, I trust?" he responded, doffing his hat.

Oh, yes sir. Never better! Very kindly of you to ask, Master Captain," she said continuing to smile and bow. Then she turned

338

back into the room and said, "Layla, Rosa! Come, it's the Master …" then she caught herself and turned toward Nathan and smiled, "I should say, 'the *Captain*' is here."

The other two women came to the door. Nathan stood back to allow them room, gesturing for them to come out onto the porch. When they stepped outside, they caught sight of Evelyn for the first time, and suddenly went silent. Now they seemed shy, looking mostly at the ground, only occasionally daring a glance upward. It was a completely different reaction from the men working in the fields. She could see them fidgeting slightly, straightening their skirts, pulling at a stray wisp of hair as if she would be judging them. Of course! She realized, it was because she was a woman, and they were women, and they were instinctively measuring themselves against the newcomer. She smiled, thinking it was no different from how the young women in Richmond behaved when a strange new woman arrived. Taking her measure, and at the same time deciding how they measured up. *I guess women are women everywhere*, she decided.

"Betsy, Layla, Rosa," Nathan began, gesturing toward each woman in turn, "I would like to introduce you to our guest Miss Evelyn." The three black women curtsied to Evelyn, and she returned the salute.

"Very nice to make your acquaintance," Evelyn said, being prepared for it this time. She'd never been introduced in the formal manner to slaves, but somehow it seemed like the correct thing to do, despite their difference in station.

The women remained shy and did not respond in kind.

"Rosa, I came to inquire if you are quite recovered from your earlier … *difficulties*?" Nathan addressed the youngest of the three women, barely more than a girl.

Evelyn noticed when Nathan addressed Rosa, the young woman lit up like a lamp. She was really quite pretty, despite her humble attire, Evelyn thought.

"Oh, I am feeling *much* better, Captain. It is very kindly of you to ask," she said, and smiled brightly. She made a quick glance toward Evelyn, continuing to smile.

Yes, very pretty, indeed, Evelyn decided.

"Good, good! I'm pleased to hear it. And I trust you believe me when I say nothing of the kind shall ever occur again?"

"Oh, yes, Captain. If you say it, then I believe it's so. We *all* do."

Evelyn found this conversation puzzling. She couldn't guess what had happened to Rosa. She seemed perfectly fit now, whatever it may have been. If Nathan didn't volunteer it, she would have to ask him about it later.

They said their goodbyes and turned to move on. If Evelyn had looked back, she would have seen Rosa lingering in the doorway, looking in their direction. Rosa gazed after Evelyn, taking in every detail: her figure, her hair, the way she dressed. Even how she walked. As Evelyn turned a corner and disappeared from sight, Rosa sighed heavily, turned, and walked back into the cabin.

They made their way through the camp and passed a cabin with the front door open. An ancient black man, with only a few wispy strands of white hair, was slowly sweeping the doorway with a broom. He was either entirely intent upon his task, or poor of sight and hearing, for he never looked up from his work as they passed. When they walked by another cabin, the door suddenly burst open with a slam. Two young children, a boy and a girl, no more than three or four years old started out the door, giggling loudly. But when they caught sight of the Captain they stopped in their tracks, slapped their hands over their mouths, and rushed back inside, pulling the door to after them.

Nathan laughed, and called out "Hello Willie and Sissy!" to which he heard only giggling through the door in response. He smiled but continued on.

"My goodness, Mr. Chambers! Do you know all their names already, even the small children?" Evelyn asked, amazed he knew the names of the little tykes. She knew he'd only been back home from the West for a few short weeks.

"Well, yes, actually. I am … quite good at remembering names, it turns out. But it's also part of my military training to learn the names of the troublemakers first. And those two …" he whistled, "They are a piece of mischief, for sure!"

Then he laughed a warm, genuine laugh. "Reminds me of when I was little. They say I was quite the terror around here, and from what I can recall, it was true."

She laughed, trying to imagine Nathan as an ornery, bare foot lad of five or six, wreaking havoc as he ran about the farm.

"Poor Miss Abbey! I guess she must have had her hands full."

"Yes, and dear old Megs too. And they're both still mothering me after all these years."

He smiled again, thinking on the vast gulf of time separating his current circumstances from that far-distant past, now a fading dream.

"Well, I suppose someone has to do it," she replied teasingly, smiling up at him.

"Yes … I understand all women believe their men need looking after. And, I will admit it's probably true. Lord knows we get into plenty of mischief when we're out on our own. Like when we were in Texas. No woman would've ever allowed her man to run off and fight Indians and outlaws, if she'd had a say in the matter, that's certain."

"I agree with that! Women have more sense!" She flashed him another smile.

They heard hammering coming from the roof of a cabin just ahead.

"Speaking of … let me introduce you to some of the men who came with me from out West."

They headed toward the sound, and when they rounded the corner of one cabin, they could see three men up on the roof. But as they moved closer, the hammering cut off, and they heard someone call out, "Ow! *Shit!* How anyone could be a *Goddamned* carpenter is beyond me! These blamed things oughta be outlawed on account of their hazard to life and limb!"

And then something came hurling through the air in their general direction, banging loudly against the wall of the cabin off to their left, before falling to the ground.

Nathan involuntarily winced. He turned toward Evelyn, shrugged, and said, "Sorry about the language … that would be our *Sergeant Jim*."

She shook her head, but smiled, "Fear not, Mr. Chambers. I grew up around farmhands; I've heard such talk before, and as far as I can tell, my ears are none the worse for the wear."

As they stepped closer, they could see a man down on one knee, sucking on his left thumb, obviously in pain. Two others were standing over him smiling as if they found his discomfort humorous. *Soldier's humor, I guess,* Evelyn thought, shaking her head.

It was at that moment the men noticed the newcomers, and Sergeant Jim snapped the sore thumb out of this mouth and immediately stood to his feet, "Captain!" he said.

The others turned in their direction as well and greeted them with kindly smiles.

"As you were, gentlemen," Nathan answered.

Evelyn noticed for the first time the man on the right was extremely large. A great giant of a man, such as she had never seen before. She let out an involuntary gasp of surprise.

"Sorry, I should've warned you about Stan. He often has that effect on people when they first meet him. He *is* rather ... *large* ... I suppose."

Stan laughed, "But Captain, you know I am never frightening even a little mouse ... on account of being so timid ... and shy!"

Sergeant Jim rolled his eyes, and the other man just shook his head and smiled, as Stan burst into another round of laughter.

"Oh my, sir! If I didn't know better, I would say you were a very giant from the storybooks I used to read as a child. Except ... I never imagined those giants to be so ... friendly!" Evelyn said, smiling up at him.

Stan returned her smile.

"Gentlemen allow me to introduce Miss Evelyn Hanson from Richmond. She and her mother are here on a visit."

"Miss Evelyn, this is Jim Wiggins from Texas, William Jenkins from ... Connecticut, isn't it, William? And, of course you have already met Stan. Stanislav Ivanovich Volkov ... all the way from Russia ... or possibly *fairyland* ... we're not quite sure which!"

Stan bowed a great sweeping bow.

"Well, carry on with your hammering, gentlemen. The cabins are coming along very nicely."

"Good of you to say, sir," Jim responded. "We should be done in another week or so, never you worry. Even if'n I have to lose a thumb doing it! *Damn!*" he said, turning and sticking the sore thumb back in his mouth, as he headed for the ladder to climb down and retrieve his hammer.

But Nathan walked over and fetched it from where it had landed, tossing it up to Jim. He caught it easily by the wooden handle, and nodded, "Much obliged, Captain."

By now they'd passed between the last of the cabins and headed toward a group of outbuildings. Barns, toolsheds, work buildings, and various other structures.

They walked between the outbuildings, Nathan describing the purpose of each, wherever description was necessary. He was hoping to meet up with Jamie and Georgie, but they weren't in the smithing shed. He couldn't imagine where else they might be, so he led Evelyn back toward the house, as the heat of the sun was getting oppressive.

Just as they reached the gravel drive, they saw two men approaching from off to their right. They stopped to await their arrival. When the men drew closer, Evelyn saw they were dripping wet—totally drenched, clothes and all! They were also young men, though not as young as the farmhand Zeke she'd met earlier. And these two were not so gangly—still lean, but also strong looking, somehow.

"Ah, that would be Jamie and Georgie. So … what have you two juvenile delinquents been up to now?"

They looked up, saw him and Evelyn and laughed. "Sorry we are, for our sodden appearance, Captain," said the read-headed one on the right, in an Irish accent.

The one on the left then added, "We were shoeing several of the horses, and it just got so blazing hot in the smithing shed. So we decided we needed to cool off."

"Yep," the other put in, "so we were after makin' our way down to yonder creek, took off our shoes, and jumped on in! What a wonder it is, sir, to be able to get cool like that. I'm remembering

343

out in Texas being hot for months on end with no respite. Made me lonesome for home, it did."

"Me too, me too," the other agreed.

"Never mind, gentlemen. I'm sure you'll dry in due time in this heat," Nathan said, unable to suppress a grin. He made introductions. The men apologized again for their unpresentable appearance and promising to look better next time.

They seemed so concerned with it, Evelyn finally said, "Please, really … think nothing of it, gentlemen. It's a perfectly wonderful idea you had to cool yourselves in the creek after your hard labors in this heat. And I have no doubt when next we meet you both shall be the very picture of properly dressed gentlemen!"

"Oh, yes, ma'am, yes ma'am, we surely will. Thank you ma'am … thank you most kindly," they both said, nearly in unison, bowing and nodding, holding soggy hats in their hands, all of which made Evelyn giggle appreciatively.

₨₧₧₧₨₧₧₧₨₧₧₧

After Nathan and Evelyn left for the house, Georgie turned to Jamie, "Well … I'll be a three-eyed toad it she ain't the prettiest gal I *ever* saw!"

"Yep, a *dotey* lass all right—sweet and kindly, too. And clearly, she's taken a liking to me already, boyo, by the way she was talking to me."

"To *you?* What're you talking about, Jamie?"

He gave his friend a playful shove at the same time.

"She clearly has a hankering for *me!* She has better taste than to fall for the likes of you!"

For which Jamie returned the shove.

They continued to push and shove and soon found themselves entangled on the ground. After a few fruitless minutes of wrestling, they gave it up. They were almost identical in size and strength, so it was of little use. They rolled back in the grass and laughed. The sun now felt good on their wet clothes. So they just lay there, looking up at the sky, enjoying the moment.

"You know she's the Captain's lass?" Jamie said, after a few minutes of silence.

"Of course! You, ninny. And they make a fine pair, don't they?" Georgie answered.

After a few more minutes, Jamie said, "I was just thinking. I remember reading a story-book story when I was a boy. It was all about kings, and knights, and fair ladies and such. I was enamored of it, and dreamed myself in shiny armor, riding a white horse into battle, waving a bright sword. Anyway, there was this one part where the bravest knight who was a loyal king's man, became the *champion* of the queen, on account o' him admiring her for being such a fine lady and all."

"A champion? What does a *champion* do, anyway, Jamie?"

"Well, in the book, he would guard her when she traveled if the king weren't about. And when the knight went into battle, he would fight in her honor, so he always won! She'd be after giving him a silken handkerchief to tie to his spear when he fought — which signified he had the queen's favor."

"Oh, yea? And what did the king think of all this *champion* business? I don't guess he was too keen on some sassy young sprout tagging along after his queen."

"Oh no! He was after *liking* it. He knew someone would always be looking out for his beloved queen when he was out doing his kingly duties and all. As I said, the knight was a loyal man o' the king, his trusted soldier, who would never betray him.

"Anyway, I was thinking … mayhap we could be Miss Evelyn's champions? I mean, after she marries the Captain and all."

"Now hold on there a minute, Jamie! How do you know she's going to marry the Captain? Did he say so?"

"Well, Georgie, lad, ain't it obvious? O' course they're gonna get married! It's just like in one of them story books I used to read. She's the most beautiful lass ever — sweet, and charming and all — like a real-life princess. And the Captain, well … he's … he's *the Captain!* O' course they'll get married!"

"Well, now you say it *that* way, I see the logic. All right, let's shake on it. When Miss Evelyn marries the Captain, we'll fight it out to see who's her champion," Georgie said.

"What? But it was *my* idea. Why should I have to be after fighting *you* for it?"

"Because I like the idea too. And besides, what good's a champion if he can't win a single fight?" Georgie said with a laugh.

"Okay, it's a deal, boyo. We'll fight over it."

Then Jamie spat in his hand and held it out to Georgie, who spat in his own. Then they shook hands with enthusiasm, completing the transaction.

⁂

Later that evening, Nathan, Tom, and the three ladies enjoyed a friendly dinner, and then moved to the veranda to enjoy the sunset.

The ladies had tea, while Nathan and Tom sipped whiskey. Out of respect for the ladies' delicate sensibilities, they did not light up cigars, as was their usual pleasure.

When the conversation lagged for a few moments, Tom recalled something he'd read in the latest copy of the Richmond newspaper, *The Daily Dispatch*. He thought to restart the conversation with it. "Say, Captain, I've been reading in the Richmond paper a little more about that Lincoln fellow. Seems like the split in the Democratic Party between Northern and Southern factions is making it more likely Lincoln may win the election. And they say the folks in South Carolina are so up in arms about it the talk of secession is everywhere." He believed it an interesting topic, one he and the Captain had been discussing a lot lately, and it never occurred to him it might be controversial amongst this group.

"Lincoln? Oh my, I've heard he's some sort of radical abolitionist or something," Miss Harriet said in a tone indicating she found such an idea repulsive. "And that Republican party of his wants to free all the slaves as soon as he gets elected."

"Oh, he couldn't really do that, could he?" Evelyn added, feeling a sudden anxiety she couldn't quite put a finger on. "That would be … a truly terrible thing … *wouldn't it?*"

She was now so uncertain about what to say on the subject, she ended her sentence weakly, turning it into a faltering question.

"Who knows what a man like *that* might try to do!" Harriet answered firmly.

Nathan and Tom exchanged looks that said this wasn't where this conversation was supposed to go.

"I'm sure the rumors about Mr. Lincoln are greatly exaggerated," Tom offered, trying to diffuse the situation. But it was too late; Nathan now had his dander up.

"Talk of secession over the election of *one* man is utter foolishness, no matter what he may say or do," Nathan said.

Miss Abbey said nothing but looked concerned. She hadn't spoken of Nathan's plans to the ladies. Nathan would do *that* when he was ready, she'd decided. But now that decision seemed to be backfiring, as Harriet and Evelyn had unwittingly touched on a very sore subject for Nathan.

"But if Lincoln tries to use the power of the federal government to tell the states what they can do, shouldn't they stand up to him?" Harriet asked him. "And if he won't listen, then don't they need to show him the states can stand on their own, by seceding?"

"Madam, I didn't fight my way across Mexico, and half of Texas just to see this country torn apart by this ridiculous notion. Even if Lincoln wants to free the slaves, he can't do it on his own. It'd take years of talking, planning, and negotiating before anything of the kind could ever happen. People are just jumping to conclusions, reacting with their baser instincts, rather than using the good minds God gave them!"

Nathan's voice had risen, and he was now clearly becoming heated.

"Yes, that's probably true … I … see what you mean, Mr. Chambers." Harriet offered, now sensing she had tread upon dangerous ground, and needed to back-peddle. "Don't you agree, dear?" she continued, turning toward Evelyn.

Harriet was trying to turn the situation to their advantage, showing Nathan they were sympathetic to his point of view. And she tried to steer Evelyn in the same direction. But it was a mistake, and Evelyn knew it. If she agreed with her mother, she was simply saying what she was told to say. If she disagreed, she would be disagreeing with Nathan, which was liable to anger him even more.

"I … I think … it's a very troubling situation. On the one hand, Mr. Lincoln could be terrible for the South, but on the other … splitting up the country? That doesn't seem like a good idea either …" she trailed off, feeling embarrassed. She'd tried to take both sides but had taken neither. She felt inadequate, and foolish. Like a little girl amid a conversation with grownups suddenly asked a question out of her depth.

An awkward silence followed. Miss Abbey attempted to change the subject. She talked about the various flowers that should be blooming in her garden in the next few weeks, how well the crops were looking, how hot the weather was, and various other innocuous topics.

But the conversation was obviously lagging, and the earlier good humor at dinner was spent. Finally, Nathan rose and made his excuses: that he had farm work early in the morning and needed a good night's sleep. They all said their polite goodnights and departed for their various rooms.

Evelyn was downcast. It had mostly been a good day until the last. But now it felt like it was all for naught. She was sure Nathan believed she was nothing more than a pretty face. Someone with no ideas or opinions of her own, just spouting what she'd been taught to say. And then she realized with a sudden shock … *if he thinks that … he's right!* It was a thoroughly depressing notion.

She had a hard time falling asleep that night. And her dreams were troubled by strange visions. Frightful, demonic creatures were clawing and grasping for her as she tried to run. But her feet wouldn't move. And when she screamed for help, no sound came from her mouth.

The next day it surprised Evelyn when Nathan did *not* join them for breakfast as he had on previous days. Miss Abbey said Mr. Chambers had risen early to attend to business out on the farm and had already had his breakfast. Further, she didn't expect him back at the house until later that evening, well after dinner.

348

A sense of dread was growing on Evelyn. She felt things had gone terribly wrong. But when she tried to talk to Harriet about it, her mother cut her off snappishly. She realized Harriet was worried and anxious as well but didn't want to speak of it. It meant Harriet was out of ideas, and that was even more troubling.

Evelyn spent a long, anxious day in the house. She went to the library and looked through the shelves of books. She picked out one that looked interesting. It was a new one by the well-known English author, Charles Dickens, titled *A Tale of Two Cities*. The story seemed promising at first, prophetic even, seemingly: *"It was the best of times, it was the worst of times ..."* But when she sat down to read it, she found she could not concentrate. She was just reading the words without absorbing what they meant. So after a time, she gave it up and put the book back on the shelf.

She tried wandering about the flower garden. But the sun beat down mercilessly, and in her current mood the flowers had somehow lost their luster.

When the maids served lunch, she had no appetite for it, taking only a few nibbles. When dinner time arrived, she was hungry and knew she must eat, so she forced herself to down as many bites as she could stand. Still Mr. Chambers had not returned.

As the three ladies sat on the veranda, politely chatting, Evelyn heard the voice of Mr. Chambers speaking with a maid just inside the back door. She didn't know whether to feel relieved, or nervous ... not knowing what his demeanor might be.

When he came outside and walked in their direction, her heart sank. He had a serious, determined expression. Not the warm, friendly look he'd shown her on previous occasions. It did not bode well, she was certain.

When he reached the table, he removed his hat and made a slight bow, "Ladies ... I trust you had a good day in my absence?"

He spoke politely, to which they made the typical, meaningless, polite replies.

"Miss Harriet, Miss Abbey ... would you be so kind as to allow me a few moments to speak with Miss Evelyn?"

Although the words were polite, it was clear he was all business.

"Oh, certainly dear. I was just thinking it would be a lovely evening for a stroll in the garden as the sun is setting. Harriet, dear, would you care to join me?" Miss Abbey intended to be calm and sweet, but somehow fell short, as if she too felt a growing anxiety.

Harriet quickly agreed, and the two ladies left down the steps toward the garden path.

Nathan took a seat at the table opposite Evelyn and placed his hat on one of the vacant chairs. He wasted no time, but immediately started in, "Miss Evelyn. As you know, I'm a military man, and I have developed the habit, good or otherwise, of coming straight to the point—telling things exactly as I see them."

Evelyn nodded, but said nothing. She didn't think she could've said anything if she tried. How had this all gone so terribly wrong?

"I still see myself as a young man, but the truth is I'm not the innocent youth I once was. I've seen and done a lot of things that've made me … more *experienced* in life and … how should I say it? More *aware* of what I want and need to be happy."

Evelyn could think of nothing to say, so she just sat and listened. Despite her trepidation, she was determined not to gaze at her feet like a schoolgirl receiving a scolding. So she forced herself to maintain eye contact with Mr. Chambers. But this time she did *not* smile.

"The point is … I can see you're a fine person … a proper lady … there can be no doubt. But … I've known many ladies in my travels and have … enjoyed their company—that I'll not deny. But I've found, after a while, their beauty and their charm … it somehow, loses its luster. And then you're left with … well, with someone you can't really talk to. And then … well, then there's nothing left to do but say your goodbyes and move on."

He paused for a moment as if to gauge her reaction or understanding. But she continued to meet his eye with a thoughtful expression. She nodded occasionally, but otherwise offered no response.

"So getting to the heart of it … I'm at a point in my life where I need to find a woman … the *right* woman … to marry, to continue the family. And … at the risk of sounding rude, I feel the way it is between you and I, it will soon grow dull. And we'll be left with nothing to say to each other. So … I believe it would be best for all concerned if you and Miss Harriet were to leave tomorrow and return to Richmond."

He sat back in his chair and waited for her response, seeming relieved to have gotten out the uncomfortable thing he'd come to say.

She sat quietly for a moment, and then bowed her head, rubbing her temples with her right hand, as if massaging a headache.

Ironically it was not the stunned silence Nathan likely assumed it was. The moment the words she'd been dreading all day actually came from his mouth, she felt a sudden sense of relief, to her own surprise. It was as if the worst that could possibly happen *had* happened, and now there was nothing left to fear. For the first time in days it felt like she could think clearly. No more doubt, no more playing a role, no more walking on too-thin ice. She had done it Miss Harriet's way, and it had failed. Utterly, and completely. Now, it was time to do it *her* way!

She lowered her hand and looked Nathan in the eye. He seemed surprised that she shed no tears, and the look on her face seemed calm.

"I agree with you, Mr. Chambers," she said.

"You do? Well, then—"

But before he could continue, she interrupted, "I agree … but I do have something more to say … and I have a favor to ask of you before I go."

"All right … well, of course, certainly … anything at all, if it is in my power to grant."

He agreed readily, likely relieved she was taking the whole thing so well.

"The truth is I have *not* been perfectly honest with you since my arrival. My words and my actions have been no more than a role; a well-practiced role, like an actor in a play. Only this play was written for a single purpose: to make you want to marry me. My Momma heard all these grand things about you and your family, and she became determined to see us married.

"Ever since my arrival I've been saying what she taught me to say and doing what she taught me to do. Other than whatever natural beauty or charm God may have blessed me with, there is nothing you've seen or heard this week that has really been *me!*"

She paused and looked at him for a moment. He said nothing, but had a shocked, wide-eyed expression. Clearly this was *not* what he'd expected. But now she had started, she decided she may as well carry it through, for better or worse.

"To tell the truth, Mr. Chambers, I've been practicing for this role so long I don't know how I really feel about things—what I really *think* about them, I should say. I've never taken the time to give it *any* serious consideration."

She paused, gathering her thoughts for what she would say next. Nathan's expression had softened, and he said, "Now the mixed feelings I've been having are beginning to make sense. But tell me if I'm correct; I *did* see the *real* you on a few occasions—in the flower garden with the little birds, and down by the duck pond. And when you noticed the repairs on the cabins?"

She looked up at him and smiled, "Yes ... that *was* me. Not an act."

"Well, that's good to know. That was the part of you I liked *best.*"

It was gratifying, and gave her hope, but she was still determined to have her say, despite his softening.

"But I also would like to offer in my defense: *you*, Mr. Chambers, have also not been entirely honest with me." She said it as a statement of fact; it was not offered as a question.

Nathan raised an eyebrow at this, and the smile left his face, but he did not interrupt.

"Despite my behavior to the contrary this week, I am *not* a complete fool. My Daddy taught me many interesting things when I was younger, and he used to discuss philosophy with me hours on end. I know enough to tell when someone is only giving partial arguments, or not saying all that's on their mind.

"I'm not accusing you of *lying* to me. At first, I was uncertain, but now I'm sure you believe every word you've said. What I've been wondering about is ... the words you *haven't* said. For example, you have said what you *believe* in the strongest terms, but you have never once said what you intend to *do* about those beliefs. For you, being a soldier—clearly a man of decisive action—that seems ... very *odd* to me."

Now it was Nathan's turn to be quiet and thoughtful. His face now had a reddish hue—not anger ... a blush of shame, maybe? Like what she was saying had struck a chord.

"Very well, Miss Evelyn. I will admit there is some truth in what you're saying. I haven't been entirely ... *forthcoming* ... with you. But I ... wasn't sure how you'd accept it ..." he finished lamely, perhaps realizing for the first time he'd also been playing a role that wasn't entirely honest.

They were both silent for a moment. Then he said, "You mentioned a favor you would ask of me?"

"Yes. I had *not* forgotten. Just this: you will allow me to spend one more day here. We will meet in this same spot at this same time tomorrow. Then you will tell me if you still wish me to go, or if you would prefer I stay a while longer. If you tell me to go, I will pack my things and leave with no further argument or discussion, and no hard feelings between us."

"And if I ask you to stay?"

"Then it will be *my* turn to decide the matter," she said, and flashed him a smile—the first true smile he had seen from her since he'd arrived that evening. He returned her smile with a quick laugh.

"What else?" A smile now touched the corners of his eyes.

"Tomorrow when you say something to me or ask me a question, I will think about it, and give you my *honest* thoughts and feelings. And if I don't know how I believe about a thing, I'll tell you *that* as well. And you will continue to tell me everything you're thinking, but *this* time you will also say what you're planning on *doing!*"

"All right. That seems fair. Anything else?"

353

"Yes. Starting tomorrow morning, you will call me 'Evelyn,' and I will call you 'Nathan,' or 'Captain,' if you prefer. But anyway, we will stop being so *awfully* formal with each other!"

"*Nathan* will do just fine."

"And please have the maids pack us some food. Then you will meet me at first light on the front drive and spend the day with me."

He tilted his head with a curious, thoughtful expression.

"All right, done."

"And one more thing ..."

"Yes?"

"Come dressed as you are now, not formal."

He looked down at himself. Well-worn riding boots, rough brown work pants. A white cotton shirt with loose sleeves—it had once been a nice dress shirt, but he had long since retired it to rougher use. And an old felt hat to top it off. Not exactly the picture of a gentleman courting a fine young lady!

"Very well, as you wish," he said with a chuckle.

Chapter 12. View from the High Road

"Before the gates of excellence
the high gods have placed sweat;
long is the road thereto
and rough and steep at first;
but when the heights are reached,
then there is ease,
though grievously hard
in the winning."
– Hesiod

Tuesday July 10, 1860 – Greenbrier County, Virginia:

After Evelyn had excused herself to retire for the evening, Nathan sat alone on the veranda sipping a glass of whiskey and blowing long puffs of smoke from a cigar. The two older ladies had finally returned from their tour of the gardens and had retired as well.

The sun had not yet set. It was the time of summer when the sky stayed bright long after people had gone to bed. Nathan was in a thoughtful mood, mulling over everything that'd been happening recently. All the emotions, up and down. Evelyn's surprising response to the difficult decision he had come to. Her unexpected revelations, and her mysterious plans for the morrow. He had to admit she was the most curious and intriguing woman he'd ever been around. No woman had ever talked to him the way she had just now. So honest and open, so forceful and … thoughtful. Yes, curious … and intriguing …

He sat staring into his glass, the whiskey in the bottom swirling lazily, and did not notice when one of the servants stepped up to his table. A voice said, "Begging your pardon, Master Captain, sir."

He looked up, and saw it was Willie, a groom who watched the front door when not caring for horses. "Yes, Willie, what is it?"

"So sorry to disturb your thoughts, sir. But they's a man out front. A messenger, sir, who arrived a moment ago by horseback. He has a letter for you. I says he can hand it to me, and I'll be sure you gets it. But he says, no, he must deliver it into your own hands hisself by his master's orders.

"Sorry to bother you sir, but he won't leave 'til he sees you. Shall I have him run off, sir?" Willie asked.

"No, it's quite all right, Willie. I'll come 'round and see him." He stood, stubbing out the cigar in a metal ash tray sitting in the middle of the table. When he swallowed the last swig of whiskey and set the glass down, it occurred to him he always left the ashtray dirty and the glasses on the table when he retired. But everything was always spotlessly clean the next evening. *Hmm ... getting a bit used to playing the king around here,* he decided.

He was enjoying the cool of the evening, so he took the long way around the house via the veranda, rather than cutting through. When he reached the front door, he saw a man standing beside a horse on the drive. He was a young white man, dressed in work clothes—a farmhand, maybe. He looked uncomfortable and anxious as he stood there. One of the other grooms stood next to him holding the reins of the horse. The two were not looking at each other nor conversing, as far as Nathan could tell.

As he came down the stairs, he said, "I am Mr. Chambers. I've been told you have a letter for me?"

"Yes, sir. Sorry to bother you, sir," he said, taking off his hat and making a slight bow. "My master, Mr. Elijah Walters, tasked me with delivering this letter into your own hands, sir, and none other. On pain of his severe displeasure, if you take my meaning, sir. Very sorry I am for disturbing you, sir, but those were his orders."

The man sputtered out the words, obviously uncomfortable he'd been placed in an awkward position by one terrifying master to potentially get on the wrong side of another.

"Think nothing of it, my good fellow," Nathan answered amiably.

Evelyn's intriguing proposition had put him in a better mood, and so the unexpected interruption had not put him off. He also felt sympathy for the nervous young man. He stepped up to the messenger and held out his hand. The man handed over a large, thick, yellow-colored envelope. The feel of it surprised Nathan. It was much thicker than a typical letter would be, no matter how wordy. And he could not imagine Walters being wordy; if anything, he tended toward the opposite. He thought to ask the messenger about it, when it occurred to him this must be the long-promised proposition for resolving the old property line dispute. Besides, from the look of him he highly doubted he was someone Walters confided in.

"Very well. Did your master expect you to return with a reply?"

"No, sir. Not that he mentioned."

"Well, then, tell your master I thank him kindly for this ... and also tell him ... I said his messenger carried out his duties in a most efficient and gentlemanly manner."

"Oh, thank you. Thank you very kindly for that, sir!" The young man smiled for the first time.

The messenger departed, and a few moments later Nathan was entering Tom's office upstairs. Tom was still working, as expected. They opened the letter, and as Nathan had suspected, it was a legal document, proposing a change in the property lines between the two plantations. A brief note accompanied it, and read

> Chambers,
>
> Enclosed are the documents I earlier promised regarding the long-standing properly line dispute between our two farms. I trust you will find this a fair settlement.
>
> E. Walters

"Not a man to waste time on any niceties," Tom said with a scoff.

"Yes, not too surprising, though, given how he behaves in person."

"I'll have a look at these documents before I turn in, sir. If you stop by in the morning, I will have an opinion for you on the matter."

"Thank you, Tom."

Nathan then headed off to his bedroom, once again wondering what the morrow would bring.

ᏽᏬᏒᏬᏝᏬᏭᏬᏱᏬᏒᏬᏝᏬᏭᏬᏱᏬᏒᏬᏝᏬᏭ

The next morning, Nathan poked his head in the doorway to Tom's office and wasn't surprised it was still empty. *Too early even for Tom*, he thought. He moved down the hall and knocked on Tom's bedroom door. A minute later it opened, and Tom appeared, the lower part of his face lathered up for shaving.

"Ah, good morning, sir," he said amiably. "Sorry I'm not yet regulation. If you'd like to come on in and sit, I won't be but a moment."

"Thanks, Tom."

He came in and sat on the edge of the bed, while Tom returned to his shaving. Tom was leaning over a basin of water, looking at his reflection in the mirror as he shaved himself clean with military precision. *Like everything else he does*, Nathan thought.

"I won't stay long. I just wanted to hear your opinion on Walters' proposal, if you had time to look it over since last night."

Tom continued his shaving, but answered, "Yes, I read it. And it seems our good friend Walters wants to continue the family feud for another generation."

"Oh? How so?"

"Well, if I read it rightly, he is offering to do us the great favor of taking the disputed area off our hands. His proposal puts the property almost entirely within his own domain."

"Hmm … not very neighborly of him. But I guess I shouldn't be surprised. We didn't exactly see eye to eye when we were there for our little visit."

"It gets worse, sir. Besides the usual legal wording about property lines vs. landmarks, and such, he added an extra

358

paragraph. It says he considers this land already his and disavows the original dispute. Further … if any of our livestock wander onto 'his' land it will be subject to seizure and forfeiture. And if any of our employees are caught on 'his' land, they'll be arrested and prosecuted."

Nathan shook his head in disgust. "And so, it continues … Well, even though it is most certainly a waste of your time, I suppose we should draft a response."

"It's no bother, sir. Won't take me long. But, how do you want to play it? Push back all the way, or do things proper and offer a compromise?"

"If he were a reasonable man, he would've offered a compromise to begin with. Although it's likely a wasted effort, we should take the high road and propose the compromise, splitting it fifty-fifty. I'll not have anyone say I willingly continued this silly feud.

"But, Tom … push back *all the way* on the other items. Tell him we dispute his claims to the property and do *not* recognize his right to seize our livestock or imprison our people. And we'll deal with such behavior in the *strongest possible* terms."

"Yes, sir!" Tom responded, wiping the last of the lather from his face with a towel. "I was hoping you'd say that."

After he departed Tom's room, Nathan headed down the back stairs toward the kitchen to collect the picnic lunch he'd requested the night before. Megs was there, handing him the bundle, and a plate with a slice of fresh, hot bread covered in butter.

"Got to keep your strength up, Captain," she said with a sly grin. "Could be you're in for a long day!"

She made a quick laugh.

"Thanks, Megs."

He wondered what she meant by *that*. He sat at the kitchen table, normally used by the servants, and wolfed down the bread. Then he drank the coffee she set down in front of him, followed by another slice of bread.

When he finished, he scooped up the lunch bundle, and headed down the hall toward the front door. The house was mostly dark and quiet as he made his way to the hallway closet where he kept his coats and hats. There he snatched up the same old felt work-hat he'd worn the previous day, still wondering what Evelyn was up to with her odd request.

It didn't entirely surprise him when he found himself alone on the veranda outside the front door. It was still a little before sunrise—light enough to see, but not yet first daylight. The air smelled clean and fresh, with a cool dampness to it that belied the heat to come, later in the day.

He stood for a few minutes, wondering if he might be in for a long wait, Evelyn still abed, sound asleep at this hour. But then in the dim, pre-dawn light he saw movement over toward the barn where the horses were kept. He could just make out two men coming toward him, leading two horses, one of which he recognized instantly as his mare Millie. The other appeared to be Tom's gelding, Jerry.

He stepped down the stairs and out onto the gravel of the drive as they approached. He wondered if this was part of Evelyn's secret scheme, though there was still no sign of her.

His questions were soon answered, however, as the "men" came closer, and their features became clear.

Nathan laughed, and called out, "Well, it appears my grooms have become much prettier since I last saw them!"

"Only one has, Captain, sir!" the one on the right answered with a laugh. Nathan could see now it was one of the regular grooms—one he'd taken a special liking to—named Cobb.

"This'n here is as ugly as ever he was, sir. Now, *that'n* over there ..." he said, nodding his head toward the other groom, "is a *whole other* matter!" He chuckled, shaking his head.

The "groom" on the left responded to this with a very unmanly giggle.

When they came to a stop, Evelyn tipped back the old straw hat covering her head, tied on with a bright yellow ribbon. "Good morning, Nathan," she said, smiling up at him.

He took a moment to respond, he was so taken aback by her appearance. She was not wearing her usual feminine attire this morning, but rather a much more masculine look. Besides the straw hat, she wore riding boots and britches, and a plain, if slightly frilly, yellow shirt.

"Good morning, Evelyn," he finally responded. It was such a shocking change Nathan didn't know what to say.

She spun around as if modeling the latest fashion from Paris. When she did so he saw she'd braided her long golden hair in a neat, single strand down her back.

"Do you like it, Nathan? I wore it just for you," she said, and giggled again.

"Well, it takes a little getting used to, I must admit ... but you look quite ... *fetching* in it," he said, returning her smile. And it was true. Unladylike or not, she looked utterly appealing in her rustic riding garb. And she definitely looked nothing like a man up close—*not at all!*

"I hope you don't mind, Nathan. Unbeknownst to Miss Harriet, I smuggled along my riding gear on the chance the opportunity might present itself. And now, it has! You ... *do* know how to ride?" she asked, teasingly.

"Madam, I've been riding horses since I was old enough to walk ... or maybe even before," he responded in mock annoyance. "I think I can hold up my end of things."

She laughed. Then taking the reins in her left hand, she turned, reached up to grasp the back of the saddle as high as she could reach, and lightly sprung up—her left boot sliding into the stirrup as her right leg gracefully swung up over the saddle. When she was properly seated, she smiled again at Nathan.

He was impressed, "That was as neatly done as I've ever seen it. I'm guessing you've done this before." He took Millie's reins from Cobb and got himself up into the saddle.

"I had to get Megs to help sneak me down the backstairs in case Miss Harriet was up early. She would've stormed like the end of creation if she'd have seen me wearing *this!* It was the one indulgence from my childhood she allowed me, but only if I promised *never* to wear it in public," she flashed him another smile.

"Yes, I can imagine she'd be quite scandalized by it, but it is ... a fine look on you, I have to admit," and he meant it. The way the riding britches fit her was … well, *flattering* was too mild a word for it, he decided.

As they walked the horses up the drive, side by side, he said, "You are also a good judge of horseflesh, it would seem. That's Tom's horse, named Jerry. Next to Millie here, the finest in the stable. But a bit high-spirited. I trust you can handle him …"

"Well, I suppose we shall see."

"So … where are we going?" he asked.

"You must lead the way, since I don't know this farm. But if it helps you decide, I'd like to see someplace wild and beautiful— like the duck pond."

He thought about it a moment, then said, "I know just the place."

"And is it in the direction we're presently going?"

"Yes."

"And will we travel for some distance along this road?"

"Well, not far … about two-and-a-half miles until we turn off to a side trail," he answered, wondering where this was leading.

"In that case, I shall meet you there, sir!" she said, and spurred her horse into action. The gelding leapt forward, pounding ahead down the gravel road at a gallop.

For a moment Nathan sat where he was, stunned, as she left him, literally, in the dust. But his competitive spirit took over, and he launched Millie into motion, a simple task as Millie was itching to run with the gelding. She was also highly competitive and loved a good race.

They pounded down the road, quickly passing by the barns and work buildings, moving past the cabins, and under the great oak tree by the wooden table. They soon left all the farm buildings behind and were passing between wide fields of cotton.

He pushed Millie hard, but still could not overtake Evelyn. The gelding had a longer stride and was a strong runner. They continued on like this, a few horse-lengths apart, for several minutes before she pulled the gelding to a sudden, jarring stop. Nathan was not expecting this, and Millie had to dodge to one side as he whisked past her. He pulled Millie to a stop, and they turned around to trot back to where Evelyn was now waiting. She sat still atop Jerry, patting him on the neck and cooing, "Oooo … you're such a fine fellow … a fine, strong runner."

When Nathan approached within a few steps, she looked up and smiled, "What took you so long?"

"It was hardly a fair race, with the head start you had, taking off like that without warning," he sniffed, but then grinned. He had enjoyed the run and was having a hard time acting annoyed.

"Not to mention you men are such great heavy loads for a horse, while I am as light as a feather … isn't that so, Jerry?" She reached down and scratched him on the side of the neck. He bobbed his head in his pleasure.

"Well, there's that too … but why did you stop so suddenly? I nearly ran right overtop of you, or broke my neck trying not to!"

"Nonsense! Millie would've never allowed that to happen, no matter how *poorly* you were riding … would you Mill?" she said, making a clicking noise to get her attention.

"Besides, you said it was two-and-a-half miles to the turn, and I didn't want to miss it. This is almost exactly two miles from where we started, so I stopped."

He stood up in the stirrups and looked around to get his bearings. "Yes, I'd say you're right … just about two miles. But … how did you know *that?* You've only been this way once before, and you were inside a carriage, so I doubt you could have remembered much of it."

She laughed, "My father was very clever, and one of his favorite things to do was to sit around and think of solutions to problems nobody else even considered. Like how to tell how far you've ridden a horse. He reasoned out, excluding the exceptionally fast, or exceptionally slow, most horses moved at basically the same speed, using the same number of strides. So if you set up markers at a measured distance apart and walked between them, or trotted, or galloped, you could then count the number of strides. From there it would be simple math to figure out any distance. So we put it to the test on our farm, using several different horses and riders. We came up with the number for a mile when walking, trotting, or galloping."

"So you just ... counted the strides?" Nathan asked in amazement.

"Don't sound so shocked, Nathan ... I *can* count!" she grinned.

"That's not what I meant ..."

"For the average horse it's approximately twenty-four feet per stride at a gallop. At 5,280 feet to the mile, that's 220 strides. So all I had to do was count 440 strides, and we had reached two miles, more or less. That's much more reliable than trying to judge time in your head or trying to look at a pocket watch when you're in the heat of a race."

He nodded his head in appreciation. "A very neat trick, Evelyn. I'm impressed. I must remember that one."

"My father came up with the idea after he read a book about Julius Caesar as a young senator. Pirates kidnapped Caesar and took him to a secret lair to hold him for ransom. The pirates allowed the young Roman free rein of their ship during the journey. They were confident no one could ever remember the way to their hideout amongst the hundreds of bays and inlets in that part of the Mediterranean. After he was ransomed back to Rome, he led the Roman navy straight to the pirate base and captured them all. When the befuddled pirates asked him how he'd found them so easily he answered, 'Simple ... I counted the number of inlets until we entered your hideout. To lead our ships back, I simply counted them again.' Daddy loved stories like that, of people solving seemingly complex problems with simple reasoning."

They'd been walking the horses along easily now as they talked, and Nathan found once again he was greatly enjoying her company. But he had done so before, he reminded himself. In the gardens and by the pond, but something had always come along to spoil the pleasant feelings. Maybe it'd be different this time ... he'd have to wait and see.

He found the side trail, a simple dirt track across a field of wild grass, the very same trail where Miss Abbey had experienced the rattlesnake incident. He kicked Millie into an easy trot, and Evelyn came along behind. They had not gone far when they heard a rustling through the grass back toward the road. Looking back, Nathan could see out a large animal moving along the trail behind them. "Ah, Harry! Had a nice run?" he called back. Harry didn't answer but now followed along behind at his usual distance.

This was another wild section of the property. Once they'd crossed the field, the trail rose, and they wound between clumps of large bushes and thickets of spindly deciduous trees. As they moved along, these gave way to larger, taller trees: maples and oaks. Nathan stopped Millie and turned to allow Evelyn to pull up next to him.

"The trail gets a little steeper here for a ways as it climbs the hill. At the top it's the highest point on the property and affords a nice view all around. Keep a tight rein on Jerry. A slip here could be disastrous."

She smiled and said, "Lead on, sir."

He turned and started Millie up the trail. They walked this part—a fairly steep dirt trail—as the footing was made somewhat treacherous by the occasional rock or root sticking up. It crossed the hill in many zig-zagging switchbacks, several of which offered a stomach-turning view on the downhill side of the narrow track.

But the Army-trained horses proved sure-footed and seemed not to mind the steep hike. They soon reached a section where the path was more level and rolling. From the point where they had begun the ascent, the trees had been so thick they could see little beyond a few dozen feet in any direction. But now the trees suddenly ended, and they found themselves once again in an area of tall grass and low brush. Evelyn asked Nathan about the many stumps amongst the grass, as if the whole area had once been wooded.

"My granddaddy used to climb this hill when he first started the farm. He wanted a grand view of his property and the surrounding countryside from up high. But the top of the hill was so heavily wooded, he could only see anything by climbing a tall tree as high as he could and peering through the branches. Well … being an ambitious and enterprising young man, you can imagine what happened next. He decided to *'kill two birds with one stone,'* as the Good Book says. So he built the trail we've just been riding on, harvested the trees, and dragged them down the hill to build the farm buildings. He cleared the whole mountain top so he would have his view. Come … let me show you how it came out."

He kicked Millie into a trot. Evelyn followed along closely.

They crested a rise, and here the ground leveled out. They could now see great distances out toward the south, rolling hills and mountains as far as the eye could see. But a low rock outcropping blocked the view to the north, so they couldn't see back toward the farm. Nathan now led her toward the rocks, which appeared to be at the summit the hill. Next to it a single, small tree still grew, affording visitors a little shade next to the rocks.

They stopped next to the tree and dismounted.

"No need to tie them." Nathan let his reins drop. "They're Army horses, trained not to wander off. Besides, they'll happily crop the grass in the tree's shade."

Evelyn looked at him a moment, shrugged, and let the reins loose.

Nathan reached up and brought down the picnic bundle he'd looped around the saddle horn. He'd have preferred to tie it to the saddle, but Evelyn's sudden departure had made that impossible. *Hopefully nothing has gotten too mangled,* he worried.

He held out his hand to Evelyn, and she took it without hesitation. He led her up to the top of the rocky knoll. These rocks were old and worn — smooth and rounded on top — not rough or jagged. Clearly this hill was ancient, wind and weather having worn the rocks smooth over many eons.

When they reached the top, Evelyn gasped with delight. Looking back to the north, Mountain Meadows Farm spread out before their eyes. Like a beautiful painting, exquisite and delicate in its fine detail. The fields of cotton and tobacco, the slave cabins, the various outbuildings. And finally, the grand house, elegant, white and shining in the distance, like the princely palace in a story book.

"It's absolutely … *magnificent!* Thank you so much for bringing me here, Nathan!"

She turned and smiled up at him.

He looked down at her and swallowed hard. She *was* something special, he had to admit. Beautiful … hair like gold … ice-blue eyes that seemed to pull a man into them. Lips soft and sweet, often with a warm smile upon them.

But … who would've guessed she could ride a horse like *that?!* Better than most men he knew.

It had been one of the hardest decisions he'd *ever* made to send her away yesterday. And yet, here she was still. He didn't think he'd be able to do it again.

"You're welcome."

They sat down on the smooth rock surface, still cool to the touch, the sun's rays having not yet warmed it from the night before.

He suddenly felt self-conscious and at a loss for words. But remembering the food he'd carried up the mountain, he said, "Hungry?"

"Oh … yes, now you mention it … I was so concerned about avoiding Miss Harriet, and surprising *you* … I forgot all about breakfast. What did you bring?"

She leaned forward to have a look at the bundle he was unwrapping.

"Well … I don't rightly know. Megs put it together. I asked her to pack us a picnic lunch and left the details to her. Hmm … let's see …" he untied the cloth and laid it out on the rock behind them. "Looks like a couple of pieces of cold chicken, a few slices of bread … cheese, and … what's this?" He unwrapped another smaller, heavy bundle inside the larger one. A green bottle rolled out and hit the rock with a clink. Nathan quickly reached out to grab it, keeping it from rolling away. When he did, the rest of the contents of the smaller package fell out with a clatter: two small, metal cups.

"Seems to me Megs has a bit of a romantic notion," Evelyn said with a grin.

"Yes, apparently so."

The bottle was full, but the cork protruded about halfway, so he could extract it without a corkscrew.

Evelyn retrieved the cups as Nathan uncorked the wine. She held them out, and he poured each about half full, before setting the bottle in a nook in the rocks where it wouldn't spill. She handed him a cup, and raised her glass, "Here's to a beautiful, new day, Nathan."

He nodded his head in response, and they clinked the metal cups together in salute. They each took a sip of the red wine. Nathan declared it a good one—a Cabernet ... bold, full flavored, with a smooth finish. It seemed Megs had pulled out one of the better bottles for the occasion.

They shared out the food and enjoyed the simple fare. The morning exercise had given them each a good appetite. They talked little during their lunch, mostly small talk about the various things they could make out in the distance: a circling hawk high in the sky, the duck pond—a shining dot on the very edge of sight.

When they finished their meal, she turned to him and said, "Nathan, please tell me what you intend to do with this place. The *whole* story this time. And then, I will think about what you say, and will give you my *honest* thoughts, for better or worse. Does that sound fair?"

"All right," he answered, gazing into her sparkling blue eyes. He found the sight distracting, so he turned away and stared into the distance to gather his thoughts.

"By now you know I was a serious trouble-maker as a boy. But more than that, I had ... an extreme temper that was ... out of control. And my father, being cold and stern, always seemed to bring out the worst of it in me. By the time I was a young man it got to where we nearly came to blows, on a regular basis. So Miss Abbey bundled me off to a school in New York—mostly to keep the peace in the family. I imagine she believed after a few years I'd mature, and learn to control my temper; and when I returned all would be well."

Evelyn leaned forward and listened intently. Nathan had a faraway look in his eyes and did not meet her gaze as he told his tale. He knew she'd heard some of this before, in bits and pieces, but he wanted her to hear the whole story, in his own words.

"I imagine she now regrets that decision, though it succeeded in *one* way; I *did* mature, and I *did* learn to control my temper—for the most part—I'm sure you'll be happy to hear." He gave her a rueful smile. She smiled back and made an appreciative chuckle.

He turned away again and continued his narrative.

"But while I was living in the North, as you can imagine, I was exposed to all the knowledge, thoughts, and ideas of the wider world. For the first time I began to think about the way things were in the South, and on this farm. How the wealth of my own family was earned on the backs of people who had no say in the matter. People who reaped little of the benefits of their own labor. The arguments I'd always heard in favor of the practice suddenly seemed shallow and self-serving.

"So when I'd completed my schooling, and it was time to return home, I balked at the idea. I pleaded with Miss Abbey to send me to a school of higher education in the North. I believe she would've agreed, but Daddy would have none of it. He offered to pay for my further schooling only if I attended the University of Virginia. I'm pretty sure by that point he'd come to suspect I'd been corrupted by Northern influence, though we'd never had any serious discussions on the subject.

"So I was at an impasse. I had no money to continue my education in the North but was now morally opposed to returning to the farm in the South, or to a Southern university. I could stay in the North by getting a job as a common laborer of some kind. And being bright and reasonably well educated, after a few years could work my way up to a higher position. I didn't mind hard work, but I was prideful and felt I was made for better things.

"But then, fortunately for me, a solution presented itself. One of my best friends at school, George Brown, told me he was planning on attending the recently founded U.S. Military Academy in New York. It wasn't far from where we'd attended boarding school, at a place on the Hudson River called West Point. He practically begged me to go with him, though he needn't have bothered. I practically jumped at the chance. You see, if you attend the military academy, you not only get one of the best educations in the country, but it's entirely free! You just have to commit to serving as an officer in the Army for four years after you graduate. My friend had an uncle who was a U.S. congressman from New York. I'd met him on a few occasions when I'd been invited to several of George's family events. This uncle provided me the needed recommendation to the academy commandant, and the next thing I knew I was being sworn in as a cadet alongside George."

He turned to look at her again. She nodded encouragingly, "And then you were in the Army?"

"Yes, when you graduate the academy, they make you a second lieutenant, the lowest rank of a commissioned officer, but higher than all the common soldiers. You feel pretty special and important at first, until you find yourself sitting at a desk in a large building in Washington City with a stack of papers, a pen, and an inkwell. Not exactly the weapons and duty a young man dreams about!"

"I should imagine not!"

"But as luck would have it, I was soon rescued from my doldrums by the war breaking out with Mexico. That was in '46, and suddenly the Army needed every man they could put in the field with a gun. Well, you can imagine the excitement for a young officer, heading off to war, his brass buttons so new they'd never needed polishing!" He paused, staring into the distance, remembering that heady moment.

He breathed a heavy sigh and then continued.

"Anyway … the long, bloody story of the Mexican War can wait for another day. After the war was over, they gave me a choice: return to my desk duty in Washington or stay in the West. The posting would be in the only place with any sort of action, out on the frontier in Texas. Young, aggressive, and fresh from the excitement of war, the idea of a dull posting back East held little appeal. So I signed up to fight Indians and arrest outlaws out West. There really was nothing else I'd rather be doing. I realize now it also kept me from thinking about coming home. My only twinge of guilt, if I ever considered it at all, was for Miss Abbey, knowing how she must be suffering my long absence."

"And then you received the news of your father's passing? That must've been quite a shock."

"Yes. For the first time in my adult life I had to face up to my family's shame: the slaves. I finally had to decide what to do about *them*," he paused, struggling with what to say next.

She remained silent, gazing up at him in quiet encouragement.

Finally, he turned to her, and looked her in the eyes. "I decided I *had* to return home ... I'd been ... running away ... my entire adult life, and it was finally time to come home. But I still didn't know what to do about the farm and the slaves. I laid awake many nights agonizing over it.

"Before we left Texas, I was convinced it would be best to sell the farm. If I sold the farm ... I'd no longer be a slaver, it's true. But the slaves ... would still be slaves."

He was quiet for another long moment, staring down at his boots.

Then he looked up at her, "In the end, I believe God has shown me the path ... through darkness and doubt, into the light. One day I'll tell you all the ... incidents ... *adventures?* Anyway, all the happenings on our long journey ... a trek of over twenty-five hundred miles from the edge of civilization back to here. And ... looking back on it now I believe our Lord God guided my steps ... not in the way one might assume—to keep me safe, as one would've prayed for. No ... he took me along a more treacherous path for a purpose. To teach me *wisdom* ... *hard* lessons ... lessons I *needed* to learn. So when I arrived here at last, and even as I rode down the very drive we just raced on, only then I decided what I *must* do. I decided ... I *must* free the slaves ... every last man, woman, and child."

Evelyn's eyes went wide, and she immediately put her hand over her mouth to suppress a gasp of shock that might otherwise have come out.

"But, Nathan ... what about the farm ... what about Miss Abbey? What will become of them?"

"Well ... that was, of course, the question I was asking myself. And the more I considered my conundrum the angrier I became. *By God!* Men had been prospering for thousands of years without

371

slavery. So why is it in these modern, industrial times, in this great, wealthy country we're so dependent upon it?

"It occurred to me; except for Mr. Whitney's Cotton Engine, there have been precious few advancements in agriculture in the South for hundreds of years. Yet in the North, without slaves, they produce enough food for a country of millions. And they do it all throughout Europe as well. So there *must* be a way to keep the farm alive without enslaving the innocents.

"Then I asked Tom his opinion. It turned out he'd already been applying his extremely clever mind to the problem and had concluded we *could* do it. So, since that day, Tom has set out to investigate every conceivable agricultural advancement meant to produce higher yields, and more profits, with less labor. He's recruited our scholar, William, to assist him. That's what he's been doing, ensconced in his office all day long: writing letters and sending telegrams to anyone and everyone who might know something about what we're looking for. Reading everything to be read, talking to everyone to be talked to. He and William have been compiling a list of every agricultural improvement known to man. New machines, new equipment, new types of crops and seeds, modern, man-made fertilizers, and so on. They're calculating the impact each advancement could have on our profitability. Measuring the cost of the improvement against the potential gain."

"Oh, my! I've been wondering what Tom was doing closed up in that room all day. I thought maybe he was writing a book! And, has all this research come up with a solution?"

"They've made tremendous progress. I believe before it's over, Tom may be the country's foremost authority on modern agricultural techniques, if not the world's. And, of course, William's contributions have been invaluable. He's really quite brilliant, you know.

"But despite our best efforts, we keep coming back to the need for labor. Not as much as before, and not necessarily *free* labor. A smaller, more skilled workforce could do the job. But even so, a farm requires relatively inexpensive labor if it's to prosper. So it all came down to a basic problem: if we free the slaves, where will we find the needed labor in a region of the country where no such labor force exists?"

Nathan paused, looking at Evelyn, as if he expected her to answer his rhetorical question. But he found her intensely interested gaze more satisfying than any answer she could have given.

"I also knew I couldn't just set the slaves free and turn them out. Doing that might be every bit as cruel as continuing to enslave them. They'd have nowhere to go and no employable skills. So I became determined that before I set them free, I would teach them how to be free men. How to survive in the wider world, so they'd have a fighting chance. That's what my Sunday sermons have been about—not just about the teachings of God and Jesus, though they always play their part, of course. Rather, I've been teaching them what to do if they leave this farm. How to stand up for themselves. How to be *men* again, like they once were, far away and long ago in Africa."

Evelyn said nothing, but Nathan could see her eyes wide, as if in wonder at what he was suggesting. Her eyes swelled with tears, and a slight smile touched the edges of her mouth. This time he did *not* misinterpret her meaning!

"Then … it finally occurred to me I'd been focusing my thoughts on the two problems separately; how to run the farm without slaves, and what would become of the slaves once I freed them. But I realized these were *not* two separate problems—they were one and the same. I just needed to convince enough of the freed former slaves to stay on and retrain to work the new, modern farm. For a wage, this time, of course.

"But the question was how to get them to stay once they'd been freed. Fortunately, my recent experiences made the solution to that problem obvious. I'd just come from out in the wilds of Texas. There I'd seen people who'd traveled thousands of difficult and dangerous miles from the East coast, or from other countries. They'd left the safety of their homes, friends, and neighbors behind just to claim a small piece of land to call their own.

"And here we sit, surrounded by a vast acreage we already own thanks to the foresight of my granddaddy, and the diligence of my daddy. And though the acreage under tillage has grown year by year, as money and resources have allowed, still the vast majority of the farm property is undeveloped. So to make them want to stay, I intend to deed each freedman—and woman—a plot of land of their own. They can till and plant this parcel as they see fit, keeping all the proceeds for themselves. I'll also gift them the cabins to live in. As you probably noticed, they built these houses simply and sturdily such that we can easily dismantle and move them if we wish. Or, the freed men can use them where they now sit, it makes no difference to me."

"Oh, but Nathan, if they're busy working their *own* farms, how will they help you with *yours*?"

"Well, that must be part of the arrangement. They must agree to work a certain number of hours during the week on the main farm—I'll pay them a wage for it, of course, but it can't be extravagant. With the remaining time they can do as they wish on their own places. And those too young or too old to work in the main farm, can be supported by the others, or spend their time working their own farms, as they wish."

"Okay ... I can see you've given this a lot of thought ... but what about things they'd need to buy? Farm implements and such ... and ... oh my goodness, food and clothing? They can't simply wait for their crops to come in!"

Nathan smiled. It pleased him to see she was now pondering the same issues he'd been struggling with himself. But she no longer seemed shocked, or self-righteous. And wasn't trying to argue him out of it.

"They can borrow the farm implements they need when they're not in use by the main farm. They'll have to coordinate their efforts at certain times of year, but it should be workable. As for the money ... I've struggled with that one. I don't want them to continue depending on me for all their needs, or they'll still be slaves in everything but name. No, I'm determined they'll learn how to make, save, and spend money wisely. In fact, I've already started teaching them about these things in my little Sabbath lessons. I intend to pay each freedman a lump sum of money— exactly how much, I don't know ... We still need to work that out.

"And ... it's important to make it clear to them I'm not *giving* them anything. They've *earned* the land grant and the money through their own hard labor, and that of their forbearers—labor we should have been paying them for all along."

"It's ... very *admirable*. But will they truly understand and appreciate the value of the land ... and of the money? They've never considered such things before. I wonder if the allure of someplace different ... up North where folks may be more welcoming, might prove too strong."

"It's possible ... and, of course, if any decide to leave, I will wish them well and give them what help and guidance I may. But I have time to get them used to the idea, and to make sure they understand the value of what I'm offering. It's going to take a couple of years, maybe longer, to put everything in place."

"Years? ... Yes, I suppose so, though it must gall you in the meantime. Well, my father always liked to say, 'Rome wasn't built in a day'—although ... now I think on it, he never told me how long it *did* take. And so, this farm having been run with slaves for more than fifty years can't be changed in a day either."

"True. And if I weren't actively doing something about it every day, it *would* gall me. But I've already started the process, with a lot of little things. You've mentioned these people seem a bit happier, smile a little more, and stand up straighter than slaves you've seen before."

"Well, yes—I'd seen it, but didn't know what to make of it at first. But then I saw how you treated them ... *decently*? No, that's not quite right ... *respectfully*? Yes, how *respectfully* you treated them every time you spoke with them. I've seen masters who were kindly, who never abused their servants. But I've never seen a master treat them with as much *respect* as you do."

"And why not? I say. They *are* fellow human beings, same as you and I. Enslaved at the moment, through no fault of their own. A different color of skin, yes. Some different facial features and whatnot, but nothing of significance. They smile, they talk, they laugh, they think, and they ... *love* ... same as you and I ..."

At the word, "love," she blushed, and for a moment looked down at her feet.

375

"Showing respect to those you have power over ... to me it's what a man *should* do ... always. In the Army it's one thing that separates *good* officers from *bad*. In war, the time may come when you must ask your men to lay down their lives for you! Respecting them ... it's the very least you can do in return. 'There but for the grace of God go I,' is a good motto to follow, in my opinion.

"If you were to ask my men why they followed me all the way from Texas to Virginia, they might say something of the sort, I reckon."

"Yes, I *know* they would ... and also ... I would say they did it because of ... their *love* for you."

There was a softness in her voice and in her eyes as she gazed up at him.

And when his eyes met hers, he could feel tears welling. "Maybe so," he answered in a voice choked with emotion, "maybe so."

"Thank you, Nathan, for opening up ... for being honest. I ... I need to do the same. But ... please don't tell Miss Harriet ..."

He smiled and nodded his understanding.

"I really *must* tell you ... I *know* my Daddy would've approved of you ... and your plan. In fact, I believe he would've become a disciple had he ever heard your ideas. He also inherited his farm, though not nearly so large, nor with so many slaves. But he always felt conflicted about it and ended up making decisions to the benefit of the slaves but to the detriment of the farm. Ultimately, he lost the farm, and we became nearly destitute. Momma and Daddy became estranged, after which he ... well, to be honest, he pretty much drank himself to death.

"Oh, Nathan. I know my Daddy was a terrible businessman ... naïve, maybe ... but I loved him so. He taught me so many things, including how to think like a man ... for better or worse."

She sighed a heavy sigh, and tears streamed down her cheeks.

"I'm ... I'm so sorry, Evelyn ... I didn't know."

"I wanted you to know the *truth* about our family, so there'd be no secrets between us. After Daddy passed, Momma and I were forced to move into a small house in Richmond, with what little money we had left. She reckoned the only way out of our

376

desperate situation was to make sure I married into a wealthy family. And, after several … well … *disasters* would not be too strong a term … she heard about you returning from the West to inherit your Daddy's farm. She decided you were the solution to all our problems. We've come here under false pretenses. We've conspired against you and … and … I'm *so* sorry. I'm *not* the daughter of a wealthy Richmond family, as you were led to believe. I'm just … *me.* And if you tell me to get back on the train for Richmond tomorrow, I won't blame you."

"Evelyn … I didn't even know you were coming, so you can't say I welcomed you under false pretenses." He laughed, "In fact, I had no *pretenses* at all!"

She smiled and wiped away her tears.

"And I've been off in the Army so long … I care nothing for your position in so-called 'polite society.' It's what's in your heart that matters. And from where I sit you have nothing to be ashamed of in that regard!"

"Thank you … for being so … *understanding*, Nathan."

"Understanding? My dear lady, there is nothing I need to *understand*. You've been through a difficult campaign, true … but you've come out with your head held high—unbeaten and still fighting. No man could ask for more.

"If anything, it brings me closer to you than before."

Evelyn couldn't contain her enthusiasm, "Oh, Nathan! Thank you for being so gracious, and for sharing your plans with me!

"Yesterday I said I'd give serious consideration to whatever you had to say and tell you what I thought. Well … I'm just … *amazed* by you—by *all* of this! I don't have to ponder it at all. It's like you've struck a match in a dark place, and suddenly my eyes can see! It's … absolutely … *wonderful!* What you're doing for these people! And … doing it wisely and with careful thought for the future. What my father was always lacking in his plans: how to do the right thing *and* still ensure the farm continues to prosper."

She was overcome with excitement, and on an impulse, leaned over and kissed him on the cheek. He sat up, and for a split second had a shocked look. Then he smiled.

"Well, I guess you *did* like it." He laughed.

She blushed, and said, "Sorry ... that was a bit ... *forward* of me. I was just ... so enthusiastic about the whole idea, and I—"

But before she could finish her sentence, he leaned in and kissed her briefly on the lips. It was her turn to be shocked. Then she smiled, "Oh! So I guess you didn't mind my little *indiscretion?*"

He laughed again.

"Nathan?"

"Yes?"

"I would like ... I would like it ... *very much* ... if ... if you would kiss me again."

She said this softly, her eyes looking down at the rock in front of her. She'd never said or done anything so bold and didn't have the courage to even look at him.

By way of answer he leaned toward her and softly touched her under the chin, lifting her head so that she met his gaze. She found herself staring into his intense brown eyes. Like falling into a deep dark pool ... she felt she might swoon again, it was so overwhelming ...

"I can't imagine anything I'd rather do," he said, and leaned in to kiss her gently on the lips. This time he didn't end it quickly, and they lingered together for a moment before she finally pulled back.

"Oh my ... Captain!" she said, smiling again. "You've taken my breath away!"

"Well, I guess that's how it's supposed to work, isn't it?" he said, smiling back at her. He slid a little closer to her and kissed her again. This time he gently placed his arm around the small of her back. It surprised her how soft and gentle he was for such a large, strong man. She'd never enjoyed this sort of thing before. *Never was the right man before,* she decided.

When they drew apart again, she was nearly overcome with emotion. On another sudden impulse, she leaned in and wrapped her arms around him, burying her head in his chest. She had never imagined she could behave this way ... he had ... such a strong effect on her. Almost completely overwhelming...

He said nothing, but put his arms around her gently and held her close to him. She could hear his heart beating, and could feel the rock-hard strength in his body, despite the tenderness with which he held her.

They stayed that way, motionless and silent for several minutes. Then she slowly pulled back, and he didn't try to stop her. When she sat up, she wiped a tear from her eyes.

"I'm sorry, Nathan … I … don't know what came over me. I feel so … *fond* of you suddenly," she whispered in a voice quivering with emotion.

"Well, whatever came over you, I won't mind if it happens again," he said, smiling. She laughed a gentle laugh, and once again stared into his dark eyes. She could see by the intense look in his eyes, he was also feeling strong emotions. And he seemed to be breathing more heavily.

As if guided by a hand other than her own, she reached up and placed her lips on his, closing her eyes. He held her close, pulling her against him. As she leaned forward into the kiss, he relaxed backward, and was now resting his head against the rock, with her on top, their lips still pressed together.

"Oh … Nathan … I feel so …" she began, but couldn't think of what to say, so she just kissed him again. A vision of her encounter with Stanley Finch back in Richmond briefly flashed through her mind but exited as quickly as it had entered. This man was something altogether *different* … so soft, and gentle, not forcing himself on her. But so much stronger and more powerful.

She felt a stirring inside, both emotionally and physically, such as she'd never experienced before. Her mind went blank as she immersed herself in the warmth of his embrace. It was wonderful—something she'd never imagined possible.

Then she seemed to come out of something like a trance … and realized she was lying on top of him. And … his body was hard and … she had an overwhelming, aching need in her most intimate, womanly parts, urging her on … to *be* with this man … to become a woman … this was the man she wanted … this was the right time …

But a part of her mind said, *No ... not yet ... too soon, wait a while ... it will be better if you wait ...*

Her breathing was coming hard, and she felt him reacting in the same strong, physical and emotional way.

And then, her logical mind, in a last desperate effort, forced her to speak the only words she could think to say, coming out in a breathless whisper, "I ... I've never *been* with a man before ..."

This simple phrase seemed to be the exact right thing to cut through the passion and emotion, into the rational part of *his* mind. He reacted almost instantly.

"*Oh!* Oh my God! Oh ... Evelyn, I'm so sorry, Evelyn, dear ... oh, I'm so sorry."

And then they were sitting upright, and he held her softly, but no longer passionately.

"Are you all right? Oh, Evelyn, I didn't mean to ..."

But she placed a finger on his lips.

"No, Nathan. There's no fault to you ... there was something ... something between us. Anyway, it was *not* your fault ... I was there too ... it's not your fault."

He looked in her eyes, and the worried look on his face began to ease. He seemed relieved not to have harmed her somehow. She smiled at him encouragingly, a smile he immediately returned.

Then he held her close again, this time very gently, "I've never known anyone like you, Evelyn. I'm ... well, I'm a bit older than you, and I've known ... a few ... women in my life. But it feels like ... like there's something *special* about you ... something *special* between you and I ..."

She smiled, relaxing, and feeling like she could breathe again.

"I feel the same way, Nathan."

৪৩৩৫৩৫৪৩৩৫৩৫৪৩৩৫৩৫

When they were off the narrow track and back on the road, they could ride side by side once again. He momentarily toyed with the idea of getting even with her by instigating another horse race. But he decided they'd better walk the horses. The animals had worked hard going up and down the hill, not to mention their earlier gallop. And he was enjoying having a little more time alone with Evelyn.

They'd been riding along in silence for a few minutes, and his mind had begun to wander, when she said, "What are you thinking about?"

He couldn't help but smile … her timing with that question had been perfect. Though he mulled over several subjects during their brief silence, at that moment he happened to be thinking about …

"Oh … I was just pondering … *the wedding.*"

"Wedding? Who's getting married?" she asked.

He'd thought to play a little trick on her with that sudden pronouncement, but based on her reaction, she apparently understood he was speaking of someone else's wedding.

"It's one of those little things I was talking about up on the hill. I actually announced the idea on the very day you arrived. If you recall, your carriage arrived just as our Sabbath talk was breaking up that day…" then he laughed.

"What's so humorous?"

"You remember when our eyes first met as you rode by in the carriage, I laughed out loud, and later you asked me why?"

"Yes, I remember. Your reaction confused me."

"Yes … I know. Sorry about that. It *was* rude of me. But, you see, in my Sabbath sermon I'd just announced the slaves on the farm could now be married … and then, the next thing I saw was *you*.

"I think … well, after the day we've had … I can tell you … that first sight of you fairly took my breath away! I thought … I should say, I *think* … you are an exceedingly beautiful woman."

She smiled and nodded at the compliment.

"And then I realized Momma had conspired against me, as it were, and it tickled me. Even as I was announcing a wedding for my people, she was attempting to arrange the same for me. She, and Miss Harriet I presume, had planned our courtship entirely without my knowledge or approval."

He chuckled, "Clearly mothers *do* know what's best, after all."

Evelyn smiled demurely, and blushed, but said nothing.

"Anyway … after telling them they were no longer forbid from marrying, I announced we would hold a wedding—a real, legal, white-dress wedding, with a real minister—for any slave couple wanting to do it."

"Oh, Nathan! What a lovely idea! You really *are* such a kindly, thoughtful man."

"Well … I must admit, I do have my moments."

They shared a smile.

"But … despite my best efforts I'm afraid I've been less than successful at winning over the majority of the slaves. From what I understand, though they appreciate I've made some improvements, and am generally kindlier than my Daddy, most of them still don't believe I'm for real. They think my talk of freeing them is just a ruse—a thinly disguised attempt to get them to work harder and more cooperatively."

"Oh … I see. That must be … a bit disheartening."

He nodded agreement.

"But … hopefully the wedding will prove your sincerity in a very *real* way?"

"Yes, that's my hope, though I would have done it anyway. It's the right thing to do after everything they've been through."

"And did any couples agree to go through with it?"

"Twelve couples … so far."

She smiled brightly, "Oh! That's wonderful! You must be so happy!"

He returned her smile, pleased she was so enthusiastic about his idea.

ಬಿಞಿಌಯಬಿಞಿಌಯಬಿಞಿಌಯ

Margaret stared out her window, taking in a sight she'd not seen before. A scene that gave her pause and increased her growing sense of unease, though she struggled to discern its purpose or meaning.

In the pasture out beyond the okra field a dozen men rode on horseback … with weapons drawn.

She recognized more than half of them as the regular farmhands—Bob, Stenson, and others. But several men were new

382

to her. Walters was with them and seemed to be instructing them in some sort of training exercise.

She was baffled by it. The men rode in two short columns led by Walters. They trotted halfway across the field and then at a shout from Walters, fired their weapons off to the sides toward various objects: barrels, hay bales, and other objects spread around on the ground in the field.

They lined up and repeated this exercise over and over, pausing between each round to reload weapons.

She pulled up a chair and sat, thinking about what it might mean. And suddenly it came to her, and a cold hand of fear clutched her heart, nearly taking her breath away.

☙℘ℭℛℭ℘℘ℭℛℭ℘℘ℭℛℭ℘℘ℭℛℭ

Nathan tied the horses to the hitching post in the drive and led Evelyn up into the house. In the foyer they'd planned to part ways, Evelyn going upstairs to change, hopefully before Miss Harriet saw her. And Nathan going back out to spend the remainder of the afternoon looking over the farm work.

They parted with a quick, but affectionate kiss, after glancing about to make sure no one was watching. They agreed to meet again at the dinner table, this time more properly attired.

Evelyn walked up the elegant, curved stairway in the foyer. She was feeling smug about getting away with her little wardrobe indiscretion, when she saw Miss Harriet at the top of the stairs. Harriet stood with her arms crossed and a scowl on her face.

"When they told me you went riding with the Captain I had a feeling I would find you dressed like this. What were you thinking, Evelyn? I'm sure it has completely scandalized Mr. Chambers!"

Evelyn did not immediately reply but removed her straw hat and calmly strolled up the stairs. This time her mother's words of reproach had no effect on her. For one, she had been expecting it and was entirely prepared. For another, she knew she was in the *right* this time. Her plan had *worked!* Nathan was no longer disgusted with her, and in fact, maybe … just maybe he …

When she reached the top of the stairs, she stopped and looked at her mother. "Momma, ever since Daddy died, I've done everything your way. I've said everything you've told me to say. I've dressed the way you've told me to dress. And I've behaved the way you've told me to behave. And yet, last evening Mr. Chambers told me to go home ... and *never* come back!"

"He said *what?!*" Harriet exclaimed, her hand covering her mouth.

"You heard me right, Momma.

"Right back there on the veranda, after you and Miss Abbey left us alone, he told me he wanted nothing further to do with me. That we should pack up and leave today."

Evelyn paused for a moment, allowing this news to sink in.

"Oh, my! Then ... how is it you've gone out riding together today?"

"Momma, in the midst of last night's disaster, it came to me. *Your* way had failed. Failed miserably, and utterly. And now it was time for me to ... well, try to just be *me!* So I begged Mr. Chambers for one more chance. I remembered Daddy used to be fond of saying 'desperate times call for desperate measures,' and so I decided to let Mr. Chambers see a different side of me. More of the *real* me, maybe."

"So you dressed up like a ... like a ... *man?!* And I supposed you rode astraddle like a man as well, not side-saddle like a decent lady?"

"Of course, Momma! Side-saddle is so ... *ridiculous!* Why ... you're likely to fall and break your neck riding that way!"

Then she couldn't help but smile. She was in such high spirits her mother's scolding had little effect.

"What are you smiling about now, child?"

"Momma ... it worked. *It worked, Momma!* He took me for a ride to the top of a high hill ... that one over there with the bald crown. And it was ... *wonderful!* The view was magnificent, and we ate a beautiful lunch Megs had packed for us. We talked and talked, and then ..."

"Then?"

"Then … *he kissed me, Momma!* A real, sweet, story-book romance kiss! The kind of kiss I used to dream of when I was a young girl, before all the Stanley Finches of the world drove such thoughts completely from my mind."

Now it was Harriet's turn to smile. "Well, I have to hand it to you, girl. I can't agree with your tactics, but I will give you credit for saving us from another disaster! Now, hurry upstairs and change into something decent, before Miss Abbey sees you and we have another crisis on our hands!"

Evelyn noticed this time Harriet's tone was much milder, and the scolding was only lukewarm. She knew she'd done well this time, and Harriet knew it too.

"Yes, ma'am!" she answered, and hurried to do as she was bid, a bright smile still lighting her face.

ಬಿಲಾಣಿ ಬಿ

Later that evening Nathan and Evelyn were once again alone together on the veranda. They had had a light-hearted meal with the older ladies, Nathan retelling the story of his granddaddy's hilltop for Miss Harriet's benefit.

On another occasion, Harriet might have objected to the young couple going off unchaperoned, but this time she knew when to leave well enough alone. The girl now seemed to have Mr. Chambers well in hand and sticking her nose into it could only cause problems. So she smiled her most pleasant smile, and nodded appreciatively at everything Mr. Chambers had to say. Propriety and her own feelings on the matter were of little consequence, with so much at stake.

The older ladies declined to join them on the veranda. They seemed to sense it was a good time to leave the young couple alone.

So they sat by themselves, enjoying the cool of the evening as the sun began to set. Nathan sipped his usual whiskey, and Evelyn enjoyed a small glass of brandy Megs had warmed for her.

"So?" Evelyn asked, looking Nathan in the eye.

"What do you mean?"

"Yesterday evening we sat in this very spot, and … well, I will skip the unpleasantries, except to say we agreed to meet today at this same time and place. And you would tell me your decision," she answered, setting her elbows on the table, resting her chin on her hands, and smiling.

"My decision?" For a moment he couldn't think what she meant. With the pleasures of the day, the events of the evening before had been driven completely from his mind. But then he remembered, "Oh … that. Well, after everything we've been through today, don't you already know my decision?"

"Well, maybe I do … but then … maybe I *don't*. Anyway, I wish to hear you *say* it."

He smiled. "All right, Evelyn. If you must hear it … then I will confess, you have entirely changed my mind today. I know now I was wrong about you … *utterly and completely* wrong about you. As wrong as a man can possibly be, in fact. And I … no longer want you to leave."

"And …?" she asked, continuing to smile up at him, her chin resting on the back side of her linked hands.

"And …" He had to think a minute about what else she wanted of him, and then it came to him. He stood and made a bow. In a mock formal tone, he said, "Miss Evelyn, would you do me the great honor of staying on as my guest, for however long you wish?"

She sat still for a moment and looked up to the sky as if mulling over her answer. Then she laughed and stood herself. She made a formal curtsey, "Mr. Chambers, I am most honored by your invitation, and I gratefully accept. I shall stay until … until … anyway, yes! I shall gladly stay!" She giggled, spoiling her attempt at formality.

Chapter 13. Plans and Preparations

*"Give me six hours to chop down a tree
and I will spend the first four
sharpening the axe."*
– Abraham Lincoln

Thursday July 12, 1860 – Greenbrier County, Virginia:

The next day, Evelyn was like a ray of sunshine after a spring shower. Her mood was so bright and sparkling it was practically contagious throughout the house. Nathan had gone out before daybreak once again, and so she had not yet seen him. But she greeted everyone else she met with such warmth and enthusiasm that soon the entire household staff seemed to be singing and humming as they went about their work.

After breakfast she sought out Megs, finding her working in the kitchen, supervising the cleanup of the morning meal, and already starting on preparations for the midday supper. She took Megs by the hand and led her out onto the veranda where they sat down at a table.

"Megs, Mr. Chambers told me of the big wedding. He didn't say so, and being a man, he probably doesn't know or care, but I'm guessing *you* are the one who's arranging the whole thing."

Megs eyed her with curiosity.

"Well, that's true, child. Me and, of course, Miss Abbey. She has the … artistic touches … me, I'm more practical, making sure the right amount of cloth gets ordered, dresses gets sewn by all the women, and so forth. With Mr. Tom arranging to purchase things and what not. Why you asking?"

"I'm just so impressed by everything the Captain has told me about what he's trying to do to improve the lives of his people. But … he told me most of the slaves are still suspicious of him, and skeptical. Do you think this will finally convince them he's sincere?"

Megs smiled, "Well ... it sure ain't gonna *hurt*. It's making it a whole lot harder for them that's still determined to speak ill of him. But ... of course, they's also skeptical about the wedding itself ... saying it ain't really gonna happen after all. That either the Captain's gonna change his mind on it, or the other white masters here-abouts are gonna put a stop to it."

"Well, all the more reason to make sure it's a great success!"

"Yes, ma'am. We can agree on that."

"And what about the couples? Are they as excited as they *should* be?"

"Yes, dear, they understand what it means. It means a real, legal marriage even the other white men must recognize, it being sacred before God n'all. It means they can't never be separated by being sold off one by one. And ... they also appreciate it's a *romantic* thing ... such as they had never dreamed possible."

"Oh, good! I'm so glad to hear it. I was worried the Captain might be disappointed. That he was doing a wonderful thing that folks wouldn't be grateful for."

"No, Miss Evelyn. Don't you go worrying about the Captain's feelings. If this wedding comes off, it should put an end to any more naysaying. I expect the people will finally start seeing him for what he is."

"Oh? And ... what exactly is *that*, Megs? When we first met you hinted at some things, but you never really said how you feel about him. Don't worry, whatever you say will be just between us."

Megs gave her a sideways look, then said, "I'm not worried about that, Miss Evelyn. If I thought ill of the farm's master, I would never say so—not to another living soul. But happily, that ain't how it is.

"I think he is more than just kindly and thoughtful ... I've come to believe he is a *great* man. Maybe the greatest any of us has ever known, or ever will know. I guess the old kings from the story books, like King Arthur and Caesar, were men like that. I don't know ... men who towered over other men without treating them that way, if you understand me."

"Yes, I think so," Evelyn answered, becoming thoughtful.

"Anyway, I reckon our Captain will cast a long shadow across the world before he's done. I don't figure him for a gentleman farmer the rest of his days. Once he gets over to Richmond and starts hobnobbing with gov'ners and senators and such lot … well, there ain't no telling where he may end up …"

Megs had a faraway look, as if trying to picture it.

"And if ever they's another great war, I reckon they'll call our Captain away to lead them armies, like a mighty Caesar."

"Anyway, child … you ain't said why you dragged old Megs out here to talk about this wedding and whatnot … my kitchen duties ain't fixing to do themselves!" she laughed.

"Sorry, Megs, I was just curious about Nathan … uh, the Captain … is all. No … what I came here to ask you was, 'how can I help?'"

"Help with *what*, dear?"

"Help with the wedding, of course! I can sew a dress, and I can … help with decorations—arranging cut flowers and such—and … I don't know … What about music, and … and dancing? A proper wedding should have music, and dancing, shouldn't it?"

"My, my, Miss Evelyn! You're getting way ahead of *me*. I figured if we had white dresses on the ladies, clean white shirts on the men, and a real preacher that'd be wedding enough!"

"Nonsense, Megs! That's no kind of *romantic* wedding! There must be food, and flowers everywhere. The men in fine clothes, and the women in beautiful gowns with veils. And it must have *music* and dancing! Leave it to me, Megs!"

"Oh … but what about the Captain, miss? I don't know if he's gonna want to pay his good money for all them *fine* things …"

But Evelyn laughed, "You leave the Captain to me as well, Megs! When I'm through with him, he'll happily pay for whatever we ask!"

"If you say so, Miss Evelyn. If you say so."

But Evelyn's good humor and enthusiasm were so infectious Megs couldn't help but smile and shake her head in appreciation.

"Now you mention it, I believe I *will* leave the Captain to you, Miss Evelyn!"

Megs stood, a mischievous grin touching the corners of her mouth, as she headed back inside.

Wonder what she meant by that, Evelyn thought. Then shrugged.

�ಬ�ಬ�ಬ�ಬ�ಬ�ಬ�ಬ

On Sunday, Evelyn and Miss Harriet accompanied them to church, which forced two of the farmhands to sit in back. Nathan was not keen on saying much of anything to Reverend Blackburn. He was still feeling unhappy with the pastor, but also a bit sheepish about his own angry response. So when Harriet and Evelyn kept the Reverend quite occupied with small talk, Nathan was perfectly fine being relieved of that uncomfortable necessity.

And again, he exchanged the bare minimal greeting with Walters in the aisle.

Nathan was wondering what he could do to make the weekly church visit more pleasant, and less tense.

On the other hand, he continued to be especially popular among the neighbors … although it looked like a few of the women with young available daughters were disappointed to see Evelyn there.

�ಬ�ಬ�ಬ�ಬ�ಬ�ಬ�ಬ

Nathan kept his Sabbath sermon brief, giving a short follow-up talk about money, mostly re-emphasizing points brought out in earlier lessons.

It was not his best performance, he realized. His heart was not really in it. To his surprise, thoughts of Evelyn were now filling his mind almost every waking hour, and often in his sleep as well. It wasn't the first time he'd ever fallen for a woman. But it was the first time in a long time he'd considered it possibly a permanent arrangement. And … he had to admit, she was, in so many ways, a cut above any woman or girl he'd ever been with before.

The evening before, after dinner, they'd taken another stroll down by the duck pond. This time nothing broke the romantic mood, and … it had been a *most* enjoyable interlude. They'd not yet consummated their relationship, but he was wondering how long that would last. He knew it'd be best to wait and be sure this

390

would really work out. But his willpower was waning. She was an extremely desirable woman, in every conceivable way, and he was no longer an inexperienced young lad. But he wanted to respect she was still innocent, and not to push her into anything.

He was now keenly aware of where she sat during his sermon, in the midst of the throng, next to Miss Abbey and Miss Harriet. He stalwartly resisted the urge to lock eyes with her during the entire speech, but still made eye contact with her often as he spoke. He was sure everyone would notice.

It took him by surprise, however, when she raised her hand and waived at him even as he was wrapping up his sermon. "Yes, Miss Evelyn? You have … a question?"

"Well, no, not a question, exactly. But I would like to say something to everyone before you send them away. If it would be all right?"

"Certainly, Miss Evelyn. Please, come up here where everyone can see you."

He gestured for her to join him by the table, in front of the gathering.

Nathan couldn't imagine what she was up to. So he waited with a bemused look on his face, as Evelyn came toward him.

"Good morning, y'all," she said, flashing them her dazzling smile. Nathan couldn't help smiling in response.

"The Captain has graciously agreed to allow the wedding couples to learn a dance for the wedding."

Her announcement was met with silence, but she noticed several couples looked at each other and smiled or rolled their eyes.

"I want y'all to know this will be the finest wedding *ever*. And … well, I believe it won't be a *proper* wedding without the grooms dancing with the brides. But don't worry and don't be shy. I will teach the lessons myself, and I promise none of you could possibly be a worse dancer than I was when I first started!"

She laughed. There was a twitter of laughter in response. "So if I could learn to dance, so can you. And … believe me … *it will be fun!* I promise. So I beg of you wedding couples … please join me right after lunch to begin our dance lessons! Thank you!"

She turned to Nathan and smiled, gesturing for him to continue.

Nathan dismissed them after wishing them God's blessing.

"Well, that was nicely done," he said as the crowd was breaking up. "You are full of pleasant surprises, Evelyn. You seem so comfortable speaking in front of a large group. Maybe you should go to Richmond and play senator instead of me."

She smiled, "Why shouldn't I be comfortable? No matter how many there are, they are all still just people. It's no different from talking to them one at a time … except one has to speak a little more loudly to be heard, of course."

Nathan shook his head in wonder, "You really *are* something special, as I've said before."

She smiled again, "I'm very gratified to hear you say so, Nathan."

He leaned in closer and whispered, "Will you walk with me?"

She nodded by way of answer, and they turned and strolled back up the road, arm in arm, in the direction opposite the house. Once again Nathan could feel her closeness. It now felt intense, like the burning heat from a fire.

After they'd walked along the road a short distance, he turned and took her on a side trail leading down toward the creek. It was an easy path, and not steep. Soon they were at the water's edge next to a huge old willow tree. As they approached the great tree, he looked around to see if anyone was watching. He led her around behind the trunk, and then, leaning her up against it, kissed her passionately on the lips. She returned the kiss with enthusiasm, and they remained locked together for several minutes.

When they finally parted, she said, "Oh my, Captain! What has gotten into *you* this morning?"

"Only you, Miss Evelyn!" he answered, and kissed her again.

When they separated, she said, "Oh! You must let me sit now, or I shall faint from lack of breath!"

So he led her over to a small, rugged wooden bench next to the water. It was a favorite spot of Miss Abbey's. He could remember swimming in the creek when he was a boy, with her watching from that same bench, or more likely its predecessor. They sat on the bench, hand in hand.

After a few moments of quiet, he said, "So … how goes the wedding planning?"

For a moment she pretended to misunderstand, toying with him, "Why … I didn't know you were ready to discuss *that* already, Captain!"

He smiled at her witticism, the same attempt he'd made the first time they'd ridden down from the hill. "You know what I mean! Megs may be your friend, but she's like a second mother to me … you think she doesn't tell me everything going on around here? In addition to the dance lessons, I know perfectly well you've practically taken over the whole thing. I understand you've even sent a telegram to Richmond, asking for musicians!"

"Well, someone had to do it! You can't have a wedding and dancing without music, can you?"

"Well … no … I suppose not—"

"And I've ordered material to make veils for the women, and suits for the men."

"Suits?"

"Of course, Nathan. You don't expect these men to go to their wedding in their worn old work clothes, do you?"

"Well, no … I just—"

"And I've sent for the cobbler from Lewisburg to come make sure the men have decent shoes to wear … you don't mind, do you? Can't very well have the grooms in bare feet!"

"All right, all right. I've been a soldier long enough to recognize when I'm entirely outgunned, completely outmanned, and have been thoroughly outmaneuvered!" He laughed. "What else will you be spending my money on?"

"Oh, nothing, really. That's *almost* all …"

"Almost?"

"Well, there's the baker …"

"Baker?"

"Well, of course. You can't have a wedding without a bride's cake!"

"Hmm … why not just take *all* my money, spend what you like, and give me back any that happens to be left over?"

"Oh … what an excellent suggestion, sir! I may just do that," she laughed, and then leaned over to kiss him one more time.

They were so intent on each other; they didn't notice their tryst was observed. From behind a tree a few yards back up the path, a young woman spied curiously. Rosa held a bemused, half smile on her face as she gazed at the couple. After a moment she shook her head, turned, and walked back toward the cabins.

ɬᴆᴄᴈᴄᴈɬᴆᴄᴈᴄᴈɬᴆᴄᴈᴄᴈ

Evelyn had decided to hold her dance lessons in a large, barn-like shed used to store wagons, Miss Abbey's formal carriage, and several large farm implements: plows, rakes, and harrows. She recruited Georgie and Jamie to move the farm equipment out and dust everything off, making it into a respectable dance hall, despite the dirt floor underneath. Considering what her "students" were accustomed to, she doubted anyone would mind that!

Leaving nothing to chance, Evelyn had gone to visit Tom before lunch to get a list of the couples to be married. Then she asked Megs to enlist a youngster or two to go around the camp locating each person on the list, making sure they knew when and where the lessons would be held and encouraging them, on her behalf, to participate.

She decided she'd start with a waltz. It was not only a beautiful, romantic dance, but it was also the easiest to learn. And if they learned nothing more in the few weeks remaining before the big event, at least they could have their one wedding couples' dance. Afterward, maybe they'd try a polka. She would save the more difficult things, like the French quadrilles, for later if time allowed. She assumed the complex German cotillion was beyond their reach, given their lack of prior experience.

Since she had no musicians, she planned to sing or hum the appropriate music while going through the steps. But to her joyful surprise, that turned out to be unnecessary.

When she returned to the impromptu dance hall after lunch, William was there waiting for her. "Hello, Miss Evelyn," she noticed he seemed shy, as he made only fleeting eye contact with her when he spoke.

"Hello, William. Are you interested in learning how to dance?" She was half teasing, and half wondering if it were true.

"Oh, no, Miss Evelyn. I am actually well educated in a number of the popular steps, from a purely academic point of view. But I'm … a poor participant, I fear. I'm … rather awkward with my feet, it seems."

"Oh, I'm sure that isn't true, William. Such a capable young man! Why, I'm sure with a little practice you'd be the talk of all the young ladies at the ball!"

She gave him a bright smile.

"It is … most kind of you to say, Miss Evelyn … but I wonder … if I were the 'talk,' exactly what would they be saying?"

She laughed. "So if you're not here to learn the dance, then why *are* you here, may I ask?"

"I'm here to offer you my services. You see, I am … among other things … reasonably proficient with the violin, and … well, I thought you might need a little music for your dance lessons."

"William! The Captain has told me all about how smart and competent you are at almost everything. It seems you're a man of many talents!"

She was so pleased she practically beamed, but she resisted the urge to kiss him. He was already blushing furiously, and she didn't want to make him any more uncomfortable.

"Please, think nothing of it, Miss Evelyn … just trying to help out."

He turned and walked over to where he had left a violin case leaning up against the far wall. Then he knelt and opened the case, standing up with a well-worn violin and bow. He ran the bow across the strings, playing a few notes. She thought it sounded lovely, but William stopped and adjusted the strings, before trying a few more notes. Soon he seemed satisfied and began playing a tune.

In just a few bars she recognized it and clapped for joy, "Oh, William, it's Chopin's *Grande Valse Brillante!* 'The Great, Sparkling Waltz,' we might say in English. I know it well—why, it's the very thing I planned to hum as my couples learned the dance! You are a God-sent *miracle*, sir!"

William stopped playing, and made a slight bow, blushing once again. "Thank you, ma'am ... maybe it's not so 'sparkling' when I play it, but it may serve ... and save you from humming."

"Nonsense, you play *beautifully!*"

William smiled and continued to blush.

"William ... you're such an intriguing mystery. I've already heard how you're knowledgeable in practically every subject and nearly saved the Captain's life with your timely and proficient medical skills. And Big Stan has told me you were a brave soldier, and really quite a good boxer, holding your own against all kinds of scoundrels out West. And now ... you play the violin like a young Mozart! Please, sir, if you will; indulge my curiosity, and tell me how such an obviously *learned* man came to be one of the Captain's soldiers, way out in Texas?"

William sat, and looked down at the floor, softly chuckling.

"You know, in all the years I was in the Army, and all the things I proved I knew, nobody ever asked me my story, not even the Captain. Oh, except Stan, of course. There's no keeping anything from him.

"I guess I take after my father. He was, like me, very ... *bookish* ... you might say. He was a high school teacher when I was born, and then he got a job teaching at Yale College in New Haven, Connecticut. So I, being a bright and curious boy, with a thirst for knowledge ... well, I basically grew up at the college. I was listening to college lectures when most children were still learning their A-B-Cs in grammar school! By the time I was officially enrolled in the college, in my early teens, I had already spent most of my life there. The normal classes were a matter of routine. So I studied at the medical school for several years, then the Sheffield Scientific School, and finally the Yale Graduate School of Arts and Sciences. I helped design the program for Yale College to be the

396

first in North America to grant a true Doctor of Philosophy degree. I'd hoped to be its inaugural recipient … but then …"

"Then, what, William?"

"My father took ill, and, after a short time he passed away. And … somehow it changed me. I'd always admired him—my whole life—looked up to him and aspired to be just like him. But on his death bed he looked at me, and said, 'William, I've learned everything I know from reading books and listening to other men speak. But I've never learned anything from being out in the world. Don't die like me … wishing you'd seen more of the wide world.'

"So after he was gone, I decided I must do as he said, and go out to see the world, instead of learning everything from books. And … well, I'd always had a desire to see the great American West but was too timid to go out on my own. So I joined the Army. That way I could travel in the relative safety of other men."

"Oh! What a bold decision! And how did it turn out for you?"

"My goodness, Miss Evelyn … it was *horrible!* I quickly realized it was the most disastrous decision I could have possibly made. I was entirely out of my element; a strange, bookish man in the middle of a group of rugged, mostly ignorant, fighting men, many of whom could barely read! They saw me as the oddest, most ridiculous, and worthless man they'd ever encountered. And, I was ready to agree with them. But then …"

"Then?"

"Well, to be honest, I have no other explanation for it than to say … then, *Stan* happened."

"Really? You mean Big Stan?"

"Yes. One day he arrived at the fort and they assigned him to our bunkhouse. And … well, my life has never been the same since. He is … well, he is the most different person from me you could possibly imagine, but also … he is the best friend I ever had.

"He turned everything around for me with all his jokes and foolishness, but also there's a compassionate side to him. I believe he recognized I needed a friend before I did.

"And then there was the Captain …

"We were out on patrol and got into a day-long skirmish with several dozen Comanche Indians. That day I fired and re-loaded my rifle more times than I could count, while scrambling up and down ridges and gullies with the other men in the platoon. By the end of it I was so exhausted I could hardly lift my gun anymore.

"But the Captain stepped up and called me out in front of the others. He said, 'Private Jenkins … today, you gave the enemy hell. Well done, mister!' Then he shook my hand, stood back, and saluted me, which I returned with great pleasure, and a newfound pride.

"After that the other men treated me with more respect, seeing I could actually fight, despite my bookishness. I finally began enjoying Army life, feeling I was good for something after all. And gradually the men appreciated my other knowledge, especially the medical training. Thanks to Stan, and the Captain, I became accepted among the men, and finally became a real soldier. And, also … more of a real *person*, I think."

"Oh, William … I'm so impressed with you. What a courageous thing you've done. You are most admirable, in so many ways. And I am so happy you found Stan. What a treasure to meet a *true* friend in this world."

"Yes … I think you're right, Miss Evelyn. And … thank you for listening to my story."

"Oh, my dear William! Thank *you* for sharing it with me! But … if you don't mind indulging my curiosity, I've been wondering what made you, and the other soldiers, decide to accompany the Captain back to Virginia, especially since you were finally enjoying the Army life."

William was quiet for a moment.

"Miss Evelyn, a person might live his whole life and never meet a *truly* great man. Someone who's head and shoulders above other men in practically every way, but who doesn't act the part, if you understand my meaning.

"I expect Washington was that kind of man, and Jackson maybe … probably a few others. Perhaps even this Lincoln fellow everyone is now talking about. Nothing the Captain does surprises me anymore. That he's now a State Senator for Virginia

… it just seems, somehow … *natural* for him. If he one day becomes governor, or even president, it won't surprise me in the least.

"It seems to me if you have the chance to even *meet* a man like that face to face, you ought to do it, even if you must travel many miles or suffer numerous hardships. And if—by some stroke of great good fortune—you're given the opportunity to become a companion to such a man, you'd be a fool not to jump at it. Miss Evelyn, Captain Chambers is *that* kind of man, in my opinion.

"So to answer your question, when Tom, that is, *Sergeant Clark*, as we called him then, asked me to join him and accompany the Captain back to Virginia, I didn't have to think on it even one minute. And I would've gone even without Stan. But of course, I was delighted he decided to come too. And if you were to ask him why, he would likely say much the same … in his own unique manner, of course."

Evelyn had expected something of the sort, but William's description of Nathan went beyond anything she'd anticipated. She now felt she'd only seen a small glimpse of all there was to see of him. "A *truly* great man," William said. Megs had called him a "great man" and had compared him to the old kings and Caesars.

It made her wonder what a future with Nathan might be like. *What would I be next to a man like that? I am … just a pretty young girl, with no special gifts or talents, who has done nothing, and is nothing extraordinary. Not great at all, let alone truly great! And if I were to marry him, what then? What would I be? Just … the wife of a truly great man? Nathan Chamber's wife … Mrs. Nathan Chambers? The wife of Governor Chambers? Who would I be? A person who is no longer herself, but only has an identity through the man she married? And … who am I now, anyway?*

This worrisome train of thought was thankfully interrupted when she saw the first of the wedding couples peeking hesitantly around the corner of one of the large doors.

"Come! Please come!" Evelyn said, giving these people her full and positive attention. "Come over here and please … tell me your names."

They entered, but proved even shyer than William had been.

"My name is George … named after the first president, Miss. And this here's Babs. I reckon we're some of those that's fixing to get married."

Although he was a very large, powerful looking man, he spoke softly, and never made more than momentary eye contact with Evelyn. Babs didn't look up at all.

"Thank you for coming, George. Thank you for coming, Babs. Oh, my goodness, Babs! You will be such a *beautiful* bride!"

This prompted a smile from both Babs and George, and Babs dared a quick look at Evelyn, "Thank you very kindly, ma'am," she said, still holding onto her grin.

But before Evelyn could quiz them, hoping to draw them out a bit more, two more couples arrived. These were followed immediately by four more. The rest then arrived, all in a bunch. Evelyn guessed they'd all been holding back, waiting for the first couple to enter.

The dirt floor of the dance hall was not ideal for dancing, but it was packed down hard, so it would likely serve the purpose. *A shame that huge old house doesn't have a ballroom*, she thought. *It has a lovely great room with a grand piano, and room enough for a dozen or more people to gather around it. But definitely not enough space for couples to dance. Oh, well … maybe someday it will, if …* then she cut short the thought. *No time for that now*, she scolded herself.

Then she reminded herself the big wedding would be outside, on the lawn, so practicing on the dirt floor was probably for the best, anyway.

Most of the couples were young people—mostly in their twenties from what Evelyn could tell. But there were a few older couples—people she assumed had already "jumped the broom" and likely had several children by now. Finally, they could make their marriages legal and official.

But of all the couples, Evelyn was especially touched by one pair. Their names were Toby and Anna.

They both had white hair, wrinkled faces, and walked partly bent over, Anna leaned on a cane and clung to Toby's arm. Evelyn would not be surprised to learn they had grandchildren, or even great-grandchildren! But Anna smiled sweetly when she looked at Evelyn, and Toby fairly beamed. Then he said, "More'n fifty-year now we been together ... why ... we've had children and grandchildren 'bout too many to count! And now, finally we's gonna get married, all legal-like, and whatnot. With a real, Godly preacher and all. God bless us all, and God bless the Captain."

Evelyn wasn't sure Toby and Anna would be able to dance, but it was a pure joy they were there, and she told them so.

Evelyn recognized several of the people from her walks with Nathan but didn't remember their names until they introduced themselves. She did, of course, recognize the groom, Cobb. He'd helped her with the horses on the morning when she had taken her ride with Nathan. And she'd spoken with him on many other occasions, since his groom duties made him a regular around the house. Cobb was accompanied by a pretty young woman named Hetty, who curtseyed politely when Cobb introduced her.

"If you'll excuse my saying so, Miss Evelyn, I likes your current attire much better'n what you was wearing the time I was helping you with them horses." Cobb grinned.

Evelyn chuckled and nodded her head in agreement.

Hetty looked at him sideways, as if wondering what in the world he was talking about. He leaned over and whispered, "I'll tell you all 'bout it later, don't you worry none!"

After the introductions were complete, Evelyn started class.

"Thank you so much for coming. I'll not promise to be able to remember all your names today, but by the time we're finished with our lessons, I will!

"As I said earlier today, this will be the most wonderful wedding ever, and you ladies ... why, you will be the most beautiful brides ever!" She said this with such honest enthusiasm, many smiled, and several giggled appreciatively. "And ... what fine-looking gentlemen, as well!"

"Especially me!" old Toby shouted out and slapped his knee with a laugh which was echoed by the group. Anna gave him a scowl, and shook her head, rolling her eyes.

Oh! They are so sweet! Evelyn thought to herself, smiling at the old couple.

"All right, class. The first dance we will learn is *especially romantic*. It's called, 'the waltz.'"

On the walk back to the cabins after the dance lesson, Cobb walked next to Hetty, explaining why he'd been discussing clothing with Miss Evelyn. Now she'd heard the story, Hetty was giggling with amusement.

"You trying to make me believe Miss Evelyn ... fancy, prettier-than-life, Miss Evelyn dressed up like one of you old grooms? Like a *man*! To go riding with the Captain? What kinda fool you take me for Cobb? Why ... I can't even picture it ... she be always so ... *perfect*! I seen white women all dressed-up-like before, but never seen one wear it so well as *that* one. Dressed like a *man*? You been sneaking into the Captain's whiskey, Cobb?"

"No ... I swears it, Hetty. It's just like I told it. She done dressed in riding boots, britches, and old straw hat, exactly like I said!"

"And the Captain never told her to go back inside and dress up decent-like? I still can't believe it," Hetty said, shaking her head, but grinning just the same.

"Come now, Hetty, darlin'. I done promised I'd tell the tale. I never promised you'd *believe* it!" Cobb then flashed her his very best, mischievous-boy smile. It had the desired effect on her, as he knew it would. She smiled and shook her head. *That smile never failed me yet,* Cobb thought with satisfaction.

He still couldn't believe they were getting married in only a few weeks. Unlike many of the others, they'd never jumped the broom, and didn't have any children together. In fact, their romance was still new when the Captain had announced the big wedding. He'd been working up the courage to ask her to jump the broom with him, but when he heard about the wedding, he figured *that* would be even better. So he had put on his best, most winning smile, and asked her the question. He was both shocked and pleased when she said, "All right, Cobb. But don't go expecting any of that 'honor and obey' nonsense. I reckon if I was to obey *you*, there'd be no end of trouble I'd be getting into!"

He couldn't disagree with that, knowing his own mischievous nature, so it was agreed.

And he was ready to get the whole thing over, now that it was decided. For one, he had a burning desire to bed Hetty. But though she'd seemed agreeable enough to the idea before, since the wedding was coming, she said it would have to wait.

He didn't understand why it all had to take so long. But the ladies said you couldn't rush a *real* wedding. There were dresses to be made, and cakes, and … all kinds of other mysterious things to be planned and arranged. Including, he discovered to his amusement, learning how to dance. *Finally,* he thought, *something worth doing in all this.* He had always liked the idea of dancing, especially in the company of an attractive woman. He'd thoroughly enjoyed the Saturday night bonfire dances that'd started up since the Captain had given them the Sabbath day off work. But that dancing was just made up on the spot, whatever steps the music called for and happened to put into one's head. The older folks spoke of dances from old Africa, but he knew nothing about those, having never seen or learned them himself.

Now under Miss Evelyn's tutelage, he was actually going to learn how to dance a *real* dance, with practiced steps and all. He'd enjoyed their first lesson immensely, even though several of the other grooms were grumbling about it and grousing as to why it was necessary. He had always loved music, and it seemed the most natural thing to move to the rhythm of it. He felt like he took to it right away, and even Miss Evelyn commented on what a good dance student he was. Hetty also seemed to enjoy it, or maybe his enjoyment was contagious to her, but either way she was also doing well.

The whole thing was almost dreamlike … but he hoped there'd never be an awakening! He'd about decided the Captain, and all his plans, were for real. Was he *really* going to free them, after all?

He figured if the wedding came off as planned, that *must* decide it, once and for all. After that, nobody would listen to the cynics any longer. *If* it came off …

A short time later, George and Babs sat together on the grass not far from Cobb and Hetty.

Babs said, "George, Mr. Tom says we that's fixing t'get married needs to choose a family name. You know, like the Captain and Miss Abbey's family name being *Chambers*. So's we can give our dear little ones that name too. Annie and Lucy are so excited about this whole wedding business they's about to burst. They'll be so pleased if we all get a real family name we can share."

"Hmm ... yeah, I been thinking on that too, Babs. And I ... well, you know how I was named for the first president, Mr. Washington?"

Babs rolled her eyes at him, "Yes, George ... I *do* recall hearing *something* of the kind."

"Oh, yes ... I guess I done said it before ... but anyway, I was thinking ... would it be okay to use his *last* name as well? Or would it be ... *blasphemous*-like?"

"No, I don't believe so ... It'd be blasphemous if we used the name of the *Christ*. Or maybe one of the saints. But Mr. Washington ... well, he was a *great* man for sure, but still just a *man* after all. I reckon that'd be a good, strong name to have."

"Oh! Thank you, Babs! Thank you. That makes me very happy. *George Washington* ... I likes the sound of that! Not that I'm fixing t'be no president, mind!"

He laughed. Babs laughed along with him, shaking her head at the thought.

Chapter 14. Love's Labour's Lost

"True love cannot be found
where it does not exist,
nor can it be denied
where it does."

– Torquato Tasso

Thursday July 19, 1860 – Greenbrier County, Virginia:

Tony had been out working in the fields as usual on the day Sickles had nearly given Rosa a beating. So by the time he returned to the cabins, the whole farm was a-buzz with the talk. Though relatively few people had actually seen it, everyone was talking about it, so the story was getting more and more muddled as it went around.

Tony heard various and conflicting versions of the tale. Mr. Sergeant Jim had taken the whip away from Sickles and had beaten *him* with it. The Captain had fought Sickles with a knife, cutting the whip into pieces as Sickles tried to whip him. The Captain had cut Sickles into pieces with a knife. And the Captain's Indian had given Sickles the evil eye, frightening him off from doing the beating. The more questions he asked, and the more he heard, the more confused he got.

One thing seemed clear: Sickles had intended to give Rosa a beating—nobody knew quite why, Rosa being a very sweet and good-natured girl—and the other white men, or possibly the Indian, had intervened and put a stop to it.

One thing he knew for sure was, Sickles, and two other white farmhands, were gone. This he knew because he'd seen it with his own eyes. These white men were riding out, looking glum, as Tony and the others were walking back in from the fields. Two of the Captain's soldier-men were riding with them, the ones called Georgie and Jamie. They did not look downcast like the others. They even smiled and winked at Tony as they rode by, which pleased him greatly. Of course, he didn't know what it was all about at the time, but later he realized he'd witnessed Sickles' forced exodus.

Like everyone else, he was happy about Sickles' departure. The man was just plain mean and generally had the bad temper of a rained-on rooster! But what had happened to Rosa—and even worse, what had nearly happened—had shaken him up more than he would have believed possible before. By now he'd seen plenty of whippings, and was well used to the idea the white masters could do whatever they wanted to the slaves. It was no use worrying about it, either before, during, or after.

But something had changed. A different wind now blew on the farm, he had to admit, despite his continued skepticism. The things the Captain had done and said had brought about a subtle change in his outlook, without him acknowledging it.

He knew in his gut things weren't the same as they'd been. The white overseers no longer treated them with utter contempt, and no longer felt free to abuse them with impunity. And the new white farmhands, the ones who'd been soldiers out in the West, treated the slaves differently than any white men he'd been around before. They seemed to view the slaves more as … well, fellow farm workers, than inferior beings. They laughed, they smiled, they made crude jokes. Though they might give orders, or offer instructions on a task, they never threatened, or berated.

Oh, for sure, the one they called Sergeant Jim could yell and curse as good as any white farmhand he had ever known. But there was no real meanness behind it. And he'd dole it out in equal measure to white men or black.

But never to the women, Tony realized, now that he thought on it. Sergeant Jim always treated the women kindly, white or black. Tipping his hat to them, smiling, and addressing them as "ma'am."

And Tony now realized, despite himself, he now felt things would continue to get better, rather than the same old sameness he'd always known.

Which made what happened to Rosa hit him like a punch in the stomach. Every time he thought about her, and imagined her innocent body violated by Sickles, or her soft flesh torn by the whip, it sent a shudder through him.

He had tried to see her several times in the days following the incident. But she wouldn't come out of her cabin, and the women watching over her wouldn't let him in.

"She don't want to see no *man!*" they said, as if he was dense for even considering it. But he couldn't see why not. It wasn't as if *he* had done anything to her. And anyway, though it was a man had caused all the trouble, wasn't it also men who'd put a stop to it, and saved her from the beating?

Eventually she did come out and looked no worse for the wear. But when he talked to her, she seemed distracted somehow. Like her mind was elsewhere, and she wasn't really focusing on him or what he was saying. He shrugged it off, trying not to take it personally. He guessed it was the aftereffects of the incident and would eventually wear off.

Lately he'd been daydreaming about her as he worked. The lines of her face, the smooth skin of her neck, the subtle curves of her slender figure. Her eyes, her smile. Her laugh. In fact, he was having difficulty thinking of anything else. It surprised him. He'd never been like this before. He'd always been level-headed, skeptical of anything new and different. But now this woman, still not much more than a girl, had his mind all … *muddled*. When he walked through the cabins, he went out of his way to pass by *her* cabin, to see if he could catch a glimpse of her. When the Captain held his Sabbath talks, he did his best to sit as close to her as possible. If not next to her, then somewhere he could look at her without being too obvious.

He finally could hold it in no longer, and one day after work he confided in Johnny, his best friend on the farm.

"Something's wrong with me, John."

"Whatcha mean, Tony? You looks perfectly fit to me," Johnny eyed him suspiciously, as if whatever it was might be catching.

"It's that girl, Rosa," Tony answered.

"Rosa? What's Rosa got to do with … oh! Oh, I sees it now! You's falling for that girl Rosa! Oooo … yeah, yeah … she be a looker all right! Oh, I sees it now," he said, slapping his forehead as if chastising himself for being dense. "Now I get why we always has to sit in a certain place, or get somewhere early and such like … you was trying to sit near that girl."

Tony growled, becoming irritated, "Don't make me wish I ain't told you, Johnny."

"Sorry, sorry, Tony! You caught me by surprise is all. Yes, sir, you's got 'fine taste,' as the white folks would say. Yes … that there's a fine young woman, that is!"

Johnny reached over and slapped Tony on the back.

"Yeah, well maybe so, Johnny. But seems she done put some kinda witchly spell on me, or something. I can't seem to think on nothing else. 'Specially with all this wedding talk, and whatnot. I ain't never felt anything of the like before. What's the matter with me?"

Johnny laughed. "I know exactly what the matter with you is, Tony! You's in love, boy! That's what that is, pure and simple. Wheewoo," he whistled. "There ain't no more fatal disease known to man, no, sir. You's *doomed*, boy!" He grinned.

"Stop enjoying my suffering else I might find a way to make you suffer too." Tony showed Johnny a fist, to emphasize his point.

"Come on now … don't get hot, Tony. I's just teasing is all. Sorry … it's a serious matter all right … but on the other hand, it won't kill you. But, does the girl return those warm kinda feelings?"

"Well, she's nice, and friendly and all … but more in a sisterly sort of way, if you get my meaning. That was what I wanted to ask you John … you think maybe she still too young for such thoughts? You know, love for a man and all?"

"Hmm …" Johnny scratched his chin thoughtfully. "Course I ain't no expert on that question, but from what I been told, once they starts to *looking* like a woman, they starts in to *thinking* like one too. And from what I been seeing lately, that-there Rosa of yours … she do *look* the part!"

"Then what's a man's gotta do to make a woman start thinking 'bout him … you know … in *that* way?"

"Well, from what I hear, if you was one of the white folks, you'd be writing her love poems, bringing her sweet-smelling flowers, and such like. Woo boy! None of that nonsense here in the cabins, thank the Lord!"

Johnny laughed.

"Can't decide if you're trying to help, or still having fun on my suffering."

"Come now, Tony! I'm just cheering you up! You gotta relax a little … stop worrying on the whole thing so much. The old men say if you gotta work too hard to get the woman … she ain't the right woman! I don't know, Tony … maybe … you could just …"

"Just what?"

"I don't know … what if you walks right up to her and tells her how you's feeling? And if this wedding business has got you all worked up, why not ask her to jump the broom with you? You both old enough. Look here, Tony … you a good-looking, strong, smart fella … why wouldn't no young woman want to love you?"

Johnny's tone had changed, and he sounded more serious, and thoughtful now.

"Hmm … maybe you're right, John. I never thought of doing that. Seems too easy … and from my experience anything too easy, don't never work."

"Well, that's true … but maybe this time it will!"

Johnny gave him an encouraging smile, and a pat on the back.

"Humph! You're a big help! Well, maybe I *will* … maybe I just will."

Tony became quiet and thoughtful again.

⚬⚬⚬⚬⚬⚬⚬⚬⚬⚬⚬⚬

There was no time to talk with her during the long workdays, so Tony had decided to wait until Sunday, after the Sabbath sermon. Then he'd have time and a more casual setting in which to speak with her.

Waiting until Sunday also gave him time to get his courage up, and to think of exactly what it was he wanted to say. He felt better once he'd decided he would do it. And since Sunday was now several days off, he could relax and not worry about it too much.

But now the momentous day had arrived, and he found himself anxious and fidgety. Like he'd sat down on a red ant hill; he couldn't stay still nor get comfortable. He positioned himself a little behind her during the Captain's Sunday afternoon talk, and afterward couldn't remember a single word of it.

When the sermon was over, the people dispersed. Tony followed Rosa a short distance behind, waiting for the right moment.

But the giant man Stan stepped up to him and pulled him to the side.

"Hey, Tony. You come fetch water for us at target practice again today? Maybe one day Captain will let you shoot guns, too."

"Well ..." Tony wavered. He greatly enjoyed the target shooting. The comradery of the soldiers, and the way they treated him — respectfully, like a ... *real* person. Plus, for some reason he didn't entirely understand, he had a burning desire to learn how to shoot a gun.

But ... he *had* to talk with Rosa, or he would explode. "Mr. Stan ... I got's something I gotta do." He tried to come up with some reasonable excuse. He looked up at Stan, who looked back at him curiously, likely wondering what Tony needed to do so badly on a day he didn't have to work. Tony decided the truth would be best. Mr. Stan, despite his great size, was also a young man like himself, so would surely understand. "Mr. Stan ... it's ... I got's to go talk to this young woman, you see ..."

Stan's face was suddenly lit with his broad grin, "Oh *ho!* So Tony ... there is young female woman, is there? Oh ... ho, ho! Very good, Tony ... very good! You go do battle with sweet young missy. Later you come give Stan full report on success of conquest, hmm?"

He slapped Tony on the back, and strode away with his great long strides, shaking his head and chuckling to himself.

Tony caught up to Rosa just as she got to the area where the cabins started. She was walking with Betsy and two other women. He was hesitant to talk with her in front of the others, but he didn't want to wait and watch her go into her cabin and shut the door. So he worked up his courage and stepped up behind her as she walked, tapping her lightly on the shoulder.

She turned and seemed surprised, "Tony?"

"Hello, Rosa. Can I talk with you?"

"What about, Tony? I was just fixing to help with the supper."

But thankfully Betsy seemed to understand and said, "Rosa, you stays and have a word with Tony, here. We'll get things started without you … come along when you may." She gave Tony a meaningful look before turning and leading the others away.

"Well, what was it you wanted to talk about, Tony?" She looked friendly, but not overly so.

That didn't seem particularly encouraging to Tony, but he was determined to see it through. "I been, thinking, Rosa. Well … you'd look mighty fine in one of them white lacey wedding dresses the women have been sewing on."

He felt an immediate sense of relief having got the words out.

But Rosa didn't seem to get his meaning, "Oh … well, no, those ain't for me Tony. Them's for the women that's gonna be in the Captain's great wedding. Though mostly they's already married by the old ways of jumping the broom. Why you been thinking a thing like that, Tony? You know I ain't one of those getting married."

"Well, Rosa, you see … it's just … I been thinking. You and I … well, we … well, it's just we get along real well. And … we're old enough and … well, I was wondering if *we* might be in that wedding too."

But Rosa still seemed confused, as if her mind were wandering, "Oh no, Tony. We can't be in the wedding on account of we ain't got nobody to marry … *yet*."

Oddly when she spoke, she had a faraway expression, as if her mind had wandered off on another road, and she sighed a heavy sigh.

Then he noticed she was looking off toward the road, where the old oak tree stood next to the big old wooden table. Tony turned and saw the Captain sitting there with his new lady friend, the one who'd been visiting the farm these past several weeks and was teaching the wedding couples how to dance. They smiled, and chatted easily, clearly happy in each other's company. Tony looked back at Rosa, but she was absorbed in the scene playing out across the road.

"Rosa …" he said, trying to regain her attention. "Rosa!"

She finally turned and looked at him.

"What is it, Tony?" She seemed annoyed by the interruption.

"Why you staring over at the Captain and his lady friend when I's trying talk with you?" It was his turn to become annoyed. "You thinking they's the ones ought to get married, 'stead of us?"

"Well, sure. Why wouldn't the Captain want to marry her? Look how beautiful she is … *perfectly* beautiful. Her hair, her face … the way she dresses. Even how she walks and talks. I overheard some of the white farmhands say she's just like a real-life princess. Course I ain't never seen one of those, but I imagine it must be so."

Tony glanced over, "Yeah … I guess so. But look, Rosa. You're … well … you're plenty pretty too."

Rosa looked at him for the first time and smiled, but shook her head, "Not next to her I ain't. If only …" she sighed.

Tony shook his head in confusion. "Rosa … about this wedding …"

"Oh, Tony. I'm still just a girl. I ain't ready for such things, can't you see?"

"No, I don't see, Rosa. You's been lookin' plenty growed up lately."

"Well, maybe so, but … not like *that*," again she gestured over toward Evelyn. "When I see her … I feel like I'm still just a little girl. I wish … I wish one day I could be like her … fancy dresses, proper manners. A lady admired by one and all. A lady who's pretty enough to be with a man like the Captain …"

"Rosa … you're … I …" Tony struggled to find the right words, but nothing would come. So he turned and walked away. Rosa had already gone back to watching the Captain and Miss Evelyn.

Though she hadn't rejected him out of hand, Tony still felt the sting of it. He strode briskly along. The mixed emotions gave way to a growing anger. As he walked along, he fed the anger with his own dark thoughts … heating it to the simmering point. Why did she want to be like the white woman? So she could have a man like the Captain? *Why not a man like me?*

The more these thoughts ran through his mind, the more he resented the Captain. The good feelings he'd been having about the man had soured. He no longer saw the Captain's smile as warm and encouraging. Now when he pictured it in his mind, it seemed smug and demeaning, as if he were secretly laughing at their simple-mindedness as he told them whatever lies pleased him and would serve him. The whole wedding business … likely it'd be postponed, put off for one reason or another, until it was eventually forgotten. Just to make the people work harder, be more loyal, and not … *run away?*

Though he burned with anger and burned with a great empty ache from Rosa's rejection, he couldn't feel anger toward *her*.

☙℞℺☙℞℺☙℞℺

Sunday July 29, 1860 – Greenbrier County, Virginia:

The following Sunday, Nathan asked Evelyn to go riding with him after they'd returned from church and he'd given his regular sermon to the farm workers. He wanted to get away from prying eyes, so he could be alone with Evelyn. But not for the usual romantic tryst. This time he was feeling an uneasiness in Evelyn he couldn't quite put his finger on. Though their relationship continued to blossom, from time to time she would go quiet, and appear thoughtful or worried. But when he'd ask her about it, she was dismissive—it was nothing, a passing headache, or some such. And she'd brighten back up, and he'd soon forget all about it … until the next time.

Today he was determined to get her to discuss whatever was troubling her, if she would. He could no longer envision a future that didn't include her. He wanted nothing to jeopardize that.

She had readily agreed to Nathan's offer, and at the risk of scandalizing her mother, she once again donned her riding clothes. When he saw her, remembering how well he'd liked her

413

appearance dressed that way, he smiled broadly, which she returned brightly. She asked if they could ride up to the top of the hill once more and enjoy the view as they'd done before.

This time they didn't race up the road. They walked the horses easily, chatting comfortably about nothing of any great import, until they reached the side trail. The narrow trail forced them to travel in single file the rest of the way to the top of the hill. And, as before, Harry the Dog followed along, at his usual distance.

When they reached the top, they left the horses in the tree's shade. Once again they climbed the great rock and sat in the same place they had the first time. There they gazed out at the grand view of the farm below.

Evelyn marveled at how comfortable she was in his company, so different from when they'd been here before, only a few weeks ago. She grasped his arm, and leaned in to kiss him, with an ease now as natural as breathing. And he returned her affections with obvious warmth and enthusiasm.

This time they'd not brought along a lunch, it being mid-afternoon, between lunch and dinner. She again gazed out at the now familiar farm below, recognizing many more of the details than she'd been able to the first time.

After a moment of quiet contemplation, Nathan said, "Evelyn, there's something I've been wanting to talk to you about …"

For an instant, she had a sudden shocked notion he was about to *propose* to her … but then the thought died as quickly as it had come. Somehow his tone was too *serious* … or concerned, maybe … for him to be preparing to ask *that* question. And besides, she had a feeling he'd want to make more of a production of it—if and when he did it.

"Yes, Nathan, dear … what is it?"

"Well, lately I've been … *worried* about you. Mostly you seem comfortable, and happy being here with me, but occasionally you seem … I don't know exactly how to describe it … distant? Thoughtful? Worried? I don't know … but not your normal happy self. And every time I ask you about it, you brush it off as insignificant, and brighten back up, and I leave off. But it has happened too many times lately for me to continue ignoring it."

She bowed her head, and looked at her feet, but didn't answer.

"Evelyn, do you remember when we first came up here? We promised to be honest with each other ... not just by what we *say*, but also by not holding back the things left *unsaid?*"

She sighed a heavy sigh and looked up at him. She was smiling, but her eyes were watery.

"You're right, Nathan. Of course, you're right. I've not been ... sharing my ... *unsaid* things lately. I ... I have no excuse other than ... my own fears."

"Fears about what, Evelyn? Don't you know by now, I mean you no ill? That I will never intentionally harm you, either by word or deed?"

"Yes, I know that, Nathan. You are a *wonderful* man. You wouldn't harm *any* woman if you could help it, and especially not me. I can feel that more strongly than ... Well, anyway, it's not *that* ... it's ... just ..."

"Just?"

"Nathan ... I don't know how to explain it, because I don't really understand it myself. Sometimes I feel so happy being here and being around you. Like I could just ... I don't know ... fly like one of your little garden birds, maybe."

"But ... *other* times?"

"Other times ... when I imagine our future together, if ... if we were to be married someday ... Oh, Nathan ... everyone goes on about how *great* you are—your men, Megs, your Momma ... I guess the Governor even ..."

He looked at her, a puzzled expression on his face. She realized she was floundering, and he was only becoming confused. So she decided to try a different tack.

"You see ... when I came here, I hadn't any expectations of who you were, or what you'd be like. So when you turned out to be ... kind, and thoughtful, and ... *everything* you are ... I couldn't have been happier. If only you'd love me, and want to be with me, I'd be the luckiest woman alive. But I wasn't honest with you at first, as you know ... not letting you see the *real* me. And so, you sent me away—rightly I will now readily admit. But ever since then it's been the *real* me ... only ... now ... I feel ..."

"Now ... you no longer want me to love you?"

"Oh no ... not *that!* No, never *that*, Nathan! That's not what I mean at all. It's that ... well, maybe William said it best. He said you are a 'truly great man,' the kind who is very rare, such that a person might meet only once in a lifetime."

"Oh, I don't know about all *that*. William may have an inflated opinion of me, from some of our absurd adventures together, out West ..."

"No, Nathan ... I don't think so. But anyway, please let me finish, or I shall not be able to get it out. Most of the time I feel good about being with you. And other times I feel like ... like ... *nothing*." She said the last word almost in a whisper, so he was unsure he heard her rightly.

"You mean sometimes you feel *nothing* for me?"

"No, no, Nathan! Sometimes I feel like *I am nothing!* You're such a great man, and I am just a *nothing*. Nothing but a pretty girl who doesn't know how to do anything and has never accomplished anything. Who am *I* next to you? What will I *be* next to you? I feel like ... like ... I'll be lost forever in your shadow, and no one will ever find me ... *not even me.*" And then it seemed as though a voice in the back of her mind whispered, *And ... who am I?*

"Oh, Evelyn, that's nonsense! You are certainly *not* a nothing! And you are *not* just a pretty girl ... I've known many pretty girls, and as I told you before, I've soon tired of them. But with you it's different, *special* somehow, like the more I'm with you the more I want to be with you. Can't you see?"

Evelyn could see the earnestness in Nathan's eyes, and she knew he was speaking his true feelings. But she also knew, with a sinking heart, he did *not* understand what she meant.

She suddenly realized he was incapable of understanding it, for the simple reason he didn't see himself as a great man at all, only an ordinary, good man. A man who always tried to do his best in any given situation, and in dealing with other people, but didn't always succeed. Part of his greatness was in how it came so naturally to him, he didn't even recognize it in himself like others could. So he couldn't possibly understand why she would feel lost next to him.

Once again, she felt foolish for having her worries and doubts. And then, looking into his serious, concerned eyes, her heart melted.

She reached up and kissed him. "Oh, Nathan, I have so much *love* for you … never doubt that … I am … just being foolish, I'm sure."

"Yes, you are being foolish, if you worry you aren't 'good enough' for me. You are—it sounds trite, but—you are head and shoulders above any woman I've ever known before, in *every* way. And I don't mean your beauty, although that is also the case, in my eyes."

"Thank you, Nathan."

Though he hadn't really understood what she'd said, she did feel better for having got the words out. Maybe it was just nervousness, and the newness of the relationship. And the fears about the future. She still saw herself as a little girl, one who now had to worry about the idea of marriage and all that goes with it. It was a bit overwhelming. Maybe it was simple nerves. Maybe all young girls went through the same thing, and it would pass.

But who am I? the little voice in the back of her mind seemed to whisper, once again. This time she tried her best to ignore it.

She'd decided another kiss would be nice, when some movement out of the corner of her eye caught her attention. The motion she'd seen was back toward the tree where they'd left their horses. She turned her head and was startled to see a gray, four-legged shape in the grass out beyond the horses. Her first instinct, being out in the wild, was it must be a wolf stalking the horses. But before she could shout the alarm, she realized this was no wolf. For one, no wolf was ever *that* big! And for another, the horses looked straight at it, and showed no fear or alarm. She had forgotten about Harry.

Nathan looked in the direction of her gaze, "Looks like Harry has found a bone to dig up."

And indeed, Evelyn now noticed Harry was digging furiously with his front paws, throwing a steady stream of dirt up in the air behind him.

"My, but he does dig with great enthusiasm!"

"Yes, too bad we can't hook him to a plow—he'd have the whole farm worked over in no time!"

She watched for a moment, then saw something else. "Nathan, do your men often camp out up here?"

"No, never since we've come here from Texas. Why do you ask?"

"Well … because it looks like there was a recent campfire right over there next to where the dog is digging his hole …"

He stood to get a better view. "I see what you mean … let's go have a look, shall we?" He reached down to offer her his hand.

She took his hand and stood to her feet. She felt a slight twinge of regret that their opportunity for another romantic moment had likely come to an end—at least for the time being. She realized now she had caused the end of it herself! *Too clever for your own good, Evelyn!* she scolded herself.

They climbed down from the rock, hand in hand, and walked over to where they'd seen the dark spot on the ground. Harry had stopped digging and was now lying on the grass. He appeared to be chewing on something. Nathan came over to have a look, and when he got close Harry bared his teeth threateningly.

"I'll have none of *that* now, Harry!" Nathan said in his most stern Captain's voice. Harry immediately snapped his mouth closed and laid his head on the ground. Nathan leaned in and examined the bone Harry had been chewing.

"Hmm … fresh meat on the bone. Strange for it to have been buried up here …"

"Look, Nathan … these coals are still hot." She had brushed aside the dirt on top of the dark spot in the ground, and he could see a wisp of smoke coming up from underneath.

"By God, you're right!" he said, coming over next to her. He held his hand over the hole in the dirt and he could feel the heat.

"Nathan, this fire was going this morning, before we arrived. In fact, it was probably put out shortly before we came up this hill. Who would've been up here, if not your men?"

Without offering an answer, Nathan ran over to the shade tree, and leaped up to reach one of the lower branches. He swung a leg over the branch and clambered up as high as he could in the tree. From a swaying branch near the top he leaned out, gazing toward the south.

"There's a haze, but … I can just make out … yes … riders … two riders, out on the road. Now they're gone from view."

Pausing for one last look, he started back down the tree.

Evelyn walked over next to the tree as he climbed back down. "Who were they, do you think? And why would they be camping up on your mountain? Deer hunters?"

"Maybe … but if they were hunting up here, I'm sure we would've heard gunshots. There are plenty of deer about. I'm sure they'd have had plenty of targets. But that bone … it's not a deer bone, it's from a cow. No … I don't believe they were hunting up here."

"Then what, do you think?"

"I don't know. Let's poke around some more and see what else we might find." He strode past her back toward the place where they'd found the remains of the fire. She followed close behind.

They looked around the fire pit but found nothing else. Then widening their search, Evelyn said, "Over here, Nathan. See how the grass is all matted down? It looks like a man slept here, if I'm not mistaken."

Nathan came over to see what she was looking at. "Yes … I believe you're right."

Then looking around he said, "And there's another."

They walked over to where he'd pointed. Sure enough, there was another patch of flattened grass, in the general shape of a man rolled up in a blanket.

Nathan strode a little farther down the hill toward where some low bushes grew. "And look here, Evelyn. The grass is all cropped and trodden—they tied horses here."

She came and looked. Examining the ground, she found a hoof print in a patch of bare dirt, the horseshoe clearly visible in the imprint.

When Evelyn started to move forward, Nathan caught her by the arm, "Wait … I want Billy Creek to investigate this, before we walk around on it anymore."

"Billy? What a strange fellow he seems. He's hardly said two words to me since I've arrived. He just looks at me with an inquisitive expression … like … like I'm a strange creature he's never seen before."

"Yes, that's Billy all right. But he's a good man, despite his oddities. Once you get to know him, you realize he's extremely intelligent, and has a lot of common sense … and wisdom … for such a young man."

"Well, then, I'm eager to know him better … if he'll ever talk to me!"

"Anyway, Billy can read the dirt on the ground like you and I can read a book. And the less we walk on it the better for him. Let's get back to the house. I want him back up here while there's still plenty of daylight."

๑๛๏๙๛๑๛๏๙๛๑๛๏๙

Although he was eager to get Billy up the hill, Nathan forced himself to walk the horses. They'd worked hard going up and down the hill, and a few minutes more or less would make little difference.

It gave Evelyn a chance to quiz him about their findings on the hill.

"Nathan, I can tell you're worried whoever it was up on your hill may have been up to no good. What do you imagine they were doing up there?"

"Spying."

"What? Spying on the farm? Why would anyone want to do *that*?"

"I fear it may be the sins of the fathers are now visited upon the sons," he answered cryptically.

420

She gazed at him inquisitively, and he laughed, "Sorry. It seems my father and our nearest neighbor, Percival Walters, had a long-running dispute about a misdrawn property line. The disagreement turned into a feud as the years went by. And I'm afraid my peace overture towards the son, Elijah, has been less than fruitful. It appears he intends to continue the conflict.

"Oh? That seems odd."

"Before my arrival he instigated several incidents in an attempt to persuade Momma to sell him the farm. Strongarm tactics intended to intimidate a helpless widow."

"Not a very decent fellow, clearly. But why the continuing animosity? Now that you're home and Miss Abbey is no longer alone, surely he'll give off causing any mischief."

"I thought so too, until I discovered what kind of man he truly is. He's murdered several of his slaves by his own hand."

"What!? How do you know he's done *that?*"

"I have it from an impeccable source who witnessed it with her own eyes!"

He then told her about the unexpected visit from Margaret Walters, and the story she told of her experiences with Walters, and the murders she'd witnessed. Finally, he told her how impressed he'd been with Margaret, and how anxious he now was about her safety and welfare.

Evelyn was quiet for a moment and seemed thoughtful. It occurred to him he may have been bragging up Miss Margaret a little *too* much. So he said, "But don't be concerned … there is nothing of the romantic kind between us. I just have a great deal of respect and admiration for how clever and courageous she's been, and all she's had to deal with."

Evelyn looked surprised, "Why should I be concerned about *that*, Nathan?"

"Well, in my experience … sometimes women become … I don't know … jealous may be too strong a word for it. But anyway, they don't much like their men noticing other women in a positive way."

She smiled, "Oh … I see. You know, I've never understood that concept. If the man I loved didn't love me more than any other …

he must *not* be the right man. Why should I waste such feelings on *him?*

"If there's truly something *incredibly special* between you and I, something you could *never* have with another woman, why would I worry if some other woman was smarter ... or prettier, or ... whatever? She still wouldn't be ... *me!*"

"Speaking of clever and admirable ..." he said, smiling at her. She blushed but returned the smile.

"Anyway ... I wasn't entertaining any of *those* thoughts, Nathan. I was worrying about poor Margaret's predicament, living with that *horrible* man. And I do wish there was a way you could get her out of there. How awful for her."

"Yes. Believe me, I'm sorely tempted to ride in there with all my men, guns blazing, kick in the front door, shoot Walters right between the eyes, and grab her. But unfortunately, we're no longer in Texas. I'm afraid that's just not how they do things here in Virginia, more's the pity."

She laughed. "You've warned me there's a dark side to you ... am I seeing a glimpse?"

"No, not at all. If you ever see *that* side, you'll know it. I won't just be *talking* about violence and mayhem, I'll be *doing* it!"

He smiled, and reached into his pocket for a cigar, but there was a cold glint in his eye, that made her believe it was so.

"Anyway, her fear is if we were to somehow affect a rescue, she would be forced to live the rest of her life in fear of Walters coming after her. She'd be always looking fearfully back over her shoulder. I must confess I have thought of no solution to *that* problem, short of his demise."

They were quiet for a moment, and her thoughts turned back to the hill and the spies they'd apparently discovered. "But Nathan ... from everything you've said, he wanted to intimidate Miss Abbey, so she'd sell the farm and leave. And he's an evil and despicable man, brutalizing his own slaves. But even so, what can he gain by spying on your farm?"

"I ... I don't know. I surely wish I could ask Miss Margaret that question ..."

"Well, since she's not here, you'll just have to *settle* for me ..."

422

He looked at her with surprise, and she grinned. He knew she'd played him.

"Touché … well said. So … *have* you any ideas?"

"No … I haven't the faintest …"

"Hmm … me neither."

He was quiet and thoughtful for a few moments, and finally concluded, "Let's wait and see what Billy has to say. Maybe we're jumping to conclusions. Anyway, don't worry over much about it—if Walters has something planned, we'll deal with it!"

Nathan had a hard, determined edge to his voice, leaving Evelyn with little doubt he could handle just about anything that came his way. She guessed Walters did not truly understand who he was dealing with. But perhaps he'd have to find out the hard way.

After they left the horses off at the stables, Nathan excused himself to go find Billy. He'd start with Sergeant Jim, who always seemed to have an idea where the other men were.

☙஭ଓଔ☙஭ଓଔ☙஭ଓଔ☙஭ଓଔ

Later that afternoon Nathan, Billy, and Jim reached the top of the hill. They stopped and dismounted. Billy asked Nathan to describe exactly where he and Evelyn had walked, and what they'd seen.

At the end of Nathan's narrative, Billy smiled.

"So … Captain, you're saying *the woman* noticed the dog digging up the remains of the camp food. *And* she discovered the campfire, *and* she figured out it was still warm. *And then* she found where the men had slept. So what were *you* doing while she was doing all this?"

There was a twinkle in his eye that said he was enjoying his little tease. Jim chuckled, and looked away, but said nothing, chewing on an unlit cigar he'd clamped in his teeth.

Nathan puffed up in mock indignation, "Well, I *did* discover where they'd tied the horses!"

"Oh, so while *the woman* was finding all the difficult little clues, you were cleverly discovering where two large, grass-eating

423

animals had been tethered for several days? Very observant of you, Captain! Ha!"

"All right … you insubordinate soldier! Get on with it … you've had your fun at my expense."

But then he had another concern, "Billy … have we spoiled your reading by our walking all about earlier?"

"It will not matter, Captain. Your stride I know perfectly well, none better. And even a child can tell a woman's tracks from those of men."

He turned and trotted away, heading toward the large rock at the top of the hill.

Nathan and Jim led their horses back to the trees at the edge of the clearing. They found a shady spot to wait out Billy's investigation. They let the horses loose to graze and sat themselves on some convenient stumps in the shade.

During the next two hours they watched Billy climb all over the large rock outcropping. Later they saw him climb up the shade tree Nathan had gone up earlier in the day. Then he seemed to wander at random all over the surrounding field, his head bent down. Occasionally he'd drop on all fours to inspect something on the ground.

When he was finally satisfied, he came trotting back. It impressed Nathan that Billy didn't seem in the least tired or winded by his exertions; rather he had an excited spark in his eyes.

"You and the woman were correct, Captain. Two men with their horses were up here for two days and nights, leaving this afternoon. The south side of this mountain is not nearly so steep. They came and went by following an old elk trail leading to this meadow. They did not hunt but spent their time observing the farm from up on the rock. The food they ate they brought with them. And, the woman was right … the men were watching when they saw your horses leave the road and come onto the path leading to the hill. Then they tried to put out their fire and hide their camp in a great hurry. This was good for us. They didn't have time to do a good job of it and left many useful signs. Although I cannot tell for sure who they were, there is nothing here making me believe you are wrong in your guess. For one, they are *not* expert riders, as soldiers, or even hunters … more like … *farmers*."

"Thank you, Billy. That is very helpful …"

"Captain, I will now track them back down the hill and see what else I may discover."

"All right … I suppose you'll not be wanting our company?" he asked, already knowing the answer.

"No, Captain. A scout must do this work alone. And I won't need the horse either."

Then Jim took over, "Okay, scout! Tell me where you may go, and when you expect to be back. And when we should send the grave digging detail," he said this last with a smirk on this face.

"I'll go down the back side of this hill, following their trail. I will go slowly to see if anything interesting fell during their flight. Then I will track them along the road to discover where they went when they left this property. After that … well, we shall see. I expect to be back tomorrow by afternoon. The next morning at the latest. If longer, you may send your grave diggers to find me."

Jim nodded in answer.

"And … Sergeant Jim? If I don't come back, send rifles with your grave detail and shoot whichever bastards have killed me!"

He smiled at his own grim humor as he walked over to his horse.

Jim laughed. It was his favorite type of humor, "That I will, Billy. That I will!"

He grinned as he continued to chew on his cigar. "In fact, I will go so far as to shoot the sons-of-bitches myself, if it'll please you!"

Billy laughed in response. He opened his horse's saddle bag and pulled out a pack he'd prepared in anticipation of this part of the expedition.

When he turned to go, Nathan said, "Billy …"

"Yes, Captain?"

"Stay clear of Walters' place if that's where they went. It'll be enough to know they came from there. I don't trust that one … he's mean as a snake and would likely take pleasure in killing you … or worse."

"I will be careful, Captain. Thank you."

"Oh, and Billy? One more thing…"

"Yes, Captain?"

"Her name is Evelyn … *Miss* Evelyn. You needn't keep calling her 'the woman.'"

"Ha!" Billy grinned, turned, and trotted away.

ℬℐℭℬℐℭℬℐℭℬℐℭ

Billy Creek returned the following morning, reporting directly to Sergeant Jim, as was his habit. They found Nathan out on the west side of the farm, conversing with the men working out there, chopping weeds in a large field of cotton.

"Ah, Billy. Not dead yet, I see, despite Sergeant Jim's foreboding …"

"More's the pity," Jim chimed in, shaking his head in mock despair, "would've enjoyed riding out and shooting someone needing it. Haven't had occasion to even unholster my sidearm since we arrived here in *civilization.*" He spat to the side, as if that last word were a curse.

"Don't worry, Sergeant Jim. Sure I'll have other chances to get myself kilt. Ha!"

"Well, that's mighty decent of you, Billy. I thank you kindly." Jim tipped his hat to Billy.

"So … what news, Billy?" Nathan asked.

"Walters' men, for certain. Tracked them right up to the start of his own road. There they turned and went down it like they lived there. Poor riders, as I said before. Farmers … *pah!*"

"Well, that settles that, at least. Now we need to figure out what he plans to do … and decide what to do about it!" Nathan said.

"Well, whatever it is … if I know you, Captain, we'll be for preparing a nice, neighborly-like greeting for him." Jim had a wicked grin, as if greatly looking forward to the event, which he was.

"Yes, *very* neighborly … if your neighbor were the *devil!*" Nathan agreed with a scowl.

426

"One more thing, Captain," Billy said, "One of Walters' men saw me up by their road. He came riding up the road when I was head-down reading tracks. He looked right in my eyes before I slipped away."

"*Oh!* Well … can't be helped, I suppose. That'll give our friend Walters something to chew on, anyway …"

Nathan gave this new information some consideration. "It's probably nothing to worry about. He can't know we discovered his spies, and he'll assume we're doing what he's doing—spying on an unfriendly neighbor. But you'll need to steer clear of Walters and his men from now on, Billy. He might hesitate to molest my other men, but he'll think an Indian's fair game. He'll either have you shot on sight or try to capture you to find out what you know."

"I will attempt to avoid both outcomes, Captain."

శు౬౧౧ఇ౸శు౬౧౧ఇ౸శు౬౧౧ఇ౸

Elijah Walters sat in his usual upright, stiff manner in a great leather chair in his library. Two of his white farmhands stood in front of him, nervously clutching their hats in their hands. He could have eased their anxiety with a smile or a kind word, but he rather enjoyed seeing them fidget nervously. He had always enjoyed the power he had to strike fear into lesser men with little effort. Saying nothing at all, showing no emotion, and staring at them with a bland expression would unnerve them more completely than any sort of angry tirade. Of course, it helped they knew he was capable of extreme violence, when it was called for.

"Did you disguise the remains of your camp as I instructed?" he began his inquisition. The men had come to report the results of their expedition to reconnoiter Chambers' farm. Walters knew the men wanted to spew forth all they'd seen and heard and leave as quickly as possible. But he would rather extract it from them slowly, and meticulously. And not in the way they wished to tell it. He knew the truth would never come out *that* way. Men would always tell you what they thought you wanted to hear, unless you were clever enough to trip them up and extract the truth from them.

"Oh yes, sir! Yes, sir!" the one on the left answered, continuing to fidget and crush his hat in his fists. The man noticed Walters had the unnerving habit of looking away from the man who was speaking. And inexplicably looking at the one who wasn't!

"Ain't that right, Tommy?"

"Oh yes, that's right, sir! We cleaned it up slick as can be … just like you told us, sir."

"Let the fire go cold, covered it with dirt, turves, and leaves? Straightened the grass where you'd slept with a branch?" Walters quizzed them, observing them intently as they answered.

"Yes, sir. That we did, just as you instructed, sir. Nobody would ever knowed we was there, sir," the one named Tommy answered, looking over at the other for confirmation.

"And while you were there, you tied the horses back in the woods, so they wouldn't leave a telltale patch of cropped grass?"

This time there was a slight pause before the one on the left, Jeremy, answered, "Well … yes sir, we done tied them back by the trees away from the camp. Only …"

"Yes?"

"Well, we didn't tie them *far* back in the trees on account of … we was worried wolves might get at them while we was asleep."

"So you didn't take turns sleeping and standing watch as I instructed," Walters said. It wasn't a question, but rather a statement. "Very well … we shall discuss this matter later," he said after a long, painful pause. The two men had a sudden dread of that future discussion.

"Let's discuss the purpose of your expedition. What are Chambers' numbers?"

Fortunately for the men, this was a question they were expecting, as it had been the reason for their expedition.

"In addition to Mr. Chambers, of course … of white men, we counted ten. Of negroes, we counted over a hundred, of which about seventy-five are field hands, the majority of which are men.

"He appears to have a full stable of horses, but it was hard to count on account of they was in and out of the barn where they's kept. But best estimate is eight. Oh, and one pack mule. They also keep a small herd of cattle, some for milkin' and others for meat, of course. We counted around thirty. Pigs, chickens, ducks, and so forth … of which we didn't keep count."

From the way the men reported this information, with precision, confidence, and lack of nervous fidgeting, Walters knew this part was true. Or as close to true as was humanly possible from a hilltop several miles distant looking through a spy glass. So he said nothing.

"And what of Chambers … his personal habits?"

"Yes, sir. Up before dawn and out and about the farm all day, checking in on the various work being done. Don't ride his horse about much, preferring to walk mostly from what we could tell."

"Interesting," Walters replied, looking thoughtful.

"And … sir? There's one other thing we seen, you might find … 'interesting,' sir."

"What would that be?" Walters asked in his bland manner.

"Well, sir, we seen one of his white hands take three hunting dogs from outta a pen where they's kept and led them off toward town. At the end of the day, we seen him come back without 'em. And nobody else ever brought 'em back, neither … at least not whilst we was there."

"And … so, apparently he has sold them off. What of it?"

"Well, sir, it appears to us they was the *last* three dogs he had in the pen. It now stands empty, sir! Meaning he's got no more hunting dogs … 'less you count that big, ugly mongrel that's always running about loose."

"Really? Hmm … yes, that *is* interesting. Seems Mr. Chambers no longer cares if his slaves run away. Very interesting."

The men were dismissed, hopeful their last little gem of information may have saved them from Mr. Walters' wrath. Only time would tell.

Walters sat and mulled over this information. He was certain the fools had left a trail a child could follow, but it didn't worry him. Likely Chambers rarely visited the hilltop anyway, and even if he did, he had no reason to suspect Walters was up to anything. Probably would assume hunters had trespassed.

But Walters intended to use the information they'd gathered to plan his intervention. To put a stop to this absurd, blasphemous mass-slave wedding Chambers was planning.

The first Walters had heard of it was the day Reverend Blackburn had come for his usual visit, just after Walters returned from Richmond. Blackburn said he was concerned Chambers might be setting a bad precedent by holding this kind of wedding. It would make it difficult, if not impossible, to sell off these married slaves separately. If such a thing were to become popular … why, it could undermine a slave master's ability to buy and sell his own property, as was his legal right.

Over the next week or two, inquiries in town had confirmed it. They'd specially ordered large quantities of white cloth and lace from the Lewisburg Mercantile—far too much cloth for a single bride, or even a half-dozen brides! And then he learned Chambers or one of his men had approached several of the local preachers asking them to perform the ceremony. They confirmed he intended it to be strictly legal, and binding! All had turned him down. But it seemed to be proceeding, nonetheless.

The more he thought about it, and Chambers' smug ideas on doing away with slavery, the angrier he became. *By God … this will not happen while I sit here doing nothing … practically in my own back yard! I must not allow it to happen. It is … blasphemous. Treating these … black-skinned animals as if they were proper human beings … unbelievable!*

Then a wicked smile crossed his usually expressionless face. *And maybe … just maybe … I'll get a shot at that self-righteous, abolitionist bastard. No one will believe he didn't shoot at me first!*

ဆပ္ဆရဆဆပ္ဆရဆဆပ္ဆရဆ

Later that evening, Walters' man Bob poked his head in the door. "Sorry to bother you, sir. But there's something I think you should hear." There was another white man standing next to Bob. Walters recognized him as one of the farmhands, *Ben* … or *Bill*, maybe …

"Yes, what is it?" Walters asked.

The two men stepped inside the library door.

"Go on, Ben, tell the master everything you just told me."

"Well sir, begging your pardon and all …" the man said, bowing nervously.

"Get on with it," Walters prodded.

"Yes, sir. I was coming back from town on an errand for Mr. Hill here. Was almost to the turn off to our place—I mean to *your* place, sir—when I sees a man walking along the edge of the road across from the start of your road, sir. He was looking at something on the ground, and hadn't seen me yet, so I paused to see what he was up to. I reckon he must've heard me as he suddenly looks up. And … well, sir, you can imagine my surprise when I finds myself looking directly into the face of an Injun!"

"An Indian? You mean an honest-to-God, feather-wearing savage? Had you stopped off for drinks in town before your return? That's preposterous. There are no longer Indians in Virginia. Hasn't been for nearly a hundred years."

"Oh, no sir! I hadn't been drinking, no sir! Not a drop. And he may've been a savage, but he weren't wearing no feathers, sir. He was dressed like a *real* man, same as us all. Only his face gave him away. Years back, before I came to be in your service, sir, I was out West for a time. And I seen my share of red Injuns. I swear on God's Holy Bible, sir, this here was a real honest-to-God Injun, or I'm a snake!"

Walters continued to stare at the man in disbelief, when Bob offered, "Sir … I heard a rumor in town. Didn't think much of it at the time, you know how people like to talk and make up wild tales. Anyway, the rumor was when he was out West, Captain Chambers had captured a wild Indian and had tamed him and dressed him up as a white man. And, they said he'd brought this tame Indian back to Virginia with him. People claimed to have seen his Indian wandering about loose. Like I said, sir, I didn't give it much credence … until now."

"Hmm … now it *is* making more sense. Perhaps I've underestimated our Mr. Chambers. So, Ben, what did you do with this Indian when you saw him?"

"Well, sir, that's the strangest part of my tale. When he looks up and sees me, I shouts out 'Hey, you there! What you be a doin' messin' around by Mr. Walters' road?'

"Then I spurs my horse forward fixing to catch ahold of him and drag him back here for you, or Mr. Hill, to have a word with. But 'fore I can catch up to where he was standing he suddenly vanishes. Like … into thin air, as they say. I spins my horse all 'round, worrying he has somehow slipped behind me … but … *nothing*, sir. He was simply … gone!"

"Nonsense! A man can't vanish like a conjurer's trick, even if he is an Indian," Walters scoffed.

"I swears it, sir! On my dear departed mother's grave, I does! And I hadn't been drinking neither, sir!"

Bob nodded, "I didn't believe him either, sir. So I actually smelled his breath to check. Horrible smell … but no whiskey on it."

"Humph! Very well, then. You may go."

After the man departed, Bob said, "Sorry to have bothered you sir, but figured you ought to hear that, crazy as it sounds."

"No, you did rightly, Bob. It seems Mr. Chambers is doing a little reconnoitering of his own. Perhaps he is not as big a fool as I'd assumed. We will have to keep a watch out for this Indian of his, and next time … *I want him caught and brought to me!* Do you understand?"

"Yes, sir. I will pass the word among the men."

"I'd like to question this fellow on what he's up to, and … maybe we shall also see what color *blood* a savage Indian has."

Bob shuddered at the look that came into Walters' eyes. Not a pleasant look at all … *not at all!*

After Bob departed, Walters sat and stared into the cold fireplace. *Sent his Indian to spy on me, did he? More of a man than I'd given him credit for. But no real man would be so soft on slavery!*

It was the second time he'd underestimated Chambers, it occurred to him.

He'd thought to bluff Chambers into giving over the disputed section of property, or at least goad him into a petulant reaction. But when he'd received Chambers' answer, it surprised him to be

432

granted neither expected response. The letter was addressed simply to "Mr. Elijah Walters, Lewisburg Virginia." He turned it over and saw it was sealed with a red blob of wax imprinted with a seal: a mountain shaped like the letter M. *Mountain Meadows*, he thought and scoffed. Such a silly, romantic notion to name your property that way. His property had always been referred to simply as Walters Farm, which ought to be good enough for anyone.

He'd unsealed the letter and spread it out on the side table next to the chair. It contained no personal note, only a proposal of property line adjustment. Despite Walters' earlier proposal to simply take the entire parcel, Chambers was offering a compromise! *Well now … he may have worn a fancy officer's uniform in the Army, but he reveals himself a weakling. No stomach for a conflict,* he'd thought. Then he continued to read … the last paragraph gave him pause, *maybe I have judged him too quickly,* he decided. It disputed Walters' claims to the property and threatened extreme measures, including physical violence as necessary, if he molested any of Chambers' livestock or employees. Walters had crumpled the paper and thrown it into the fireplace, the same he now stared into.

Yes, I have underestimated you twice now … I shall not do so again …

❦❧❦❧❦❧❦❧❦❧❦❧

On Wednesday of the week of the wedding, rumors swept through the cabins once again. They'd seen a large black carriage arriving at the great house, and five white men—strangers, neatly dressed—had emerged and been welcomed into the house. They also appeared to have a great deal of luggage. The rumor was these were preachers come to perform the wedding ceremony. Or government officials come to put a stop to it. Or a half-dozen other things.

It wasn't until Cobb came out to the cabins after his work shift the true story became known. It turned out they were the musicians who'd play at the wedding. The unusual amount of luggage included their musical instruments.

433

The musicians were a chamber music quintet from Richmond. Evelyn had sent a telegram to her best friend Belinda back in Richmond, saying that she needed excellent musicians for a wedding she was arranging. To prevent unnecessary rumors, she made a point of telling Belinda it was not *her* wedding, but rather a wedding for *"someone else of Mr. Chambers' acquaintance."* But telegraph messages being what they were, she did not elaborate, leaving Belinda to make the necessary arrangements.

When the musicians arrived at Mountain Meadows, they were given rooms and invited to join the usual Chambers' party for dinner. It was a *most* pleasant dinner, with a lively conversation. Having five new guests, fresh from all the goings-on in Richmond high society was a real treat for those isolated in western Virginia for so long. The elder of the musicians was the leader, Max Sherman, a violinist of some renown, who appeared to be in his mid-fifties. The youngest, James Banner, a cellist, looked to be in his early twenties. Playing the regular circuit of balls for the elite of Richmond, they were extremely well informed about much of the news of interest among the upper crust. And they were happy to spread whatever gossip they may have heard at the many functions where they had performed.

After dinner, the company moved to the veranda to enjoy another spectacular summer sunset. The servants had set out extra tables and chairs to accommodate the guests. Nathan had invited Jim to join them as well.

The guests had spread themselves out amongst the tables, and James Banner ended up at the table with Nathan, Tom, and Jim. He proved to be a very intelligent, interesting young man, and they all got along famously. They were well into their second glass of whiskey when Max Sherman approached the table.

"Good evening, Mr. Sherman. Beautiful sunset, is it not?" Nathan greeted Sherman with a raised glass.

The response, however, was somewhat less than cordial. "Mr. Chambers ... may I have a word with you ... in private?"

Nathan was taken aback by this response. The evening had been so pleasant and light-hearted up to that moment, Sherman's sudden change of mood was surprising.

"Well, Mr. Sherman … anything you have to say, you can say in front of my men."

Sherman stood for a moment, as if weighing Nathan's response, and then shrugged. "Very well. James, please move to one of the other tables so I may discuss a business matter with these gentlemen."

James immediately stood, and moved away, obeying Sherman's wishes.

Sherman sat, and looked up at Nathan, "Mr. Chambers, as much as I hate to intrude on an otherwise exceedingly pleasant evening, I must tell you I feel we were brought here under false pretenses."

"Oh? How so?"

"Well … I've just been informed … by your mother, Mrs. Chambers, this wedding … well … this wedding is *not* what we had believed it would be."

"And how is that?" Nathan was bristling at what he assumed was coming.

"I have come to understand, this wedding is … is somewhat of a *farce*. That it involves some sort of mass ceremony. For any number of … well, not to put too fine a point on it Mr. Chambers, but it seems to involve a large number of negro slaves."

Nathan didn't immediately respond to this but raised his glass and took another sip.

"Let me ask you this, Mr. Sherman: when you were hired, did you ever ask *who* was getting married?"

"Well … no … but we assumed—"

"So … did anyone *lie* to you, or mislead you in any way as to *who* was getting married? Did they say, for instance, it was *I* who was getting married, or tell you any particular person was getting married?"

"Well, no. They *did* say it was not *you* per se getting married, but—"

"Did anyone, at any time tell you the persons being married were of the *white* race?"

Nathan was beginning to enjoy the debate, despite his annoyance, knowing he was on the high moral ground.

"No, no, and no. Of course not. Nobody in their right mind would assume anything other than a *normal* wedding. A normal wedding with a *normal* white man and woman. Why would anyone think of anything else?" Sherman was becoming exasperated.

"Well, sir ... I'm not particularly keen on doing what's *normal*. I much prefer doing what's *right*."

This answer tickled Jim. He smiled, and silently raised his glass in salute, taking another swallow.

"But ... Mr. Chambers ... be *reasonable* ... we *can't* do this wedding ... what if word got back to Richmond ... that we performed at a wedding for a bunch of negro slaves? We'd be the laughingstock of the city. No one would ever hire us again. We'll be ruined. I *won't* do it. I'd rather forgo the fee, and eat the cost of the travel, than to have that smear on our good reputation."

Nathan was simmering. Evelyn had gone to all the trouble and cost of arranging for these musicians. And now this ... *person* ... wanted to back out just because he didn't agree with who was getting married? Even though he'd never once thought to ask who that might be? It could've been any kind of miscreant or criminal, as long as he was white, and these musicians would have happily performed, no questions asked. But because these good, honest, hardworking people happened to be black-skinned slaves, he refused to do what he'd already agreed to do. On top of which, it was too late to arrange anyone else! The simmer was working up to a boil ...

"Excuse me, Captain ..." Jim interjected. "I'm thinking I could have a private word with this fine gentleman. Perhaps we can settle this matter in a friendly, amicable way that will be to the mutual benefit of all concerned." He grinned at Sherman and then turned toward Nathan and gave him a wink.

Nathan looked at Tom, who just shrugged.

"All right, Jim. I will leave it in your capable hands. Mr. Sherman ..." he said, once again raising his glass toward Sherman.

"Mr. Chambers," Sherman said, bowing slightly.

Jim rose from his seat, and extended his arm, pointing out toward the gardens, "Shall we walk, Mr. Sherman?"

"Very well," Sherman responded, rising, "as you wish."

They departed, stepping down the back stairs of the veranda, and strolling along the path to the flower garden. Nathan could see Jim was speaking to Sherman. Jim seemed in good humor. He held a broad smile on his face as he spoke.

"What d'you suppose that's all about?" Nathan asked Tom once Jim and Sherman were out of earshot.

"Well, sir ... you may not be entirely aware of Jim's *particular* skills when it comes to ... *persuasion*. When we were in the Army, I saw him negotiate any number of different ... *arrangements*. With everyone from the tinker who mends the pots, to the outlaws roaming the hills, and hostile Indian chiefs. And he always seemed to ... well, to know what would convince them to see things his way."

"Oh?"

"Yes. In fact, I will be *very* surprised ... if he doesn't convince our reluctant musician to perform as agreed—to enjoy doing it, and to pay *you* the fee for the privilege!"

Nathan considered this for a moment, and again raised his glass, "Well, then, here's to Sergeant Jim, and success on his present campaign."

They clinked glasses and had another sip.

In less than half an hour the two men returned. Jim, still smiling, returned to the table with Nathan and Tom. Sherman, looking somewhat glum, went to the table he'd previously occupied with Miss Abbey and the other ladies.

"So ..." Tom prompted, "successful mission, Jim?"

Jim sat down, picked up his glass, and took a long swallow. "Yes, Mr. Clark. You could say so."

"I hope you don't mind, Captain, sir, but I did increase his pay a bit ... to compensate him for the ... *misunderstanding*, and all."

Nathan waved his hand, a motion meant to show the fee was of little significance.

"And that was all it took?" Tom asked, "You just offered him more money?"

"Oh, yes. That was all."

He paused a moment, taking another sip. Then he said, "Well ... that and ..."

"And?" Nathan asked.

"Well sir ... begging your pardon, but it did take a little bit of Texas-style persuasion to get him to see reason on the matter."

"Yes?"

"Well, Captain, sir, I hope you won't mind, but I told him you had a mighty fearsome temper. And when we was in the Army, we got awful tired of the grave digging detail for them who crossed you."

"Humph! Killing outlaws and hostile Indians out in Texas is one thing, Mr. Wiggins ... but you didn't honestly expect him to believe I would start killing ... *musicians?!* Just because they'd caused me annoyance and inconvenience?"

Nathan wasn't sure whether to feel insulted or amused.

"Oh *no*, sir! Certainly not *that!* And he even said, 'Oh, come now Mr. Wiggins, you don't honestly expect me to believe Mr. Chambers will have us shot for not performing at this wedding, do you?'

"To which I answered, 'Well, of course not, he would *never* do such a thing! I was only trying to make the point you ought not to cross him and invoke his temper. Because, what he *is very likely to do* is to make you *walk* back to White Sulphur Springs Hotel, carrying all your luggage. And, just for spite, he'll likely send a telegram to all the Richmond newspapers telling about what a lovely performance you put on at his negro slaves' wedding. Or ... you could accept the extra fee the Captain has generously offered as recompense for any misunderstanding and go ahead and perform as you already promised you'd do.'"

Nathan shook his head and smiled, "You are quite something, Mr. Wiggins. And did this complete the transaction?"

"Well, sir ... he drives a hard bargain ... for a *musician!* I'm afraid he took to the idea of a telegram to the newspapers from you extolling his virtues. I may have agreed to something of the sort ..." Jim trailed off, reaching for his glass and taking a quick swallow.

"And, aren't the papers going to want to know *who* it was got married?" Nathan asked.

"Oh, yes I reckon they'll be more than happy to report on the wedding of your dear second cousin, Elspeth from up Jackson County way." He smiled a broad grin and took another swallow.

"Hmm … I see. Never mind I don't have a second cousin up Jackson County way, or any other way for that matter …"

"Oh, well … that may be so, but the people over to Richmond don't know that!"

Tom started chuckling, "I told you sir, leave the negotiating to Sergeant Jim! He does have a knack for it."

"Yes … I'm beginning to see what you mean. Well, Jim, I guess I owe you thanks for straightening out this mess, even if you did besmirch my good name in the process."

"Oh, never mention it, Captain! It was my pleasure," Jim replied with a wink.

Nathan raised his glass in salute. Tom and Jim returned the gesture, and they all took another drink.

ഇരുവരുടെ

As the big day approached, Evelyn was thrilled to have the musicians play for her dance lessons. She even got permission from Nathan to excuse the brides and grooms from their usual work duties, so they could practice for a couple of hours during the day.

Now that he was recommitted to the event, Sherman was most cooperative … even offering helpful suggestions to the dancers as they practiced. And when he discovered William, who'd been sitting and watching, was a violinist, he invited him to sit in with the group. It seemed to Evelyn that William held up his end perfectly, as there was no noticeable degradation in the music's quality when he took part. If anything, the sound seemed deeper and richer to her ears.

And Evelyn and Nathan's relationship seemed to blossom as the wedding drew nearer. They were often seen strolling out to the flower gardens, returning hours later. They also spent a lot of time together discussing various details of the upcoming event.

And everyone now deferred to Evelyn on any decisions or arrangements concerning the wedding, even Miss Abbey. It occurred to Nathan she was acting more and more like the lady of the house. He was starting to believe it might not be a bad thing to make it so.

When he mentioned that notion to Tom one evening when they were going over farm business in Tom's office, he responded, "And … why not? You two seem to be getting on famously. Aside from her obvious natural attributes, she's proven herself intelligent, capable, and warm-hearted. She's now enthusiastically on board with all your ideas and plans. And she gets along perfectly with Miss Abbey, and everyone else, for that matter. I can see no downside to such an arrangement."

Nathan couldn't find any fault in Tom's reasoning and was considering when to ask her the "big question."

"You know, sir, the wedding, with its sacred ritual, the music, the dancing and all … would be an auspicious and proper moment to make such a proposal."

"Hmm … not a bad notion, Tom."

At that very moment, Evelyn sat on her bed in her room. Miss Harriet sat next to her. They were discussing what Evelyn would wear to the wedding. They'd decided to go "all out". She would wear the formal, gold-colored gown from Miss Dupree's dress shop, along with the hat and all the trimmings. Miss Harriet would also apply the makeup they'd bought there as well.

"You'll look like a princess! The Captain will be dazzled by your elegance and beauty."

"Well, hopefully he is already much taken by me," she responded, still a little reticent about making herself out to appear something other than she really was.

"Of course he is, of course. But I've been thinking … this will be a *very* romantic event. The ladies all dressed, the music, the dancing. The Captain will be wearing his very finest, and you'll be a beauty such as he has never seen before. Wouldn't it be the perfect time for him to propose marriage?" Harriet asked.

"*Oh!* Oh, do you really think so? I ... I've been so wrapped up in the preparations, it never occurred to me ... it might turn into something more. *Oh my ...*"

"What's the matter, girl? Isn't it what you want? Mr. Chambers ... is he not everything I told you he would be?"

"Oh, yes, Momma! He's ... he's everything and *more*, a *wonderful* man ... so much more than any man I ever met before. He is ... he is a *great* man. A man other men admire and respect. A tall, strong man, and yet so kind and gentle ... and so handsome and heroic! I ... I can't imagine ever loving another man now I've met *him!*

"But, Momma ... I just wonder ..."

She was about to tell Harriet about her doubts and fears ... how she wasn't important enough for him, how she would be lost in his shadow. But then, it occurred to her Harriet was even less likely to understand it than Nathan was, so she changed what she was going to say.

"Well ... it just seems like a dream, is all. Like it's not real. Like I'll wake up back in our little house in Richmond and this will have all been a dream."

"It's *real*, all right! And if you play your cards right, we may never have to leave this place!"

"Oh, Momma. That just seems ... well, too good to be true," Evelyn concluded. But the voice in her mind would not relent, *But then who will I be? And ... who am I ... now?*

Chapter 15. The Flight of Icarus

"It was the best of times,
it was the worst of times."
– Charles Dickens
(A Tale of Two Cities)

Saturday August 4, 1860 – Greenbrier County, Virginia:

A bright smile lit the young woman's face as she held her hands in the air above her head. An older woman standing behind reached up, holding a bundle of white cloth. She quickly slipped the white bundle down over the outstretched arms, pulling the dress down around the younger woman. After another moment of pulling and straightening, the older woman stood back to have a look. The sparkling white dress, trimmed with lace, was in striking contradiction to the dingy, humble surroundings of their cabin. But, the woman decided, it made a most beautiful contrast to the lovely dark skin of the young lady wearing it. The older woman nodded her head appreciatively, and she too smiled. She was older than the first woman—enough to be her mother, which in fact she was. She reached up and placed a white lacy veil on her daughter's head, and the two shared a long, intense look. Tears welled up in both sets of eyes, a perfect complement to their growing smiles—like a sparkling rain shower in a beam of dazzling sunshine. Mother and daughter overflowed with emotion, understanding the significance of this momentous day.

ಬಿಎಂಎಲ್ಎಬಿಎಂಎಲ್ಎಬಿಎಂಎಲ್

In another dark cabin nearby, men were putting on suits, laughing and smiling as they did so. Among the men, humorous insults were exchanged, and there was a good-natured pushing and shoving, all adding to a general sense of comradery. A fly watching from the wall would have noticed one man in the room was clearly different from the others. For one, his face was white, in stark contrast to the others. And for another, his dress coat was a dark blue rather than black, and it had red and gold trim and a decided military cut to it with epaulets on the shoulders. It was an army master sergeant's dress uniform, and the man wearing it, whom the other men referred to as "Mr. Tom," was busily helping to tie up ties, and straighten collars. If the fly had understood the social norms of humans of the day, he might have found it extremely unusual and ironic; the white man was the one rendering service to the black men on this day. But the man in the blue suit seemed no different in one sense: he shared in the general good humor and comradery of the moment.

ༀ☙ඣⓍ☙ඣⓍ☙ඣ

Miles away, in a dark barn, oil lanterns hung from several hooks providing dim illumination. Black-colored men, their skin beaded with sweat, worked to saddle up horses in the pre-dawn darkness. White men, dressed in drab, workman-like clothes and boots, were busily loading rifles, shotguns, and pistols, and strapping on holsters. Several had large hunting knives in sheaths at their belts. Two men coiled up long, braided leather bullwhips and tied them carefully to their saddle horns. There was but little talk, and that was subdued, and pointed—instructions on preparation of various pieces of equipment or harness. The men were serious and went about their business efficiently amid an air of tension and nervous energy. When all was ready, the black men threw open the large barn double-doors and stood to the side. The white men led their horses out onto the gravel drive, walking toward the great house looming ahead in the darkness. Light shone from several windows, though the house was mostly dark. When the group of men and their horses reached the front of the house, they stopped and waited. Not a word was spoken, and the men did their best to quiet the nervousness of fidgeting horses.

After a few moments, the front door swung open and a stream of light shone out, momentarily dazzling the men who stood there in near darkness. When the door swung to once again, and their eyes readjusted, they could see a man step out. He was a stout man, dressed in similar fashion to the other men, except he wore expensive riding boots and a fine felt hat. A pistol holster on his

443

left hip in the stylish cross-draw fashion marked him as a gentleman. He walked slowly down the stairs. When he reached the ground, he stood and looked at the men in front of him as if performing an inspection, which he was. He had an entirely bland, unreadable expression on his face. But those few among them who dared make eye contact noted there was an unusual fire in those eyes this morning.

After a few tense moments, he stepped forward and took the reins offered him by a man who was leading two horses. The horse offered was a magnificent, dappled gray gelding—an exceptionally fine animal. Without a word, the man reached up to grasp the saddle horn. He raised his left foot up into the stirrup and neatly swung his right leg up and over the saddle. The others immediately followed suit. Some performed the act nearly as efficiently as their master, while others were less proficient and required several attempts, or even required help from their fellows. The master, ignoring the efforts of his men, turned his horse and slowly walked up the drive. Soon the whole group of men were walking their horses behind their master in a double column, as neatly as unskilled riders could manage. As if he sensed his men were now in proper order behind him, the leader kicked his horse into a slow trot. He seemed eager to get on with the task at hand. The other men followed his lead.

A lonely young woman, willowy thin and elegantly dressed, stared out an upstairs window, watching the riders depart. A frown creased her features as she breathed a heavy sigh, clutching at her heart, silently saying a prayer—but not on behalf of the riders …

ༀ஌ଔ௴ༀ஌ଔ௴ༀ஌ଔ௴

Miles away, on the lawn in front of a great, white house, black men in clean, white uniforms busily set out chairs, and straightened arrangements of flowers set on tables. The sun was nearly up, so they had no difficulty seeing while going about their business. A tall, thin black woman also dressed neatly in a pale blue dress directed the efforts of the men. Though she performed her duties with a serious demeanor and wasn't hesitant chastising

444

any deficiencies in the men's efforts, she held a tone of good humor in her voice. And she let slip a smile of satisfaction between harangues.

Nearby, in the barn where they'd held the dance lessons, five musicians quietly tuned their instruments in a manner producing a sound which might seem chaotic, to the uninitiated. After a few moments, however, the leader of the group raised his bow, and smiled, as if satisfied with these strange-sounding efforts. The room suddenly became silent. Then he struck a note with his bow, and the others joined in, the resulting sound much more recognizable and pleasing to any ears that might be listening.

In one of the smaller rooms in the great house, a man looked at himself in a brass-framed mirror hanging on the wall. He had dark hair, graying at the temples, but otherwise wore his forty-some years well. Today he donned a simple, loosely fitting black robe, and was concentrating on securing a white, tie-like accouterment around his collar. Once tied, the traditional preacher's tabs hung partway down the breast of his robe in two separate rectangular strands. The ends of the sleeves of his white shirt were the only other contrast to the darkness of his garment. He breathed a heavy sigh, picked up his Bible from the nightstand by the bed, and headed for the door.

A young man lay on his back looking up at the stars as they slowly faded in the lightening dawn sky. He lay on a rough wool saddle blanket spread on the ground to cover a patch of grass, wet with morning dew. The field of grass in which he lay was uncut and several feet tall, so from his present position he could see nothing but sky. From that vantage point it was easy to imagine he was alone in the universe, floating like an angel among the heavens. A quick, quiet cough off to his right brought him out of his reverie and reminded him he was *not* alone out here in the pre-dawn darkness. Aside from the man to his right he knew there were several others, not far off. He reached down with his right hand and patted something hard and cold laying alongside him in the darkness: his rifle. *No, not alone,* he thought and grinned, then went back to enjoying the stars.

🙰ಏ)ಌ೮ಣ🙰ಏ)ಌ೮ಣ🙰ಏ)ಌ೮ಣ

A young woman, her long golden-blond hair hanging down her back in curling locks, sat in a chair, looking at herself in a mirror. For the second time in her life she saw a person looking back she didn't entirely recognize. Her, but *not* her somehow. More … *something* … alluring? *Seductive*? She couldn't decide exactly, but she had to admit the French makeup made a difference. But with a subtlety not easily discerned by a casual observer.

An older woman standing next to her, a small brush in hand, took a step back to admire her handiwork.

The young woman stood and performed a pirouette as the older woman inspected. The long, flowing golden gown, with just the right amount of cleavage, was elegantly embroidered and outlined in lace. It twirled out around her in a lovely circle as she spun. A sparkling golden necklace with a glittering green gemstone enhanced the overall appearance of elegance and affluence.

She stopped. The two women locked eyes, smiled and laughed.

Absolutely perfect, the older woman beamed at the thought. *Figure of a Greek goddess, face of a fairy princess, and golden hair of an angel. All wrapped up in the elegant gown and jewelry of a queen!*

The older woman placed a lacey, yellow colored hat on the younger woman's head, tying it on with a long ribbon. She again stepped back to take in the entire effect. The elegant hat topped all, a necessity for keeping the summer sun off delicate white skin, but also a fashion statement in its own right.

The mother leaned in and gave her daughter a gentle kiss on the cheek. She turned, and donned her own stylish hat, and the two headed for the door, arm in arm.

446

The group of rough-looking, armed riders stopped after their leader held up his hand. He stood in his saddle and turned to look back at his men. They returned his expressionless stare in like manner, as they'd learned to do through hard experience. Satisfied with what he saw, he turned and sat back down in his saddle. He kicked his horse into motion, turning left heading north on a side road leading off the main east-west road. This side road lead to Mountain Meadows Farm. Once the entire troop was on the road, he moved into a fast trot, the others immediately doing the same.

A tall, handsome man, with dark hair and broad shoulders stood at attention as if for inspection. He'd dressed in military finery, an army captain's dress uniform. Long navy-blue frock coat with a high collar, a double row of sparkling brass buttons down the front, and gold epaulets on the shoulders. A glossy black leather belt trimmed in red circled his waist, fastened by a gold belt buckle emblazoned with the stylized American eagle, complete with olive branch, arrows, and banner reading *E Pluribus Unum.* The trousers were sky blue with a red stripe down the side. But rather than running all the way to the floor, as would have been the norm for an officer in formal dress, these trousers were tucked inside riding boots.

The black knee-high boots were polished to a high gloss. It was an acceptable variation, if somewhat unusual. It caused the "officer" performing the inspection to raise a questioning eyebrow, to which the man being inspected just smiled.

The "superior officer" was a middle-aged woman, slim, and still very much in the flower of her beauty. She'd dressed formally as well, in a long, elegant gown of a light pink color. It had a high collar and long, close-fitting sleeves, richly embroidered and trimmed in lace.

She leaned in and picked a piece of lint from the frock coat, then stood back for another look. Now satisfied, she turned and walked over to the closet, returning with something held out in front. She held it out to the man, as if it were an offering. He looked down and saw it was his cavalry saber, its finely wrought brass hilt resplendent in the brightly polished, enameled sheath trimmed with brass, shining with a mirror-like finish. He gazed at it a moment but shook his head. She returned a puzzled expression, not expecting this reaction. He moved over to the dresser, opened a drawer, and pulled something out. She could see he was fastening something around his waist and over his shoulder. When he turned around, she saw he'd strapped on his pistol harness. It was of black leather, highly polished like the rest of his accouterments. This belt had a simpler, more worn brass buckle with only the large letters *US* on the front. A black leather strap ran over his left shoulder, under the epaulet on that side. And on his right hip was a holster with button down flap, inside of which was his large, beautifully engraved Colt revolver. The woman raised an eyebrow once again. She thought the sword a much nicer addition for a formal event. In her mind the pistol had a more serious connotation. Something an officer might wear at a formal gathering in an active war zone, for example. But again, he just smiled, and shrugged his shoulders, so she let it go. The gentleman held out his hand toward the door, inviting the lady to exit with him.

"Oh! Wait …" she said and hurried back to the closet. In a moment she stepped back out and placed something on his head. It was his fine, dress officer's hat in the style called "Hardee." It was of black felt with a wide brim, stylishly pinned up on one side, an ostrich plume on the other. It had a gold braided hat band, and a brass pin in front depicting a pair of crossed bugles: the symbol of an infantry officer. It was the ideal thing to top off his attire, giving him a handsome, rakish look.

He tipped his hat to her, and smiled, "Thank you kindly, ma'am. I'd nearly forgotten it." He held out his arm, and smiling brightly, said, "Shall we go, Momma?"

She reached out and took the offered arm, "Yes, let's do."

৪৩১৫৪৫ঝ৪৩১৫৪৫ঝ৪৩১৫৪৫ঝ

Nathan had decided to hold the event precisely at sunrise. He had several reasons for doing so. For one, he liked the symbolism of it. Somehow the dawning of a new day seemed most apropos. And also, those who had to dress up for the wedding wouldn't have to dress twice, or risk soiling their fine clothes waiting around for an afternoon event. But most important, he wanted the darkness to cover *all* the preparations he'd arranged.

He and Miss Abbey passed through the front door, still arm in arm. They paused when they reached the top of the stairs on the veranda, surveying the scene spread out before them. The wedding had been laid out on the lawn, to the left of the circular drive. It appeared everyone except the brides and grooms were already in their places. The musicians sat on the left in the front. When they saw the Captain at the top of the stairs, they recognized their cue to begin playing. They'd arranged two sections of chairs toward the front with an aisle in between. Since there were insufficient chairs on the farm to seat the entire population of well over a hundred, there'd been much discussion about how many chairs there ought to be, and exactly who should occupy them. After much discussion, Nathan had made the final decision. They would seat the parents of the brides and grooms, if they still lived on the farm. Also, Miss Abbey, Miss Harriet, and Miss Evelyn would sit on chairs. Although they protested, he refused to relent—he would *not* have women dressed in their finest sitting on the grass! He also included Megs in that list, and insisted she dress as finely as the other ladies, to which only Megs protested.

Nathan, Tom, and the bride grooms would stand at the front along with the minister. The musicians, of course, would also sit on chairs. Everyone else would sit on the grass behind the chairs and to the side. Nathan could now see they'd arranged everything as he'd ordered. He could also see the pastor standing in the front in his dark robes, holding his Bible. Evelyn, Harriet, and the parents of the wedding couples occupied the chairs up front. It turned out there were nine of these parents still living on the farm. This included a mother and father who were marrying each other, while their own daughter married a young man in the same ceremony! So nine chairs were now occupied. Megs had not yet arrived, as she still had wedding duties to attend, and Miss Abbey, of course, was entering with him.

Out past the musicians on the lawn, they'd laid out tables, with white linen tablecloths. Arrangements of flowers and enough food and drink for all in attendance entirely covered the tables. *Also, bridal cakes, no doubt,* Nathan reminded himself with a grin, thinking of all the arrangements Evelyn had been making; not to mention all the *money* she'd been spending!

Nathan and Miss Abbey walked deliberately down the stairs and across the lawn, down the aisle between the people seated on the grass and those up front in the chairs. It was traditional in a formal wedding ceremony for the members of the wedding party to adopt a serious demeanor, walking in a stately fashion and looking straight ahead. But Nathan chose instead to smile, make eye contact, and briefly converse with those he encountered along the way. When he was partway through the crowd, someone called out, "God bless you, Captain!" to which he nodded his head and said, "Thank you." There followed a veritable chorus of the same, "God bless you, God bless you, sir, God bless you, Captain," and now those seated closest to him were reaching up to touch him with extended arms. As he moved through them, he reached down to clasp those hands he passed, saying, "Thank you, thank you, thank you," over and over. When he finally reached the front and passed through the chairs, he made brief eye contact with the pastor who seemed surprised at the reception Nathan had received.

Nathan turned to face the crowd, and said in a loud, clear voice, "May God bless all of you!"

Then he turned and led Miss Abbey to her chair in the front, next to Miss Harriet. After Miss Abbey took her seat, Nathan leaned down toward Miss Harriet, took her extended hand and kissed it. "God bless you, and good morning to you, Miss Harriet."

She smiled and replied, "Good morning, Mr. Chambers."

He moved in front of Miss Evelyn and likewise leaned forward to take her hand. But when he looked at her fully for the first time that day, his heart skipped a beat. He wouldn't have believed it possible beforehand, but he thought her even more beautiful than she'd ever been before. She'd dressed elegantly, true—but there was something else … something *magical* about her today. He smiled and gently kissed her hand. He detected a slight tremble from her through the elbow-length white gloves she wore. Then he looked in her eyes and said, "God bless *you*, Evelyn … as he has clearly blessed *me* with your presence."

She suddenly seemed shy, and looking down, answered, "Thank you, Nathan. I … feel the same way. And God bless *you*, sir."

He turned and walked up to the front to stand a few feet away from the minister, leaving room between them for the grooms. And as that was the next cue, Tom suddenly strode forth from the door, in all his military finery. He was followed closely by the twelve grooms all in a row, led by old Toby. They were all neatly dressed in black frock coats, with black trousers and shiny black shoes. Their shirts were as white as snow, and a long bow tie of red topped the whole thing off. Evelyn had to choke back tears at such a wonderful sight. Try as they might to appear serious, the grooms couldn't keep the grins from their faces, as friends quietly called out to them from the audience.

As they came closer, Evelyn decided Tom looked almost as splendid as Nathan, though he was not nearly so tall and handsome. Then she realized there was something not quite right about his appearance. After a moment it came to her; he was wearing a pistol holster instead of a military sword! She had seen soldiers at formal affairs often before, and they always wore the sword when they arrived, unbuckling and setting it to the side when the dancing started. She thought it gave them a dashing, heroic look. Then a sudden thought hit her, and she glanced back at Nathan standing in the front. For the first time she noticed he too wore the pistol holster instead of the sword. *How odd*, she thought, and felt a twinge of disappointment. All week she'd imagined what Nathan would look like in his officer's uniform. And the image in her mind had always included that darned sword! *Well, no time to ask him about it now*, she decided.

Tom led the bridegrooms down the aisle and up to the front, where they lined up to Nathan's right, facing the audience, with Tom nearest Nathan.

As soon as the grooms were in place, the musicians paused in their playing and began a new piece. It was the Bridal Chorus from Wagner's opera *Lohengrin*, which had become popular at weddings in the previous decade, a song future generations would come to know simply as "Here Comes the Bride." And with that, the doors to the great house once more swung wide. This time Megs stepped out, followed by the brides. Everyone seated on chairs or on the grass turned their heads to watch as the women came slowly down the stairs. The brides never tried to adopt a serious countenance; they all smiled from ear-to-ear. The effect of the white dresses, dark complexions, and bright smiles was a dazzling sight those in attendance would never forget.

Megs reached the bottom of the stairs, followed closely by Anna and Babs together, the older woman leaning heavily on the arm of the younger for support. The rest of the women came behind in double file. Each carried a white lily in her hand.

When they stepped out onto the drive to cross over onto the lawn, several things happened, almost simultaneously.

As if the very heavens were smiling on the event, the first rays of the dawn lit the front of the house. The white dresses of the brides seemed to explode in a sparkling whiteness. It was so bright it was almost painful to the eyes of those watching from the darkened lawn.

And then, inexplicably, a woman in the audience gave out a long, loud scream of terror. This sound was immediately followed by the unmistakable sound of pounding hooves. And, if anyone would have been looking anywhere other than toward that sound, they would have seen both Nathan and Tom move quickly and purposefully in that direction, Nathan snatching up an empty chair as he went. A large group of riders, a dozen or more, approached the house at a steady trot. A stern looking man led them. All but the leader had weapons in hand—rifles, pistols, and shotguns. The music stopped, as did the scream. Nobody moved, nobody spoke. It was as if time stood still, and everyone was frozen in place where they were.

Everyone except for the approaching riders, Nathan, and Tom. The two men trotted out to the driveway to intercept the horsemen.

But before he reached the edge of the lawn, Nathan turned toward the wedding audience, and said, in a loud, commanding voice "Everyone ... stay where you are, and be *silent!*" It was a voice that expected to be obeyed and allowed no arguments.

Evelyn was filled with terror at the sight of the approaching men, clearly armed for violence. But even so, somehow Nathan's voice had reassured her and eased her fears. A man was in charge who knew how to deal with such things. The others seemed to sense it too. Nobody moved or spoke, waiting breathlessly to see what would happen next.

Nathan continued to trot out onto the drive, Tom closely behind. When he reached the point where the circular drive met the main road, Nathan stopped and set the chair in the middle of the road, back facing the approaching men. He hopped up onto the chair, resting his left foot on the top of the back of the chair, his right foot on the seat. Evelyn could see the chair rocking precariously, but Nathan seemed unconcerned, perfectly at ease and balanced.

As the riders approached, he rested his left hand on his left knee, and raised his right hand, gesturing for them to halt and make parley.

And, inexplicably, the riders came to a halt, only a few feet from where Nathan stood on the chair. Nathan and the leader of the horsemen faced each other at almost the same eye level.

For a moment it was silent, as the dust settled and the horses fidgeted. Then Nathan spoke, in the same loud, clear voice, "Walters ... why have you come uninvited to my home, with men armed for war?"

It was a clearly worded formal challenge and appeared to catch Walters off guard. Then, recognizing Chambers was not only addressing him, but speaking so all present could hear, Walters seemed to accept the verbal challenge.

"Chambers ... I've come to put a stop to this blasphemous travesty. I'll not sit idly by, mere miles away, while my neighbor commits atrocities against God, man, and nature. These ..." he waved his hand toward the grooms and the brides, "... these, *persons*, have no right to be legally wed as if they were decent white folks. They're no better than jungle animals!"

But then, as if by a conjurer's trick, Nathan's pistol was in his right hand, pointed directly at Walters' face. He drew the hammer back with an audible *click*.

"You seem to mistake me, *sir*, for a man who'd allow another man to tell him what he can or can't do in his own house!"

For a moment Walters seemed startled, suddenly staring down the barrel of the Colt revolver, inches from his face. But he gathered his composure and turned his head to the side, speaking to his own men this time, "He's bluffing. He knows he's outnumbered and outgunned. He'll do nothing."

But Walters appeared surprised when Nathan chuckled.

"What do you find so amusing, pray tell, Chambers?"

"Well, for one ... unless I miss my guess, I'd bet most of your men would be very happy if you called that bluff, and I answered it, based on how poorly you treat them."

Nathan noticed several of Walters' men looking down, as if he'd guessed exactly what they were thinking.

"And for another, I'm *not* outnumbered."

Although he was tempted to smile after this remark, he decided instead to return Walters' bland expression with one of his own.

This seemed to set Walters on edge, and he gazed around nervously. "If you mean to include this rabble of jungle savages in your number, you'll be sorely disappointed. I have no fear of such creatures, besides which they are unarmed, and my men, as you can see, come entirely prepared."

"Oh no, I was not speaking of *them*. As you say, they carry no weapons—the innocents in this contest. Walters, I'm surprised at you ... though, you not being a military man I suppose it can be forgiven ..."

454

"I tire of this, Chambers … make plain what you have to say, that I might get on with my business …"

"I had assumed, from your *spying*, you knew my numbers," Nathan said. The mention of the word "spying" caused Walters to flinch.

"So, Walters … where are my men?"

This time Nathan *did* smile, the wicked predatory smile of a crocodile.

Walters' eyes widened, finally realizing his fatal mistake.

Tom gave a loud whistle. From out of the tall grass on both sides of the drive, six men stood, rifles in hand, pointed straight at the horsemen. They'd dressed in plain work clothes, so did not look especially soldierly. But at only thirty yards away there was no mistaking the bayonets attached to four of the rifles.

They heard galloping hooves. Two riders came around the corner of the nearest outbuilding, up onto the road, and down toward the waiting group, cutting off any chance of escape. Both riders held revolvers in their hands.

Tom's pistol was also now in his hand, pointed at the intruders.

Evelyn held her hand over her mouth to stifle a gasp of amazement. She also hadn't noticed the glaring absence of Nathan's men until that very moment.

"And, in case you think you still have us outnumbered," Nathan continued, "My men are veteran soldiers who've killed enemies in battle. I promise they'll not hesitate to do so again." It was a minor lie, since two of his men were the original farmhands, and he couldn't be sure all the soldiers had actually killed anyone. But Walters had no way of knowing any of that. "They can knock you off the saddle from that distance with their eyes closed. And lest you're tempted to think they have only one rifle shot each, I will point out each also carries a six-shot revolver. And … if any are left alive after the gunfire, I expect the bayonets will finish the business."

This was too much for several of Walters' farmhands, who'd never been in a gunfight. Four or five tossed their guns to the ground and held up their hands in surrender.

The two riders pulled up to the rear of the group, Sergeant Jim and Billy Creek. Each held a pistol in his right hand, and the reins in his left. But when they came to a stop, freeing their other hand, each pulled out a second pistol that'd been tucked into his belt.

And to add an exclamation point to the whole affair, Harry the Dog chose that moment to make his appearance. He was always suspicious of strangers, but generally left them alone. But this particular bunch seemed to have his master all riled up, and so they riled *him* up, too. He came slinking up, and stood near the Captain's chair, baring his teeth and emitting a low, threatening growl. The fur down the center of his back was standing on end. The effect made him appear even larger and more ferocious than usual.

This display set Sergeant Jim to chuckling. "And if the bayonet don't finish you off, the Captain's hound will likely just go ahead and eat you!"

The rest of Walters' men threw their guns to the ground and raised their hands. All but Walters himself. He sat staring at Nathan, his bland expression restored.

"You're not the man you claim to be, Chambers. So soft on your slaves ... not a *real* man at all. I expect out West you let your men take all the risks, let them do the real fighting? Taking the bullets ... while you sat back at your desk taking all the credit?"

Nathan glared at him but didn't answer. He felt the old familiar rage rising ... the man had abused and imprisoned his own wife, beaten to death several of his slaves. He'd terrorized Miss Abbey, and had the gall to come onto Nathan's own property, threaten his people and now accuse him of cowardice ...

"Nothing to say in your defense, Chambers? Just as I suspected ... no stomach for a *real* fight ... no balls, clearly. Does the young lady know *that* about you? That you're not a *real* man? Maybe I should take her with me when I go. Teach her what a real man is made of ... make a *woman* of her?"

Nathan was reaching the boiling point ... Walters had now dragged *Evelyn* into it, threatening *her*.

456

His sight seemed to blur … his face was burning … his trigger finger quivered …

"Sir … *don't* …" Tom warned, "… remember what happened with Moat Kangly … and Gold-tooth …"

But Tom's words were distant and devoid of meaning. The uncontrollable wrath was taking hold of him … he fought to control it.

But then an image of Evelyn appeared in his mind, triggered by Walters' implied threat against her. She stood smiling up at him, beautiful, loving, innocent. A dazzling star shining like the sun. The light of her vision cut through his darkness. *She is watching … the woman you love … Do you want her to see … that side of you?*

He shook his head. As the vision began to fade, a faint, distant voice seemed to whisper, *Evelyn is watching …*

After another tense moment, Nathan spoke. His voice quavered, and his face was a dark, threatening storm cloud, "Drop your weapon, *sir* … or … I shall be forced to pull this trigger …"

The two men stared each other down for another long tense moment. Each seemed coiled as tightly as a clock spring.

Finally, Walters slowly reached down with his left hand, unbuttoned the cover to his holster, lifted the revolver out with two fingers, and dropped it to the ground. "This is *not* over, Chambers," Walters said.

"It is for today!" Nathan turned away, hopped down off the chair, and lowered the hammer on his pistol. He spun it in a full circle and holstered it, all in one, smooth motion. He strode away, never looking back. Tom stayed where he was, continuing to eye Walters with suspicion, his pistol still aimed at the man's chest.

Then Sergeant Jim took charge, and the rest of the Captain's men trotted up, still aiming their bayoneted rifles at the horsemen. "Gentlemen, if you will be so kind as to dismount, and follow me back to the barns, we shall soon be on our way. Please do leave all your weapons on the ground. I shall not think kindly of anyone who holds back on me," at which point several knives and two whips were thrown down.

The horsemen quickly dismounted, and the Mountain Meadows' men took charge of their horses. The former soldiers knew how to take dangerous captives in hand and had it down to a routine. Georgie and Jamie quickly gathered together the horses, tying them end to end in a group that could be easily led by one or two men. Stan and William did a quick, thorough search of the captives for weapons. They found none. Zeke and Benny quickly gathered up the discarded weapons into a pile. At Jim's instruction they carefully removed all the percussion caps and lowered the hammers, so there'd be no accidents. Jim and Billy continued to guard the prisoners from horseback, pistols raised. When all was ready, they moved the group, weapons, horses, and men away from the Big House and back toward the barns.

ᏕᎧᏋᎧᏡᏋᏕᎧᏋᎧᏡᏋᏕᎧᏋᎧᏡᏋ

The people watching appeared to breathe a collective sigh of relief as Nathan and Tom returned to the front of the wedding area next to the groomsmen.

But now there was much talking, murmuring, and a general restless fidgeting among the gathering. The fear of the unexpected intruders seemed to have swept away the bright, happy mood of a few moments earlier.

So Nathan stepped forward in front of the minister, and raised his hands for silence. He spoke in the same strong projecting voice he'd used before, "It says in the Good Book, Isaiah chapter forty-one, verse ten, the Lord God said to his people *'Fear thou not, for I am with thee. Be not dismayed; for I am thy God. I will strengthen thee; yea. I will help thee; yea. I will uphold thee with the right hand of my righteousness,'*" and Nathan held up his right hand in a fist. He paused and looked out over his people. "Have no fear of these evil men. Rather, trust in God, and all will be well …"

Then he looked back at the minister, as if for affirmation, to which Reverend Holing responded simply, "Amen!" nodding his head, and smiling.

Nathan signaled to the musicians to resume playing and waved to Megs to bring the brides forward. And with that, the wedding was back on, as if nothing at all had happened.

458

And once the brides had resumed their march, Nathan glanced over at Evelyn for the first time since he'd kissed her hand. To his surprise, she was not looking back to watch the brides' entrance like everyone else. Instead, she was looking right at him. Their eyes met, and she smiled. She shook her head as if to say, "I can't believe what just happened!" He returned her smile, and shrugged, as if to answer, "It was *nothing*, really …"

But inside Nathan was feeling exceedingly pleased with himself. Although the rage had boiled, he'd controlled it this time and hadn't killed Walters, as he'd feared he might. He never wanted Evelyn to see *that* ugly side of him. He feared it might turn her away. And in the end, the thought of *her* had helped him regain control. Now, he felt confident he *could* control it, even under the worst circumstances!

And … he also knew from experience it was extremely rare, in fact uncommonly lucky, for any military operation to go off as planned, without a hitch. And the timing of this one could not have been more perfect. After deciding Walters' spying must be for the purpose of disrupting the wedding, Nathan had baited the trap. He'd instructed his men to spread the word about the date and time of the event to anyone who'd listen whenever they were in town, at church, or visiting one of the local taverns.

Of course, Billy had been watching Walters from a distance, ever since the enemy troop entered the main east-west road. So the Mountain Meadows men had plenty of warning, and knew almost exactly when their adversaries would arrive, and what their numbers would be.

But there was no guarantee Walters would cooperate so nicely by stopping right where Nathan had set his trap. It could have easily degraded into a running gun fight, with unarmed civilians scattering in every direction. *Thank God that had not happened,* he thought, saying a quick prayer of gratitude.

In fact, there'd been much debate about where to spring the trap, with Sergeant Jim pushing for doing it back up the road, away from the house where there'd be no possibility of collateral damage. But Nathan thought it was important he personally face down Walters and send him packing. He had to be at the wedding and couldn't be in two places at once!

He also liked the idea of witnesses to whatever happened. Important for the future free men to see what their enemies were capable of, and also to see there were also good men willing to stand up for them.

He'd hoped the humiliation might discourage Walters from trying anything again. That last part, he had to admit, was not likely to work out the way he'd hoped, based on Walters' calm reaction at the end. And … he reminded himself, lest he become too smug, his adversary had never trained in military tactics, and so had easily fallen into his trap. Next time might not be so simple.

But his own personal performance also pleased him. By resisting the urge to put a bullet through Walters' forehead, he'd done as well as he possibly could've under the circumstances. And, to do it in front of a beautiful lady like Evelyn, dressed in his best military finery … well, that was beyond common good fortune. He imagined it'd made quite a heroic spectacle. Like a prince out of a fairy tale story book, driving off the evil villain!

The brides had lined up on the opposite side of the minister from the grooms. The smiles weren't quite as bright as they'd been. But those bright flames were slowly re-kindling, as the brides looked out at the spectators, catching the eyes of friends and loved ones in the audience.

The musicians finished the bridal march, and once again a hush fell over the gathering. The pastor, Reverend Steven Holing, stepped forward, and began the ceremony.

"Dearly beloved … we have come together in the presence of God to witness and bless the joining together of these men and these women in Holy Matrimony."

Although he held the Bible open in his hands, he didn't read from it. He'd performed the ceremony so many times he could do it in his sleep. The only challenge this time was remembering to use plurals when referring to the brides and grooms.

He was happy to be once more on familiar footing. This was the first time in over a week he'd donned the traditional dress of his calling. During his journey south from Wheeling, a city in the very northernmost point of western Virginia, he'd been forced to travel incognito.

In his younger days he'd traveled freely throughout the South, stopping to enjoy the hospitality of every Methodist Episcopal pastor along the way. He had very fond memories of those days, now long gone.

In 1844 the church had split, North and South, on the issue of slavery. To those in Wheeling, Richmond was a city so far distant as to be virtually meaningless in everyday life. There were very few slaves, and little interest in the propagation of the institution. Most people in Wheeling considered themselves Northerners, with little love for their distant, and governmentally controlling, cousins to the southeast.

When Captain Chambers' telegram arrived, asking for a pastor willing to perform a proper, legal wedding for a group of slaves, the church was happy to oblige. The Chambers family had been longtime members of the church and preferred having a Methodist minister for the ceremony. But clearly, none of the ministers of the Methodist Episcopal Church, South would oblige him. So Reverend Holing had packed away his robes, dressed as a common laborer, saddled up a horse, and started upon the road to … *here*—this peculiar place that didn't quite fit with what one expected of Virginia. For starters, young Mr. Chambers, who made no secret of his opposition to slavery, was himself a slave owner whose family had clearly built its fortune upon the institution. And he seemed to have surrounded himself with a company of like-minded young men from the military service.

The whole place had a different feel from any plantation he'd ever visited in the South. Perhaps the spectacular natural setting had something to do with it. Not the humid, flat, featureless landscape of the Southern coastal lowlands. This place had hills, and trees, and rivers. A pleasant breeze often blew, and even in the heat of the day the temperature never felt stifling.

And the slaves … was it just the excitement of the wedding ceremony, or did these slaves seem more … *interested*? More *alive*, maybe? Whatever it was, it had a *good* air about it. And it made him happy he'd come and could take part in this most memorable event in these people's lives. Jesus Christ would approve, ministering to the most downtrodden people of the earth, and making their lives more … Christian, proper, and righteous—not to mention happier!

"The union of husband and wife in heart, body, and mind is intended by God for their mutual joy. For the help and comfort given one another in prosperity and adversity. And, when it is God's will, for the procreation of children and their nurture in the knowledge and love of the Lord."

As he spoke, he alternated looking toward the brides, the grooms, and audience. He enjoyed performing the wedding ceremony. He had a fine, strong baritone voice people enjoyed listening to. He'd always thought he might have made a good actor or singer if life had led him in a different direction.

Then he came to the part of the ceremony where it was traditional to ask for the father to give away the brides. So again he had to use plurals, "Who shall give *these* women to be married to *these* men?"

With that, Nathan stepped forward and said, "Their fathers, and I," and he motioned for the men seated in the chairs to make their way forward. They were also joined by one of the bride grooms, who was the father of one of the brides. So there were four fathers, plus Nathan. But Megs had neatly lined up the brides so at the beginning every other bride had a father. So Nathan would have time to escort a bride and return for the next while one of the fathers brought over his daughter. Nathan stepped up to the first bride, bowed, and smiled at Anna, whose own bright smile made her face even more wrinkled than usual. He held out his left arm to her, and she took it with her right, and gently patted his arm with her other. They walked across to where old Toby stood next to the minister, beaming from ear-to-ear. When Nathan set Anna's hands in Toby's he leaned in and said, "God bless you two with all His joy and happiness."

"Oh, thank you, Captain. Bless you, bless you, sir," they answered, and grasped his hands firmly in theirs. And then he turned back to where the other brides waited, as Babs came over

462

to where George waited, escorted by her father, named Pete. They smiled at Nathan as they passed.

They repeated this routine until they had run out of fathers, after which Nathan continued to escort the remaining brides one at a time. But despite the numbers, he seemed in no hurry. He appeared to give each bride and groom the same attention, words of encouragement, and blessing he had at the beginning.

Now each bride stood facing her groom, and the fathers returned to their seats while Nathan took his place at the end of the row of grooms.

The minister turned to the audience. "If any man can show just cause why these couples may not lawfully be married, speak now, or else forever hold your peace."

Nathan made a show of stepping forward, leaning to gaze toward where Walters and his men had recently departed, shrugging his shoulders, and smiling. There followed a twitter of laughter, lightening the mood.

The minister turned toward the couples and said, "Now, to you grooms I will ask a question, and if you agree, it is traditional to answer, 'I will.'"

"Wilt thou have this woman to thy wedded wife, to live together after God's ordinance in the holy estate of matrimony? Wilt thou love her, comfort her, honor, and keep her, in sickness and in health, and, forsaking all others, keep thee only unto her, so long as ye both shall live?" To which all the grooms responded, "I will."

"Now, you brides, I will likewise ask you a question, and if you agree, the traditional answer is, 'I will.'"

"Wilt thou have this man to thy wedded husband, to live together after God's ordinance in the holy estate of matrimony? Wilt thou obey him, and serve him, love, honor, and keep him, in sickness and in health, and, forsaking all others, keep thee only unto him, so long as ye both shall live?"

Most of the brides immediately answered, "I will," but Hetty paused, and scowled at Cobb. He knew how she felt about that "obey" part, so he just smiled, and shrugged, which made her laugh. Finally, she relented, saying, "Oh, all right. I will!" She shook her head and seemed to be wondering if she would regret it later.

"Very good!" Reverend Holing said with a smile.

"And now, I shall read from the Holy Bible, the first book of Corinthians, chapter thirteen."

> *If I have prophetic powers, and understand all mysteries and all knowledge, and if I have all faith, so as to remove mountains, but have not love, I am nothing. If I give away all I have, and if I deliver up my body to be burned, but have not love, I gain nothing.*
>
> *Love is patient and kind; love does not envy or boast; it is not arrogant or rude. It does not insist on its own way; it is not irritable or resentful; it does not rejoice at wrongdoing but rejoices with the truth. Love bears all things, believes all things, hopes all things, endures all things.*
>
> *Love never ends.*
>
> *So now faith, hope, and love abide, these three ... but the greatest of these ... is love.*

When the minister read these words, Evelyn felt strong emotions welling up inside her, and she began to tear up. She found her eyes drawn toward Nathan and wasn't surprised to find he was also looking at her. Now he did not smile, but had a serious, thoughtful expression. Their eyes met and held there for a long moment. She sensed a very strong connection with him ... he was everything a woman could ever wish or desire ... but was it true *love*? How did one *know*?

The minister paused, and looked up, saying, "This is the Holy Gospel of our Lord Jesus Christ ... all praise and glory be unto his name." And he looked down for a moment and was still, as if in silent prayer.

After a moment he looked up and smiled. Turning toward the couples, he said, "Now, this next part is for you grooms to say. It is rather lengthy, so we will do it a bit at a time. First, I will say it, and then you will repeat, until we get to the end. Ready?"

He recited, "I take thee to my wedded wife," which the grooms repeated. Then "to have and to hold, from this day forward," which was also repeated. And then "for better for worse, for richer, for poorer", "in sickness and in health", "to love and to cherish, till death us do part", "according to God's holy ordinance", "and thereto I plight thee my troth."

The grooms seemed quite relieved to have gotten through that part, without too many missed words. There were grins and raised eyebrows exchanged between the men, and Nathan and Tom looked at each other, rolled their eyes, and smiled.

Then it was the brides turn to repeat the vows. They generally did much better, although Hetty again paused and was late repeating when it came time for the phrase "to love, cherish, and *obey*." By now those in the bridal party were expecting it. There were a lot of smiles, and a smattering of laughter from the wedding party, the loudest of which came from Cobb himself!

The minister said, "Now that these men and these women have given themselves to each other by solemn vows, I pronounce they are husbands and wives, in the name of the Father, and of the Son, and of the Holy Spirit."

This pronouncement was met with the same respectful silence. But Nathan applauded, along with Tom, and the seated ladies quickly joined in. Nathan raised his hands high, and nodded to the audience to encourage them, and they quickly took the hint. Soon a thunderous applause broke out, mixed with shouts of joy, and peals of laughter. The brides and grooms at first looked around in bewilderment at what was happening. And then, realizing the significance of the moment, the couples hugged each other, laughing, and kissing. The grooms turned and shook hands, patting each other on the back with great warmth and enthusiasm. The brides exchanged hugs and kisses.

After a few moments of this, the minister raised his hands for quiet. When the noise died back down, he said, "And those whom God has joined together *let no man put asunder!*"

He turned toward Nathan, and they shared a meaningful look. *Well, that's the whole point of this, isn't it?* Nathan thought and smiled. The pastor, seeming to read his thoughts, nodded and returned the smile.

Finally, Reverend Holing stepped forward, and raised his hands to the audience, saying "The peace of the Lord be always with you."

To which those used to hearing such things, namely the white people in the front responded, "And also with you."

"Amen!" he answered. And with that one simple word the wedding was over, and the celebration began.

ဢၢၣၧၩၪၧၩၪၧၩ

Evelyn immediately sprang to her feet and trotted out in front of the couples. It was now time for her to play her part. She motioned to the newly wedded couples to follow her. She led them to the open lawn area between the musicians and the tables with the food and the flowers. They obediently followed, arm in arm. When they arrived in the designated area, Evelyn made sure they were all spread out and in their assigned positions, just as they'd practiced. The couples stood a few feet apart from each other. All the men faced in one direction, and the women in the other, facing them.

Evelyn turned and waved over those seated on the grass and on the chairs. Soon a large circle of people were standing around the newlyweds. They ushered the small children up to the front, so they could see.

She turned toward the dancers, and at a signal the grooms all made a formal bow to their brides, and the brides returned a low curtsey. Then the dancers all struck a pose. Each man stretched out his left-hand high overhead and toward his bride, tucking his right hand behind his back. Each bride reached up to grasp his left hand with her right. They stood still, waiting. Evelyn signaled to Mr. Sherman … and the music began.

Per her request, it was Chopin's "Great Sparkling Waltz," as Evelyn had called it. The same William had played on his violin on the night of their first dance lesson.

When they struck the first note, the brides each did a pirouette, spinning around while still grasping the groom's upraised hand. When each woman completed the circle, she ended facing her partner. Then they joined, her right hand in his outstretched left, and her left hand resting lightly upon his upper right arm, just below the shoulder. They all performed this move beautifully — even Anna had managed it without a hitch. Evelyn clapped her hands, beaming with enthusiasm, "Oh! Nicely done, nicely done!"

She hovered around the dancers as they progressed through their steps, giving little quiet words of encouragement or instruction where needed; but mostly she just smiled, and laughed, covering her mouth with her hands to not distract the performers. Although there were a few missed steps here and there, her students' performance delighted her. And they seemed to enjoy themselves as well. Especially Cobb, she noticed. He had a real knack for it — he was very graceful on his feet and appeared to thoroughly love dancing. In fact, his enthusiasm seemed contagious to those around him, especially Hetty, who'd gone from looking nervous and tense, to smiling and laughing as they executed their steps. The couples moved around and around, mixing in various steps they'd learned. To the untrained eye, the dance seemed very complex, though actually each step was quite simple when broken down and practiced. It was the combination of steps in different sequences that made the whole seem like more than the sum of its parts.

And then, even as the dancers seemed to be warming to their task, the waltz was over. The couples stopped, let go of one hand and continued holding the other, as they turned to face the audience. The men bowed, and the ladies curtseyed. When they rose, Evelyn was the first to clap, and the rest of the audience quickly joined in. A spontaneous cheering, hooting, and laughing came from the awestruck audience making the performers smile and bow again, waving to special friends or loved ones. Several of the brides had to stop to wipe tears from their eyes, their emotions overflowing. And several of the grooms had inexplicably gotten dust in their eyes requiring the use of a sleeve to rectify.

But before the audience could move forward and overflow the dance floor, Evelyn held up her hands for quiet and attention. After several minutes of shushing, a respectful silence came over the group.

"That was ... *absolutely lovely!*" Evelyn exclaimed. "I'm so happy for all of you, and so proud of you. You've done wonderfully today, on this *most* wonderful day! I know you will treasure this memory 'as long as you both shall live,' as the saying goes.

"Please now, everyone continue to leave a space for dancing. The couples may dance again, as much as they like, but now I would like to invite anyone else who knows how to waltz to come forward and join the dance! Maestro, if you please?" she said, turning once again toward Mr. Sherman, who nodded in acknowledgment.

The music started again. She looked over toward the front area where Nathan had been standing, half expecting to see him coming toward her to ask her for the next dance. And he was coming forward, but already arm in arm with another woman, his mother, Miss Abbey. And right behind him came Tom, with Miss Harriet. *That's very gallant of Tom,* she thought, *I shall have to remember to thank him later.*

When Evelyn looked back at Nathan, once again her heart skipped a beat. He looked so handsome and ... and *magnificent!* The morning was warming up, so he'd stripped off his coat, setting it aside, along with the pistol holster. He now wore a snowy white, long-sleeved shirt, with slightly puffy sleeves and shining brass buttons at the cuffs. Around the collar he wore a loose black bow tie, like those worn by the grooms. But the thing that most caught her eye was the vest he wore over top of all. It was a dark, velvety purple cloth, the entire front covered in embroidery, swirling patterns of a shiny gold thread. The back was a satiny, gold material. The overall effect, with the military style pants and boots was almost ... *princely,* she thought.

She enjoyed watching Nathan and Miss Abbey dance the waltz, which they performed beautifully, Miss Abbey beaming with delight. Tom and Miss Harriet were also doing very well. About half the wedding couples were still dancing, while the others were enjoying talking with people in the gathering.

Evelyn stood back this time, letting the dancers alone to do as they would. She was assuming she'd sit out this dance, when she felt a tap on her shoulder. She turned and saw it was Cobb. But instead of his usual broad smile, he was looking ... shy, almost?

"Hello, Cobb. How can I help you?" she asked, puzzled what could be amiss with him.

"Well, you see, Miss Evelyn ... I was standing over there talking with some of the folks, and Miss Hetty, of course ... oh! The new 'Mrs. Cobb,' I should say!" His little faux pas made him break into a smile briefly, but he quickly resumed his serious expression. "Anyways, as I was saying, I was talking about how wonderfully you had taught us to dance, and when I looked over, I saw everyone but you was dancing—the Captain, and Miss Abbey and all. And it ... well, it just didn't seem right ma'am. So of course with Mrs. Cobb's permission, I wanted to ask if ... well, if you would not be terribly offended to dance with me ... just once, is all!" Cobb seemed relieved to have gotten out what he came to ask and was having a hard time making eye contact with her.

"Well, dear me, Cobb! What a gallant, gentlemanly thought. Of course, I would be greatly honored to dance with you," she said, and smiled at him brightly. "You are, after all, my very best student!"

Cobb seemed to relax, and he laughed as well. "Well, since you put it that way, I will have to try special hard to hold up my end of things!" he said with his own bright smile.

They moved into the dance area and joined in. Cobb appeared hesitant and unsure at first, but Evelyn smiled at him and nodded reassuringly, whispering, "Relax, you dance beautifully. There is nothing to fear," after which he did much better.

At one point during the dance she caught Nathan's eye, and he smiled at her. It was a smile of warmth, and amusement.

Clearly, he did not disapprove of her dancing with one of his grooms! *Not a typical Southern gentleman at all,* she decided.

And as she danced, her mind wandered ... surely, he would ask her to dance the next dance, now he had satisfied his obligations to his mother. But ... if Miss Harriet was right, would he ...? Would he ask her *the big question?*

It was a most auspicious occasion, a wedding, after all, with everyone dressed in their finest. And Nathan must be very pleased with how everything had turned out. Even the interruption by the nefarious neighbor had turned to his advantage. In the end, he'd proved himself wise, courageous, heroic, and even merciful. With seeming ease, he'd made his large, frightful neighbor look small and foolish, along with all his men. Nathan had been a man among boys. A lion among sheep.

Her mind continued to run down that path ... Nathan was *clearly* something special ... No! More than merely *special* ... *extra*-ordinary! One in a million? The kind of man other men looked up to and wanted to be like. And women ... women would be drawn to him like iron shavings to a lodestone! Already a war hero, heir to a family fortune, and a state senator. There was no telling where a man like that might go, what he might do ...

And am I the woman this great man wants to marry? How can that be? After all, what am I, really? I am pretty, that I know. Plenty of people have told me so, and I can see it for myself in the mirror. But what of it? What am I? Who am I? And what would I become if I married Nathan? Only "that pretty woman on the arm of the great man?"

She'd been down this road before, but today it seemed to hit her with greater force. As if the further her mind raced down this track, the larger Nathan loomed, and the smaller she became. *When I came here, I didn't even know what I thought about anything ... I only repeated whatever Momma told me to say to ensnare the perfect husband. And now ... now am I only doing and saying whatever I think will please Nathan? What do I think? What do I want? Who ... am I?*

These thoughts continued to run through her mind, growing stronger and stronger. And this time she could not seem to brush them off or push them back down. She felt on the verge of panic.

What if he asks me? What shall I say? What do I want? What will I become? Who am I?

By the time the dance ended, her bright smile had faded, and she had a worried expression. Even Cobb noticed and thought he might have done something wrong. Or possibly she wasn't feeling well.

"Is something troubling you, Miss?" he asked, a frown of concern touching his typically sunny face. "Did I step on your foot, or something?"

"Oh, no! No, Cobb … *dear me!* You danced wonderfully! You take to it so naturally … what a fine student you've turned out to be. No, maybe it is … just a touch of the heat …"

She tried to come up with some plausible explanation for her sudden change of mood, but it sounded lame even to her own ears.

Thanking Cobb for the dance she turned toward the others. She could see Nathan had already escorted Miss Abbey to her seat. They were exchanging a few quiet words with each other, laughing and smiling.

Evelyn watched as if in a dream. Nathan turned and looked at her, and their eyes met. He started toward her. He was smiling, but there was something else there too—a serious, determined look. *Is this the moment? Oh, how shall I answer … what shall I do? … Who am I?* She felt a panic rising in her and didn't know how to quell it.

€ʒɔɔΣɔΣʒɔɔΣɔΣʒɔɔΣ

Evelyn fought down the growing panic through sheer force of will. She made herself focus on the dance, *left forward, right forward and out, left slide over, right back …* and the rhythm of the music, and soon she was feeling calm again, and enjoying herself. She realized she'd hadn't danced since that horrible night back in Richmond with Stanley Finch, and it was her first time *ever* dancing with Nathan. And, like everything else he did, he danced wonderfully. He had the easy, natural grace of a man with great athleticism. Maybe not the natural feel for the rhythm and music

Cobb seemed to have, but there was an unmistakable strength, control, and power there.

Then suddenly the music ended, and the dance was complete. Nathan took her arm in his, with an ease and familiarity that now seemed natural, even though it really hadn't been that long since they'd first met. He led her through the crowd, away from the dance area, out onto the lawn a little way beyond the tables where they'd set out the food and flowers.

He paused and turned toward her, and with no preamble said, "Evelyn, I find I've completely fallen in love with you."

Although she'd expected something of the kind, it still seemed shocking to hear those words coming from his mouth. For a moment she stood motionless, as if stunned.

Then, as through a thick fog, a voice in her head was saying, *Say something ... a thing like that needs an answer ... say something, fool girl!*

And so, she said the thing most natural to say, "I'm in love with you too, Nathan." She was surprised the words had come so easily, especially since she realized for the first time, with no doubts, they were absolutely true.

She leaned into him, and laid her head against his chest, and he put his arms around her, and held her there gently. It felt so good hugging him, so warm and comforting. With his strong arms holding her, nothing in the world could harm her. She closed her eyes and let her mind drift ... the sounds of the music, the low chatter of the voices ... off toward the garden the sound of birds chittering in the trees. And she could feel Nathan's heart beating next to her. It was a moment she wished would never end.

But then he pushed back from her, and gently lifted her head with a hand under her chin, so she was looking up into his eyes. "Evelyn ... it's such a fine day ... and much of it thanks to you. Why, the couples' dancing ... it was quite astounding! And the musicians play beautifully. It is all very ... well, it has made for a very memorable day. And I ... I would like to make it even more meaningful, and memorable. I would like to ask you a question ..."

But with these words, the panic attack she thought she'd suppressed came back in full force, and she felt her head spinning. *What do I think? What do I believe? What do I want? ... WHO AM I?*

"Evelyn! Evelyn! Are you all right?" Nathan's voice came through the darkness of a dream. His voice seemed so clear and real, but when she opened her eyes, all she could see was blue sky, with little puffy clouds in it. And then, Nathan's face was there, looking down at her. He had a concerned expression.

"Nathan? What happened?" she asked, feeling disoriented and fuzzy headed.

"Hurry over with that water!" he called out, looking away from her for a moment. He turned back down and said, "We were talking, and suddenly you just went limp and I had to catch you to keep you from falling. I laid you down on the grass, and ... here you are. I guess you fainted ... too much heat and ... excitement, maybe? How are you feeling now?"

Just then someone came running up and handed Nathan a glass filled with water. He leaned down and supported her head. "Here, Evelyn, have a sip of water."

She took a sip, and it felt good, though she had difficulty swallowing lying down, and nearly choked on it. It seemed like a fog was swirling around inside her head. And she could hear a voice in her mind, like an echo far in the distance repeating, *Who am I ... who am I ... who am I?* over and over. She sat up, placing one hand down on the grass to hold herself, rubbing at her forehead with the other. Nathan immediately put an arm around her back to steady her.

"How are you feeling?" he repeated.

"Strange ..." she answered truthfully, "I ... don't feel well, Nathan." And then, like water gushing from a broken pipe, uncontrollable emotions welled up in her, and shook her. She said, "Oh, Nathan! I'm so terribly sorry ... I have ruined everything ... everything you planned ... I've ruined it. I'm so sorry, so sorry, so terribly sorry," and now she was sobbing, and repeating the word "sorry" over and over, sobbing great sobs.

She felt herself lifted from the ground. Nathan had swept her up in his arms and was now hurrying toward the house. She closed her eyes and leaned into his chest, and continued to cry, whispering "Sorry, Nathan, so sorry. Oh, Nathan, I'm *so sorry*," while all the while the voice now far away in the distance kept muttering, *Who am I … who am I … who am I?*

She heard a jumble of voices, concerned sounding, consoling, trying to comfort. And then Nathan in a commanding voice saying, "Quickly Megs, make up a bed in the darkest, coolest room in the house! And somebody bring a damp cloth!" She felt him leap up the stairs, two or three at a time. And then the sun vanished, and she was in cool darkness.

It was quiet, and she was lying on something soft. Someone laid a damp cloth over her forehead. She heard a soothing, comforting voice. But not Nathan this time … a woman. It was a familiar voice, and it seemed like she should know who it was, but just now it escaped her. She drifted off to sleep, but even as she did, she heard that strange voice in her mind once again, now far away and faint, whispering, *Who am I?*

                              

Although Nathan felt obligated to return to the party, congratulating the newlywed couples, and making small talk, Evelyn's unexpected collapse and departure had cast a pall over the proceedings. And especially over Nathan's mood. He'd gone from a glorious feeling of joy, victory, and excited anticipation, to one of worry and dread.

He'd never seen anything like it before, although he'd heard of such things. Yet, Evelyn had always seemed so stout-hearted — riding a horse like a man, hiking all over the farm with him in the hot sun. Even the day he'd told her to leave and never come back, she'd hardly even flinched, defiantly tossing it back in his face.

But now, just as everything was going so beautifully, and he was getting ready to ask her hand in marriage, she suddenly fainted. And right before he could get the words out of his mouth! It left him confused, concerned, and frustrated.

It was not even yet the heat of the day. And he knew she'd been raised on a farm by a father who clearly wanted a boy and treated her as such. So she was no delicate flower to wilt with a little heat. It was confounding and frightening. Could she really have a serious illness? The thought gave him a chill of fright such as he had rarely ever experienced. He shook his head, to clear away the evil thoughts.

He felt an arm on his shoulder and turned. It was the minister, Reverend Holing. "Mr. Chambers, I can see you're concerned. I am very sorry your lady friend, Miss Evelyn is not feeling well. Has she had such … spells … before?"

"No … as a matter of fact, I was just thinking she's shown a very stout constitution up 'til this moment …"

But a voice said, "That's not true, Nathan. There was one other time …" It was Miss Abbey, who'd stepped up behind him as he was talking with the minister.

"What do you mean, Momma? Another time?"

"Yes, it was the day she arrived, in fact. Why … it was right after she first met you in the library. You had come in and introduced yourself. And when you left, she suddenly felt light-headed, and looked very pale. Megs had to take her to a bedroom to lie down. But later she seemed better, and I hadn't thought about it since … until just now."

"Oh! That *is* news. Very strange … she's seemed so stalwart all the rest of the time she's been here. Riding horses, giving dance lessons, going for long walks, and … well … many other kinds of activities …" he trailed off, a blush coming to his cheeks, as he remembered those *other* activities.

"Is there anything I can do for you?" the minister asked.

"Pray for Evelyn, if you would," Nathan said, then turned and strode back toward the house.

Miss Abbey stood for a moment, watching as he departed. She turned to the pastor and said, "And pray for Nathan too, I think." The minister raised an eyebrow, but Miss Abbey did not elaborate on what she was thinking.

Later that afternoon Nathan sat alone at his usual table on the veranda. He was leaning back in his chair slowly puffing on a

475

cigar, watching the smoke drift up into the blue sky. There was no glass of whiskey, although the servants had offered. *Too early in the day for that,* he thought, *though it is sorely tempting ...*

Miss Abbey came out onto the veranda and sat in the chair opposite him.

"What news, Momma?" he asked before she even sat.

Nathan had tried to drop in on Evelyn earlier to see how she was doing but had been turned away. Megs seemed embarrassed, and was extremely apologetic, but Evelyn had insisted on no visitors while she was recuperating. Nathan had had to bite back an angry response to that. He had become very accustomed to getting his way in his own house and was not used to being told he could *not* do something he wanted to do. But he chided himself for being too high and mighty, and reminded himself people had a right to their privacy, even within his house.

So he'd retreated, defeated for the moment, but not ready to give up on it. He sought out Miss Abbey and asked her to see what she could find out about what was going on with Evelyn. He assumed a woman might very well succeed in this sort of task, where a man would fail.

"Well, I've not seen her myself, but I spoke with Megs. She said Evelyn was sitting up and seemed better after having slept for a few hours and—"

"Oh! That's good to hear. But should I send William in to examine her, do you think?" he asked, his voice still filled with concern.

"Well, maybe, but ... before you interrupted my story, I was going to tell you, after speaking with Megs, and being turned away myself, I made further inquiries."

She paused and looked at Nathan to see if he would interrupt again, but he waved his hand in a gesture meaning, "go on with your story," so she continued. "I found out she had also turned Miss Harriet away, which I found most surprising. So I went to see the pastor."

"The pastor? Why? Did you want to ask if he thought his prayers had been efficacious?"

"No, Mr. Knows-everything, I did not go to ask him *that!*" she said, reaching over to slap his hand in mock reproach, and smiling.

But he was in no mood for humor, and responded simply, "Sorry, please do go on…"

"Well, it occurred to me in his line of work he must spend a great deal of his time tending to the sick. There are plenty of folks who can't afford a doctor, or who live far from where one is available. And a pastor is at least an educated man and may be a comfort in such times. Anyway, I asked him if he would look in on her, and he agreed. Apparently, she will turn everyone else away, but can't quite bring herself to turn away God's own servant, which was the other reason I sought him out."

"Very clever of you, Momma," he said sincerely. "And what did he discover? Is she suffering some illness?"

"I don't know … he said she'd regained her color and seemed *physically* fit to him."

"Oh, good … that's a relief."

"But he also said something odd … he said *physically* she seemed fine, but she seemed to be very troubled of mind …"

"Troubled? What could possibly be troubling her? Everything has been going along so beautifully."

"Nathan … I need to say something and ask you something that is … of a *very personal* nature …"

"Yes, Momma? What is it?"

"Well, there *is* one thing can make an otherwise healthy young woman suffer fainting spells … and trouble her mind …"

She paused to see if he understood where she was going with this. But he returned a blank look, so she continued, "… and that is … if she is *with child.*"

"Oh! Oh, you don't think …?" he stammered.

"Well, dear, *that* is the uncomfortable thing I wanted to ask you … is it possible? You know, that she is with child?"

"Possible?" For a moment he didn't understand what she was asking, but when it came to him, he blushed. *"Oh!* No … no, Momma. I didn't … we didn't … we … No, it is *not* possible, Momma!"

"Oh, good. Not that a child would be a *bad* thing, mind," she said with a smile, "but all things in their proper time and order, don't you think, dear?"

But his mind was already off on a different track, and instead of answering her, he said, "At least it is not possible by *me*. You don't suppose she ... she was already ... *you know* ... before she arrived here?"

"Well, I had actually considered that as well, and so I had a nice little talk with Miss Harriet. Hopefully I was tactful about it, but I needed to know the truth. But after talking to her, I am convinced Evelyn was *not* with child when she arrived."

"How do you know for sure, may I ask? Of course, Miss Harriet is going to vouch for Evelyn's chastity, but how do you *know* it's true?"

Then it was Miss Abbey's turn to blush. "Well, dear ... it's a bit of a delicate subject, actually. But since you insist on knowing ... you are, I assume, aware of a woman's ... monthly cycle?"

Nathan nodded, but said nothing.

"Well then, you will know if the woman has her regular cycle, it means she cannot be with child. As soon as she is, the cycle stops until sometime after the birth. And Miss Harriet assures me Miss Evelyn, most inconveniently as you can imagine, suffered her monthly cycle while riding on the train from Richmond to here. So you can see, there is no way she was with child when she arrived."

"Oh ... yes, I see," he said, almost sorry he'd asked. "But then, what could be worrying her so much she suffers these spells?"

"I really can't imagine, dear. Like you, from what I could see everything seemed to be going along wonderfully. It has been such a joy to watch the two of you together ... ever since that day you went out riding you've both seemed so happy with each other. I've already been planning the wedding in my mind ..." she said, sounding wistful.

He surprised her by saying, "Yes ... me too. And I was about to ask her that very thing when she fainted. Now, as you can imagine, I'm eager to talk with her so I can finish that conversation, only ... she won't let me into that damned room!"

"Well, the good news is she can't stay in there forever, and when she comes out, you can ask her all the questions you want. And hopefully she will have some answers!"

But Evelyn did *not* come out, the rest of the afternoon, and well into the evening. She didn't come to dinner, and Megs said she barely touched the food brought in to her. Other than the pastor, and the maids, she had let no one into her room all day. Finally, late in the evening Megs came out to tell Nathan that Evelyn had asked for Miss Harriet. The two of them were even now in the room by themselves with the door shut. Megs did not know what they were discussing, or if she did, she wouldn't say. Miss Abbey went inside the house to await Harriet's exit from the room to see what she could discover.

Nathan found the whole thing maddening and frustrating beyond anything he could recall. He'd always been able to tackle his problems head-on—make a plan, fight a battle. But this ... this felt as if the world was spinning out of control. He could no longer sit, so he paced back and forth on the veranda. As if sensing his ill humor, everyone left him alone with his thoughts.

Finally, after what seemed like hours, Miss Harriet came out onto the veranda, followed by Miss Abbey. Nathan thought Harriet suddenly looked old, and tired, not at all her usual, fiery self. And Miss Abbey had a look of pain and sadness on her face.

Nathan had a sense of dread as he ushered the ladies to a seat at his table. "What is it, Harriet?" he demanded, "What is wrong with Evelyn?"

For a moment she did not respond but held her hand up to her forehead as if her head pained her. When she spoke, it was in a quiet voice, "I'm sorry, Mr. Chambers ... I truly am. I really don't know what is the matter with her ... she ... I ... I've never seen her like this before. She is ... not of her right mind, maybe ... I don't know. I've heard of such things, but I never imagined, *my* Evelyn ... oh, dear ..." She put her hands over her face and cried.

Nathan looked at Miss Abbey questioningly, and Miss Abbey said, "Harriet, please tell Mr. Chambers what you just told me ... what Evelyn intends to do." She said it in a commanding, almost angry voice, which was very unusual for Miss Abbey.

"Oh … oh, I'm so sorry Mr. Chambers … I've tried, believe me I have, but she won't listen, she won't listen," Harriet said, between more sobs.

"Won't listen about what?" Nathan demanded, "Please speak plainly, Miss Harriet. What is it Evelyn intends to do?"

Harriet sat up and wiped away the tears with a handkerchief.

"We are leaving for Richmond in the morning, and she does not intend to come out of her room until it's time to leave."

ༀ৯ᨠ৪ৡৠৣৢᨠ৪ৡৠৣৢᨠ৪ৡৠৣৢᨠ৪ৡ

They could get not get much more useful information out of Miss Harriet. She was clearly distraught, but if she knew any more about what Evelyn was thinking, she wouldn't say. Harriet did say at one point she'd refused to leave, but Evelyn had said she would simply go home by herself. It was clear no amount of Harriet's persuasion had prevailed upon Evelyn to change her mind.

After Harriet had gone back inside, Miss Abbey turned to Nathan and said, "We shall refuse to give her the carriage, until she comes to her senses! She can hardly walk back to town."

"Hmm … I suspect that is *exactly* what she would do, Momma," Nathan said. He'd become quiet and thoughtful. "No … if she wants to leave, we must let her go … I have sworn an oath to free my people from bondage, Momma. I can hardly start building my household by forcing someone to stay here against their will!"

"Humph! You're *right* of course, but it is … so … so confounding! What is she thinking? Why is she doing it? Did you say something when you walked off together at the wedding? Something to make her so upset?"

"Yes … yes, I suppose I did," he answered, distractedly, going back over the moment in his mind. "I told her …" his voice broke, choked with emotion, "… I told her … I was in love with her."

He turned and looked at Miss Abbey, his eyes once again clear and focused, "But … Momma … do you know how she answered me? She said, 'I'm in love with you too, Nathan!' How *that* could make someone want to run away, I can never imagine!

480

"Has the world gone mad, Momma? People are talking about destroying this great country our fathers fought and died for, because they don't like the man who's running for president. A man rides onto my property under force of arms to stop a holy ceremony between good, decent, God-fearing people. And a woman faints and runs away after telling a man she loves him? *Damn it, Momma!* What is going on?"

But she had no answer, slowly shaking her head, wiping tears from her eyes.

He stood and strode off across the veranda, down the stairs, and headed out across the lawn. Miss Abbey sunk down in her chair, put her face in her hands, and continued to cry quietly.

ᏚᏬᏏᏣᏎᏬᏏᏣᏎᏬᏏᏣᏎ

After Harriet's departure from the room, and her subsequent announcement they would leave in the morning, Megs' demeanor suddenly changed. She was no longer friendly, no longer doting on Evelyn. She was matter-of-fact and spoke only the least amount required to perform her duties.

It didn't surprise Evelyn, but it made her sad. She'd made a very strong connection with Megs, and now she'd broken that connection. She couldn't blame Megs. She'd helped raise Nathan. He was like a son to her, and she was fiercely loyal. Now she thought Evelyn had done him wrong, so she'd turned cold.

In the morning, she came in to help Evelyn get dressed, and continued her stony coldness.

Finally, Evelyn stopped dressing, wiped away the tears streaming down her face, and turned to face Megs.

"I'm so sorry ... I don't know what's happening ... but I want to tell you ... to say ... thank you for all you've done. And for ... for ... being my *friend.*"

She became choked with tears and couldn't continue.

Then Megs stony look softened somewhat. She grasped Evelyn's hands in hers and sat her down on the bed. She looked into her eyes and said, "But, *why*, child? Why are you leaving? Nathan is the best man in this whole world. Why, now the big wedding's come off so beautifully, the people on this farm are

481

finally convinced of how good he is. But though he's brave and strong, he is so gentle and kindly. And I've seen how he looks at you ... why, I'd not be surprised if he were to ask you to marry him straightaway. Then you'd be, well, the wife of a *truly great man!*"

But though Megs had meant well, she unknowingly said the one thing Evelyn could not bear to hear or think about. Evelyn suddenly pulled her hands away and buried her face in them. But before she lost all control, she wanted desperately to explain to Megs, as much as she could, the 'why' of it. Between building sobs, she managed to get out, "Oh Megs ... that's it ... he's so great. He's ... he's a *giant* of a man ... and I'm ... I'm ... nothing ... nothing. Just pretty and ... and ... *nothing.*" Then the sobs shook her, and she could say no more. But the voice in her head was again whispering, scolding, accusing, repeating, over and over, *Who am I? Who am I? Who...?*

ᏗᏒᎧᎤᏣᎤᏗᏒᎧᏣᎤᏣᏒᎧᏗᏒᎧᏣᎤ

Evelyn still felt shaken and wobbly when she left her room to get in the carriage, so Megs walked alongside to steady her. She half expected to see Nathan standing outside her bedroom door when it was finally opened but was relieved to see no one there. She dreaded seeing him, seeing the pain she'd inflicted on him, not knowing what to say. And a part of her dreaded he would ask her to marry him, right there on the spot. She honestly didn't know how she would answer, and it gave her great fear. And she prayed he wouldn't ask it. She never wanted to answer no to *that* question from *him*. Maybe she could answer it later. Maybe, in another time ... another place ... after ... *after what?*

Who am I?

But when she still hadn't seen him all the way down the stairs, down the hall, and out into the carriage, she felt an incongruous disappointment. Would he let her go without even seeing her again? But she was already so empty and devastated, it hardly seemed to matter.

Who am I? Who am I?

482

Then, just as the driver climbed up to his seat, Nathan came out the front door of the house. He came down the stairs and walked straight up to the window of the carriage. There he stood, eye to eye with Evelyn, not two feet away. She knew she must look awful, from all the crying, but her heart sank when she saw *his* face. His eyes were red, as if he'd not slept all night or had been crying. And he had the look of a man in great pain.

"*Why*, Evelyn?" he whispered. "Why? If I did or said something to offend or hurt you, I will apologize and beg forgiveness on bended knee. Please don't leave like this ... at least tell me ... *why*?"

The pain in his voice broke her heart, and the tears once again flowed. But she was determined not to fall apart right now ... not yet, not without speaking to him one last time ...

Who am I?

"Nathan ... you've been ... everything ... you've done *nothing* wrong ... nothing ... to hurt me. It's all my fault ... all my fault ... I'm so sorry ... I ... I just can't stay ... I'm sorry ... so, so sorry."

She could see the tears welling up in his eyes, and before she lost all control, she choked out the last words she could manage in a raspy whisper. She never knew if he heard or not, "I love you, Nathan ..."

Then she turned and grabbed Harriet's arm, motioning for her to get the carriage started. Harriet called out to the driver, "If we must leave, then we'd best get on with it. Driver let's go now. Miss Abbey, Mr. Chambers. Farewell."

The driver snapped the reigns, and the horses started off. Evelyn laid her head down on the seat and allowed the emotions to flow over her, and soon her mind was lost somewhere far away.

Nathan stood still where he was for a long time, staring off after the carriage.

Miss Abbey was there, and Megs of course. Cobb was also there, having helped get the carriage ready and all the luggage stowed. Tom had also come. When he'd heard she was leaving, he could hardly believe it, and he wanted to be there to comfort Nathan if possible. But now everyone just stood still, staring off into the distance, stricken dumb. These were the people who loved Nathan the most, and now they suffered for him, but did not know what to say to ease his pain.

Finally, he turned around, and looked at them. He said, "What happened? What has just happened? Can someone explain it to me, because I don't understand what just happened?"

Tom shook his head and turned away, fighting down his own tears. Cobb gazed at his feet and could not meet the Captain's eyes. He felt heartbroken but couldn't find any words to say. And Miss Abbey was wiping her eyes and nose with her handkerchief.

Only Megs returned his look with a thoughtful expression. She was piecing together an idea about what had happened, and to her surprise, was no longer angry at Evelyn. She was, however, heartsick about the whole thing. And she felt a burning desire to hug and comfort Nathan like she used to when he was a little toddler suffering a stubbed toe. But he was a grown man now, and it was no longer her place.

Nathan climbed the stairs to the veranda and then turned for one last look.

Evelyn was gone.

Chapter 16. New Beginnings

"You've got to be willing
to lose everything
to gain yourself."
– Iyanla Vanzant

Tuesday August 7, 1860 – Greenbrier County, Virginia:

When Rosa heard about Evelyn's departure, she felt an odd, aching emptiness. Like something bright and shining had suddenly been swept from view, leaving darkness in its wake.

But mostly she felt a great sadness for the Captain. Such a good, kindly man; he did not deserve to suffer such loss.

Then she smiled ruefully and shook her head in wonder as she recalled all the ridiculous rumors about him that'd been circulating through the farm before his arrival. Some monster he turned out to be!

But now she suffered for him. She'd thought Evelyn was so perfect, that they were so perfect together. Rosa had dreamed of being like that, dressed in finery, walking and talking like a princess. With a fine, handsome, heroic man like the Captain on her arm.

She knew she was just a field slave, but a part of her felt she was something more. Or … maybe less.

She'd always felt different, and she was acutely aware she *looked* different. And there'd always been plenty of people ready to remind her. Though the white masters mostly treated her no differently than the others, ironically the other black folks were the ones who made her feel odd. Calling her "light-skinned," or "half-white," or sometimes "half-black." They made sure she knew she wasn't totally one of them, that her Daddy had been a white man, though no one seemed to know who he was or had been.

But the Captain had treated her special. After the near-whipping incident he'd gone out of his way to check on her, to make sure she was well and wasn't too upset over what had happened.

He'd been there for her when she was suffering. She wanted to return the favor. To be there to help him with his. But now that the effects of the incident with Sickles had passed, she was back to her regular duties. She rarely even saw the Captain, except from a distance on Sundays when he preached.

She could think of only one solution; she'd have to become a house slave. If she asked the right way, she was fairly sure the Captain would say yes—out of guilt over the whipping incident, if nothing else. Then she could be there to help comfort him, as he had been there for her.

ৰ৩৪৩৫৩৪৩৫৩৪৩৫৩৪৩৫৩৪৩৫

Nathan was vaguely aware a sudden bright light shone into his eyes, despite his best efforts to keep them closed. He also realized someone had pulled the covers from his bed, since he felt a sudden chill. The chill became infinitely worse, when a heavy splash of cold water hit his face, arms, and chest.

He sat up and shook his head, spitting water from his mouth and blowing it from his nose. But before he could utter the curse building on the tip of his tongue, another wave of cold water hit him hard in the face. It ran down the front of his shirt in an ice-cold stream. He sprang from the bed.

"Goddamn it! Who's the poxy, motherless, son-of-a-whore who …"

Before he could finish his curse, another cold splash hit, driving water into his open mouth, nearly choking him.

Now he stood on unsteady feet, shaking water from his face, spitting it from his mouth, and coughing it from his lungs.

He gazed around him and everything seemed fuzzy and indistinct. Water streamed from his hair into his eyes. He shook his head and his sight cleared. He was standing in his own bedroom beside his bed, fully dressed. He'd been sleeping in his clothes, which were now soaking wet. He looked up and saw Tom and Jim a few feet away. Each held a bucket in his hands, now empty, thankfully.

"Oh … good morning, gentlemen," he said. They apparently, found this humorous, for some reason he couldn't quite grasp. They both grinned at him.

"Good morning, sir!" Jim said, cheerfully. "Though it is now, in fact, afternoon, sir! Did you enjoy your little bath, Captain?"

Nathan looked down at his sodden clothes, water still dripping onto the floor. He shook the cold liquid from his hands.

"Yes … thank you, Jim … Tom. That was … very refreshing …"

Jim laughed. "Oh, you are *most* welcome, sir! It was … well, it was *our* pleasure, though I doubt very much it was *yours!*"

"Sir …" Tom said, in a more serious tone, "You've been dead drunk for three days now, and it's time you stopped and pulled yourself out of it. You have a farm full of people who need you. You can't just drink yourself to death, no matter how badly you feel. So please get yourself up and dressed, sir."

Nathan looked at Tom and nodded. His head pounded, and the room seemed to be moving around, but what Tom was saying got through to him.

"Yes … you're right, Tom. Sorry. Would you … would you please have a bath drawn for me? I feel … and likely *smell* … like I've not bathed in weeks. Cold water will be fine … in fact, it's probably for the best."

An hour later Nathan was clean—though cold—and dressed, sitting in the sunlight on the veranda with Tom and Jim.

"I'm feeling embarrassed, and … remorseful, gentlemen. I've never done anything of the like before … not even when they murdered Maria. When *that* happened, I was too angry … and too determined … to spend any time feeling sorry for myself.

"Anyway, I feel … rather … *empty* … and ashamed. I imagine I've let everyone down who's looked up to me, starting with you two."

"Oh, think nothing of it, Captain," Jim said, jovially. "By God sir! You're the only man I know who's never 'tied one on,' as they say, 'til now. It was bound to happen sometime. You *are* a human being after all … ain't you, sir?"

"Yes, Mr. Wiggins. My aching head makes that *abundantly* clear."

Jim laughed again. He sat back and took a puff on a cigar. Nathan had declined the offer to smoke one of his own. Though his head had, thankfully, eased off its pounding somewhat, his stomach was still feeling weak, and the thought of a cigar just now did not appeal.

Then Tom spoke, the concern in his voice plain to hear.

"Sir … I think I can speak from most recent, *personal* experience. Suddenly losing a woman you love, is … well, probably the hardest thing a man can endure. I think it's harder than suffering a great injury or illness, or even the death of a close family member. It's something a man … feels down into the depths of his soul. I feel for you sir, I truly do, but I also know there is nothing any of us can do for you. You must tough your way through it. And come out the other side."

"Yes, you're right, as usual, on all counts, Tom. It does feel … I don't know … like a cross between a hard punch in the gut and a complete aching emptiness."

He was quiet for a moment, staring ahead as if seeing something that wasn't there. His eyes teared up.

Then he shook his head, wiped his eyes, and looked at Tom, "And, Tom … I owe you another apology. I'd nearly forgotten about your own recent loss … back in New Orleans with—"

He paused mid-sentence and glanced over at Jim, realizing he might be giving away a confidence.

"It's okay, sir. Jim knows all about Adilida and has given plenty of helpful advice on the matter."

"Oh, good. So I wanted to say, I'm sorry I've all but ignored your troubles, being absorbed in my own. Tell me Tom, truly, are you still feeling badly about that? Does it still trouble your mind?"

"Yes, sir. The more I think on it the more I believe I may have been wrong about her. I know what I saw … what you and I *both* saw. But my heart tells me … she was *not* playing me false, and there must be a good, reasonable explanation for it, despite appearances. So now I'm feeling like the worst sort of cad, as you can imagine."

"Yes, I understand, Tom. And I'm sorry for you. But at least … well, at least you know what you may have done wrong … whereas I have … *no idea*. Why did she leave? She seemed so happy here. She is … an *enigma* to me.

"But … by God, *what a woman!* Oh, I've been with other women, of course. Just between us men … I've been with *many* other women …" he blushed and met their grins with a shrug.

"But they're as tin, next to her gold, she's so far above the others. Her smile, her eyes, the wit and wisdom she has in abundance … the *life* in her! And there's something else … a thing I can't even describe … glimpses of something *extraordinary* …"

He became quiet again, and once again his eyes watered.

"Yes, sir. I can see she was a special woman. It must be somewhat like how I've been feeling about Adilida. Not to compare them, sir. I'm sure your Evelyn is … a whole other matter …"

"No, no, Tom. Once again, I must apologize. It is … a very *personal* thing. To you … your Adilida is, above all others … as it should be."

"Yes, sir. Thank you, sir."

Jim laughed and said, "Well … thankfully, I've never known a woman like *either* of those! Sounds like a whole lot of mischief to me!"

"You're right about that, Jim," Nathan said, and forced a smile. It was comforting talking about what had happened, and feeling a bit of good humor, with men whose companionship he greatly valued.

"I have an idea, Captain," Tom said, "If you're willing, let's make a pact to write a heartfelt letter to our respective women, such as they are. And … well, I guess … tell them how we feel … *honestly* feel, and see … if just maybe … they feel the same way too. Maybe your Evelyn will say why she left so suddenly, and my Adilida will explain why she was sitting at a table, hugging and kissing some other man."

Nathan, seeing the earnestness in Tom's eyes, said, "All right, Tom. I agree. We'll write our letters … and then …"

"Then, we'll see, sir."

"All right. God help us, Tom, but ... I guess then we'll see ..."

ᏚᏰᏱᏫᏣᏓᏳᏰᏱᏫᏣᏓᏳᏰᏱᏫᏣᏓ

"Excuse me, Mr. Walters, sir. Sorry to disturb your repose ... but there's a gentleman here I think you should speak with. He's, well ... I believe he is seeking employment, and ... yes, sir, I know we're not in need of any more hands at the moment, but ..."

"Bob ... why would I wish to talk to this man?"

"Well, his name is Sickles, sir."

"Sickles? The kind made of ice, or the cutting kind?"

"What? Oh, I see ... yes, very clever, sir ... very clever. Well, from what I know of him, the *cutting kind*, I'd say."

"Why does that name sound ... *familiar*, somehow, Bob?"

"Oh, well, sir, that's because I'd hired him to do a ... *service* ... on our behalf a few months back. You see, until recently he was head overseer at Mountain Meadows Farm."

"Oh, yes ... and none too successful at that *service*, clearly."

"I've spoken with him about that at length, and I believe the failure was purely bad luck and not his fault. Apparently, unbeknownst to us, it very nearly succeeded."

"Humph! I'm not convinced ... men who've failed at a task typically say something of the sort. Well, be that as it may ... why is he no longer employed there? Did they catch him at it?"

"Oh, no sir. If they'd done that ... well, I doubt very much he'd be standing here at our door today."

"*Pah!* You give Chambers too much credit. He's not as tough as he tries to pretend."

"Yes, sir. I'm sure you're right. Anyway, it seems Mr. Sickles had a ... *disagreement* with Mr. Chambers about how to discipline the slaves, sir."

"I see. Well, then ... yes, bring him in, Bob. I would like to hear what he has to say about our *beloved* neighbor, Mr. Chambers."

Eavesdropping from the top of the stairwell, Margaret winced when she heard those words.

ᏚᏰᏱᏫᏣᏓᏳᏰᏱᏫᏣᏓᏳᏰᏱᏫᏣᏓ

The Captain had finished his sermon, and the people were dispersing to various locations around the cabins.

Among them were Tony, Johnny, and Ned. Tony walked with a steady, determined stride the others were finding hard to match.

"Hey, Tony … what's the big ol' hurry, anyways? We gots nowhere we needs to be in such an all-fired rush!" Johnny said, almost trotting to keep up with Tony's long strides.

But Tony strode on, as if he hadn't heard. Johnny glanced over to Ned, who just shrugged his shoulders in response, so they both just followed along.

When they reached the very last cabin in the far northeast corner, Tony stopped. He sat against the side of the cabin, facing out toward the woods.

The others sat down on either side of him, happy to catch their breath.

"Man, Tony … what kinda bur got up under your backside today?" Johnny prodded. But Tony just glared at him, so Johnny gave it up, and just leaned back to relax.

They sat there for several minutes without talking.

Then Ned said, "Hey … you fellas seen that young gal … Rosa? Saw her come outta the Big House with them house slaves today! Wouldn't never've 'spected that. I thought her a nice, decent girl. Never figured her for one of them white's whores."

When Ned started talking, Johnny had a bad feeling about the topic, and tried to think of a way to signal him to shut up and leave off.

In an instant Tony was on top of Ned, pounding his fists into Ned's face. Ned squawked, rolling up into a ball, trying to protect his face with his hands and arms. But Tony was stronger and faster, and Ned was taking a serious beating.

By the time Johnny could pull Tony off, for which he also received several hard punches, Ned was bleeding out his nose, and from his mouth with a split lip.

Ned was crying and whimpering, "What you go'n do that for, Tony? Ain't never done nothing to you. Damn. That done hurt … *damn!*" He was spitting blood from his mouth.

491

Johnny was furious with Tony, though he understood what had triggered it.

"Damn it, Tony! Ned don't deserve nothing of that kind from *you*. Bad enough what the slavers done to him ... now you gonna do it too? Damn, boy! I know he said something set you off, but he don't know 'bout none of that. He oughtn't to have none of that from you!"

Tony sat again and buried his face in his hands. He was still a long time. Johnny wasn't sure if he was thinking, crying, or still hot tempered and working to control it.

Finally, Tony got up and walked over to Ned. Ned flinched back, worried Tony might hit him again. But Tony knelt in front of him, and said, "I'm powerful sorry and ashamed of myself, Ned. I had no call to do anything of the sort to you. Now I owe you in *blood*. I wish you'd just stand up and hit me back, just as hard as you can. I promise, on God's honor, I won't fight back."

Ned looked up at him, and seeing he was sincere, said, "I ain't got no mind to hit you Tony. You's my friend ... or at least you *was*. I just wanna know what I did to you."

But Tony just sat down hard on the ground and hung his head. So Johnny answered for him, "Look, Ned. It ain't your fault on accounta you weren't never told. But," he glanced over toward Tony to make sure of his reaction, then continued, "you see ... Tony had ... *feelings* for the young woman ..."

Then it was Ned's turn to feel ashamed. "*Oh!* Oh, damn ... I's terrible sorry, Tony. I won't never say nothing about her ..."

"You ain't got no reason to be sorry, Ned. You ain't done nothing wrong. She *is* a whore now. A damned whore to the white slavers. *Dammit!* I reckon I've *earned* the right to say it ... but, I'd ... rather nobody *else* said it ..."

"Oh, yes'sir, Tony. I reckon I ain't never gonna say any such thing again," Ned said, shaking his head.

Johnny sat back against the cabin wall and sighed a heavy sigh, happy his two friends had worked things out, and all was now well again.

After a while, Tony moved back over to where he'd been before, and Ned sat up next to him. A person passing by might not have known anything had happened, unless they looked closely and noticed Ned's battered and bleeding face.

"I reckon the Captain's all talk … he ain't never gonna free us. Look at that … that whore … now that fancy white woman is gone, she done throwed herself at his feet like she got no shame. And he … he happy to let her. Smiling at us, acting all holy and kindly, but all the while taking our women for his pleasure, whenever he pleases. And then toss 'em out, no doubt, when he tire of 'em. And all that sweet Jesus talk. Just to make us work harder and make them slavers more money.

"*Freedom* …" he sighed, and shook his head slowly.

"He gonna dangle it out in front of our eyes like a shiny dollar, just outta reach … for as long as he can still get one of us to believe it. Then he gonna snatch it away, and we be right back where we started. But I say … I got a mind to make an honest man of him, whether he want it or no."

"What you mean by that, Tony?" Johnny asked, not sure he liked where Tony was headed with this.

"I mean … I been thinking we ought to get our own selves outta here and grab our own freedom. Y'all have heard if we just go far enough north the folks'll help us be free, and not put us back in chains."

"Yeah, but Captain says we don't know nothing 'bout how things is up in them parts … that we gonna just go up there and starve ourselves …"

"More lies to keep us here … if them folks up North wants to see us free, it don't make no sense they'd be for letting us starve ourselves. I reckon there'll always be a job for a strong young man willing to work hard. Maybe them others'd starve, but not the likes of us three. We got strong arms and backs. Somebody's gonna want to pay us to work hard."

"Hmm … maybe you got a point there, Tony …" Ned spoke up for the first time. "Maybe Captain's just been saying that stuff to keep us here."

"Yeah, and I was talking with one of them grooms, and he said Captain done sold off all them hunting dogs. So if we run off into the woods, they won't be no way to track us."

493

They were quiet for a moment, thinking about this, when Johnny's eyes suddenly widened, "Not all!"

"What's that, John?"

"Not *all* them dogs … Captain's still got that one big ol' crazy dog, and he's worse'n all them others put together, I reckon. Maybe that's why he done sold off the others … don't figure on needed 'em with that big ugly monster about. That thing's like to eat a man for breakfast and come back for another'n at dinner!"

"Yeah … I ain't forgot about *him*, but I been thinking up an idea about that too."

"What idea, Tony? How you gonna get rid of that big ol' hound?"

"Y'all know I been watching them soldiers shoot the guns, and I figure by now I know how it all works. And … I learned from one of them grooms where they keeps the guns and powder, and such. It's in a closet downstairs in the house. He says it ain't even kept locked up, and the front door ain't never locked neither. I reckon if I was to sneak in there real quiet-like late in the night, I could get me one of them guns, and all the fixin's. Then if that old hound come after us … *boom!* I just shoots him dead."

"Wheew …" Johnny whistled, and leaned back against the wall. "That-there's a pretty bold plan, Tony, that is. But … don't you reckon they's more likely to be tracking us down if they knows we took a gun?"

"Well, they only takes 'em out for the shooting on Sundays, so if we make our run, say … Sunday night … they may not notice it missing for a whole week. By then, we's over to the North and gone. And if'n that hound come after us, we put an end to him, and keep right on running."

Tony had another thought he didn't care to share with the others. *And if the Captain comes after us, maybe I'll just put an end to him as well …*

ଔଽୈଔଔ୫ଔଔ୫ଔଔ୫ଔଔ

Evelyn sat in the carriage, looking out the window, watching people passing by.

Harriet had asked the driver to stop off at the general store on their way home from the train station, so they'd have food in the larder. She'd left it empty when they'd departed for western Virginia, now more than a month ago, not knowing when they'd return. Now she was inside the store, purchasing whatever essentials they'd need, while Evelyn waited outside.

Evelyn felt … a great, empty nothingness. She'd cried so many tears, she had no more left. It felt like she couldn't feel any emotions at all. Her life was an empty, burned-out shell. Her father was gone … buried in the cold earth for the rest of eternity. She'd never see him again. Never again talk with him. He'd no longer be there with his comforting hug, and warm, reassuring smile.

And now Nathan was gone, too. That was her own doing. She still didn't understand it. *What have I done? I was so … happy … and … in love. And then … who am I?*

She shuddered at the thought. That strange voice in her head. Her, and yet … *not* her. Was she going insane? She'd heard of such things happening but had never really believed it. Now she wasn't so sure … had she lost her mind? Mostly she didn't think so. But after what had happened with Nathan … maybe …

She watched as a steady stream of people flowed past on the sidewalk. Gentlemen, in fine suits, ladies with parasols, and many black faces—usually following behind a white master, carrying their goods. But occasionally a trusted slave would be allowed to shop unattended and would be seen walking alone with a parcel or several bags. It was a scene she'd become familiar with since they'd moved into town from the farm, but she still found it fascinating. So many people! All going about some business of their own. But after a while it became much of a blur, like watching a stream of water, always slightly different ripples, but always the same flow.

But then, as her mind had begun to wander, something unusual caught her eye. An especially pretty young black woman suddenly turned and darted into the alleyway as she came level with Evelyn's carriage. A slave she assumed, though unaccompanied. It was such an anomaly, it pulled Evelyn from her dark reverie. She watched the girl look around to see if anyone was observing, then duck down behind some barrels.

The analytical part of Evelyn's mind immediately took over and worked the problem. Hiding, obviously ... but from whom? Only one possibility ... from a master or overseer, which means ... she's a runaway! Then, searching her mind she realized the thing that'd caught her attention wasn't the sudden movement into the alley—it had happened before that ... fear on a pretty young face. Not what she expected in broad daylight in downtown Richmond. Why was this woman afraid? Why had she run away?

Then she recalled Nathan telling her about what had occurred on his own farm, just before Evelyn's arrival. A young slave girl had narrowly escaped being raped and whipped by the head overseer.

Evelyn was suddenly alive and awake, as she'd not felt for several days. What if this girl was running from the same predicament—escaping a master, or overseer, who intended to rape her ... or already had?

With no more conscious thought, Evelyn stepped from the carriage, and strode into the alley. She looked around to make sure no one was watching, just as the slave girl had done. Then she stepped up next to the barrels where she'd seen the girl hide. She looked down, and saw a huddled form, squeezed as far back as possible next to the brick wall where they'd stacked barrels. She'd covered her head with a garment of some kind. So someone walking past who glanced over would've noticed nothing out of the ordinary, just a pile of discarded clothing or other goods.

Evelyn also ducked down behind the barrels. She shuffled her way over to within a foot of the covered form.

"I won't harm you, nor give you away," she said, in what she hoped was a reassuring voice. "My name is Evelyn. Why are you hiding here?"

There was no response, so she tried another tack, "*Listen* … I … will help you if I can, but you must talk to me."

The cloth came down, revealing the frightened, pretty young face she'd seen back on the street. "I'm called, Violet, miss."

"I can see you're in trouble, Violet. You've run away from your master."

The girl nodded but said nothing.

"If you want my help, you must tell me *why*, Violet."

Now Evelyn could see tears welling up in the girl's eyes. "The master he … he … took me to his bedroom and … he did … you know … things a man ought do only with his proper wife. And, I ain't never been to a man's bed before. And now … he's like to keep me in the house all the time. But then the missus … she done got angry with me and say she gonna skin me alive if'n he touch me again. But I know he gonna do such, on account of he told me so hisself. I's sorry causing you any trouble miss, but I'm just a girl, and terrible afraid of the master and the missus. So when we was shopping and the overseer turned away I just ran."

Tears were streaming down her face.

Evelyn reached in front of her neck and unclasped the cape she wore around her shoulders. She leaned over and wrapped the garment around the girl, fastening the clasp.

"Come with me."

At first the girl stared at her, as if not comprehending. But then their eyes met; Violet nodded, and rose to her feet.

"Keep your head down, looking at your feet. I will lead the way to my carriage. You must walk slowly, and act as if everything were normal. You're my servant, and we're returning to our carriage—just as we *always* do."

They walked back down the alley toward where the carriage was parked out on the street, the girl walking a half pace behind. Evelyn paused for only a moment as they reached the street, glancing in both directions. Seeing nothing unusual, she stepped over to the carriage, opened the door, and ushered the girl inside.

The driver was either daydreaming or had nodded off. He sat still in his seat and never looked down at them.

Once they were inside the carriage, Evelyn whispered, "I'm sorry, but you must crawl under the seat, and be as small and still as you may. My mother will return in a moment, and she must *not* see you."

"Yes, ma'am," she whispered, and crawled underneath the seat, behind Evelyn's legs. Evelyn leaned down and covered the girl's form with the cape. It was dark enough inside the carriage it just might work.

Evelyn found her heart was beating wildly, and she had to consciously work to calm herself, and slow her breathing. When her mother returned, nothing must seem out of the ordinary. As the minutes ticked by, she could feel herself relaxing, and her heartbeat returning to normal.

She noticed a man coming down the street acting unusual — looking into store windows, and down side alleys between buildings. He glanced over and saw her watching him. She looked away, but it was too late. From the corner of her eye she could see him crossing the street toward her. He stood next to the carriage and waved at her through the window. She opened the carriage window and said, "Yes … how may I help you, sir?"

"Sorry to disturb you miss. But I was wondering if you saw a young slave woman come by here recently. She'd have been by herself, and … I assume acting in a big hurry."

Evelyn's mind raced … did he *know* something? Had he seen her rescue the girl? No … no, he'd have been too far away. He only came to ask her because she was the one person on the street who was stationary and, presumably, watching people as they passed. What to say? What to say?

And then it came to her; use Harriet's training … *act the part!*

"My good sir … do I *look* like a lady who would pay any notice to a slave girl passing by? Why … there must be hundreds walking past this very spot every hour. And, to be perfectly honest, they all tend to look alike to me. There could've been a dozen slave girls just as you've described come past and I would've paid them no mind.

"Why? Have you misplaced one of your slaves, sir?"

"Yes, ma'am, so it would seem. Just turned my back for a moment, and … she was gone. Don't understand it, neither. Never caused no trouble before. *Damn* … oh, sorry for the language, miss! But I reckon my master's gonna be terrible angry about it. Well, none o' your concern, of course. Thank you for your time, miss."

He tipped his hat, and continued down the street, still looking from side to side, and into every window.

Evelyn said nothing but reached down and gently patted the bundle behind her legs. Then she sat back and tried to relax, awaiting Harriet's return.

But as she sat, the strange voice in the back of her mind seemed to whisper, *Maybe … this … is who I am …*

\<End of Book 2\>

If you enjoyed *Enigma*
please post a review.

SEDITION
ROAD TO THE BREAKING BOOK 3

Nathan strode back toward the boardinghouse, head down, deep in thought. He nearly walked right into a man standing on the street in front of him, speaking his name.

He stopped and looked up. *Three* men, in fact. He immediately recognized the one on the left as Peter Stevens, the handsome young gentleman who'd escorted Evelyn to the ball where he'd last seen her. He was also a former army officer, and a member of Wise's cadre. Nathan fought down a very strong desire to strangle the man, a feeling he'd also experienced that night at the ball.

Stevens grinned, but Nathan didn't return the smile. The other young men, also dressed as gentlemen, did *not* smile. They looked nervous and gave him non-committal looks.

"Stevens ..."

"Mr. Chambers. Well met, sir. May I introduce Mr. Miller and Mr. Baker?"

Nathan nodded toward them but didn't offer his hand. Miller and Baker tipped their hats to him, but likewise didn't extend their hands.

"Well, I'm sure it's my pleasure to see you again, Mr. Stevens. But if you'll excuse me ... I'm in a hurry just now and have important matters to attend."

"Please, Mr. Chambers ... I've been looking for you and wish but a moment of your time."

Nathan eyed him with suspicion. He could think of no *good* reason for Stevens to seek him out but could easily imagine several *bad* ones.

"Oh? And what is it you wish to speak with me about, pray, Stevens?"

"Mr. Chambers ... now the secession is a ... *fait accompli* ... as they say ... some friends of mine would like to know your thinking on certain topics, sir."

"Hmm … by 'friends' I assume you mean our *esteemed* former governor, Henry Wise? I can see no reason why Mr. Wise would seek my opinion on *any* subject whatever. He certainly has shown no inclination for doing so in the past."

"Mr. Chambers … he knows you're a man … such as myself … of great military experience—even heroic service to the country. He begs you to consider lending your … considerable martial talents … to the wellbeing of Virginia in her hour of need."

Nathan gave him a bland look, then said, "I was unaware *you* had served during the late Mexican War, sir …"

Stevens blushed. "Did I say so? No … I simply refer to my time doing my duty in the military, same as you."

"Maybe not *quite* the same. But be that as it may … I believe I will keep my own counsel concerning my future plans, if it's all the same to you … and Henry Wise."

"But, sir … will you not at least do me the honor of allowing me be the first to hear your intention to come to the defense of the Commonwealth? I should be most honored, sir, if I could give the good news to my friends and associates regarding this matter."

Nathan knew he was being baited into disclosing his true intentions, but at this point he was having a hard time caring. After all the recent calamitous events, he was feeling disgusted with the whole affair and not particularly inclined to equivocate.

He reached into his pocket and pulled out a cigar. It seemed to him one of the men flinched when he did this. But it'd been out of the corner of his eye, so he couldn't be sure. He stuck the cigar in his mouth but didn't light it.

"Mr. Stevens … you may tell Mr. Wise and the rest of your *friends* I have no intention of fighting for Virginia—now, or *ever.*"

Stevens frowned at him, "Then … you will fight against us, sir? You will be a traitor to your own home of Virginia?"

Nathan took the cigar from his mouth and pointed it at Stevens.

"Let me tell you the difference between you and I, Stevens—aside from the fact I actually fought in a war, while I understand you took to your sick bed. *I don't break my sacred oaths!* You and I swore an oath to protect the United States and obey their

President. I won't break my oath, sir! While you … you dare call *me* traitor, when in fact, it is *you*, sir, who is the traitor! You and all your friends speak nothing but treasonous sedition."

Stevens went red in the face. Nathan could see he'd struck a nerve.

"Gentlemen, I tire of this conversation. In fact, I am sick at heart, and wish only to return to my home and there pray to God cooler heads prevail. Good day to you, sirs."

But when Nathan put the cigar back in his mouth, and attempted to move past them, he found himself staring down the barrels of three pistols.

Stevens glared at him, "I'm sorry you feel that way, Chambers, as it will not go well for you. Now you will please just hand over that Colt you keep in your pocket and come with us … *sir!*"

Nathan met eyes with each of the three. The looks they returned told him Stevens was the only one who'd drawn a gun on a man before. The other two had no experience, neither military nor police.

"Or *what*, Stevens? Will you murder me, right here in broad daylight, on this street in the middle of town? With … God knows how many people watching out their windows, or from down the street? Secession or not, there'd be a *noose* in it for you."

Stevens hesitated a moment, then said, "Of course not, sir. We only wish you to accompany us, that we might discuss this matter more thoroughly … in private."

Nathan could readily imagine the subject of that "conversation," and had no wish to take part.

But Stevens and company had unwittingly stepped into Nathan's trap. He'd forced them to consider how bad it might go for them if they murdered an unarmed man in the street. It was the slight edge he needed.

"Now, if you would be so good, Mr. Chambers, please just reach in your pocket and hand me that Colt … nice and easy like …"

Nathan glowered at him for a moment, then shrugged. He carefully pealed back the right side of his jacket and slowly reached across with his left hand. Then he lifted the small pistol out of his waistcoat pocket with two fingers.

He held it out by the barrel in his left hand. Stevens reached forward to take it. As his hand touched the handle Nathan lunged forward and punched him hard in the face. The blow *crunch*ed bones in the man's nose and staggered him backward.

Nathan swung the pistol at the middle man to pistol whip him. But the man's cowardice saved him; he'd already backed away, so the strike missed his face by mere inches.

Nathan's mind raced, already on to the third man, behind him and to the right. He imagined the man already pulling the trigger.

A sudden blinding pain struck the top of his head: a searing hot bolt of lightning. It streaked down his back and through his arms even to his fingertips. Excruciating agony like knives and needles shot down his arms and legs. His knees buckled, and his sight grew dark. Bright, dazzling, many-colored lights flashed and sparkled in the darkness. The world became a swirling dream, and the ground rushed up to meet his face.

Acknowledgments

I'd like to thank the following individuals for assisting in the writing and editing of *Enigma*, including reading the beta version and providing invaluable feedback: Angela Thompson, Bruce Wright, Charlie Carman, Craig Bennett, Gay Petersen, Jeff Kaye, Larry Zinkan, Leslie Johns, Marilyn Bennett, Mike Bennett, Nick Bennett, Patricia Bennett, Rachel Bennett, and Tessa Wyrsch.

And special thanks to my editor, Ericka McIntyre, who keeps me honest and on track, and my proofreader Travis Tynan, who makes sure everything is done correctly!

And, last but not least (at all!), the experts at New Shelves Books: my trusted advisor on all things "bookish," Keri-Rae Barnum, and the guru Amy Collins!

Get Exclusive Free Content

The most enjoyable part of writing books is talking about them with readers like you. In my case that means all things related to *Road to the Breaking*—the story and characters, themes, and concepts. And of course, Civil War history in general, and West Virginia history in particular.

If you sign up for my mailing list, you'll receive some free bonus material I think you'll enjoy:

- A fully illustrated *Road to the Breaking* **Fact vs. Fiction Quiz.** Test your knowledge of history with this short quiz on the people, places, and things in the book (did they really exist in 1860, or are they purely fictional?)

- **Cut scenes from** *Road to the Breaking.* One of the hazards of writing a novel is word and page count. At some point you realize you need to trim it back to give the reader a faster-paced, more engaging experience. However, now you've finished reading the book, wouldn't you like to know a little more detail about some of your favorite characters? Here's your chance to take a peek behind the curtain!

- I'll occasionally put out a **newsletter with information about the Road to the Breaking Series**—new book releases, news and information about the author, etc. I promise not to inundate you with spam (it's one of my personal pet peeves, so why would I propagate it?)

To sign up, visit my website:
http://www.ChrisABennett.com

ROAD TO THE BREAKING SERIES:

Made in the USA
Monee, IL
10 May 2023

33363214R00298